BACH PERSPECTIVES

VOLUME SIX

J. S. Bach's Concerted Ensemble Music,
The Ouverture

BACH PERSPECTIVES

VOLUME SIX

Editorial Board

Bach
Perspectives

VOLUME SIX

J. S. Bach's Concerted Ensemble Music,
The Ouverture

Edited by Gregory G. Butler

UNIVERSITY OF ILLINOIS PRESS · URBANA AND CHICAGO

ISSN 1072-1924
ISBN 0-252-03042-7

Bach Perspectives is
sponsored by the
American Bach Society
and produced under the
guidance of its Editorial
Board. For information
about the American Bach
Society, please see its
Web site at this URL:
www.americanbachsociety.org

CONTENTS

PREFACE

This series, *Bach Perspectives*, was begun in 1995 as a forum for exploring various facets of the life and works of the composer Johann Sebastian Bach. Three volumes are devoted to studies of the reception of Bach's music in subsequent generations. Contributions in BP 2 focus on the Leipzig publishing house of Breitkopf and the dissemination of Bach's music in the eighteenth century; those of BP 3 trace the impact of Bach's creativity on the compositional activity of composers "from Mozart to Hindemith"; and essays in BP 5 collectively explore many facets of Bach reception in America, from *Dwight's Journal* to Brubeck's jazz. Other volumes deal more directly with Bach's music.

In BP 1 the authors investigate compositional issues, such as the role of improvisation in the keyboard works, and address cyclic structures and parody in cantatas, and concerto styles in instrumental works. In BP 4 the studies center on analysis and interpretation regarding specific forms and styles of a wide range of Bach's music. In this and the following volume (*Bach Perspectives* 6 and 7), concerted ensemble music by Bach takes center stage, and in many respects this topic further develops the issues raised in both BP 1 and BP 4.

Many of the works discussed in these two volumes would have been heard in Zimmermann's coffee house or garden, as part of performances of the Leipzig Collegium Musicum directed by Bach. Heinrich Zedler's *Grosses Universal Lexicon* included the following entry in 1739:

> *Musicum collegium* is a gathering of certain musical connoisseurs who, for the benefit of their own exercise in both vocal and instrumental music and under the guidance of a certain director, get together on particular days and in particular locations and perform musical pieces. Such collegia are to be found in various places. In Leipzig, the Bachian *Collegium musicum* is more famous than all others.[1]

The fame of the Leipzig Collegium Musicum was not simply due to the technical proficiency and musicianship of its members but also, and in large measure, arose from the superlative and ingenious creativity of its director, Johann Sebastian Bach, whose music they performed. Such works continue to be appreciated and applauded, and the studies presented in BP 6 and BP 7 investigate their respective origins, characteristics, forms, and significance.

Robin A. Leaver, past President
The American Bach Society

1. *Grosses Universal Lexicon* 22 (Leipzig: Zedler, 1739), col. 1488; trans. NBR, 203.

EDITOR'S PREFACE

This volume of *Bach Perspectives*, along with its sister volume, to be published next in the series, marks the extension of a project begun with my early collaboration on volume 4 of the series, edited by David Schulenberg and published in 1999. The intention to bring out a collection of essays devoted entirely to Bach's concerted ensemble music, only partly realized in two studies by Jeanne Swack and myself in the earlier volume, has now come to fruition in volumes 6 and 7. The first of these focuses on the ouverture, a genre of concerted ensemble music that has received remarkably little attention in the scholarly literature of late.

The opening essay by Joshua Rifkin is a seminal study of the early source history of the B-minor orchestral suite BWV 1067. It not only elaborates on his discovery that the work in its present form for solo flute goes back to an earlier version in A minor, ostensibly for solo violin, but also takes this discovery as the point of departure for a wide-ranging discussion of the origins and extent of Bach's concerted ensemble music. The other two studies in the present volume mark a continuation of the focus of the two earlier studies in volume 4, referred to above—that of genre. Jeanne Swack presents an enlightening comparison of Georg Phillip Telemann's and Bach's approach to the overture as concerted movements in their church cantatas, highlighting the somewhat idiosyncratic approach of the former. Finally, Steven Zohn views the ouverture BWV 1067 from the fascinating generic standpoint of the "concert en ouverture."

This volume is innovative in at least one respect. Zohn's study acts as a response to Rifkin's in suggesting that the early version of the B-minor suite may also have been scored for flute. Thus *Bach Perspectives* 6 continues not only to present issues at the heart of Bach studies, but also to reflect the atmosphere of healthy scholarly debate that informs and animates the field.

Gregory Butler
Vancouver, British Columbia

ABBREVIATIONS

BDOK Werner Neumann and Hans-Joachim Schulze, eds. *Bach-Dokumente.* 4 vols. Kassel: Bärenreiter; Leipzig: VEB Deutscher Verlag für Musik, 1963–78.

BG [Bach-Gesamtausgabe.] *Johann Sebastian Bach's Werke.* Edited by the Bachgesellschaft. 47 vols. Leipzig: Breitkopf & Härtel, 1851–99.

BJ *Bach-Jahrbuch.*

BOM Siegbert Rampe and Dominik Sackmann. *Bachs Orchestermusik: Entstehung, Klangwelt, Interpretation.* Kassel: Bärenreiter, 2000.

BOW *Bachs Orchesterwerke*, ed. Martin Geck and Werner Breig. Dortmunder Bach-Forschungen 1. Witten: Klangfarben-Verlag, 1997.

BWV [Bach-Werke-Verzeichnis.] Wolfgang Schmieder, ed. *Thematisch-systematisches Verzeichnis der musikalischen Werke von Johann Sebastian Bach.* Rev. ed. Wiesbaden: Breitkopf & Härtel, 1990.

KB Kritischer Bericht (critical report) of the NBA.

NBA [Neue-Bach-Ausgabe.] *Johann Sebastian Bach: Neue Ausgabe sämtlicher Werke.* Edited by the Johann-Sebastian-Bach-Institut, Göttingen, and the Bach-Archiv, Leipzig. Kassel: Bärenreiter; Leipzig: Deutscher Verlag für Musik, 1954–.

NBR Hans T. David and Arthur Mendel, eds. *The New Bach Reader: A Life of Johann Sebastian Bach in Letters and Documents.* Revised and enlarged by Christoph Wolff. New York: W. W. Norton & Co., 1998.

P Berlin, Staatsbibliothek zu Berlin, Mus. ms. Bach P (Partitur).

ST Berlin, Staatsbibliothek zu Berlin, Mus. ms. Bach St (Stimmen).

TVWV [Telemann-Vokalwerke-Verzeichnis.] Werner Menke, ed. *Thematisches Verzeichnis der Vokalwerke von Georg Philipp Telemann.* 2 vols. Frankfurt am Main: Klosterman, 1981–83.

TWV [Telemann-Werke-Verzeichnis.] Martin Ruhnke, ed. *Georg Philipp Telemann: Thematisch-Systematisches Verzeichnis seiner Werke: Instrumentalwerke.* 3 vols. Kassel: Bärenreiter, 1984–.

The "B-Minor Flute Suite" Deconstructed

New Light on Bach's Ouverture *BWV 1067*

Joshua Rifkin

Johann Sebastian Bach's Ouverture for Flute, Strings, and Continuo (BWV 1067)—in common parlance, "the B-Minor Flute Suite"—has long enjoyed a favored position both within his own instrumental output and in our musical practice at large. Indeed, for generations of performers and listeners, the work has become virtually emblematic of the flute itself. As its continued preeminence reminds us, moreover, the ouverture has evaded the scholarly scythe that has so painfully diminished the body of Bach's instrumental music with flute—identifying this piece as a transcription from a different medium, disqualifying that one as a product of his authorship altogether.[1] If anything, recent scholarship seems only to have heightened the ouverture's sig-

This essay, originally scheduled for publication in *Bach Perspectives* 4 and completed in something very close to its present form by the autumn of 1997, became a casualty of editorial upheavals and software problems; it appears now thanks to the persistence, encouragement, and, in the end, forbearance of Gregory Butler. I presented a version at the Bach Symposium held at the University of Dortmund in January 1996; I thank my colleagues there, especially Werner Breig and Martin Geck, for several valuable observations. Reports of my findings surfaced at various places soon after the Dortmund meeting, among which I would note references in BOW 5, 29 n. 4, and 31, and Wolfgang Hirschmann's report in *Die Musikforschung* 49 (1996): 407–8, at 408; these accounts made it possible for some to retro-engineer essential portions of my work even as it remained unpublished (cf. BOM, 258–60). Other authors have drawn on my research with my cooperation; see, for instance, Jeanne Swack's entry "badinerie" in *J. S. Bach*, ed. Malcolm Boyd and John Butt, Oxford Composer Companions (Oxford: Oxford University Press, 1999), 58. In preparing my final text, I have benefited greatly from the kindness of Helmut Hell and his co-workers at the Music Division of the Staatsbibliothek zu Berlin—Preußischer Kulturbesitz in providing access to the original sources. My relationship to BWV 1067, and Bach's flute music in general, would no doubt have remained an essentially passive one if not for the good fortune of performing these works with Christopher Krueger in concerts of the Bach Ensemble. Though not unmindful of a certain irony, I thus offer the present article to Chris as a token of gratitude for many years of friendship and musical collaboration. Plates 1–4 appear by permission of Berlin, Staatsbibliothek zu Berlin—Preußischer Kulturbesitz—Musikabteilung mit Mendelssohn-Archiv.

1. See Section V. Irving Godt, "Politics, Patriotism, and a Polonaise: A Possible Revision in Bach's Suite in B minor," *Musical Quarterly* 74 (1990): 610–22, has in fact posited an early version of the

nificance: with most authorities now agreed on placing its creation in the late 1730s, it ranks as the very latest of Bach's original compositions for larger instrumental ensemble, the capstone to a rich succession of works stretching back at least as far as the Brandenburg Concertos.[2]

The present study will upset—or at least seriously qualify—this gratifying picture. Let me immediately forestall any worry that I shall seek to remove BWV 1067 from the canon of Bach's works: both the transmission and, surely, the music itself leave no room for doubt that he composed it.[3] But on every other count, we shall see that the evidence tells a very different story from the one familiar to us.

I

The ouverture BWV 1067 survives in only one source from Bach's lifetime, a set of six parts preserved—together with several more added later by Carl Friedrich Zelter—in ST 154.[4] Table 1 lists the original parts in detail.[5] As it makes clear, Bach himself wrote

---

B-minor ouverture lacking both some of its present movements and the solo flute part. But his arguments, though not without insight on a number of points, strike me as far-fetched; and in any event, as I hope the present study will show, they rest on presuppositions that we can no longer regard as tenable.

2. See Section II, which begins on p. 12.

3. Although Bach's parts to the ouverture (see immediately in the main text) no longer have their original wrapper, leaving us without an attribution in his own hand or that of a scribe directly associated with him, all the eighteenth-century manuscripts carry his name, as do entries plainly referring to BWV 1067 in the catalogues of C. P. E. Bach's estate and the library of Princess Anna Amalie of Prussia; Peter Wollny, moreover, has identified the script of the existing wrapper as that of C. P. E. Bach's daughter, Anna Carolina Philippina. See, for details, NBA VII/1 (*Vier Ouvertüren Orchestersuiten*), ed. Heinrich Besseler and Hans Grüß, KB, 23, 37–39; BDOK 3:384 (no. 887) and 492 (no. 957); and Peter Wollny, "Zur Überlieferung der Instrumentalwerke Johann Sebastian Bachs: Der Quellenbesitz Carl Philipp Emanuel Bachs," BJ 82 (1996): 7–21, at 16 n. 46.

4. Cf. the descriptions in NBA VII/1, KB, 34–37 and 40–41. The editors of NBA VII/1 call the six original parts "incomplete," as they lack duplicate copies of the violins and a third continuo part (ibid., 36). This assumption, however, rests on patterns of transmission in Bach's Leipzig church music that do not necessarily apply to his instrumental output. None of the surviving sources for Bach's instrumental music includes duplicate violin parts or a third copy of the continuo, and for most of them, at least, there seems little reason to imagine that they ever did; see Joshua Rifkin, "More (and Less) on Bach's Orchestra," *Performance Practice Review* 4 (1991): 5–13, at 7–9, as well as idem, "Besetzung—Entstehung—Überlieferung: Bemerkungen zur Ouvertüre BWV 1068," BJ 83 (1997): 169–76, at 172–76. On a possible original score of BWV 1067, see the Postscript.

5. In the table and elsewhere, I follow the numbering of the parts adopted in NBA VII/1, KB, which differs from that used by the library. References to movement titles follow Bach's orthography, as seen in the two autograph parts as well as in revisions to parts nos. 2, 3, and 6, rather than the normalized

the flute and viola parts; each of the rest shows the hand of a different, anonymous copyist.[6] Yoshitake Kobayashi's investigation of the paper and script assigns the set as a whole to "ca. 1738–39"; but Bach's viola part, although written on the same paper as the others, appears to postdate them by some years—presumably it replaces an earlier copy that had suffered damage or got lost.[7] No. 5, the unfigured continuo, also occupies a secondary position, but of a somewhat different sort: as a direct copy of no. 6, it offers no independent testimony on the origins or readings of the music.[8] For obvious reasons, therefore, the discussion that follows will concern itself essentially with parts nos. 1, 2, 3, and 6.

---

forms used in NBA VII/1 and elsewhere today. The form *Bourée* comes from the viola; other autograph versions (not all reported accurately in NBA VII/I, KB, 53) read *Bourèe* (Flute, Continuo no. 6), *Bouree*, or *Boureè* (both Violin 2).

6. Yoshitake Kobayashi, "Zur Chronologie der Spätwerke Johann Sebastian Bachs: Kompositions- und Aufführungstätigkeit von 1736 bis 1750," BJ 74 (1988): 7–72, at 29, labels the scribes of Violin 1 and the unfigured continuo "Anon. N 2" and "Anon. N 3," respectively. NBA VII/1, KB, 36, suggests that the scribe of the figured continuo did not draw his own F-clefs in the margins of the part, as clefs written within the staff for Bourée 2, Menuet, and Battinerie show a different form; but since—as the editors in fact note—the clef at the start of Bourée 1 matches the shape of the clefs in the margins, we may better explain the discrepancies by assuming that the copyist drew these in advance of writing the actual notes. See also n. 11.

7. See Kobayashi, "Zur Chronologie der Spätwerke Johann Sebastian Bachs," 21–22 and 53. For more on the dating of the parts, see Section IV.

8. NBA VII/1, KB, 42, describes no. 5 as "probably a copy" of no. 6, "evidently made before the correction" of this latter part. This does not quite describe the situation accurately: although no. 5 omits the figuring and many other additions—it lacks all of Bach's trill signs after the first twenty measures and has no dynamic indications except for that of the Double and the possibly nonautograph indications in the Polonoise and at m. 36 of the Battinerie (see nn. 103 and 212)—it incorporates an altered reading at mm. 45 and 176 in the first movement (cf. NBA VII/1, KB, 48 and 50, also the Postscript in this essay) as well as the autograph movement titles (see also n. 188) and even the marking *tasto solo* at m. 198 of the Ouverture. These items, indeed, confirm the dependency of the one part on the other, which might otherwise seem open to question, as the two do not show the same line endings; see also the observations on clefs in NBA VII/1, KB, 42, and in n. 11. No. 5 does not, however, reflect the correction to no. 6 at m. 27 of the Sarabande detailed in Table 2, nor the ones at m. 179 of the first movement and mm. 15 and 20 of Bourée 1 reported in n. 12, even though tablature letters in all but the third of these—and Bach's figures in the second and third—leave no ambiguity concerning the intended pitch (see also n. 184), and the figures confirm further that the scribe had at least half of the newer readings before him. At m. 51 of the opening movement, moreover, Anon. N 3 initially followed the uncorrected reading of his model (cf. Table 2), although here, too, the figuring makes the intended version plain; and in m. 14 of the Sarabande, he overlooked both a sharp placed very high and very far to the left of the first note by the scribe of the unfigured part and a natural, by the same scribe, in front of the last note (cf. NBA VII/1, KB, 52, but noting the following modifications: the sharp

Table 1. Ouverture BWV 1067: Original parts

Part	Scribe[a]
1. Traversiere	JSB
2. Violino 1	Anon. N 2 + JSB (heading, title, clef, time and key signatures + revision)
3. Violino 2	Singular + JSB (heading, title, clef, time and key signatures + revision)
4. Viola	JSB
5. Continuo (unfigured)	Anon. N 3 + JSB (heading, title, clef, time and key signatures)
6. Continuo (figured)	Singular + JSB (heading, title, clef, time and key signatures + figuring and revision)

[a] JSB = Johann Sebastian Bach; on Anon. N 2 and N 3, see Kobayashi, "Zur Chronologie der Spätwerke Johann Sebastian Bachs," 29.

All parts on paper with watermark of crossed hammer and iron in ornamental shield (NBA IX/1, no. 105)

Of these, we must first consider the three nonautograph parts. In each instance, Bach himself appears to have got the copyist started: not only did he write the heading at the top of the page, but he also entered the movement title, clef, key signature, and time signature. We may perhaps take this as more than a simple courtesy. On several occasions where Bach provided the initial elements of a part, he did so to signal a notational change—usually to tell the scribe to copy the music in a key different from that of the parent manuscript. I might cite two examples here. In 1724, Bach amplified the scoring of the Weimar cantata *Gleichwie der Regen und Schnee vom Himmel fällt* (BWV 18) with a pair of recorders that double Violas 1 and 2 of the original instrumentation at the upper octave. While the violas, tuned to the high Chorton pitch standard inherited from the original version, play in G minor, the recorders play in A. The wind parts thus involved transposition to both a new register and a new key, not to mention a new clef; Bach eased his copyist's task by writing out the opening bars of each part as a guide.[9] In the 1740s, Bach prepared a version of the cantata *Liebster Gott, wenn werd ich sterben* (BWV 8) that transposed the work from E major to D. Although he wrote

on the *custos* at the end of the preceding system remains intact, and I would think the sharp directly before the first note of m. 14—rather thickly squeezed in but not crossed out—the later addition).

9. For a facsimile of the second recorder part, see NBA I/7 (*Kantaten zu den Sonntagen Septuagesimae und Sexagesimae*), ed. Werner Neumann, p. vi. For details of the copying—including information on the preparation of a further such transposed part—cf. ibid., KB, 105; on the date of the performance, see Alfred Dürr, *Zur Chronologie der Leipziger Vokalwerke Johann Sebastian Bachs*, 2nd edition, Musikwissenschaftliche Arbeiten 26 (Kassel: Bärenreiter, 1976), 9 and 64.

most of the instrumental parts himself, the three that he did not all show autograph title, clef, and signatures.[10]

I do not mean to imply that the entry of initial clefs by Bach inevitably denotes transposition; indeed, the unfigured continuo part of BWV 1067 offers a useful reminder on this very point.[11] Nevertheless, in light of the other examples just considered, we

10. See NBA I/23 (*Kantaten zum 16. und 17. Sonntag nach Trinitatis*), ed. Helmuth Osthoff, KB, 65; in the viola part, Bach wrote the first four bars of music, as well. For the date, see Kobayashi, "Zur Chronologie der Spätwerke Johann Sebastian Bachs," 55. The practice continued right up to the end of Bach's life; see the discussions of Johann Christoph Bach's motet *Lieber Herr Gott, wecke uns auf* in Hans-Joachim Schulze, *Studien zur Bach-Überlieferung im 18. Jahrhundert* (Leipzig: Edition Peters, 1984), 179, and, more fully, Daniel R. Melamed, *J. S. Bach and the German Motet* (Cambridge: Cambridge University Press, 1995), 182–84, and Christoph Wolff, *Johann Sebastian Bach: The Learned Musician* (New York: W. W. Norton, 2000), 451–53.

11. Compare Table 1 with the discussion on pp. 2–3 and, particularly, n. 8. Bach provided a similar non-transposing guide, again with autograph heading, for the same copyist in a violoncello part to Locatelli's Concerto Grosso op. 1 no. 8; cf. Hans-Joachim Schulze, *Katalog der Sammlung Manfred Gorke: Bachiana und andere Handschriften und Drucke des 18. und frühen 19. Jahrhunderts*, Bibliographische Veröffentlichungen der Musikbibliothek der Stadt Leipzig 8 (Leipzig: Musikbibliothek der Stadt Leipzig, 1977), 15 and plate 2 (p. 170), as well as Kobayashi, "Zur Chronologie der Spätwerke Johann Sebastian Bachs," 29, and Kirsten Beißwenger, *Johann Sebastian Bachs Notenbibliothek*, Catalogus Musicus 13 (Kassel: Bärenreiter, 1992), 120–21 and 302–3. Perhaps this means that the scribe simply lacked experience—something we might infer as well from the way he apes the different clef forms of his model in BWV 1067, where Bourée 2, Menuet, and Battinerie all adopt the variant design of the figured continuo part (cf. n. 6; the Locatelli part shows this latter clef throughout, which suggests that it became the scribe's normal form after BWV 1067—a point, incidentally, that helps resolve the problem of chronology raised in Kobayashi "Zur Chronologie der Spätwerke Johann Sebastian Bachs," 29 and 42). Yet with the Locatelli concerto, the title and incipit still indicate a deviation from the copyist's source, as the new part depends on one meant for violone (see Beißwenger, *Johann Sebastian Bachs Notenbibliothek*, 120 n. 47). Much the same applies to the one further example of a nontransposing incipit from this period known to me, the violone part of the Harpsichord Concerto in A Major (BWV 1055, ST 127), which presents a reduced version of an older part labeled simply "Continuo"; see principally the illustrations in Christoph Wolff, "Bach's Leipzig Chamber Music," *Early Music* 13 (1985): 165–75, at 171–72, or as reprinted in idem, *Bach: Essays on his Life and Music* (Cambridge, Mass.: Harvard University Press, 1991), 223–38, at 232–33, as well as the discussion in Werner Breig, "Zur Werkgeschichte von Johann Sebastian Bachs Cembalokonzert in A-Dur BWV 1055," in *The Harpsichord and its Repertoire: Proceedings of the International Harpsichord Symposium Utrecht 1990*, ed. Pieter Dirksen (Utrecht: STIMU, Foundation for Historical Performance Practice, 1992), 187–215, at 205–6. So the situation with the unfigured continuo of BWV 1067 remains unclear; could Bach at first have meant Anon. N 3 to copy the part directly from the parent manuscript of the ouverture while he himself figured the other part? In any event, whether or not this scribe needed Bach's assistance to get parts started, the same does not apply to the scribe of Violin 1, who also wrote the recorder parts to the Harpsichord Concerto in F Major (BWV 1057), ST 129; cf. NBA VII/1, KB, 35 n. 3, and Kobayashi, "Zur Chronologie der Spätwerke Johann Sebastian Bachs," 29):

may well suspect that Bach and his assistants took the music of BWV 1067 from a source notated in a key other than B minor. It does not, in fact, take much effort both to confirm this suspicion and to establish the key in question. As we see from Table 2, the violin and continuo parts show a number of corrections and other features suggestive of transposition up a tone.[12] The autograph flute part, although it does not contain any clearly altered notes, reveals an unusually high percentage of accidentals placed squarely a degree too low, as well as a single appoggiatura written as f#" instead of g" and two more on a" that lack their leger lines.[13] As the viola part could in principle

both of these show the copyist's hand from the very start, including the part titles, the designation "Concerto" in the second recorder, and the fairly uncommon French violin clefs. We should note, however, that this scribe too evidently gained some experience between his work on BWV 1067 and BWV 1057; see Section IV, which begins on p. 43.

12. Unless otherwise indicated, references to the continuo always denote no. 6. Obviously, not every one of the examples necessarily indicates transposition; taken together, however, they hardly seem to allow any other interpretation. In Violin 1, a rather heavily written accidental at m. 144 of the first movement looks at first sight like a flat changed to a natural; closer inspection reveals, however, that Anon. N 2 in fact started to draw the symbol as a natural sign, although further details of the correction remain unclear. NBA VII/1, KB, 50, reports a revision up a tone—from g to a—in the continuo at m. 179 of the opening movement; but whereas the greatly thickened note head does not allow an unambiguous reading, the length of the stem sooner implies a revision down from b, and the unfigured part reads b at this juncture. I should note, in any event, the presence of several revisions down a tone elsewhere in the continuo—Ouverture, m. 106 (nn. 2 and 3); Bourée 1, mm. 15 and 20 (last note in both); and Battinerie, mm. 28 and 29 (last note in both)—and an even greater number in Violin 2: Ouverture, mm. 17 (note 8), 36 (last note), 51 (last note), 88 (last note; see the Postscript, and esp. n. 184), and 196 (first note); and Rondeaux, mm. 17 (first note) and 36 (note 4). In this part, too, the first note of m. 176 in the opening movement, although not altered in any way, lies unusually high. At least some of these corrections—in the continuo, those in Bourée 1; in Violin 2, those at mm. 17, 36, and 51 of the first movement—seem to show the scribe simply maintaining a pattern set in the previous notes or writing the linearly more "obvious" note rather than the one actually called for. Taken as a whole, however, the corrections in the violin could equally suggest that this part derived from a model in soprano clef, a notation commonly used in French ouvertures—not least those of Johann Bernhard Bach, which J. S. Bach performed at Leipzig (cf. Section II); if so, we could see these downward revisions, too, as indications of an A-minor source. Beyond these problem cases and the musical changes referred to in nn. 8 and 17 (see also Table 6 in the Postscript), the parts contain other corrections, as well, but most of these at least do not seem liable to shed any significant light on the copying history of ST 154; for a possible exception, see n. 16.

13. For the accidentals, see Ouverture, mm. 5, 25, 48, 58, 70, 73, 74, 76, 102, 109, 122, 152, 153, 158, 163, 167, and 205; Rondeaux, mm. 15, 32, and 39; Sarabande, mm. 12 and 14; Bourée 1, m. 11; Double, m. 10; Menuet, mm. 6 and 17; and Battinerie, mm. 12, 13, 14, and 15. For the appoggiatura written a tone low, see m. 213 of the opening movement; for those missing leger lines, see m. 198 of the same movement, m. 36 of the Rondeaux and m. 18 of the Menuet. Readers can readily check

derive from its lost predecessor in the set—and hence from a model in B minor—we might not so readily think to investigate it for hints of transposition. Yet not only does it contain its own share of misplaced accidentals, but the composer unmistakably thickened the first note in m. 9 of the Sarabande upward from a low start, and he just as unmistakably wrote the third note of m. 8 in the Battinerie as e' rather than the f♯' that the harmony demands.[14]

A final, if more circuitous, pointer arises from a detail in the second-violin part. At m. 15 of the Menuet, the first note as entered by the copyist read g'; as Plate 1 makes clear, someone other than the copyist, no doubt Bach himself, carefully excised it and replaced it with the same note an octave lower.[15] With the original reading restored, the string and continuo parts descend to exactly one tone above the lowest limit of the violin, viola, and cello: A, D, and D, respectively. By all indications, therefore, Bach and his copyists drew the parts to the ouverture from a source—more likely than not a score—that presented the music in A minor.[16]

What can we establish about the A-minor version of the ouverture other than its key? As Bach entrusted the string and continuo parts of the transposed version to copyists, we

---

some of these observations through the facsimile reproductions in NBA VII/1: viii–ix—although I should note that these show what look like many thickened notes not in fact altered in the manuscript. While more than a few things can, of course, affect the placement of accidentals—meaning that not every low accidental may indicate transposition—the overall picture does seem clear.

14. Accidentals placed a tone too low occur at mm. 35, 38, and 118 of the opening movement, and m. 21 of Bourée 1; the part as a whole contains far fewer accidentals than that of the flute. On m. 8 in the Battinerie, cf. NBA VII/1, KB, 55.

15. My thanks to Werner Breig for valuable discussion on this matter. The correction, although visible even in photocopy, goes unreported in NBA VII/1, KB, 55.

16. A curious double-stop at the end of the Menuet in Violin 2—f♯'–b', which the close of every other movement indicates should have read f♯' alone (cf. NBA VII/1, KB, 55)—could imply a parent score that compressed the final measures of Violin 1 and Violin 2 into a single staff. A score would seem indicated as well by the fact that none of the parts lower than Violin 1 contains movement titles in the scribe's hand; that Violin 1 alone contains a scribal *piano* at the start of Bourée 1 or m. 18 of the Battinerie (although cf. n. 103), where the entire ensemble would reduce its volume; and that Bach inserted virtually all of the performance indications, including the continuo figuring, in the parts that he did not copy himself (see the Postscript, and esp. n. 188). Further evidence of a score model possibly comes from m. 208 of the first movement, where the first note of Violin 2 originally read a' rather than e' with a preceding tie (cf. NB VII/1, KB 50), perhaps a sign that the scribe's eye wandered to the viola part, or that his exemplar compressed Violin 2 and Viola onto one staff; in this instance, however, the difference in rhythmic values—underscored by the dot of augmentation directly after the a' in Violin 2 as first entered—makes the argument harder to sustain. Whatever the case, the strong possibility remains that an "original score" of the B-minor ouverture—in the sense of an autograph composing document—never existed. But see the Postscript, p. 73.

Table 2. Indications of transposition in the violin and continuo parts of вwv 1067

Movement, Measure Ouverture	Part	Remark
8	Violin 2	Last note originally a step lower
15	Violin 2	5th note originally a step lower
47	Violin 2	3rd note begun a step lower
51	Continuo	4th note originally a step lower
81	Violin 2	4th note originally a step lower
97	Violin 1	Last note begun too low[a]
109	Violin 2	2nd note probably begun a step lower
146	Violin 2	2nd note begun a step lower
158	Violin 2	Whole note placed considerably too low
208	Violin 2	2nd note possibly begun a step lower
Rondeaux		
11	Violin 2	Last note originally a step lower
18	Continuo	1st note originally a step lower (?)
40	Violin 1	Second half of measure stemmed as if a step lower (cf. m. 42, as well as Ouverture, m. 88)
Sarabande		
23	Violin 2	3rd note originally a step lower
27	Continuo	1st note originally a step lower
30	Violin 2	Last note originally a step lower
Bourèe 1		
19	Violin 2	2nd note originally a step lower
Menuet		
1	Violin 1	4th note originally a step lower
24	Violin 2	Lower note of double-stop (cf. n. 16) originally a step lower
Battinerie		
2	Violin 1	Notes 2–3 stemmed as if a step lower
12	Continuo	2nd note placed considerably too low
39	Continuo	Last note placed considerably too low

[a] Misreported in NBA VII/1, KB, 49, as a correction down a tone; but while the g' understood by Besseler and Grüß as the final reading, and correspondingly printed in the score, does not create an unacceptable dissonance, it both breaks the upper pedal held from m. 96 to m. 98 and produces a needless doubling of the seventh.

Plate 1. ST 154, Violin 2, f. 2ᵛ and Menuet, mm. 14–16

can assume that they simply followed their model verbatim; in this respect, therefore, the ouverture as we know it—barring any revisions made after copying—would not have differed at all from its predecessor.[17] But the solo part, clearly, did not go unchanged, otherwise Bach would hardly have gone to the trouble of writing it out himself.[18] This fact obviously raises the question of the original solo instrument. We can safely eliminate the flute. Even if we could imagine the solo line written in a way that would avoid the present occurrences of d'—the lowest note on the Baroque flute—in both solo and tutti passages, the overall tessitura would still put the music uncomfortably low for the instrument;[19] and in any event, it seems hardly credible that Bach would have written a concerted work with so little regard for the properties of its featured instrument that he ultimately felt obliged to transpose it to a more favorable key.[20]

The next obvious candidate, the oboe, also appears unlikely. Here, the lower end of the range poses no problem, although a single d#' in a tutti section would have had to read differently—c#', as it would have become in A minor, does not lie within the capabilities of the Baroque oboe.[21] But the particular sorts of agility required have no parallel in any oboe music of Bach's that I know; and we would have to imagine both

17. See, however, the Postscript, and esp. n. 229. If, as Godt ("Politics, Patriotism, and a Polonaise") contends, the immediate precursor of BWV 1067 had a different succession of movements, we might surely expect to find some trace of this in the parts themselves, such as autograph indications analogous to those by which Bach evidently signaled transposition. Among revisions actually present, the most important, aside from the octave shift in Violin 2 just described, affect the first movement: the measures in the continuo line already referred to in n. 8, and two passages in Violin 2 discussed in NBA VII/1, KB, 35, and also in the Postscript. The lost viola part at these latter places presumably underwent a similar correction; for other possible readings from this part, see n. 183. For Bach's other revisions to the parts, see the Postscript.

18. The various discrepancies between Flute and Violin 1 in unison passages—most notably at m. 36 of the first movement (cf. Example 11 and the discussion there)—no doubt reflect changes undertaken by Bach while copying the solo part; presumably, the original readings matched those still preserved in Violin 1.

19. In solo passages, d' occurs in m. 78 of the Ouverture and m. 4 (first and second endings) of the Double to the Polonoise; in tutti, d#' occurs in unison with Violin 1 in m. 115 of the Ouverture.

20. Admittedly, the prominent flute part of BWV 8 appears as originally composed to have lain beyond the capabilities of the instrument or player at Bach's disposal, occasioning several revisions in the original performing materials and ultimately, it would seem, leading to the downward transposition discussed earlier; cf. NBA I/23, KB, 76–78. But since the composing score no longer survives, several details of the process remain unclear; and in any event, considerations not present in a purely instrumental piece would no doubt have contributed to the initial choice of key. On the problem of whether some of the Violin Concerto in A Minor (BWV 1041) may have originated in a different key, see n. 52.

21. Although c#' occurs even in some autograph oboe parts, its presence would clearly seem a matter of oversight rather than intention, as Bach's numerous and well-known efforts to avoid the note make plain.

the Polonoise and its Double in a form more radically different from the surviving one than the neat script of the autograph flute part gives us any warrant for doing.[22]

Barring the remote possibility of an instrument in another register entirely, only one alternative remains: the violin. Admittedly, the part does not seem to contain much distinctively idiomatic writing; even the most determined attempt to locate opportunities for multiple stops comes up empty, and places where Bach might have exploited the lowest string prove almost as hard to find.[23] But the relative absence of display may reflect conventions specific to the genre. Johann Adolph Scheibe, for one, drew a distinction between the relatively modest demands on the solo instrument in what he called the *Concertouverture* and the greater virtuosity typical of the Italianate concerto.[24] An ouverture in G minor for violin and strings by Bach's cousin Johann Bernhard Bach illustrates the point nicely: here, too, the solo part lacks any multiple stops, and it descends beyond the d' string in only a single measure.[25] Within BWV 1067 itself, moreover, a passage heard initially within a few bars of the first solo entry effectively removes any doubts about the original instrumentation; as Example 1 makes clear, Bach surely conceived mm. 60–62 and 124–26 of the opening movement with a play on the open e" string in mind.[26] Should this evidence not suffice, I might draw attention to a detail in the autograph flute part noticed by Klaus Hofmann after I sent him an early draft of this paper: even a fleeting glance at Plate 2 reveals unmistakably that Bach fashioned the first letter of the heading "Traversiere" out of a "V."[27]

22. I would take the difficulties with the Double as self-evident. As for the Polonoise, unless Bach had the oboe pause here he would have had to have it double the first violin at the unison rather than the upper octave used by the flute; but unison doubling would have led to trouble in the final measure, which goes out of the oboe's range.

23. Following the readings of the existing version, the solo part would have gone below the d' string only in the places listed in n. 19, and, presumably, at mm. 4 and 12 of the Polonoise—the doubling of the melody at the upper octave surely belongs exclusively to the flute adaptation. One could also imagine mm. 94³–102¹ of the Ouverture and much of the Double an octave lower.

24. Johann Adolph Scheibe, *Critischer Musikus*, 2nd ed. (Leipzig, 1745; reprint, Hildesheim: Georg Olms, 1970), 672, quoted by Hans-Werner Boresch, *Besetzung und Instrumentation: Studien zur kompositorischen Praxis Johann Sebastian Bachs*, Bochumer Arbeiten zur Musikwissenschaft 1 (Kassel: Bärenreiter, 1993), 78.

25. The violin reaches b♭ and g with the last two notes of the Loire; cf. Hans Bergmann, ed., *Johann Bernhard Bach: Ouverture in g, Carus-Verlag 40.527/01* (Stuttgart: Carus, 1988).

26. Nor does it take much fantasy to perceive a chain of arpeggios shimmering behind mm. 152–62 of the same movement; mm. 133–37³ and 139⁴–143¹ could offer further possibilities for open-string work, although not without some shuffling of octave positions. But neither these speculations nor those in n. 23 can count as evidence in the way the measures cited in the main text surely do.

27. My thanks to Dr. Hofmann for spotting what I so embarrassingly missed. In principle, of course, the correction could mean only that Bach started work with the intention of copying one of the

Ex. 1. Ouverture in B Minor (BWV 1067), mvt. 1, mm. 59–63 (= mm. 123–27),
flute, transposed.

II

My reference in the last paragraph to the G-minor ouverture of Johann Bernhard
Bach had more behind it than simply the wish to lend substance to some comments
of Scheibe. Johann Bernhard's ouverture owes its survival to J. S. Bach: it comes down
to us through a set of parts written largely in his hand.[28] Andreas Glöckner has dated
their copying to 1730; some of the evidence he presents could even suggest limiting
the time frame to the later months of the year.[29] Bach clearly intended the materi-

two ensemble violin parts; but given the availability of scribes for this task, the weakness of such an
explanation would appear self-evident.

28. For details of the parts (ST 320), see Bergmann, *Johann Bernhard Bach: Ouverture in g*, 3; or
Beißwenger, *Johann Sebastian Bachs Notenbibliothek*, 234–35. Bach's parts clearly served as the model
for the only other known source of Johann Bernhard's ouverture, a score copied by the Berlin musicians Hering in the second half of the eighteenth century (P 291; cf. Beißwenger, 117; Bergmann,
Johann Bernhard Bach: Ouverture in g, 3).

29. For the assignment of the parts to 1730, see Andreas Glöckner, "Neuerkenntnisse zu Johann
Sebastian Bachs Aufführungskalender zwischen 1729 und 1735," BJ 67 (1981): 43–75, at 48–49.
C. P. E. Bach's script in the continuo part stands particularly close to his flute and oboe parts for the
cantata *Gott der Herr ist Sonn und Schild* (BWV 79), which Glöckner can fix to October 31, 1730; see
"Neuerkenntnisse zu Johann Sebastian Bachs Aufführungskalender," 49, as well as the excerpt from
the continuo part reproduced in Bergmann, *Johann Bernhard Bach: Ouverture in g*, 4. A late-summer
or autumn dating for ST 320 might also seem indicated by the appearance in the second Violin 1
part of the scribe Anon. Vb, whose scarce contributions to Bach's performance materials include one
of the parts for the cantata *Jauchzet Gott in allen Landen* (BWV 51), a work supposedly performed on
September 17, 1730 (cf. Glöckner, 48 n. 9, and Dürr, *Zur Chronologie der Leipziger Vokalwerke Johann
Sebastian Bachs*, 101 and 154). But whereas the parts to BWV 51 all but certainly belong to 1730 (cf.
Dürr, 53–54, 101), their dating within the year rests on a liturgical assignment that Bach seems to
have added only as an afterthought, possibly in conjunction with a later performance; see Klaus Hof-
mann, "Johann Sebastian Bachs Kantate 'Jauchzet Gott in allen Landen' BWV 51: Überlegungen zu
Entstehung und ursprünglicher Bestimmung," BJ 75 (1989): 43–54, at 44 n. 7, although not without
reference to the qualifying comments in Hans-Joachim Schulze, ed., *Johann Sebastian Bach: Jauchzet
Gott in allen Landen (BWV 51). Faksimile nach dem Partiturautograph der Deutschen Staatsbibliothek Berlin*
(Leipzig: Zentralantiquariat der Deutschen demokratischen Republik, 1988), 3–4.

Plate 2. ST 154, Traversiere, f. 1ʳ and Ouverture, Heading

als for use with the student Collegium Musicum that he had taken charge of in the spring of 1729.[30]

Given this background, we may find it more than a little provocative that the opening movement of Johann Bernhard's ouverture displays a striking number of resemblances to the first movement of BWV 1067, both in the overall rhythmic character of the quick fugal sections and in specific details of structure and thematic material.[31] Example 2a, for instance, shows a passage heard near the end of the fast section in Johann Bernhard's piece; its alternation of rocking solo figures and tutti interjections inevitably recalls the passage from BWV 1067 reproduced in Example 2b. A still more telling relationship links Example 3a and Example 3b, which show the end of the first tutti and start of the first solo episode in their respective movements. Like his cousin, J. S. Bach has the solo instrument enter running, so to speak. This itself might not seem especially noteworthy; much the same thing occurs in the first movement of Bach's ouverture BWV 1068, as well.[32] But what happens next brings home the connection. Johann Bernhard's solo lead-in settles onto a decorated version of his fugal theme; as we see from Example 3c, J. S. Bach, while disguising his tracks more art-

30. On Bach and the Collegium, see Werner Neumann, "Das 'Bachische Collegium Musicum,'" BJ 47 (1960): 5–27, esp. 5–6, or the reprint in *Johann Sebastian Bach*, ed. Walter Blankenburg, Wege der Forschung 170 (Darmstadt: Wissenschaftliche Buchgesellschaft, 1970), 384–415, esp. 384–85. Leipzig parts from 1730 survive for two further ouvertures of Johann Bernhard Bach (ST 318 and 319; cf. Glöckner, "Neuerkenntnisse, zu Johann Sebastian Bachs Aufführungskalender," 66, and Beißwenger, *Johann Sebastian Bachs Notenbibliothek*, 232–33), and J. S. Bach presumably had materials prepared for two more—a fourth still extant in a copy by Hering, and a fifth listed along with the others in the catalogue of C. P. E. Bach's estate (cf. ibid., 105–6, and Hermann Max's preface to Bergmann, *Johann Bernhard Bach: Ouverture in g*, esp. 2 n. 4, where he raises the possibility of identifying the fifth ouverture with BWV 1070—an ingenious suggestion, but one I think contradicted by the style of the music; cf. also NBA VII/1, KB, 11).

31. Karl Geiringer already offered a summary reference to these resemblances in his article "Artistic Interrelationships of the Bachs," *Musical Quarterly* 36 (1950): 363–74, at 366–67, and noted them once more in passing in his and Irene Geiringer's book *The Bach Family: Seven Generations of Creative Genius* (London: Allen & Unwin, 1954), 101. Hermann Max has also spoken of "manifold . . . similarities between the ouvertures of both cousins . . ., most strikingly between Bernhard's . . . ouverture with concerted violin and that in B minor of Johann Sebastian"; see Bergmann, *Johann Bernhard Bach: Ouverture in g*, 2.

32. I should point out, however, that I have not discovered this feature in the—admittedly relatively few—works that I have managed to examine among the ouvertures of Telemann, Graupner, and other composers referred to elsewhere (see esp. nn. 42 and 49). The parallel between BWV 1068 and Johann Bernhard's ouverture, incidentally, reinforces the suspicion that Bach meant the first-violin part of BWV 1068 for a single player; cf. Rifkin, "Besetzung—Entstehung—Überlieferung," 174–76.

fully, does exactly the same.[33] Given these similarities, it hardly comes as a surprise to find a more than passing degree of kinship between the fugal themes themselves, with their upbeat kickoffs, prominent syncopation, and descent from the fifth degree—something readers comparing Example 4a with Example 4b can hardly fail to notice.[34] The initial rhythmic gesture, moreover, not only cements the bond between the two themes but also sets BWV 1067 apart in a small but significant respect from the rest of Bach's French ouvertures. In every one of these, the subject of the central fugal section begins within the final cadential measure of the introduction, creating a rather breathless transition of the sort illustrated in Examples 5a–c; in BWV 1067 and Johann Bernhard's ouverture, on the other hand, the upbeat start produces the more relaxed cadential articulation illustrated in Examples 5d–e.[35] The difference even extends to note values of the music that follows: although BWV 1067 and the work of Bach's cousin have the same time signature as BWV 1066 and 1068, they move in values twice as large—eighths, quarters, and halves instead of sixteenths, eighths, and quarters.

I would think these examples go beyond the similarities that we might expect to find in any two works adopting the format of the concerted ouverture. At minimum, we may take them as further—if supererogatory—confirmation that Bach composed the original version of BWV 1067 for violin. But the affinities between BWV 1067 and Johann Bernhard's ouverture may have other implications, as well. In 1961, Martin Bernstein challenged the longstanding tradition that assigned the B-minor ouverture to Coethen.[36] The demands on the soloist, he observed, greatly exceed anything we can infer about the capabilities of the flute players there; and "Kast and von Dadelsen

33. Compare, too, the counterpoint of the solo line and first violin with the harmonization of the fugue subject in mm. 107–10 and 175–78.

34. For more on these themes, see pp. 27–28.

35. For a convenient list of all Bach's pieces in the style of the French ouverture, see Matthew Dirst, "Bach's French Overtures and the Politics of Overdotting," *Early Music* 25 (1997): 35–45, at 38. Upbeat fugal starts and a pause on the last chord of the introduction occur with some frequency in Telemann's ouvertures; cf. the thematic catalogue in Adolf Hoffmann, *Die Orchestersuiten Georg Philipp Telemanns* TWV 55, *mit thematisch-bibliographischem Werkverzeichnis* (Wolfenbüttel: Möseler, 1969), 79–183; or, slightly less informative in this regard, 3: 89–250.

36. For an extreme manifestation of this tradition, see the critical report to NBA VII/1, which—although published in 1967—begins its chapter on the chronology of the ouvertures with the unqualified assertion that "the material used in Köthen no longer exists" (12, similarly 7).

Ex. 2. *a*, Johann Bernhard Bach, Ouverture in G Minor, mvt. 1, mm. 137–58
(figuring omitted).

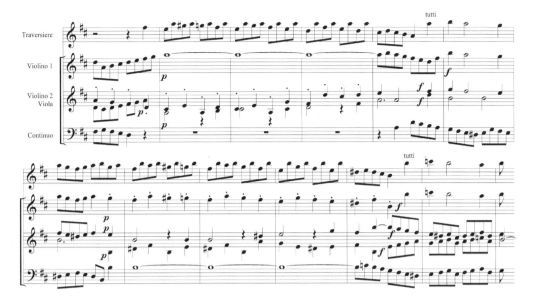

Ex. 2. *b*, Ouverture in B Minor (BWV 1067), mvt. 1, mm. 133–44 (figuring omitted).

Ex. 3. *a*, Johann Bernhard Bach, Ouverture in G Minor, mvt. 1, mm. 44–50
(figuring omitted).

Ex. 3. *b*, Ouverture in B Minor (BWV 1067), mvt. 1, mm. 53–59 (figuring omitted).

Ex. 3. *c*, Ouverture in B Minor (ʙᴡᴠ 1067), mvt. 1, fugal theme compared with
mm. 55–59, flute.

Ex. 4. *a*, Johann Bernhard Bach, Ouverture in G Minor, mvt. 1, fugal theme.
b, Ouverture in B Minor (ʙᴡᴠ 1067), mvt. 1, fugal theme.

Ex. 5. *a*, J. S. Bach, Ouverture in C Major (ʙᴡᴠ 1066), mvt. 1, mm. 15–16
(strings only; first ending, figuring omitted).
b, J. S. Bach, Ouverture in D Major (ʙᴡᴠ 1068), mvt. 1, mm. 23–24
(strings only; first ending, figuring omitted).
c, J. S. Bach, Ouverture in D Major (ʙᴡᴠ 1069), mvt. 1, mm. 23–24
(strings only; first ending, figuring omitted).

Ex. 5. *d*, Johann Bernhard Bach, Ouverture in G Minor, mvt. 1, mm. 17–18
(first ending, figuring omitted).
e, J. S. Bach, Ouverture in B Minor (bwv 1067), mvt. 1, mm. 19–20
(strings only; first ending, figuring omitted).

agree that the few autograph parts . . . show Bach's late hand, no earlier than 1735." The ouverture, he concluded, "is certainly not an early work, copied late."[37] Although the critical report to the edition of the ouvertures in the nba passed over these remarks in silence, by 1979, Hans-Joachim Schulze—who also does not mention Bernstein—could write that "according to the present state of knowledge the orchestral suite counts as a late work."[38] Six years after that, Christoph Wolff drove home the point with an argument that in effect recapitulates and extends the considerations first brought into play by Bernstein:

37. See the panel report "Bach Problems," in *International Musicological Society: Report of the Eighth Congress New York 1961*, ed. Jan LaRue, 2 vols. (Kassel: Bärenreiter, 1961–62), 2:127–31, at 127; also in German translation as "Bach-Probleme" in Blankenburg, ed., *Johann Sebastian Bach*, 416–24, at 417. The remarks on Bach's script—now superseded by Kobayashi, "Zur Chronologie der Spätwerke Johann Sebastian Bachs" (cf. n. 7)—depend on Paul Kast, *Die Bach-Handschriften der Berliner Staatsbibliothek*, Tübinger Bach-Studien 2/3 (Trossingen: Hohner, 1958), 76, and Georg von Dadelsen, *Beiträge zur Chronologie der Werke Johann Sebastian Bachs*, Tübinger Bach-Studien, 4/5 (Trossingen: Hohner, 1958), 113.

38. See Hans-Joachim Schulze, "Johann Sebastian Bachs Konzerte—Fragen der Überlieferung und Chronologie," in *Bach-Studien 6: Beiträge zum Konzertschaffen Johann Sebastian Bachs*, ed. Peter Ahnsehl, Karl Heller, and Hans-Joachim Schulze (Leipzig: veb Breitkopf & Härtel, 1981), 9–26, at 10; the volume contains the proceedings of a colloquium held at Rostock in May 1979. See also n. 117.

A comparison of the flute parts of the fifth Brandenburg Concerto . . . and BWV 1067 demonstrates immediately that there are worlds between them, but not merely on technical grounds. There is no indication that Bach experimented in Cöthen with hybrid forms combining the idea of a suite with that of a concerto. . . . The conflation of genres in BWV 1067 seems to reflect a trend characteristic of Bach's compositional concerns in the later 1730s, namely that of presenting unprecedented and often daring approaches to musical genres of a rather conventional nature. . . . Apart from this general overview, various features of this intricate, polyphonic score—namely, a fine balance between dense and transparent textures, rhythmic refinement and penetrating use of dissonance and consonance, especially in the *Grave* [*sic*] of the *Ouverture*—show a degree of sophistication without equal in any earlier period of Bach's compositional life.[39]

Wolff's synthesis of instrumental, source-critical, and stylistic evidence has, for all practical purposes, crystallized the present consensus on the dating of BWV 1067.[40] As we now see, however, the subject hides a complication previously unsuspected. On the one hand, we can affirm the late origin of the B-minor ouverture: by every indication, the parts document the actual creation of the piece, not merely its copying. But with the revelation that the music had already existed in an earlier version, the question of chronology shifts to a different plane; and here, it would seem, we have even less to go on than before. The flute writing no longer has any bearing on the issue. Nor, on reflection, does the "conflation of genres" remain compelling. Although we cannot demonstrate that Bach in Coethen did indeed essay "hybrid forms combining the idea of a suite with that of a concerto," he certainly pursued other hybrids during this period—witness, if nothing else, the remarkable synthesis of fugue, concerto grosso,

39. Wolff, "Bach's Leipzig Chamber Music," 174–75 (*Bach: Essays on his Life and Music*, 37); Wolff, too, makes no reference to Bernstein. Bernstein's point about the flute writing, incidentally, had already received strong, if indirect, support from the remarks on Coethen flute parts in Robert L. Marshall, "J. S. Bach's Compositions for Solo Flute: A Reconsideration of Their Authenticity and Chronology," *Journal of the American Musicological Society* 32 (1979): 463–98, at 477–78, or as reprinted, with revisions and slightly altered title, in idem, *The Music of Johann Sebastian Bach: The Sources, The Style, The Significance* (New York: Schirmer Books, 1989), 201–25 and 316–28, at 211 and 321; these observations seem to have gone unnoticed by Ardal Powell, who challenges Bernstein's assessment of the flutists at Coethen in "Bach and the Flute: The Players, the Instruments, the Music" (with David Lasocki), *Early Music* 23 (1995): 9–29, at 10. In light of the present article, of course, the issue becomes moot.

40. Martin Geck, "Köthen oder Leipzig? Zur Datierung der nur in Leipziger Quellen erhaltenen Orchesterwerke Johann Sebastian Bachs," *Die Musikforschung* 47 (1994): 17–24, at 21–22, has raised some pertinent questions about the details of Wolff's case but seems inclined nevertheless to accept a late origin for the ouverture.

and solo concerto in the final movement of the Fourth Brandenburg Concerto (BWV 1049).[41] Even if Scheibe may have coined the name *Concertouverture*, moreover, his treatment of it as a phenomenon evidently requiring no special introduction alerts us to the fact that the specific generic combination encountered in BWV 1067 reflects a tradition established at least a decade before Wolff's "later 1730s." Telemann wrote a substantial number of ouvertures with concerted solo parts, many of which—as Table 3 makes clear—survive in manuscripts from the 1720s.[42] Whether or not Bach knew

41. Cf. Carl Dahlhaus, "Bachs konzertante Fugen," BJ 42 (1955): 45–72, esp. 45–50 and 58–59. Malcolm Boyd has also taken issue with Wolff's formulation, citing the First Brandenburg Concerto as counterevidence; see in his review of Wolff, "Bach: Essays on His Life and Music," *Music & Letters* 73 (1992): 446–47, at 447. I think, however, that this misreads the spirit, if not the letter, of Wolff's remark: surely, Wolff meant the infusion of concerted elements into the suite rather than the other way around.

42. Independently of me, Geck ("Köthen oder Leipzig," 21) has also drawn attention to Telemann's concerted ouvertures. The roster of pieces in Table 3 depends essentially on the two catalogues cited in n. 35, collated with Horst Büttner, *Das Konzert in den Orchestersuiten Georg Philipp Telemanns. Mit einer Bibliographie der Orchestersuiten*, Veröffentlichungen der Niedersächsischen Musikgesellschaft 1 (Wolfenbüttel: Georg-Kallmeyer-Verlag, 1935), 80–81; and Ortrun Landmann, *Die Telemann-Quellen der Sächsischen Landesbibliothek: Handschriften und zeitgenössische Druckausgaben seiner Werke*, Studien und Materialien zur Musikgeschichte Dresdens 4 (Dresden: Sächsische Landesbibliothek, 1983); see also, more recently, the list in Steven Zohn, "Telemann, Georg Philipp," in *The New Grove Dictionary of Music and Musicians*, ed. Stanley Sadie, 2nd edition, 29 vols. (London: Macmillan, 2001), 25:199–232, at 224–25. As I have not inspected every one of these ouvertures—at the time of writing most did not have modern editions—I cannot assert without qualification that each puts its solo instrument to featured use in the opening movement, as does BWV 1067; but of those that I have examined (TWV 55: D 6, D 8, Es 2, and a 2 in editions cited by Hoffmann, *Die Orchestersuiten Georg Philipp Telemanns*; D 7 as ed. Ian Payne, Severinus Urtext Telemann Edition 33; A 8 as ed. Willi Maertens, Breitkopf & Härtels Partitur-Bibliothek 3949), only TWV 55: D 7 does not do so. Apart from two pieces—D 8, for trumpet, and A 8, for violin—all of the solo concerted ouvertures survive at the Hessische Landesbibliothek in Darmstadt or the Sächsische Landesbibliothek in Dresden. The datings in the table for the former group of sources come from a study of the papers in Darmstadt manuscripts carried out by Brian Stewart in the summer of 1988 and communicated by him to a circle of colleagues later that year ("Penn State Telemann-Nachrichten," October 18, 1988); my thanks to Dr. Stewart for sharing this information. Dates for the Dresden manuscripts rely essentially on Landmann, *Die Telemann-Quellen der Sächsischen Landesbibliothek*; Manfred Fechner, *Studien zur Dresdner Überlieferung von Instrumentalkonzerten deutscher Komponisten des 18. Jahrhunderts: Die Dresdner Konzert-Manuskripte von Georg Philipp Telemann, Johann David Heinichen, Johann Georg Pisendel, Johann Friedrich Fasch, Gottfried Heinrich Stölzel und Johann Gottlieb Graun. Untersuchungen an den Quellen und thematischer Katalog*, Dresdner Studien zur Musikwissenschaft 2 (Laaber: Laaber, 1999), 134–35; and Steven Zohn, "Music Paper at the Dresden Court and the Chronology of Telemann's Instrumental Music," in *Puzzles in Paper: Concepts in Historical Watermarks. Essays from the International Conference on the History, Function and Study of Watermarks, Roanoke, Virginia*, ed. Daniel W. Mosser, Michael Saffle, and

Table 3. Telemann's concerted ouvertures with one solo instrument

TWV 55 No.	Solo Instrument	Source[a]	Date
C 2	Oboe	Darmstadt 1034/25	?
D 6	Viola da gamba	Darmstadt 1034/18	ca. 1730
D 7	Trumpet	Darmstadt 1034/43	ca. 1725
D 8	Trumpet	Darmstadt 1034/48	1724
		Schwerin 5399/6	?
D 14	Violin	Darmstadt 1034/81	1726–30
		Dresden 2392-O-5	ca. 1725?[b]
Es 2	Recorder	Darmstadt 1034/14	ca. 1725–30
E 2	Oboe d'amore	Darmstadt 1034/96	1736 and later
E 3	Violin	Dresden 2392-O-7	ca. 1740
e 10	Flute/oboe	Dresden 2392-O-23	ca. 1725?[b]
F 13	Violin	Dresden 2392-O-10[a]/10[b]	ca. 1730?/ca. 1725–33[c]
G 6	Violin	Darmstadt 1034/47	ca. 1725
G 7	Violin	Darmstadt 1034/63	1726–30
G 13	Violin	Dresden 2392-O-2 (lost)	—
g 7	Violin	Dresden 2392-O-16[a]/16[b]	ca. 1730?/ca. 1725–33[c]
A 4	Violin	Darmstadt 1034/34	ca. 1725
A 7	Violin	Dresden 2392-O-6	1741
A 8	Violin	Schwerin 5399/7	Before 1730[d]
a 2	Recorder	Darmstadt 1034/5	1725
h 4	Violin	Dresden 2392-O-15	Before 1741

[a] Darmstadt = Hessische Landes- und Hochschulbibliothek, Mus. Ms.

Dresden = Sächsische Landesbibliothek, Mus.

Schwerin = Wissenschaftliche Allgemeinbibliothek, Mus.

[b] See n. 42 above.

[c] Cf. Landmann, *Die Telemann-Quellen der Sächsischen Landesbibliothek*, 145–46 and 151, as well as Fechner, *Studieren zur Dresder Überlieferung*, 66–91, and the information on two of the papers used by the scribe of 2392-O-10a and 16a in Zohn, "Music Paper," 158 (no. 18) and 161 (no. 325).

[d] Date from Hoffmann, *Die Orchestersuiten Georg Philipp Telemanns*, 19.

Ernest W. Sullivan II (New Castle, Del.: Oak Knoll Press; London: British Library, 2000), 125–68, which Prof. Zohn kindly made available to me before its publication and has had the further kindness to discuss since. I must differ, however, over the dates he proposes for the manuscripts of TWV 55 D 14 and e 10 (ibid., 148–49). Zohn describes the watermark of these sources—his no. 10, a posthorn in a crowned shield—as "probably a variant of the very similar Watermark 9," which he assigns to the decade 1710–20; noting further that it "appears only in manuscripts copied by Pisendel and an unidentified Dresden copyist" apparently "active in the years around 1720," he suggests that its use falls roughly between 1712, when Pisendel arrived in Dresden, and 1720. But the two watermarks

these pieces, Johann Bernhard's ouverture leaves no doubt that by 1730 at the latest, he had become familiar with the type they represent.[43]

This said, however, I do not mean to suggest that we should push the original version of BWV 1067 all the way back to Coethen. Surprising as it may seem, even Spitta never came right out and claimed that Bach composed this music there, although he did strongly imply it; and I can think of no real grounds on which such a case might rest.[44] Whatever qualifications I may have expressed about some of Wolff's observations, moreover, intuition tells me that his point about texture, rhythmic refinement, and dissonance treatment still holds. Certainly, a considerable distance separates the B-minor ouverture from its generic siblings in Bach's output—a distance already apparent in our discussion of Example 5, and more palpable still in the broader span of music that leads to the measures considered there. In the three other ensemble ouvertures, the harmonic motion of the opening section remains confined almost exclusively to the level of the half note and whole note; BWV 1067, on the other hand, moves predominantly in quarters or halves, expanding to dotted halves only rarely and to whole

---

do not resemble one another so closely as to encourage the assumption of contemporaneous, or even directly successive, use, nor can I find any source among the manuscripts cited by Zohn that mixes them; and our only real chronological anchor for the unidentified copyist—or rather copyists: the hands listed by Fechner as "P(1)" and "P(2)" (*Studien zur Dresdner Überlieferung*, 134–35 and 194–97) all but certainly belong to different scribes—comes from a paper type that neither Fechner nor Zohn can trace before the mid-1720s (see Zohn, "Music Paper," 142–43 and 167 n. 34, and Fechner, *Studien*, 60–63, 128–29, 212–13, and 229).

43. The impetus for Johann Bernhard's ouverture no doubt came directly from Telemann: the obituary for J. S. Bach of 1754 explicitly states that Johann Bernhard "wrote many fine *ouvertures* in the manner of Telemann"; see NBR, 298, and, for the original text, BDOK 3:81 (no. 666). Johann Bernhard and Telemann both worked at Eisenach in the years 1708–12; given what we shall see about the dating of Telemann's concerted ouvertures, however, I would hesitate in attributing Johann Bernhard's work too directly to contacts in this period.

44. Spitta placed his discussion of BWV 1067 and Bach's three other ensemble ouvertures within the division of his biography devoted to the Coethen period, and he characterized the script of the autograph parts in BWV 1067 as conforming to Bach's "Köthen type"; see Philipp Spitta, *Johann Sebastian Bach*, 2 vols. (Leipzig: Breitkopf & Härtel, 1873–80; reprint, Wiesbaden: Breitkopf & Härtel, 1979), 1:748–51 and 833–34. On the other hand, in a discussion of the Leipzig Collegium Musicum, he goes no further than to write (ibid., 2:616), "Which of his orchestral partitas he composed afresh for the musical society cannot be said with certainty. It is very probable that Bach already involved himself with this form in Köthen as well." Godt, "Politics, Patriotism, and a Polonaise," 617, writes that Forkel "assigned all four orchestral suites to Bach's work in Cöthen." But Godt appears to have credited Forkel with the work list appended to the English-language version of his biography; cf. Johann Nikolaus Forkel, *Johann Sebastian Bach: His Life, Art, and Work*, trans. Charles Sanford Terry (London: Constable and Company, 1920; reprint, New York: Da Capo Press, 1970), 158.

notes only at the approach to the first and second endings.[45] The imitative treatment of the outer voices in the first two measures has no parallel elsewhere, nor does the neatly articulated bipartite structure created by the firm cadence on the mediant and restatement of the opening material at m. 11.[46] Even the harmonic language reveals a significant difference: BWV 1067 relies considerably less on suspension figurations, considerably more on overt fifth progressions than do BWV 1066, 1068, or 1069.[47] BWV 1066 and 1069 without question date from Bach's Coethen years, and BWV 1068 most likely comes from Coethen, as well.[48] As it hardly seems possible that BWV 1067

45. The opening section of BWV 1066 moves in quarters only when approaching the cadence at m. 15; BWV 1068 quickens the harmonic pace at mm. 6 and 9, BWV 1069 at mm. 7–8, 16, and 22.

46. Although BWV 1069 restates the opening music on the dominant at m. 9, the approach through a half-cadence, with an attendant reinterpretion of the harmony, effectively vitiates the articulation; a similarly masked return of opening material occurs in the keyboard ouverture BWV 831 at m. 13.

47. If we discount "ornamental" dominants such as those in BWV 1068, mm. 3, 6, 13, and 15, or BWV 1069, mm. 4, 7, 12, and 14, the basses in these two ouvertures move all but entirely by step. BWV 1066 has a clear string of dominant bass patterns in mm. 3–6 but otherwise remains prevailingly linear in its progressions.

48. The use of music from BWV 1069 in the cantata *Unser Mund sei voll Lachens* (BWV 110) means that at least an early version of the ouverture must have existed by December 25, 1725. BWV 1066 survives in a non-original set of parts copied late in 1724 or early 1725 but clearly dependent on another set written at an earlier time; see Joshua Rifkin "Verlorene Quellen, verlorene Werke—Miszellen zu Bachs Instrumentalkomposition," in BOW 59–77, at 59–61 and 69–71. Although the surviving original parts for BWV 1068 date from 1731, the work itself—in a version without trumpets, drums, and oboes—probably has an earlier origin. See Rifkin, "Besetzung—Entstehung—Überlieferung," as well as Werner Breig, "The Instrumental Music," in *The Cambridge Companion to Bach*, ed. John Butt (Cambridge: Cambridge University Press, 1997), 123–35, at 135, and BOM, 261–64; the objections registered by Hans-Joachim Schulze, "Probleme der Werkchronologie bei Johann Sebastian Bach," in *"Die Zeit, die Tag und Jahre macht": Zur Chronologie des Schaffens von Johann Sebastian Bach. Bericht über das Internationale wissenschaftliche Colloquium aus Anlaß des 80. Geburtstag von Alfred Dürr, Göttingen, 13.-15. März 1998*, ed. Martin Staehelin, Abhandlungen der Akademie der Wissenschaften zu Göttingen, Philologisch-Historische Klasse, Folge 3, 240 (Göttingen: Vandenhoeck & Ruprecht, 2001), 11–20, at 19, confuse—not for the first time—personal and aesthetic bias with historical evidence, and wind up implying as well that the Preludio to the E-major violin partita (BWV 1006) does not exist. The stylistic distance between BWV 1067 and BWV 1068—which we can see further exemplified in their rhythmic profiles as defined by the shortest consistent note values (see Dirst, "Bach's French Overtures and the Politics of Overdotting," 36, 38)—strengthens the case for assigning the latter piece to Coethen rather than Leipzig, as do similarities between BWV 1068 and BWV 1069 observed in Joshua Rifkin, "Klangpracht und Stilauffassung: Zu den Trompeten der Ouvertüre BWV 1069," in *Bach und die Stile: Bericht über das 2. Dortmunder Bach-Symposion 1998*, ed. Martin Geck and Klaus Hofmann, Dortmunder Bach-Forschungen 2 (Dortmund: Klangfarben Musikverlag, 1999), 327–45, at 339 and 344 n. 47. The rhythmic profile of BWV 1067, I might note, separates it not only from BWV

would have preceded the other three ouvertures in origin, its stylistic differences from them surely argue for placing it in Leipzig.

We may also wonder if the concerted ouverture as a genre itself existed much before the end of Bach's Coethen period. By all available indications, Telemann's pieces of this sort had no real predecessors—the rather sparse literature on the history of the ouverture does not identify any, nor have I succeeded in doing so on my own.[49] Sig-

---

1068 but from Bach's other ouvertures or movements in French ouverture style, as well (cf. Dirst, "Bach's French Overtures," 38); significantly, all but two of these pieces—the opening chorus of the cantata (BWV 97) *In allen meinen Taten* and Variatio 16 of the Goldberg Variations (BWV 988)—date from before 1730. While the introductory sections of both the keyboard variation and the cantata movement exhibit the slower harmonic motion that I associate with Bach's earlier practice, the former merely follows the pattern of the underlying theme in this regard, and the latter resembles the opening of BWV 1067 in its reliance on root motion in the bass and its tendency towards imitative treatment of the outer voices.

49. I sought to trace the early history of the ouverture as an autonomous multimovement instrumental genre in an unpublished paper, "Bach und die 'Französische Art': Gedanken zu den Ouvertüren BWV 1066–1069," read at the Dortmund Bach-Symposion of January 1998; readers will find essential portions summarized in BOM, 252–55. I would also draw attention to the useful recent discussions in Christoph Großpietsch, *Graupners Ouvertüren und Tafelmusiken: Studien zur Darmstädter Hofmusik und thematischer Katalog*, Beiträge zur mittelrheinischen Musikgeschichte, 32 (Mainz: Schott, 1994), 39–50, and Ewan West, "The Ouvertüren of Johann Friedrich Fasch in Historical Context," in *Fasch und die Musik im Europa des 18. Jahrhunderts: Bericht der Internationalen Wissenschaftlichen Konferenz 1993 zu den III. Internationalen Fasch-Festtagen in Zerbst*, ed. Guido Bimberg and Rüdiger Pfeiffer, Fasch-Studien 4 (Weimar: Böhlau, 1995), 97–111. The incorporation of concerted elements requires further investigation. Although trio episodes for oboes and bassoon enjoyed long familiarity in dance movements of operas or even some early German ouverture suites, their first appearance known to me in a French ouverture proper—if still not within a fully worked-out structure or ritornello-like repetitions—does not occur until Agostino Steffani's *Orlando generoso* (1691) and *La liberta contenta*, or *Alcibiade* (1693); cf. Colin Timms, *Polymath of the Baroque: Agostino Steffani and His Music* (Oxford: Oxford University Press, 2003), 202–5, and Hugo Riemann, ed., *Agostino Steffani: Ausgewählte Werke, Dritter Teil*, Denkmäler der Tonkunst in Bayern 23 (Leipzig: Breitkopf & Hrtel, 1912), 100–102 and 117–19. Among multimovement instrumental works not drawn from operas, I find both the first comparable use of wind trios and the first truly concerto-like formal layouts in the ouverture movements of Francesco Venturini's *Concerti da camera* of ca. 1714; my thanks to Michael Talbot for bringing this publication to my attention and sharing transcriptions of its contents with me. David Schulenberg reminds me that Handel uses solo instruments in the ouvertures to three of his early operas: *Agrippina* (1708–9) has passages for both oboe and violin; *Rinaldo* (1711) includes solos for recorder, oboe, and violin; and *Il pastor fido* (1712) contains extensive dialogues between oboe and orchestra. But even leaving aside the fact that only this last piece features a single instrument throughout, none of them shows a regular concerted layout of the sort encountered in Venturini or later composers. So far as I can tell from the discussion and thematic catalogue in Großpietsch, *Graupners Ouvertüren und Tafelmusiken*, 85–118 and 301–86, as well as the remarks in Colin Lawson, "Graupner and the Chalumeau," *Early*

nificantly, few of the works listed in Table 3 have a source that seems likely to predate even the mid-1720s, and none of the admittedly few Telemann ouvertures we can definitely trace to the previous decade puts a solo instrument to concerted use.[50]

All in all, then, Coethen would seem to remain a distant possibility for even the first version of BWV 1067. The best guess for its creation would put it in the later

---

Music 11 (1983): 209–16, at 214, and Michael Jappe, "Zur Viola d'Amore in Darmstadt zur Zeit Christoph Graupners," in *Basler Studien zur Interpretation alter Musik*, ed. Veronika Gutmann, Forum Musicologicum 2 (Winterthur: Amadeus, 1980), 169–79, at 170, Graupner wrote only a single concerted ouverture in the sense understood here, the work with recorder catalogued by Großpietsch as F 5 and ed. Klaus Hofmann, Nagels Musik-Archiv 220 (Kassel: Nagel, 1983); otherwise, he used concerted instruments only in occasional dance movements but rarely if ever in the opening movement, nor consistently throughout an entire work. None of his ouvertures, moreover, survives in a source dating from much before 1730 (cf. Großpietsch, *Graupners Ouvertüren und Tafelmusiken*, 283–93, although also n. 68). Graupner's Darmstadt colleague Johann Samuel Endler composed no true concerted ouvertures; see Joanna Cobb Biermann, "Johann Samuel Endlers Orchestersuiten und suitenähnliche Werke," BOW 341–53, at 344–45. Among other contemporaries of Telemann, Fasch seems to have left only one piece of the type, FWV: A 1—and this, according to Rüdiger Pfeiffer, *Verzeichnis der Werke von Johann Friedrich Fasch (FWV): Kleine Ausgabe*, Dokumente und Materialien zur Musikgeschichte des Bezirks Magdeburg 1 (Magdeburg: Rat des Bezirkes Magedburg, 1988), 63–64, dates from ca. 1740. Großpietsch (*Graupners Ouvertüren und Tafelmusiken*, 85–86) mentions the existence of four *Ouverture alla Concerto* with solo violin by J. C. Hertel among the manuscripts of the Hessische Landes- und Hochschulbibliothek destroyed in World War II; but given Hertel's dates (1699–1754), these surely did not precede Telemann's contributions to the genre. I can locate only a single further concerted ouverture, thanks to the now-defunct RISM online database of music manuscripts after 1600: a work for violin and strings by Johann Martin Doemming, dated "Limburg, 1733," in Rheda, Fürstlich zu Benttheim Tecklenburgische Musikbibliothek, Ms. 172.

50. A keyboard transcription of the ouverture TWV 55: Es 4 figures among the earlier entries of the Andreas Bach Book (MBLPZ III.8.4), for which Robert Hill appears to suggest a date of ca. 1710 or even earlier; cf. *Keyboard Music from the Andreas Bach Book and the Möller Manuscript*, ed. Robert Hill, Harvard Publications in Music 16 (Cambridge, Mass.: Department of Music, Harvard University, 1991), xxii–xxiii, although in the light of idem, "Johann Sebastian Bach's Toccata in G Major BWV 916/1: A Reception of Giuseppe Torelli's Concerto Form," in *Das Frühwerk Johann Sebastian Bachs: Kolloquium veranstaltet vom Institut für Musikwissenschaft der Universität Rostock 11.–13. September 1990*, ed. Karl Heller and Hans-Joachim Schulze (Cologne: Studio-Verlag, 1995), 162–75, at 165 n. 10. Stewart (see n. 42), can date Darmstadt sources for the following pieces from TWV 55 to before 1720: D 16 (1716), d 1 (1716), e 6 (1716), and G 5 (1715 or earlier); in addition, he provides early dates for the two smaller-scale ouvertures formerly numbered among TWV 55 but now listed as TWV 44: 7 (= TWV 55: F 4; 1714 or earlier) and 44: 8 (=TWV 55: F 5; 1714–16). Hoffmann, *Die Orchestersuiten Georg Philipp Telemanns*, suggests placing TWV 55: c 3, Es 5, e 6, G 11, g 3, and B 2 before 1716, as treble-bass versions of their dance movements all appear as partitas in Telemann's *Kleine Cammer-Music*, published that year.

1720s or early 1730s.[51] At this point, the full relevance of Johann Bernhard Bach's ouverture becomes clear. For it would seem an obvious, if unprovable, inference that J. S. Bach composed what eventually became BWV 1067 under the direct impact of his cousin's composition; and in all probability, this means at the time he performed Johann Bernhard's ouverture and had its music "in his ear." With due caution, therefore, we might assign the original version of BWV 1067—the lost Ouverture in A Minor for Violin and Strings—to the latter part of 1730 or to 1731. Thus situated, the ouverture becomes one of a flush of instrumental pieces traceable to the year or so immediately following Bach's accession to the directorship of the Leipzig Collegium Musicum; in particular, it now lies close to a series of works featuring the violin—the D-major ouverture BWV 1068 and, above all, the A-minor concerto BWV 1041 and the double concerto BWV 1043.[52] To these compositions, moreover, we may surely

51. See also n. 62.

52. Cf. Wolff, "Bach's Leipzig Chamber Music," 169 and 175 (*Essays*, 228–29); on the dates, see Glöckner, "Neuerkenntnisse zu Johann Sebastian Bachs Aufführungskalender," 49–51, 71. As already mentioned (see n. 48), the version of BWV 1068 prepared in 1731 more likely than not represented an instrumental amplification of an earlier composition. Geck, "Köthen oder Leipzig," 19, emphasizes that BWV 1041, too, might have a pre-history. Dietrich Kilian argues in NBA VII/3 (*Konzerte für Violine, für zwei Violinen, für Cembalo, Flöte und Violine*), ed. Dietrich Kilian, KB, 17, that the distribution of hands in the original parts (ST 145), as well as the relationship between these parts and the autograph of the later harpsichord arrangement BWV 1058, could suggest that Bach took the first two movements of BWV 1041 from a source other than that used for the last movement; according to Kilian, too, copying errors in the second-violin part could suggest that the first two movements originally stood in G minor. But while the possibility that Bach assembled the concerto from disparate sources would indeed seem considerable, the hypothesis of transposition from G minor appears less promising, as all three nonautograph parts—Violin 1, Violin 2, and Continuo (from movement 1, m. 141)—reach their lowest note at least once in the first two movements: Violin 1 hits g in mvt. 1, m. 130, Violin 2 in mvt. 2, m. 16, and the continuo descends to C at m. 166 of the first movement and the very last note of the second. Whatever the internal history of BWV 1041, I would suggest that its outer movements at least cannot have originated at great distance from BWV 1043—the Leipzig origin of which, I might note, Geck does not bring into question. The first movements of both works share a formal property unique in Bach's concertos. Not only do they close without a full restatement of the opening ritornello—a characteristic found otherwise only in the da capo movements BWV 1042/1, 1049/1, 1050/3, 1053/1, and 1053/3, and the fugal finale of BWV 1049—but they reach their conclusion by "sliding into" a ritornello epilogue that itself lies embedded in the transposition of an earlier passage: in BWV 1041/1, mm. 146^2–171 equal mm. 59^2–84, which in turn present an expanded version of mm. 8^2–24 (with exact correspondence in the last six measures; hence mm. 19–24 = 79–84 = 166–171); for BWV 1043, see Hans Eppstein, "Zum Formproblem bei Johann Sebastian Bach," in *Bach-Studien 5: Eine Sammlung von Aufsätzen*, ed. Rudolf Eller and Hans-Joachim Schulze (Leipzig: VEB Breitkopf & Härtel, 1975), 29–42, esp. 32–34 and Table 1 (p. 40), and also Jeanne Swack, "Modular Structure

add the G-minor sonata BWV 1030a, which also shares thematic affinities to Johann Bernhard's ouverture.[53] Spitta long ago called attention to the resemblance between the fugue subject of the ouverture and the opening theme of the sonata.[54] Hans-Joachim Schulze subsequently extended Spitta's observation with the suggestion that the sonata theme—in the B-minor transposition of the final version with flute, BWV 1030—in turn served as an inspiration for the fugal theme in BWV 1067.[55] Schulze, however, proceeded on assumptions concerning the origin of BWV 1067 that we can now recognize as invalid; we can more simply understand BWV 1030a and the earliest version of BWV 1067 as part of a chronologically contiguous nexus centered around the G-minor ouverture of Johann Bernhard Bach—all the more so as Klaus Hofmann has pointed to other considerations suggesting a date around 1730 for BWV 1030a, as well.[56]

---

and the Recognition of Ritornello in Bach's Brandenburg Concertos," BP 4 (1999), 33–53. In the last movements, too, the closing ritornello, while stated fully, blurs the demarcation between solo and tutti through the absence of a strongly articulated preceding cadence—again, a trait not often found elsewhere; the nearest parallels occur in the outer movements of BWV 1060. I see no reason to think, incidentally, that BWV 1043 ever existed in the form of a trio sonata, as recently argued in BOM, 108–9. The assertion that the solo parts and continuo can stand entirely on their own (ibid., 109) overlooks not only the observation on the slow movement in Rifkin, "Verlorene Quellen, verlorene Werke," 71–72 n. 28, but also mm. 31, 35, 70, and 74 of the first movement, where the solo violins lack the necessary third supplied by the ripieno. In these measures and their immediate predecessors, moreover, the hypothesis makes it hard to explain the juxtaposition of rather neutral melodic material in the soloists with citations of the head motive in the ripieno; nor can it very well account for mm. 80–85 and 199–122 of the last movement, in which Bach not only manages to insert a derivative of the principle theme as an accompanying figure but in so doing keeps the prevailing rhythmic motion from breaking down, or for the rhythmic and motivic lacuna that the absence of the ripieno would create at m. 4 of the same movement.

53. On the scoring of BWV 1030a, see Klaus Hofmann, "Auf der Suche nach der verlorenen Urfassung: Diskurs zur Vorgeschichte der Sonate in h-Moll für Querflöte und obligates Cembalo von Johann Sebastian Bach," BJ 84 (1998): 31–59 (with a "critical postscript" by Hans Eppstein, 60–62), esp. 50–53; my thanks to Dr. Hofmann for sharing this work with me before its publication.

54. See Spitta, *Johann Sebastian Bach*, 1:26.

55. See Schulze, "Johann Sebastian Bachs Konzerte," 22 n. 7. Peter Schleuning, *Johann Sebastian Bachs "Kunst der Fuge": Ideologien—Entstehung—Analyse* (Munich: Deutscher Taschenbuchverlag; Kassel: Bärenreiter, 1993), 88, and Klaus Hofmann ("Auf der Suche nach der verlorenen Urfassung," 55–56 n. 67) have both located further themes similar to that of BWV 1030, but these seem less likely to have any real significance.

56. See Hofmann, "Auf der Suche nach der verlorenen Urfassung," 53–57, esp. 55–56 n. 67.

III

Placing the original form of BWV 1067 in 1730 or not long afterward exposes two further relationships of interest not only for themselves but because they reinforce, and possibly even tighten, the chronological net around the ouverture. The Polonoise marks one of the rare appearances in Bach's output of the sharply rhythmic version of this dance sometimes considered under the rubric "mazurka."[57] His other instrumental polonaises—those in the First Brandenburg Concerto (BWV 1046) and the Sixth French Suite (BWV 817)—belong to a more smoothly rhythmicized type lacking the distinctive dotted figure at the start of the first measure; so, too, do most of his vocal movements based upon the polonaise.[58] Provocatively, we can discern something like a small flurry of interest in the mazurka on Bach's part right at the end of the 1720s. His first known reference to the idiom occurs in a piece composed in January 1729, the aria "Großer Herzog, alles Wissen" from the secular cantata *O! angenehme Melodei* (BWV 210a).[59]

57. Cf. Doris Finke-Hecklinger, *Tanzcharaktere in Johann Sebastian Bachs Vokalmusik*, Tübinger Bach-Studien 6 (Trossingen: Hohner, 1970), 54 and 58. Although the musical example ibid., 54, seems to imply that the term "mazurka" already appears in Sperontes' *Singende Muse an der Pleiße*, the various editions of the original in fact label the piece in question "Tempo di Pol." or "Air en Polon."; see *Denkmäler deutscher Tonkunst* 35/36 (Leipzig: Breitkopf & Härtel, 1909; repr. Graz: Akademische Verlags-Anstalt, 1968): xxx, 27. According to Jan Steszeswki, "Mazurka," in *Die Musik in Geschichte und Gegenwart*, 2nd ed., ed. Ludwig Finscher (Kassel: Bärenreiter and Stuttgart: Mezler, 1994), *Sachteil*, vol. 3, cols. 1699–1708, at 1699, the term "mazurka" does not actually surface until 1753.

58. Cf. Finke-Hecklinger, *Tanzcharaktere in Johann Sebastian Bachs Vokalmusik*, 54–58, and Meredith Little and Natalie Jenne, *Dance and the Music of J. S. Bach* (Bloomington: Indiana University Press, 1991), 194–98. The Polonaise in BWV 817 bears the title "Menuet. Poloinese" in one of its sources; see NBA V/8 (*Die sechs französischen Suiten BWV 812–817, 814a, 815a. Zwei Suiten a-Moll, Es-Dur BWV 818, 819, 818a, 819a*), ed. Alfred Dürr, KB, 153, and David Schulenberg, *The Keyboard Music of J. S. Bach* (New York: Schirmer Books, 1992), 274.

59. For the date, dedicatee, and text of BWV 210a, see Hildegard Tiggemann, "Unbekannte Textdrucke zu drei Gelegenheitskantaten J. S. Bachs," BJ 80 (1994): 7–22, at 7–9 and 11–14; Bach subsequently reused the music of "Großer Herzog" in the secular cantata *Angenehmes Wiederau* (BWV 30a) as well as in further variants of BWV 210a and its final version, *O! holder Tag, erwünschte Zeit* (BWV 210); (cf. p. 50 and nn. 101 and 119). Werner Neumann, "Johann Sebastian Bachs 'Rittergutskantaten' BWV 30a und 212," BJ 58 (1972): 76–90, at 80, and Klaus Häfner, *Aspekte des Parodieverfahrens bei Johann Sebastian Bach: Beiträge zur Wiederentdeckung verschollener Vokalwerke*, Neue Heidelberger Studien zur Musikwissenschaft 12 (Laaber: Laaber, 1987), 97–106 and 566, have raised the possibility that he actually composed the aria as early as 1725 to a text beginning "Großer Flemming, dein Vergnügen," which appears under the inscription "Aria tempo di Polonaise" in a serenata by Picander. I see no reason to believe this, however. Both the A and the B section of "Großer Herzog" begin with a pair of rhyming lines, and Bach's setting clearly reflects this feature. Picander's text, on the other hand, leaves its first line unrhymed, resulting in a shorter A section; attempting to match it with Bach's music

Later that year, he exploited the same rhythmic hallmarks in the aria "Aufgeblasne Hitze," the penultimate solo movement of *Der Streit zwischen Phoebus und Pan* (BWV 201).[60] Beyond these two pieces, we might also point to the G-minor polonaise (BWV anh. 119) copied no later than 1732 by Anna Magdalena Bach in the second of her two music books and all but identical with a composition found in a manuscript dated "Leipzig, 1729."[61] After this, the mazurka remains absent from Bach's music until the aria "Fünfzig Taler bares Geld" in the Peasant Cantata (BWV 212) of 1742. Its return here, of course, warns us against relying too strongly on the Polonoise of BWV 1067 as a chronological indicator; but one cannot deny that the movement would seem more at home around 1730 than at a much later date.[62]

(cf. the examples in Häfner, 100–102) leads both to an unidiomatic repetition and to a discrepancy in prosody between the A and B sections.

60. "Aufgeblasne Hitze" in effect maps the rhythmic profile of the mazurka onto the harmonic and phraseological model of the *folia*. Just where in 1729 BWV 201 falls remains uncertain; cf. Glöckner, "Neuerkenntnisse zu Johann Sebastian Bachs Aufführungskalender," 47–48, 64, 66, 70, and 73. But Bach surely did not compose it before he took over the Collegium Musicum in the spring of the year.

61. For the concordance, see Karol Hlawicka, "Zur Polonaise g-Moll (BWV anh. 119) aus dem 2. Notenbüchlein für Anna Magdalena Bach," BJ 48 (1961): 58–60. The copy of BWV anh. 119 shows what Georg von Dadelsen calls Anna Magdalena's early script, the transition from which to her later hand he places in the years 1733–34; see Dadelsen, *Bemerkungen zur Handschrift Johann Sebastian Bachs, seiner Familie und seines Kreises*, Tübinger Bach-Studien 1 (Trossingen: Hohner, 1957), 27–37, esp. 33, as well as NBA V/4 (*Die Klavierbüchlein für Anna Magdalena Bach*), ed. Georg von Dadelsen, KB, 70–72, and the facsimile *Johann Sebastian Bach: Klavierbüchlein für Anna Magdalena Bach 1725*, ed. idem (Kassel: Bärenreiter, 1988). But BWV anh. 119 precedes by a good five items—including two in other hands—a series of entries by C. P. E. Bach (BWV anh. 122–25) that Glöckner ("Neuerkenntnisse zu Johann Sebastian Bachs Aufführungskalender," 46–53) assigns to 1732. Even this dating, moreover, may err slightly on the late side, as the various forms of the F-clef in Emanuel's pieces would seem if anything to fall between those of the two cantatas BWV 29 and BWV 70, which date from August 27, 1731, and November 18, 1731, respectively (cf. ibid., 45–46, and especially Table 1, nos. 10 and 11). The quarter-note rests, of a type found in no dated manuscript between BWV 29 and the *Missa* of 1733 (cf. ibid., 46, and Table 1, no. 6), do not argue against this assumption, as Emanuel's contribution to BWV 70 does not include any. With due caution, then, we may narrow the date of BWV anh. 119 to 1729–31.

62. Godt, "Politics, Patriotism, and a Polonaise," 617–22, attempts to set the Polonoise—which he regards as a later addition to the ouverture—in the context of Bach's campaign to win favor from the Saxon-Polish crown in the mid-1730s. Since, as already indicated (cf. n. 17), we have no reason to think that BWV 1067 did not have the present sequence of movements from the start, Godt's interpretation of the Polonoise would lead to a substantially later dating for the entire ouverture than the one advanced here. But the examples cited in the main text surely rob his thesis of any compelling force.

Ex. 6. *a*, Ouverture in B Minor (BWV 1067), Battinerie, mm. 1–8, transposed
(figuring omitted).

Ex. 6. *b*, Scherzo in A Minor (BWV 827/6), mm. 1–7.

Ex. 7. Wilhelm Friedemann Bach (?), Scherzo in E Minor (BWV 844a), mm. 1–5.

The second relationship will require more extensive discussion but may have more powerful consequences. As Example 6 makes clear, the Battinerie—especially when read in its original key—has a close counterpart in the Scherzo of the A-minor keyboard partita (BWV 827). Beyond the common tonality and meter, we may observe a more specific connection in such things as the anacruistic opening built on an ascending tonic arpeggiation in the bass, or the pervasiveness of the snap-like rhythmic figure exposed at the start of the Scherzo and from m. 6 onward in the Battinerie. The names, too, provide a link—surely no one will fail to recognize that both titles mean the same thing in their respective languages. Further evidence of the affinity between the two pieces comes from the scherzo BWV 844a/br ii a 55b, a work attributed in some late sources to J. S. Bach but almost certainly composed by his son Wilhelm Friedemann.[63] More than one scholar has recognized a close similarity between BWV 844a and the scherzo of BWV 827; indeed, David Schulenberg has called the latter work "the probable 'starting point'" for the former.[64] Yet the opening of BWV 844a, reproduced in Example 7, suggests that the E-minor scherzo in fact had a dual parentage, for the nervously syncopated chains and wide melodic leaps of mm. 2–3 unmistakably bring mm. 6–8 of the Battinerie to mind. The same rhythmic gesture confronts us as well in a third scherzo by a composer of the Bach circle, a short piece included by Johann Ludwig Krebs in his *Clavier-Übung* II.[65] As Example 8 makes plain, the beginning shows no particular resemblance to any of the other music just considered; but the final measures of the B section bring us once more into the realm of BWV 827/6, BWV 844a, and the Battinerie.

Bach's use of the title Battinerie presents something of a mystery. Not a single composition labeled "badinerie"—to restore the word to unaccented French—survives in a source dating from much before 1730.[66] As we see from Table 4, the term then makes what looks like a fairly concentrated succession of appearances in three ouvertures by Telemann and two by Graupner.[67] At first sight, this could appear to signal the

63. On the authorship of BWV 844a, see Hartwig Eichberg, "Unechtes unter Bachs Klavierwerken," BJ 61 (1975): 7–49, at 20–28, and Peter Wollny, "Studies in the Music of Wilhelm Friedemann Bach: Sources and Style" (Ph.D. dissertation, Harvard University, 1993), 91–92; the alternate br numbers cited here and elsewhere refer to Wollny's forthcoming *Thematisch-systematisches Verzeichnis der Werke Wilhelm Friedemann Bachs*, Bach-Repertorium 2, as cited in idem, "Bach, Wilhelm Friedemann," in *The New Grove Dictionary of Music and Musicians*, 2nd edition, 2:382–87, at 386.

64. See Schulenberg, *The Keyboard Music of J. S. Bach*, 384, and Eichberg, "Unechtes unter Bachs Klavierwerken," 27–28. Eichberg, however, speculates that the dependency may have run in the opposite direction—a suggestion not terribly plausible in and of itself and weakened both by the observations in Wollny, "Studies in the Music of Wilhelm Friedemann Bach," 91–92, and by the considerations raised in my later discussion of early scherzos.

65. I owe my knowledge of this piece to Andrew Talle, whom I gratefully thank for his assistance. The work appears in *Clavier-Übung | bestehet | in einer nach den heutigen Gout | wohl eingerichteten Svite | . . . | componiret | von | Johann Ludwig Krebs | . . . | Zweyter Theil* (Nuremberg: Johann Ulrich Haffner, n.d.).

66. Erich Schwandt, "Badinage, Badinerie," in *The New Grove Dictionary of Music and Musicians*, ed. Stanley Sadie, 20 vols. (London: Macmillan, 1980), 2:10, reproduced almost unchanged ibid., 2nd ed., 2: 457–58, found no "badineries" at all beyond the last movement of BWV 1067; but see the discussion immediately following.

67. Cf. Großpietsch, *Graupners Ouvertüren und Tafelmusiken*, 234–35, as well as Hoffmann, *Die Orchestersuiten Georg Philipp Telemanns*, 60; I wish to thank Dr. Großpietsch for calling these examples to my attention. Catalogue numbers for Graupner's ouvertures come from the thematic inventory in

Ex. 8. Johann Ludwig Krebs, Scherzo from *Clavier-Ubung* II. *a*,
mm. 1–8. *b*, mm. 25–32.

Table 4. Badineries by Telemann and Graupner

Composer	Title	Key, Meter	Parent Work	Source[a]	Date
Telemann	La Badinerie	F major, $\frac{2}{4}$	Ouverture TWV 55 F 3	Darmstadt 1034/12	ca. 1730
Telemann	La Badinerie italienne	F♯ minor, ¢	Ouverture TWV, 55 fis 1	Darmstadt 1034/52	1729–1730
Telemann	Badinerie	G major, ¢	Ouverture TWV 55 G 8	Darmstadt 1034/68	1738 or later
Graupner	Badinerie	B♭ major, $\frac{2}{4}$	Ouverture B 3	Darmstadt 464/78	ca. 1735–1737
Graupner	Badinerie	B♭ major, $\frac{2}{4}$	Ouverture B 7	Darmstadt 464/20	ca. 1735–1737

[a] Darmstadt = Hessische Landes- und Hochschulbibliothek, ms mus.

emergence of a newly fashionable genre, with predictable repercussions for Bach. Yet caution would seem in order. For one thing, the provenance and chronology of the existing manuscripts suggest that Graupner wrote his badineries in direct response to Telemann's lead; and in any event, Graupner's music seems hardly to have circulated outside his native Darmstadt.[68] Beyond the use of binary form and a lively duple meter, moreover, I find it hard to see any resemblance between the Battinerie of BWV 1067 and the badineries of either Telemann or Graupner. Those that I have managed to examine in their entirety lack the distinctive snap figure. Graupner's examples both start on the downbeat, and while Telemann's have upbeat starts, these belong either to the short quarter-bar variety or echo the simple two-note pickup of the gavotte.[69] It would seem more than likely, then, that Bach wrote his Battinerie without any im-

---

Großpietsch, 301–86. A search through all the ouvertures registered on the RISM online database (cf. n. 49) uncovered no further instance of the badinerie. The title does occur considerably later among the harp and keyboard pieces of Johann Ludwig Köhler's *XXIV. Leichte und angenehme* Galanterie-*Stücke . . . Erster Theil* (Nuremberg: Johann Ulrich Haffner, [1756]); see Mark A. Radice, "The Nature of the *Style galant:* Evidence from the Repertoire," *Musical Quarterly* 83 (1999): 607–47, at 618 and 633. Köhler's badinerie—a copy of which Prof. Radice kindly placed at my disposal—shows no discernible resemblance to Bach's Battinerie.

68. The sources of all five ouvertures originated at Darmstadt during Graupner's tenure there; Hoffmann, *Die Orchestersuiten Georg Philipp Telemanns*, 15, identifies the scribe of TWV 55: F 3 as Johann Samuel Endler, that of TWV 55: fis 1 as Graupner himself. The dates given in Table 4 for the Telemann manuscripts come from Brian Stewart (cf. n. 42); on the date of the Graupner sources—both of them autograph scores—see Großpietsch, *Graupners Ouverturen und Tafelmusiken*, 287–93. Großpietsch suggests that Graupner may have composed many of his ouvertures some time before the preparation of the existing fair copies, but we have no real evidence on the matter one way or the other; see *Graupners Ouvertüren und Tafelmusiken*, 289, as well as "'in Deutschland nicht mehr üblich'?—Suite, Gattung, Zeit, Geschmack in Orchesterwerken Bachs und Graupners," in BOW, 321–28, at 323–24. On the circulation of Graupner's music, we may note that virtually nothing by him survives anywhere but Darmstadt; see the overviews in anon., "Graupner," in *Die Musik in Geschichte und Gegenwart*, 2nd ed., *Personenteil*, vol. 7, cols. 1525–32, at 1527–28, or Andrew D. McCredie, "Graupner, Christoph," in *The New Grove*, 2nd ed., 10:312–14, at 313–14, as well as the observations in Großpietsch, *Grapners Ouvertüren und Tafelmusiken*, 51 and 281.

69. For a complete reproduction of the badinerie from Graupner's ouverture B 3, see Großpietsch, *Graupners Ouvertüren und Tafelmusiken*, 235; for a modern edition of TWV 55: fis 1, see Friedrich Noack, ed., *Georg Philipp Telemann: Musikalische Werke* 10 (*Sechs ausgewählte Ouvertüren für Orchester mit vorwiegend programmatischen Überschriften*) (Kassel: Bärenreiter, 1955), 101–14 (Badinerie: 108–10). For the rest, see the incipits in Großpietsch, 386, and Hoffmann, *Die Orchestersuiten Georg Philipp Telemanns*, 124 and 143. Großpietsch, 232–83, draws attention to a close thematic resemblance between the Bach's Battinerie and the Réjouissance of Graupner's ouverture E 8; the latter piece, however, starts on the downbeat, producing a wholly different metric orientation.

mediate reference to other pieces of similar title. Indeed, given his heavily Teutonic orthography, we may well think that he never even saw the word *badinerie* but only heard it and thus in effect coined it himself—as a Gallic equivalent for *scherzo*.

This reasoning suggests, of course, that Bach composed his scherzo before the Battinerie. But once again, we must proceed carefully. Bach's Scherzo itself has a murky generic background. Although some have proposed that he borrowed the title from Francesco Bonporti's *Inventioni* of 1712, which has three movements so labeled, nothing in Bonporti's music implies even a superficial kinship with the Scherzo of the A-minor Partita.[70] Nor has an obvious antecedent emerged thus far from other quarters.[71] Table 5 lists the few scherzos beyond BWV 827/6, BWV 844a, and Krebs's piece that research has managed to locate in the years separating Bonporti from the later Viennese products of Wagenseil and Haydn.[72] All come from the pens of com-

70. Cf. Schulenberg, *The Keyboard Music of J. S. Bach*, 286 and 419 n. 19, as well as ibid., 407 n. 50, and *Francesco Antonio Bonporti: Invenzioni per violino e basso continuo Opera Decima—1712*, ed. Roger Elmiger and Micheline Mitrani, 2 vols., Collana per la storia della musica nel Trentino 7/1–2 (Trent: Società Filarmonica di Trento—Sezione studi musical trentini, 1983), 1:16–17 and 60, and 2:90–91 and 106–7. For the early history of "scherzo" as a musical designation, see, most fully, Tilden A. Russell, "Minuet, Scherzando, and Scherzo: The Dance Movement in Transition, 1781–1825" (Ph. D. dissertation, University of North Carolina at Chapel Hill, 1983), 30–37; grateful thanks to Prof. Russell for placing his dissertation at my disposal. See also Wolfram Steinbeck, "Scherzo," in *Handwörterbuch der musikalischen Terminologie*, ed. Hans Heinrich Eggebrecht and Albrecht Riethmüller (Wiesbaden: Franz Steiner, 1972–), 13. Auslieferung (Winter 1985–86), 5–7; and idem, "Scherzo," in *Die Musik in Geschichte und Gegenwart*, 2nd ed., *Sachteil*, vol. 8, cols. 1054–63, at 1058.

71. Cf. Russell, "Minuet, Scherzando, and Scherzo," 38–39; but note that Steinbeck ("Scherzo," *Die Musik in Geschichte und Gegenwart*, col. 1058) points to possible links with the "pohlnische Styl" and explicitly describes the snap figure at the start of BWV 827/6 as Polish in rhythm. To Peter Williams, "Is There an Anxiety of Influence Discernible in J. S. Bach's *Clavierübung I?*" in *The Keyboard in Baroque Europe*, ed. Christopher Hogwood (Cambridge: Cambridge University Press, 2003), 140–56, at 143, the very title *scherzo* seems "of questionable aptness."

72. The list of pieces—restricted to single movements or single-movement compositions, and hence excluding collections like Telemann's *Scherzi melodichi* of 1734 (cf. Zohn, "Telemann," 227), the individual items of which have different titles anyway—derives principally from Russell, "Minuet, Scherzando, and Scherzo," 37–38. For the scherzos in Scheuenstuhl's *Clavier-Übung*, Part 2, and Köhler's *Galanterie-Stücke*, see Radice, "The Nature of the *Style galant*," 625 and 633; Prof. Radice kindly furnished me with copies of both works. The scherzos BWV anh. II 134 and 150 survive among a series of musical-clock pieces that oral tradition assigns with little credibility to J. S. Bach. Wollny has identified two members of the group as works of Wilhelm Friedemann Bach (BWV anh. ii 133 = f. 22 = br ii a 63; BWV anh. ii 150 = f. 13/2 and f. 6/2A = br ii a 80), finds another (BWV anh. ii 146 = br ii a 56) in a manuscript very likely devoted wholly to works of Friedemann, and, indeed, credits the entire set to Friedemann—although the basis for the blanket attribution seems less than entirely

posers belonging either to the same generation as Bach or the one immediately following: Johan Agrell, Conrad Friedrich Hurlebusch, Johann Ludwig Köhler, Michael Scheuenstuhl, and perhaps Wilhelm Friedemann Bach. All but one share the same minimal identifying traits as BWV 827/6, BWV 844a, Krebs's scherzo, and the various badineries: duple meter and binary form.[73] In principle, therefore, this entire body of music could spring from a common forebear or set of forebears not yet identified; and on that basis, we could just as well reverse the proposed sequence of Bach's Scherzo and Battinerie. Considering the repercussions that such a move would have for the chronology of the ouverture, we might surely hope to find a way of resolving the impasse. Fortunately, a closer look at the pieces in Table 5 makes such a resolution possible.

Even a casual glance at the table reveals a curious imbalance among the composers represented: Hurlebusch uses the term *scherzo* with a frequency that almost implies a proprietary interest. Given the publication date of his sonatas, the appearance of the snap figure in several of them may not seem especially noteworthy.[74] But the scherzo in the suite that opens Part II of Hurlebusch's *Compositioni musicali* demands closer attention.[75] Unlike the composer's later scherzos—but like BWV 827/6, BWV 844a,

clear; see "Studies in the Music of Wilhelm Friedemann Bach," 98–103, 189–90, 208, 415, and 443. The first of the two pieces credited to Agrell, while catalogued under his name in Joachim Jaenecke, *Die Musikbibliothek des Ludwig Freiherrn von Pretlack (1716–1781)*, Neue musikgeschichtliche Forschungen 8 (Wiesbaden: Breitkopf & Härtel, 1973), 92, very likely does not belong to him; it occurs in a keyboard miscellany written at Darmstadt in 1743 (cf. ibid., 50, 57, 236) among a series of pieces without attribution that follow an "Allegro del Sigr. Agrell" but do not seem to make up a suite. The catalogue number for the Agrell symphony comes from the thematic index by Jeannette Morgenroth Sheerin in *The Symphony, 1720–1840: A Comprehensive Collection of Full Scores in Sixty Volumes*, ser. c, vol. 1 (New York: Garland, 1983), xxxix–xliv; for the date of the manuscript cited in Table 5, see ibid., xli. The table omits the "scherzo" movements of Telemann's late *divertimenti* TWV 50: 22 and 23, as these date from after the period of concern to us here and in any event show no real similarity to any of the pieces from the Bach circle; cf. Zohn, "Telemann," 227.

73. The exception, the Scherzo from the Sonata op. 6 no. 1 of Hurlebusch, stands apart as well in its position as the opening number of a multimovement work.

74. For the duple-meter scherzos among the sonatas, see *Keyboard Sonatas by Conrad Friedrich Hurlebusch (1696–1765)*, ed. Agi Jambor, 2 vols. (Philadelphia: Elkan-Vogel, 1965–66), 1:5, 23, and 27–28, and 2:15, 25, and 34; the snap figure occurs in op. 5 nos. 1 and 4 and op. 6 nos. 3 and 4. Although Hurlebusch obviously could have composed his sonatas considerably earlier, at least some of this music must surely postdate his move to Amsterdam in 1743; see William S. Newman, *The Sonata in the Classic Era*, vol. 2 of *A History of the Sonata Idea*, 2nd ed. (New York: W. W. Norton, 1972), 781.

75. Cf. *Compositioni musicali per il cembalo divise in due parti di Corrado Federigo Hurlebusch, Hamburg (ca. 1735)*, ed. Max Seiffert, Uitgave XXXII der Vereeniging voor Nederlandsche Muziekgeschiedenis

Table 5. Scherzos between Bonporti and Wagenseil (excluding BWV 827/1, 844a, and Krebs)

Composer	Title	Key, Meter	Parent work, medium	Source	Date
Agrell (?)	Scherzo	G major,	—(Suite?), keyboard	SBB MUS. BP 711	1743
Agrell	Scherzo	D major,	Symphony D:135175, orchestra	Uppsala, Universitetsbiblioteket, Instr. mus. i hs. 12:2	before 1748
W. F. Bach (?)	Scherzo (BWV ANH. II 134/ BR II A 64)	G major, $\frac{2}{4}$	—, keyboard (?)	Musical clock, Köthen (anon., attr. orally to J. S. Bach)	ca. 1750?
W. F. Bach (?)	Scherzo (BWV ANH. II 148/ BR II A 78)	G minor, $\frac{6}{8}$	—, keyboard (?)	Musical clock, Köthen (anon., attr. orally to J. S. Bach)	ca. 1750?
Hurlebusch	Scherzo	D major, $\frac{2}{4}$	Suite, keyboard	*Compositioni musicali per il cembalo . . . parte seconda*	1735
Hurlebusch	Scherzo	G major, c	Sonata op. 5, no. 1 (E major), keyboard	*VI Sonate di Cembalo*, op. 5	ca. 1746
Hurlebusch	Scherzo	F major, ¢	Sonata op. 5 no. 3, keyboard	*VI Sonate di Cembalo*, op. 5	ca. 1746
Hurlebusch	Scherzo	G major, c	Sonata op. 5 no. 4, keyboard	*VI Sonate di Cembalo*, op. 5	ca. 1746
Hurlebusch	Scherzo	A minor, $\frac{3}{4}$	Sonata op. 6 no. 1, keyboard	*VI Sonate di Cembalo*, op. 6	ca. 1746
Hurlebusch	Scherzo	G minor, ¢	Sonata op. 6 no. 2, keyboard	*VI Sonate di Cembalo*, op. 6	ca. 1746
Hurlebusch	Scherzo	G major, ¢	Sonata op. 6 no. 3, keyboard	*VI Sonate di Cembalo*, op. 6	ca. 1746
Hurlebusch	Scherzo	B♭ major, ¢	Sonata op. 6 no. 4, keyboard	*VI Sonate di Cembalo*, op. 6	ca. 1746
Köhler	Scherzo	G major, ¢	—, harp or keyboard	*XXIV Leichte und angenehme Galanterie-Stücke*	1756(?)
Scheuenstuhl	Scherzo	G major, $\frac{2}{4}$	—, keyboard	*Gemüths- und Ohr-ergötzende Clavier-Übung . . . IIter. Theil*	1744(?)

and that of Krebs—it uses $\frac{2}{4}$ rather than c or ¢ as its time signature, and as Example 9 makes clear, it cultivates the snap figure almost to the point of obsession.

Although Hurlebusch did not publish the *Compositioni* until the mid-1730s, at least a good portion of its contents originated considerably earlier.[76] As Hans-Joachim Schulze first noticed, two pieces survive in copies by Bach's Leipzig scribe Christian Gottlob Meißner that seem to date from about 1727.[77] Hellmut Federhofer, moreover, has found the suite to which the scherzo belongs in an Austrian manuscript all but surely written before 1725.[78] Since the scribe who made the copy contributed nothing else to the manuscript but an otherwise unknown work by the Viennese court musician Nicola Matteis, Federhofer suggests that the inclusion of the suite reflects the composer's visit to Vienna in 1716–18 and his contacts there with members of the imperial musical establishment.[79]

The early date for the Hurlebusch scherzo and the transmission of his music in

---

(Amsterdam: G. Alsbach & Cie; Leipzig: Breitkopf & Härtel, 1912), 53–54; my thanks to Gregory Butler for providing me with a copy of this volume.

76. The publication itself came in response to an unauthorized, and highly corrupt, edition brought out by the Amsterdam organist Witvogel in 1733 or 1734; cf. BDOK 2:262–63 (no. 373).

77. See Hans-Joachim Schulze, "Johann Sebastian Bach und Christian Gottlob Meißner," BJ 54 (1968): 80–88, at 86–87 (also *Studien zur Bach-Überlieferung im 18. Jahrhundert*, 107). To judge from the C clefs, quarter rests, and eighth rests on a sample page, Meißner's script forms in the Hurlebusch copies (both in SBB Mus. ms. 30 382) fall between those of the cantatas *Ich will den Kreuzstab gerne tragen* (BWV 56), performed October 27, 1726, and *Vergnügte Pleißenstadt* (BWV 216), from June 5, 1728; my thanks to Klaus Hofmann for valuable assistance on this matter.

78. See Hellmut Federhofer, "Unbekannte Kopien von Werken Georg Friedrich Händels und anderer Meister seiner Zeit," in *Festschrift Otto Erich Deutsch zum 80. Geburtstag am 5. September 1963*, ed. Walter Gerstenberg, Jan LaRue, and Wolfgang Rehm (Kassel: Bärenreiter, 1963), 51–65, at 52 and 59–60. The manuscript—Graz, Diözesanarchiv, Bestand St. Lambrecht, Ms. 24—includes contributions by three scribes, the first of whom wrote the Hurlebusch suite; a companion volume written by the third scribe on identical paper, Bestand St. Lambrecht, Ms. 25, carries an ex libris dated 1725 (cf. ibid., 55–56). Ms. 24 labels the Hurlebusch scherzo "Villanela"; whether this represents the composer's original title or a scribal variant remains uncertain. According to Federhofer, the musical readings of the suite also differ from those in the *Compositioni musicali*.

79. See Federhofer, "Unbekannte Kopien," 59; for Hurlebusch in Vienna, see Johann Mattheson, *Grundlage einer Ehren-Pforte* (Hamburg, 1740), new ed. with original pagination ed. Max Schneider (Berlin: Leo Liepmannssohn, 1910; reprint, Kassel: Bärenreiter, 1969), article "Hurlebusch," 120–25, at 121. The possible Viennese connection for Hurlebusch's suite could help explain the curious bifurcation of scherzo transmission, which appears to follow independent courses in Germany and Austria; perhaps the two branches stem from a common root.

Ex. 9. Conrad Friederich Hurlebusch, Scherzo in D Major, mm. 1–18.

Leipzig obviously provoke the question of a possible tie to Bach.[80] This possibility brings us back to the well-known account—published anonymously but unmistakably by C. P. E. Bach—of a meeting between the two composers "of which I was witness":

> Bach once received a visit from Hurlebusch, a clavier player and organist who was then quite famous. The latter was prevailed upon to seat himself at the harpsichord; and what did he play for Bach? A printed minuet with variations. Thereupon Bach played very seriously, in his own style. The visitor, impressed with Bach's politeness and friendly reception, made Bach's children a present of his printed sonatas, so that they might, as he said, study them, although Bach's sons were already able to play pieces of a very different kind.[81]

The narrator does not reveal when this episode took place. As more than a few commentators have emphasized, Hurlebusch published nothing for keyboard before

---

80. Contacts with Hurlebusch or his music, incidentally, might well account for the appearance of the term *scherzo* in Agrell's symphony and in the keyboard piece ascribed to him by Jaenecke (cf. n. 72): Hurlebusch served from 1722 to 1725 as chapel master to the king of Sweden, the brother of Agrell's patron Prince Maximilian of Kassel, and he visited Kassel itself in 1725; Kassel had close dynastic and musical ties, moreover, with Darmstadt, where the manuscript containing the questionable scherzo originated. For Hurlebusch in Sweden and Kassel, see principally Mattheson, *Grundlage einer Ehren-Pforte*, 121–23; for Agrell, Kassel, and Darmstadt, see *The Symphony, 1720–1840*, c/1, pp. xvi–xvii and xxi–xxiv.

81. NBR, 408; for the original, see BDOK 3:443 (no. 927). On the authorship, see principally Dragan Plamenac, "New Light on the Last Years of Carl Philipp Emanuel Bach," *Musical Quarterly* 35 (1949): 565–87, at 575–87, as well as *The Bach Reader: A Life of Johann Sebastian Bach in Letters and Documents*, ed. Hans T. David and Arthur Mendel, rev. ed. (New York: W. W. Norton, 1966), 281 (NBR, 401), and David Schulenberg, "C. P. E. Bach and Handel: A Son of Bach Confronts Music History and Criticism," *Bach* 23, no. 2 (1992): 5–30, at 11.

the *Compositioni*, which appeared in the spring of 1735.[82] Bach served as agent for this collection; thus it would seem plausible to imagine Hurlebusch stopping at his house with a consignment of the volumes, then giving one of the copies to Bach's children. But this reading has its problems. For one thing, Carl Philipp Emanuel left Leipzig for Frankfurt-an-der-Oder at or near the beginning of September 1734, some eight months before the announcement of the *Compositioni* in May 1735.[83] More important, the reference to "children" and "sons"—no doubt meant synonymously—makes little sense in the context of the early 1730s. Wilhelm Friedemann, already older than twenty, moved to Dresden in the spring of 1733; and of Bach's other sons alive at the time, only Gottfried Heinrich, born in 1724, comes into question as a recipient of Hurlebusch's generosity—Johann Gottfried Bernhard, born 1715, would no longer have counted as a "child," and Johann Christoph Friedrich, born 1732, could surely not yet "play pieces of a very different kind." Even if we expand the circle to include Bach's daughters, the picture hardly changes: only Elisabeth Juliana Friderica, born in 1726, would qualify for consideration.

The reference to Bach's sons would fit perfectly, however, in 1726, which Hans-Joachim Schulze has also brought into play as a possible date for the Hurlebusch visit.[84] In this year, Hurlebusch would have encountered Wilhelm Friedemann at the age of fifteen or sixteen, Carl Philipp Emanuel at the age of eleven or twelve, and Johann Gottfried Bernhard at ten or eleven. Indeed, the version of the incident transmitted by Forkel says explicitly that Hurlebusch presented his sonatas to Bach's "eldest sons."[85] Whether Forkel added this information on his own or got it from Philipp Emanuel,

82. See particularly *The Bach Reader*, 457–58, and BDOK 3:444. For the date of the *Compositioni*, as well as Bach's involvement in their distribution, see BDOK 2:256–57 (no. 363) and 262–63 (no. 373).

83. Cf. BDOK 1:235, 2:256–57 (no. 363), and 3:444. Philipp Emanuel enrolled at the University of Frankfurt-an-der-Oder on September 9, 1734.

84. See BDOK 3:444. In his autobiography, Hurlebusch noted that he went to Bayreuth in January 1726 for a stay of two months and from there traveled to Dresden, a route that would have taken him through Leipzig; see Mattheson, *Grundlage einer Ehren-Pforte*, 123. Gregory Butler, *Bach's Clavier-Übung III: The Making of a Print. With a Companion Study of the Canonic Variations on "Vom Himmel Hoch," BWV 769* (Durham, N.C.: Duke University Press, 1990), 4, also considers the possibility of a meeting between Hurlebusch and Bach in 1726 but treats this as a different occasion from the episode reported by C. P. E. Bach.

85. J.[ohann] N.[ikolaus] Forkel, *Ueber Johann Sebastian Bachs Leben, Kunst und Kunstwerke: Für patriotische Verehrer echter musikalischer Kunst* (Leipzig: Hoffmeister und Kühnel [Bureau de Musique], 1802), 46, translation in NBR, 460; Arthur Mendel (in *The Bach Reader*, 457) already emphasized the absence of just such a formulation from Emanuel's report.

or even Wilhelm Friedemann, remains uncertain—no reference to the episode appears, at any rate, in Emanuel's surviving letters to Forkel.[86] But whatever the case, Forkel's account certainly bears out what logic would seem to indicate. Perhaps, then, we should read Philipp Emanuel's reference to "printed" works as a shorthand for compositions that eventually did appear in print.[87]

Needless to say, assigning Hurlebusch's visit to 1726 would make sense as well in regard to Meißner's copies, especially as one of them contains the very set of variations that Hurlebusch played for Bach.[88] The dating also fits neatly—almost too neatly, one could think—with the history of Bach's Scherzo. As copied by the composer into Anna Magdalena's music book of 1725, the A-minor Partita stills lacks this movement; Bach evidently added it for the publication of bwv 827 in the late summer of 1727.[89] Given the entire confluence of circumstances, it seems hard to avoid the conclusion that he got the idea for his Scherzo from the Hurlebusch piece; the unmistakable distance in quality between them probably does nothing more than remind us yet again that Bach cared less about where he found useful ideas than about what he could make of them.[90]

---

86. Cf. bdok 3:263–64 (no. 785), 276–79 (nos. 791–95), and 284–90 (nos. 801 and 803). Only a single letter of Wilhelm Friedemann's to Forkel appears to survive; see ibid., 291 (no. 805). Forkel did state, however, that he also gathered information in conversations with Friedemann and Carl Philipp Emanuel; see *Ueber Johann Sebastian Bachs Leben*, x. For more on Forkel's treatment of his sources, see recently Hans-Joachim Hinrichschen, "Forkel und die Anfänge der Bachforschung," in *Bach und die Nachwelt*, ed. Michael Heinemann, Hans-Joachim Hinrichsen, and Joachim Ldtke, interpretation, 4 vols. (Laaber: Laaber-Verlag, 1997–2005): 1:193–253, at 209–13.

87. Nevertheless, this raises the question of the form in which Hurlebusch would have given his music to the Bach sons: surely he could more readily dispose of a printed copy than of a manuscript.

88. Cf. Schulze, as cited n. 77. As Schulze points out, the readings of the Meißner copies do not derive from the printed edition.

89. For the history of bwv 827, see, most conveniently, Schulenberg, *The Keyboard Music of J. S. Bach*, 284–86; for the announcement of the publication, dated September 19, 1727, see bdok 2:169 (no. 224). As Schulze has demonstrated, Bach probably did not begin work on Anna Magdalena's book—in which the A-minor Partita stands as the first entry—until the second half of 1725, possibly as a gift for her birthday (September 22) or the couple's anniversary (December 3); see Hans-Joachim Schulze, "Ein 'Dresdner Menuett' im zweiten Klavierbüchlein der Anna Magdalena Bach: Nebst Hinweisen zur Überlieferung einiger Kammermusikwerke Bachs," bj 65 (1979): 45–64, at 63–64.

90. Cf. the well-known report of Theodor Lebrecht Pitschel on Bach's recourse to the music of other composers as a stimulus for his own, bdok 2:397 (no. 499; transl. nbr 333–34). Butler (*Bach's Clavier-Übung III*, 4–9) has already suggested that Bach took a greater interest in Hurlebusch than the tone of Philip Emanuel's report would lead us to suspect. The argument, however, rests on chronological presuppositions different from those adopted here, and the evidence strikes me as equivocal. In Butler's

With the lineage of Bach's Scherzo finally clarified, the implications for BWV 1067 fall readily into place. The dependence of BWV 827/6 on Hurlebusch means that the creation of the Battinerie—and with it, obviously, the entire ouverture—must indeed come after the expansion of the A-minor Partita in 1727. Unlike the duple meter and snap figure, moreover, the extended anacrusis at the opening of both the Scherzo and the Battinerie belongs to these pieces alone; the very specificity of this relationship surely means that a great deal of time cannot have separated them.[91] The date of the scherzo, of course, already brings it into broad proximity with the A-minor ouverture. But without wishing to indulge in undue speculation, I think we can see a more immediate point of focus in 1731, when Bach brought out all six partitas in a single, revised edition.[92] Some of the changes made to the plates concern the Scherzo of BWV 827, so this piece clearly came under Bach's eyes at the time.[93] Perhaps, then,

view, Bach took essential ideas for the Prelude and in Fugue in E♭ (BWV 552) that frame the third part of the *Clavier-Übung* from pieces in the *Compositioni*; the fugue allegedly draws on a fugue in D major in Part II (*Compositioni*, ed. Seiffert, 78–80), the prelude on the ouverture that directly precedes the scherzo under discussion here (ibid., 47–52). Although the subjects of the two fugues do indeed show considerable similarity, Butler fails to persuade me that their elaboration does, as well—and as he observes, "this particular fugue subject is not unique to Hurlebusch and Bach" (*Bach's Clavier-Übung III*, 8). I have similar misgivings about the relationship between Bach's prelude and Hurlebusch's ouverture. Despite the evident resemblances in Butler's single-line examples (ibid., 4, example 1a), the melodic and gestural configurations have quite different harmonic underpinnings—which surely weakens the supposed connection no less than the similarities of texture and diastemic succession argue for it. To my eyes and ears, moreover, the putative formal correspondences between the two pieces (ibid., 4–5) make greater sense in Butler's Figure 1 than in the actual music: not only does the designation of mm. 94–111 in Hurlebusch's ouverture as A¹ seem optimistic, but the undifferentiated succession of elements labeled A, B, and C obscures the difference between the standard ouverture form employed by Hurlebusch—with B, C, and A¹ all falling within the quick middle section—and Bach's rotation of ideas within a single-tempo structure.

91. The scherzos in Hurlebusch's op. 5 nos. 1 and 4 begin with half-measure upbeats; those of op. 5 no. 3 and op. 6 no. 3 have a bourrée-like pickup of two eighths, and the scherzo of op. 6 no. 4 starts like a gavotte with an upbeat of two quarters. But not only does the date of these pieces make their relevance to Bach questionable, they also reach a strong accent on the downbeat of the first measure.

92. Cf. NBA V/1 (*Erster Teil der Klavierübung*), ed. Richard Douglas Jones, KB, 17; Christoph Wolff, "The Clavier-Übung Series," in *Essays*, 189–213 and 416–17, at 196–200 and 416; or Schulenberg, *The Keyboard Music of J. S. Bach*, 276–78. The precise date of the edition remains unknown, as no announcement appears in any contemporary newspaper or fair catalogue.

93. Cf. NBA V/1, KB, 20. I distinguish these changes from the handwritten corrections found in some exemplars; see particularly ibid., 27, as well as Christoph Wolff, "Textkritische Bemerkungen zum Originaldruck der Bachschen Partiten," BJ 65 (1979): 65–74, translated as "Text-Critical Comments on the Original Print of the Partitas," in *Essays*, 214–22 and 417–18.

this renewed contact with his earlier composition left its mark in the creation of the Battinerie. If nothing else, this possibility would accord nicely with the hints that the performance of Johann Bernhard Bach's ouverture took place in the later months of 1730 rather than earlier in the year.[94]

IV

Barring unexpected discoveries, we shall probably never succeed in dating the A-minor ouverture with greater precision. Before leaving matters of chronology, however, we might pause over the creation of the existing version in B minor with flute. As already indicated, Kobayashi assigns all but the viola part of ST 154 to the late 1730s—"ca. 1738–39," he writes at two places, "ca. 1739" at a third, and in a related proviso at yet another location, "1738 is . . . not to be excluded."[95] A fresh examination of the subject, drawing in part on evidence not yet available to him, refines his conclusions to a slight—yet, we shall see, not insignificant—degree.

The paper of ST 154 appears in two items of secure, or reasonably secure, date: an autograph letter of January 18, 1740, and the aborted fair copy of the St. John Passion that Bach evidently undertook in anticipation of a performance in March 1739.[96] Other sources with the same paper include the four autograph parts to the Harpsichord Concerto in A Major (BWV 1055); the three remaining original parts to the concerto for the same instrument in F major (BWV 1057); and twelve bifolios in the so-called London autograph of the second Well-Tempered Clavier.[97] Don Franklin has

94. See n. 29. Obviously, we would wish also to know more in this connection about the origins of BWV 844a; but in the absence of early sources, these remain cloudy. See, however, the remarks in Wollny, "Studies in the Music of Wilhelm Friedemann Bach," 91–92.

95. Cf. n. 7, and Kobayashi, "Zur Chronologie der Spätwerke Johann Sebastian Bachs," variously at 11, 23, 45, and 53.

96. See Kobayashi, "Zur Chronologie der Spätwerke Johann Sebastian Bachs," 11 and 44, also NBA IX/1–2 (*Katalog der Wasserzeichen in Bachs Originalhandschriften*), ed. Wisso Weiß and Yoshitake Kobayashi, Textband, 96, and Abbildungen, 95 (no. 105). Whether or not the fundamentally circumstantial evidence for assigning the Passion score to 1739—for which see NBA II/4 (*Johannes-Passion*), ed. Arthur Mendel, KB, 75, as well as BDOK 2:338–39 (no. 439), and Alfred Dürr, *Die Johannes-Passion von Johann Sebastian Bach: Entstehung, Überlieferung, Werkeinführung* (Munich: Deutscher Taschenbuchverlag; Kassel: Bärenreiter, 1988), 24–25—should ultimately prove correct, the source cannot realistically date from any other year; see Kobayashi, "Zur Chronologie der Spätwerke Johann Sebastian Bachs," 20 and 44, as well as the discussion immediately following in the main text.

97. See principally Kobayashi, "Zur Chronologie der Spätwerke Johann Sebastian Bachs," 11 and 45–46, and Don O. Franklin, "Reconstructing the *Urpartitur* for *WTC* II: A Study of the 'London autograph' (BL Add. MS 35021)," in *Bach Studies*, ed. Don O. Franklin (Cambridge: Cambridge University Press, 1989), 240–78, at 247 (Table 2) and 248; also the source descriptions in NBA VII/4

observed that three members of this complex—the ouverture, the F-major concerto, and the bifolios from the Well-Tempered Clavier—have the same rastrum, as well; and although I have not had a chance to measure the originals, it looks as if BWV 1055 and the relevant pages of the St. John Passion also share a rastrum, one distinguished by a slightly smaller gap between the two uppermost lines than in the lower portions of the staff.[98]

As Kobayashi in particular has shown, the entire group of manuscripts documents a major evolution in Bach's hand, which we can most easily follow in his manner of drawing downstemmed half notes.[99] Until the end of 1737, these virtually always show the stem to the right of the note head unless the note sits above the staff on a leger line, in which case the stem will sometimes descend from the center or the left—although this in fact seems to become very rare precisely in the mid-1730s.[100] By the summer

---

(*Konzerte für Cembalo*), ed. Werner Breig, KB, 123–24 and 179–80, and NBA V/2.2 (*Das Wohltemperierte Klavier II—Fünf Präludien und Fughetten*), ed. Alfred Dürr, KB, 25–27, as well as the facsimile *Das Wohltemperierte Klavier II / Johann Sebastian Bach*, introd. by Don Franklin and Stephen Daw, British Library Music Facsimiles 1 (London: British Library, 1980).

98. See Franklin, "Reconstructing the *Urpartitur*," 247 (Table 2) and 248; although the author noted the difference between the Passion and most of the other manuscripts with the same paper, he did not have access to BWV 1055 at the time he wrote. My thanks to Prof. Franklin for sharing with me this and other details of his work.

99. See Kobayashi, "Zur Chronologie der Spätwerke Johann Sebastian Bachs," 20–21.

100. The score and autograph performance materials for BWV 30a, from September 1737 (SBB Mus. ms. Bach P 43, ST 31), provide the last secure *terminus* for this phase of Bach's script; both show the older form of the half note exclusively, at least on notes within the staff. Cf. *Johann Sebastian Bach: Angenehmes Wiederau, freue dich in deinen Auen, Drama per Musica* BWV 30a. Faksimile der autographen *Partitur*, ed. Werner Neumann, Faksimile-Reihe Bachscher Werke und Schriftstücke 16 (Leipzig: veb Deutscher Verlag für Musik, 1980), and the reproduction of a page from the oboe d'amore part in NBA I/39 (*Festmusiken für Leipziger Rats- und Schulfeiern—Huldigungsmusiken für Adlige und Bürger*), ed. Werner Neumann, ix, noting that an apparent exception in the tenth system actually represents a correction. Among manuscripts definitely or probably written in 1736 or 1737, I find no half notes above the staff with stems from the left or center in the autograph score of the St. Matthew Passion (P 25; note, however, that this does not include the repairs to the manuscript made in the 1740s; cf. Kobayashi, "Zur Chronologie der Spätwerke Johann Sebastian Bachs," 52) or the dual autograph of the Concerto for Two Harpsichords in C Minor (BWV 1062) and Flute Sonata in A Major (BWV 1032, P 612), and only one in the flute sonata BWV 1030 (P 975; see mvt. 3, m. 74, flute). For these works, readers may usefully consult the facsimile reproductions *Johann Sebastian Bach: Passio Domini nostri J. C. secundum Evangelistam Matthaeum*, ed. Karl-Heinz Köhler, Faksimile-Reihe Bachscher Werke und Schriftstücke 7 (Leipzig: veb Deutscher Verlag für Musik, n.d.); *Johann Sebastian Bach: Konzert c-Moll für zwei Cembali und Streichorchester* BWV 1062—*Sonate A-Dur für Flöte und Cembalo* BWV 1032, ed. Hans-Joachim Schulze, Documenta musicologica, ser.

of 1740 or at most a year later, the stems have shifted definitively to the left of the note head regardless of staff position.[101] On this basis, we can safely place the bifolios from the Well-Tempered Clavier later than either the Passion, the ouverture, or the two harpsichord concertos; among these four pieces, in turn, BWV 1057 clearly occupies the latest position, as it alone uses the newer form of the half note more than sporadically. Beyond this point, however, things become harder to pin down. The Passion, for example, slightly exceeds the ouverture in its representation of half notes with left-hand stems, and the—admittedly very few—downstemmed half notes in the A-major concerto include none whatever with the stem to the left, even when they go above the staff.[102] Conversely, both the A-major and F-major harpsichord concertos tend to abbreviate the *piano* sign to *p*, which occurs at most once in the ouverture and not at all in the Passion; whether alone or in combination, moreover, the *p* itself assumes a fairly unusual form—marked by a vertical downstroke and uncommonly large

<hr>

II, vol. 10 (Kassel: Bärenreiter, 1980); and *Sonata a Cembalo obligato e Travers. solo di J. S. Bach*, ed. Werner Neumann, Faksimile-Reihe Bachscher Werke und Schriftstücke 4 (Leipzig: VEB Deutscher Verlag für Musik, n.d.).

101. The first *terminus* comes from the autograph oboe and viola parts to *Schleicht, spielende Wellen* (BWV 206, SBB Mus. ms. Bach ST 80), whose script enables Kobayashi ("Zur Chronologie der Spätwerke Johann Sebastian Bachs," 47) to assign the revival of the work from which they stem to August 1740. The second, and more certain, one comes from BWV 210 (ST 76), which—as Michael Maul has now shown—Bach wrote for the wedding of the Berlin doctor Georg Ernst Stahl on September 19, 1741; see Maul, "'Dein Ruhm wird wie ein Demantstein, ja wie ein fester Stahl beständig sein': Neues über die Beziehungen zwischen den Familien Stahl und Bach," BJ 87 (2001): 7–22, esp. 16–19. The autograph voice and violone parts in ST 76 show left-hand stems exclusively; cf. *Johann Sebastian Bach: O holder Tag, erwünschte Zeit. Hochzeitskantate* BWV 210, ed. Werner Neumann, Faksimile-Reihe Bachscher Werke und Schriftstücke 8 (Leipzig: veb Deutscher Verlag für Musik, 1967), and NBA I/40 (*Hochzeitskantaten und weltliche Kantaten verschiedener Bestimmung*), ed. Werner Neumann, viii. After 1741, Bach's downstems move to the center of the note head, where they remain in all further autographs; cf. Kobayashi, "Zur Chronologie der Spätwerke Johann Sebastian Bachs," 21.

102. For the Passion, see the reproduction of the autograph pages included as a supplement to NBA II/4; among the fair overall number of downstemmed half notes in this portion of the manuscript, those on the staff show a left-hand stem only at no. 10, m. 25, Continuo, and—as the continuation of a similarly stemmed pair of tied notes above the staff—no. 1, m. 38, Oboe 1. Further half notes above the staff with stems drawn to the left or from the middle of the note head occur in the oboe parts of the opening chorus at mm. 4, 10–11, and 24; the movement includes thirty-two half notes above the staff in all. The flute part of the ouverture has a single half note with a downstem in the center of the note, almost to its left (Ouverture, mm. 177), and one other (Polonoise, m. 4) that shows the stem moving decisively toward the center of the note; in all its half notes above the staff—thirteen, by my tally—the stems keep solidly to the right. The Concerto has eleven downstemmed half notes in its first movement, all but two of them (Violin 1, mm. 69–70) on the staff. See also n. 104.

loop—again found nowhere in the Passion and at best rarely in the ouverture.[103] In a time of transition, of course, we cannot necessarily expect an absolutely consistent progression from one manuscript to the next.[104] The small size of the sample further reduces the prospects of achieving an airtight chronology. But assuming my eyes have not deceived me about the ruling of the Passion and the parts to the A-major concerto, we can still narrow the options to some degree. For one thing, even if the script leaves open some chance of dating the ouverture and the concerto before the Passion, the use of a clearly later rastrum for the ouverture suggests that neither of the instrumental works could have anticipated the Passion by a significant margin. Indeed, if we consider the script and the ruling together, it would seem more plausible than not to arrange the ouverture and its related manuscripts in the sequence BWV 245, 1055, 1067, 1057. At most, the dynamics could suggest reversing the position of the middle two pieces; but this has no effect on the overall picture. Whatever the case, I think it safe to abandon 1738 as a possible terminus for anything in this group.[105]

---

103. The use of *p* for *piano* does have precedents in Bach's manuscripts from at least the fair copy of the Brandenburg Concertos (SBB Am.B. 78), often with the letter in much the same form as in BWV 1055 and 1057; cf. *Johann Sebastian Bach: Brandenburgische Konzerte. Faksimile des Autographen* (Frankfurt/M: C. F. Peters, 1996). In the immediate context, however, the differences remain striking. The single isolated *p* in BWV 1067—Polonoise, m. 10, Continuo—requires some comment on its own. For one thing, its use may reflect nothing more than a concern to avoid the figures immediately to its right (cf. also n. 212). More important, the letter itself, though not unlike its counterparts in the harpsichord concertos, does not entirely match them, either; indeed, at first sight, none of the dynamics in the continuo for the Polonoise and Battinerie would seem assuredly autograph: both the abbreviation *f* and the written-out *piano* show an uncharacteristic upright orientation in their script, and the *piano* lacks the hiatus between the second and third letters customary in Bach (cf. Kobayashi, "Zur Chronologie der Spätwerke Johann Sebastian Bachs," 18). Nevertheless, the *forte* at m. 20 of the Battinerie, the first letter of which matches exactly the abbreviated signs elsewhere in both movements, seems unquestionably his, and the *p* of the *piano* at m. 36 in the Battinerie looks precisely like the first letter in the manifestly autograph marking at the same spot in Violin 1. Violin 2 also has *piano* markings with a similar *p* at mm. 95 and 152 of the first movement, but these appear less likely to come from Bach's hand and could even date from a later time. See also n. 188.

104. As if to emphasize the point, the two half notes above the staff in the autograph score of the A-major concerto—which quite obviously originated before the parts (cf. NBA VII/4, KB, 127)—both have left-hand stems; cf. n. 102, as well as the reproduction in Breig, "Zur Werkgeschichte von Johann Sebastian Bachs Cembalokonzert in A-dur BWV 1055," 197. BWV 1055 occupies the fourth position among the six harpsichord concertos (BWV 1052–57) entered as a series on pp. 1–94 of P 234; cf. Werner Breig, "Zum Kompositionsprozeß in Bachs Cembalokonzerten," in *Johann Sebastian Bachs Spätwerk und dessen Umfeld: Perspektiven und Probleme. Bericht über das wissenschaftliche Symposium anläßlich des 61. Bachfestes der Neuen Bachgesellschaft Duisburg, 28.-30. März 1986*, ed. Christoph Wolff (Kassel: Bärenreiter, 1988), 32–47, at 44–47, and NBA VII/4, KB, 19–20. See also following note.

105. On the basis of this discussion, and given the date for the St. John Passion score (see n. 96), we can also refine the chronological estimates for both the parts to BWV 1057 and the second Well-

This conclusion all but shuts the door on one scenario for the creation of the ouverture that has gained some currency, at least in the English-speaking world. In his discussion of bwv 1067, Martin Bernstein speculated that Bach composed the work for the Dresden court, home of the great flute virtuoso Pierre Gabriel Buffardin.[106] Robert Marshall, too, has flirted with a Dresden connection, suggesting more than once that Bach "had Buffardin in mind" in this music.[107] Yet even allowing for the fact that Bach could at most have arranged bwv 1067 for Buffardin rather than actually have composed it for him, he can hardly have intended the piece for Dresden. So far as we know, he made no journey there after May 1738, nor do we have any evidence that he planned to visit Dresden in the months that followed.[108] We also have no grounds for thinking that he prepared the parts with the idea of sending them to the Saxon capital; in any event, they clearly remained in his possession.[109] The entire idea of linking bwv 1067 with Dresden, moreover, rests on a premise that no longer holds water. Bernstein developed his hypothesis in the context of biographical research that set the end of Bach's involvement with the Leipzig Collegium Musicum in 1736 or

---

Tempered Clavier in Kobayashi, "Zur Chronologie der Spätwerke Johann Sebastian Bachs," 45–46, and Franklin, "Reconstructing the *Urpartitur*," 247: for the concerto, Kobayashi's "ca. 1739" might better read "1739–40" or even, if we accept his dating for the oboe and viola parts of bwv 206 (cf. n. 101), "April 1739–August 1740"; this in turn could well mean that the earliest layer of the London autograph should now have the date 1740–41, the second 1741–42—indeed, the latter estimate looks all the more likely in view of the new findings on bwv 210 (cf. n. 101), which shares its rastrum, and at least a closely related paper type, with the second layer of the London autograph (cf. Franklin, "Reconstructing the *Urpartitur*," 247–49, and Kobayashi, "Zur Chronologie," 45–46, although also 16–17; in an e-mail of September 16, 2003, Prof. Franklin informed me that a beta-radiogram of one leaf in the London autograph appears to show small differences against his tracing of a mark from bwv 210). It would now appear all but certain as well that at least the latest items in p 234—bwv 1055, 1056, and 1057—belong to 1739 rather than the previous year (cf. Breig, "Zum Kompositions-prozeß in Bachs Cembalokonzerten," 44–47, and Kobayashi, "Zur Chronologie der Spätwerke," 41). See also n. 112.

106. See "Bach Problems," 127 (*Johann Sebastian Bach*, ed. Blankenburg, 417).

107. See Marshall, "J. S. Bach's Compositions for Solo Flute," 487 (*The Music of J. S. Bach*, 217), as well as idem, "Bach the Progressive: Observations on his Later Works," *Musical Quarterly* 62 (1976): 313–57, at 335–36 (*The Music of J. S. Bach*, 23–58, at 38).

108. Cf. *Kalendarium zur Lebensgeschichte Johann Sebastian Bachs*, ed. Hans-Joachim Schulze, 2nd, rev. ed. (Leipzig: Bach-Archiv, 1979), 50–51.

109. Wollny's identification of the script on the wrapper confirms the long-held suspicion that the parts to bwv 1067 went from J. S. Bach to C. P. E. Bach; cf. n. 3, as well as nba VII/1, kb, 36. On the possibility of an early score copy—which in principle could have gone to Dresden, but which in actuality would seem hardly likely to have done so—see the Postscript.

not long afterward.[110] From this perspective, it clearly seemed necessary to seek the impetus for the ouverture outside of Leipzig. Yet at almost the same time Bernstein presented his case for Dresden, Werner Neumann established that Bach in fact returned to the Collegium before the close of the decade—although as we shall see, this fact, too, does not resolve every potential issue.[111] Nevertheless, with the suppositions changed, the need to look elsewhere obviously diminishes.[112]

We might bear this point in mind when considering a more recent suggestion about the origin of the B-minor ouverture. According to Martin Geck, "Bach was intensely involved with works for the flute" in the later 1730s. Like Peter Schleuning before him, Geck sees a connection here with C. P. E. Bach's "call to the court of the crown prince and subsequent Prussian king Frederick II in 1738"—and that "the B minor ouverture in particular would have cut a fine figure at Potsdam goes without saying."[113] Unfortunately, none of this withstands scrutiny. As evidence for Bach's involvement with the flute in the late 1730s, Geck cites "some of the sonatas in the sequence BWV 1030–39."[114] Yet not only, as we shall see, do the pieces in question include several of at best dubious authenticity, but with at most one exception—BWV 1035, which a note on a nineteenth-century copy links to a visit of Bach's to Potsdam in the 1740s—the flute works among them demonstrably or all but definitely predate the start of Philipp Emanuel's employment by Frederick.[115] In other words, we have no more reason to

110. Cf. "Bach Problems," 127 (*Johann Sebastian Bach*, ed. Blankenburg, 417), and Neumann, "Das 'Bachische Collegium Musicum,'" 6 (*Johann Sebastian Bach*, 386).

111. See Neumann, "Das 'Bachische Collegium Musicum,'" 6–8 (*Johann Sebastian Bach*, 386–88). Although Neumann's article nominally appeared in 1960, I hardly consider it a foregone conclusion that Bernstein would have had access to it before the presentation of his arguments in September 1961 (cf. *International Musicological Society: Report of the Eighth Congress* 2: xiii).

112. The refined chronology for the ouverture and the instrumental works closest to it, and especially the observations in n. 105, also cuts the ground from under speculations connecting the harpsichord concertos to Dresden; cf. Schulze, "Johann Sebastian Bachs Konzerte—Fragen der Überlieferung und Chronologie," 12–13, and, on the supposed identity between one of the papers in P 234 and a receipt of Bach's from May 5, 1738, NBA IX/1: 51 (no. 48).

113. Geck, "Köthen oder Leipzig," 21–22, with reference to Schleuning, *Johann Sebastian Bachs "Kunst der Fuge,"* 85–88.

114. Geck, "Köthen oder Leipzig," 21; in n. 16, Geck adds, "I cite these sonatas as a whole, as I would otherwise have to discuss the transmission of every individual sonata."

115. On the problems of authenticity, see Section V, p. 54ff. For the dates of BWV 1030 and 1032, see p. 53; on those of BWV 1031 and 1034, cf. nn. 136 and 140, respectively, and the literature cited there. On the dating of BWV 1033, see Glöckner, "Neuerkenntnisse zu Johann Sebastian Bachs Aufführungskalender," 50; for BWV 1035, see NBA VI/3 (*Werke für Flöte*), ed. Hans-Peter Schmitz, KB, 22–24, as well

associate the B-minor ouverture with Potsdam than we do with Dresden. The search for its origins might better at least begin closer to home.

In this connection, the relationship between BWV 1067 and the harpsichord concertos in F and A major can hardly go unnoticed. Although the gap separating the F-major concerto from the other two works reminds us of a need for circumspection, it does not seem extravagant to suppose that all three sets of parts originated with a common purpose. Considering the extent to which the paper and script focus our attention on 1739, one event of that year immediately stands out: Bach's return to the Collegium Musicum on October 2.[116] Hans Grüß, in fact, proposed such an association for BWV 1067 some thirty-five years ago, and Don Franklin has more recently brought BWV 1057 into the picture, as well.[117] Just as Bach had presumably composed the original version of the ouverture for the Collegium in the early period of his directorship, we might think it tempting to imagine that he now prepared its transposed and rescored version, together with at least some of his harpsichord concertos, in connection with his resumption of activities. Still, especially given the leeway that remains in the dating, we cannot exclude a private occasion beyond our knowledge.

As for the motivation behind the rescoring, we do not have to look beyond a consideration already implicit in Bernstein's and Marshall's speculations about Buffardin—namely, the stimulus of a particular flutist. If anything, this argument becomes more compelling in conjunction with the arrangement than with an original work. In principle, after all, Bach could have felt moved to compose the ouverture even without a distinguished soloist at hand; but surely he would not have taken the trouble to adapt it to a new instrument unless spurred by the availability of a first-rate player. Wherever this player originally came from, Bach would most likely have encountered him in the circle of predominantly student instrumentalists who flocked to the Collegium; to quote the well-known account of Leipzig concert life published by Lorenz Christoph Mizler in October 1736, "there are always good musicians among them, so that sometimes they become, as is known, famous virtuosos."[118] At least one secular

---

as Hans Eppstein, "Über J. S. Bachs Flötensonaten mit Generalbaß," BJ 58 (1972): 12–23, at 18–20, and Marshall, "J. S. Bach's Compositions for Solo Flute," 491–94 (*The Music of J. S. Bach*, 220–22). For BWV 1038 and 1039, cf., respectively, Marshall, "J. S. Bach's Compositions for Solo Flute," 471 n. 17 (*The Music of J. S. Bach*, 318 n. 17), and NBA VI/3, KB, 48.

116. Cf. Neumann, "Das 'Bachische Collegium Musicum,'" 7–8 (*Johann Sebastian Bach*, ed. Blankenburg, 388).

117. See Grüß's preface to the Bärenreiter miniature score of BWV 1067 (Bärenreiter-Ausgabe TP 193, forward dated 1973), and Franklin, "Reconstructing the Urpartitur," 248 n. 17.

118. Translation from NBR, 186; for the original, see BDOK 2:278 (no. 387). The report appears in

vocal work of this time—*Angenehmes Wiederau* (BWV 30a), performed in September 1737—requires a flutist of no small attainment, and so does the music of the solo cantata BWV 210a, a version of which seems likely to have figured in the activities of the Collegium.[119] Admittedly, we have no evidence for the participation of Collegium members in the performance of BWV 30a, nor can we say for sure when BWV 210a might have received a hearing; but we may still read Mizler's report as indicating that Bach had no need to rely on imported talent for the flute parts.[120]

Mizler, in fact, may have more to do with our story than simply providing some background color. As a student in the early 1730s, he received instruction from Bach in keyboard playing and composition; his dissertation, completed in June 1734, names Bach as one of its four dedicatees; and on returning to Leipzig in the autumn of 1736 after an extended period of travel and study, he soon established himself as one of Bach's most trusted associates.[121] In the context of this relationship on the one hand,

---

the first volume of Mizler's *Musikalische Bibliothek oder Gründliche Nachricht*, the forward to which bears the date October 20, 1736.

119. Cf. Kobayashi, "Zur Chronologie der Spätwerke Johann Sebastian Bachs," 40. The solo part of BWV 210a, although written in 1729 (cf. n. 59), contains a textual revision addressing its music to "esteemed patrons" ("werte Gönner"); cf. NBA I/39 (*Festmusiken für Leipziger Rats- und Schulfeiern—Huldigungsmusiken für Adlige und Bürger*), ed. Werner Neumann, KB, 99–100.

120. BWV 30a actually fell in the interregnum between Bach's two periods as leader of the Collegium; but see the comments in NBA I/39, KB, 75–76.

121. For Mizler's lessons, see BDOK 3:88–89 (no. 666); for the dissertation, cf. BDOK 2:247–48 (no. 349). Thanks largely to the exemplary edition of Johann Gottfried Walther's correspondence by Klaus Beckmann and Hans-Joachim Schulze, we can clarify the account of Mizler's whereabouts during the years 1734–36 in Franz Wöhlke, *Lorenz Christoph Mizler: Ein Beitrag zur musikalischen Gelehrtengeschichte des 18. Jahrhunderts*, Musik und Geistesgeschichte: Berliner Studien zur Musikwissenschaft 3 (Würzburg-Aumühle: Konrad Triltsch, 1940), 10–14. By all indications, Mizler returned to his native Franconia immediately after completing his dissertation at the end of June 1734 and remained there without significant interruption until late February 1735; see his letter dated "Heidenheim im Anspachischen. d. 25 Octob: A. 1734" in *Johann Gottfried Walther: Briefe*, ed. Klaus Beckmann and Hans-Joachim Schulze (Leipzig: VEB Deutscher Verlag für Musik, 1987), 177–78, and the information on the dedication of his *Lusus ingenii de praesenti bello* communicated ibid., 202–3. The letter would seem to bear out Wöhlke's suspicion (*Lorenz Christoph Mizler*, 10) that the "Reise ins Reich" mentioned in the autobiography written for Mattheson's *Grundlage einer Ehrenpforte* ("Mizler," 228–33, at 229) in fact refers to this stay, as Franconia formally belonged to the Holy Roman Empire. The subsequent visit to Leipzig also referred to in the autobiography (ibid.) cannot have lasted more than a few weeks, as Mizler matriculated at the University of Wittenberg on March 22, 1735; cf. *Walther: Briefe*, 291. Wöhlke (*Lorenz Christoph Mizler*, 13) probably errs in assuming that Mizler made further visits to Leipzig from Wittenberg: Walther's comment, in a letter to Heinrich Bokemeyer of August 3, 1735, that "Herr Magister Mizler is once again in Leipzig" (*Walther: Briefe*,

and our inquiry into BWV 1067 on the other, a passage in a letter of November 6, 1736, to Johann Gottfried Walther in Weimar cannot help but arouse interest:

> I have only been back in Leipzig for six weeks, and still in the greatest disarray; but as soon as I've unpacked, I'll send you a cantata of mine on love and monastic life. If I may kindly ask something of you, I would like a concerto for the *traversiere* that's quite difficult. I am a great devotee of beautiful concertos for the flute, and when

---

186: "der Hr. *M.* Mizler sich wiederum in Leipzig . . . befindet") probably depends on a letter that Mizler had sent some months earlier—the reissue of the *Lusus ingenii de praesenti bello* appeared in Wittenberg precisely in August 1735 (cf. ibid., 202–3). For the time of Mizler's return to Leipzig in 1736, see the letter cited further in the main text, as well as Mattheson, *Grundlage einer Ehrenpforte*, 230; see also Walther's letter of January 1737 quoted in the following note. Evidence for Mizler's subsequent relationship with Bach, too well known to rehearse in detail here, comes chiefly from his participation in the dispute with Johann Adolph Scheibe and the activities of the Societät der musikalischen Wissenschaften. Klaus Hofmann, "Alte und neue Überlegungen zu der Kantate 'Non sa che sia dolore' (BWV 209)," BJ 76 (1990): 7–25, has proposed that Bach wrote the Italian cantata BWV 209 to honor Mizler on his departure from Leipzig in the summer of 1734. While much about the argument seems persuasive—though not to Andreas Glöckner; see NBA I/41 (*Varia: Kantaten, Quodlibet, Einzelsätze, Bearbeitungen*), ed. Andreas Glöckner, KB, 41—some problems remain. The cantata survives only in a score by an unknown scribe to which Johann Nikolaus Forkel added both the text and the attribution to Bach (P 135; cf. Hofmann, "Alte und neue Überlegungen," 7 n. 1, and NBA I/41, KB, 38–40). Not only does Forkel's underlay often contradict the beaming of the voice part (cf. ibid., 48–49), but at several points, especially in the first aria, "Parti pur e con dolore," the musical phrases appear to demand a poem of more lines than the text now contains. In both this and the concluding movement, moreover, the verses and their setting violate norms of aria writing so basic that even a poet or a composer with only a minimal knowledge of Italian could scarcely have ignored them unless working under special constraints: in neither of the two arias does the last line of the second section rhyme with one from the first; and the second aria commits a further solecism in splitting its borrowed Metastasian lines between the A and B sections, causing the first to end without syntactic closure. All this raises the possibility that the cantata originally had another text, and that the version transmitted in P 135 represents a none too skillful adaptation undertaken—very conceivably by Forkel himself—for a special set of circumstances. A further detail in the manuscript suggests, too, that Bach can hardly have written this music as early as 1734. The opening Sinfonia contains a number of *pizzicato* markings—more, indeed, than we find preserved either in BG 29.45–66 (*Kammermusik für Gesang*, vol. 3), ed. Paul Graf Waldersee, or in NBA I/41, 45–68 (cf. ibid., KB, 46)—that make little or no musical sense. All occur, however, at places where Bach would routinely have asked for soft playing; and Bach's manuscripts of the later 1730s often show the abbreviation *pia* written in a fashion that the unsuspecting eye could read as *piz* (cf. Kobayashi, "Zur Chronologie der Spätwerke Johann Sebastian Bachs," 21, and esp. Figure 6b on p. 18). A score of the harpsichord concerto BWV 1056 (P 239) copied by Forkel from manuscripts based on the lost original—and, we may assume, at least partially autograph—parts would appear to confirm that scribes could fall prey to this danger; cf. the table in NBA VII/4, KB, 166–68, and mm. 8, 15, 38, 56, etc. of the third movement as they appear in NBA VII/4:208–17, or the edition by Hans-Joachim Schulze (Leipzig:

I am exhausted from studying, I can give myself virtually new powers through this instrument. Surely, there will be a virtuoso of the *traversière* in the Weimar chapel. I'll send back the copying charges immediately, and ask that it be written out quite cleanly and large.[122]

By his own testimony, Mizler, a self-taught flutist, "often made himself heard" on the instrument during his student days.[123] The letter to Walther suggests that he did not wholly abandon public performance after his habilitation as a lecturer at the university.[124] Indeed, since the letter follows close on both his return to Leipzig and his description of the Collegium concerts—where, in his words, "Any musician

---

Edition Peters 9386a, 1977). The odd *pizzicato* markings in BWV 209, therefore, could well derive from a misreading of an autograph source; and while Bach's potentially ambiguous *piano* indications occur in isolation as early as 1734 (cf. Kobayashi, "Zur Chronologie der Spätwerke," 21), they do not appear in the frequency necessary to produce a situation like that encountered in BWV 209 until the second half of the decade. For more on the problems of the cantata, including that of its authorship, see my notes to the recording L'Oiseau-Lyre 421 424–2.

122. *Walther: Briefe*, 201–2: "Ich bin erst 6 Wochen wieder in Leipzig, u. noch in der größten Unordnung, so bald ich aber ausgepacket, werde Ew. WohlEdl. eine *Cantata* vom Kloster-Leben und der Liebe von mir zusenden. Wenn ich mir etwas von Ew. WohlEdl. gehorsam ausbitten darf, so bitte um ein *Concert* auf die *Traversiere*, so etwas schwehr ist. Ich bin ein großer Liebhaber von schönen *Concerten* auf die Querflöte, und wenn ich vom Studieren müde bin, kan ich mir durch dieses Instrument gleichsam neue Kräffte schaffen. Es wird ohnefehlbar in der Weymarischen Capelle ein *Virtuose* auf der *Traversiere* seyn. Die Schreib-Gebühren werde sogleich zurücksenden, bitte es etwas sauber und groß abschreiben zu lassen." Just when—even whether—Mizler received the concerto, which Walther presumably obtained from a member of the Weimar chapel, remains unclear; on January 21, 1737, Walther wrote to Heinrich Bokemeyer, "At the New Year's fair just passed I answered the Herr Magister's letter and sent him a concerto for flute; but he has traveled back to his home and is not returning from there to Leipzig until this March, according to the word of the agent he has left there, who received the package" (ibid., 199: "An verwichener Neü-Jahrs-Meße habe des H. *M.* Schreiben beantwortet, und demselben ein *Concert* auf die Quer-Flöte geschicket; er ist aber in seine Heimath verreiset, und kömt erst im Merz *a. c.* von da wieder zurück nach Leipzig, laut der Aussage des hinterlaßenen *Mandatarii*, welcher das Paquetgen in Empfang genomen"). Credit for introducing Mizler into the larger discussion of Bach and the flute goes to Michael Marissen and Ardal Powell; cf. Powell, "Bach and the Flute," 14, 20, and 27 n. 70. Powell does not, however, venture any suggestions about associations with specific works. Whether, as Hofmann suggests ("Alte und neue Überlegungen," 18 n. 40), the prominent role accorded the flute in BWV 209 strengthens the case for linking the cantata to Mizler must remain open.

123. See Mattheson, *Grundlage einer Ehren-Pforte*, 231.

124. Mizler held his inaugural disputation on October 24, 1736, and announced a series of lectures on Mattheson's *Neu-eröffnetes Orchester*—which, in the event, he seems not to have held until the following May; cf. Wöhlke, *Lorenz Christoph Mizler*, 16–17, and *Walther: Briefe*, 199 and 203.

is permitted to make himself publicly heard"[125]—we may wonder specifically if he intended to present the requested concerto with Bach's ensemble; and this speculation, in turn, leads to the question of whether Bach might have written some of his own flute compositions for Mizler. As his request for something "quite difficult" reveals, Mizler plainly relished music that demanded a more than an ordinary degree of prowess.[126] It would appear striking, therefore, that two of Bach's most ambitious pieces for the flute—both, like BWV 1067, adapted from earlier music—originated in close proximity to Mizler's renewed presence on the Leipzig scene.[127] The double autograph containing the Sonata in A Major (BWV 1032) and the Concerto for Two Harpsichords in C Minor (BWV 1062) shows two papers whose datable use by Bach all but certainly occupies a period ranging from August 13, 1736, to January 13, 1737; and the paper of the Sonata in B Minor (BWV 1030) covers a range extending only from October 7, 1736, to September 28, 1737.[128] Hence we must seriously entertain the possibility that these works owe their origin to Bach's association with Mizler; and clearly, we cannot avoid asking if the same could not also hold true for BWV 1067.[129]

---

125. NBR, 186; original BDOK 2:278 (no. 387).

126. The partial translation in Powell, "Bach and the Flute," 20—"please send me a flute concerto— one that is difficult to play"—overlooks the qualifier; presumably, Powell failed to recognize Mizler's "so" as a relative pronoun and thus read "etwas" as a substantive rather than an adverb. Strictly speaking, one could perhaps read Mizler's formulation as indicating "not too hard" rather than "not too easy"; but note his use of "etwas" in the reference to copying near the end of the quoted passage.

127. On the original form of both sonatas, see Section V; it begins on p. 54.

128. For BWV 1032, see Schulze's preface to the facsimile of P 612 (see n. 100), 10–11 (English translation, 17–18), as well as Kobayashi, "Zur Chronologie der Spätwerke Johann Sebastian Bachs," 10 and 40—the implicit hesitation in which over the later terminus (cf. ibid., 39) I find difficult to share. For BWV 1030, see ibid., 12, 40, and 46; on the papers of both works, see also NBZ IX/1–2, Textband, 50 (no. 46), 68 (no. 86), and 72 (no. 95).

129. If Bach intended BWV 1032 for Mizler, then he presumably also had Mizler in mind for one of the solo parts in BWV 1062; indeed, this could explain the singular combination of these two pieces in the same manuscript. Previous hypotheses concerning the two flute sonatas have focused on Dresden. According to Marshall, "J. S. Bach's Compositions for Solo Flute," 484–87 (The Music of Johann Sebastian Bach, 216–17), "the inordinate difficulty" of the concluding double movement in BWV 1030, "along with the fact . . . that Bach's connections with Dresden had increased considerably during the 1730s and indeed culminated in November 1736 with his receiving the title of Composer to the Royal Court Chapel, suggest that Bach prepared the final version of his greatest and most difficult flute composition . . . for the master flautist Buffardin." Schulze (see the preceding note) has speculated that Bach intended BWV 1032 and its sister work BWV 1062 for a visit to Dresden in December 1736; again, he points to Buffardin as the probable intended performer. For a variation on this hypothesis, see n. 138. Needless to say, none of these suggestions has any more evidence

Of course, we cannot foreclose other options, either. Leipzig surely had more than one good flutist, even if none but Mizler has yet to emerge from anonymity.[130] Nor can we wholly rule out a visiting artist. This latter possibility could, paradoxically, reopen the door to Buffardin. Carl Philipp Emanuel Bach wrote that Buffardin visited the elder Bach at Leipzig; and though we have no real idea when this occurred, a ray of hope remains for those who would still like to imagine the Dresden virtuoso displaying his mettle in what Marshall has called "the whirlwind badinerie."[131] But here, even more than with Mizler, caution remains in order; and in any event, we do not really have to know who inspired the B-minor ouverture to feel grateful to him.

V

The "deconstruction" of BWV 1067—as a work in B minor, as a work for flute, and as a work untouched by the process of recycling so prevalent in Bach's instrumental output—has implications that reach beyond the piece itself. These begin with the matter of key. One often hears that Bach had a special attachment to B minor. I have yet to trace this notion to its source; but I need hardly remind anyone of the principal exhibits: apart from BWV 1067, these include the *Trauerode* (BWV 198); the Mass BWV 232; the Ouverture in the French Style (BWV 831); the flute sonata BWV 1030; the prelude and fugue for organ BWV 544; and perhaps the violin pieces BWV 1002 and BWV 1014. Of these, however, we now see that most originated in other keys. BWV 1030 derived from a model in G minor.[132] BWV 831 started life in C minor, and it has become apparent that the opening Kyrie of the B-minor Mass did, as well.[133] If we

---

behind it than do ours concerning Mizler—which at least have the virtue of economy, as they keep the music in Bach's immediate surroundings.

130. Although the survey of flutists known, or possibly known, to Bach in Powell, "Bach and the Flute," 19–20, includes other musicians active in Leipzig, none of these except the oboist Johann Caspar Gleditsch—whose flute-playing in any event remains hypothetical—resided there after 1735.

131. See BDOK 3:287–88 (no. 400), and Marshall, "J. S. Bach's Compositions for Solo Flute," 487 (*The Music of Johann Sebastian Bach*, 217).

132. Cf. Werner Neumann's afterword to the facsimile cited in n. 100, or Marshall, "J. S. Bach's Compositions for Solo Flute," 484 (*The Music of J. S. Bach*, 216 and 324 n. 66), and, most comprehensively, Hofmann, "Auf der Suche nach der verlorenen Urfassung."

133. For BWV 831, cf. NBA V/2 (*Zweiter Teil der Klavierübung—Vierter Teil der Klavierübung—Vierzehn Kanons* BWV 1087), ed. Walter Emery and Christoph Wolff, KB, 48–51; on the Kyrie, see my notes to the recording Nonesuch 79036, and John Butt, "*Bach's Mass in B Minor*: Considerations of Its Early Performance and Use," *Journal of Musicology* 9 (1991): 109–23, at 111–12. Alfred Dürr, "Zur Parodiefrage in Bachs h-moll-Messe: Eine Bestandsaufnahme," *Die Musikforschung* 45 (1992): 117–38, at 119, objects that the assumption of a transposition from C minor "is supported by only a single

bear in mind that the two B-minor preludes and fugues in the Well-Tempered Clavier owe their specific tonality as much to necessity as to anything else, then we really have little basis for imagining that Bach had a particular affinity for B minor—at least more than he did for any other key.

Our findings on BWV 1067 also continue—and may bring to completion—a process of attrition that has affected Bach's flute music perhaps more severely than any other part of his output. The past four decades have witnessed a considerable amount of discussion concerning both the authenticity of the works themselves and the extent to which Bach actually conceived them for flute.[134] In both areas, the results have proved largely negative. One piece that long hovered around the edges of the canon, the sonata with obbligato harpsichord BWV 1020, has definitively fallen by the way-side.[135] Robert Marshall has prodded us to worry about the weak transmission and

---

correction of an accidental" (Tenor, m. 35,5) in the autograph of the Mass (P 180). But this argument overlooks at least three further instances of sharps corrected from naturals: m. 11, Continuo, note 2 (cf. Butt, 111–12); m. 63, Violin 1, note 4; and m. 116, Soprano 2, note 4. Cf. *Johann Sebastian Bach: Messe in h-Moll* BWV *232: Faksimile-Lichtdruck des Autographs*, ed. Alfred Dürr, 2nd ed., Documenta musicologica, ser. II, vol. 12 (Kassel: Bärenreiter, 1983).

134. Three studies above all got the current phase of the debate underway: Hans Eppstein, *Studien über J. S. Bachs Sonaten für ein Melodieinstrument und obligates Cembalo*, Acta Universitatis Upsaliensis: Studia musicologica Upsaliensia, Nova series 2 (Uppsala: Almqvist & Wiksell, 1966); idem, "Über J. S. Bachs Flötensonaten mit Generalbaß"; and Marshall, "J. S. Bach's Compositions for Solo Flute." While the specific findings of both authors have not always sustained closer scrutiny, their role in exposing the issues remains inestimable.

135. On BWV 1020, see particularly Yoshitake Kobayashi, "Neuerkenntnisse zu einigen Bach-Quellen an Hand schriftkundlicher Untersuchungen," BJ 64 (1978): 43–60, at 53–54; Marshall, "Bach's Compositions for Solo Flute," 464–67 (*The Music of Johann Sebastian Bach*, 202–4); Ulrich Leisinger and Peter Wollny, "'Altes Zeug von mir'. Carl Philipp Emanuel Bachs kompositorisches Schaffen vor 1740," BJ 79 (1993): 128–204, at 194–96; and Jeanne Swack, "Quantz and the Sonata in E♭ Major for Flute and Cembalo, BWV 1031," *Early Music* 23 (1995): 31–53, at 45–47 and 52–53, which Prof. Swack kindly shared with me before publication. The sources in fact transmit BWV 1020 as a work for violin, but scholarly consensus has long considered flute the more likely solo instrument; indeed, we may well suspect that the piece began its existence as a trio sonata for flute, violin, and continuo—the harpsichord discant never descends below g, and the frequent parallel thirds and sixths in the middle movement contain nothing contrapuntally essential. Whether in this supposed original form or in the version presently transmitted, the authorship of the music continues to present uncertainties. Although J. S. Bach clearly did not write it, Swack and, more forcefully, Leisinger and Wollny have shown that a seemingly unimpregnable attribution to C. P. E. Bach in the hand of his Hamburg copyist Michel does not really resolve matters, either: on the evidence they put forth, it seems clear that Michel relied in this instance on a Breitkopf manuscript of dubious authority. See also the following note.

anomalous style of the continuo sonata BWV 1035, while Jeanne Swack and Siegbert Rampe have uncovered a connection between the obbligato sonata BWV 1031 and the trio sonata QV 2:18 of Quantz so close as to persuade any but the most recalcitrant that Quantz must have written both works—or, if he didn't, that BWV imitates him with a slavishness few would think typical of Bach.[136] The trio sonata BWV 1038 rests

136. For BWV 1035, see Marshall, "J. S. Bach's Compositions for Solo Flute," 491–92 (*The Music of Johann Sebastian Bach*, 220); although he ultimately comes down in favor of accepting the sonata—and although the discovery of new compositional activity connected with Bach's presence in and around Berlin in 1741 (see Maul, "'Dein Ruhm wird wie ein Demantstein'") could well increase its plausibility—I would take his cautions seriously. On BWV 1031, see Swack, "Quantz and the Sonata in E♭ Major"; Siegbert Rampe, "Bach, Quantz und das Musicalische Opfer," *Concerto* 84 (June 1993): 15–23, esp. 17–19; and Dominik Sackmann and Siegbert Rampe, "Bach, Berlin, Quantz und die Flötensonate Es-Dur BWV 1031," BJ 83 (1997): 51–85. Swack also finds procedures typical of Quantz in BWV 1020, which previous scholarship had recognized as a virtual sibling of BWV 1031; she expands the circle of relationships, moreover, with a demonstration of similarities between BWV 1031 and the indisputably authentic sonata BWV 1032 strong enough to indicate that whoever composed one of these two pieces must at least have known the other. To the arguments on BWV 1031, I might add that I find it even harder than Swack does to imagine Bach going so far in emulating Quantz as to restrict the flute to a range characteristic of the latter composer but vastly narrower than that otherwise exploited in his own pieces for the instrument (cf. "Quantz and the Sonata in E♭ Major," 32). I should note, too, that the recapitulation form employed in the last movement of both BWV 1031 and QV 2:18 has no real counterpart in Bach's unquestionably authentic sonatas—the late "Cembalo solo" in the violin sonata BWV 1019 might appear at first to have the same structure, but Bach approaches the recapitulation from a half-cadence on the dominant, a not insignificantly different gambit; cf. Alfred Dürr, "Johann Gottlieb Goldberg und die Triosonate BWV 1037," BJ 40 (1953): 51–80, at 77–78, or as reprinted idem, *Im Mittelpunkt Bach: Ausgewählte Aufsätze und Vorträge* (Kassel: Bärenreiter, 1988), 36–57, at 54. Finally, it seems hard to understand how Bach could have composed both BWV 1031 and BWV 1032. If BWV 1031 came first, BWV 1032 represents a leap in compositional sophistication all but impossible to reconcile with even the most optimistic view of the time-frame involved—QV 2:18 appears not to date from before 1724, and probably not until about 1730, while the original version of BWV 1032 originated no later than the early months of 1736 (cf. p. 53). If BWV 1032 came first, Bach need hardly have relied so directly on Quantz for BWV 1031; and in any event, the incomparably lesser sophistication of BWV 1031—which I do not confuse with the more "modern" style noted by Marshall, "J. S. Bach's Compositions for Solo Flute," 473 (*The Music of J. S. Bach*, 208)—would mark this sonata as an incomprehensible regression. The attempt in Sackmann and Rampe, "Bach, Berlin, Quantz und die Flötensonate Es-Dur," 60–66, to place BWV 1031 in the 1740s not only bypasses this last question but rests on premises dubious in themselves: the supposed resemblances to the trio sonata from the *Musical Offering* and two other pieces allegedly of the same decade—the Prelude, Fugue, and Allegro for Lute (BWV 998) and the triple concerto BWV 1063—look tenuous at best, and we have no evidence to date the composition of BWV 1063 this late. On strictly musical grounds—to which, besides those already adduced by Swack, we might add the choice of key (cf. BOM, 66–75)—the simplest explanation for the entire complex would assign BWV 1020 and BWV 1031 as well as QV 2:18 to Quantz and assume that J. S. Bach wrote the original version of BWV

in limbo, and so, despite an ingenious rescue attempt on Marshall's part, does the solo sonata BWV 1033.[137] Of the few works with apparently unassailable credentials, three turn out to have begun life in different instrumental guises from the ones familiar to us today. Michael Marissen has exposed the obbligato sonata BWV 1032—or at least its outer movements—as an arrangement of a lost trio for recorder, violin, and continuo.[138] Klaus Hofmann has shown that Bach originally composed the solo part of

---

1032 under the impact of an acquaintance with these new *Sonaten auf Concertenart* of his younger Dresden colleague; in this connection, the "strong resemblance" between the opening theme of BWV 1032 and the aria "Halleluia, Stärk' und Macht" from the cantata *Wir danken dir, Gott, wir danken dir* (BWV 29, noted in Marshall, "J. S. Bach's Compositions for Solo Flute," 490–91) (*The Music of J. S. Bach*, 219) becomes newly provocative, as the composition of BWV 29 closely preceded Bach's visit to Dresden in September 1731 (cf. *Kalendarium zur Lebensgeschichte Johann Sebastian Bachs*, 40). If BWV 1020 and 1031 indeed derived from trio sonatas, then the arrangements conceivably stem from the Bach household—a thought also recently entertained by Hofmann ("Auf der Suche nach der verlorenen Urfassung," 59). As Swack has already implied in connection with BWV 1031 ("Quantz and the Sonata in E♭ Major," 47), this could point toward an explanation for the admittedly still problematic transmission. See also n. 139.

137. On BWV 1038, see particularly Ulrich Siegele, *Kompositionsweise und Bearbeitungstechnik in der Instrumentalmusik Johann Sebastian Bachs*, Tübinger Beiträge zur Musikwissenschaft 3 (Neuhausen-Stuttgart: Hänssler, 1975), 23–46, and David Schulenberg, "Composition as Variation: Inquiries into the Compositional Procedures of the Bach Circle of Composers," *Current Musicology* 33 (1982): 57–87, at 65–74. On BWV 1033, see Marshall, "J. S. Bach's Compositions for Solo Flute," 467–71 (*The Music of J. S. Bach*, 204–6), and Hans Eppstein, "Zur Problematik von Johann Sebastian Bachs Flötensonaten," BJ 67 (1981): 77–90, at 79–83 (Marshall's brief response in *The Music of J. S. Bach*, 225, does not address Eppstein's crucial demonstration that BWV 1033 could not, as Marshall contends, really have originated as a composition for unaccompanied flute); also the new source observation in Leisinger and Wollny, "Altes Zeug von mir," 192–94, as well as the remarks on possible relationships to sonatas of Christoph Förster and C. P. E. Bach in, respectively, Jeanne Swack, "On the Origins of the *Sonate auf Concertenart*," *Journal of the American Musicological Society* 46 (1993): 369–414, at 399–401, and Leta Miller, "C. P. E. Bach's Instrumental 'Recompositions': Revisions or Alternatives?" *Current Musicology* 59 (1995), 5–47, at 15 n. 2.

138. See Michael Marissen, "A Trio in C Major for Recorder, Violin and Continuo by J. S. Bach?" *Early Music* 13 (1985): 384–90, at 387–88; idem, "A Critical Reappraisal of J. S. Bach's A-Major Flute Sonata," *Journal of Musicology* 6 (1988): 367–86; Jeanne Swack, "Bach's A-major Flute Sonata BWV 1032 Revisited," *Bach Studies 2*, ed. Daniel R. Melamed (Cambridge: Cambridge University Press, 1995), 154–74, at 171–74; and Klaus Hofmann, "Ein verschollenes Kammermusikwerk Johann Sebastian Bachs: Zur Fassungsgeschichte der Orgelsonate Es-Dur (BWV 525) und der Sonate A-Dur für Flöte und Cembalo (BWV 1032)," BJ 85 (1999): 67–79, esp. 76–78. Swack ("Bach's A-Major Flute Sonata," 172) finds the transposition of the sonata from C major—the unquestioned original key of at least its outer movements—to A "puzzling"; in her view, the uppermost line, even if composed for recorder, would have remained playable on the transverse flute in C. Taking her cue from Schulze's speculations

the obbligato sonata BWV 1030 for violin; and the researches of Hans Eppstein and Russell Stinson have made it evident that the trio sonata BWV 1039 derives from a lost piece most likely for two violins.[139] With the B-minor ouverture also exposed as an arrangement, the list of securely authentic instrumental works destined from the outset

on BWV 1032, 1062, and Dresden (see n. 129), she suggests that Bach intended the A-major version for Johann Joachim Quantz, whose apparent preference for a lower tessitura the transposition would thus have reflected. But as Marissen has pointed out ("A Trio in C Major," 387), the transposition would in fact have cost little effort—virtually no more, certainly, than if Bach had left the piece in C, as the change of the top part from French violin clef to treble clef would still have obliged him to shift every note down a "third"; and however well the transverse flute could negotiate the music in C major, A major more naturally preserves the fingerings and resonances of the presumed recorder part. On the sequence of movements, both Marissen ("A Trio in C major," 390 n. 15) and Hofmann ("Ein verschollenes Kammermusikwerk," 76–77) have pointed to evidence suggesting that the present Largo e dolce might not originally have belonged to the same work as the surrounding Vivace and Allegro. But Hofmann's argument for tracing this movement back to a supposed antecedent of the Organ Sonata no. 1 in E♭ Major (BWV 525) strikes me as less than compelling. The outer movements of BWV 525 and the middle movement of BWV 1032 occur together only in a "Concerto" in C major for the unlikely combination of violin, violoncello, and bass assembled by an unknown hand in the mid eighteenth century (ST 345). While the octave variants in the bass cited by Hofmann (ibid., 73 n. 21; for details, see NBA IV/7 [Sechs Sonaten und verschiedene Einzelwerke], ed. Dietrich Kilian, KB, 71–72) make a plausible case for thinking that the arranger took the outer movements from a source deriving from the same parent as BWV 525, the wide discrepancy in range between them and the central movement—C–b on the one hand, AA–e' on the other—hardly supports the assumption that all three came from the same place, not least as Hofmann ("Ein verschollenes Kammermusikwerk," 72–73) has shown that the trio version followed its model literally in restricting the upper end of the bass part in the third movement to b♭, and as the readings of mm. 46–50 in the first movement seem designed to avoid anything that would go below C. The arranger, moreover, would have had good reason to seek another slow movement than the one in BWV 525: this would not only have created uncomfortably dense textures in the lower register at more than a few spots, but would also have taken the cello repeatedly as high as a', whereas the present sequence of movements only twice takes it even to e'—once in the second movement (m. 68), and once in the third (mm. 46–47). See also n. 146.

139. On BWV 1039, see most prominently Hans Eppstein, "J. S. Bachs Triosonate G-dur (BWV 1039) und ihre Beziehungen zur Sonate für Gambe und Cembalo G-Dur (BWV 1027)," Die Musikforschung 18 (1965): 126–37, and the chapter "Kellner as Copyist and Transcriber? A Look at Three Organ Arrangements" in Russell Stinson, The Bach Manuscripts of Johann Peter Kellner and his Circle: A Case Study in Reception History (Durham, N.C.: Duke University Press, 1989), 71–100 and 165–68, also published in essentially identical form as "Three Organ-Trio Transcriptions from the Bach Circle: Keys to a Lost Bach Chamber Work," in Bach Studies, 125–59. For BWV 1030, see Hofmann, "Auf der Suche nach der verlorenen Urfassung." Marissen's and Hofmann's findings on BWV 1030 and 1032, incidentally, increase the distance between these works and BWV 1031, as the uppermost line of this sonata clearly belonged to the flute from the outset—a further reason for doubting Bach's authorship?

for the flute becomes very modest indeed: the solo partita BWV 1013; the continuo sonata BWV 1034; the trio sonata and canon perpetuus from the Musical Offering (BWV 1079); and, in the realm of music for larger ensembles, the Fifth Brandenburg Concerto (BWV 1050).[140]

An even more important consequence of our findings concerns Bach's instrumental production as a whole. If the history of the B-minor ouverture provides yet another example of Bach's familiar propensity for adapting his compositions to new use, it also reduces the already exiguous number of works among his instrumental music that remained untouched by such intervention.[141] As things now stand, we can identify hardly a concerto, an ouverture, or a sonata of more than two obbligato parts that did not either undergo some kind of reworking—from changes in readings to transcription for another medium—or owe its very existence to it. The trio sonata of the Musical Offering, of course, went quickly from conception to publication not long before the end of Bach's life and thus had no real chance of further evolution;[142] and the six violin sonatas BWV 1014–19, although revised in greater or lesser degree between their earliest appearance in the mid-1720s and the version fixed some twenty-five years later in a copy by Bach's pupil and son-in-law Johann Christoph Altnickol, stand apart as a closed set evidently designed as such and intended from the outset for its present medium.[143] With these exceptions, however, the list of authentic multivoice pieces

140. Even this list could require some qualification, as some have felt inclined to question the scoring of BWV 1013, and Frans Brüggen's notes to a recording of Bach's flute compositions issued by Seon in 1976 and since, available in a variety of other forms, express uneasiness about the music of BWV 1034; my thanks to Michael Marissen for this latter reference. On BWV 1013, however, see Marcello Castellani, "Il 'Solo pour la flûte traversière' di J. S. Bach: Cöthen o Lipsia?" *Il flauto dolce* 13 (1985): 15–21, translated as "J. S. Bachs 'Solo pour la flûte traversière': Köthen oder Leipzig?" *Tibia* 14 (1989): 567–73, and also Yoshitake Kobayashi, "Noch einmal zu J. S. Bachs 'Solo pour la flûte traversière,'" *Tibia* 16 (1991): 379–82. As for BWV 1034, the attribution, in a manuscript of Johann Peter Kellner's assignable to the years 1726–27, strikes me as more powerful than Brüggen's reservations; cf. Stinson, *The Bach Manuscripts of Johann Peter Kellner and his Circle*, 22–23, and Marshall, "J. S. Bach's Compositions for Solo Flute," 474–75 (*The Music of J. S. Bach*, 209).

141. Indeed, the period between the inception and completion of this study saw the number grew smaller still; see Rifkin, "Besetzung—Entstehung—Überlieferung," and Klaus Hofmann, "Zur Fassungsgeschichte des zweiten *Brandenburgischen Konzerts*," in BOW, 185–92.

142. Even here, however, we should not overlook the fragmentary transcription for melody instrument and harpsichord begun—at his father's behest?—by Johann Christoph Friedrich Bach; cf. NBA VIII/1 (*Kanons, Musikalisches Opfer*), ed. Christoph Wolff, KB, 74–75.

143. On the history of the violin sonatas, see Marshall, "J. S. Bach's Compositions for Solo Flute," 475–76 (*The Music of Johann Sebastian Bach*, 210, 319–20), and, more fully, Schulze, *Studien zur Bach-Überlieferung im 18. Jahrhundert*, 97–98, 110, 112, and 115–19; readers of the latter might want to

not presently known in more than a single version, or not known ever to have had one, includes nothing more than the ouvertures BWV 1066 and, perhaps, 1069, and very possibly the Sixth Brandenburg Concerto (BWV 1051).[144] If we reduce the various clusters of pieces and versions to their underlying common forms, Bach's instrumental output boils down to the rather modest body of music shown in Figure 1.[145]

As the figure makes clear, of course, the multiple forms of each individual piece have rarely all come down to us intact. Early versions in particular seem to have vanished to an alarming degree; too often, as with BWV 1067, we can merely deduce their existence through paleographic or, sometimes, analytic evidence.[146] To make things worse, much

---

note the minor correction concerning the scribe Schlichting in Joshua Rifkin, "'. . . wobey aber die Singstimmen hinlänglich besetzt seyn müssen . . .'—Zum Credo der h-Moll-Messe in der Aufführung Carl Philipp Emanuel Bachs," *Basler Jahrbuch für historische Musikpraxis* 9 (1985): 157–72, at 160 n. 9, as well as the new information on the copyist Anon. 300 in Peter Wollny, "Ein 'musikalischer Veteran Berlins': Der Schreiber Anonymus 300 und seine Bedeutung für die Berliner Bach-Überlieferung," *Jahrbuch des Staatlichen Instituts für Musikforschung Preußischer Kulturbesitz 1995*, ed. Günther Wagner (Stuttgart-Weimar: Mezler, 1996), 80–133. See also, most recently, Frieder Rempp, "Überlegungen zur Chronologie der drei Fassungen der Sonate G-Dur für Violine und konzertierendes Cembalo (BWV 1019)," in *"Die Zeit, die Tag und Jahre macht,"* 169–83.

144. Although two versions of BWV 1069 supposedly existed—a lost early one for winds and strings alone, and the known version with trumpets—I have suggested that we have reason to question the authenticity of this latter form; see Rifkin, "Klangpracht und Stilauffassung." On the question of a precursor for 1051 see, most fully, Ares Rolf, *Das sechste Brandenburgische Konzert: Besetzung, Analyse, Entstehung*, Dortmunder Bach-Forschungen 4 (Dortmund: Klangfarben, 2002), 82–92 and 130–31.

145. The list omits the following works as questionable or inauthentic: BWV 1020, discussed in nn. 135 and 136; BWV 1022 and its close relative BWV 1038, on which see the literature cited in n. 137; BWV 1025, an arrangement of a piece by Silvius Leopold Weiss with evidently minimal involvement by Bach—see principally Karl-Ernst Schröder, "Zum Trio A-Dur BWV 1025," BJ 81 (1995): 47–59; BWV 1036, on which see Siegele, *Kompositionsweise und Bearbeitungstechnik*, 44, and Leisinger and Wollny, "Altes Zeug von mir," 174–79; and BWV 1037, for which see Dürr, "Johann Gottlieb Goldberg und die Triosonate BWV 1037." See also the following note.

146. We should note, however, that some "lost" instrumental works probably never existed. As shown in Rifkin, "Verlorene Quellen, verlorene Werke," 65–68, 72–74, the Sinfonia to the cantata *Am Abend aber desselbigen Sabbats* (BWV 42) comes not from a concerto but from the Coethen serenata *Der Himmel dacht an Anhalts Ruhm und Glück* (BWV 66a); nor, as argued ibid., n. 57, do we have any reason to assume an earlier instrumental model for the first three movements of the secular cantata *Entfliehet, verschwindet, entweichet, ihr Sorgen* (BWV 249a). Alfred Dürr, "Zum Eingangssatz der Kantate BWV 119," BJ 72 (1986): 117–20, proposes that Bach took the opening chorus of *Preise, Jerusalem, den Herrn* (BWV 119) from a French ouverture that no longer survives; but while the evidence clearly points to the reuse of an earlier composition, I would question the specifics of Dürr's identification. All of Bach's instrumental ouvertures (cf. Dirst, "Bach's French Ouvertures and the Politics of

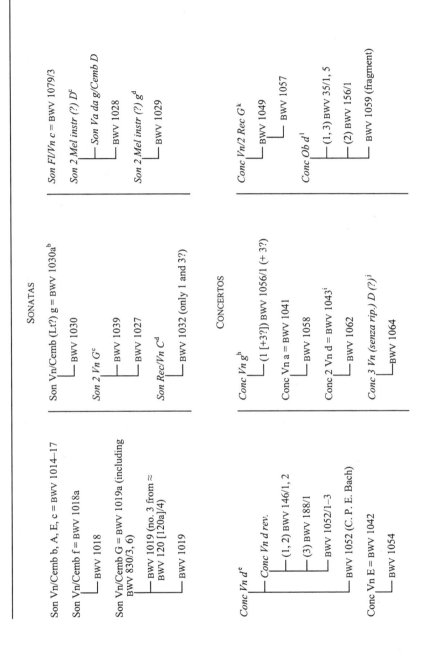

Figure 1. Bach's Instrumental Music in Three or More Parts

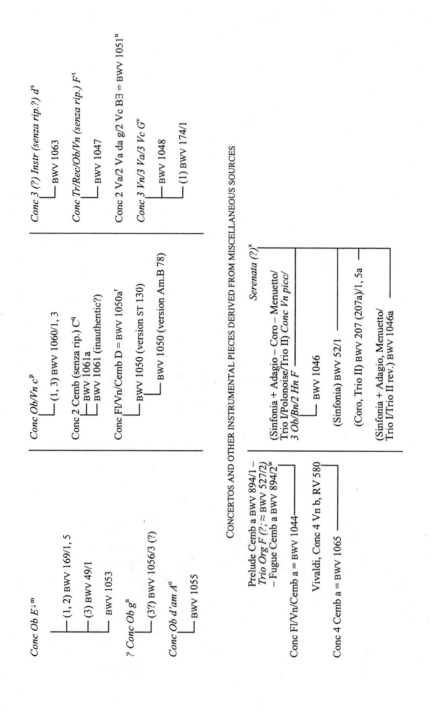

Figure 1. Continued.

OUVERTURES

Ouv Str D^y
  └ BWV 1068

Ouv Vn/Str a
  └ BWV 1067
Ouv 2Ob/Bn/Str C = BWV 1066?

Ouv 3Ob/Bn/Str D^aa
  ├ (1) BWV 110/1
  └ BWV 1069 (inauthentic?)

WORKS BY BWV NUMBER

BWV 1027 → *Son 2 Vn G*
BWV 1028 → *Son 2 Mel instr (?) D*
BWV 1029 → *Son 2 Mel instr (?) g*
BWV 1030 → *Son Vn/Cemb (Lt?) g*
BWV 1032 → *Son Rec/Vn C*
BWV 1039 → *Son 2 Vn C*
BWV 1041 = Conc Vn a
BWV 1042 = Conc Vn E
BWV 1043 = Conc 2 Vn d
BWV 1044 → BWV 894, ≈ 527/2
BWV 1046a → *Serenata*
BWV 1047 → *Conc Tr/Rec/Ob/Vn (senza ripieno) F*

BWV 1048 → *Conc 3 Vn/3 Va/3 Vc G*
BWV 1049 → *Conc Vn/2 Rec G*
BWV 1050 → Conc Fl/Vn/Cemb D
BWV 1050a = Conc Fl/Vn/Cemb D
BWV 1051 → *Conc 2 Va da g/2 Vc B♭*
BWV 1052 → *Conc Vn d*
BWV 1053 → *Conc Ob E♭*
BWV 1054 = BWV 1042
BWV 1055 → *Conc Ob d'amore A*
BWV 1056 → *Conc Vn g – Conc Ob d – Conc Ob g*
BWV 1057 → *Conc Vn/2 Rec G*
BWV 1058 = BWV 1041
BWV 1059 → *Conc Ob d*

BWV 1060 → *Conc Ob/Vn c – Son (Conc? Sinfonia?) 2 Vn c/b?*
BWV 1061 → Conc 2 Cemb (senza rip.) C
BWV 1061a = Conc 2 Cemb (senza rip.) C
BWV 1062 = BWV 1043
BWV 1063 → *Conc 3 Instr d (?)*
BWV 1064 → *Conc 3 Vn (senza rip.) D (?)*
BWV 1065 = Vivaldi RV 580
BWV 1066 = Ouv 2 Ob/Bn/Str C
BWV 1067 → Ouv Vn/Str a
BWV 1068 → Ouv Str D
BWV 1069 → Ouv 3 Ob/Bn/Str D

a. Within each group—sonatas, concertos, ouvertures—the order of items follows scoring (in sonatas and ouvertures, number of instruments; in concertos, solo instrument and number), then key (upper case = major, lower case = minor). *Italics* = lost version; if two sources appear to transmit an essentially identical version of the music (e.g., BWV 1047 in Am.B. 78 or Penzel's copy ST 637), these appear as a single entry; ≈ = early version or model. Abbreviations: Bn = Bassono; Cemb = Cembalo; Conc = Concerto; Fl = Flute; Hn = Horn; Lt = Lute; instr. = melody instrument; Ob = Oboe; Ob d'am = Oboe d'amore; Org = Organ; Ouv = Ouverture; Rec = Recorder; rev. = revised; rip = ripieno; Son = Sonata; Str = Strings; Tr = Trumpet; Va = Viola; Va da g = Viola da gamba; Vc = Violoncello; Vn = Violin; Vn picc = Violino piccolo;

b. See Hofmann, "Auf der Suche nach der verlorenen Urfassung."

c. See Eppstein and Stinson as in n. 139.

d. See n. 138.

e. See Eppstein, *Studien über J. S. Bachs Sonaten für ein Melodieinstrument und obligates Cembalo*, 122–36, and idem, ed., NBA VI/4 (*Drei Sonaten für Viola da gamba und Cembalo*), KB, 20–26.

f. See Laurence Dreyfus, "J. S. Bach and the Status of Genre: Problems of Style in the G-minor Sonata, BWV 1029," *Journal of Musicology* 5 (1987): 55–78, revised and expanded as "The Status of a Genre" in idem, *Bach and the Patterns of Invention* (Cambridge, Mass.: Harvard University Press, 1996), 103–33 and 251–54, but in the light of the evidence for a trio sonata presented variously in Siegele, *Kompositionsweise und Bearbeitungstechnik*, 97–100; Walter Emery, "A Neglected Bach Manuscript," *The Music Review* 11

Figure 1. Continued.

(1950): 169–74, at 172–73; Eppstein, *Studien*, 112–19; and NBA IV/5–6 (*Präludien, Toccaten, Fantasien und Fugen für Orgel*), ed. and Dietrich Kilian, KB, 142–44.

g. See principally Breig, "Bachs Violinkonzert d-Moll"; idem, "Zum Kompositionsprozeß in Bachs Cembalokonzerten," esp. 33–38; and Dreyfus, *Bach and the Patterns of Invention*, 195–208, 257–58. Given the highly literal approach to his model displayed by Philipp Emanuel in much of BWV 1052a (see Breig, "Bachs Violinkonzert d-Moll," 9–16), his singular readings in the viola at mm. 81–90 of the first movement (esp. mm. 81–83), or in the solo part at mm. 244–49 of the third movement (cf. BWV 188/1, m. 249) and throughout the second movement, especially at m. 57, indicate that he worked from a source different from that drawn on by Bach for both BWV 1052 and the various cantatas—and given particularly the ornamented reading of the solo line at mm. 7–11 and 22–23 of both BWV 1052/1 and BWV 146/1, we may surely consider the version available to Emanuel the earlier of the two.

h. On this work and its problems, see NBA VII/7, KB, 81–86; Bruce Haynes, "Johann Sebastian Bachs Oboenkonzerte," BJ 78 (1992): 23–43, at 37–38; Werner Breig, "Zur Werkgeschichte von Bachs Cembalokonzert BWV 1056," *Bachs Orchesterwerke*, 265–82, esp. 267; and Rampe and Sackmann, *Bachs Orchestermusik*, 143–44. The identification of the middle movement with the cantata fragment BWV ANH. 2 suggested by Pieter Dirksen (cf. Breig, "Zur Werkgeschichte von Bachs Cembalokonzert BWV 1056," 267) does not strike me as persuasive. The music looks far more typical of an aria than the slow movement of a concerto: even in those few instances when such a movement begins with a ritornello (BWV 1041/1058, 1042/1054, 1050, 1052, 1053, 1055, and 1064), the music never shows a medial cadence on the dominant,

as occurs here in m. 4 and in numerous arias. Nor does the absence of a voice line necessarily indicate an instrumental movement; see, for instance, the reproduction from the autograph of *Ich bin vergnügt mit meinem Glücke*, BWV 84 (SBB Mus. ms. P 108), in NBA I/7 (*Kantaten zu den Sonntagen Septuagesimae und Sexagesimae*), ed. Werner Neumann, vii. Finally, the corrections leave no doubt that Bach did not take this piece from an earlier source: if, as it appears, he changed the first note of the second staff in m. 6 from a♭'' to g'', then the original reading already presupposes the correction at the end of m. 5 (a♭'' from f'); similarly, nothing could really have preceded the f' on the second eighth of m. 6 but the g''. Cf. *Johann Sebastian Bach: Der Geist hilft unser Schwachheit auf, Motette BWV 226. Faksimile-Lichtdruck des Autographs*, ed. Konrad Ameln (Kassel: Bärenreiter, 1964), and Marshall, *The Compositional Process of J. S. Bach* 2:148–49.

i. See n. 52.

j. See Werner Breig, "Zur Chronologie von Johann Sebastian Bachs Konzertschaffen: Versuch eines neuen Zugangs," *Archiv für Musikwissenschaft* 40 (1983): 77–101, at 83–90.

k. See Marissen, "Organological Questions and Their Significance in J. S. Bach's Fourth Brandenburg Concerto," 46–47, and Gregory Butler, "The Question of Genre in J. S. Bach's Fourth Brandenburg Concerto," BP 4 (1999): 9–32, at 15, 27, 29 n. 10, and 31–32 nn. 28 and 30.

l. See Joshua Rifkin, "Ein langsamer Konzertsatz Johann Sebastian Bachs," *Bach-Jahrbuch* 64 (1978): 140–47; also Steven Zohn with Ian Payne, "Bach, Telemann, and the Process of Transformative Imitation in BWV 1056/2 (156/1)," *Journal of Musicology* 17 (1999): 546–84. The suggestion that the two instrumen-

tal movements in BWV 35 might not have come from the same work as one another (see Rampe and Sackmann, *Bachs Orchestermusik*, 124), while obviously impossible to disprove, overlooks the fact that the scribes of the cantata took the continuo part of the first, and most of the remaining instrumental parts (Oboes 1, 2, Taille; first copies of Violin 1 and 2; Viola) for the second, not from the autograph of the cantata but from an otherwise unknown source—surely the score or parts of the original concerto; cf. NBA I/20 (*Kantaten zum 11. und 12. Sonntag nach Trinitatis*), ed. Klaus Hofmann and Ernest May, 188–90.

m. For the key and the solo instrument, see principally Siegele, *Kompositionsweise und Bearbeitungstechnik*, 136–42; NBA VII/7 (*Verschollene Solokonzerte in Rekonstruktionen*), ed. Wilfried Fischer, KB, 132–37; and Rifkin, "Verlorene Quellen, verlorene Werke," 72 n. 34, to the evidence in which I might now add the correction of a♭ to a♮ in the harpsichord at m. 169 of the third movement (cf. NBA VII/4, KB, 77). The speculations in Wolff, *Bach: The Learned Musician*, 318 and 497 n. 41, and Konrad Küster, "Orchestermusik," in *Bach-Handbuch*, ed. Konrad Küster (Kassel: Bärenreiter, 1999), 898–935, at 923–24 and 930 (also idem, "Die Vokalmusik," ibid., 96–513, at 327), on an organ concerto as possible model ignore the manuscript evidence cited in "Verlorene Quellen"; and against the reservations about the suitability of this music to the oboe expressed in Haynes, "Johann Sebastian Bachs Oboenkonzerte," 31–32, I would note that more than one Baroque oboist of my acquaintance finds this piece eminently playable, and even a gratifying challenge. Of the corrections in the autograph of BWV 1053 that Rampe and Sackmann (*Bachs Orchestermusik*, 131 and 465 n. 22) interpret as signs of a model written a tone lower, only those at mm. 32, 46, and 55 of the first

Figure 1. Continued.

movement possibly have this implication; the rest either alter readings identical to those in BWV 169/1 as they would appear in E or E♭ (no. 1, mm. 3 and 4; no. 2, m. 3) or do not involve revisions of a second (cf. NBA VII/4, KB, 66–72).

n. See Haynes, "Johann Sebastian Bachs Oboenkonzerte," 37, and Rampe and Sackmann, *Bachs Orchestermusik*, 143–44.

o. See chiefly Werner Breig, "Zur Werkgeschichte von Johann Sebastian Bachs Cembalokonzert in A-Dur BWV 1055," and idem, "Zur Gestalt von Johann Sebastian Bachs Konzert für Oboe d'amore," *Tibia* 18 (1993): 431–48. The attempt in Rampe and Sackmann, *Bachs Orchestermusik*, 135–36 and 138–41, to sustain arguments for the viola d'amore as the original solo instrument rests essentially on a failure to read the autograph of BWV 1055 very knowledgeably: not only the frequent corrections (see Breig, "Zur Werkgeschichte," 192–93) but also the character of Bach's script (see the reproduction in NBA VII/7, ix) exclude any realistic chance that the arpeggio figures of the harpsichord in the ritornellos come from the model.

p. For the double concerto BWV 1060, see chiefly Rifkin, "Verlorene Quellen, verlorene Werke," 61–65 and 71–72; the attempted refutation in Sackmann and Rampe, *Bachs Orchestermusik*, 161–64, presents such a partial and distorted account of my arguments as to verge on wilful misrepresentation.

q. See NBA VII/5 (*Konzerte für zwei Cembali*), ed. Karl Heller and Hans-Joachim Schulze, KB, 92–94; Wolff, 228; and Rampe and Sackmann, *Bachs Orchestermusik*, 155–56.

r. While the version of BWV 1050 in Am.B 78 unquestionably derives from the one notated in ST 130, the score of Am.B 78 probably did not depend directly on ST 130. See Dürr and Marshall as in n. 207; note,

too, in amplification of the latter's points, that the correspondence between copyist's marks and page turns in the score falls down midway through the first movement—the parts show a mark at m. 98, but the score has a page turn a measure later.

s. See NBA VII/6 (*Konzerte für drei und vier Cembali*), ed. Rudolf Eller and Karl Heller, KB, 26–31; NBA VII/7, KB, 141–43; Karl Heller, "Eine Leipziger Werkfassung und deren unbekannte Vorlage: Thesen zur Urform des Konzerts BWV 1063," *Bach in Leipzig—Bach und Leipzig: Konferenzbericht Leipzig 2000*, ed. Ulrich Leisinger, Leipziger Beiträge zur Bachforschung 5 (Hildesheim: Georg Olms, 2002), 90–108; and Rampe and Sackmann, *Bachs Orchestermusik*, 170–75.

t. See Hofmann, "Zur Fassungsgeschichte des zweiten Brandenburgischen Konzerts," which I continue to find persuasive despite the objections in Rampe and Sackmann, *Bachs Orchestermusik*, 94.

u. Cf. n. 144.

v. See principally NBA I/14, KB, 69–71, 96, and 106–7, and Marissen, "Penzel Manuscripts of Bach Concertos," 80–84.

w. See Peter Wollny, "Überlegungen zum Tripelkonzert a-Moll BWV 1044," *Bachs Orchesterwerke*, 283–91; Hans Eppstein, "Grundzüge in J. S. Bachs Sonatenschaffen," BJ 55 (1969): 55–30, at 23–24 and 30; and n. 147 in this essay.

x. See n. 151.

y. See n. 48; the further details and speculations in Rampe and Sackmann, *Bachs Orchestermusik*, 261–64, strike me as mostly questionable, but as they do not affect the basic facts of the matter I need not consider them here.

z. See Rifkin, "Verlorene Quellen, verlorene Werke," 59–61.

aa. See Rifkin, "Klangpracht und Stilauffassung." The objections in Rampe and Sackmann, *Bachs Orchestermusik*, 85, do not present the original argumentation completely or accurately, nor do the counter-arguments provide wholly accurate information—while the authors rightly draw attention to a nest of parallel octaves in BWV 1068/1 that went unremarked in "Klangpracht und Stilauffassung," 343 n. 36 (Ouverture, m. 86, Trumpet I/Violin 1, and mm. 86–87, Trumpet 2/Violin 2 and Trumpet 3/Continuo), the other place they mention (Ouverture, mm. 55–56) in fact contains no parallels.

Figure 1. Continued.

of the music that we do have survives only in secondary sources, and the transmission even of works for which original manuscripts exist displays painful lacunae—only in the rarest case do we have both the autograph score and the accompanying parts.[147] Yet without wishing to minimize the extent of the damage, I would suggest that these losses have created something of a misleading impression. Scholars have generally read the fragmentary transmission of Bach's instrumental music as a sign that his production in this domain originally encompassed a far greater number of compositions than we

---

Overdotting," 38) follow the traditional pattern of starting the quicker central section with a fugal exposition unsupported by the bass until the final entry; BWV 119/1, by contrast, maintains continuo involvement throughout and lacks a thoroughgoing imitative structure. Nor do the instrumental ouvertures contain anything remotely like the call-and-response entry of the voices at m. 44. I would think it more likely, therefore, that the movement derives from a chorus in ouverture style, such as Bach wrote in BWV 21, 61, 97, and 194. The instrumental trio that Hofmann ("Ein verschollenes Kammermusikwerk"; see n. 138) proposes as the source of the organ sonata BWV 525 might represent another such phantom. Without the slow movement of BWV 1032, nothing in the music really presupposes ensemble realization—all the more so as Hofmann's reading of the middle line in the outer movements as an oboe part (cf. "Ein verschollenes Kammermusikwerk," 69) depends on a questionable interpretation of some variants in the late trio arrangement (ibid., 73 n. 21): surely, we may better understand the octave transfers in the middle voice at mm. 32–33 of the first movement and mm. 15–17 of the third as attempts to avoid some particularly ungainly part crossing, especially as the second of these introduces an otherwise unmotivated break in the imitation between the upper two voices. Accordingly, I find no reason to believe that the first movement ever began with anything but an idiomatic pedal line of the sort the piece now has (see ibid., 71 n. 14), and even less to imagine any medium but the organ for the last movement, whose principal theme seems designed not least to show off the player's pedal technique. Two further supposed instrumental trios associated with the organ sonatas also merit comment. According to Dietrich Kilian (NBA IV/7, KB, 74), the copy of BWV 527/1 in an early version by Johann Caspar Vogler (P 1089) shows signs of dependency on a set of parts. But while the alignment of treble and bass in mm. 1–7 could give this impression, other features—such as the stemming of the top voice in mm. 3–7 or the spacing of the two upper voices in m. 11—indicate strongly that Vogler worked from a score; and the sextuplet passages at mm. 57–60 and 85–92, ideally suited to the keyboard, do not fit well on flute, oboe, or violin. Hofmann ("Ein verschollenes Kammermusikwerk," 67 n. 1) suggests that the slow movement of BWV 528 comes from a piece with oboe, as the top line of an early version avoids c♯' in a context where we might sooner have expected it; but I find the spot ambiguous at best, not least because it introduces other variations as well into material it restates. Finally, the trio sonata considered as a source for the slow movement of the concerto BWV 1060 in Rifkin, "Verlorene Quellen, verlorene Werke," 63, 65, and 72, remains too vague a possibility to count without question as a lost composition. On the trio hypothesized as the model for BWV 1043, see n. 52.

147. See Christoph Wolff, "Die Orchesterwerke J. S. Bachs: Grundsätzliche Erwägungen zu Repertoire, Überlieferung und Chronologie," in BOW, 17–30.

can account for today.[148] Surely, however, the very intensity with which Bach recycled his instrumental works tells us precisely the opposite—that he in fact wrote only a limited number of such pieces, which he then had constantly to adapt to ever new situations.[149] If, therefore, we orient ourselves to the basic compositional substance and not to each particular manifestation and transformation that it may undergo, it seems fair to suppose that we in fact know the greater part of what Bach created in the instrumental realm.

Two examples may show how this assumption fits with the source situation. The first concerns the Brandenburg Concertos. Manuscripts written after 1750 transmit Concertos 2, 3, and 5 as independent pieces, in versions that clearly represent an earlier—if not necessarily very much earlier—stage of development than those preserved in the dedication score of 1721; a close relative of the first concerto, moreover, survives in a copy of 1760 whose readings also point to models predating the dedication score.[150] These posthumous sources, in other words, show no recognizable connection to the six concertos as a set but derive ultimately from Bach's original manuscripts of the individual pieces. Yet should we assume that Bach assembled the contents of the dedication copy from a larger supply of similar works, then we must ask at the same time why the very items he selected turn up in the second half of the century but the putative rejected candidates fail to appear—for the surviving corpus of Bach's music contains not a single further composition of analogous profile.[151]

148. See, for example, the recent discussion in Peter Wollny, "Abschriften und Autographe, Sammler und Kopisten: Aspekte der Bach-Pflege im 18. Jahrhundert," in *Bach und die Nachwelt* 1:27–62, at 33–34.

149. The degree to which Bach recycled his instrumental music has no match among at least his sacred vocal works, nor, so far as I can tell, among the instrumental works of any of his contemporaries.

150. Cf. Alfred Dürr, "Zur Entstehungsgeschichte des 5. Brandenburgischen Konzerts," BJ 61 (1975): 63–69, and Michael Marissen, "Penzel Manuscripts of Bach Concertos," in BOW, 77–87. Marissen has established elsewhere that manuscripts thought by Heinrich Besseler to contain independent versions of the fourth and sixth concertos in fact derived from the dedication score; see Michael Marissen, "Organological Questions and Their Significance in J. S. Bach's Fourth Brandenburg Concerto," *Journal of the American Musical Instrument Society* 15 (1991): 5–52, at 45–47, and idem, *The Social and Religious Designs of J. S. Bach's Brandenburg Concertos* (Princeton, N.J.: Princeton University Press, 1995), 121–27.

151. Malcolm Boyd has voiced similar suspicions in *Bach: The Brandenburg Concertos*, Cambridge Music Handbooks (Cambridge: Cambridge University Press, 1993), 16–17. Bach approaches the manner of the Brandenburg Concertos most closely in the sinfonia BWV 42/1—and this piece, as pointed out in n. 146, does not come from a concerto. The supposition that Bach more likely had a fairly narrow base of works on which to proceed when assembling the Brandenburg Concertos receives further

As a second example, I would mention the Violin Concerto in E Major (BWV 1042). In contrast to the Brandenburg Concertos, we know this work solely through manuscripts copied after Bach's death.[152] Against this, however, we have the harpsichord arrangement BWV 1054 in the autograph volume P 234. Once again, the late transmission—which we must surely regard as random—brings us a work that already reaches us, even if in different form, through other channels.

The idea that a large stock of instrumental music by Bach has disappeared without a trace would thus compel us to imagine not one, but two bodies of lost sources—original manuscripts and at least some later copies. Unless, moreover, the missing compositions led an existence utterly different from that of the surviving ones and never underwent recycling, we would in effect have to imagine something like two bodies of lost pieces, as well.[153] Such a rapidly expanding population of ghosts cannot strike very many as something credible. By every indication, therefore, we can define the scope and nature of Bach's instrumental output to a much greater degree than previously imagined. True, we lack this or that version of this or that work, and doubtless not every concerto, every ouverture or sonata of his has come down to us even through a single representative.[154] But on the whole, I think it safe to say that relatively little has escaped us completely.

---

support from the findings of Hofmann, "Zur Fassungsgeschichte des zweiten *Brandenburgischen Konzerts*," and from the heterodox genesis of the first concerto arrived at independently by Michael Talbot and myself; see his "Purpose and Peculiarities of the *Brandenburg Concertos*," in *Bach und die Stile*, 255–89, at 271–76 and 287–88.

152. Cf. NBA VII/3, KB, 21–23, as well as the supplementary information in Wollny, "Ein 'musikalischer Veteran Berlins,'" 102 and 106.

153. Responding to a preliminary version of these findings in "Verlorene Quellen, verlorene Werke," 67–69, Hans-Joachim Schulze observes that their "optimistic conclusion . . . will not win the allegiance of every author"; see his review of BOW in BJ 85 (1999): 201–4, at 202. Yet if, as the context suggests, he rates the number of lost compositions considerably higher than I do, he rates the number of lost versions considerably lower: "The complicated processes of creation or arrangement assumed by various authors for individual concertos presuppose that these various stages would have taken written form. Where all this material could have remained, whether it still existed at the division of Bach's estate or whether Bach during his lifetime had let it out of his hands, made a gift of it, sold it, or lent it and not got it back—these questions have not yet had a satisfactory answer." Schulze does not explain how "these questions" differ from the question of the entirely unknown instrumental pieces whose existence he appears to take for granted.

154. For an apparently "new" lost instrumental work, see the remarks on the slow movement of the double concerto BWV 1060 in Rifkin, "Verlorene Quellen, verlorene Werke," 62–63, 65, and 71–72, but also the cautions in n. 146.

VI

Let us come back to our point of departure—the "B-Minor Flute Suite." Does all that has emerged in the course of the present exploration change our understanding of the piece? If we choose to listen self-critically, we shall no doubt have at least to qualify the extent to which we hear it as somehow embodying the essence of both B minor and the flute. Less obviously, we may find our perceptions affected by the latest—and presumably last—shift in its chronological position. For a very long time, after all, the musical community associated the ouverture with Coethen and its princely court, a station in Bach's career when the still relatively young composer seemed to have enjoyed a degree of contentment never equaled in the remainder of his life.[155] With its assignment to the late 1730s, the work moved to a very different milieu: the conflicted world of Leipzig on the cusp of Bach's late period—the world of the battle with Ernesti, the attacks of Scheibe, and the trouble over the Passion music in 1739.[156] Now, although pushed back only a few years and still in Leipzig, it appears once again in new surroundings: while following closely on a time of mounting tension with his civic employers, it nevertheless comes at what we might see as the height of Bach's middle period—indeed, in the first flush of his involvement with an ensemble that more than a few scholars have seen as betokening a revitalization of his powers after a period of increasing tribulation in his ecclesiastical and scholastic duties.[157] To the extent that we think of music as reflecting the circumstances of its creation, we face the prospect that the ouverture will somehow take on a different guise with each new dating.

Of course, we can take such things only so far. As Laurence Dreyfus reminds us, Bach resists easy contextualization; indeed, it seems almost better to place him dialectically against contexts than within them.[158] Not only that, but the very sort of context

---

155. Wolff's assessment in *Bach: The Learned Musician*, 202, can stand for many: "Bach found himself in a musically ideal situation."

156. Cf., variously, n. 96 and BDOK 1:82–91 (nos. 32–35) and 95–106 (nos. 39–41); 2:267–76 (nos. 380 and 382–83) and 286–88 (no. 400), as well as the further items cited 287; and 3:314 (no. 820). Among modern biographical accounts, that of Arno Forchert comes closest to bringing these episodes into conjunction; see his *Johann Sebastian Bach und seine Zeit* (Laaber: Laaber, 2000), 142–47 and 156–65.

157. As Wolff has put it, Bach "must have felt that, as director of the collegium, he would be able to establish an area where he would be completely independent and free to pursue his own ideas"; see Walter Emery and Christoph Wolff, "Bach, III: (7) Johann Sebastian Bach," in *The New Grove* 1:785–840, at 798, lightly modified in *The New Grove*, 2nd ed., 2:309–82, at 323.

158. See Laurence Dreyfus, *Bach and the Patterns of Invention* (Cambridge, Mass.: Harvard University Press, 1996), esp. the chapters "Bach as Critic of the Enlightenment," 219–44, and, from a more autonomously musical vantage point, "Composing against the Grain," 33–58.

routinely invoked in connection with Bach belongs to a rather different world from those in which I have just situated the ouverture: whereas few will read, say, Handel without reference to specific constellations of patrons, friends, and collaborators in Rome or London, Bach has a habit of winding up not so much in Weimar, Coethen, or Leipzig as in an abstract German universe governed by the overarching concepts of Lutheranism, Enlightenment, and absolutism.[159] Even allowing for a strong dose of religious, philosophical, and national ideology, I think we may see this tendency as rooted more than a little in the powerfully self-willed logic of Bach's compositional invention and its mechanisms; and that logic, to complete a kind of hermeneutic circle, leaves the ouverture untouched not only by vagaries of dating, but also by revelations about its key and instrumentation.

But this conclusion, and indeed the entire train of reasoning behind it, may well miss the point. For one thing, if we can now recognize the Ouverture for Flute and Strings in B Minor as a derivative of another composition—an epiphenomenon, if you will, rather than the phenomenon itself—then questions of understanding must inevitably shift to a different object: the Ouverture in A Minor for Violin and Strings. Admittedly, some may continue to regard the distinction as trivial. As the ouverture itself reminds us, Bach transposed and transcribed his earlier works often enough to make us wonder if he really cared very much about scoring and key. I see no reason, however, to draw such an inference: a readiness to alter the sonority of music already composed does not inevitably translate into an indifference toward sonority when actually conceiving and composing that music. Indeed, in this era of "historical performance," the point would hardly seem to require a strenuous defense; and in any event, no matter what Bach himself might have thought, we have no obligation to consider specifics of tonality and instrumentation as matters of incidental significance.[160] Even leaving aside facile notions of key characteristics, no one will deny that strings playing in A minor produce, simply by virtue of fingering and resonance, something very different from what the same group will produce in B minor; nor, just as obvious, does an ensemble of strings alone really sound anything like a mixed ensemble of strings and flute. The differences may not register dramatically on the page, nor in an analytic discourse—and an attendant sense of compositional logic—all but inevitably concentrated on internal relationships of pitch and duration. Yet in the

---

159. See, to name just three familiar examples, Ulrich Siegele, *Bachs theologischer Formbegriff und das Duett F-Dur: Ein Vortrag*, Tübinger Beiträge zur Musikwissenschaft 6 (Neuhausen-Stuttgart: Hänssler, 1978); Eric Chafe, *Tonal Allegory in the Vocal Music of J. S. Bach* (Berkeley: University of California Press, 1991); and Marissen, *The Social and Religious Designs of J. S. Bach's Brandenburg Concertos*.

160. Cf. Rifkin, "Klangpracht und Stilauffassung," 340.

reality of performance, they prove anything but negligible. As more than a few who have heard the reconstructed A-minor ouverture have remarked, the darker, more uniform color and the lower pitch together lend the music a gravitas unknown in what has become its familiar garb.[161] The solo instrument, too, exposes meanings previously unsuspected. To take just two: the bariolage on its very first entry lends a newly assertive undercurrent to the deportment of the principal actor; and at the opposite end of the work, the imploring gestures in mm. 18–19 and 36–37 of the Battinerie speak now with an urgency that few would have recognized before.

These observations, however, could raise another objection: that to supplant, if only in the realm of critical inquiry, the B-minor ouverture with that in A minor risks fetishizing Bach's original conception over its subsequent evolution. Yet without wishing to deflate the nimbus of the "Fassung letzter Hand," I would ask just how well "evolution," and all that it implies, really fits the present situation.[162] In line with the bias confronted in the last paragraph, we typically locate those revisions of Bach's that we regard as genuine compositional enhancements in the domain of pitch and rhythm: elaborations of melodic lines, intensifications of harmonic density, sharpening of rhythmic gestures. Changes of key or scoring have a more contingent status, and nowhere more so than when they occur not within a piece otherwise left fundamentally intact—as with, for instance, the addition of flutes to the cantata *Gott der Herr ist Sonn und Schild* (BWV 79), or the final version of the aria "Zerfließe, mein Herze" in the St. John Passion—but on the level of transferring an entire composition from one medium to another.[163] Hence Bach's keyboard adaptations of the three extant concertos with one or two violins have never really established a place comparable to the originals either in the repertory or in scholarly reception, even though, strictly speaking, they embody his final thoughts on the music. Conversely, we may wonder if the D-minor

---

161. Much of what I write here reflects the experience of performing the A-minor ouverture with the Bach Ensemble at concerts in the U.S. and elsewhere in 2000 and 2002; my thanks especially to the violin soloists Linda Quan and Emlyn Ngai.

162. I have already touched on the underlying theme of the following remarks elsewhere: see Joshua Rifkin, "More (and Less) on Bach's Orchestra," 10–11; "From Weimar to Leipzig: Concertists and Ripienists in Bach's *Ich hatte viel Bekümmernis*," *Early Music* 24 (1996): 583–603, at 594; and "Klangpracht und Stilauffassung," 340.

163. On BWV 79, see particularly Michael Marissen, "Aufführungspraxis und Bedeutung in zwei Instrumentalwerken Johann Sebastian Bachs," in *Bach und die Stile*, 291–301, at 295–96; on "Zerfließe, mein Herze," see Joshua Rifkin, "The Violins in Bach's St. John Passion," in *Critica Musica: Essays in Honor of Paul Brainard*, ed. John Knowles, Musicology 18 (Amsterdam: Gordon and Breach, 1996), 307–32, at 322–28.

harpsichord concerto BWV 1052 would ever have achieved its iconic, if sometimes contentious, status if the underlying composition for violin had survived.[164] At least among the music for instrumental ensemble, in other words, our inherited approach has indeed tended to elevate the original above the transformation.[165]

Obviously, much of what I describe here has to do less with articulated preferences, or even unconscious prejudices, than with accidents of transmission, the development of what we might call the working Bach canon in the nineteenth century, and a considerable amount of inertia since. But some of it surely reflects a more deeply perceived truth, as well; for we do not have to restore the entire analytic and critical hierarchy whose consequences I have sought to qualify to recognize that modifications of pitch and rhythm on the one hand, and of key and instrumentation on the other, have very different meanings in Bach's reworking of his music. If nothing else, it would seem clear that he regarded changes of the former sort as an improvement on what he had formerly written and meant them to supersede what they replaced—even if he did not always hold absolutely to this in practice.[166] But in principle as well as in practice, I doubt anyone would contend that he regarded the transfer of a sonata, concerto, or ouverture from one medium to another in the same light: whatever the attractions of the new scoring, and however many revisions of internal detail he may have introduced, Bach surely did not consider the very fact of adaptation as an evolutionary step effacing its precursor any more than subsequent reception has done. This would seem all the more the case when the newer incarnation leaves the inner fabric of the music largely or completely untouched—precisely the situation, as we have seen, with the B-minor ouverture. Especially under this circumstance, we may surely think it reasonable to grant the original not only parity with, but even primacy over, the arrangement.

Not, I should add, that I expect any of this to have much consequence in the real world; if nothing else, the inertia alluded to not many lines above means that the A-minor ouverture stands about as much chance of edging out its celebrated B-minor

---

164. See, for some early manifestations, Werner Breig, "Bachs Violinkonzert d-Moll: Studien zu seiner Gestalt und seiner Entstehungsgeschichte," BJ 62 (1976): 7–34, at 22–23; Bodo Bischoff, "Das Bach-Bild Robert Schumanns," in *Bach und die Nachwelt* 1:421–99, at 465; and Hans-Joachim Hinrichsen, "Zwischen Bearbeitung und Interpretation: Zum praktischen Umgang mit Bachs Instrumentalwerk," ibid., 2:341–89, at 355.

165. In vocal music things have tended to work differently, as the relative position of many sacred cantatas and their secular models—not least those relegated in BWV to the shadow world of "a" numbers—indicates; but this, as I need hardly emphasize, has different reasons yet again.

166. To mention a particularly well-known example, Bach's last performance of the St. John Passion incorporated barely any of the revisions he had made in the abandoned autograph score of 1739; cf., most readably, Dürr, *Die Johannes-Passion von Johann Sebastian Bach*, 23–24.

progeny in either musical practice or scholarly consciousness as a new typewriter layout has of spelling the end to the qwerty keyboard.[167] But in fact no one—and not merely flutists—would really want to see the ouverture as we have known it fade from view. After all, Bach arranged it. Nor, despite its secondary status, can we deny its appeal. Awareness that the octave doubling of the Polonoise represents both an afterthought and a matter of virtual necessity makes the resultant sonority no less arresting; and only the hardest of hearts could fail to take pleasure from hearing the flute scamper through even the very passages in the first movement or the Battinerie where only the violin can reveal all that the music has to say. Whatever its origins, moreover, BWV 1067 documents a clearly important side of Bach's musical concerns of the later 1730s: for whatever reason, he turned to the flute often in the period, even if not as a medium for new composition. So the gain of a significant new work by Bach does not mean the loss of another; deconstructing the "B-minor Flute Suite" does not mean destroying it.

Postscript: Christian Friedrich Penzel and a Lost Source for BWV 1067

In the critical report to their edition of BWV 1067 in the *Neue Bach-Ausgabe*, Heinrich Besseler and Hans Grüß draw special attention to a score and set of parts—P 1065 and ST 639, respectively—written by the Oelsnitz cantor and former Leipzig prefect Christian Friedrich Penzel. Unlike two other secondary sources from the eighteenth century, these manuscripts do not show obvious signs of dependence on the surviving original parts; on the contrary, they offer singular readings at several points.[168] Since the first page of P 1065 shows the inscription "J.J.," often found in Bach autographs, Besseler and Grüß suggest that Penzel's copies derive from "an autograph score of Bach's."[169] If we take this to mean a composing document, then the suggestion runs into conflict with our findings in Section I, which seemed to indicate that Bach and his copyists created the B-minor ouverture directly in parts. Indeed, such a score would in effect remove all but the most tenuous evidence for the supposed early version of the work. Obviously, the matter demands closer consideration.

We must begin with the Penzel manuscripts themselves. As Yoshitake Kobayashi has established, the two copies did not originate at the same time: the parts date from circa

---

167. See also, in a similar connection, Breig, "Bachs Violinkonzert d-Moll," 34.

168. For the other eighteenth-century sources, as well as nineteenth-century copies dependent on Penzel, see NBA VII/1, KB, 37–38, 40–42, 45, and 122. For the readings, see further in the main text.

169. NBA VII/1, KB, 39. The description of the first page ibid., 38, reverses the positions of the composer attribution and the inscription: "J.J." stands to the left of the title, "di J. S. Bach" to the right.

1755, the score from circa 1760.[170] In contrast to what we might expect, therefore, the parts cannot have derived from the score. Indeed, well before Kobayashi's investigations, the readings had led Besseler and Grüß to exactly this conclusion.[171] According to the two editors, Penzel must have copied score and parts independently from the same parent source. Yet especially if we follow Besseler and Grüß in identifying this source as the putative original score of BWV 1067, their scenario runs into more than a few difficulties. The gap in time now opened up by Kobayashi between ST 639 and P 1065 presents one. Although we cannot entirely rule out the possibility that Penzel made two separate copies from the same manuscript at widely spaced intervals, it does not appear immediately plausible that he should have done so: if he had a score in his possession over a longer period of time, he would scarcely have had to write P 1065; and if he had extended access to a set of parts, he would have had no need to produce ST 639. More important, certain features of P 1065 reveal that Penzel did not copy this manuscript from another score but rather assembled it from parts.

A single example should suffice to make this clear. Plate 3 shows the second page of P 1065, which contains mm. 25–59 of the opening movement. As the reader will immediately note, Penzel reversed the two violin lines in the uppermost system. His method of copying makes the error easy to understand. In both this movement and the Rondeaux, he wrote out the flute in its entirety but restricted the first violin to occasional cues except for the relatively few places—such as the last five measures of the page reproduced here—where it proceeds independently of the solo instrument.[172] For large stretches, therefore, the staff immediately below the flute remained blank, which makes it hardly surprising that the second violin should occasionally have wandered into it at the start of a new page or system. In principle, of course, a scribe copying from a score could have fallen prey to such a mistake, at least if his model also contained nothing in the first-violin staff. But surely, no one with a score before him would have felt impelled to count up rests so painstakingly where instruments remain silent. The numbers could not very well have served as a guide for a future copyist extracting parts from P 1065. If Penzel had this in mind, he would presumably

170. See Yoshitake Kobayashi, "Franz Hauser und seine Bach-Handschriftensammlung" (Ph.D. dissertation, Universität Göttingen, 1973), 174–83, esp. 179 and 181. According to Kobayashi, P 1065 has a watermark found otherwise only in a manuscript dated 1754 (P 1053, BWV 211) and in a further source lacking a date but characteristic of Penzel's script ca. 1755 (P 1055, BWV 1068); see also n. 204. Nevertheless, the handwriting of P 1065 surely justifies Kobayashi's dating; perhaps the watermark in the manuscript—which I have not had the chance to compare with other sources—in fact represents a variant form of the one documented in the mid-1750s.

171. See NBA VII/1, KB, 45–46.

172. For details of this in the first movement, see NBA VII/1, KB, 47.

Plate 3. P 1065, f. 1ᵛ

have entered a "12" in the continuo at the start of the second system rather than the "11" at the end of the first; and he also would have had no reason to write a "3" in the same part at the bottom of the page, as the continuo has a further four measures' rest before it enters again. Penzel, in other words, numbered the rests for his own orientation—to keep himself from getting lost when transferring parts to score.[173]

The remainder of P 1065 essentially bears out the lessons of our sample page. For the Sarabande, Bourée, and Polonoise, Penzel switched the notational roles of the two lead instruments, copying Violin 1 in full and the flute in abbreviated form. If, by this measure, he hoped to avoid the problem of errant instrumental lines, the strategy did not always succeed; on fol. 5r, in the last system of the Sarabande, Violin 1 occupies the uppermost staff and the other parts follow immediately below, meaning that the flute remains absent and the lowest staff remains empty. At no point, however, does the order of priority between flute and violin shift within a movement, as we could expect if Penzel had a score before him; and the Sarabande, although composed in only four real parts, maintains the five-stave layout of the preceding music.[174] From the Double to the end, Penzel appears to have copied once more from the flute. The Double, of course, left him no other option, as the violins and viola fall silent for the entire movement. Presumably, a tacet marking in Violin 1—Penzel's own part, for example, reads, "Violino 1. tac"—alerted him to the change in scoring; as Penzel notated the movement on two staves instead of five, we can surmise that he cast a glance at the other string parts before proceeding.[175] Somewhat puzzlingly, the Menuet does not return to the five-stave layout, but places flute and violin together on the top staff with the inscription "Flauto con Violino. 1." Although this could obviously revive suspicions that Penzel worked from score, we shall see evidence in the next paragraph suggesting that he copied the line from a separate flute part; and in the Battinerie, an error in the continuo again suggests dependence on parts: near the end of the move-

173. A similarly telling instance, again in the continuo, occurs at the three bars of rest occupying mm. 134–36 of the first movement (fol. 3r): mm. 134–35 come at the end of a line and carry the number "2," m. 136 begins a new line and marks the total "3" as it appears in the corresponding part. Similarly, when reaching the end of a line at m. 9 of the Rondeaux (fol. 4r), Penzel augmented the rest with a surely superfluous "1." A copyist would scarcely have had a great need for such low measure counts, which Penzel entered with obsessive consistency.

174. This point remains unaffected by the accident in the final system; here, too, Penzel had drawn a brace of five staves.

175. Besseler and Grüß (NBA VII/1, KB, 39) cite the reduced layout of the Double as support for their assertion that Penzel copied from a score. As Michael Marissen has shown, Penzel's copy of the sinfonia BWV 1046a (P1061), another manuscript with systems of varying size, also derives from parts; see "Penzel Manuscripts of Bach Concertos," 77–78.

ment, Penzel copied only two of the three identical measures 33–35 into P 1065 but nevertheless continued to write the bass line until just before its conclusion five bars later—only then, it seems, did he realize that he had come to the final note ahead of the other instruments.

Notwithstanding the slight uncertainty created by the layout of the Menuet, therefore, the conclusion that P 1065 derives from a set of parts would appear unshakeable. Indeed, having established that P 1065 derives from a set of parts, it takes little effort to identify Penzel's model. Michael Marissen has shown that Penzel copied scores of the Second and Third Brandenburg Concertos from parts that he himself had prepared at earlier times; a comparison of readings in the ouverture leaves no doubt that he followed the same procedure here, as well.[176] The variants shared by P 1065 and ST 639 include more than a few outright errors. A particularly notable one occurs in the second half of the Battinerie: from the start of this section in the middle of m. 16 until m. 21, the second-violin line contains the parts of both Violin 1 and Violin 2. To imagine that P 1065 could owe this reading to anything but ST 639 would presuppose the existence of a second set of parts containing exactly the same mistake—hardly a credible proposition.[177] In at least one instance, moreover, a discrepancy between P 1065 and ST 639 plainly reflects an attempt by Penzel to rectify something that had gone wrong in the part. At m. 208 of the opening movement, Violin 2 should read as shown in Example 10a. In ST 639, however, Penzel transformed this into the reading reproduced in Example 10b; and in P 1065, the measure assumed the form shown in Example 10c.[178] The readings of ST 639 also help resolve the questions about the Menuet raised in the last paragraph and explain the error in the continuo of the Battinerie. At m. 8 of the Menuet, Penzel's flute part and the combined treble line of P 1065 have an appoggiatura on b' instead of the d'' found both in Violin 1 of ST 639 and in Bach's flute and violin parts; the chances that a common parent score for ST 639 and P 1065 would have written out the two lines and had different appoggiaturas for each would appear slender indeed. At m. 33 of the Battinerie, an inexplicable sharp sign in the continuo of ST 639 obscures the first note; Penzel could have momentarily read this as canceling the entire measure.

---

176. See ibid., 79–82; we no longer have the set of parts from which Penzel copied BWV 1046a.

177. Besseler and Grüß (NBA VII/1, KB, 45) already commented on this reading but saw it as indicating the dependence of both P 1065 and ST 639 on a common parent in score form.

178. Similar attempts at correcting problematic readings in ST 639—not all of them reported, or reported fully, in NBA VII/1, KB—occur in the Continuo at m. 39 of the first movement (erroneous sharp before the fifth note rubbed out in P 1065), and in Bourée 1, mm. 15 (first and last note in ST 639 E♯; P 1065 adds a sharp to change the third note from G to G♯, then cancels both this sharp and the one beside the last note) and 22 (last note in Continuo A in ST 639, in P 1065 A changed to C♯).

Ex. 10. *a*, Ouverture in B Minor (BWV 1067), mvt. 1, m 208, Violin 2.
a, ST 154. *b*, ST 639. *c*, P 1065.

Penzel's score, P 1065, thus derives from his parts, ST 639.[179] This means, obviously, that the "J.J." at its head cannot have the significance imputed to it by Besseler and Grüß. In point of fact, more than one further manuscript by Penzel also shows "J.J.," or the related invocation "I.N.I.," independently of its model.[180] Bach's pupil Johann Ludwig Krebs, moreover, used "J.J." to begin at least one of his autograph scores.[181] Perhaps the habit of starting manuscripts in this fashion came from Bach; but musicians of his school clearly adopted it as their own. Bach himself, we might note, used "J.J." far less often in secular compositions than in sacred works, and even more infrequently in instrumental music; indeed, among his admittedly not plentiful instrumental manuscripts, I find it only in large collective volumes, never in individual scores, whether of keyboard, organ, or ensemble pieces.[182] So we have little reason to

179. Unless otherwise indicated, all further citations of readings in Penzel refer solely to ST 639.

180. Apart from BWV 1067, Penzel used "J.J." in his scores of BWV 112 (P 1033), 113 (P 1034), and 129 (P 950); "I.N.I." appears in his scores of BWV 41 (P 1026), 133 (P 1039), 137 (P 1040), 140 (Oxford, Bodleian Library, c61 No. 7), and 149 (P 1043). Although most of these seem indeed to depend on Bach's autograph scores, Alfred Dürr has shown that the copies of BWV 129 and 140 all but certainly derive from the original parts, and Andreas Glöckner has asserted without qualification that Penzel's score of BWV 133 does so, as well. See NBA I/15 (*Kantaten zum Trinitatisfest und zum 1. Sonntag nach Trinitatis*), ed. Alfred Dürr, Robert Freeman, and James Webster, KB, 77–83; NBA I/27 (*Kantaten zum 24.-27. Sonntag nach Trinitatis*), ed. Alfred Dürr, KB, 133 and 140–41; and NBA I/3.1 (*Kantaten zum 2. und 3. Weihnachtstag*), ed., Klaus Hofmann, Andreas Glöckner, et al., KB, 132.

181. Cf. Ulrich Leisinger and Peter Wollny, *Die Bach-Handschriften der Bibliotheken in Brüssel: Katalog*, Leipziger Beiträge zur Bach-Forschung 2 (Hildesheim: Olms, 1997), 190.

182. Among secular vocal compositions, "J.J." appears mostly in large-scale works from Leipzig: BWV 30a (see n. 100), 36c (P 43), 201 (P 175), 206 (P 42), 207 (P 174), 214 (P 41), and 215 (P 139); Bach also used it in the moralizing solo cantata BWV 204 (P 107), but not in the Coffee Cantata (BWV 211, P 141), or the Peasant Cantata (BWV 212, P 167). Instrumental manuscripts headed with "J.J." include those of the organ sonatas BWV 525–30 and the late chorales BWV 651–68 and 769 (both in P 271), or the harpsichord concertos BWV 1052–57 and the evidently abandoned set beginning with BWV 1058 (P 234; see Breig, "Zum Kompositionsprozeß in Bachs Cembalokonzerten," 45). For a complete list of autograph instrumental sources, see NBA IX/12 (*Die Notenschrift Johann Sebastian Bachs: Dokumentation ihrer Entwicklung*), ed. Yoshitake Kobayashi, 206–11.

think that an autograph of BWV 1067, in whatever version would have included "J.J." in its title. Even indirectly, therefore, the likelihood of tracing Penzel's "J.J." to Bach would appear slim. As the error in Violin 2 of the Battinerie tells us, Penzel must have taken ST 639 from a score; we have nothing to indicate, however, that that score came from Bach's own hand. Its identity and character remain open to question. The search for an answer yields contradictory results. To start with the simplest evidence, Penzel's viola part differs in pitch and rhythm from Bach's at a handful of places in the first and last movements.[183] Without exception, the readings in Penzel make as much sense musically as those in ST 154; hence in all probability, they stem from the part that the composer replaced in the 1740s. So autograph or not, the score behind Penzel's copies must go back to quite an early point in the history of BWV 1067. But defining that point exactly proves more difficult. The musical text transmitted by ST 639 and, secondarily, P 1065 shows a complex relationship to the parts of the late 1730s. At the most basic level, it has the correct readings for the great majority of the apparent transposition errors and other wrong notes listed in Table 2 and notes 12 and 16; yet at three places—summarized, along with other readings that we shall mention, in Table 6—it retains incorrect pitches subsequently rectified in Bach's parts: a discordant note in the second violin at m. 88 of the first movement; the untransposed final note at m. 30 of the Sarabande in the same part; and a dissonance created when the scribe mistakenly perpetuated the ostinato pattern of the continuo at m. 20 in Bourée 1.[184] Of the more substantive revisions to ST 154, Penzel fails to incorporate an alteration

---

183. See the variants listed in NBA VII/1, KB, for Ouverture, mm. 86, 156, and 187, and Battinerie, m. 12.

184. While the scribes themselves appear to have corrected most of the actual wrong notes, tablature letters, seemingly in Bach's hand, added to the following emendations suggest that these initially went unchecked (for locations within the measure, see NBA VII/1, KB, 48–55): Ouverture, mm. 8, 17, 36, 81, 88 (all Violin 2), 179 (Continuo), and 196 (Violin 2); Rondeaux, mm. 11 (Violin 2) and 18 (Continuo); Sarabande, mm. 27 (Continuo) and 30 (Violin 2); Bourée 1, m. 20 (Continuo); and Menuet, m. 1 (Violin 1). According to NBA VII/1, KB, 49, the second-violin part of ST 154 could originally have had g' rather than f#' as the last note of m. 88 in the Ouverture; but a fresh examination of the original suggests that Besseler and Grüß did not adequately distinguish the note head—which does not go sufficiently above the line to count as a g' (cf. m. 196 in the same movement)—from the somewhat higher-placed cross that cancels it. Two places in Violin 2 further complicate the relationship between Penzel and ST 154. In the penultimate measure of the Sarabande, Penzel's first note reads b rather than e'; although this seems clearly preferable in terms of dissonance treatment and because of its closer parallel with the cadence ending in the first section, I cannot imagine a circumstance that could have led Bach's scribe to write e' if his model read b—compression of two parts into a single line, for example, does not seem likely here—and in any event, Bach left the e' unchanged. At the end of the Menuet, Penzel has the single f#' clearly called for rather than the double stop of P 154 (see n. 16). See also n. 202.

Table 6. Possible connective readings in ST 154 (Bach) and ST 639 (Penzel)

a) Readings shared by Penzel with ST 154 before correction

Movement, Measure	Part	Remark
Ouverture		
45, 176	Continuo	Last note a (changed in ST 154 to d')
88	Violin 2	Error; last note f#', corrected in ST 154 to e'
Sarabande		
30	Violin 2	Error; last note e', corrected in ST 154 to f#'
Bourée 1		
20	Continuo	Error; last note c#', corrected in ST 154 to b

b) Revisions to st 154 shared by Penzel

Movement, Measure	Part	Remark
Ouverture		
64–69, 168–73	Violin 2	Rhythm altered (see NBA VII/1, KB, 35)
Menuet		
15	Violin 2	1st note transposed down an octave (g' to g)

made to the continuo line at mm. 45 and 176 of the first movement but transmits three significant modifications to Violin 2: the octave shift at m. 15 of the Menuet, and a change in rhythm at mm. 64–69 and 168–73 of the opening movement.[185] Elsewhere in Violin 2, moreover, he has a variant reading at a place—m. 16 of Bourée 1—where ST 154 shows an unclear correction.[186]

If we turn from note content to performance indications—still restricting our attention to the violin and continuo parts—the picture shifts again. Compared with ST 154, Penzel's text looks spartan in the extreme: not only does it lack figuring, but it has no tempo markings or instructions like the *staccato* in the continuo at the start of the Battinerie; no dynamics beyond a *piano* that Bach added to Violin 1 in ST 154 at m. 55 of the opening movement; no staccato dots whatever; and relatively few slurs, trills, and appoggiaturas.[187] Since the figuring, the indications of tempo and performance style,

185. For the changes in the continuo, see also n. 8; for m. 15 of the Menuet, see also Plate 1. Penzel's viola part transmits mm. 64–69 and 168–73 of the opening movement in the same rhythmic shape as the revised second violin; cf. n. 17.

186. Cf. NBA VII/1, KB, 53.

187. For details of Penzel's articulation and ornaments, see especially nn. 189–91 and 219; for the autograph *piano* in ST 154, cf. the following note.

and even, it would appear, the staccato dots in ST 154 all come from the composer's hand—and because most of the dynamics, at least a portion of the slurs, nearly every trill, and no doubt most of the appoggiaturas do so, as well—we may readily suspect that whatever Penzel does include simply mirrors the state of the ouverture before the parts underwent any but the most cursory intervention by the composer.[188] The single *piano*, after all, can hardly weigh very heavily in this context. Nevertheless, a closer look reveals some curious inconsistencies. Among the slurs, Penzel transmits none of the admittedly few attributable with any security to Bach, while including most of those recognizable as the work of the scribe in the first-violin part of the Rondeaux

188. For the figuring, see Table 2 and n. 212. Apart from the tempo markings, Bach's verbal entries in ST 154 include all movement titles and small performance directions ("Da Capo," "doucement," "Double tacet," etc.) in Violin 2, and everything in the Continuo but perhaps the headings of the Double, Menuet, and Battinerie—whose uncharacteristically perpendicular lettering may nevertheless show a sufficient affinity with both the unquestionably autograph inscription "Boure 1mo da Capo" on the same page and the dynamics discussed in n. 103 to warrant an attribution to him. I infer the autograph character of the staccato dots not only from their characteristic slanted shape but also from spatial irregularities of the kind detailed in n. 224, which show that their entry must have come at a later time than the original copying. Among the dynamics, Bach added all of those in Violin 1 except at Bourée 2, m. 1, and Battinerie, m. 18; in Violin 2 with at most four exceptions (Ouverture, mm. 79 and 102, possibly also mm. 95 and 152; cf. n. 103); and most if not everything in the continuo (cf. ibid.). Of the trills, he wrote all but a handful in Violin 1 (cf. NBA VII/1, KB, 47, 50–51, and 54–56, at Ouverture, mm. 1 and 198; Sarabande, m. 8; Bourée 2, m. 11; and Battinerie, mm. 8, 10, 30, and 32); all but at most one (Ouverture, m. 4) in Violin 2; and everything in the continuo (readers comparing the score in NBA VII/1: 27–46, should note that the trill there at m. 200 of the first movement comes from a later source, not ST 154). The slurs pose some difficulty of attribution. In Violin 1, both the inward curl at the left of the copyist's ties and a comparison with his recorder parts to BWV 1057, in which he would appear to have written all the slurs (cf. NBA VII/4, KB, 182–83), enable us to identify Anon. N 2 at the following places (NBA VII/1 includes slurs from later sources in Rondeaux, mm. 8, 10, and 40, and Bourée 1, m. 23): Ouverture, m. 202; Rondeaux, throughout; Sarabande, mm. 7–8, 10–12, 19, 29–30, and probably all further slurs not attributable to Bach; Polonoise, mm. 2 and 7 (second slur); and Menuet, all except perhaps mm. 22–23. Against this, Bach would appear responsible for the slurs at mm. 130, 132, and possibly 197 of the first movement, and we may also recognize his hand in the Sarabande at mm. 14 and 23–26, perhaps mm. 3, 4, and 6, as well; Polonoise, m. 9, perhaps also m. 7 (first, third and fourth slurs), and possibly mm. 1, 8, and 10 (although these could equally belong to Anon. N 2); Menuet, mm. 22–23; and in the Battinerie probably at m. 12, more certainly at m. 24. In Violin 2, the copyist appears more likely to have written the single pair of slurs in the first movement (m. 195), those in the Rondeaux, and most of those in the remaining movements—I would feel hesitant in attributing anything more than Sarabande, m. 27, or Polonoise, mm. 10–12, to Bach, and even these strike me as less than certain. I think it probable, too, that the scribe of the figured continuo wrote some or most of his own slurs; in particular, the ductus of those in Double, m. 9, and Menuet, mm. 16 and 18, strikes me as close enough to his ties or fermatas to suggest a common hand. For the appoggiaturas, see the following paragraph in the main text.

and Menuet; yet he provides barely any slurs for either violin in the Sarabande, even though the copyists, and not Bach, appear to have written most of these, as well.[189] Penzel's trills also fall puzzlingly between those of Bach and the scribes, if in a slightly different way. He incorporates most but not all of the trills entered by Anon. N 2 in Violin 1—Violin 2 contains at best one trill by its copyist, the figured continuo part none.[190] In all three parts, however, he goes beyond what the scribes wrote; and although the extra trills in the violins neither approach those of Bach in number nor coincide with them in every instance, the continuo part reveals a provocative correspondence: after the first eight measures, which he leaves completely bare, Penzel has precisely the same trills as Bach.[191]

The appoggiaturas, too, raise questions. In ST 154, anomalies of spacing—in Violin 1, for instance, at mm. 5 and 6 of the first movement, or in m. 23 of the Menuet—make it clear that someone other than the copyist squeezed in many of these, which allows us to attribute them safely to the composer. It may come as no surprise, therefore, that Penzel's violin parts have none of the frequent appoggiaturas in the first move-

189. Penzel's first-violin part shows no slurs in the opening movement; the same slurs for the Rondeaux as ST 154 (cf. the preceding note) except at m. 12 (lacking), plus additional slurs at mm. 4 (first half) and 10 (second half); slurs at Sarabande, mm. 6 (notes 1–3; ST 154, notes 1–2) and 11; in Bourée 1, m. 23 (nn. 4–7; ST 154 without slur); and essentially the same slurs as NBA VII/1 in the Menuet (lacking mm. 5, 7, 13, 14, 17, and 21, and with a single four-note slur in m. 23 rather than the possibly autograph pairs). In Violin 2, Penzel has no slurs at all except for one covering all six notes of Menuet, m. 23 (paired eighths in ST 154). Penzel's continuo part has none of the slurs in the Sarabande or Battinerie; the same slurs as ST 154 in Double, mm. 7 and 9, plus slurs on the third quarter of mm. 1 and 5; and the slurs in the Menuet at mm. 10, 12, 16, and 18, but not those at mm. 2 and 20.

190. Of the trills written by Anon. N 2 (see n. 188), Penzel transmits those of the Ouverture and Battinerie, but not the Sarabande and Bourée 2; his copy also lacks the probably non-autograph trill in Violin 2 at m. 4 of the first movement (cf. ibid.).

191. Beyond the trills identical with those of Anon. N 2 (see the previous note), Penzel's first-violin part shows trills at several places in the first movement (cf. NBA VII/1, KB, 47–48 and 50, with reference to mm. 3, 8, 10, 11, 13, 14, 15, 16, 209, 210, and 211, to which readers should add m. 10, first note, and m. 19, sixth note as transcribed—cf. the remark on notation ibid., 48, which applies to Violin 1 rather than Violin 2), and two in the Polonoise (neither recorded ibid., 54): m. 4, note 1, and m. 5, note 5. Of these, the ones at mm. 10, 11 (note 4), 19, 209, 210, and 211 of the Ouverture correspond to autograph additions in ST 154, and so does the trill at m. 4 of the Polonoise. Penzel has a single trill in Violin 2, at m. 202 of the Ouverture, which also corresponds to one entered by Bach in ST 154. In the continuo, the trills common to Penzel and Bach occur at mm. 20, 206, and 209 of the opening movement, and m. 9 of the Sarabande. In Bach's continuo part, we might note, the trills at mm. 2, 4, 6, and 8 of the first movement all lie beneath figures, which would presumably have made them easier to overlook—although the scribe of the unfigured part in ST 154 does in fact include them; see n. 8. See also n. 206.

ment or the Sarabande, nor the single appoggiatura in both violins at m. 36 of the Battinerie. His continuo part, too, lacks the one appoggiatura in ST 154, a note clearly added by Bach at m. 2 of the Menuet. With the upper lines of the Menuet, however, things grow more complicated. Violin 2 has no appoggiaturas in any source. But Penzel's copy of Violin 1 has five of the seven appoggiaturas found in ST 154, lacking only those at mm. 12 and 23. As we have already observed, the small note at the latter spot unquestionably represents an addition from Bach's hand, and we might well feel inclined to assume the same with the one in m. 12. Yet neither in their shape nor in their spacing do the remaining appoggiaturas of the Menuet show any consistent difference either from these two or from any of the numerous small notes elsewhere in ST 154; indeed, throughout the movement, the appoggiaturas in ST 154 look, if anything, more cramped than the ones mentioned at the start of this paragraph. Nor do the ink colors encourage a division of scribal labor along the lines of Penzel's copy; at least to the naked eye, the appoggiaturas in mm. 2, 8, and 12 seem to have the same ink as the notes they precede, while those in mm. 10, 20, and 23 appear to differ, and the appoggiatura in m. 18 does not allow a decision either way. We must reckon, therefore, with the very real possibility that Bach added all or most of the small notes in the Menuet rather than merely the two missing from Penzel; and in that case, we must wonder why Penzel would have copied the appoggiaturas here more or less in their entirety but ignored them consistently everywhere else. The puzzle remains even if, as the ink could suggest, Bach inserted only the appoggiaturas in mm. 10, 20, and 23; then we must ask why Penzel included the first and second of these but omitted the third, and also omitted the one in m. 12 presumably written by Anon. N 2.

The solo part harbors problems of its own. At m. 36 of the first movement, the flute and first-violin lines in ST 154 show a curious discrepancy. As we see from Example 11, both fit equally well with the rest of the texture, and the accidental in the

Ex. 11. Ouverture in B Minor (BWV 1067), mvt. 1, mm. 36–37
(figuring omitted) as in ST 154.

violin surely means that the scribe did not write e♯" inadvertently but took it from his model. The original solo line, therefore, must also have read e♯"—Bach presumably opted for the d" in the flute as he wrote out the part. Penzel, too, gives the flute d" rather than e♯"; indeed, he writes d" in the violin, as well. But on the whole, his flute part seems to have little in common with Bach's beyond the bare notes. Much like the string parts, it contains very few trills and hardly any of the numerous appoggiaturas or careful articulation that enrich the autograph copy—and what articulation it does have sometimes conflicts directly with the composer's: in place of Bach's scrupulously differentiated phrasing in Bourée 2, for instance, Penzel slurs the eighth notes in pairs or, in m. 3 and the second half of m. 5, in four-note groups, and he includes no slurs after m. 6.[192] Even the notes do not always conform to those in Bach's part. In the second half of the Double, both the start and the close vary to a more than routine degree from the version in sт 154, as shown in Example 12.[193] Penzel's reading in the final measure could possibly have its roots in an error of beaming, and an error in transmission could equally account for the way he lops off the second ending. But in m. 6, we might sooner imagine his simple arpeggio giving rise to Bach's florid scale than the other way around.[194]

These variants alert us to a further problem; for whether or not either of them can count as evidence of textual deterioration, at least one other reading of Penzel's unquestionably does. At m. 4 of the Polonoise, he provides a version of the continuo

192. Penzel has trills in the flute only at the following places (location within measure as in the autograph part of sт 154 unless otherwise noted): Ouverture, mm. 1 (second and third quarters, as in Violin 1 of both sт 154 and sт 639; see also the discussion near the end of the main text), 13 (first quarter; not in sт 154, but in sт 639, Violin 1), and 198; Sarabande, mm. 8 and 31; Polonoise, m. 4 and m. 10 (not in sт 154). His only appoggiaturas occur at m. 10 of the first movement (also in sт 639, Violin 1); Rondeaux, m. 36; Polonoise, m. 4; and in the Menuet at the same places as in his first-violin part (see the foregoing paragraph in the main text). Apart from the slurs in Bourée 2 detailed in the main text, he has essentially the same slurs as Bach in the Rondeaux, lacking only those in mm. 12–13, and with a single four-note slur instead of the two-note slurs at m. 28; slurs in the Sarabande only at mm. 6 (three notes, as in sт 639, Violin 1; cf. n. 189) and 19 (notes 1–3, 4–6); in the Polonoise on the third quarter of mm. 1, 5, 7, 9, and 10, as well as on the first quarter of mm. 2 and 7; in the Double on the first quarter of mm. 2, 10, and 11, and the first and second quarters of m. 7 and—in the slightly more differentiated form shown in ex. 12—m. 12; in the Menuet at mm. 1, 5–7, 9, and 11; and in the Battinerie at mm. 18, 36 (over four notes), and 37.

193. Cf. nba VII/1, kb, 46. The first half of the Double has a minor variant, as well: the last note of the first ending reads c♯" instead of e".

194. Beyond the Double, Penzel's flute part has singular readings at Ouverture, m. 194, and Bourée 1, mm. 21–22, neither of which would appear to have any particular significance; for these, see nba VII/1, kb, 45–46.

Ex. 12. Ouverture in B Minor (BWV 1067), Double (figuring omitted).
a, mm. 5–6. *b*, mm. 12–13.

that both effaces a clear parallel with the close of the movement and—as we see from Example 13—produces extremely dubious counterpoint with the upper lines.[195] To judge from the corrections visible in Plate 4, Penzel himself created the bass line here, no doubt seeking to repair a faulty source; the change of the third note from F♯ to G suggests that his model lacked the first quarter note of the measure.[196] Given the high degree of fidelity with which Penzel transfers the ouverture from parts to score, other

195. Besseler and Grüß (NBA VII/1, KB, 46) have already drawn attention this variant, although without exploring its implications; Penzel's score has a different reading in the viola. Another variant in Penzel's continuo part may also provide some relevant evidence, although I have no ready explanation for it (see, however, n. 202): at m. 12 of the first movement, the penultimate note reads d instead of B; while we may well consider this musically preferable—B leaves the chord without a third—Bach's figuring clearly presupposes B, and he would surely have recognized a wrong note here. At m. 15 of the same movement, I might also mention, the sixth note reads a instead of g; presumably, however, this reflects only an inadvertent substitution of an octave leap for the less obvious seventh.

196. Most likely, then, the alteration of the fourth note from G to F♯ means that Penzel at first intended to fill in the missing beat with eighth notes G and A. The notation in ST 154 presumably reflects a

Ex. 13. Ouverture in B Minor (ʙᴡᴠ 1067), Polonoise,
m. 4 strings only (figuring omitted).

questionable details in his copies most likely reflect problems in his model, as well.[197] At m. 206 of the first movement, for instance, he transmits an implausible line for the second violin—barely acceptable in its dissonance treatment, and not even that in the hollow sonority it produces on the second beat; although the absence of a correction means that we cannot necessarily credit Penzel with the reading itself, the spot surely betokens something gone awry in a manuscript previous to his.[198] Even the dynamics, it would seem, represent a symptom of decline: as the omissions include not only the many added by Bach but also the few—including the prominently situated *piano* in Violin 1 for Bourée 2—written by the scribes of sᴛ 154 and hence part of the text before they copied it, someone along the way must have chosen to ignore *forte* or *piano* indications more or less on principle.[199] Much the same, we might think, could have

----

line break in its model, not least because the final cadence has the dotted quarter one would expect here, as well. That Penzel himself could have made the mistake appears less plausible, as he clearly gave some consideration to the measure and would surely have noticed an omission of his own.

197. I have located no wrong notes, for instance, in Penzel's score not already in his parts; and while the score contains some corrections of such mistakes, these all seem to postdate the actual copying.

198. See ɴʙᴀ VII/1, ᴋʙ, 50; the first three notes in Penzel read e'–e'–e', with the second-beat chord thus e–e'–a♯'–f♯" rather than Bach's e–c♯'–a♯'–f♯". A number of other singular readings must also surely count as corruptions or slips of the pen, whether by Penzel himself or one of his antecedents; beyond those in ex. 10b and nn. 178 and 193–95, these occur at several places in the Ouverture—mm. 2, Viola (last note f♯' rather than g'; from transposition error?); 72, Violin 1 (last two notes a third low); 146, Continuo (notes 5 and 6 f♯–b; corrected in part, but evidently after score copied); and 182, Violin 2 (last note b'; later correction in score)—and in the remaining movements as follows: Sarabande, m. 3, Violin 2 (first two notes a'–g'); and Menuet, mm. 16, Continuo (D–E–F♯–A–d–f♯), and 18, Continuo (last note B).

199. For dynamics entered by the copyists in sᴛ 154, see n. 188.

Plate 4. ST 639, Continuo, f. 2ᵛ and Polonoise, mm. 3–4

happened with the slurs in the Sarabande.[200] Hence whatever source Penzel ultimately drew on, its readings passed through at least one intermediary before reaching him; and the very loss of quality that this process obviously entailed only adds to the difficulty of making our way back to its starting point—and with that, of course, of establishing just where these readings fit in the transmission of the ouverture.

How can we resolve all these contradictions? I can think of two possible scenarios. On the one hand, we could imagine that Penzel's version of the ouverture had its origins in a score drawn up from the original parts before the composer subjected them to any extensive revision. Alternatively—and contrary to what our earlier investigation suggested—we could surmise that the creation of the B-minor ouverture began with a score, after all, and that st 154 and Penzel's copies descended more or less independently of one another from this model.[201] I say "more or less" because this putative score must have undergone some intervention based on the parts in their fully corrected state; otherwise Penzel could not have transmitted such things as the rhythmic and registral alterations to the second violin discussed earlier, or the substitution of d" for e#" in the flute and first violin at m. 36 of the first movement.[202] For that matter, a score copied from the parts in their precorrected state would have had to undergo much the same process.[203] If we recall the further intermediary stage indicated by the deterioration of the readings before they reached Penzel, we can

200. Cf. ibid.

201. In principle, we could add a third possibility: a score transposed directly from that of the A-minor ouverture and revised to incorporate some of the revisions in the parts. Counterintuitive as this may seem, something not wholly dissimilar must in fact have occurred in the transmission of the Harpsichord Concerto in F Minor (bwv 1056; cf. nba VII/7, kb, 86–88, also nba VII/4, kb, 154); in the present instance, however, the hypothesis cannot account for the errors shared by Penzel and st 154, especially the one in the Sarabande.

202. The scores of the harpsichord concertos bwv 1053–57 show a number of revisions that postdate the copying of the parts, although not incorporating readings from them; cf. nba VII/1, kb, 23, and the relevant lists of corrections for the individual works. A later revision to a score of bwv 1067 could perhaps help account for the otherwise puzzling readings in Violin 2 and Continuo discussed in nn. 184 and 195.

203. Theoretically, one could imagine a score copied at a stage where Violin 2 and Continuo had both undergone only partial revision—the former with mm. 64–69 and 168–73 of the first movement, and m. 15 of the Menuet, already in their newer readings, but the wrong notes in the first movement and the Sarabande (cf. Table 6) still uncorrected; the latter with most of the wrong notes listed in n. 12 already emended, but with an error remaining in Bourée 1 (cf. Table 6), and still without the newer reading in the opening movement at mm. 45 and 176 (cf. ibid. and two paragraphs below in the main text). But while we shall see that the revision of the parts may indeed have encompassed more than one layer, the picture sketched here would seem needlessly complex against the hypothesis of a later revision to the score.

represent the two scenarios as shown in Figure 2.[204] On purely textual grounds, I see little reason to prefer one version of the events over the other.[205] Both explain things such as the uncorrected errors in the second-violin and continuo parts or the near-total absence of Bach's added performance markings. Both mean that we must consign the occasional agreement between Penzel's trills and Bach's to the realm of coincidence.[206] Neither, as we see, can stand without the auxiliary hypothesis of subsequent revision on the basis of the fully corrected parts. The question essentially comes down to how plausible each looks in the wider context of Bach's practice; and here, again, the matter resists an easy solution.

If, as it has originally appeared and as our first scenario presupposes, Bach and his scribes produced the A-minor ouverture directly in parts, it would have made sense—whether for the composer himself or for another interested party—to have a score prepared at an early opportunity.[207] We might think it odd for this task not

204. Strictly speaking, Figure 2b could do without the second score copy. But eliminating this manuscript would mean that the first score copy already contained the various corruptions discussed in connection with Penzel; and if so, we might expect Bach or whoever transferred the changes from ST 154 to have restored more of the correct readings in that process. In addition, we might recall that the dispersal of Bach's manuscripts among his heirs meant that few original sources remained in Leipzig after his death; cf. Wollny, "Abschriften und Autographe," 47–51 and 59–60, esp. 47–48. Not by chance, perhaps, Penzel's score and parts of BWV 1068 (P 1055, ST 636), written about the same time as ST 639 (cf. Kobayashi, "Franz Hauser und seine Bach-Handschriftensammlung," 179 and 181), derive from a lost score of clearly secondary character (cf. NBA VII/1, KB 63–65); a handful of shared errors or otherwise questionable readings in the first movement—some eventually corrected in the extant manuscripts, some not—strongly suggest that this source in turn depended on Bach's parts (ST 153): cf. NBA VII/1, KB, 68–70 and 72, at mm. 31–32 (Violin 2), 34 and 40 (Oboe 2), and 51 and 92 (Violin 1; in both instances read "C 7" rather than "D 7" or "D 7a"), also the rather different reading of the evidence in BOM, 262–64.

205. See, however, our discussion of the flute part at pp. 83–88. At first sight, the fact that Penzel's continuo part has the right notes at places demonstrably corrected during or before the figuring of ST 154 (Ouverture, mm. 51 and 179, Bourée 1, m. 20; cf. n. 8) but transmits mm. 45 and 176 of the opening movement in the form already superseded when Anon. N 3 copied the unfigured part could appear to favor the scenario in Figure 2b; but see pp. 80–83.

206. The additional trills in Penzel (cf. nn. 191–92) all occur at places where an experienced musician would in fact have had little trouble inferring their presence. Indeed, Penzel's score has a handful of trills not found in his parts—including at least two (Ouverture, m. 4, Continuo; Polonoise, m. 12, Violin 1) corresponding with those of Bach. See also n. 226.

207. Bach evidently had scores drawn up from the parts to several Weimar cantatas—BWV 21, 61, 63, 185—more or less directly after copying, and even, in the case of BWV 185, demonstrably before the first performance; in Leipzig, his student Bernhard Christian Kayser began a score of the cantata *Mein liebster Jesus ist verloren* (BWV 154, P 130), all but certainly on the basis of the original parts,

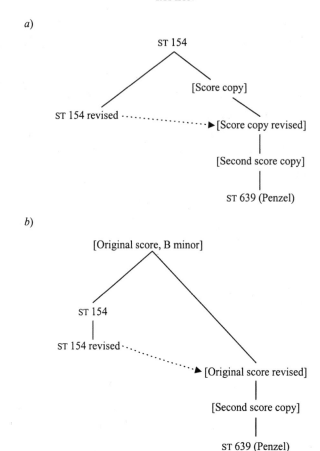

Figure 2. Ouverture in B minor, BWV 1067:
Possible stemmata

within months of the first performance. See, for BWV 21, NBA I/16 (*Kantaten zum 2. und 3. Sonntag nach Trinitatis*), ed. Robert Moreen, George Bozarth, and Paul Brainard, KB, 107 and 114–15, and Paul Brainard, "Cantata 21 Revisited," in *Studies in Renaissance and Baroque Music in Honor of Arthur Mendel*, ed. Robert L. Marshall (Kassel: Bärenreiter; Hackensack, N.J.: Joseph Boonin, 1974), 231–42, at 232 and 235; for BWV 63, NBA I/1 (*Kantaten zum 1. Weihnachtstag*), ed. Alfred Dürr, KB, 19–21; for BWV 185, NBA I/17.1 (*Kantaten zum 4. Sonntag nach Trinitatis*), ed. Yoshitake Kobayashi and Kirsten Beißwenger, KB, 28–30; for BWV 61, Rifkin, "From Weimar to Leipzig," 600 n. 36; and for BWV 154, NBA I/5 (*Kantaten zum Epiphaniasfest bis zum 2. Sonntag nach Epiphanias*), ed. Marianne Helms, KB, 68–69 and 73–75, and Andrew Talle, "Nürnberg, Darmstadt, Köthen—Neuerkenntnisse zur Bach-Überlieferung in der ersten Hälfte des 18. Jahrhunderts," BJ 89 (2003), 144–72, at 155–62. Unlike the parts of BWV 1067, those to BWV 21, 63, and 185—we lack the parts for BWV 61—contain dots, small crosses, or similar marks indicating page turns in the score copy, and marks of this sort occur as well in other parts of Bach's used, or probably used, as exemplars for early scores; see, variously,

to have waited until Bach could revise his copyists' work in every detail. But in that regard, a look at what other parts for instrumental compositions we have from his Leipzig years proves instructive. Bach barely supplemented the nonautograph portions of BWV 1041; left those in the three remaining original parts to BWV 1068 completely untouched; added nothing to the original continuo part of BWV 1043; and never corrected the two parts of BWV 1057 copied by Anon. N 2.[208] Nor did he furnish the string parts he wrote out for Johann Bernhard's G-minor ouverture with much in the way of performance indications: beyond the relatively complete, if mostly schematic, dynamics, they contain scarcely any articulation, very few trills, and even fewer appoggiaturas.[209] Indeed, compared with these examples, BWV 1067 stands noticeably apart in its wealth of detail. It seems worth asking, therefore, if Bach might not at first have edited the ouverture more sparingly, or if something could even have forced him to leave it for a time without any revision at all.

Admittedly, the parts to the Ouverture show no palpable sign of an interruption between their copying and at least their first revision. Nor could such an interruption, should it have occurred, have lasted very long: with at most a handful of exceptions,

---

NBA I/10 (*Kantaten zum 2. und 3. Ostertag*), ed. Alfred Dürr, KB, 82–85; NBA VII/3, KB, 17; and Alfred Dürr, "Zur Entstehungsgeschichte des 5. Brandenburgischen Konzerts," BJ 61 (1975): 63–69, at 68, although in the light of Robert L. Marshall, review of *Johann Sebastian Bach: Brandenburgisches Konzert Nr. 5 D-dur* BWV *1050. Faksimile des Originalstimmensatzes nach dem Autograph der Deutschen Staatsbibliothek zu Berlin*, ed. Hans-Joachim Schulze (Leipzig: Edition Peters, n.d.), *Music & Letters* 58 (1977): 236–39, at 237–38, and the further observations in Figure 1, n.r. Nevertheless, Kayser's score of BWV 154 lacks any such markings, nor did Penzel make use of them when transferring BWV 1067 from parts to score or leave any markings in the original parts of BWV 1055, which served as the model of his score copy (P 1060; cf. NBA VII/4, KB, 128).

208. For BWV 1043, 1057, and 1068, see, respectively, NBA VII/3, KB, 32–33; NBA VII/4, KB, 182–83; and NBA VII/1, KB, 58. For BWV 1041, see NBA VII/3, KB, 12–13, but noting that Bach surely did not write the heading of Continuo 2, and that his musical revisions, other than the possible clarification of individual pitches and rests, seem not to extend beyond two trills in Violin 2 (mvt. 1, mm. 17 and 72) and a handful of dynamics in this part (mvt. 2, mm. 17 and 31) and Continuo 2 (mvt. 1, m. 166; mvt. 2, mm. 11 and 15). Admittedly, the copyists' portions of BWV 1041 already incorporate more dynamics, and perhaps more articulation, than those of BWV 1067 in their unrevised state; but the second violin and continuo of BWV 1068 lack the *piano* and *forte* markings that the concerted structure of the opening movement surely allows us to expect in at least mm. 42, 58, 71, and 89.

209. Cf. the reproduction of the autograph violin on p. 4 of the edition cited in n. 25. The lack of articulation becomes especially noticeable if we compare the passages from Johann Bernhard's ouverture and BWV 1067 reproduced in exx. 2a and 2b—surely, the staccato markings on virtually all the quarters in the latter example suggest similar treatment of Violin 1 in the former at mm. 139–44 and 152–54.

Bach's dynamics cannot date from much after 1739.[210] Yet the parts do hint in spots that some revisions may have taken place at a later stage than others. Our consideration of the appoggiaturas, for instance, could encourage the suspicion that Bach added them to the first-violin line of the Menuet before providing them anywhere else.[211] In the continuo, anomalies of spacing and appearance suggest that he did not enter the dynamics for the Polonoise and the Battinerie until he had already completed the figuring and several other revisions.[212] The changes in the same part at mm. 45 and 176 of the first movement could also document a layer of correction subsequent to the figuring. Read strictly, the altered version demands a 6 over the last note, whereas the note as originally written need not have had anything above it; given the thoroughness of Bach's figures in this movement especially, the absence of the 6 could imply something more than carelessness.[213] For that matter, the very manner in which Bach executed this pair of revisions—carefully excising the original note and then drawing

210. Cf. Kobayashi, "Zur Chronologie der Spätwerke Johann Sebastian Bachs," 21–22, and the details on BWV 206, 210, 1055, 1057, and 1067 ibid., 42, 45, and 47–48; for the possible exceptions in ST 154, cf. n. 103 and the following note.

211. On the appoggiaturas, see p. 82.

212. See n. 103, as well as Battinerie, m. 18, where the irregular placement of the *piano*—above rather than below the staff, and well to the right of where the music dictates (cf. NBA VII/1, KB, 56)—clearly reflects a concern to avoid the figures both here and on the staff below; the seemingly anomalous position of the figures in m. 19 does not indicate otherwise, as those on the first two notes merely continue a linear plane already begun before the *piano*, and the descent to a lower plane at the third note seems motivated by the very long downstem of the note on the system above. Elsewhere in the part, Bach entered the dynamics before or together with the figuring, as we see from the way figures avoid dynamics on the staff above them at Ouverture, mm. 74, 78, and 151; Rondeaux, m. 28, and the start of Bourée 2. Conceivably, the extreme compression of the figures under the direction "moderato e staccato" at the beginning of the Polonoise means that the figuring as a whole represented a distinct stage of revision; but as Bach would appear to have written trills and figures more or less simultaneously in mm. 6 and 206 of the first movement, I think it more likely that trills, figures, and all but the manifestly later dynamics formed part of a single process. Nevertheless, it seems worth pointing out that no figures appear in the surviving continuo parts of BWV 1041, 1043, and 1068 (BWV 1055 has figures, but from a later date, and in any event not for a directly comparable purpose; cf. Breig, "Zur Werkgeschichte von Johann Sebastian Bachs Cembalokonzert in A-Dur BWV 1055," 205–8, and NBA VII/4, KB, 124–25 and 133–34), although Bach's copies of Johann Bernhard's ouvertures do all include figured continuos (cf. Beißwenger, *Johann Sebastian Bachs Notenbibliothek*, 232–35).

213. Cf. Table 6. Although Bach does put a horizontal stroke over the second quarter of m. 45 and uses a stroke or figures to guard against a change of harmony in two similar instances of descending stepwise motion (see mm. 92 and 150), he provides no such indication in the first half of m. 176; neither here nor in m. 45 does the altered note cover any figuring. Conversely, he almost never leaves an ascending third on the second of two quarters unfigured; cf. mm. 47, 74, 76, 106, 157, 159, and 161 in the first movement, or mm. 1, 5, 6, 9, 11, 13, and 14 in the Menuet.

in the new one—distinguishes them from virtually all the other changes in sᴛ 154, where he or the scribes tended to alter notes simply by thickening them or crossing them out. The same unusual fastidiousness, however, marks the emendation of the second violin in the Menuet; perhaps, then, Bach made all three changes sometime after he had first reviewed his copyists' work.[214]

Should the revision in sᴛ 154 in fact embody more than one phase of work, it would not represent the only such instance in Bach's parts; to take one noteworthy example, the aria "Ich will auch mit gebrochnen Augen nach dir, mein treuer Heiland, sehn" in the cantata *Mit Fried und Freud ich fahr dahin* (ʙᴡᴠ 125) evidently went through several revisions stretching over the course of more than a decade.[215] How many stages the ouverture might have gone through, and how much time elapsed between them, would seem impossible to determine—in theory, the process could have extended at least to the repeat performance revealed by the viola part. But whatever the case, we may think it possible that Bach did not initially make very extensive changes to the parts but restricted himself essentially to the correction of wrong notes—even if he did not catch every one of them, the addition of dynamics, most likely the figuring, and conceivably the provision of appoggiaturas in the Menuet.

Still, these speculations encounter a major stumbling block in the flute part. For one thing, we must consider the variants in Example 12: as already indicated, we cannot so easily dismiss Penzel's readings here as corruptions. Perhaps more important, while we have seen that scribes could well reduce the quota of performance directions with each new copy, even the most liberal understanding of this process seems hard put to travel the distance between Bach's thoroughly articulated and decorated flute part and

214. The rhythmic alteration in Violin 2 at mm. 64–69 and 168–73 of the first movement, although not involving actual erasure, could form part of this same hypothetical layer, as could the erasure and rewriting of Violin 1 in the same movement at mm. 170–71 (cf. ɴʙᴀ VII/1, ᴋʙ, 50); this latter instance, however, merely rectifies a mistake in copying. The altered notes and added dynamics in the continuo have obvious consequences for the unfigured continuo of sᴛ 154, as this includes both the new readings in the first movement (cf. n. 8) and the *piano* and *forte* markings in the Polonoise, as well as the *piano* at m. 36 of the Battinerie; significantly, we have no real evidence to exclude the possibility that this part, not unlike that for the viola, originated later than its paper would suggest—cf. n. 11, as well as Kobayashi, "Zur Chronologie der Spätwerke Johann Sebastian Bachs," 24 n. 24, and Schulze, *Katalog der Sammlung Manfred Gorke*, 15 and plate 2 (p. 170).

215. For ʙᴡᴠ 125, see ɴʙᴀ I/28.1 (*Kantaten zu Marienfesten I*), ed. Matthias Wendt and Uwe Wolf, ᴋʙ, 32 and 54, as well as Uwe Wolf, "Überlegungen zu Bachs Kommunionsmusiken," ʙᴊ 85 (1999): 133–41, at 138–41, and Kobayashi, "Zur Chronologie der Spätwerke Johann Sebastian Bachs," 37; for general observations and some further examples, see ibid., 22, 48 (ʙᴡᴠ 114), 56 (ʙᴡᴠ 91 and 137), and 63–64 (ʙᴡᴠ 187, 29), also ɴʙᴀ I/5, ᴋʙ, 67, and 78. Obviously, the number of later autograph insertions in Bach's parts could well exceed those identified, as not all added items will involve elements of Bach's script that changed measurably over the years.

the version transmitted by Penzel.[216] But could the autograph flute part in fact have replaced one produced by a copyist—or by Bach and a copyist in tandem—together with the string and continuo parts of BWV 1067? The note content of the existing solo line gives no indication of having differed to any significant extent from that of the violin part from which it apparently derives; hence aside from the octave transposition in the Polonoise—which Bach could very easily have signaled with an annotation in the parent source or even a verbal instruction—a scribe would have had no problem transferring the music directly to the flute.[217] Admittedly, the piano markings show that the existing part cannot postdate Bach's added dynamics elsewhere in ST 154 by any significant margin, and the preparation of two flute parts in quick succession does not, on the face of it, make much sense: although Bach did occasionally substitute one part for another before the first performance of a new cantata, such instances seem always to have involved issues of playability or a change of instrumentation, neither of

216. Up to a point, we could account for the discrepancies through the assumption that Penzel's model—like his own eventual score of BWV 1067—did not usually notate both Flute and Violin 1 in full. Indeed, the correspondence between Penzel's flute and violin parts in such details as the ornaments in mm. 1 and 10 of the first movement or the appoggiaturas in the Menuet (see n. 192) makes this virtually certain, and even suggests that the exemplar—again, like Penzel himself in much of his own score (see n. 174)—tended to write out the violin rather than the flute. But this explanation breaks down in the solo portions, most notably in Bourée 2 (see p. 84) and in the Battinerie, where Penzel's text retains the copyist's trills in the first-violin part of ST 154 but lacks any of those in the autograph flute part.

217. Cf. nn. 23 and 26. Under the assumption of a discarded flute part, the d' at m. 36 of the first movement would have entered the score copy as a later revision—precisely as it would have under the stemma in Figure 2b. The provision of *solo-tutti* markings in the first movement of Penzel's flute part—at all places where Bach has them, and at mm. 102, 143, and 151 besides (cf. NBA VII/1, KB, 49)—could strengthen the assumption that it derives ultimately from another part, not a score. We have, admittedly, few sources against which to test this: no autograph scores of any solo concertos have survived other than those for the harpsichord concertos BWV 1052–59. Nevertheless, these contain not a single marking of this sort beyond a lone *tutti* in the D-major concerto (BWV 1054) at m. 33 of the last movement; cf. *Johann Sebastian Bach: Konzert D-Dur für Cembalo und Streichorchester BWV 1054. Faksimile der autographen Partitur,* ed. Hans-Joachim Schulze, Faksimile-Reihe Bachscher Werke und Schriftstücke 11 (Leipzig: Deutscher Verlag für Musik, 1972). Bach may, on the other hand, not have thought such indications needed as much in a harpsichord concerto as in a work for another solo instrument; in contrast to the autograph solo parts for BWV 1041, 1043, and 1067, the harpsichord part to BWV 1057 has no *solo-tutti* markings at all—not even the two present in at least the dedication copy (SBB Am.B. 78) of its model, the Fourth Brandenburg Concerto (mvt. 1, mm. 83 and 89; cf. *Johann Sebastian Bach: Brandenburgische Konzerte. Faksimile des Autographen*). Michael Marissen reminds me, however, of a *solo* marking in the Coethen harpsichord part of the Fifth Brandenburg Concerto (ST 130) at m. 154 of the first movement; cf. the facsimile cited in n. 207.

which could really apply to the ouverture.[218] On the other hand, instrumental works need not have followed so tight a schedule as that governing the production of Bach's Leipzig sacred music; especially with a demanding solo piece like BWV 1067, Bach could have felt inclined to give the player advance access to his part—which obviously opened the door to loss or damage. But if it does not take much effort to imagine such a story, we might nevertheless hesitate to pursue it without a compelling reason for doing so.

This brings us to the second of our proposed scenarios. At first sight, the version of events represented in Figure 2b would seem to have the advantage of greater simplicity. Yet if, as it asks us to believe, the errors shared by Penzel and ST 154 in its unrevised state preserve the readings of a common parent, complications emerge here, as well. These begin with the question of who wrote the supposed original score and what sort of document it represented. All but certainly, we can reject the hypothesis of a composing manuscript. Bach could no doubt have fallen prey to a slip like that in the continuo of Bourée 1 when copying from another source, or even in the process of setting down the music for the first time, but in the latter instance, he would surely have corrected the final note by the time he had worked out all four voices. Under no circumstance, moreover, might we think he ever meant the f♯ in Violin 2 at m. 88 of the first movement or the e' near the end of the Sarabande to form part of the harmonic fabric.[219]

Regardless of its place on the stemmatic chain, then, an early score of the B-minor ouverture will have depended on an exemplar of some sort. Under this presupposition, the error in the Sarabande could still imply a model a whole tone lower; hence even in the context of Figure 2b, many of what we have read as signs of transposition in ST 154 remain just that—although not newly created by the scribes copying the parts but taken over by them from the still uncorrected parent source.[220]

The assumption, however, of a fair copy as the model for ST 154 and, ultimately, Penzel creates difficulties of its own. As became clear in Section I of this study, the

---

218. See, for example, the discussion of the flute part to BWV 8 in n. 20.

219. In principle, of course, errors in the extant sources could have resulted from ambiguities in the exemplar—corrections or notes placed unclearly; cf. Robert L. Marshall, *The Compositional Process of J. S. Bach: A Study of the Autograph Scores of the Vocal Works*, 2 vols., Princeton Studies in Music 4 (Princeton, N.J.: Princeton University Press, 1972), 2:4. But although we could account for m. 16 of Bourée 1 (see pp. 76–80) in this fashion, it can hardly explain why Penzel and ST 154 share the same mistakes in the three places just discussed.

220. This would not apply, obviously, to notes nudged upward during the actual copying of the parts.

new version of the ouverture would not have required a score unless Bach meant it to differ from the earlier one in more than just its key and its solo instrument. Yet in such an instance, he would surely have had to write all or most of the manuscript himself; and here, no less than with a composing score, the wrong notes raise troubling questions.[221] The questions increase, moreover, if we consider the autograph scores of other works adapted from older music. These not only reinforce the suspicion that Bach would have emended most if not all of any lapses committed in the process of writing but suggest that he would have enriched his text with considerably more performance indications—dynamics, certainly, and most likely articulation and ornamentation as well—than either the scribes of ST 154 or Penzel have given us reason to think their exemplar contained.[222] Indeed, a score in Bach's hand presumably would have included at least a good portion of what he subsequently felt impelled to add to the parts or change in them.[223] Whether or not the new accompanimental rhythm at mm. 64–69 and 168–73 of the first movement or the registral shift in the second violin at m. 15

221. The well-known case of the Sinfonia to the cantata *Ich liebe den Höchsten von ganzem Gemüte* (BWV 174), in which Bach reworked the first movement of the Third Brandenburg Concerto by adding wind and ripieno parts to a score written out largely by a colleague, hardly offers a parallel to the hypothetical situation presented here, as nothing in BWV 1067 implies such a clear-cut division between old and new material; cf. NBA I/14 (*Kantaten zum 2. und 3. Pfingsttag*), ed. Alfred Dürr and Arthur Mendel, ix–x and KB, 69–71 and 109–13. See also n. 229.

222. Several of Bach's fair and revision copies of the 1730s—especially those of instrumental compositions—have appeared in facsimile editions; to those of BWV 244, 1030, 1032 and 1062, and 1054 mentioned in nn. 100 and 217, I might add the autograph of the Mass in A Major (BWV 234), for which see *Johann Sebastian Bach: Messe A-dur* BWV 234. *Faksimile der autographen Partitur und Continuo-Stimme*, ed. Oswald Bill and Klaus Häfner (Wiesbaden: Breitkopf & Härtel, 1985). Although not available in complete facsimile, the autograph of the cantata *Freue dich, erlöste Schar* (BWV 30, P 44) also provides telling evidence when compared with its model, BWV 30a; cf. the facsimile of the latter cited in n. 100, and the page from BWV 30 in NBA I/29 (*Kantaten zum Johannisfest*), ed. Frieder Rempp, x, or *Die Handschrift Johann Sebastian Bachs: Musikautographe aus der Musikabteilung der Staatsbibliothek Preußischer Kulturbesitz Berlin. Ausstellung zum 300. Geburtstag von J. S. Bach, 22. März bis 13. Juli 1985*, ed. Rudolf Elvers and Hans-Günter Klein, Staatsbibliothek Preußischer Kulturbesitz Ausstellungskataloge 25 (Wiesbaden: Dr. Ludwig Reichert, 1985), 129. As already noted, the systematic omission of dynamics in Penzel's copies means that we can draw no inferences from them about the dynamics of our putative score; but in this regard, we can surely rely on ST 154.

223. In principle, this might seem to contradict the supposition that Bach could have left the parts largely untouched on an early revision. But I think we can take it as a rule that Bach subjected his musical texts to considerably more elaboration and modification when writing them out himself than when dealing with copyists' work. In the F-major harpsichord concerto, for instance, the score shows many details elaborated beyond the readings of his model, and the autograph solo part carries the process of evolution still further; yet Bach did not bother to revise Anon. N 2's recorder parts (cf. NBA VII/4, KB 182–83).

of the Menuet occurred to him immediately when reviewing a copyist's part, I find it hard to imagine that either possibility would have escaped him as he wrote out the music in full; and if, in the Rondeaux, he scrupulously placed a dot under every two-note slur of the autograph flute part, would he not have thought to do the same with the unison violin line in a score produced immediately beforehand?[224]

Even a modest detail of ornamentation seems to have significant implications in this regard. At the very start of the ouverture, Penzel and Anon. N 2 place trills on both the second and third quarters of the first-violin line, and Penzel's viola part has trills on the same beats in m. 2.[225] Assuming that a common model stood behind their copies—and that Penzel or one of his predecessors did not simply embellish the viola part on his own initiative—this source must have had the same trills.[226] Yet Bach's version of the motive, whether in the autograph flute and viola parts or in his additions to the violins and the continuo, consistently has a trill on the second beat alone.[227] The flute part, as we have seen, means that he cannot have waited very long after the creation of the B-minor ouverture to have opted for this form of the theme.[228] But if he wrote the ouverture in score, would he have altered the shape of the opening gesture so soon afterward? A change of mind about music composed several years earlier certainly appears well within the realm of possibility; but we may think it less likely for Bach to adopt two such different versions in quick succession.

These observations leave us with a paradox. If Bach did not need to write a score of the ouverture himself, he would have had little purpose in having a copyist prepare one in advance of the parts, either. Moreover, a score already identical to BWV 1067 in key and instrumentation leaves us hard put to explain the starting cues for the copyists and—perhaps even more so—Bach's slip of the pen in the heading of the solo part. So in the end, our second scenario for the history of Penzel's copies proves no more straightforward than the first—it, too, leaves us with problematic assumptions and

---

224. Obviously, the absence of the staccato dots in Penzel's copy suggests that his model did not include them; and the cramped spacing of slurs, dots, and note heads in ST 154 confirms that Bach added the staccato markings to Violin 1.

225. Cf. NBA VII/1, KB, 47.

226. Penzel decorates the theme similarly in the flute part and on subsequent appearances in the violins, as well (ibid., 47–48); but given the observations on his trills and on the relationship between his flute and violin parts in nn. 191, 215, and 206, not to mention the absence of further copyists' trills in the violins of ST 154, none of this allows us to infer anything more about his model.

227. See mm. 1 (Flute), 2 (Viola, Continuo), 4 (Violin 2, Continuo), 6 (Continuo), 8 (Flute, Violin 1, Continuo), 11 (Flute, Violin 1), and 20 (Continuo).

228. This would remain effectively the same even if some time elapsed before Bach entered the trills in the violin and continuo parts.

unanswered questions.[229] But if we cannot provide an airtight explanation for the relationships among the sources, we can at least affirm the fundamental thrust of what we read from the parts: the Ouverture in B Minor represents Bach's adaptation of an earlier work, all but certainly one for violin in A minor.

229. A B-minor score as the model for ST 154 would open the way for a hypothesis advanced in a number of lectures and concert commentaries by Werner Breig, who argues that the original version of BWV 1067 called for only two violins in all, with the first of them moving back and forth between solo and ensemble roles in a manner akin to the opening movement of BWV 1068; my thanks to Prof. Breig for sharing his thoughts with me on various occasions over the years and for informing me of a forthcoming article on the subject. Breig himself had earlier proposed a similar disposition for the violin concerto that served as the model for BWV 1052, and I have suggested something much like this for the original version of the double concerto BWV 1060; see Breig, "Bachs Violinkonzert d-Moll," 61–65, and Rifkin, "Verlorene Quellen, verlorene Werke," 25–30, where I also draw attention to a related use of the first violin in the harpsichord concerto BWV 1053 and its putative model. While I find Breig's suggestion ingenious and musically attractive, other considerations make me skeptical. First, insofar as we can establish their dating, the pieces mentioned here—to which we may add the Fifth Brandenburg Concerto—seem all to belong to an earlier phase of Bach's career than BWV 1067: the Fifth Brandenburg dates from before 1721, BWV 1068 more likely comes from Coethen than from Leipzig (see n. 48), and the models of BWV 1052 and 1053 can date from no later than 1726 (see Figure 1). Second, Johann Bernhard Bach's concerted ouverture also calls for solo violin and two ripieno violins, and also contains extensive duplication of solo and ripieno lines; not only that, but a brief passage in unison between the first and second violins in mm. 107–12 of the first movement inevitably puts us in mind of the unisons between Violin 2 and Viola in the opening movement of BWV 1067 at mm. 59–63 and 123–27. In principle, we could read these features, too, as a sign of J. S. Bach's editorial hand; indeed, while he left the copying of Johann Bernard's other ouvertures largely to family members and students, Bach himself wrote the violin and viola parts to the G-minor ouverture (cf. Beißwenger, *Johann Sebastian Bachs Notenbibliothek*, 232–35). But none of these parts shows any trace of revision; and even if Bach should have expanded the complement of violins in his cousin's ouverture, Breig's hypothesis would still force us to imagine this adaptation taking place at more or less the same time as the creation of BWV 1067 with only two violins or, failing that, to posit a history for both works far more complex than either the music or the sources give us any warrant for doing. Whatever the circumstances, moreover, the transformation of BWV 1067 envisaged by Breig goes beyond anything actually documented in Bach's instrumental output, as it entails not merely the addition of a new part to an existing complex but the rewriting and internal reapportionment of that complex itself. All this, finally, presupposes a score largely or entirely written by the composer himself—and as the foregoing discussion has shown, we have more than a few reasons to doubt that such a manuscript could have existed.

A Comparison of Bach's and Telemann's Use of the Ouverture as Theological Signifier

Jeanne Swack

A spirit of stylistic and generic experimentalism is central to the compositional methods of both Johann Sebastian Bach and Georg Philipp Telemann, Bach's most significant German contemporary. This exploration of the possibilities afforded by the plethora of national styles and genres and their combinations informs not only a large portion of both composers' instrumental outputs, but a significant number of their vocal works, as well. The implementation of a systematic encoding of signals for various national styles and genres permitted these two composers, and doubtless many of their contemporaries, to play with and manipulate these signs in order to layer a complex web of references onto the more commonplace conventions of style and genre.

In order to clarify the relationship of the genre of the individual work as a whole vis-à-vis the allusions to genres in individual movements which lie outside the customary parameters of the genre itself, I shall use the term *mode* for the outside genre, borrowing from Alistair Fowler's *Kinds of Literature: An Introduction to the Theory of Genres and Modes*.[1] Fowler defines *mode* as a borrowing of characteristics from the repertoire of a genre outside the main genre, and then using these characteristics to enrich the main genre.[2] Thus, for example, a sonata movement that borrows formal and stylistic conventions from an operatic aria would be said to be a sonata move-

An earlier version of this paper ("Telemanns Vokalmusik: Klangrede der Aufklärung") was read at the second Frankfurter Telemann-Symposium, Frankfurt, October 24–27, 2001. I would like to thank Michael Marissen, Robin Leaver, and Mark Louden for their comments during the preparation of this essay.

1. Alistair Fowler, *Kinds of Literature: An Introduction to the Theory of Genres and Modes* (Cambridge, Mass.: Harvard University Press, 1982).

2. See ibid., 106–8. Fowler points out that the term for the mode is generally adjectival, and that it is never complete in itself. The designation for the main genre, on the other hand, is always a noun.

ment in the operatic mode. Such a movement would still remain within the genre of sonata: the genre would be delineated by scoring, movement succession (tempos, key relationships), whereas the mode would be delineated by formal gestures and large-scale schemes such as the use of a motto and da capo. It is possible for a movement to allude to more than one mode, either simultaneously or in succession. The exploration of the possibilities afforded by the interplay between genre and mode was the basis for large numbers of Telemann's instrumental and vocal works.

Although Bach's cantatas have received much attention in recent scholarship, it has been difficult to assess his achievements without placing these works within the context of the broader cantata repertoire of the time. Telemann's cantatas provide fertile ground for the study of the development of the Lutheran cantata in the first half of the eighteenth century, as well as the achievements of one of the major proponents and key developers of the genre itself. Further, the study of these works allows us to explore Telemann's experimentation with genre, experimentation that is echoed, though not duplicated, in far better-known cantatas of Bach. The majority of Telemann's cantata movements are in keeping with the still-developing conventions of the new genre of the Lutheran madrigalian cantata (a genre in whose development he himself played a pivotal role), but a number of movements show evidence of the same sort of genre experimentation so evident in his instrumental works as well as in Bach's, although the latter's output in both respects is considerably smaller, even taking into consideration the likelihood of numerous lost works. In addition, some of Telemann's cantatas demonstrate thematic connections with his instrumental works, adding another layer to the interconnections between the vocal and instrumental repertoires.

I am basing the study of genre in the cantata repertoire on a sampling of about three hundred and fifty cantatas from the collection of Telemann's sacred vocal works in the Stadt- und Universitätsbibliothek, Frankfurt am Main. I will not explore all of the genres to which Telemann referred in his cantatas here but will focus my analysis on three examples of his allusions to the French ouverture or to the style of the opening section of ouvertures, all in cantatas composed during his period of employment in Frankfurt. In so doing, I will show that Telemann's cantatas actually employ allusions to the ouverture in ways that are more unexpected and idiosyncratic than in the cantatas of Bach.

Six of Bach's surviving cantatas—*O Ewigkeit, du Donnerwort* (BWV 20) (First Sunday after Trinity, 1724); *Nun komm, der Heiden Heiland* (BWV 61) (First Sunday in Advent, 1714); *In allen meinen Taten* (BWV 97) (liturgical occasion unknown, 1734); *Unser Mund sei voll Lachens* (BWV 110) (Christmas, 1725);[3] *Preise Jerusalem, den Herrn* (BWV 119) (inauguration of Leipzig town council, 1723); and *Höchsterwünschtes Freudenfest* (BWV

3. The opening movement is a reworking of the Ouverture in D Major (BWV 1069).

194) (organ dedication in Störmthal, 1723)—make use of the ouverture.[4] In each case, the Ouverture is the initial movement of the cantata, prompted by the liturgical ordering of the cantata as the first of a yearly cycle, the first of a season, the birth of Christ, or a general festive occasion.[5] In three of these cantatas, BWV 20, 61, and 97, a chorale tune is overlaid on the ouverture, a procedure also used by Telemann.

The most obvious ways in which Telemann's use of the ouverture in his cantatas differs from Bach's have to do with the placement of the ouverture movement and the integration of ouverture and aria forms in the cantata, as well as in the details of adapting chorale melodies to the ouverture structure in opening choruses. Consider, for example, the cantata *Wie der Hirsch schreiet nach frischem Wasser* (TVWV 1: 1616) (Sixteenth Sunday after Trinity, 1717), from the Frankfurt *Italienischer Jahrgang*, in which Telemann not only placed the ouverture in an unusual position in the cantata, but also devised a hybrid form. Gottfried Simonis was the author of the madrigalian sections of this cantata, and he assembled the complete text. The movement types and texts for the cantata are given in Figure 1.

The Gospel reading for the Sixteenth Sunday after Trinity, Luke 7:11–17, recounts the story of Christ's revival of a dead man, the only son of a widow, in the town of Nain. Thus, the theme of the cantata text, a longing for death and eternal life, echoes the idea of resurrection expressed in the Gospel reading. The use of the untexted chorale, "Ich hab mein Sach Gott heimgestellt," parallels the similar use of this chorale melody in Bach's *Actus tragicus, Gottes Zeit ist die allerbeste Zeit* (BWV 106), where the viols and recorders softly play the same tune over the text "Es ist der alte Bund. Mensch, du mußt sterben" [It is the old covenant. Man, you must die.], in an older contrapuntal style contrasting with the soprano's modern presentation of the text "Ja, ja, ja komm Herr Jesu komm," with its promise of eternal life.[6] Indeed the entire cantata, like BWV 106, is permeated with ideas of longing for death and the expectation of eternal life as expressed in the eighteen strophes of the chorale, a chorale classified as a "*Sterbelied*" in the Schemelli *Gesangbuch*.[7] The first recitative, "Was ist die Welt? Ein Labyrinth"

---

4. Of course there are other allusions to the style of the dotted section of the ouverture elsewhere in Bach's cantata repertoire. For instance, the second half of BWV 20 opens with an aria, "Wacht auf, wacht auf, verlorne Schaafe," which invokes the style of the A section of the ouverture.

5. See Richard D. P. Jones, "Ouverture," in the *Oxford Composers Companions: J. S. Bach*, ed. Malcolm Boyd and John Butt (Oxford: Oxford University Press, 1999), 355.

6. Alfred Dürr has shown how the entire text of BWV 106 echoes themes presented in the eighteen strophes of the chorale "Ich hab mein Sach Gott heimgestellt." See Alfred Dürr, *Die Kantaten von Johann Sebastian Bach* (Kassel: Bärenreiter, 1985), II, 837.

7. Georg Christian Schemelli, *Musicalisches Gesangbuch* (Leipzig: Breitkopf, 1736), facs. ed. Hildesheim: Georg Olms Verlag, 587–88.

Figure 1. Disposition of G. P. Telemann, "Wie der Hirsch schreiet nach frischem Wasser" (TVWV 1: 1116) (16th Sunday after Trinity, 1717).

---

1. Opening chorus: (Psalm 42):

Wie der Hirsch schreiet nach frischem Wasser, so schreiet meine Seele, Gott, zu dir.

Meine Seele dürstet nach Gott, nach dem lebendigen Gott.

Wann werde ich dahin kommen, daß ich Gottes Angesicht schaue?

As the deer yearns after fresh water,

So yearns my soul after Thee, O God.

My soul thirsts for God, for the living God.

When shall I come there, so that I can see God's visage?

(*stile antico*)

2. Bass aria:

Ich sehne mich nach meinem Grabe,

Weil ich auf der verleerten Welt

Doch keinen Trost zu hoffen habe

Der meinen Geist zufrieden stellt

Nur durch den Tod komm' ich zum Friede

Und an den lusterfüllten Platz,

Wo Jesus meiner Seelen Schatz

Mir alle Seligkeit beschieden

Der ich mich schon in Gedanken labe,

Drum sehn' ich mich nach meinem Grabe.

I long for my grave,

Because I have no hope of finding consolation

In an empty world

That would give my spirit satisfaction.

Only through death do I come to peace,

And at that joyous place,

Where Jesus, my soul's treasure,

Grants me all blessedness,

That I already refresh my thoughts,

Therefore I long for my grave.

($\frac{6}{8}$ or $\frac{12}{8}$, depending on part, pizzicato cello, with soft chorale in strings and oboe above, "Ich hab mein Sach Gott heimgestellt," not da capo, ends with a brief recitative underscoring the text "nach meinem Grabe.")

3. Soprano recitative:

Was ist die Welt?

Ein Labyrinth, wo man an seiner Not kein Ende findet;

Ein Kerker, wo man uns gefangen hält,

Die Folterbank vor Gott ergebnen Seelen;

Ein Mordplatz uns zu quälen;

Ein Lazarett, wo man stets siech und krank;

Ein Schreckrevier, wo stets ein kläglicher Gesang in die erschrock'nen Ohren fällt;

Figure 1. Continued.

Ein ungestümes Meer, das uns an keinen Hafen stellt
Das ist die Welt.
What is the world?
A labyrinth, where one finds no end to his misery;
A prison, where we are held captive,
The torture rack for souls devoted to God,
A murder place to torture us;
A hospital, where one is always ill;
A territory of horror, where always a lamenting song
Falls in the horrified ears,
A monstrous sea, that gives us no harbor,
That is the world.

4. Tenor aria:
   Was mich erfreuet das ist im Himmel,
   Was mich ergötzt das find ich dort.
   Was mich vergnügt, was mich kann laben,
   Das alles werd ich droben haben.
   Hier in dem wüsten Weltgetümmel
   Erblickt man keinen sicheren Hort.
   ($\frac{3}{4}$, polonaise allusion, da capo aria)
   What makes me joyful is in heaven,
   What gives me delight I will find there.
   What gives me pleasure, what can refresh me
   All will have over there.
   Here in the desert-like tumult of the world,
   One glimpses no safe shelter.

5. Bass recitative:
   Drum komm nur komm geliebter Tod!
   Du meiner Marter süßes Ende!
   Komm reiche mir die kalten und verfallnen Hände.
   Ich will sie dir mit grössten Freuden küssen,
   Und meine Augen willig schliessen.
   O come, O come beloved death!
   You sweet end to my martyrdom!
   Come reach to me the cold and decaying hands.
   I will kiss them with the greatest joy,
   And will close my eyes willingly.

6. Alto aria:
   Öffnet euch ihr Himmels Pforten,
   Zeiget mir bald eure Pracht.
   Daß ich mög in Salems Auen
   Bald das Licht der Freuden schauen,

Figure 1. Continued.

---

das der Auserwählten lacht.
Open ye gates of heaven,
Show me soon your majesty.
So that I may in Salem's meadows
Soon see the light of joy,
That the chosen one smiles on.
(¢-¾-¢, French ouverture), a text that combines the Gospel theme of resurrection with echoes of
   the text of Psalm 42.

7. Chorale:
   Amen mein lieber frommer Gott,
   Bescher uns alle ein sel'gen Tod,
   Hilf daß wir mögen allzugleich,
   Bald in dein Reich,
   Kommen und bleiben ewiglich.
   Amen, my dear pious God,
   Grant us all a blessed death,
   Help that we may all equally
   Soon come in your realm,
   And remain forever.
(Verse 18 of "Ich hab mein Sach Gott heimgestellt")

[What is the world? A labyrinth] plays off of the text of the fourth strophe of the
chorale, "Was ist der Mensch? Ein Erdenkloß, von Mutterleib kömmt er nackt und
bloß, bringt nichts mit sich auf diese Welt, kein Gut noch Geld, nimmt nichts mit sich,
wenn er hinfällt" [What is man? A lump of mortal clay, who comes from the womb
naked and bare, brings nothing with him into this world, neither goods nor money,
and takes nothing with him when he decays.][8]

The sixth movement of this cantata offers an ingenious play on genre, combining
the formal structures of both the da capo aria—the "default" form for a cantata aria
and clearly the form expected by the librettist—with a complete ouverture. Ex 1a provides an annotated score to the opening, dotted section of the ouverture movement.
Departing from the customary placement of ouverture movements, which usually
form the opening chorus of cantatas, this movement serves as the cantata's penultimate
movement immediately preceding the concluding four-part chorale harmonization.
The ouverture, however, perfectly suits the text, which calls for the opening of the
gates of heaven— "Öffnet euch ihr Himmels Pforten, zeiget mir bald eure Pracht"

---

8. Another version of this recitative text occurs in an undated funeral cantata, *Du aber Daniel, gehe
hin* (TVWV 4:17).

[Open, ye gates of heaven, show me soon your majesty]—and the word "Öffnet" at the beginning of the text of the A section must have been the word that inspired this hybrid form. In fact, the ouverture form aptly suits not only the pomp and majesty of the text of the A section, but of that of the B section, as well: "Daß ich mög in Salems Auen bald das Licht der Freuden schauen das der Auserwählten lacht" [That I may in Salem's meadows soon see the light of joy that smiles on the chosen one], a text well served by the rapid movement of the fast, imitative section.

Of course a conventional ouverture cannot simply be mapped onto a standard da capo aria without structural compromises; nor is the reverse possible without similar adjustment. Telemann took into account the features common to both genres, tampering with both structures to produce a hybrid. Because of the almost totally French style

Ex. 1a. G. P. Telemann, "Öffnet euch ihr Himmels Pforten" (TVWV 1: 1616/6), mm. 1–42.

Ex. 1a. Continued.

Ex. 1a. Continued.

of the movement, however, the impression is that of a somewhat peculiar ouverture with an overlaid vocal part largely doubling the violins. The texture is typical of an Italian aria.

The aria opens with a ritornello ending in the tonic (mm. 1–10), which likewise serves as the first statement of the ouverture's opening dotted section, with an imitation of a typical first ending in m. 10. This already causes a difficulty with the ouverture form, as the first dotted section customarily ends in the dominant or relative major. The first vocal section, including the first presentation of the text of the A section (mm.11–26), ends with a cadence in the dominant. This section begins as though it were a repeat of the opening ten measures, with the vocal part doubling the violins and the treble part lowered an octave, but in the second half of m. 13 it veers away. After the cadence in the dominant at m. 26, the ensuing measure and a half function as a brief ritornello in the da capo aria structure. But had the ouverture structure actually begun in m. 11, its opening dotted section would have been perfectly in keeping with the characteristic A section of an ouverture. The first half would then extend from m. 11 to m. 27^2, and the putative ritornello would supply the first ending. Because mm. 27^3–42 repeat mm. 11–27, in an actual French overture this section would constitute the customary repeat of the dotted section, ending properly on the dominant. In the context of the A section of a da capo aria, this repetition functions as the second statement of the A text following the internal ritornello but is compromised because it is not normal either for the music of the second statement of the A text to be the same as that of the first, or for the second A text (with or without a concluding ritornello) to end in the dominant. Thus, both the A section of the da capo aria and the first section of the ouverture are essentially complete, but each is disturbed to support the other. Most crucially, the slow, dotted portion of the ouverture has three sections instead of two, and the A section of the da capo aria fails to end in the tonic.

The B section of the da capo aria (mm. 43–114) corresponds to the fast, imitative section of the ouverture, and the style belongs to the French ouverture rather than to the Italian aria, in keeping with the style of the piece as a whole. Figure 2 provides a schematic diagram of this section. However, whereas Telemann's da capo arias contain one or two statements of the B text, with either no or only one internal ritornello, the B section of this aria comprises three statements of the B text separated by two ritornellos. The B sections of Telemann's da capo arias are generally shorter than the A sections, but the ouverture genre requires a longer fast section than the opening slow section, and the three statements of the text and three loose expositions of the subject provide proportions more in keeping with the ouverture. The ritornellos, which introduce the only triplet figures in the movement, stand quite apart from the style of the fast section and appear to provide the typical ritornello separation of statements of the B text. There are precedents, of course, for the appearance of ritornellos in some

Figure 2. Analysis of "Öffnet euch ihr Himmels Pforten," mm. 43–114.

	Measures				
	43–61	61–65	65–81	81–85	85–114
French ouverture	Fast imitative section, first set of entries	Ritornello 1 in concerted ouverture	Fast imitative section, second set of entries	Ritornello 2 in concerted ouverture	Fast imitative section, third set of entries
Da capo aria	First presentation of B text	Ritornello 1	Second presentation of B text	Ritornello 2	Third presentation of B text (not conventional)

concerted ouvertures in which the B section is cast in ritornello form. A good example is Telemann's Ouverture for Solo Recorder, Strings, and Continuo in A Minor (TWV 55: a2). The "extra" statement of the B text and second ritornello of the B section in this case compromise the B section of the da capo aria in much the same way as the appearance of a third section (really the first section, as it is the "extra" section) in the opening dotted section compromises the ouverture.

The return to the dotted music in m. 114, given in Ex. 1b, constitutes both the modified da capo of the da capo aria, with its return to the opening A text, and the return of the opening style in the French ouverture. Here, it is the da capo form that is the more compromised. This section is a repetition of the opening ritornello (mm. 1–10) with the voice now doubling the violin. It lacks the dual iteration of the A text found in the first A section. Ironically, whereas most da capo arias either bypass the opening ritornello or shorten it in the da capo, this da capo really consists entirely of ritornello, although the ritornello was originally partially duplicated at the beginning of the first A-text section. On the other hand, considered as a return to the dotted opening of the ouverture, this section follows the customary conventions. The entire imitative section and concluding dotted section are repeated, in keeping with the ouverture structure but completely at odds with that of the da capo aria.

Is this movement, then, an ouverture or a da capo aria? Its context, as an inner movement of a cantata, is that of a da capo aria, and this is the genre for which the text appears to have been conceived. In form, however, the piece is more nearly a texted French ouverture, with an extra ten-measure section at the beginning and two strongly contrasting ritornellos in the fast, imitative section. The style is almost entirely that of the ouverture. In Fowler's conception of genre, it would be difficult to assign mode and genre to this movement if one were to view it in isolation from the expectations of

Ex. 1b. G. P. Telemann, "Öffnet euch ihr Himmels Pforten"
(TVWV 1: 1616/6), mm. 114–23.

the cantata genre and of the librettist, as neither of the two competing genres seems to have the upper hand. According to Fowler, "modal terms never imply a complete external form." By his definition, then, this aria likely encompasses too much of the external form of the second genre, the ouverture, to justify being classified as a da capo aria "in the mode of an ouverture."[9] Indeed, the ouverture structure threatens to overwhelm the movement's generic status as a da capo aria, rather than enrich it. Further, both competing forms are equally compromised, although the scoring and function privilege the da capo aria. Nor does it really form a subgenre: it fails to give birth to much in the way of imitators, unlike, for example, the concerted ouverture.

Although this movement finds no counterpart in the repertoire of Bach cantatas and no regular place in Telemann's own cantatas, its form was one that the composer did later employ occasionally. Most prominently, he was to return to it many years later in his oratorio *Die Auferstehung und Himmelfahrt Jesu* (1760), in the duet aria for two sopranos "Ihr Tore Gottes, öffnet euch!" [Ye gates of God, open up!].[10] Here again, it must have been the "opening" topos of the text that inspired Telemann to choose the ouverture as a mold in which to cast the duet. The style, of course, is quite typical of Telemann's late style in its employment of Lombardic rhythms in place of some of the dotted rhythms in the opening section (a device, however, that he had used nearly thirty years before in the *Musique de Table* of 1733). Again, the B text's more lively sentiments, "Werft eure Diademe nieder, so schallt der weite Himmel . . ." [Throw down your diadem, so resounds the broad firmament], fit the quick, dance-like music Telemann supplied for it, with its allusions to the bourrée.

Bach's ouverture-choruses with chorale melodies stated as cantus firmi have clear counterparts in Telemann's cantatas, although the latter's treatment of such movements differed from that of the Thomascantor. Telemann's cantata from the *Französischer Jahrgang, Christ ist erstanden* (TVWV 1: 136) (Easter, 1715), sets a text from Neumeister's fourth yearly cycle.[11] Neumeister based his text on that of the chorale "Christ ist er-

9. See Fowler, *Kinds of Literature*, 107.

10. I am grateful to Wolfgang Hirschmann and Ralph-Jürgen Reipsch for pointing out this aria to me.

11. The texts were printed in Neumeister's *Geistliche Poesien mit untermischten Biblischen Sprüchen und Choralen*, to be set by Telemann for the 1714–15 cycle both in Frankfurt and Eisenach. The cycle was reprinted in Erdmann Neumeister, *Fünffache Kirchen-Andachten* (Leipzig, 1716). "Christ ist erstanden" appears on pp. 206–8 of the latter. See also Georg Phillip Telemann, *Christ ist erstanden*, ed. Martin Hertel (Frankfurt: Habsburger Verlag: 1999), Preface. Hertel transcribed the piece in *Chorton*, and I have transcribed it in *Kammerton* (*Chorton* and *Kammerton* are a minor third apart in the sources for this piece, which are largely copied for a 1722 Frankfurt performance by Johann Christoph Bodinus, who was Telemann's successor as Kapellmeister from 1721 to 1727 at the Barfüßer-Kirche.)

standen von der Marter alle" (a *Leise* based on the Medieval Easter sequence, *Victimae Paschali laudes*), and on a passage from Psalm 118, "Man singet mit Freuden vom Sieg in den Hütten der Gerechten," a text also set by Bach in the opening parody movement to his eponymous cantata, BWV 149. Neumeister constructed the chorus text in such a way that the first and second lines of the chorale text are presented followed by the psalm text, and finally, the second, third, and fourth lines of the chorale text. Thus, the text is given a tripartite shape whose outer parts require the setting of the chorale tune as some kind of cantus firmus. By juxtaposing the two texts, he interprets the psalm text: the victory of the righteous is achieved through the resurrection of Christ, and the word "froh" at the end of the second line of the chorale is linked with the word "Freuden" in the Psalm.

Drawing upon this three-part design, Telemann conceived the chorus as a vocal French ouverture, in which the slow A sections set the chorale tune and the fast B section sets the psalm. The overall disposition of the movement is given in Figure 3.

Although the implied tripartite structure maps well to the design of the French ouverture, as do the affects of the texts, Telemann has not simply overlaid the chorale onto an ouverture. His ouverture itself is somewhat idiosyncratic because of his need to present a theological interpretation of the text. To begin with, the opening section of the chorus is ostensibly in F minor, yet Telemann begins the movement with a brass-like fanfare for strings in C major over a C pedal point, symbolically proclaiming the resurrection. The opening nineteen measures of the first section of the movement are given in Ex. 2a. It is only after the opening fanfare that the proper key of the movement makes its appearance for the minor-key setting of the chorale tune.[12] Further, Telemann does not present the chorale tune in all four voices, but only in the tenor, perhaps a reference to the tradition of tenor cantus firmus settings of chorale tunes in the first generation of composers of polyphonic chorale settings. At any rate, the effect

---

12. A cantata once attributed to Telemann set to the Neumeister text *Nun komm, der Heiden Heiland* (TVWV 1: 117), the same text as that set by Bach in BWV 61 (Neumeister, Cycle 4), begins in a nearly identical manner. The cantata is transmitted in Mügeln, No. 355 and 395, and bears an attribution to TEL. See Ute Poetzsch, "Neues über den Telemannbestand im Kantoreiarchiv zu Mügeln," in *Auf der gezeigten Spur: Beiträge zur Telemannforschung, Magdeburger Telemannstudien*, 13 (Ochsersleben: Dr. Ziethen Verlag, 1994), 106–11, 121; and Werner Menke, TVWV, I, xiii–xiv. Poetszch points out that this cantata stands apart from the other Mügeln cantatas attributed to "TEL" or "T.E.L.," in that all of the others are strophic *Odenkantaten* with introductory sonatas or sinfonias, with texts largely taken from the fifth yearly cycle of Neumeister's *Fünffache Kirchenandachten*. If Telemann is not the composer of TVWV 1: 1178, then the actual composer was certainly familiar with Telemann's opening chorus to *Christ ist erstanden*, although it is possible that the sources are in the reverse chronological order. To complicate the issue, Telemann did indeed set Neumeister's text as *Nun komm, der Heiden Heiland* (TVWV 1: 1175), but in a wholly different style.

Figure 3. Disposition of the opening movement of G. P. Telemann,
"Christ ist erstanden" (tvwv 1: 136) (Easter, 1715).

I. Dotted, with chorale cantus firmus: Christ ist erstanden von der Marter alle. Deß sollen wir
alle froh seyn.
Christ is arisen from all the torment. For this we should all be happy.

II. Fast, partly imitative section, F major, triple meter: "Man singet mit Freuden vom Sieg in
den Hütten der Gerechten. Die Rechte des Herrn behält den Sieg. Die Rechte des Herrn ist
erhöhet. Die Rechte des Herrn behält den Sieg.
*Shouts of joy and victory resound in the tents of the righteous: "The Lord's right hand has done mighty
things [maintains the victory]! The Lord's right hand is lifted high; the Lord's right hand has done
mighty things!"*

III. Four-part chorale: "Deß soll'n wir alle froh seyn. Christus will unser Trost seyn. Kyrie eleis."
For this we should all be happy. Christ will be our consolation. Kyrie eleis.

Ex. 2a. G. P. Telemann, "Christ ist erstanden von der Marter alle"
(tvwv 1: 136/1), mm. 1–19.

Ex. 2a. Continued.

Ex. 2a. Continued.

of the single-voice cantus firmus, an archaic reference, set against the modern, pompous ouverture is startling here as it is at the beginning of BWV 140 and BWV 20. As dictated by the libretto, the chorale is interrupted after the second line, and there is no repeat of the slow section of the ouverture (as is often the case in cantata settings).[13]

The fast section of the ouverture sets the psalm excerpt, with the change in mode to F major and the fast $\frac{3}{8}$ meter underscoring the joy of victory. This section presents each line of the text as a separate subsection with the appropriate word painting, producing far more motivic contrast than in a real Lullian ouverture. Ex. 2b presents the opening of the fast section. For example, the text "Die Rechte des Herrn behält den Sieg" is illustrated by sustaining the notes, whereas the text "Die Rechte des Herrn ist erhöhet" underscores the raising up of the hand of God by means both of ascending notes and melismas. Further, the repetition of the text "Die Rechte des Herrn behält den Sieg" in the psalm imparts a rondeau-like structure to the corresponding music.

13. In the Bach examples, BWV 20 has no repeat of the first section; BWV 61 has no repeat; BWV 97 has a repeat but the opening dotted section is entirely instrumental; BWV 110 has no repeat, and the opening dotted section is entirely instrumental; BWV 119 has a repeat but the opening dotted section is entirely instrumental; BWV 194 has a repeat but the opening dotted section is entirely instrumental. Thus, Bach never repeated the opening section when the opening dotted section is set for chorus, but sometimes did so when the chorus is silent throughout the opening section.

Ex. 2b. G. P. Telemann, "Christ ist erstanden von der Marter alle"
(TVWV 1: 136/1), mm. 28–65.

Ex. 2b. Continued.

Ex. 2b. Continued.

Ex. 2b. Continued.

Ex. 2b. Continued.

It is at the moment of the expected return to the dotted section of the ouverture where Telemann's setting most crucially breaks from its generic fetters to free the chorus from the pomp of its putative model. At this point, the listener familiar with the conventions of the ouverture would expect a return of the slow, dotted music of the A section, in this case in conjunction with the chorale cantus firmus. But as Ex. 2c reveals, Telemann brought back only the opening tempo, dispensing with the dotted rhythms of the orchestra altogether and bringing back the chorale as a simple four-part setting (beginning with line 2, in accordance with the libretto). Thus, the stark harmonization of the chorale substitutes for the worldly splendor of the opening section, at exactly the point where the return of the dotted music is expected. The simple congregational joy at the resurrection of Christ thus takes precedence.

A particularly puzzling example of Telemann's use of the ouverture occurs in the cantata *Jesus sei mein erstes Wort* (TVWV 1: 986) (Fifth Sunday after Trinity, 1715), a work from the *Französicher Jahrgang* with a text taken from Neumeister's fourth cantata cycle. In this cantata, a choral dictum in the mode of an ouverture appears as the *last* of ten movements, standing on end the normal function of the ouverture as a movement signifying openings or beginnings. In fact, the placement of the ouverture at the end of the work violates one of the functional hallmarks of the genre.[14] The layout of the cantata is presented in Figure 4. A particular oddity in the performing materials for this cantata is that for the first two chorales, the two separate sets of performance material provide completely different melodies, even though the texts are the same. I have labeled these according to the copyists of the two scores, Beck and König.

One must consider this cantata as part of a larger theological tradition in which Christ is referred to as the "A" (alpha) and "O" (omega), the beginning and the end. Eric Chafe[15] discusses four of Bach's cantatas in terms of their use of the "A" and "O" metaphor, which derives from the book of Revelation.[16] In addition, Chafe also

14. Johann Gottfried Walther stresses the relationship of the term *ouverture* with its placement at the beginning of the work: "Ouverture [gall.] hat den Nahmen vom Eröffnen, weil diese Instrumental-Piéce gleichsam die Thür zu den Suiten oder folgenden Sachen auffschliesset." Johann Gottfried Walther, *Musikalisches Lexikon* (Leipzig, 1732), facs. ed. (Kassel: Bärenreiter Verlag, 1953), 456. Scheibe also defines the ouverture by its opening function: "Es sind aber die Ouverturen eigentlich zum Anfange theatralischer Stücke erfunden und verfertiget worden." Johann Adolph Scheibe, *Critischer Musikus*, 2nd ed. (Leipzig, 1745), 668.

15. See Eric T. Chafe, "*Anfang und Ende:* Cyclic Recurrence in Bach's Cantata *Jesu, nun sei gepreiset,* BWV 41," in *Bach Perspectives* 1, ed. Russell Stinson (Lincoln, Neb.: University of Nebraska Press, 1995), 103–34.

16. See Chafe, "*Anfang und Ende,*" 103–4. The relevant verses are Rev. 22:13, "I am the Alpha and the Omega, the first and last, the beginning and the end"; 1:8, "'I am the Alpha and the Omega,'

Ex. 2c. G. P. Telemann, "Christ ist erstanden von der Marter alle"
(TVWV 1: 136/1), mm. 118–31.

Figure 4. Disposition of G. P. Telemann, "Jesus sei mein erstes Wort"
(TVWV 1: 986) (5th Sunday after Trinity, 1715).

1. Soprano aria (da capo): Jesus sei mein erstes Wort (numbered 1).
2. Chorale: All Tritt und Schritt in Gottes Nam' [two different but as yet unidentified melodies].
3. Chorus: Wer Jesum bei sich hat, was will der bessers haben?
4. Bass aria: Jesus sei mein täglich Wort (numbered 2).
5. Chorale: Und wenns gleich wär dem Teufel sehr [Melodies: Beck: "Wer Gott vertraut, hat wohl gebaut," Zahn 8207b; König: "Was mein Gott will, das gescheh allzeit," Zahn 7568]. The text is the second strophe of "Wer Gott vertraut, hat wohl gebaut."
6. Chorus: Wer Jesum bei sich hat, hat alles Wohlergehen.
7. Chorale: Auf Ihn will ich vertrauen in meiner schweren Zeit [Melody: "Von Gott will ich nicht lassen," Zahn 5265, *Telemann, Fast Allgemeines Evangelische-Musicalisches Lieder-Buch* (Hamburg, 1730), No. 152]. Melody in König is a variant of Beck's, which is closest to Telemann's melody. The text is the third strophe of the chorale.
8. Tenor aria: Jesus sei mein letztes Wort (numbered 3).
9. Chorus: Wer Jesum bei sich hat, kann nicht im Tode sterben.
10. French ouverture: Alles was ihr tut, mit Worten oder mit Werken (Col. III, 17).[a]

a. Mislabeled as II:17 in *Fünffache Kirchen-Andachten*, p. 347.

treats cantatas that set texts that use the beginning-end metaphor in some way. One of these, *Gott, wie dein Name, so ist auch dein Ruhm* (BWV 171) (New Year's Day, 1729?), with a text by Picander, includes an aria for soprano whose text draws on the idea of the name "Jesus" being both the first and last word of the speaker (in the case of the Picander text, the first word of the New Year):[17]

Jesus soll mein erstes Wort
In dem neuen Jahre heißen.
Fort und fort
Lacht sein Nam in meinem Mund,

says the Lord God, 'who is, and who was, and who is to come, the Almighty'"; and 21:6: "He said to me: 'It is done. I am the Alpha and the Omega, the Beginning and the End. To him who is thirsty I will give drink without cost from the spring of the water of Life.'" (New International Version); see also Melvin Unger, *Handbook to Bach's Sacred Cantata Texts* (Lanham, Md.: Scarecrow Press, 1996), 593. The "A" and "O" trope also finds its way into chorale texts, such as "In dulci jubilo" and "Wie schön leuchtet der Morgenstern."

17. See Chafe, *"Anfang und Ende,"* 104–5. This aria is a parody of an earlier aria from BWV 205 beginning with the text, "Angenehmer Zephyrus."

Und in meiner letzten Stunde

Ist Jesus auch mein letztes Wort.

[Jesus shall be my first word

In the New Year.

On and on

His name makes my mouth rejoice.

And in my final hour

Is Jesus also my final word.][18]

The puzzling dissonance between the placement of the choral ouverture and its own genre expectations can be explicated only by a study of the text, for the placement of the ouverture at the end of the cantata itself forms part of the text's exegesis. The text gives rise to four distinct elements: (1) three arias (set by Telemann for soprano, bass, and tenor) which form the linchpins of the cantata, (2) three choruses accompanied only by continuo in which each line begins with the words, "Wer Jesum bei sich hat" [He who has Jesus with him], set to the same music in the manner of a litany, (3) three chorale settings, and (4) a fourth choral setting of the concluding text from Colossians.[19] Except for the final chorus, Neumeister provided three strophic texts based on a traditional Lutheran trope of Jesus as the first, lifelong, and last word,

---

18. The translation is amended from Unger, *Handbook*, 593.

19. The Frankfurt set of scores and parts, D-Ff Mus. 1192, includes an additional inserted movement copied in score (not included in the scores by Beck and König) setting the text, "Wer Jesum bei sich hat," in a more modern style with concerted instrumental parts. Only the text of the first strophe is underlaid beneath the music. The copyist of the score insert is Frankfurt copyist 58, Johann Christoph Fischer, music director at the Barfüsserkirche from 1759 until his death in 1769. A set of inserted parts for "Canto," "Alto," "Tenore," and "Basso" vocal parts, as well as "Violin 1mo," "Violino secondo," "Viola," "Violoncello," "Oboe 1mo," "Oboe 2do," and "Organo" (both *Chorton* and *Kammerton* parts), also survives as part of the same performance materials with only the three "Wer Jesum bey sich hat" movements (written out each time in the vocal parts with the three texts underlaid), but no other movements. The copyists of this set of inserted parts are Fischer and Frankfurt copyist 88, whose hand appears from 1744 on and who often copied with Fischer (Frankfurt copyist 88's hand appears in a set of manuscript copies of Telemann's *Musicalisches Lob Gottes* of 1744). Rubrics in the instrumental parts direct the performers to use the substitute sheets for the choral movements. The authorship of the substitute music is unclear. Telemann may have supplied more modern music later, or it may be the work of another composer. On the identification of these copyists, see the sample pages from various Frankfurt cantata manuscripts illustrating copyists' hands in Joachim Schlichte, *Thematischer Katalog der kirchlichen Musikhandschriften des 17. und 18. Jahrhunderts in der Stadt- und Universitätsbibliothek Frankfurt am Main* (Frankfurt: Stadt- und Universitätsbibliothek, 1979), and Eric Fiedler, *Telemann-Konkordanz*, 2nd ed. (Frankfurt: Habsburger Verlag, 2000), Preface.

the chorus texts, and the chorale texts. The libretto, however, presents the composer with distinct challenges.

Unusual in a cantata text of Neumeister, which normally presents a mix of recitative and aria, no text is provided for recitative, and Telemann included no recitative in the cantata. Nor does the libretto include texts designed for setting as da capo arias. Thus, the operatic hallmarks of the madrigalian cantata are missing. Even more crucially, the text closes, rather than opens, with the Biblical dictum; the libretto itself contains a reversal in form, with the choral dictum shifted from the beginning to the end. The three arias, whose texts draw upon a traditional Lutheran trope, each begin a section of the cantata in which the name Jesus is pronounced by the speaker as his first, lifelong, and last word. Oddly, whereas Neumeister numbered the text of the "Jesus sei" strophes in a manner that suggests they were intended to be set strophically, possibly indicating an origin in a preexistent strophic hymn, Telemann completely ignored the strophic origin of the text and sets each as a da capo aria as though composed to madrigalian poetry; in each he sets the first line of text to the A music and the remainder to the B music. An especially nice touch is afforded by Telemann's setting of the opening motto of the first aria for unaccompanied soprano, thus providing a simple, childlike beginning to the cantata, one completely devoid of instrumental accompaniment. The last word of the speaker in the final aria is illustrated by the most virtuosic melisma of the entire cantata.[20]

The texts of the arias make clear a progression in time from the birth of the believer, whose first word is Jesus, until his death:

> Aria 1 (soprano):
>
> Jesus sei mein erstes Wort
>
> Bei der Arbeit meiner Hände,
>
> Daß Er mir den Segen sende.
>
> Kann ich dessen mich erfreuen,
>
> So wird alles wohl gedeien,
>
> Und mein Werk geht glücklich fort.
>
> Jesus sei mein erstes Wort.
>
> [May Jesus be my foremost word
>
> At the work of my hands,

20. This melisma evidently caused problems for the tenor in a later performance, for Fischer later sketched in another version of the melisma, with more opportunities to breathe, above the original version in Beck's score.

Such that he may bestow his blessing upon me.

If I can take comfort in this,

All will thrive

And my work will proceed with good fortune.

May Jesus be my foremost word.]

Aria 2 (bass):

Jesus sei mein täglich Wort.

Hab' ich Jesum zum Geleite,

Und an meiner rechten Seite,

So kann ich in allen Fällen

Freudig meinen Weg bestellen.

Denn Er ist mein starker Hort.

Jesus sei mein täglich Wort.

[May Jesus be my daily word.

If I have Jesus as my guide,

And at my right side,

I can in every case

Secure my way with joy.

For He is my strong shelter.

May Jesus be my daily word.]

Aria 3 (tenor):

Jesus sei mein letztes Wort.

Ihn behalt' ich in dem Munde

Bei der letzten Lebensstunde.

Könnt Ihn auch der Mund nicht nennen,

Soll Ihn doch das Herz bekennen.

Und so fahr' ich selig fort.

Jesus sei mein letztes Wort!

[May Jesus be my final word!

His name will remain on my lips

In my last hour of life.

Even if my mouth were unable to pronounce his name,

My heart should still profess it.

And thus I will travel forth with blessing.

May Jesus be my final word!]

The texts of the choruses likewise begin with the evocation of earthly life and end with reflections on death. But now the Christian will not really die, but rather will inherit eternal life:

Chorus 1:

Wer Jesum bei sich hat, was will der bessers haben?

Wer Jesum bei sich hat, hat mehr als alle Gaben.

Wer Jesum bei sich hat, ist immer gutes Muts.

Wer Jesum bei sich hat, geniesset tausend Guts.

Wer Jesum bei sich hat, hat Rat in allen Dingen.

Wer Jesum bei sich hat, dem muß es wohl gelingen.

[He who has Jesus with him, what better could he want?

He who has Jesus with him has more than all gifts.

He who has Jesus with him is always of good cheer.

He who has Jesus with him enjoys a thousand good things.

He who has Jesus with him has counsel in all things.

He who has Jesus with him, for him everything must succeed.]

Chorus 2:

Wer Jesum bei sich hat, hat alles Wohlergehen.

Wer Jesum bei sich hat, kann unerschrocken stehen.

Wer Jesum bei sich hat, acht't Kreutz und Leiden nicht.

Wer Jesum bei sich hat, hat stets ein Freuden-Licht.

Wer Jesum bei sich hat, kann sich geduldig fassen.

Wer Jesum bei sich hat, wird nimmermehr verlassen.

[He who has Jesus with him has health and happiness.

He who has Jesus with him can stand unafraid.

He who has Jesus with him fears not the Cross and suffering.

He who has Jesus with him has always a joyful light.

He who has Jesus with him can endure with patience.

He who has Jesus with him will never be left alone.]

Chorus 3:

Wer Jesum bei sich hat, kann nicht im Tode sterben.

Wer Jesum bei sich hat, der muß das Leben erben.

Wer Jesum bei sich hat, wird froh zu Grabe gehn.

Wer Jesum bei sich hat, wird herrlich auferstehn.

Wer Jesum bei sich hat, krönt sich mit diesem Namen.

Wer Jesum bei sich hat, der glaubt und saget Amen.

[He who has Jesus with him cannot die.

He who has Jesus with him must inherit (eternal) life.

He who has Jesus with him will go happily to the grave.

He who has Jesus with him will gloriously be resurrected.

He who has Jesus with him is crowned with his name.

He who has Jesus with him believes and says "Amen."]

The three chorale verses (from different chorales) likewise progress from earthly living and work (Chorale 1) to Christ's protection (Chorale 2) to giving over the body and soul to God in death (Chorale 3):

Chorale 1:

All Tritt und Schritt in Gottes Nam', was ich fang an, teil mir dein' Hilfe mit, und komm mir früh entgegen mit Glücke, Heil und Segen. Mein' Bitt' versag mir nicht.

All mein Arbeit in Gottes Nam' was ich fang an, gereich zur Nutzbarkeit. Mein Leib, mein Seel, mein Leben, was du mir hast gegeben, lobt dich in Ewigkeit.

[With every step I take in the name of God, impart to me your help, and bestow on me in good time success, redemption, and blessing. My petition do not deny me.

May all the work in God's name that I take on be of some usefulness. My body, my soul, my life, which you have given me, praise you in eternity.]

Chorale 2:

Und wenns gleich wär dem Teufel sehr und aller Welt zuwider; dennoch so bist du, JESU Christ, der sie all schlägt darnieder. Und wenn ich dich nur hab' um mich mit deinem Geist und Gnaden, so kann fürwahr mir ganz und gar wed'r Tod noch Teufel schaden.

[And though it were displeasing to the Devil and the whole world, it is you, Jesus Christ, who defeats them all. And even if I have only your spirit and mercy by me, indeed neither death nor the Devil can harm me.]

Chorale 3:
Auf Ihn will ich vertrauen in meiner schweren Zeit. Es kann mich nicht gereuen, Er wendet alles Leid. Ihm sei es heimgestellt. Mein Leib, mein Seel, mein Leben sei Gott dem Herrn ergeben. Er mach's, wie's Ihm gefällt.

[I will trust in him in my difficult time. I cannot regret it, He turns away all sorrow. It (sorrow) is left to Him. My body, my soul, my life are surrendered to God the Lord. He acts as it pleases Him.]

The three-by-three construction of the text culminates in the passage from the third chapter of Colossians:

Ouverture:
Alles was Ihr tut, mit Worten oder mit Werken, das tut alles in dem Namen unsers Herrn Jesu Christi, und danket Gott und dem Vater durch Ihn.

[All that you do, in words or in deeds, do it all in the name of the Lord Jesus Christ, and thank God and the Father through him.]

Although there is nothing specific in this text to inspire Telemann's setting of it as an ouverture—indeed, its terminal position in the text would seem to argue against such a setting—in light of the preceding movements, Telemann's interpretation is wholly fitting. For the "opening" topos associated traditionally with the ouverture itself sets the normal movement ordering on its head: the cantata ends with an ouverture because the three movements preceding it focus on death. But in the Lutheran conception, death represents not the end, but the beginning, the beginning of eternal life, and is something to be longed for and desired. The ouverture is the prelude to eternal life beginning with the death of the believer.

Telemann divided the text in such a way that "Alles was Ihr tut" through "Jesu Christi" forms the A section of the putative ouverture, and the remainder of the text forms the B section. But the A section is somewhat peculiar in itself. Ex. 3a gives the first, dotted section of the ouverture and the beginning of the second, quick imitative section.

Ex. 3a. G. P. Telemann, "Alles was ihr tut" (TVWV 1: 986/10), mm. 1–14.

Ex. 3a. Continued.

Ex. 3a. Continued.

Ex. 3a. Continued.

Ex. 3b. A. Corelli, Sonata in A Major, op. 3, no. 12, final mvt., mm. 1–13.

The typical dotted rhythms that are the hallmark of the ouverture extend only through "Alles was Ihr tut, mit Worten oder mit Werken," that is, that segment of the text treating the worldly deeds of the faithful Lutheran whose redemption will be brought about not by deeds but by faith through grace. The text, "das tut alles in dem Namen unsers Herrn Jesu Christi," is set quite unconventionally for an ouverture, homophonically in even rhythm over a long dominant pedal in the bass almost as if it were a chorale, driving home the point that the worldly acts are not for the believer, but for Christ. The quick imitative section of the ouverture is more straightforward, emphasizing a joyous affect, with giga-like rhythms, long melismas, syncopations, and hemiolas inspired by the joy of giving thanks. The fugue theme is quite similar to that in the final movement of Arcangelo Corelli's Trio Sonata in A Major, op. 3 no. 12, and may be derived from it.[21]

* * *

Telemann and Bach both were drawn to experimenting with vocal movements based on the ouverture in their sacred cantatas, probably beginning around the 1714–15

21. See Ex. 3b. Telemann's cantata repertory shows a considerable amount of borrowing from his instrumental works. The extent of his borrowings both from himself and from other composers remains to be studied.

liturgical cycle.[22] Although it remains to be discovered how many of their contemporaries also experimented with the ouverture in cantata compositions and how early this happened, it is reasonable to expect that vocal movements based on the ouverture also spread eventually to the Lutheran cantata repertoire as a whole.

It is worth pointing out that Bach and Telemann met in March of 1714, when Telemann stood godfather to C. P. E. Bach in Weimar, and the two composers could have discussed their experiments with the madrigalian cantata at that time.[23] Further, as Peter Wollny has pointed out, the opening to Agostino Steffani's opera *Enrico Leone* (Hanover, 1689) offers a precedent for the use of the ouverture in secular vocal music.[24] In his 1718 autobiography, Telemann testified to having heard the Hanover court ensemble while a student in the Gymnasium at Hildesheim,[25] and he also named Steffani as a composer whose music he studied and emulated during this period.[26] Whereas Bach maintained the association of the "opening" topos of the ouverture genre with its traditional position as the first movement of a multimovement work, Telemann extended the ouverture allusion to later movements of the cantata, as well, even to closing movements, in order to make either relatively simple analogies expressed in texts referring in some way to "opening," or to make more complex theological arguments. In his da capo arias "auf Ouvertürenart"—to coin a modern term in the spirit of Johann Adolph Scheibe's sonata "auf Concertenart"—Telemann also drew upon structural analogies between the tripartite structure of the da capo aria and the combination of both the bipartite and tripartite forms of the ouverture with a return of the dotted material at the end. The combination of da capo aria and ouverture is in keeping with Telemann's fascination with generic hybrids as a whole, a fascination he shared with Bach.

22. Without a thorough study of all his early cantatas, it is not yet known when the ouverture first appears in a cantata of Telemann. It should be remembered that Telemann was already an experienced composer of ouvertures by the time he took up his position in Eisenach in 1708 (because such pieces were the core of the repertoire at the Sorau court of Erdmann von Promnitz in Poland, where he was employed from 1705 to 1708), and that the 1714–15 yearly cycle was designed to emphasize the French style.

23. Peter Wollny has also made this point in his introduction to *Johann Sebastian Bach, Nun komm, der Heiden Heiland BWV 61*, facs. ed. Peter Wollny (Laaber: Laaber-Verlag, 2000), xv.

24. See Wollny, *Nun komm*, xiv.

25. This appears in the autobiography printed in Johann Mattheson, *Grosse General-Bass-Schule* (Hamburg, 1731), 171–72; facs. ed. in *Georg Philipp Telemann: Autobiographien 1718–1729–1739, Studien zur Aufführungspraxis und Interpretation von Instrumentalmusik des 18. Jahrhunderts, Heft 3*, ed. Günter Fleischauer et al., 14–15.

26. This appears in the autobiography printed in Johann Mattheson, *Grundlage einer Ehrenpforte* (Hamburg, 1740), 357; facsimile in *Georg Philipp Telemann: Autobiographien 1718–1729–1739*, 39.

Bach and the
Concert en ouverture

Steven Zohn

As Bach's de facto flute concerto, the Ouverture in B Minor (BWV 1067) is at once the most frequently heard of the composer's ouverture-suites and among the least typical examples of the genre. Part of the work's appeal no doubt centers on its finely calibrated tension between style and scoring, a subtle generic friction in which the detached suavity of the French suite and the assertive display of the Italian concerto rub together in several movements. This dynamic, also present to some degree in the Ouverture in D Major (BWV 1068) is of course absent in most ouverture-suites, where concertante instruments tend to be highlighted antiphonally rather than as virtuosic soloists, as, for example, with the "French trio" of two oboes and bassoon in the Ouverture in C Major (BWV 1066). Although the special properties of BWV 1067, in particular, have long been recognized and justly celebrated, the compositional tradition to which it belongs has remained very much in the background; the tacit assumption seems to have been that the work transcends the norms of its type. This essay aims to situate BWV 1067 and 1068 within a larger repertory of concerto-like ouverture-suites, revealing some ways in which Bach's compositional choices may have been shaped by the works of his contemporaries.

In fact, few eighteenth-century composers besides Bach dealt in such concerto-suite hybrids, and only one writer of the time has left us a prescription for how these works ought to proceed. In his 1740 discussion of the "Concertouverture" in *Der critische Musikus*, Johann Adolph Scheibe repeatedly stressed that concertante instruments in an ouverture-suite must not substitute Italianate bravado for Gallic order:

> With regard to the concertante instruments, one easily observes their free, playful, and jocular singing in places where they are prominent. It is not their numbers that must stand out; rather, it is the varied entrance, the lively and natural parsing of the harmony's principal chord, and the cheerful, more or less flowing modulation of the concertante voices that give the Concertouverture a true beauty and the requisite fire. Of course, one must at the same time be mindful of the instruments' nature. But one must also avoid proceeding in a manner that is as concerto-like, long-winded, and forceful as would be appropriate in a proper concerto. Here there is a certain balance to maintain, so that one does not overshadow the true disposition and nature

of the Ouverture and lapse from a French style of writing into an Italian one, and consequently render the style of such a piece confused and disorderly.

A Concertouverture with a concertante violin must therefore be distinguishable in its elaboration from an ordinary violin concerto; the same goes for Ouverturen with other concertante instruments. In particular, such Ouverturen are most pleasing if, during their course, a pair of oboes and a bassoon alternate now and then with a harmonizing trio. [These instruments] must not, however, work very hard, but proceed together in clear harmony or simply imitate each other; the rest of the instruments then alternate with them.[1]

The term *Concertouverture*, then, may be applied broadly to any ouverture-suite with at least one concertante string or wind part, which is to say that it describes many—perhaps even a majority—of the works written during the 1720s and 1730s. Some years earlier, Scheibe had more pointedly articulated his warning against undermining a suite's French identity through excessive virtuosity: "If there are concertante voices [in an ouverture], such as oboes or recorders [*Flauten*], then they may be heard alone from time to time, with the violins or a bassoon providing the bass. If there is a concertante violin, no Italianate concerto figurations [*Passagen*] must be introduced; rather, one must adhere strictly to the French style."[2]

We may gather from Scheibe's strongly worded disapproval of concerto-like Concertouverturen that "confused and disorderly" works such as BWV 1067 and 1068 were not uncommon around 1730. Because my concern here is with this soloistic subset of ouverture-suites, I shall eschew Scheibe's general term (and the modern term *Konzertsuite*) in favor of *concert en ouverture*, an eighteenth-century formulation connected with a work scored similarly to BWV 1067: Telemann's Suite for Violin and Strings in E Major (TWV 55:E3).[3] For the purposes of the following discussion, a *con-*

1. Johann Adolph Scheibe, *Der critische Musikus*, "Drei und siebenzigstes Stück. Dienstags, den 19 Jenner, 1740" (Hamburg: Thomas von Wierings Erben, 1740), 372–73; second revised edition as *Critischer Musikus* (Leipzig: Breitkopf, 1745; repr. Hildesheim and New York: Georg Olms Verlag, 1970), 672. The quoted passage is from the 1745 edition.

2. Johann Adolph Scheibe, *Compendium Musices Theoretico-Practicum* (Leipzig, unpublished manuscript, 1728–36), transcribed in Peter Benary, *Die deutsche Kompositionslehre des 18. Jahrhunderts*, Jenaer Beiträge zur Musikforschung, III (Leipzig: Breitkopf & Härtel, 1961), *Anhang*, 84.

3. This work is listed below in Table 1. The heading, *Concert en ouverture*, obviously a reference to the violin's soloistic role in the work's Ouverture and in each of the following dance movements, appears at the top of the *Violino concertato* part prepared at the Dresden court by Copyist A (Johann Gottfried Grundig). Horst Büttner, *Das Konzert in den Orchestersuiten Georg Philipp Telemanns* (Wolfenbüttel and Berlin: Georg Kallmeyer, 1935), 17, divided Telemann's ouverture-suites into *Streichersuiten* and *Konzertsuiten*, the latter category including works with one or more concertante instruments. Adolf Hoffmann, in his editions of three other Telemann ouverture-suites for soloist and strings, TWV 55:

cert en ouverture may be understood as an ouverture-suite in which a soloist assumes a concertato role in the ouverture and in most, if not all, subsequent movements.

* * *

As a first step toward exploring the generic context of BWV 1067 and 1068, I wish to take stock of some startling findings with regard to the former work by Joshua Rifkin and, to a lesser degree, by Siegbert Rampe and Domenik Sackmann.[4] It so happens that a close reading of the parts for BWV 1067 prepared by Bach and several anonymous copyists during the late 1730s (ST 154, 1–6) yields a number of transposition errors that can mean only one thing: the work was originally conceived in A minor and transposed up a tone by Bach's scribes during the act of copying. Rifkin, unlike Rampe and Sackmann, sees a number of carelessly placed accidentals in the note-perfect autograph flute part as further confirming this act of transposition (though the evidence here, in comparison to that of the non-autograph parts, seems less than clear-cut). But whether Bach himself was transposing as he copied or reading from a source already in B minor, the main point is that the work's lower range and tessitura in A minor seem to imply a solo instrument other than the flute. If one assumes that the lost A-minor solo part closely resembled the later B-minor one, as all three scholars do, then the violin comes readily into play. Rampe and Sackmann find the solo part full of "typical violin figurations," whereas Rifkin considers it something less than idiomatic owing to its lack of multiple stops and general avoidance of the G-string (notwithstanding figuration suggesting a highlighting of the open E-string in mm. 60–62 and 124–26 of the Ouverture). To explain the solo part's curiously modest technical demands, and to confirm that Bach was indeed writing for the violin, Rifkin appeals to Scheibe's definition of the *concert en ouverture* and to Johann Bernhard Bach's G-minor ouverture-suite for violin and strings, with which BWV 1067 shares not only a number of compositional details but a lack of multiple stops and the near-total absence of pitches below d' in the solo part. On the paleographic side of the ledger, Rifkin notes that at the top of Bach's flute part a "V" (for "Violino"?) has taken on a new life as the "T" in "Traversiere."

D6 (Wolfenbüttel: Möseler Verlag, 1955), Es2 (Kassel: Nagels Verlag, 1954), and A4 (Wolfenbüttel: Möseler Verlag, 1963), gives each work the title *Konzertsuite*. And Willi Maertens refers to TWV 55: A8 as a *Konzertsuite* in the preface to his edition of the work (Leipzig: Breitkopf und Härtel, 1967).

4. See Joshua Rifkin, "The 'B-Minor Flute Suite' Deconstructed: New Light on Bach's Ouverture BWV 1067" in this volume. Since the initial presentation of Rifkin's thesis at the first Dortmund Bach Symposium in 1996, Siegbert Rampe and Domenik Sackmann have argued some of the same points in BOM, 258–60. I am grateful to Joshua Rifkin for allowing me to read a draft of his article, and for several stimulating discussions relating to BWV 1067 and similar works.

It is not my intention here to challenge the one-time existence of an A-minor version of BWV 1067; nor will Rifkin's dating of the piece to 1730–31 get any argument. But I wish to consider, in a preliminary digression with implications for the rest of this essay, the possibility that Bach's "flute suite" was always a flute suite, or that the putative solo violin part would have made better use of the instrument's capabilities than does the B-minor part. I will, in effect, be agitating not so much *against* the violin as *for* the flute as a viable solo instrument in the earliest manifestation of BWV 1067.

One of the principal arguments against the flute concerns the instrument's compass, which in Bach's time normally extended down to d'. In BWV 1067, a literal transposition of the B-minor solo part a step lower produces c' in four measures of the Ouverture (mm. 11, 36, 78, and 86) and in single measures of both the Polonoise-Double (m. 4) and Menuet (m. 16). There is, moreover, a c#' in m. 115 of the Ouverture. Thus the low range of the hypothetical solo part in A minor would seem to constitute prima facie evidence that it was intended for violin. (The oboe may be ruled out primarily on the basis of the c#' in the Ouverture, the e'''s in the Polonoise [mm. 5, 7] and the unidiomatic leaps in the Polonoise-Double.) Yet a closer look at these measures reveals that in all but two, the soloist is doubled by the first violin, the exceptions being m. 78 of the Ouverture and m. 4 of the Polonoise-Double—places where the lone c's might easily have been avoided in the A-minor part (or in performance) though octave displacement.[5] In other words, a flute soloist playing the work in its original key could steer clear of all seven pitches below d' without altering the substance of the music in any meaningful way and with the unsuspecting listener being none the wiser.

Related to the issue of compass is the flute's status during tutti passages in the middle section of the Ouverture. Bach's B-minor part, of course, includes nearly all of the tutti music—all, that is, except for one brief passage at mm. 127^4–133^4 that Rampe and Sackmann view as the composer's sole concession to his soloist's breathing requirements. But this one break seems less than strategically placed: far greater need for a breath arises at mm. 78, 162, and 174, which come at the midpoint or end of the two longest solo episodes. In fact, the most difficult aspect of the movement for the flutist is not the episodic material itself—comfortably negotiated by a "capable but not unusually virtuoso player," as Rampe and Sackmann put it—but the sheer number of notes without pause, especially if the middle section is repeated in performance. The lack of places to breathe could be taken as further evidence for the violin (or of Bach's indifference to the flutist's need to breathe), but there is another possibility;

5. In the "Ouverture," the first three beats of m. 78 could be taken up an octave, though this would slightly upset the parallelism with mm. 75–76. Similarly, the descending contrapuntal voice that culminates in c' in m. 4 of the "Polonoise-Double" (g'–f'–g'–e'–e'–c')—or just the c' itself—might be placed an octave higher.

namely, that Bach intended the tutti notations in the B-minor part as cues. Having the flutist rest during tuttis certainly would bring the piece in line with the majority of contemporaneous concertos and *concerts en ouverture* featuring wind soloists (including Telemann's ouverture-suites, TWV 55:Es2, e10, and a2, discussed below), while eliminating the need for the soloist to play c's in mm. 36 and 86 and a c#' in m. 115 in the A-minor version.[6] But even if the notated tuttis were not intended as cues, Bach might have expected that a flute soloist would tailor them to suit his needs.

Instructive in this respect are the practices of flutists doubling violin lines at the Darmstadt, Dresden, Berlin, and Karlsruhe courts during the period 1720–50. As extant performance materials make clear, Dresden flutists were frequently called upon to reinforce violins in the ritornellos of concertos and opera arias, even though the violin parts do not always make concessions to the limited range of their instruments. In the absence of much rehearsal time, they must have become accustomed to "arranging" violin parts at sight. Interestingly enough, Johann Joachim Quantz, unlike many of his contemporaries, habitually wrote out the tutti material in solo parts to his flute concertos, more often than not failing to adjust the first-violin line to fit the flute's compass.[7] What—or whether—the soloist(s) played during ritornellos is impossible to determine in most cases, but in the outer movements of a concerto for two flutes, QV 6:7, composed at Berlin and sent to the Dresden court circa 1741–50, Quantz (or at least the copyist of the parts) took extraordinary care to rewrite or simplify the first-violin part so as to render the ritornellos manageable on the flute: pitches below d' have been replaced with rests or transposed up an octave, and multiple stops have been eliminated or turned into arpeggio figures.[8] Yet in the opening and concluding ritornellos of the first movement, both flute parts still have isolated c's that, one presumes, were simply omitted in performance. Similarly, the solo part to the opening movement of Sebastian

---

6. In TWV 55:Es2 and a2, the soloist doubles the first violin in the outer sections of the Ouverture and plays none of the tuttis in the middle section. In the E-minor suite, the soloist also doubles the first violin during the opening and closing tuttis of the middle section.

7. On flutes doubling violin parts in Dresden operas and in Quantz's concertos, see Mary Oleskiewicz, "Quantz and the Flute at Dresden: His Instruments, His Repertory and Their Significance for the *Versuch* and the Bach Circle" (Ph.D. dissertation, Duke University, 1998), 280–81. A counterexample cited by Oleskiewicz is the concerto for two flutes, QV 6:6, where the ritornellos are abbreviated or rewritten in the Dresden flute parts. See Oleskiewicz, "Quantz and the Flute," 272.

8. D-Dlb, Mus. 2470-O-8. On the dating and provenance of the manuscript, see Manfred Fechner, *Studien zur Dresdner Überlieferung von Instrumentalkonzerten deutscher Komponisten des 18. Jahrhunderts: Die Dresdner Konzert-Manuskripte von Georg Philipp Telemann, Johann David Heinichen, Johann Georg Pisendel, Johann Friedrich Fasch, Gottfried Heinrich Stölzel, Johann Joachim Quantz und Johann Gottlieb Graun: Untersuchungen an den Quellen und thematischer Katalog*, Dresdner Studien zur Musikwissenschaft, II (Laaber: Laaber-Verlag, 1999), 342–43.

Bodinus' A major ouverture-suite for flute or violin and strings includes five pitches below the flute's compass (four a's and one c♯') that must have been omitted or played up an octave.[9] At Darmstadt in the late 1720s or early 1730s, Christoph Graupner called upon two flutes to replace violins in the Menuet of his D-major *Entrata per la Musica di Tavola*, despite parts with an ambitus reaching below d'.[10]

In terms of range, then, the A-minor solo part to BWV 1067 would have presented no serious obstacle to an eighteenth-century flutist. But before gauging the part's suitability for flute in other respects, we might briefly view the issue from an organological perspective. As Ardal Powell and David Lasocki have shown, efforts to extend the flute's range down to c' (but not to c♯') were apparently widespread among European woodwind makers around 1720; several surviving three- and four-joint flutes from this time, including two made by Jacob Denner (Nuremberg) and one apiece by Johan Just Schuchart (Germany) and Pierre Jaillard Bressan (London), have C-foots.[11] Quantz mentions the invention of such flutes some thirty years after the fact in his *Versuch* (though his somewhat confusing description of the extended footjoint design—including a key for c♯' but not for c'—suggests an imperfect recollection), and the flute fingering chart in the 1732 and 1741 editions of J. F. B. C. Majer's *Museum musicum theoretico practicum* illustrates a flute with a C-foot, strongly implying that this was a common enough configuration for the instrument at the time.[12]

---

9. The flute/violin doubles the first ripieno violin throughout the movement, and no pitches below d' are found in any of the following movements. Worth noting is the unusual formulation on the title page in the sole manuscript source for the work (D-KA, Ms Hs 54): "OUVERTURE ex A.# / à / Flauto Traverso ò Violino Principale / Violino Primo / Violino Secondo / Alto Viola / Cembalo ò Violoncello / è / Violon / del Sig: Bodino / [possessor mark:] "Ch: W: von Weiss." On the photocopy I examined, it is evident that the third line of the title originally read "Flauto Traverso obligato [solo (?)]." The first "o" in "obligato" was altered to read "ò," and the rest of the designation erased and replaced with "Violino Principale." The solo part, in a different copying hand from the title page, is labeled "Flaut Traverss. ò Violino Principale," with no alterations visible. Bodinus worked at the Karlsruhe court off and on between 1718 and 1752, and the A-major ouverture-suite could have been composed at any time during this period. Although this work cannot be considered a *concert en ouverture* according to the criteria laid out above, it does include one solo movement (see below).

10. Christoph Großpietsch, *Graupners Ouvertüren und Tafelmusiken: Studien zur Darmstädter Hofmusik und thematischer Katalog* (Mainz: Schott, 1994), 105 and 319.

11. Ardal Powell with David Lasocki, "Bach and the Flute: The Players, the Instruments, the Music," *Early Music* 23 (1995): 9–29, at 13. See also Martin Kirnbauer and Peter Thalheimer, "Jacob Denner and the Development of the Flute in Germany" and Friedrich von Huene, "A *flûte allemande* in C and D by Jacob Denner of Nuremberg," both in *Early Music* 23 (1995): 82–100 and 102–12. One of the Denner flutes did not survive World War II.

12. Johann Joachim Quantz, *Versuch einer Anweisung die Flöte Traversiere zu spielen* (Berlin: Quantz, 1752; repr. Kassel: Bärenreiter, 1992), 28; trans. Edward R. Reilly as *On Playing the Flute*, 2nd ed.

Now, we have no evidence that any musicians associated with Bach played a flute with a C-foot, much less that he ever composed with such an instrument in mind. But if flutes like Denner's really were in vogue around 1720, it is hard to imagine that they were unknown in Leipzig, Dresden, and other locations within Bach's sphere of activity. Would not many flutists have availed themselves of the new invention, especially when their repertory at the time consisted in large measure of works for oboe (lowest note c') or violin?[13] It is worth noting, in this connection, that the Sonata in G Minor (BWV 1030a), the early G-minor version of Bach's other famous B-minor flute piece, fits rather well on an instrument with a C-foot.[14] Then, too, a number of surviving one-key flutes at very low pitches (*flûtes d'amour* or standard C-instruments supplied with unusually long *corps de rechange*) can produce c' through transposition.[15] So there

(New York: Schirmer, 1985), 34; Joseph Friedrich Bernhard Caspar Majer, *Museum musicum theoretico practicum, das ist: Neu-eröffneter Theoretisch- und Practischer Music-Saal* (Schwäbisch Hall: Georg Michael Majer, 1732; repr. Kassel: Bärenreiter, 1954), 33; Majer, *Joseph Friedrich Bernhard Caspar Majers . . . Neu-eröffneter Theoretisch- und Pracktischer Music-Saal, das ist: Kurze, doch vollständige Methode . . . Zweyte und viel-vermehrte Auflage* (Nuremberg: Johann Jacob Cremer, 1741); repr. Michaelstein: Kultur- und Forschungsstätte Michaelstein, [1991]), 45. The two editions of Majer's treatise used the same engraved plate for the fingering chart. For discussion of Quantz and Majer, see Kirnbauer and Thalheimer, "Jacob Denner," 90–91; and von Huene, "A *flûte allemande*," 109–10 (including a facsimile of Majer's chart).

13. In his 1754 autobiography, Quantz recalled that in 1718, when he abandoned the oboe in favor of the transverse flute at the Dresden court, "there were few compositions written especially for the flute. One had to manage, for the most part, with compositions for the oboe and violin, which one had to arrange as well as possible for one's purpose." Johann Joachim Quantz, "Herrn Johann Joachim Quantzens Lebenslauf, von ihm selbst entworfen," in Friedrich Wilhelm Marpurg, *Historisch-kritische Beyträge zur Aufnahme der Musik*, I, "Stück 5" (Berlin: J.J. Schützens sel. Wittwe, 1755), 200–201; repr. in Willi Kahl, *Selbstbiographien deutscher Musiker des XVIII. Jahrhunderts* (Cologne: Staufen, 1948), 116–17; trans. in Paul Nettl, *Forgotten Musicians* (New York: Philosophical Library, 1951), 289.

14. This point is made by Powell with Lasocki, "Bach and the Flute," 17. Whether any type of flute at all was intended for BWV 1030a has recently been called into question by Klaus Hofmann, who argues that the G-minor version of the piece was scored for the "duo" combination of violin, lute, and sustaining bass instrument. See his "Auf der Suche nach der verlorenen Urfassung: Diskurs zur Vorgeschichte der Sonate in h-Moll für Querflöte und obligates Cembalo von Johann Sebastian Bach," BJ 84 (1998): 31–59, especially 50–53. However, if one takes the readings of the B-minor part at face value, then a transposition down to G minor yields only two, easily avoidable, instances of c' and c♯' in the first movement (mm. 50 and 108). The issue of whether the piece was intended for a flute with a C-foot (briefly considered and dismissed by Hofmann, 53, n. 58) therefore becomes moot, as the sonata would be playable on an instrument with the standard D-foot.

15. Kirnbauer and Thalheimer ("Jacob Denner," 96) suggest that an unusually long *corps de rechange* for one of Denner's extant four-joint instruments of ca. 1720 (producing a' at about 360 Hz) may have been intended to make the flute a transposing instrument in c' with a' at 402 Hz.

are grounds for imagining that the A-minor version of BWV 1067 was written for a flutist who could produce c', and that the later transposition to B minor was made to accommodate one who could not. Still, the notion that BWV 1030a and 1067 were conceived specifically for a flute with an extended range must remain squarely in the realm of conjecture. What seems clear, however, is that the hypothetical original versions would have been playable on many flutes of the time.

All of the foregoing speculation would of course amount to little if the transposition to A minor made BWV 1067 a significantly more challenging work for the player of a one-key flute. But in fact, just the reverse is true: a number of the most difficult passages in the B-minor part now lie much more comfortably under the fingers, and no equally problematic spots are introduced.[16] An already low tessitura becomes even lower, to be sure, but remains comparable to that of the Sonata for Flute and Continuo in E Minor (BWV 1034) and the Sonata for Two Flutes and Continuo in G Major (BWV 1027). For the solo violinist, as already mentioned, the suite is far less than the virtuoso showpiece we might expect. This could be due to the model of Johann Bernhard Bach's G-minor *concert en ouverture*, but if so, then we must ask why Bach's writing for the soloist is less challenging, on the whole, than that of his cousin. Johann Bernhard's violin spends much of its time playing widely spaced broken-chord figurations that would transfer awkwardly, at best, to a wind instrument, whereas Bach's soloist never has to contend with such athletic skips or unrelieved waves of arpeggio figures. Not that Johann Bernhard makes too many demands on his violinist's technique; the point is that we would expect Bach to make more, not fewer. We must ask, too, why Bach was content to let the solo violin/flute double the first violin throughout the Rondeau (except for mm. 32–36), Sarabande, and Menuet when Johann Bernhard's violinist has an independent part (or at least a solo *alternativement* dance) in each movement. The alternative explanation for the restrained nature of the solo writing in BWV 1067—Bach's concern to maintain a French *goût*, à la Scheibe, by reining in his violinist—becomes less attractive when one realizes that Telemann, no great lover of virtuosic display and generally more in sympathy with Scheibe's views, regularly surpassed the technical demands of BWV 1067 in his *concerts en ouverture* with concertato violin.[17]

16. Among the trickiest places in the B-minor solo part with regard to fingering and intonation are the e#"–f#" alternations in mm. 72–73 of the Ouverture, the g#"–f#"–e#" sequences in mm. 34 and 39 of the Rondeau, and the infamously awkward f#"–e#" alternations in mm. 12–14 of the Battinerie, which almost invariably force the player to choose between an awkward alternate fingering (g♭" for f#") or playing intervals that are too narrow.

17. Nearly all of these works, incidentally, make ample use of the violin's G-string. (The exception is TWV 55:E3, which contains a handful of c#"'s and b's, but no lower pitches.) Telemann's apparent disagreement with Scheibe regarding the virtuosity of concertato parts in ouverture-suites is noted in

Ex. 1. a) J. S. Bach, Ouverture-suite in B Minor (BWV 1067), first mvt., mm. 55–70 (Traversiere, transposed to A minor); b) J. B. Bach, Ouverture-suite in G Minor, first mvt., mm. 105–19 (Violino concertato); c) G. P. Telemann, Ouverture-suite in B Minor (TWV 55: h4), first mvt., mm. 56–69 (Violino concertino).

d)

e)

Ex. 1. d) J. F. Fasch, Ouverture-suite in A Major (FWV K:A1), first mvt., mm. 62–79 (Violino concertino); e) J. M. Doemming, Ouverture-suite in F Major, first mvt., mm. 41–66 (Violino concertato); f) J. S. Bach, Ouverture-suite in D Major (BWV 1068), first mvt., mm. 71–79 (Violino 1)

The type of virtuosity expected of violin soloists in the genre is illustrated by Example 1. Here one notes that the A-minor Ouverture's first episode, containing some of the most violinistic writing in the movement, requires notably less of the soloist than do episodes by Johann Bernhard, Telemann, Johann Friedrich Fasch, and Johannes Martin Doemming.[18] It is also significantly tamer than either of the two episodes played by the soloistic (but non-concertato) first violin in the Ouverture of BWV 1068. The solo part to Bach's Bourrée II is also curiously restrained—*concerts en ouverture*, including Johann Bernhard's suite, normally tax the violin soloist in the second dance of an *alternativement* pair to a much greater degree. What this means, I believe, is either that the B-minor flute part is an arrangement of a more idiomatic violin part in A minor, or that BWV 1067 was indeed originally conceived for flute.

*   *   *

Even during its apparent heyday in the 1720s and 1730s, the *concert en ouverture* seems to have found relatively few adherents. Table 1 lists all such works known to me.[19] Though the surviving repertory is slight, there are indications that the genre was familiar in many parts of Germany. Beyond Saxony and Thuringia (represented by the

---

Karen Trinkle, "Telemann und Scheibe: Unterschiedliche Vorstellungen von der Konzertouvertüre," in *Die Entwicklung der Ouvertüren-Suite im 17. und 18. Jahrhundert: Bedeutende Interpreten des 18. Jahrhunderts und ihre Ausstrahlung auf Komponisten, Kompositionsschulen und Instrumentenbau: Gedenkschrift für Eitelfriedrich Thom (1933–1993)*, Konferenzbericht über die XXI. Internationale Wissenschaftliche Arbeitstagung zu Fragen der Aufführungspraxis und Interpretation der Musik des 18. Jahrhunderts, Michaelstein, 11. bis 13. Juni 1993 (Michaelstein: Institut für Aufführungspraxis, 1996), 31–37.

18. Doemming, who is represented by a number of instrumental and vocal works in the library of the Prince of Bentheim-Tecklenburg at Rheda, appears to have been active as a composer and cellist at the Hohenlimburg court of Duke Moritz Casimir I between the 1730s and 1770s (to judge from the dates on many of the manuscripts). Unavailable to me during the preparation of this essay was Siegfried Gumpp, "Graf Moritz Casimir I. und Johannes Martin Doemming: Betrachtungen zum Musikleben am Hohenlimburger Hofe," *Hohenlimburger Heimatblätter für den Raum Hagen* 54 (1993): 502–5 and 507–11. I am grateful to Joshua Rifkin for pointing out the existence of Doemming's F-major *concert en ouverture*.

19. Dates for the Darmstadt manuscripts (D-DS) derive from an unpublished study by Brian D. Stewart of the paper types and copyists' hands in the Telemann manuscripts at the Hessische Landes- und Hochschulbibliothek (manuscript in the library's Musikabteilung). On the chronology of the Dresden Telemann manuscripts (D-Dlb), see Steven Zohn, "Music Paper at Dresden and the Chronology of Telemann's Instrumental Music," in *Puzzles in Paper: Concepts in Historical Watermarks*, Essays from the International Conference on the History, Function, and Study of Watermarks, Roanoke, Virginia, ed. Daniel W. Mosser, Michael Saffle, and Ernest W. Sullivan II (New Castle, Del.: Oak Knoll Press; London: The British Library, 2000), 125–68.

Table 1. The *Concert en Ouverture*

Composer	Work	Solo Instrument(s)	Principal Source(s)	Date
Anon. (attrib. Telemann)	TWV 55:A4	Violin	D-DS, MUS. ms 1034/34 (anon.)	ca. 1725
	TWV 55:A8	Violin	D-SWl, Mus. 5399/7	before 1730?
Johann Bernhard Bach	Ouv-suite in G	Violin	D-MÜu, Rheda Ms. 780 (anon)	ca. 1730–40?
Johann Sebastian Bach	BWV 1067	Flute/violin	D-B, Mus. ms. Bach St. 320	1730
	BWV 1068	[Violin]	D-B, Mus. ms. Bach St 154 1–6	1738–39 and later
Johannes Martin Doemming	Ouv-suite in F	Violin	D-B, Mus. ms. Bach St. 153	1731/1734–38
Johann Friedrich Fasch	FWV K:A1	Violin	D-MÜu, Rheda Ms. 172	dated 1733
Georg Philipp Telemann	TWV 55:D1	Oboe, trumpet, 2 violins	D-Dlb, Mus. 2423-N-44	ca. 1740
			Musique de table	1733
	TWV 55:D6	Viola da gamba	D-DS, Mus. ms. 1034/18	ca. 1730
			D-B, Mus. ms. 21784/3	ca. 1725?
	TWV 55:D14	Violin	D-DS, Mus. ms. 1034/81	1726–30
			D-Dlb, Mus. 2392-O-5	ca. 1725
	TWV 55:Es2	Recorder	D-DS, Mus. ms. 1034/14	ca. 1725–30
	TWV 55:E3	Violin	D-Dlb, Mus. 2392-O-7	ca. 1730–35
	TWV 55:e1	2 flutes, 2 violins	*Musique de table*	1733
	TWV 55:e10	Oboe or flute	D-Dlb, Mus. 2392-O-23	ca. 1725
	TWV 55:F13	Violin	D-Dlb, Mus. 2392-O-10a/b	ca. 1725–35
	TWV 55:G6	Violin	D-DS, Mus. ms. 1034/47	ca. 1725
	TWV 55:G7	Violin, 2 oboes	D-DS, Mus. ms. 1034/63	1726–30
	TWV 55:g7	Violin	D-Dlb, Mus. 2392-O-16	ca. 1725–35
	TWV 55:g8	2 violins	D-Dlb, Mus. 2392-O-41	1728–37
	TWV 55:A7	Violin	D-Dlb, Mus. 2392-O-6	dated 1741
	TWV 55:a2	Recorder	D-DS, Mus. ms. 1034/5	1725
	TWV 55:B1	2 oboes, 2 violins	*Musique de table*	1733
	TWV 55:h4	Violin	D-Dlb, Mus. 2392-O-15	ca. 1729?

Bachs and Fasch), examples were composed by Telemann in Frankfurt and Hamburg (with many performed at Darmstadt), and by Doemming in Hagen-Hohenlimburg; the origins of two ouverture-suites evidently misattributed to Telemann are unknown.[20] To be sure, a certain number of works have been lost, including four ouverture-suites by Johann Christian Hertel (1699–1754) entitled *Ouverture alla Concerto* or *Ouverture alla Concertino* (another interesting hybrid title) and scored for *Violino Concertato* or *Violino Principale* with strings.[21] And the boundary between the *concert en ouverture* and what is sometimes called the concerto-suite—in which a fast movement in ritornello form (or at least one not cast as an ouverture) precedes a suite of dance-based movements featuring one or more soloists—appears to have been rather fluid.[22] Still, it is unlikely that *concerts en ouverture* and similar works were ever composed in great numbers. That both BWV 1067 and 1068 exhibit traits of the genre places Bach at the forefront of composers experimenting with the style, scoring, and structure of the ouverture-suite during this period.

20. Although TWV 55:A4 has been cataloged, published, and recorded under Telemann's name, its weak invention, unimaginative solo writing, and unusual movement titles (e.g., "Minuetta") argue strongly against this attribution. The sole manuscript source, a score in the hand of Darmstadt Copyist B (Johann Gottfried Vogler?), bears no composer's name. TWV 55:A8, ascribed to "Tehleman" at Schwerin and unattributed at Rheda, is no more likely to have come from Telemann's pen: its unusually brief movements are melodically impoverished and marked by simplistic solo writing.

21. The nature of the solo violin writing in these suites, which perished in the Allied bombing of Darmstadt in 1944, is unclear. Hertel was employed as a violinist at the Darmstadt court in 1717–18. See Großpietsch, *Graupners Ouvertüren und Tafelmusiken*, 52 and 85–86. Mention also should be made here of a few lost works by Telemann—TWV 55:D26, for flute, violin, three trumpets, timpani, and strings, advertised in the 1763 Breitkopf thematic catalog, and TWV 55:G13, for violin and strings. The latter work, however, may have been identical to TWV 55:G6, which not only has the same scoring and key, but almost the identical succession of movements (ouverture, entrée, bourrée, loure, menuet, and rondeau in G6; ouverture, entrée, bourrée, loure, rondeau, and menuet in G13). Among the *Ouvertüren di Telemann* listed in the 1743 inventory of the Zerbst Hofkapelle under Fasch are five works including a part for "Violino Concertat[o]" (Nos. 4, 6, 12, 14, and 29); No. 21 in the list is described as "à Viola Concert[ato] 2 Violini Viola Rip[ieno] et Cembalo." Under the category "Ouvertüren von verschiedenen Meistern" are two works with "2 Violini Concertat[o]" by "Monseig. le Comte de Lippe" and one work with a "Violino Conc[ertato]" part by "Frey" (Nos. 1, 2, and 34). A facsimile of the inventory has been published as *Concert-Stube des Zerbster Schlosses: Inventarverzeichnis aufgestellt im März 1743* (Michaelstein: Kultur- und Forschungsstätte, 1983).

22. Examples of the concerto-suite include Telemann's TWV 43:g3, 51:F4, and 54:F1, and Johann Melchior Molter's A-major *Concerto en Suite* for "Violino Concerto" and strings, MWV VI/Anh. 1. The First Brandenburg Concerto, BWV 1046, is related to these works through its concluding *alternativement* complex of dances (Menuet–Trio–Menuet–Polonaise–Menuet–Trio–Menuet).

When and where the *concert en ouverture* arose is difficult to ascertain. A prototype for some examples could have been furnished by Francesco Venturini's twelve Concerti da camera, op. 1 (Amsterdam, ca. 1713). Featuring concertante writing for oboe, violin, or a pair of oboes with bassoon, these works follow an Ouverture or Concerto with a series of dances, arias, and characteristic pieces.[23] But the idea of writing for a soloist throughout an ouverture-suite may also have been a natural outgrowth of the inclusion in many conventionally scored works of one or two solo movements following the ouverture. The Bodinus A-major ouverture-suite mentioned above is typical in this respect: the solo flute/violin is concertato only in a florid Adagio (soloist and continuo) and in a single couplet of the Ciacone; it doubles the first violin in the Ouverture, Entrée, and concluding pair of Bourrées. Fasch's ouverture-suite (FWV K:G2), featuring several concertante winds, also contains one movement (the second Air) highlighting a solo violin. A number of works by Graupner also include solo movements.[24] Still other suites include soloists only in the first movement: the Ouverture of TWV 55:D4, like the first movement of the overture to Handel's *Rinaldo* (1711), includes two episodes with soloistic figuration for a concertato violin (later episodes in the Telemann movement add a second solo violin and two oboes).

To judge from the extant sources, Telemann was not only the most prolific composer of *concerts en ouverture*, but also very possibly the first. And considering how influential his ouverture-suites were during the eighteenth century, it would hardly be surprising if all the works by other composers in Table 1 owe their inspiration to him, at least indirectly.[25] Probably the earliest among Telemann's concerted suites are TWV 55:D14 and G7, works that almost certainly originated at Eisenach (1708–12) or Frankfurt (1712–21).[26] The latest, on the other hand, are likely the three *Musique de table* suites and TWV 55:A7, with its notably *galant* rhythmic language. Most of the other works seem to fall within the period 1715–30. It would appear, then, that the

---

23. See Janice B. Stockigt, *Jan Dismas Zelenka (1679–1745): A Bohemian Musician at the Court of Dresden* (Oxford: Oxford University Press, 2000), 52–53.

24. Großpietsch, *Graupners Ouvertüren und Tafelmusiken*, 85–118.

25. Carl Philipp Emanuel Bach's and Johann Friedrich Agricola's recollection that Johann Bernhard Bach "wrote many fine *ouvertures* in the manner of Telemann" (NBR, No. 306) may in part reflect Johann Bernhard's interest in the *concert en ouverture*. As already intimated in note 21, Fasch at Zerbst probably performed several examples of the genre by Telemann.

26. TWV 55:D14 is transmitted in a set of parts copied ca. 1725 by the Dresden violinist Johann Georg Pisendel, whereas TWV 55:G7's five-part string ensemble (including two violas) links it to a number of Telemann vocal and instrumental works written up to about 1715. The G-major suite is also noteworthy for its pairing of the solo violin with two concertante oboes, though it is the violin that assumes the role of principal soloist.

idea of crossing the ouverture-suite with the concerto occurred to Telemann a decade or more before Bach composed BWV 1067 and 1068.

Some norms for the genre, insofar as the modest repertory allows us to generalize, may be established by a survey of Telemann's *concerts en ouverture*. First, and most obviously, the violin was the instrument of choice for the solo role. Wind instruments make a few appearances in Table 1, but as discussed below, some of the works in question are likely arrangements of more conventionally scored ouverture-suites. Aside from the fast section of the ouverture, usually in ritornello form with two to four episodes, the soloist is often featured during the second dance in each of two or three *alternativement* pairs, where it either plays divisions of the first violin's melody or takes the leading role in a duet or trio texture; this is also the pattern in Johann Bernhard's and Doemming's suites. In rondeau forms, the soloist is usually featured in the episodes. Apparently reflecting the relative modernity of the *concert en ouverture* as a generic offshoot is the paucity of older dance types such as the allemande and courante, which turn up only in TWV 55:D6 and F13. On the other hand, the presence of a soloist seems in many works to have foreclosed the possibility of including characteristic movements, which are more common in Telemann's overture-suites without a soloist.

Aside from BWV 1067, the *locus classicus* for the *concert en ouverture* is surely Telemann's Suite for Recorder and Strings in A Minor (TWV 55:a2), one of his best-known works. Unlike Bach, Telemann displays his soloist in every movement, following the Ouverture with *Galanterien* (paired menuets, passepieds, and polonaises), dance-like characteristic pieces (*Les Plaisirs* and *Rejouissance*), and a slow movement in ritornello–da capo form (*Air à l'Italien*). This last is one of relatively few ritornello-based "dance" movements in Telemann's ouverture-suites, and its presence here points up the concerto-like style of the work as a whole.[27] One is of course tempted to imagine Bach's contact with TWV 55:a2, given its similar scoring to BWV 1067 and inclusion of two polonaises (a dance not otherwise found in the works listed in Table 1). But Telemann's suite seems not to have circulated very widely: its only eighteenth-century source is a score copied at the Darmstadt court around 1725, probably not long after the work was composed. Another remarkable work that may or may not have been known to Bach is the Suite for Viola da gamba and Strings in D Major (TWV 55:D6), also likely written during Telemann's Frankfurt or early Hamburg years. If the recorder suite emphasizes the soloist's facility in the Italian concerto style, this one seems consciously to exploit the association of the viola da gamba with French music by adopting an unusually Gallic

---

27. Though not in ritornello form, the "Sicilienne" of TWV 55:E3 is allied to a type of slow concerto movement: opening and closing tuttis act as a ritornello frame for a main section in which the solo violin's melody is accompanied by a *Bassetchen* bass and punctuated by brief tutti interjections.

style, particularly in the Sarabande, Courante, and Gigue; Scheibe would no doubt have approved. Bach could, of course, have encountered some of Telemann's *concerts en ouverture* with violin soloist at the Dresden court, and works such as TWV 55:F13, A7, and h4 might easily have impressed him as particularly effective examples of the genre. He is even more likely to have known the extraordinary ouverture-suites published with the *Musique de table* in 1733. These works, despite scorings that resemble more conventional ouverture-suites with multiple concertante instruments, align themselves with the *concert en ouverture* through their concerto-like handling of the soloists in each movement. They also embody, with a Bachian systematism, the three most common suite types: *Galanterie* dances (TWV 55:e1), characteristic pieces (TWV 55:B1), and "airs" (TWV 55:D1). In the D-major work, Telemann came closest to breaking down the barrier between suite and concerto when he followed his Ouverture with a bourrée and giga in ritornello–da capo form (Air. Tempo giusto and Air. Allegro), a passepied *en rondeau* (Air. Vivace), and what is essentially a fast concerto movement in ritornello–da capo form lacking any dance associations whatsoever (Air. Presto).

Measured against the practices just outlined, BWV 1067 will strike us as unusual in several respects. It has, for instance, only one *alternativement* dance pair (instead of the usual two or three), and includes a solo *double*, otherwise found only in TWV 55:A4, D6, and F13 (the last suite being unique in having two). More unusual is the limited use to which Bach put his soloist, for although the flute/violin plays in each movement, only four of six dances following the Ouverture have concertato parts. Of the other works listed in Table 1, just three, FWV K:A1, TWV 55:D6, and TWV 55: h4, fail to include a solo part in every movement (or *alternativement* movement pair), and only one of these, FWV K:A1, allows the soloist to remain mute, as it were, for longer than one movement. Following his Ouverture, Bach holds the soloist in check for almost all of the Rondeau and the entirety of the Sarabande. The absence of solo writing in Bach's Menuet is particularly striking, for the conventions of the *concert en ouverture* would seem to dictate the inclusion of a second menuet featuring the soloist. This is the case with all thirteen of Telemann's works to include the dance, as it is with Doemming's suite. It is perhaps less surprising that Bach writes exclusively for the tutti in his Sarabande, given that this dance normally lacks an *alternativement* partner. All five of Telemann's sarabandes (TWV 55:D6, D14, Es2, E3, g8) nevertheless feature the soloist(s) to some degree.

Whereas Bach's Ouverture, Bourrée II, and Polonoise-Double fully exploit the presence of a concertato instrument, the Rondeau and Battinerie feature textures in which the concertato flute/violin is closely tied to the Violin 1 line. The only solo writing in the Rondeau, in fact, comes more than midway through the movement in a brief passage (mm. 32 through 36²) where the texture is suddenly reduced to three parts: soloist, Violin 1, and Violin 2. The emergence here of the concertato flute/violin is incongruous, even musically unmotivated, and indeed there is no reason why Bach could not have scored the passage more conventionally for Violin 1 and Violin 2 with Viola. This may, in fact, have been the movement's original reading; for if Bach had been concerned from the outset with including a soloist in his Rondeau, it would have been more natural to have the concertante instrument dominate the episodes, as is almost invariably the case with rondeau movements in *concerts en ouverture*.[28] Similarly, for much of the Battinerie the concertante flute/violin is closely shadowed by Violin 1, which even overshadows the soloist at times (mm. 6–9 and 28–31). It is as if Bach has created two parts from one, especially because only one brief passage toward the end of the movement (mm. 33–37) takes real advantage of the five-part scoring. Perhaps, then, an early version of the Battinerie was also scored for four-part strings. The implications of this line of argument are clear enough: BWV 1067 could have been assembled in part from movements originally lacking a concertato instrument, two of which (the Rondeau and Battinerie) Bach revised to accommodate one.

The idea of arranging an ouverture-suite to include a concertante part may have been relatively widespread during the eighteenth century. As is well known, two mid-century copies of BWV 1068 in the hand of Christian Friedrich Penzel rechristen Bach's Violino 1 as Violino Concertato and include a new Violin 1 part that doubles Violin 2 during the Ouverture and following Air, the two movements featuring soloistic writing.[29] The anonymous copyist of the Berlin set of parts to TWV 55:D6 took a similar approach when he created a flute part that doubles the first violin almost continuously but replaces the violin in the minore section of the Sarabande and alternates with it (dividing up a single musical line) in the Bourrée.[30] Two other Telemann *concerts en ouverture* with wind soloists turn out to be arrangements—probably not by the composer—of works for string ensemble. In TWV 55:E2 the oboe d'amore doubles Violin 1 or, as in the fast section of the Ouverture, all three upper string parts in turn. Oddly, it does not play at all in the Rigaudon II, where the running eighth notes in Violin 1 might have been turned into a wind solo. Another work for oboe and strings, TWV 55:C2, resembles the Bodinus suite in following an ouverture lacking solo episodes with a slow movement for soloist and continuo, then making little subsequent use of the

28. See the suites by Johann Bernhard Bach, Doemming, and Telemann (TWV 55:D14, Es2, G6, g7, g8, and A7). An exception is TWV 55:D6, where the rondeau is the only movement not to include a solo line for the viola da gamba.

29. See Heinrich Besseler and Hans Grüß, eds., NBA VII/1 (*Vier Ouvertüren [Orchestersuiten]*), KB, 59–61, 65. See also Rifkin, "Besetzung—Entstehung—Überlieferung," 175–76.

30. The title page to the parts, owned by J. Ditmar, Cantor of the Berlin Nikolaikirche, reads: "Ouverture / à 7 / Viola da Gamba / Flute Allemande / 2 Violini / Viola / Violoncello / ex / Cembalo / di / Telemann."

soloist.[31] And it seems unlikely that Telemann was responsible for the non-concertante trumpet parts of TWV 55:D7 and D8, which mostly double Violin 1 and are tacet in a number of movements.

Three works listed in Table 1, TWV 55:Es2, e10, and g8, seem to bear witness to a rather more sophisticated arranging process. Both the Flûte Pastorelle (recorder) soloist in the E-flat major suite and the concertante oboe/flute in the E-minor suite have independent solo writing in the Ouverture movement but are often tied to the Violin 1 line during the following dances. In a number of movements (including the E♭ Menuet I, Passepied II, and Gigue; and the E-minor Carillon, Menuet I, and Gigue) the soloist either doubles Violin 1 or alternates with it. Elsewhere in these two suites there is evidence of the rewriting of ripieno string parts to accommodate the addition of a soloist.[32] In both works, the most soloistic writing outside of the Ouverture movements occurs in *alternativement* dances (the E♭-major Bourrée II and the E-minor Rigaudon II) scored for soloist and continuo. The G-minor suite is unique among *concerts en ouverture* in having only three real parts throughout: two solo violins, doubled in tutti passages by ripieno violins and by continuo. Although both the Ouverture and Passacaglia contain soloistic writing, elsewhere the two lead violins seem underemployed, often repeating (Sarabande) or echoing (Eccho) music played by the tutti. This unusual scoring, when considered alongside the unusually prominent role assumed by Violin 2 throughout, suggests that the work may be an orchestral arrangement of a trio.[33]

Two unusual features of FWV K:A1 raise doubts as to whether its present form reflects Fasch's original conception of the piece. First, the Violino Concertino doubles the Violino 1mo for much of the work, receiving solos only in the Ouverture, Gavotte I, and Air. Andante (the suite also includes another air, a second gavotte, a bourrée, and three minuets). Stranger still, the solo passage in the Gavotte occurs in the "wrong" dance of this *alternativement* pair, for without exception, concertante instruments in other *concerts en ouverture* assert themselves only in the second of paired dances. Given that the Dresden violinist Johann Georg Pisendel did not hesitate to recompose the

---

31. Most of the brief solos in the *Amener* and *Les Trompettes* movements could have been drawn by an arranger from the putative original part for Violin 1, which usually falls silent during these passages.

32. In the E♭-major Bourrée I, the recorder echoes Violin 1 above a strangely rudimentary Violin 2 part, suggesting that the echo effects were originally between Violin 1 and 2. In the Gavotte, the Violin 2 and Viola parts are in unison throughout. The E-minor Air is also in four real parts: when the soloist has independent material, Violin 1 and 2 double each other.

33. In this respect, it may be significant that the solo parts (*Violin 1*[mo] and *Violino 2*[do]) are not described as "Concertato" or "Concertino," whereas the (added) string parts are all labeled *in Ripieno.*

solo violin part in the Air of Fasch's ouverture-suite ғwv K:G2, by turning sixteenth notes into thirty-seconds, we should not be surprised if the A-major suite was also subjected to an arranging process at the court.

A further possible instance of arrangement in ʙwv 1067 deserves mention here. Rampe and Sackmann propose, sensibly enough, that a violin soloist in the A-minor version would have played the Polonoise in unison with Violin 1.[34] Indeed, Bach may have taken the solo part up an octave in the B-minor version solely to avoid two pitches in m. 12 (c♯ and b) that lie below the flute's compass. But might not the octave doubling have been designed, in both versions, to convey its own musical meaning—perhaps a rustic effect characteristic of the Polish style? (One thinks, for instance, of the "Polish" fourth movement of Telemann's Concerto for Flute, Recorder, and Strings in E Minor [ᴛwv 52:e1], in which the two soloists double Violin 1 at the octave in each statement of the rondeau refrain and are themselves heard in octaves during the third and final solo episode.) Alternatively, Bach's octave doubling might have been intended simply to distinguish the soloist from the full ensemble, as is apparently the case in the Menuet I movement of Telemann's ᴛwv 55:D4, where the *Violon 1 concert* frequently doubles *Dessus* and *Hautbois 1* at the octave.

*   *   *

That the *concert en ouverture* seems to have enjoyed a briefer and less widespread popularity than other hybrid genres such as the *Sonate auf Concertenart* is hardly surprising, for it was essentially a generic dead end, simultaneously choking off the suite's programmatic potential and diluting the French style through what seemed, at least to those in sympathy with Scheibe's view, like gratuitous displays of virtuosity. Indeed, by the early 1730s Telemann appears virtually to have exhausted the possibilities offered by the *concert en ouverture*, and his *Musique de table* suites may be viewed from this perspective as late attempts at reinvigorating the genre. Bach's confinement of soloistic writing in ʙwv 1067 and 1068 to selected movements might therefore be due in part to his acknowledgement of the genre's intrinsic limitations.

When placed within the small constellation of *concerts en ouverture*, ʙwv 1067 appears all the more remarkable for the complexity of its relationship to generic convention. If the solo instrument was originally violin instead of flute—and the flute cannot be ruled out in the A-minor version of the work—then ʙwv 1068 and suites by Bach's contemporaries suggest that the solo part was more idiomatic than what has come down to us. Bach's inclusion of a flute soloist in ʙwv 1067, at least in the B-minor version, may be connected to a practice of arranging string suites to include a wind soloist, and perhaps to his familiarity with Telemann's ᴛwv 55:a2. And the tentative

34. See ʙᴏᴍ, 258.

nature of the solo writing in both the Rondeau and Battinerie points toward a version of the work in which a concertante violin or flute appeared only in the Ouverture, Bourrée II and Polonoise-Double. Though such a revised view of the piece may leave us, at least for the time being, with more questions than answers, it also deepens our appreciation of Bach's genius for reinventing his music and, not incidentally, of the works that evidently helped inspire it.

CONTRIBUTORS

JOSHUA RIFKIN has performed and recorded many of J. S. Bach's vocal and instrumental works with The Bach Ensemble, most recently inaugurating a series of Weimar cantatas at the Kunstfest Weimar. He also has appeared as guest conductor with many leading orchestras and opera companies from the U.S. to Japan, and has published historical studies on Bach, Josquin des Prez, and other topics.

JEANNE SWACK is a professor of musicology at the University of Wisconsin–Madison, where she also directs the Early Music Ensemble and teaches traverso. Her research has centered on the music of Bach and Telemann and the study of anti-Semitism in German Baroque vocal music. She has edited numerous vocal and instrumental works of Telemann and is completing a book on Telemann's cantatas and instrumental music.

STEVEN ZOHN is an associate professor of music at Temple University. His most recent work on the music of the German late Baroque includes a study of the *Sonate auf Concertenart* (*Eighteenth-Century Music*) and a forthcoming book entitled *Music for a Mixed Taste: Style, Genre, and Meaning in Telemann's Instrumental Music.* He serves on the editorial board of *Georg Philipp Telemann: Musikalische Werke*, and is currently editing a volume of chamber music for *Carl Philipp Emanuel Bach: The Complete Works*. A noted performer on historical flutes, he is the recipient of the American Musicological Society's Noah Greenberg Award and has recorded works by Bach, Telemann, and Vivaldi.

GENERAL INDEX

General Index

Powel, Ardal, 142

Quantz, Johann Joachim, 56, 141

Rampe, Siegbert, 56, 139, 140, 155
Rifkin, Joshua, 139

Sackmann, Domenik, 139, 140, 155
Scheibe, Johann Adolph, 11, 12, 69, 135, 144, 155
   concert en ouverture, 11, 21, 137–39
Schemelli, Christian Friedrich
   Musicalisches Gesangbuch, 101
Scheuenstuhl, Michael, 36–37
Schleuning, Peter, 48
Schuchart, Johan, 142
Schulze, Hans-Joachim, 19, 28, 40
Simonis, Gottfried, 101
Sperontes
   Singende Muse an der Pleisse, 29 n. 57

Spitta, Philipp, 23 n. 44, 28
Steffani, Agostino, 25 n. 49, 135
Stinson, Russel, 58
Swack, Jeanne, 56

Telemann, Georg Philipp, 21–22, 25–26, 32–34, 34 n. 68, 69

Venturini, Francesco, 25 n. 49, 150

Wagenseil, Johann Christoph, 35
Walther, Johann Gottfried, 51–52
Wolff, Christoph, 19–20, 23
Wollny, Peter, 35 n. 72, 47 n. 109, 89 n. 204, 135, 135 n. 23

Zelenka, Jan Dismas, 150 n. 23

INDEX OF BACH'S
COMPOSITIONS

The University of Illinois Press
is a founding member of the
Association of American University Presses.

———————————————————————

Composed in 10/14 Janson Text
by Jim Proefrock
at the University of Illinois Press
Designed by Dika Eckersley
Manufactured by Thomson-Shore, Inc.

University of Illinois Press
1325 South Oak Street
Champaign, IL 61820-6903
www.press.uillinois.edu

BACH PERSPECTIVES

VOLUME 4
The Music of J. S. Bach
Analysis and Interpretation

BACH PERSPECTIVES

VOLUME FOUR

Editorial Board

Published by the
University of Nebraska Press
in association with
the American Bach Society

Bach
Perspectives

VOLUME FOUR

The Music of J. S. Bach
Analysis and Interpretation

edited by David Schulenberg

University of Nebraska Press Lincoln and London

ISSN 1072-1924
ISBN 0-8032-1051-5

CONTENTS

Contents

PREFACE

The present volume of *Bach Perspectives*, like its predecessors, is a collection of essays on topics of great interest in current Bach studies. It falls into two parts, each treating a distinct theme. Part 1 is devoted to Bach's activity in the concerto genre, with two contributors focusing on the use of ritornello form in these works. Part 2 turns to issues of interpretation, in both the general sense of musical and textual criticism and the more specific sense of contemporary as well as historical performance practice.

Alfred Mann, one of the founding members of the American Bach Society, provides an introduction to part 1 that raises questions about the definition and development of Bach's "orchestral" music. Issues of genre and structure are the subjects of the two following essays, which discuss what are no doubt Bach's best-known works of this type, the Brandenburg Concertos. Gregory G. Butler considers the precise genre assignment of the Fourth Brandenburg Concerto, and Jeanne Swack offers a close study of the first movement of that work.

Part 2 opens with two essays on the material culture of Bach's world as embodied in musical instruments of the period. John Koster reinterprets the history of harpsichord building in early eighteenth-century Germany, whereas Mary Oleskiewicz examines surviving instruments as well as music by the flutist-composer Johann Joachim Quantz, gaining a new perspective on one of Bach's best-known flute works, the trio sonata from the Musical Offering. The present writer then considers certain changing aspects of performance in Bach's keyboard works, and William Renwick takes a close look at a hitherto neglected collection of preludes and fugues attributed to Bach in an eighteenth-century manuscript. Fugue is also the subject of Paul Walker's reexamination of traditional views on the relationship of contrapuntal composition to rhetoric. Finally, John Butt offers a survey of trends in Bach performance during the past two decades, paying particular attention to the sacred cantatas and the Brandenburg Concertos.

This volume has been a collaborative effort in several senses of the word.

Part 1 was originally assembled by Gregory G. Butler, and the appearance of the volume as a whole is due in large measure to the organizational efforts of George B. Stauffer, president of the American Bach Society. I am most grateful to both for their cooperation and assistance.

David Schulenberg

ABBREVIATIONS

AMB   Amalien-Bibliothek. The music library of Princess Anna Amalia of Prussia (on permanent loan to the Musikabteilung of the Staatsbibliothek zu Berlin–Preussischer Kulturbesitz, Berlin).

BDOK   Werner Neumann and Hans-Joachim Schulze, eds. *Bach-Dokumente*. 4 vols. Kassel: Bärenreiter; Leipzig: VEB Deutsche Verlag für Musik, 1963–78.

BG   [Bach-Gesamtausgabe.] *Johann Sebastian Bach's Werke*. Edited by the Bachgesellschaft. 47 vols. Leipzig: Breitkopf & Härtel, 1851–99.

BJ   *Bach-Jahrbuch*.

BP   *Bach Perspectives*.

BR   Hans T. David and Arthur Mendel, eds. *The Bach Reader: A Life of Johann Sebastian Bach in Letters and Documents*. Rev. ed. New York: Norton, 1966.

BUXWV   [Buxtehude-Werke-Verzeichnis.] Georg Karstädt, ed. *Thematisch-systematisches Verzeichnis der musikalischen Werke von Dietrich Buxtehude*. Rev ed. Wiesbaden: Breitkopf & Härtel, 1985.

BWV   [Bach-Werke-Verzeichnis.] Wolfgang Schmieder, ed. *Thematisch-systematisches Verzeichnis der musikalischen Werke von Johann Sebastian Bach*. Rev. ed. Wiesbaden: Breitkopf & Härtel, 1990.

BWV ANH.   Anhang (appendix) to the BWV.

DL   Dresden, Sächsische Landesbibliothek.

F.   Martin Falck. *Wilhelm Friedemann Bach: Sein Leben und seine Werke mit thematischen Verzeichnis seiner Kompositionen*. Studien zur Musikwissenschaft, vol.1. Leipzig: C. F. Kahnt, 1913. Reprint, Lindau: C. F. Kahnt, 1956.

Abbreviations

H.	E. Eugene Helm, ed. *Thematic Catalogue of the Works of Carl Philipp Emanuel Bach*. New Haven, Conn.: Yale University Press, 1989.
Hz	hertz (in measurements of pitch, the number of acoustic vibrations per second).
KB	Kritischer Bericht (critical report) of the NBA.
m./mm.	measure/measures; millimeters (in Koster article).
mvt.	movement.
NBA	[Neue Bach-Ausgabe.] *Johann Sebastian Bach: Neue Ausgabe sämtlicher Werke*. Edited by the Johann-Sebastian-Bach-Institut, Göttingen, and the Bach-Archiv, Leipzig. Kassel: Bärenreiter; Leipzig: Deutscher Verlag für Musik, 1954–.
P	Partitur [music score, abbreviation used by the SSB].
QV	[Quantz-Verzeichnis.] Horst Augsbach, *Thematisch-systematisches Verzeichnis der Werke von Johann Joachim Quantz*. Stuttgart: Carus, 1997.
RV	[Ryom-Verzeichnis.] Peter Ryom, ed. *Répertoire des oeuvres d'Antonio Vivaldi: Les compositions instrumentales*. Copenhagen: Engstrøm & Sødring, 1986.
SBB	Staatsbibliothek zu Berlin–Preussicher Kulturbesitz, Berlin.
W.	Alfred Wotquenne. *Catalogue thématique des œuvres de Charles Philippe Emmanuel Bach (1714–1788)*. Leipzig: Breitkopf & Härtel, 1905. Reprint, Wiesbaden: Breitkopf & Härtel, 1972.
WTC	Well-Tempered Clavier.

PART ONE

Concepts of Ritornello and Concerto

Introduction

Bach's Orchestral Music

Alfred Mann

During the century now drawing to a close, Bach's instrumental ensemble music has become standard repertoire, as Bach's choral music had become during the last century. When the year 2000 marks another Bach anniversary, however, the critical observer will find that the present century's achievements have left a general reception of this repertoire with questions relatively unsettled.

How are we to judge today Paul Henry Lang's statement made at midcentury: "While Bach as a vocal composer shows indisputable limitations in spite of his almost oppressive greatness, in his instrumental music he stands before us unrivaled and beyond any criticism, aesthetical or technical."[1] The context deals primarily with the organ music. How are these words to be understood with regard to Bach's orchestral music? In a penetrating essay, Robert L. Marshall has placed the very word "orchestral" into question.[2]

The Brandenburg Concertos have become a cornerstone of the orchestral literature, but we have also come to realize that Bach referred to the works merely as "Concerts . . . à plusieurs Instruments." What is Bach's "Concert"? The word signified no more than "ensemble"—its rightful translation (and we know that it had reached "grosso" connotations early in its history). From the vantage point of our time, "Concert" seems to remain as elusive as "orchestral."

The standard terms change their meanings in history. In principle, it is futile to attempt applying them without reservation to the great works of the literature. We come closer to a true understanding when we realize that it is in no small measure through Bach's work that the modern concept of "orchestral" style arose. The argument "ensemble music for several instruments" versus "orchestral music" may have been clarified: we have learned that Bach's early concertos were conceived and performed with one instrument for each part (with the exception of the continuo, which developed in what Marshall defined as orchestral, i.e., theatrical, practice). But nowhere is the constant transition from single instrument to orchestral section more subtly ever-present than in Bach's works.

Bach's first original concertos show already a remarkable integration of solo and tutti not previously known, and in their involved fabric the violin concertos in A minor and E major show further differences between one another. The score of the Double Concerto in D Minor offers in the dissimilarity of its first and last movements a striking reflection of the growing orchestral language: after the sublime middle movement, the texture of chamber music gives way to an interchange in which the solo instruments are doubled for moments and in which veritably symphonic interjections combine all accompanying string parts. (There are corresponding climactic moments toward the ends of the opening movements in the Second and Third Brandenburg Concertos, and we find similar passages elsewhere—though never rivaling the dense texture of the Double Concerto.)

The emergence of a genuinely orchestral style is founded as much on aspects of structure as on aspects of texture. The form of the E Major Violin Concerto's opening movement suggests a sense of recapitulation more strongly than the influence of the da capo principle; its middle section is no longer that so much as a development. Tutti and solo passages of the Fifth Brandenburg Concerto reflect the new function of thematic dualism.[3] And it remains significant that the scoring of the First Brandenburg Concerto anticipates that of the early classical symphony.

Thus when we single out Bach's concertos against others of the High Baroque, we do so not only because of their overwhelming wealth of invention and great virtuosity but also because of features that indicate the maturing of an orchestral idiom. A turning point was reached with the composition of the last of Bach's early concertos, the Brandenburg Concerto No. 5. True, the "orchestra" was reduced by one part—likely because Bach, the violinist, changed his role to that of harpsichord soloist. For the first time, he blended his immense experience as organist into the ensemble situation. But the very opening shows what Charles Burney later described in Handel's Concerto Grosso Op. 6, No. 5, as "a very early specimen of the symphonic style of Italy," with its "rapid iterations of the same note" (present also in the first movement of the E Major Violin Concerto and in earlier examples of Italian literature).

Bach's ingenious raising of the keyboard concerto to a new genre altered the orchestral situation: since the harpsichord was not a melodic instrument drawn into the interplay of tutti and solo but an instrument that could vie with the contrapuntal complexity of its orchestral partner, it gained a measure of independence that in the end enhanced the independence of the latter as well. It meant a division of solo and orchestra that Bach had not been able to achieve before, and the evolution of this process was a slow one.

We are aware that in the Fifth Brandenburg Concerto the role of the harpsichord is at the outset that of one member in a concertino of three. And we witness its astounding emergence as an unqualified solo instrument in what became the first major written concerto cadenza. The sixty-four measures that Bach entered with the note "solo senza stromenti" were not contained in the original score. They constitute almost a movement within itself, one of the amazing cases in which Bach took the trouble to retrace one of his vast improvisations.

In probing the rise of the concomitant orchestral role, we are led back to the work of the Italians, especially Vivaldi, whose writing provided the young German master with a decisive impetus. This influence is evident even in the overtures (orchestral suites), which otherwise provide strong witness to Bach's indebtedness to French court composition and German *Spielmann* tradition. Addressed to a wider audience—in the Leipzig use of the Cöthen sources— these works are "orchestral" to begin with and their scores grow to the full instrumental complement that Bach used for his most festive church works. But the first and second of them suggest the same intimate sphere of *Gesellschaftsmusik* as do the concertos, and they are, in fact, the latter's true siblings. The Third Overture, as well, appears in an alternate version as a veritable violin concerto. Although the source situation here is insecure, the work's inherent orchestral nature speaks from every measure, from the ever-recurring doublings.

The evolution of the orchestral ensemble is more sophisticated, and more veiled, in the keyboard concertos. It is entirely characteristic of Bach's creative career that the breakthrough of the Fifth Brandenburg Concerto was not to remain without further elaboration of its principle. But Bach's return to the genre after the unparalleled outburst of productive activity in the 1720s must be seen in connection with two qualifying considerations: for the first time in Bach's instrumental ensemble oeuvre we are dealing with works of greatly differing scope and quality, and for the first time with works in which the technique of parody becomes the rule.

The first phase of Bach's involvement with the form of the concerto was marked by parodies. And the flow of new works intended for Collegium Musicum performances was subject to the needs and circumstances of a new situation. Yet very soon we find ourselves on shifting ground. An enigma pervades most of the new concertos: these works are apparently based on models that we do not have. What determined the exceptional stature of the D Minor Concerto, BWV 1052? It must have been, in its original form, a violin concerto. Was it by Bach? There is no doubt that, in the version we have before us, it is and could only have been Bach's creation, whatever its history.

The use of the *unisono* texture in the ritornellos of its first and second movements, a texture that recurs in the D Minor Concerto for Three Harpsichords (and, to some extent, in the C Major Concerto for Three Harpsichords), lends greater emphasis to the orchestral sound. In the last movement of BWV 1052 this principle begins to pervade the entire orchestral score: all thematic statements now find the various string sections combined.

Bach consciously probed, one might say struggled with, the disparities in the melodic sustaining power of solo and orchestral instruments. Nowhere is this more convincingly shown than in the A Minor Triple Concerto, BWV 1044, a work to which great injustice has been done. Schmieder's note "Alle drei Sätze . . . gehen auf Werke Bachs zurück" is not an unarguable statement so much as a challenge.[4] Can the derivation in any way be considered in the sense of that of Bach's other keyboard concertos? Was it Bach's last concerto?

Bach dealt remarkably with the relatively evanescent sound of the solo instrument in the slow movement. It is a prime example of what C. P. E. Bach described in his letter of 7 June 1777 to Johann Nicolaus Forkel: "Thanks to his greatness in harmony, he accompanied trios on more than one occasion on the spur of the moment and, being in a good humor and knowing that the composer would not take it amiss, and on the basis of a sparsely figured continuo part just set before him, converted them into complete quartets, astounding the composer of the trios."[5] As so often, Bach turned in the middle movement to a pure chamber music setting. But the thematic substance of the added fourth voice shows, as applied to both the violin and flute parts, the plucked sound of the solo instrument, resulting in a heretofore unattained integration of sonority. This device surprisingly takes over in the tutti sound of the other movements, as early as the opening section of the first movement, leading to complete thematic pizzicato expositions in the last. It is enhanced by the chord strokes—powerful, but related in nature to the plucked chords—which introduce an orchestral sound that is of totally novel character.

Was Bach's return to the scoring of the Fifth Brandenburg Concerto a conscious gesture? One could not imagine a greater contrast of orchestral textures than that exhibited by these two pieces—the alpha and omega of Bach's work in the genre. It needs to be considered that in the A Minor Triple Concerto Bach resorted, exceptionally, to the model of keyboard works. But any attempt at tracing the transcription process leaves the observer in a maze of unending new invention. In the third movement, Bach composed an altogether new framework in the form of a double fugue that joins with the adopted keyboard part in a triple fugue. The solo violin part is no longer that of a *violino concertato* but clearly that of the concertmaster. The flute part, in the highest register of the instrument, is no longer a solo part; it has become truly orchestral.

Bach returned to the old concerto grosso late in life, with the incomparable sinfonia for Part 2 of the Christmas Oratorio. Bach's orchestral works lead us here to the concert of shepherds and angels—flutes doubling the violins, with a quartet of oboes. It seems a logical gesture that the orchestral phrases of the composer, now in his fiftieth year, accompany and echo the cantata's chorale:

Wir singen dir in deinem Heer
Aus aller Kraft: Lob, Preis und Ehr.

NOTES

1. Paul Henry Lang, *Music in Western Civilization* (New York: Norton, 1941), 504.

2. Robert L. Marshall, *The Music of Johann Sebastian Bach: The Sources, the Style, the Significance* (New York: Schirmer Books, 1989), 54 ff.

3. Cf. Curt Sachs, *Our Musical Heritage* (New York: Prentice-Hall, 1948), 265: "The most striking anticipation of the future, however, seems to the present author to be the beautiful heartfelt melody of the Brandenburg Concerto in D major, which anticipates the characteristic allegro cantabile of the later eighteenth century, of his youngest son Johann Christian, and of Mozart himself." The remark was modified in the 2d ed. (1955), 220, to read: "Another unexpected trait is the beautiful, affec-

The Question of Genre
in J. S. Bach's Fourth
Brandenburg Concerto

Gregory G. Butler

Among the most fruitful and exciting avenues of Bach research in recent years has been the exploration of generic mixing: the composer's often complex and always ingenious play on, and play with, certain generic characteristics in the context of another genre.[1] Malcolm Boyd has observed that "Bach, in his melding of musical structures, as in his merging of genres, created no stereotypes."[2] Nowhere is this truer than in the case of the Fourth Brandenburg Concerto. Important recent research on this concerto has focused on such aspects as Bach's approaches to scoring and structure.[3] In this study I explore the ways Bach merges genres and subgenres in the opening movement of this work as he draws simultaneously on a number of different concerto traditions.

Studies to date on Bach's mixing and melding of genre have dealt almost exclusively with his dressing of works entitled sonata in the clothes of the concerto—the sonata "nach Concertenart."[4] Bach applies the reverse process in the opening Allegro of the Fourth Brandenburg Concerto, a highly sophisticated example of what, for want of a better term, might be referred to as a concerto "nach Sonatenart."

This movement is cast in what I refer to as sonata da capo form and not, as might be expected, in concerto da capo form (table 1). The main formal difference between these two constructs lies in the relative proportions of the A and B sections.[5] In sonata da capo form the A section is invariably shorter, often very much shorter, than the B section. Here, for example, the A section (mm. 1–83) is less than one-third the length of the B section (mm. 83–344). In general, one encounters similar proportions in allegro movements in sonata

TABLE 1. Gross Formal Structure of BWV 1049, 1

A

| measure | $\mid$ 1–23 : 23–57 : 57–83 $\mid$ |
| tonality | $\mid$ I → V : → I : I $\qquad\mid$ |

B

$\mid$83–105 : 105–37 : 137–57$\mid$157–85 : 185–209 : 209–35$\mid$235–51 : 251–85 : 285–323 : 323–44$\mid$
$\mid$→ V : → vi : vi $\quad\mid$→ ii : → IV : IV $\quad\mid$→ I : → I : → iii : iii $\qquad\mid$

A da capo

$\mid$ 345–68 : 368–402 : 402–27 $\mid$
$\mid$I → V : → I : I $\qquad\mid$

Solid vertical lines indicate major articulations—invariably perfect full closes; colons indicate weaker articulations of various kinds. Lowercase and uppercase Roman numerals indicate minor and major tonalities respectively. Arrows preceding them indicate modulation to the tonality in question.

da capo form, for example the second movement of the Sonata for Solo Violin in C, BWV 1005; four of the six preludes that open the English Suites;[6] most of the allegro movements in the Six Sonatas for Violin and Cembalo Obbligato, BWV 1014–19; and a number of those in the Six Sonatas for Organ, BWV 525–30. Bach also adopts this formal construct for one other allegro movement from the Brandenburg set, the third movement of the Fifth Brandenburg Concerto.

In concerto da capo form, on the other hand, the relative proportions are more in keeping with those of the da capo aria, where the A section generally is considerably longer than the B section. An example of concerto da capo form from the Brandenburg set—among the earliest allegro ritornello-form movements cast in concerto da capo form by Bach—is the third movement of the Sixth Brandenburg Concerto, where the A section (mm.1–45) is over twice as long as the B section (mm.46–65). The point here is that the opening movement of the Fourth Brandenburg Concerto is closely allied formally with similar movements that either are specifically labeled sonata or are formally consistent with such movements. At least on the basic level of formal structure, Bach's point of departure for this movement is the sonata, not the concerto.

In its more detailed formal structure, as well as in its tonal planning, this

movement also closely follows the general model encountered in those movements in sonata da capo form already referred to. In these movements the short
A section is generally subdivided into two or three rather weakly articulated
periods. (The articulation is often formal rather than cadential, involving the
beginning of successive fugal expositions.) The first period contains a modulation to the dominant, the second a return to the tonic. If present, the third
period usually remains in the tonic. The long B section is almost always subdivided into three quite distinct periods. The outer ones present a new subject
in imitation and focus on the mediant keys, whereas the central period most
often returns to motivic elements from the A section and explores subdominant tonal regions. Structurally and tonally, this describes accurately the first
movement of the Fourth Brandenburg Concerto. It is in the surface application of concerto-like modules, in place of the usual sonata-like ones, to this
underlying structural framework that this movement departs so radically from
its sonata models.[7]

The close formal links between the opening movement of the Fourth Brandenburg Concerto and other allegro movements in sonata da capo form go
beyond the general tonal and structural proportional relationships outlined
above. The opening movement of the Fifth Organ Sonata, BWV 529, may
have been a companion work, possibly even the model for this movement
(ex. 1). Like BWV 1049,1, BWV 529,1 is in sonata da capo form. Both movements
are in triple time, a feature normally reserved for allegro finales; it is rather
unusual in opening movements of concertos by Bach, and these are its sole instances in the two collections.[8] The opening gestures in both movements are
strikingly similar. An initial flourish consisting of arpeggiated sixteenth-note
figuration is followed by a trio of two soprano voices with eighth-note figuration moving in parallel thirds over a bass. In both cases this same module is
repeated immediately, with the voices of the two soprano instruments in the
trio inverted contrapuntally at the octave to produce parallel sixths. In each
case a sequence rising by step from tonic to dominant follows. The melodic
configuration, descending by broken thirds through the interval of a seventh
in the highest voice in both instances constitutes a striking parallel.

The similarity between these two movements extends beyond the superficial
level of surface detail to the deeper level of formal structure (table 2). In both
cases the general harmonic ground plans are the same: a self-enclosed opening section modulating from tonic to dominant is followed by a progression

Ex.1. *a*. J. S. Bach, Organ Sonata in C Major, BWV 529, mvt.1, mm.1–9;
b. J. S. Bach, Fourth Brandenburg Concerto, BWV 1049, mvt.1, mm.1–17. © 1950
by C. F. Peters Musikverlag, Leipzig. Reproduced by permission of C. F. Peters
Corporation on their behalf.

13

TABLE 2. A Comparative Structural Analysis of the A Sections of BWV 529, 1 and BWV 1049, 1

BWV 529, 1, mm. 1–51

measure	1–5,	5–12,	12–17	17–21,	21–28,	28–32 \	32–39,	39–46,	46–51
module	*t1*	*s1 p1*	*s2 c1*	*t1*	*s1 p1*	*s2* \	*s3 p2*	*s3 p2*	*s2 c1*
tonality	I	→V	V	V	→V/V	V/V \	→IV	→I	I

BWV 1049, 1, mm. 1–83

measure	1–13,	13–23 :	23–35,	35–47,	47–57 :	57–69,	69–81,	81–83
module	*t1*	*s1* :	*t1*	*s2*	*s1* :	*t1*	*s3*	*c1*
tonality	I	→V :	V	→IV	→I :	I	→I	I

Lowercase letters in italics refer to categories of modules: thematic (*t*), sequential (*s*), pedal (*p*), cadential (*c*).

from the dominant through the subdominant back to the tonic. Both sections are subdivided into three subsections. In BWV 529,1 the first of these is a complete period concluding with a full close, whereas in BWV 1049,1 the weaker articulations between subsections are formal and tonal in nature, and the perfect full close is held off until the end of the section as a whole. In BWV 529,1 the first clause is repeated verbatim in the dominant (mm. 17–32), but the expected concluding cadence in the dominant of the dominant (mm. 32–34) is suppressed, as indicated in table 2 by slashes, and the sequence-pedal complex (*s3p2*) follows without a break. In BWV 529,1 the concluding sequence-cadence complex (mm. 46–51) is a recapitulation in the tonic of that which closes the opening subsection (mm. 12–17), whereas in BWV 1049,1 a new, greatly extended sequential complex (*s3*) leads to the concluding cadence. The repetition of the opening head-motive module in the dominant, together with the use of the sequence-cadence complex that concludes the first period as a ritornello-like refrain in different keys later in the A section, forms the strongest structural parallels between these two movements. Thus the close identification of the opening movement of the Fourth Brandenburg Concerto with the sonata extends far beyond abstract, large-scale formal construction to include more specific elements of both surface detail and structural design in the A section.

Before considering the various generic allusions in the opening Allegro, it will be necessary to clarify Bach's original intentions regarding the scoring of the movement. In the process of transcribing this movement into the autograph score (SBB AMB 78) from his now lost *Vorlage*, Bach further obscured and minimized the contrast between ripieno and concertino groups through revisions made to the continuo part.[9] Taken in their entirety, these revisions indicate that, as in the other two movements of the concerto, the continuo in the original version of the opening Allegro doubled the violone and as such was part of the ripieno.[10] With two notable exceptions, the continuo, like the violone, did not play during concertino passages. With the revisions that he made to the continuo part in the process of transcribing from his *Vorlage*, Bach seems to have been intent on adding to the concertino a basso continuo that at any given moment would be doubling the lowest notated part in the ensemble. This is evident from corrections in the continuo part at m.13 in the autograph score.[11]

Here Bach, transcribing from the viola part (at this point functioning as *Bassätchen*) into the continuo part, notated the first eighth note of m.13 with a tail. Realizing immediately—even before entering the two eighth rests from the viola part—that the lowest notated pitches appeared subsequently in the violoncello part, he entered the two eighths on the second and third beats from that part, connecting them to the first eighth with a beam that incorporates the previously notated tail. An even clearer instance occurs at mm.53–54. Bach first entered two eighth rests into the continuo part, mechanically following the violone part, and then, immediately realizing that the lowest notated part had shifted from violone to violoncello, he copied the passage in sixteenth notes from that part over the incorrectly entered rests.[12] In making these revisions, Bach applied a thick coat of continuo varnish that somewhat obscured the clear concerto-grosso textural contrasts of the original version. If the original scoring is restored by removing the material subsequently added in the continuo part, the concertato procedure in the first movement is identical to that in the second movement, although handled here in a more complex manner. The same rapid alternation of tutti passages for full orchestra and concertino sections in reduced scoring, without continuo, is the dominant feature in both movements.

This is clearest in the division of the head-motive module that opens the movement into tutti and concertino submodules. The contrast between these submodules is heightened not only by their scoring but by their characters. The brilliant, fanfarelike opening submodule is strongly profiled as the initial enunciatory gesture of the ritornello. Strongly disjunct, it is vehement and forceful in its affect. Since later, in another structural context, Bach marks it "Tutti" in the autograph score (m. 89) to indicate where the full orchestra is to enter, it is clear that he views this submodule as a tutti block and as the head motive, given its clear formal function in the solo *Devise* at this point.[13] The concertino submodule, on the other hand, is closely identified not with the concerto genre but with the sonata. Besides its clear trio-sonata scoring, the progression in parallel thirds in the two soprano instruments and their subsequent contrapuntal inversion bear close generic associations to the trio sonata. In sharp contrast to the ripieno submodule, the concertino submodule is noticeably conjunct and soft, even pastorale-like in its affect.

In the sequential modules that follow, the alternation between tutti and concertino is even more rapid, involving two-measure segments in *s2* (mm. 35–43) and one-measure segments in *s1* (mm. 13–23, 47–57). The same sort of tutti sequential complex that leads up to the cadences concluding both the first period and the A section as a whole in the second movement is delayed here until the end (mm. 69–83) of the extended tripartite opening period. This concluding sequential module, although labeled in table 2 simply as *s3*, is in reality made up of three sequential submodules (see table 3 below). The last of these is a climactic intensification of the quick tutti-concertino alternations in the form of a rapid sequence leading up to the cadence (mm. 79–81); in this passage the duration of each tutti or concertino segment is reduced to an eighth note. The recognition of this sequential submodule as the last in a series of tutti-concertino alternations, accelerating climactically, suggests that even here, in Bach's original scoring, *flauti* I and II function as concertino parts, no matter how brief their statements.[14]

With its marked lack of differentiation in style between tutti and concertino material (with the notable exception of the expository ripieno and concertino submodules of the *t1* module) this Allegro is a sonata-like movement in which, for the most part, the musical material is simply divided between smaller and larger groups of instruments. As such, it strongly resembles nothing so much as a Corellian concerto-grosso movement. More specifically, given its rapid alternation of brief tutti and concertino sequential units (often echoing one another), it recalls Georg Muffat's adaptation of the Corellian style of concerto grosso, as seen first in compressed notation in his *Armonico tributo* of 1682 and subsequently in expanded scoring in his *Ausserlesene Instrumental-Music* of 1701 (ex. 2).

Notice the rapid alternation, here at one-measure intervals, of concertino and concerto grosso, marked respectively S(oli) and T(utti) in the parts. Muffat divides each of the two sequential units (mm. 14–15, 16–17) into one-measure segments for concerto grosso and concertino in turn, framing the whole by statements of the same cadential structure, first for concertino in the upper register, and then for concerto grosso at the octave below. Such details are similar to those adapted by Bach in the first two movements of the Fourth Brandenburg Concerto.

There are cases in which Bach's and Muffat's treatments resemble one another even more closely. In the excerpt from Muffat's Ciacona shown in example 3*a*, the descending sequence is treated similarly to that of the first sequential module in the opening movement of the Fourth Brandenburg Concerto (ex. 3*b*). In both works, sequences descending by third are divided into one-measure segments, and these sequential units are stated alternately by concerto grosso and concertino (in that order). Bach's version is extended by an additional sequential unit, and there is a climactic thickening of texture not present in the Muffat excerpt.

Muffat's concertos circulated widely in central Germany after their publication in 1701, and Bach could have encountered them in either Weimar or Cöthen, if not elsewhere. Whatever the case, Bach here drew on the Corellian concerto grosso, if not directly, then as received through the works of German intermediaries such as Georg Muffat.[15] As with Corelli and his imitator Muffat, Bach's point of departure here is not the concerto but rather the sonata.

A more detailed examination of the opening movement of the Fourth Brandenburg Concerto confirms that it is in the surface overlay applied to its underlying structural framework that this movement departs so radically from its sonata-movement models. In the Violin Sonatas, BWV 1014–19, for example, the tonally static thematic segments almost always take the form of fugal expositions. In the A sections of both this movement and BWV 529,1, Bach has replaced these with the contrasting tutti and concertino submodules discussed above. At the beginning of the outer framing periods of the B section, where fugal expositions of a new subject are the norm—this is the case even in BWV 529,1 (mm. 51–72, 84–105)—Bach substitutes what are perhaps the most overt allusions to the concerto (in this case not the concerto grosso but the solo

Ex. 2. Georg Muffat, *Ausserlesene Instrumental-Music*,
Concerto No. 4 in G Minor, Grave, mm. 12–19.

Ex. 3. *a*. Georg Muffat, *Ausserlesene Instrumental-Music*, Concerto No. 12 in G Major, Ciacona, mm. 233–37; *b*. J. S. Bach, Fourth Brandenburg Concerto, BWV 1049, mvt. 1, mm. 18–23.

TABLE 3. Modular Structure of BWV 1049, 1

A

measure	1–13,	13–23	: 23–35,	35–47,	47–57	: 57–69,	69–81,	81–83
module	t1	s1	: t1	s2	s1	: t1	s3	c1

B

83–105	: 105–25,	125–37	: 137–43,	143–55,	155–57
t2	: t2	s2	: t1	s3	c1

157–85	: 185–97,	197–209	: 209–21,	221–33,	233–35
t3	: t1	s4	: t1	s3	c1

235–51	: 251–63,	263–75,	275–85	: 285–311,	311–23	: 323–29,	329–41,	341–44
t2	: t2	s2	s1	: t3	s2	: t1	s3	c1

A da capo

345–57,	357–67	: 367–79,	379–91,	391–401	: 401–13,	413–25,	425–427
t1	s1	: t1	s2	s1	: t1	s3	c1

concerto): extended solo *Devise* structures (mm. 83–125 and mm. 235–63). The tonally unstable sequential passages have also been "concertized" by articulating them into blocklike submodules in which the sequential units are divided into clearly profiled concertino and tutti segments. In the sonata, the articulations between periods are understated and anything but overt, often dovetailing with one another through elision. Here the articulations, in keeping with the concerto genre, are very strong, in each case taking the form of a full close. That the same tutti cadential complex closes each of the five periods gives these articulations the ritornello-like authority that is so much a part of the concerto dynamic.

Bach here deploys a rather limited number of modules, quite distinct both in character and in function (table 3). Three groups or families of modules can be discerned here, each clearly differentiated by function as thematic, sequential, or cadential.

There are three distinct thematic modules. The first, *t1* (the concerto-grosso module), is the expository, head-motive module described earlier. It is the only module that is tonally stable, and its function is twofold. First, it establishes and underlines the tonality; second, it establishes the essential tutti-concertino contrast of the concerto grosso in its two complementary submodules, the opening tutti intonation (mm. 1–3) and the concertino continuation (mm. 3–7). Module *t2* (the solo *Devise* module) is marked "Solo" by Bach at its first entry (m. 83). It features the *violino principale* playing in the style of the first solo entry in a violin concerto. Finally, *t3* (the trio-sonata thematic module) follows the sonata principle of continuous expansion by means of imitative counterpoint and is greatly extended in length and thus not modular in the same way as the other modules.

Module *s* is the sequential module. In reality, it constitutes a family of four submodules, *s1*, *s2*, *s3*, and *s4*. Like *t1* it also has two primary functions. It can, as in the case of *s1*, *s2*, and *s4*, modulate to new tonalities or, as in the case of *s3*, present a circular sequential complex that remains diatonically grounded in the established local tonic. In all cases it serves to highlight further the concertino-tutti contrast, not in two contrasting submodules as in *t1* but within continuous homogeneous modules.

Each of the five periods in the movement concludes with the same perfect full close, the cadential module *c1*. This constitutes in each case along with the concerto-grosso and third sequential modules, a modular complex *t1–s3–c1* that functions as a ritornello-like closing clause to each period (mm. 57–83, 137–57, 209–35, 323–43, and 401–27).[16]

If the element of modular construction just outlined is the most important, it is nevertheless only one of a number of elements in the process of concerto overlay with which Bach is playing so imaginatively in this movement. A basic element critical to the very identity of the concerto as a genre is the ritornello. Normally in a concerto, the ritornello is a self-contained, tonally stable, tonally closed structure that is stated in its entirety by the tutti at the beginning and is then restated periodically, at least in part, in different tonalities in alternation with modulatory solo sections in the course of a given movement. The identity of the ritornello in this movement is ambiguous—intentionally so, for it underlines and amplifies the generic blurring at work here.[17]

If we take the first complete period in the movement to be the ritornello, we are immediately confronted by a host of irregularities. First, as ritornellos go it is inordinately long, about a fifth of the total length of the movement. Second, the repetition of the self-contained concertino-tutti expository *t1* module at periodic intervals throughout this period represents a significant departure from normal ritornello construction. Third, although the clear modulation to the dominant in the first clause is perhaps not so troubling, that to the subdominant in the course of the second is. Fourth, the rather long tonic prolongation at the conclusion of the period (twenty-seven measures, accounting for one-third of the total length) contradicts the strong thrust to the cadence, which is a central dynamic in ritornello construction. Fifth, the pervasive presence of concertino passages, not only in *t1* but also in *s1* and *s2*, serves to weaken the strong sense of contrast between ritornello and solo sections so important in defining the concerto.

Yet Michael Marissen's argument that the A section can be perceived as the opening ritornello cannot be dismissed out of hand. He suggests that its three clauses correspond respectively to the three divisions commonly found in the usual Vivaldian ritornello structural scheme (*Vordersatz, Fortspinnung, Epilog*).[18] In support of his hypothesis he points out quite rightly that it is followed immediately (m. 83) by the type of dramatic, flamboyant statement by the *violino principale* that one would normally expect to lead off the opening solo period in a violin concerto, immediately following the opening ritornello. In addition, in keeping with Bach's normal procedure, the opening period is repeated in its entirety only at the beginning and end of the movement. Further, the concluding clause of this period, recurring as it does at the end of each of the three periods of the B section, takes on a clear ritornello function.

In fact, an examination of the structure of this concluding clause indicates that it too has all the requisite elements of the typical tripartite ritornello, and here they are presented in a more conventional manner (table 4). The *t1* module, presenting the head motive (mm. 57–68), constitutes the *Vordersatz;* the series of three sequential submodules that make up the *s3* module (mm. 69–81) is the *Fortspinnung;* and the cadential module that closes the period, *c1* (mm. 81–83), is the *Epilog.*[19] At twenty-seven measures in length, the proportions of this clause are more in keeping with those of a typical ritornello; the *t1* module occurs only once, and there is no modulation in the *Fortspinnung* segment so that the whole, in keeping with the normal tonal profile of the ritornello, is tonally stable.

A central issue concerning this work has been its precise generic classification: is it a concerto grosso, a solo concerto, or even a triple concerto?[20] The question arises as a natural consequence of Bach's scoring, in which all three

TABLE 4. Detailed Structure of the Concluding Clause
of the Opening Period of BWV 1049, 1

	Vordersatz	*Fortspinnung*	*Epilog*
measure	: 57–62, 63–68,	69–74, 75–78, 79–81,	81–83 │
module:	: *t1*	*s3*	*c1* │

concertino instruments, various combinations of two of them, or each of them singly at different times act in the capacity of soloist.[21] Even more unusual are cases in which concertino instruments adopt the role of accompaniment while the ripieno violins are elevated to obbligato status within the ensemble as, for example, at mm. 31–35.

In a study of the "concerti senza orchestra" of Antonio Vivaldi, Noriko Ohmura isolates stylistic criteria for the works in this subgenre and for the varied scoring of the works in her Group D: those with three or more obbligato instruments where "the solo parts are superimposed, intersecting one with the other in various instrumental combinations."[22] She links the works in this group closely to the concerto grosso, commenting that "the emphasis placed on the expressive effect of contrasting timbres is symptomatic of the adherence to the writing in the concerto grosso." In her conclusion, Ohmura refers to one of the compositions from her Group D, Vivaldi's Concerto for Viola d'Amore, Two Oboes, Two Horns, Bassoon, and Basso Continuo in F Major, RV 97, as representing "one of the best examples [by Vivaldi] of writing proper to the concerto grosso."[23] The criteria for the concertos in her Group D would seem to apply remarkably well to certain details of scoring in the first two movements of the Fourth Brandenburg Concerto.

The switching of roles by instruments that Ohmura underlines as characteristic of the Vivaldian *concerto senza orchestra* takes on a typically Bachian complexity in both the first and second movements of the Fourth Brandenburg Concerto, particularly in the former. Here instruments assume not only double identities but in some cases even triple identities. The *violino principale* acts in both violin solo and violin obbligato capacities, but in tutti sections it more often than not takes on the role of ripienist, playing the principal part along with violin I. It not only acts as *Bassätchen* in the concertino but on one occasion, by means of double stops, takes on the role of the entire concertino (mm. 217–21). Violins I and II abandon their identities as ripieno instruments and slip into the roles of concertino instruments (mm. 31–35, 129–32, 193–203, 263–66) and obbligato instruments (mm. 235–41, 251–57) in their canonic imitation of *violino principale* in a trio texture. In the opening movement the role of *Bassätchen* is not limited simply to the *violino principale*, as in the second movement, but extends to ripieno instruments as well, most notably violoncello and viola. Bach's blurring of concertino and ripieno suggests that he is drawing on scoring practices characteristic of another concerto tradition, the chamber concerto for obbligato instruments of Vivaldi, if not received directly, then through one or another Saxon composer as agent.[24]

The opening movement includes references to two further concerto subgenres and one entirely different genre of chamber music. The internal structure of the *t2* module indicates that Bach viewed the tutti opening of the *t1* module as a ritornello head motive in the context of the double solo *Devise* structures that open the second and fourth periods (mm. 83–125 and 235–63). The double *Devise* is a structural feature characteristic of Tomaso Albinoni's da capo arias that he takes over into the works for one and two solo oboes from his opus 7 concertos, published in 1715.[25] It seems to have been one approach to the opening solo period with which Bach was experimenting at the time, under the influence of Albinoni.

The typical Albinonian double *Devise* structure follows immediately after the opening ritornello and is made up of two periods. The first of these, in the tonic throughout, presents a strongly profiled solo module followed by a tutti statement of either the head motive module or the cadential module from the opening ritornello. The second period begins with a restatement of the initial solo module, followed by a sequential module, also for solo instrument, which modulates away to cadence in a related key (table 5). If the strong articulation between the two periods of the typical Albinonian double *Devise* is eliminated and the whole is fused together in a continuous single period, the result is very close to the procedure adopted in the second period of the so-called *Devisenarie*. This is precisely what Bach does in the first four phrases (mm. 83–103) of his adaptation, which constitutes a double *Devise* structure in a continuous, linked presentation. The solo motto (mm. 83–89) is interrupted by the head motive of the ritornello (mm. 89–91), after which the solo motto is repeated, in this case in varied form (mm. 91–97), and extended in a modu-

TABLE 5. Comparison of a Typical Albinonian Double *Devise* and Bach's Elaboration in BWV 1049, 1, mm. 83–125 and 235–63

Tomaso Albinoni, Op. 7, No. 3

measure	9–11,	11–15	15–17,	17–22
Tutti-Solo	s	T	s	s
tonality	I	I	I	→V
submodule	x	y	x	z

BWV 1049, 1, mm. 83–125 and 235–63

module	t2					t2			
measure	83–89,	89–91,	91–97,	97–103,	103–5 :	105–11,	111–13,	113–19,	119–125
Tutti-Solo	s	T	s	s	T :	s	T	s	s
tonality	I	I	I	→V	V :	V	V	V	→V/V
submodule	a	b	a	c	b :	a	b	a	c

module	t2				t2	
measure	235–41,	241–43,	243–49,	249–51 :	251–57,	257–63
Tutti-Solo	s	T	s	T :	s	s
tonality	IV	IV	IV	→I :	I	→V
submodule	a	b	c	b :	a	c

lation to the dominant (mm. 97–103). The only departure structurally is the concluding statement of the ripieno head-motive module (mm. 103–5) in the new key. Not only does this serve to consolidate the newly established dominant tonality and balance the clause structurally, but it also clearly articulates this clause from the transposed repetition that follows (mm. 105–25). The resulting double solo *Devise* is subsequently transposed to the subdominant and repeated in abridged and varied form later (mm. 235–63), where for the opening statements of the motto in each of the *Devise* structures (mm. 235–41 and mm. 251–57) Bach adds violins I and II (marked *pianissimo*) as soloists in interrupted canon at the unison with the *violino principale*. The structure at which Bach arrives here, by doubling the typical Albinonian double solo *Devise*, represents a considerable expansion of the presumed model and shows the composer playing with a recently established solo concerto tradition in a particularly imaginative way, wedding the idea of the Albinonian double solo *Devise* with his own procedure in the vocal aria.[26]

The appearance of the solo *Devise* is one of the most overt references in the movement to the solo concerto and to the vocal aria that was infusing it with new life at this time. On the other hand, the placement of these two double *Devise* periods at the beginnings of the outer periods of the B section is very much in keeping with Bach's formal procedure in allegro movements in sonata da capo form, where prominent entries of a new subject in strongly profiled fugal expositions occur at these same points in the structure.

The other two instances in which the *violino principale* is treated in an overtly soloistic manner (mm. 187–208 and 215–28) are fundamentally different, for they occur in concerto-grosso modules. Jeanne Swack refers to Bach's procedure here as a "transfer of solo technique into the ritornello [that] temporarily weakens the identity of this passage as ritornello" and points out that it is typical of many of Bach's arias but not of his concertos. For this reason she suggests that it "may be a subtle reference to the da capo structure of the movement."[27] It may also suggest that Bach is making conflicting allusions to two distinct genres, the concerto grosso and the solo concerto, in simultaneously unfolding layers.

In the central B section are two statements (mm. 165–84 and 293–310)—the second a varied version of the first—of what are by far the longest modules in the movement, the third of the three thematic modules (*t3*). They are dominated by the three-part texture of two equal soprano instruments (*flauti* I and II) over the basso continuo. (In the varied restatement, *violino principale* joins with *flauti* I and II to create a quartet texture, although it does not take part in the close contrapuntal imitation.)[28] The same type of module appears at the analogous point in the B section of the third movement (mm. 159–75). In both movements these modules begin with a sequential submodule not previously heard featuring rapid solo-tutti alternations. In the first movement, the solo phrases of *flauto* I are echoed by the tutti, and in the submodule that follows, as at the analogous point in Bach's other allegro movements in sonata da capo form, the upper two voices proceed in close imitation, often in strict canon. These passages constitute a clear reference to another genre entirely, the genre from which the movement derives its formal structure: the trio sonata.

Johann Adolph Scheibe's description of the trio sonata is most pertinent here: "In all voices, but especially in the upper voices there must be an orderly melody and a fugal working out. . . . there must be present throughout a concise, flowing, and natural melody. . . . the one voice must be distinguished from the other throughout; however, all voices must work with the same strength, so that among them one can discern no principal voice in particular."[29] The basso continuo in particular, like the upper voices, is concise or succinct (*bündig*) and participates in the "fugal working out," in contrast to its more subservient, largely supportive role in the concerto grosso and solo concerto.

That this view seems to have been shared by Bach is borne out not only by his treatment of the basso continuo in his trio sonatas but also by his treatment of the continuo part in this concerto. The only instances of concertino passages in the opening and closing movements in which the continuo part differs appreciably from the lowest sounding part occur in these trio-sonata modules, where the continuo part presents a diminution of the cello part in running notes of shorter value.

Problems arise at only one point in the first movement as a result of the restorative suppression of the continuo part in non-tutti passages: in the sequential submodule that opens the first trio-sonata module (mm. 161–65), where this suppression leaves *flauto* 1 sounding alone on the downbeats to mm. 162 and 164. This may indicate that what is included in the continuo part in the autograph score from this point to the end of this trio-sonata module (and by extension throughout the parallel section of the second trio-sonata module) was also present in the *Vorlage* from which Bach was transcribing, the only instances in the original version of the movement where the continuo part would have been involved in concertino passages.[30] Whatever the case, it would be critical for the realization of the intended trio-sonata effect to include these rhythmically and motivically integrated continuo passages *senza Violone* in any edition of the work aiming to restore Bach's original scoring.[31] In these trio-sonata modules the stress is on the almost absolute equality of the two treble instruments spinning out an orderly, metrically regular melody—as opposed to the free, rhapsodic one implied in the solo *Devise* modules—in a continuous, imitative web: elements that taken together typify Bach's trio-sonata style.

Any such analysis as this can give, at best, only an imperfect and incomplete idea of the generic mixing that permeates this work and is so vital for understanding the various levels on which it operates. Nevertheless, it underscores a facet of Bach's compositional approach that, under close scrutiny, can be seen to be operative in virtually all his music. It seems increasingly clear that any attempt to force this work, or indeed virtually any work of Bach's, into any one generic pigeonhole is highly misrepresentative and ultimately futile. Consequently, in answer to the question as to whether this work is a concerto grosso, a solo concerto, or even a triple concerto, one might answer: It is all three, at times separately, at others simultaneously. Yet it is more, given its numerous and varied allusions to other concerto subgenres such as the chamber concerto, to related genres such as the sonata, and to such compositional processes as canon. At times one is simply at a loss to say exactly what it is generically, for this work, like so many of Bach's, presents an ambiguous, elusive, constantly shifting face, a quicksilver intangibility that defies analysis.

NOTES

1. In particular, see Laurence Dreyfus, "J. S. Bach and the Status of Genre: Problems of Style in the G-Minor Sonata BWV 1029," *Journal of Musicology* 5 (1987): 55–77.

2. Malcolm Boyd, *Bach: The Brandenburg Concertos* (Cambridge: Cambridge University Press, 1993), 58.

3. On scoring, see Michael Marissen, "Organological Questions and Their Significance in J. S. Bach's Fourth Brandenburg Concerto," *Journal of the American Musical Instrument Society* 17 (1991): 5–52; revised version in Marissen, *The Social and Religious Designs of J. S. Bach's Brandenburg Concertos* (Princeton, N.J.: Princeton University Press, 1995), 62–76. My citations are from the original version, since material germane to my analysis either appears only in the original publication or in an expanded version there. On structure, see Gerd Reinäcker, "Kurven, Widerspiele: Zum ersten Satz des 4. Brandenburgischen Konzerts," in *Bachs Orchesterwerke: Bericht über das 1. Dortmunder Bach-Symposion 1996*, ed. Martin Geck and Werner Breig (Witten: Klangfarben, 1997), 193–202.

4. See Dreyfus, "J. S. Bach and the Status of Genre"; Michael Marissen, "A Critical Reappraisal of J. S. Bach's A-Major Flute Sonata," *Journal of Musicology* 6 (1988): 367–86; and Jeanne Swack, "On the Origins of the Sonata auf Concertenart," *Journal of the American Musicological Society* 46 (1993): 369–414.

5. The distinction between sonata and concerto da capo forms is treated at length in a monograph on Bach's concertos by the author, presently in preparation, and more summarily in a paper given at the Internationales Wissenschaftliches Symposion zum Thema "J. S. Bachs Orchestermusik," 19 January 1996, "Toward a More

Precise Chronology for Bach's Concerto for Three Violins and Strings BWV 1064a: The Case for Formal Analysis," in *Bachs Orchesterwerke*, 235–47.

6. BWV 807,1, 809,1, 810,1, and 811,1. The prelude to the Third English Suite, BWV 808,1 is not cast in da capo form but rather in ritornello concerto form; see my study "An Early Minor-Key Ritornello Concerto Movement by Bach: The *Prélude* to the Third English Suite BWV 808/1" (in preparation). On sectional proportion in these preludes, see Alfred Dürr, "Zur Form der Präludien in Bachs Englischen Suiten," in *Bach-Studien 6: Beiträge zum Konzertschaffen Johann Sebastian Bachs*, ed. Peter Ahnsehl, Karl Heller, and Hans-Joachim Schulze (Leipzig: Breitkopf & Härtel, 1981), 101–2.

7. Jeanne Swack takes up the question of modular construction in the following essay in this volume.

8. Marissen, "Organological Questions," 29, sees in the movement's $\frac{3}{8}$ time and its rhythmic organization in two-measure units an allusion to the minuet. Opening allegro movements in triple time are not uncommon in the mature concertos of Tomaso Albinoni.

9. I would like to thank the staff of the Musikabteilung of the former Deutsche Staatsbibliothek, Berlin (now Staatsbibliothek zu Berlin–Preussischer Kulturbesitz) for kindly allowing me access to the autograph score of the Brandenburg Concertos during the summer of 1994.

10. The scoring of the opening movement differs from that of the other two movements in that here the violoncello has a separate part, since it frequently functions as *basso senza continuo* in concertino passages. Marissen, "Organological Questions," 47, goes so far as to suggest "that Bach added the part marked 'Continuo' for the AMB 78 version, i.e., that his exemplar had eight staves, not nine." Given that both of the other movements in the Fourth Brandenburg Concerto have continuo parts, I think it highly unlikely that in the *Vorlage* from which Bach was transcribing there was no such part. It is possible, however, that continuo and violone originally shared a single staff, in which case the *Vorlage* would indeed have had eight staves. Whatever the case, it seems clear that substantial revisions were made to a part that almost certainly existed in the original version.

11. Bach's corrections are clearly visible in the facsimile of the autograph published by C. F. Peters (Berlin, n.d., ca. 1947–50).

12. Marissen, "Organological Questions," 45–46, includes the second correction referred to above in his list of corrections, but not the first.

13. On this structural feature, see below.

14. A similar passage featuring the same very brief ripieno-concertino alternations at a highly climactic point recurs in the second movement (mm. 59–61). Here Bach clearly marks each of the alternations *f*[orte] and *p*[iano] respectively (he neglects to enter *f* for the ripieno segment and *p* for the solo segment in m. 60). The ripieno instruments, as elsewhere, are silent during the segments marked *p*.

15. German contemporaries close to Bach were writing concertos after the manner of Corelli. Sometime during the Weimar years, Bach copied Georg Philipp Telemann's Concerto for Two Violins and Orchestra in G Major, 2v. G(1). According to Robert Hill this work creates "a concerto grosso along Corellian principles out of what is essentially trio sonata texture." See Robert Hill, "Johann Sebastian Bach's Toccata in G Major BWV 916/1: A Reception of Giuseppe Torelli's Ritornello Concerto Form," in *Das Frühwerk Johann Sebastian Bachs*, ed. Karl Heller and Hans-Joachim Schulze (Cologne: Studio, 1995),164.

16. Boyd refers to my *t2* and *t3* as episodes, but otherwise our analyses diverge fundamentally only once. Whereas he hears a ritornello at mm. 263–85 (largely, I suspect, because it articulates two of his episodes), I hear this simply as an extended recapitulation of the statement of *s2* at mm. 125–37, which effects a return to the tonic.

17. The ambiguity surrounding the ritornello in Bach's concertos has been dealt with by Laurence Dreyfus, "J. S. Bach's Concerto Ritornellos and the Question of Invention," *Musical Quarterly* 71 (1985): 327–58.

18. See Marissen, "Organological Questions," 28–30. He has adopted the terminology invented by Wilmhelm Fischer for the analysis of his *Fortspinnungtypus* ritornello. See Wilhelm Fischer, "Zur Entwicklungsgeschichte des Wiener klassischen Stils," *Studien zur Musikwissenschaft* 3 (1915): 24–84. Boyd, *The Brandenburg Concertos*, 52, also adopts this position.

19. Boyd, *The Brandenburg Concertos*, 56, analyses this clause in precisely the same way.

20. This debate is concisely summarized by Marissen, "Organological Questions," 5–6.

21. Eclecticism as a guiding principle in the concerto compositions of Bach and Telemann has been addressed in a paper given at the Internationales Wissenschaftliches Symposion zum Thema "J. S. Bachs Orchestermusik," 18 January 1996, by Wolfgang Hirschmann: "Eklektischer Imitationsbegriff und konzertantes Gestalten bei Telemann und Bach," in *Bachs Orchesterwerke*, 305–19.

22. Noriko Ohmura, "I 'Concerti senza orchestra' di Antonio Vivaldi," *Nuova rivista musicale italiana* 13 (1979): 121.

23. Ibid., 147.

24. Swack, "On the Origins," 376, points to the reception of the chamber concertos of Vivaldi by Georg Philipp Telemann as early as ca.1715, describing the scoring of such works "in which the instruments take turns in the roles of 'tutti' and 'solo' or 'soli.'" Klaus Hofmann argues convincingly that the Second Brandenburg Concerto was originally conceived as a *concerto senza orchestra* and that Bach added the ripieno strings in transcribing the work into the autograph SBB AMB 78 in a paper read at the Internationales Wissenschaftliches Symposion zum Thema "J. S. Bachs Orchestermusik," 18 January 1996, "Zur Fassungsgeschichte des 2. Brandenburgische Konzerts," in *Bachs Orchesterwerke*, 185–92.

25. See Gregory Butler, "J. S. Bach's Reception of Tomaso Albinoni's Mature Concertos," in *Bach Studies 2*, ed. Daniel R. Melamed (Cambridge: Cambridge University Press, 1995), 40–66. I suggest here (26–30), based on certain details of scoring in the third movement of the First Brandenburg Concerto, that Bach had come into contact with Albinoni's opus 7 concertos before 1721.

26. A somewhat different approach to the double solo *Devise* can be seen in the two clauses that make up the first solo period in the third movement of the Sixth Brandenburg Concerto (mm. 9–14 and 15–22). This period falls in the A section of this concerto da capo form movement.

27. See Swack, "Modular Structure," in this volume.

28. This may be explained by the fact that in Bach's adaptation of the *violino principale* part for *cembalo solo* in BWV 1057, the original passage is replaced by a different one in the right hand of the *cembalo solo* part, suggesting that the reading found in BWV 1049,1 does not stem from the *Vorlage*.

29. "in den Oberstimmen ein ordentlicher Gesang, und eine fugenmäßige Ausarbeitung seyn muß. . . . es muß durchaus eine bündige, fließende und natürliche Melodie vorhanden seyn. . . . Eine Stimme muß sich von der andern durchaus unterscheiden; alle Stimmen aber müssen mit gleicher Stärke arbeiten, daß man auch darunter keine Hauptstimme insbesondere erkennen kann" (Johann Adolph Scheibe, *Critischer Musicus*, 2d ed. [Leipzig, 1745; facs. rpt., Hildesheim: Olms, 1970], 675–76); translation by the author.

30. It is surely significant that in Bach's arrangement of the Fourth Brandenburg Concerto as the Concerto for Harpsichord, Two Recorders, and Strings in F Major,

BWV 1057, the left hand of the cembalo part, which throughout closely follows the violoncello part of BWV 1049, takes up the rhythmically more active continuo part in these two instances. Further, the violoncello part for these passages seems to have been added in the autograph score (SBB Mus. ms. Bach P 234). See Marissen, "Organological Questions," 46.

31. In the one trio-sonata module in the closing presto (mm.159–74), as in the trio-sonata passage here, the violone, as a ripieno instrument, drops out.

Modular Structure and the Recognition of Ritornello in Bach's Brandenburg Concertos

Jeanne Swack

The idea that some movements of Bach's Brandenburg Concertos represent a fusion of Vivaldian concerto form with his intensely personal musical language is a commonplace in modern Bach scholarship. Nevertheless, analytical discourse on these works has traditionally tended to focus on their more overtly Vivaldian aspects, accounting for the works' structures by means of analysis according to the alternation of ritornello and solo sections. Recent commentators, especially Michael Marissen, Susan McClary, and Laurence Dreyfus, have also provided political, social, and theological interpretations on the one hand, and detailed mechanistic analysis on the other hand.[1] Yet the assumption of a Vivaldian ritornello structure as the true structural foundation of most of the fast movements has remained.[2]

But to read these works analytically according to a ritornello structure is often to miss both the deeper structural processes and the play of musical identities at work in the music. Central to Bach's working method is the employment of musical modules that return, most often intact, at various transposition levels, often in new structural contexts. This modular construction often traverses musical sections delineated on the surface by ritornellos, forming deeper structures. The use of modular construction can even cast a structural ambiguity upon the movement, either as a whole or in part, causing "ritornello" segments to function as "solo" segments, or vice versa. Thus the modular structure can undermine the surface ritornello structure. In this sense, some of the concerto movements form a binary opposition to such movements as the first Kyrie of the Mass in B Minor, BWV 232, in which a surface feature, in this case a fugal texture, disguises a deeper, well-concealed ritornello structure.

TABLE 1. Structural Levels in the Concerto in D Minor for Two Violins, BWV 1043, First Movement

Level A: Ritornello Structure

Section	R1	S1	R2	S2	R3	S3	R4
Measures	1–21/3	21/3–45	46–49/3	49/3–53	54–58/3	58/3–84	85–88
Key	i	i–v	v	v–iv	iv	vi–i	i
Disposition of fugue subject	fugal exposition, 5 entries		1 entry		1 entry (m.55)		1 entry

Level B: Modular Structure

R1	S1	R2	S2	R3	S3	R4
5–8/3 _a_	21/4–29 _c_	46–49/3 _a_	49/4–53 _e_	54–58/3* _b_	58/4–62 _e_	85–88 _a_
9–13/3* _b_	37/4–45 _c_				69–88 _d_	
	30–49/3 _d_				76/4–84 _c_	

*cadential pattern at end differs

* * *

One of Bach's overriding interests in his instrumental music is the articulation of genre. The sonata, by its very flexibility, lent itself to the evocation of, and even merging with, other genres, especially the Vivaldian concerto.[3] The latter, as exemplified in Vivaldi's own concertos published as *L'Estro armonico,* op. 3 (Amsterdam, 1711), however, was a genre with strong and specific conventions, especially for its fast movements. These included, most crucially, construction by means of a partitionable, tonally closed ritornello alternating with modulatory solo sections that featured virtuosic passagework, and the thinning of the orchestral texture during solo passages.[4] The deployment and partitioning of the ritornello, the central marker of the genre, formed Bach's starting point in the composition of his concertos, as well as many of his other instrumental and vocal genres from about 1713 on.[5] Yet Bach's treatment of essentially Vivaldian material differs so radically from Vivaldi's own procedures that attempts to apply the same modes of analysis to works of both composers often show only the superficial features of the piece, that is, the most overtly Vivaldian features, while ignoring the fascinating things that Bach does with them.

In order to signify the genre "Vivaldian concerto," Bach must present a surface level that is defined by the apparent alternation of ritornellos, usually tonally stable, with episodes, usually tonally unstable. But in a characteristic sleight-of-hand, Bach often sets up a ritornello structure that gives only the appearance of being the true scaffolding of the piece, hiding the movement's true structure at a deeper level. A relatively simple but elegant case in point is afforded by a work outside the Brandenburg set, the first movement of the Concerto in D Minor for Two Violins, BWV 1043.[6] Table 1 shows both levels of construction: the surface level of ritornello and episode (level A) and the deeper level of recurring modules (level B). The movement is composed of five modules of varying lengths, two of which (*a* and *b*) are segments from a longer ritornello, although their original context—a densely contrapuntal, apparently seamless fugal exposition—is not a traditionally Vivaldian setting for such treatment. Almost all the material of the movement is accounted for in the five recurring segments shown in the level B analysis, with the exception of mm. 1–4 (the initial statement of the ritornello subject) and mm. 13/3–21/3.[7] Thus all of the nonrecurring material in the movement consists of those sections of the initial ritornello that are not later used as ritornello segments. It is crucial that the modules sometimes cross the boundaries of surface structures; the recurring module *d*, the longest in the movement, includes a solo passage (begun by a tutti interjection) and then a complete ritornello. Module *d* also incorporates modules *a* and *c* but does not include all occurrences thereof. Furthermore, the two occurrences of *d* reflect the entire harmonic structure of the movement: a move from i to v, and the transposed repetition of the same material moving from iv to i.

The first movement of Brandenburg Concerto No. 4, BWV 1049, represents a much more complex use of musical modules, reattaching the latter in new orderings and contexts at further points in the movement. This reordering and reattachment both forms the structural underpinning of the movement and gives rise to some of its structural ambiguities. The movement is remarkable for its complex ritornello, which presents three distinct instances of *Fortspinnung* in the opening long ritornello, in the configuration V–F1–V–F2–V–F3–E.[8] The very richness of the ritornello, with its five distinct sections, gives rise to the multiplicity of permutations later in the movement.[9]

This thematically lavish ritornello provides ample material for playing with the identities of ritornello and solo material, and in fact all of the segments except F1 and E are treated in a functionally ambiguous manner at some point in the movement. The movement is further complicated by the unusual treatment of the two recorders, which sometimes occupy a third level of function between the solo violin and the ripieno strings.[10]

As table 2 shows, most of the movement is made up of recurring modules, and from R3 on Bach presents only twelve measures (mm. 235–40, mm. 258–62, and m. 310) that have not occurred before in some guise. Thus there is almost no new material presented in the second half of the movement. Although the movement can be successfully diagrammed into an alternation of ritornellos and solo episodes coupled with a da capo structure,[11] there are sufficient ambiguities involving the identity of solo and ritornello material to point to Bach's playing upon expectations of genre.

One of the most interesting of these peculiarities comprises two passages that are reciprocal in effect: the use of ritornello material in a solo episode, followed by the reference to soloistic writing for the violin in the next ritornello. The second solo contains a quotation from the *Vordersatz* beginning at m. 185.[12] This quotation, however, differs sharply from other such *Vordersatz* quotations in the movement, which take the form of tutti interjections (ex. 1). Here a quo-

TABLE 2. Structural Levels in Brandenburg Concerto No. 4, First Movement

Section	Measures	Key
Level A: R1	1–83/1	I
(V–F1–V–F2–V–F3–E)		
Level B: 1–83/1		
Level A: S1	83–136	I–vi
Level B: tutti interjections of V, long stretch of F2		
Level A: R2	137–57/1	vi
(V–F3–E)		
Level B: mm. 137–42 = variant of mm. 57–62;		
mm. 143–57/1 = mm. 69–83/1		
Level A: S2	157–208	vi–IV
Level B: mm. 185–96 presents mm. 1–12 plus solo violin;		
mm. 191–92 (equivalent of mm. 7–8) are a modification		
of mm. 7–8		
Level A: R3	209–35/1	IV
(V–F3–E)		
Level B: mm. 209–35/1 = mm. 57–68, with the V material		
presented in the principal violin in double stops		
Level A: S3	235–63/1	IV–V
Level B: mm. 241–42 = mm. 1–2; mm. 243–48 = mm. 119–24;		
mm. 249–50 = mm. 1–2; mm. 251–56 = mm. 235–40		
Level A: R4	263–85/1	I
(F2)		
Level B: mm. 263–70 = mm. 125–32 plus doublings;		
mm. 271–84 = mm. 43–56		
Level A: S4	285–322	I–iii
Level B: mm. 285–309 = mm. 157–81, with some recomposition;		
m. 310 new; mm. 311–22 = mm. 125–36		
Level A: R5		
(V–F3–E)	323–44	iii

TABLE 2. (*continued*)

Section	Measures	Key
Level B: mm. 323–44 = mm. 137–57, plus one-bar extension		
Level A: R6 (da capo)		
(V–F1–V–F2–V–F3–E)	345–427	I
Level B: mm. 345–427 = mm. 1–83		

R = *Ritornello*
S = Solo
V = *Vordersatz*
F = *Fortspinnung*
E = *Epilog*

tation begins as though it is to be another tutti interjection such as that in mm. 89–90, for example, but the recorders and ripieno strings present six bars from the *Vordersatz* while the principal violin plays virtuoso thirty-second-note figuration against it.[13] This figuration is the most overtly "concerto-like" passagework in the movement, ironically presented over the *Vordersatz*. The quotation seems to break off in mm. 191–92, where the ripieno strings present what appears to be a simple accompaniment figure instead of the reiteration of the *Vordersatz*'s initial arpeggiated figure. The ritornello quotation resumes again in m. 193 and continues until m. 196.

The *Vordersatz*, however, only gives the illusion of disappearing here. The original initial *Vordersatz* motive consists of an ascending and descending arpeggiation, a pedal point on scale degree $\hat{5}$, and a sparse accompaniment. The pedal point is present in mm. 191–92, as it was in mm. 185–86 (shifting from the principal to the first ripieno violin). The other instruments present a simplified version of mm. 185–86, which now resemble more closely a typical light accompaniment pattern than the principal *Vordersatz* motive. The quotation then continues more literally in m. 193, and when it drops out for good in m. 197 the ripieno strings continue with a more elaborate version of the variation of the *Vordersatz* previously presented in mm. 191–92. Thus the solo status of the virtuosic principal violin is initially weakened by a twelve-bar quotation from the *Vordersatz*, including two bars that constitute a simplification of the *Vordersatz*'s initial motive.

Ex. 1. Brandenburg Concerto No. 4, mvt. 1, mm. 185–96
(violoncello and violone parts omitted).

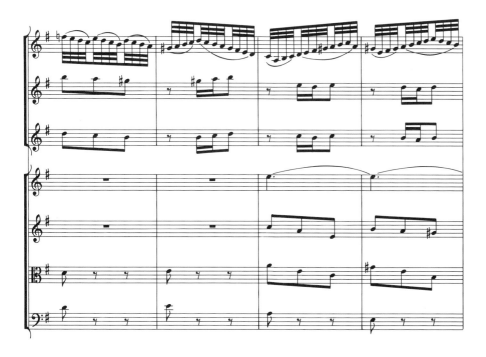

The complement to this passage is somewhat more subtle. In the next ritornello, R3 (mm. 209–35/1), Bach presents segments V–F3–E, as he had done in
R2. Although the segments presented are identical (except for some simplification of the *Fortspinnung*), the scoring is not, and for this reason the end of the
Vordersatz and the *Fortspinnung* sound ambiguous structurally.

The scoring of double stops for the solo violin is a soloistic technique that
may be seen as a signifier of virtuosity. This transfer of solo technique into
the ritornello temporarily weakens the identity of this passage as ritornello,
a disturbance that is righted only at the more conventionally scored *Epilog*
(mm. 231–35). This ambiguity was, however, prepared by the scoring of the initial *Vordersatz* of the movement for the recorders and principal violin, with
only a sparse accompaniment by the ripieno.

At this point I would like to return to the paradox caused by the reiteration of musical modules in new contexts. For in this movement Bach presents
a substantial musical module that appears to change function according to its
context, even though its musical materials remain the same. This idea stands

on its head the paradigm of the concerto movement delineated by ritornellos. The module in question first occurs in mm. 125–36, where it represents a tutti interjection in the form of *Fortspinnung* 2, played in the recorders and then in the ripieno strings beneath solo passagework in the violin. This passage is, however, still clearly solo, occurring as it does immediately before the entrance of R2 in m. 137.

The first restatement of the module is only partial and occurs not in a solo passage but as the beginning of R4 in mm. 263–70, corresponding to mm. 125–32. The difference between the restatement of this passage and its first occurrence (aside from the key) lies in its scoring. The recorders and ripieno violins have exchanged roles, so that the passage begins with the ripieno violins, bolstering its credentials as a ritornello. Furthermore, the solo violin part, identical to its first appearance except for key, is now doubled in tenths and sixths by the cello and continuo in mm. 264–65, intensifying the feeling that we have arrived at a ritornello. Thus Bach has presented essentially the same passage in two different functional guises: as solo material preceding a ritornello, and as the beginning of a ritornello.

In its third occurrence, this module reverts in function to that of a solo passage, preceding R5 (which begins in m. 323) just as its initial iteration preceded R2 (that is, mm. 311–22 = mm. 125–36). Following so closely upon the use of the same module as the beginning of a ritornello, this produces an effect rather different from that of the module in its first hearing, since the formal function of the module has already been called into question. Here, however, it is part of a large complex of modules assembled by means of permutation: a more complex example of the kind of permutation we saw in the D Minor Concerto for Two Violins. Here, too, we see the use of large modules that do not correspond with the apparent surface divisions of the piece. This process of permutation begins in R4 (mm. 263 ff.), with the reiteration of the segment we have been discussing. After the latter breaks off in m. 271, Bach proceeds with a reiteration of mm. 43–56, which concludes R4. S4 then continues with a repetition of mm. 157–81 (mm. 285–309, with some rewriting in mm. 288–91 and an alteration of interval in m. 300), comprising most of what had been S2, followed by a one-bar extension (m. 310) that then attaches to a reiteration of mm. 125–58, corresponding to mm. 311–44. The entire block of restated material comprises R4, S4, and R5, together with the da capo, R6 (mm. 345–427).

Although the first movement of Brandenburg Concerto No. 4 can be heard on one level as a somewhat eccentric Vivaldian concerto movement, its many strata of references and construction set it apart from its Vivaldian prototype.[14] In this respect, the use of a modular construction that at times calls the surface ritornello construction of the movement into question adds another layer of complexity to a movement already remarkable for its web of allusions.

* * *

The first movement of the Second Brandenburg Concerto, BWV 1047, offers a complex example of Bach's blurring of the function of segments that are demarcated at the outset of the movement as ritornello segments. It is, in fact, the extreme subtlety of the movement that has led two such perceptive analysts as Malcolm Boyd and Laurence Dreyfus to reach such different conclusions about its construction. Boyd asserts:

> The opening movement . . . leaves behind the straightforward ritornello form of the Italians. The main tonal outlines are, as usual, clear enough, with well articulated "rhyming" cadences embracing all the keys most nearly related to that of the movement as a whole: F major (bar 8), C major (28), D minor (39), B-flat major (59), G minor (83), A minor (102), and again F major at the end (118). But there is no regular alternation of solo and tutti throughout the movement, and without these cadential landmarks it would be very difficult for the listener to find an aural path through an extremely varied musical terrain, which is coloured by practically every combination of the instruments used, from the simple violin and continuo of the first episode (bars 9–10) to such densely-textured passages as bars 77–81, in which nearly every line is thematic.[15]

Dreyfus, on the other hand, following a cogent assessment of the peculiar properties of the movement's ritornello, indeed reads the structure of the movement as a consistent alternation of ritornellos and solos, with nine ritornellos.[16]

A mean between the two views expressed here might come closer to explaining the peculiar processes at work in the movement. Klaus Hofmann has presented a convincing case for the work's having originated as a chamber concerto for trumpet, recorder, oboe, violin, and basso continuo, with the ripieno parts—which contribute no real independent material—added later.[17] As would have been typical of the chamber concerto of Bach's time, the non-continuo parts would have played dual roles as both soloists and the constituents of the tutti.[18] Although this putative origin does not significantly affect a reading of the piece at hand, it does provide a possible explanation for the structural ambiguities in the piece. At the same time, the addition of ripieno strings provides a textural reinforcement of the tutti/solo dichotomy that would have been only simulated in a chamber concerto version.

A tabular listing of ritornello and solo sections suits the movement only uncomfortably, at best. The opening ritornello comprises mm. 1–8/3 and divides into four two-measure segments, which can be designated R[1], R[2], R[3], and R[4]. Bach begins to play with expectations of Vivaldian ritornello structure almost immediately after the initial ritornello. In fact, the material is presented with almost mathematical organization, and it is this organization that is in conflict with the putative Vivaldian structure.

At the end of m. 8 a two-measure solo is presented by the principal violin, which is interrupted by what appears to be a tutti interjection consisting of R[1].[19] A pattern is established whereby a two-measure solo is followed by a two-measure ritornello segment. In m. 13 the same solo material is presented in the oboe, now with an accompaniment figure in the violin. The tutti interjection again follows, with the voices interchanged and in the dominant. The solo theme moves yet again to the recorder (mm. 17–18), and again R[1] is presented in the dominant (mm. 19–20).

But now the identity of the tutti interjection material begins to be called into question. Where does the dominant ritornello begin? Measures 19–20 are simply a repetition of mm. 15–16, which are themselves a transposition (with voice exchange) of mm. 11–12. Measure 23 seems to initiate a ritornello, beginning with segment R[2], continuing with R[3], and concluding with R[4]. This would appear to be the expected dominant ritornello. If, however, mm. 20/4–22/3 were simply left out, then mm. 23 ff. would be simply a continuation of the material begun in mm. 19–20, with some adjustments to keep the material in the appropriate octave register. Measure 18/4 could be considered the beginning of the dominant ritornello, and mm. 20/4–22/3 could thus be explained as a solo interjection, turning the idea of tutti interjection on its head. That is, mm. 18/4–20/3 would no longer constitute a tutti interjection; the interjection would be the solo material in mm. 20/4–22/3. In fact, one becomes aware of the function of mm. 18/4–20/3 only in hindsight, after the material in mm. 22/4 ff. has been played. One is being asked to listen, as it were, backward.[20]

What, then of mm. 14/4–16/3? This passage is identical with mm. 18/4–20/3 and stands in the same context, between two iterations of the solo theme. Is this material really a tutti interjection? If mm. 18/4–20/3 are not, then is an analysis of mm. 14/4–16/3, comprising exactly the same material, as tutti interjection justified? And what of mm. 10/4–12/3, again the same material? Does the repetition of a segment perform the same function as its first statement? When does the solo material begin to be perceived as an interruption in the ritornello? In this regard, Bach has presented us with a structure that in some ways is analogous to certain drawings of Escher, in which material seems to transform itself from one form into another.[21]

Two further examples of modular structure from the final section of the movement show how the omission or insertion of modules contributes to the play upon the idea of the Vivaldian concerto (see table 3). The first of these examples concerns the juxtaposition of two ritornellos at the end of the movement. A similar juxtaposition in the first movement of Brandenburg Concerto No. 4 is a result of the da capo structure. In the case of the Second Brandenburg, however, the effect is quite startling, all the more so because of the sudden unison texture at the beginning of the final ritornello.

To understand this juxtaposition it is necessary to trace the modules involved back to their initial iterations. Measures 93/4–102/3, constituting the penultimate ritornello, are a reiteration of mm. 30/4–39/3.[22] This is the minor-key form of the ritornello, containing a true *Fortspinnung*.[23] In its original context, this module was followed by a solo section (mm. 39/4–45/4), a ritornello module (mm. 45/4–49) consisting of the first two original ritornello segments, and another solo (mm. 50–55/4).

Now, however, mm. 93/4–102/3 (= mm. 30/4–39/3) lead directly to the final ritornello, corresponding to a module beginning with a variant of m. 45/4. Thus the original material from the end of m. 39 to m. 45/4 has been left out, and two modules that were originally nonadjacent have been placed consecutively. This omission of the solo material from the earlier iteration of this passage will be compensated by the insertion of solo material into the continuation of the passage, that is, the final ritornello. The omission of the solo passage allows Bach to alter the original harmonic course: instead of moving up a third or down a sixth (originally from D minor to F major), Bach now is free to juxtapose two somewhat more distantly related keys: A minor and F major (moving either up a sixth or down a third). This tonal relationship is identical to the one between the two adjacent ritornellos at the end of the

Table 3. Structural Levels in Brandenburg Concerto No. 2,
First Movement, mm. 67–118

Section	Measures	Key
Level A: R6	67/4–71	v
(R¹, R²)		
Level B: ritornello motives		
Level A: s6	72–74/4	V/ii
Level B: variant of mm. 50–52		
Level A: R7	74/4–83/3	ii
(R¹–F–R⁴)		
Level B: mm. 74/4–83/3 = mm. 30/4–39/3		
Level A: s7	83/4–93/4	ii–iii
Level B: derived from R¹, R²		
Level A: R8	93/4–102/3	iii
(R¹, *Fortspinnung*, R⁴)		
Level B: mm. 93/4–102/3 = mm. 30/4–39/3		
Level A: R9	102/4–118	I
(R¹, R², solo interjection, including variant of R³ on V⁷, R³, R⁴)		
Level B: mm. 102/4–106 = variant of mm. 45/4–49;		
mm. 107–12 = variant of mm. 50–55;		
mm. 113–14 (variant of R³ on V⁷) occur in same place		
as ritornello did in m. 56;		
mm. 115–18 = mm. 5–8		

first movement of the Fourth Brandenburg Concerto and is a common tonal motion at the return of the A section of a da capo aria.

The second example, the final ritornello itself, invokes once again the idea of the solo interjection. This final ritornello (mm. 102/4–118) is remarkable for its initial sudden shift to a unison texture. But this ritornello also presents an example of modular reordering that calls its ritornello status momentarily into question. The opening of the ritornello presents the first two two-bar ritornello segments, R1 and R2. Bach then inserts a six-bar module taken from a solo section. Thus mm. 107–12 are a reiteration of mm. 50–55, with the important difference that a subtle alteration in m. 112 now prolongs a secondary dominant rather than the dominant.[24] This is accomplished, in part, by changing the bass line so it descends a semitone rather than a tone as in m. 55, producing the outline of the BACH motive in the bass.[25] Comparing this passage (ex. 2*b*) with its original context (ex. 2*a*), one can consider mm. 102/4–106 to be a variation of mm. 45/4–49; that is, both present the first two ritornello segments in some guise, and both are followed by a statement of the passage first heard in mm. 50–55.

The material that follows the module comprising mm. 50–55 in each case is different, and the different conclusions each cast a different light upon the passage. In the first case (mm. 55/4–59/3, comprising segments R3 and R4 of the ritornello), one perceives this as a new ritornello in the subdominant, following a brief solo section. This effect is likely due to the shift in key with respect to mm. 45/4–49, which are in the tonic. In the second case, mm. 113–14, Bach presents a two-measure variant of R^3 prolonging a dominant seventh chord, which is perceived as a continuation of the solo interjection owing to its unstable harmony and lighter texture, at least in the transmitted orchestral version (note that this variant of R^3 occurs exactly where R^3 had occurred in the analogous passage in m. 56). This is followed by the true continuation of the ritornello (R^3 and R^4) in the tonic. Since one perceives this passage as the continuation of the ritornello begun in m. 102/4, the effect is that of demoting mm. 107–12 from their original function as a solo to a solo interjection, an interruption of the ritornello analogous to that in mm. 21–22 (with the interruption now after R^2 instead of R^1). The strong effect of the unison texture coinciding with the arrival at the tonic in m. 103 as a signal of the final ritornello is undermined by the insertion of mm. 107–14, which, if omitted, would have resulted in a more conventional closing ritornello.

* * *

Although the use of modular composition is part and parcel of the structuring of ritornellos in Vivaldi's concertos, there the technique is generally used locally, to shorten internal ritornellos. The structure of a typical Vivaldian concerto is generally the structure articulated on the surface. This is one of the innovations of Vivaldi's own concertos: the ritornello segments serve as

Ex. 2 *a*. Brandenburg Concerto No. 2, mvt. 1: *a*. mm. 46–59; *b*. mm. 103–18 (ripieno parts, including viola and violone, omitted).

structural markers that guide the listener and anchor each new key as it is presented. The structural underpinnings of such concertos are clear.

In Bach's concerto movements, on the other hand, the superficially articulated structure may mask a deeper underlying formal foundation of the movement. This is true in many of the genres involving ritornellos in which Bach composed. In the genre of Vivaldian concerto, Bach seems more interested in the possibilities of a complex interplay of generic expectations than in the already conventional opposition and alternation of ritornello and solo. Thus his concerto movements constitute an exegesis of the Vivaldian concerto, rather than the emulation thereof.

Ex. 2 *b.*

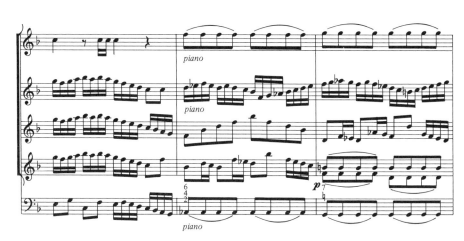

Whereas Bach uses modular construction in other genres — indeed, it seems to be an integral part of his musical language — in his concertos the manipulation of modules allows for a complex manipulation of the specific expectations that arise from the genre at the hands of a composer exploiting the very notion of genre. Modular structure serves this purpose by accommodating the partitioning of the ritornello in the traditional Vivaldian sense, but also by allowing modules initially employed in ritornellos to be placed into solo sections, or vice versa, and by juxtaposing modules that initially did not share the same tutti or solo function or that were not originally adjacent or even proximate. The modules are thus reinterpreted, and this change in meaning serves to blur the outlines of the concerto structure, calling into question the genre of the piece. Although ritornellos are unquestionably crucial to the construction of Bach's concertos, they must be considered together with modular construction in order to arrive at the true structural foundations of the work.

NOTES

1. See, for example, Michael Marissen, *The Social and Religious Designs of J. S. Bach's Brandenburg Concertos* (Princeton, N.J.: Princeton University Press, 1995); Susan McClary, "The Blasphemy of Talking Politics during Bach Year," in *Music and Society: The Politics of Composition, Performance, and Reception*, ed. Richard Leppert and Susan McClary (Cambridge: Cambridge University Press, 1987), 21–41; and Laurence Dreyfus, *Bach and the Patterns of Invention* (Cambridge, Mass.: Harvard University Press, 1996), 59–83.

2. Previous commentators, such as Heinrich Besseler and Martin Geck, have cited a presumed absence of Vivaldian features in the first, third, and sixth concertos as pointing to a dating prior to Bach's first encounter with Vivaldi's concertos. See Heinrich Besseler, "Zur Chronologie der Konzerte Joh. Seb. Bachs," in *Festschrift Max Schneider zum 80. Geburtstag*, ed. Walther Vetter (Leipzig: VEB Deutscher Verlag für Musik, 1955), 115–28; NBA VII/2 (*Sechs Brandenburgische Konzerte*, ed. Besseler), KB, 23–28; and Geck, "Gattungstraditionen und Altersschichten in den Brandenburgischen Konzerten," *Die Musikforschung* 23 (1970): 337–42.

3. See Jeanne Swack, "On the Origins of the Sonate auf Concertenart," *Journal of the American Musicological Society* 46 (1993): 369–414.

4. An excellent summary of the salient features of the Vivaldian concerto is given in Dreyfus, *Bach and the Patterns of Invention*, 59–60.

5. Scheibe, for example, logically considered the ritornello to be the *Hauptsatz* of the concerto. See Johann Adolph Scheibe, *Critischer Musikus*, 2d ed. (Leipzig: Breitkopf, 1745; facs. rpt., Hildesheim: Georg Olms, 1970), 631.

6. Hans Eppstein provides a perceptive reading of this movement in "Zum Formproblem bei Johann Sebastian Bach," in *Bach-Studien 5: Eine Sammlung von Aufsätzen*, ed. Rudolf Eller and Hans-Joachim Schulze (Leipzig: Breitkopf & Härtel, 1975), 32–34, 40.

7. References in the form "m. 13/3" refer to measure and beat respectively; where no beat number is given, beat 1 is assumed.

8. V = mm. 1–12, F1 = mm. 13–22, V = mm. 23–34, F2 = mm. 35–56, V = mm. 57–69/1, F3 = mm. 62–79/1, E = mm. 79/1–83/1. The commonly used terms *Vordersatz* (opening

segment), *Fortspinnung* (spinning out), and *Epilog* (closing segment) first appeared in Wilhelm Fischer, "Zur Entwicklungsgeschichte des Wiener klassischen Stils," *Studien zur Musikwissenschaft* 3 (1915): 24–84.

9. In the labeling of ritornello segments in this movement I follow Malcolm Boyd, *Bach: The Brandenburg Concertos* (Cambridge: Cambridge University Press, 1993), 54. Gregory Butler, in his essay in this volume, questions whether mm. 1–83 constitutes a single ritornello. By the word "permutation" I mean the setting out of a series of modules that appear in new orderings and contexts later in the piece.

10. See Marissen, *Social and Religious Designs*, 62–64.

11. See the diagram in Boyd, *Bach*, 56–57.

12. Cf. Ibid., 56.

13. See also Marissen, *Social and Religious Designs*, 72, for a discussion of this passage in terms of the apparent stylistic inappropriateness of the principal violin part.

14. Marissen, *Social and Religious Designs*, 65ff., provides a more extended discussion of possible allusions in this movement to the minuet and the social hierarchy of the court ensemble.

15. Boyd, *Bach*, 75.

16. Dreyfus, *Bach and the Patterns of Invention*, 78–83.

17. Klaus Hofmann, "Zur Fassungsgeschichte des 2. Brandenburgischen Konzerts," in *Bachs Orchesterwerke: Bericht über das 1. Dortmunder Bach-Symposium Witten*, ed. Martin Geck and Werner Breig (Dortmund: Klangfarben, 1997), 1185–92.

18. On the dual roles played by the instruments in chamber concertos of Vivaldi and Bach's German contemporaries, see Swack, "On the Origins," 376ff.

19. In the context of the piece as a chamber concerto, a tutti interjection would be performed by the solo instruments simulating an orchestral tutti.

20. Dreyfus, *Bach and the Patterns of Invention*, 81, begins the ritornello in m. 23, without offering the possibility that it begins in m. 19.

21. See, for example, Escher's "Day and Night" (1938), reproduced in Douglas R. Hofstadter, *Göodel, Escher, Bach: An Eternal Golden Braid* (New York: Vintage Books, 1980), 252.

22. This module also recurs as mm. 74/4–83/3.

23. As Dreyfus, *Bach and the Patterns of Invention*, 82–83, has pointed out.

24. An abbreviated variant of this solo module also appears in mm. 72–74.

25. One could consider the passage from m. 107–12 as presenting two overlapping BACH motives in the bass, with the first (mm. 107–10) transposed and the second

(mm. 110–12) at the proper BACH pitch. The transposed version had also been present in mm. 50–54, while mm. 52–56 comprised a faulty version, with a whole step between the final two pitches. Elke Lang-Becker, *Johann Sebastian Bach: Die Brandenburgischen Konzerte* (Munich: Fink, 1990), 43, has pointed out the BACH motive in mm. 109–12.

PART TWO

Interpretation

The Harpsichord Culture
in Bach's Environs

John Koster

lthough Bach scholars have gradually accumulated and interpreted considerable evidence about Bach's stringed keyboard instruments during the past two centuries, much of the information is essentially irrelevant to musical matters—for example, that the most valuable harpsichord
in Bach's estate was veneered. Objective methods of analysis often provide trivial answers; it can, for example, be positively stated only that the "Goldberg"
Variations were written for two-manual harpsichord, of some unknown type,
with keyboards including the notes GG to d'''. Subjective methods, on the
other hand, vary so greatly from study to study that, one suspects, each answer
reflects the prejudices of its author;[1] the Well-Tempered Clavier is variously
thought to have been written for harpsichord, fretted or unfretted clavichord,
organ, or even the early piano. Broadly based inquiries incorporating a multiplicity of types of evidence and methods of analysis are equally problematical.
Even so brilliant a study as that of Sheridan Germann cannot demonstrate
conclusively that the Fifth Brandenburg Concerto was written with a harpsichord by Michael Mietke in mind, and a fundamentally important question
about the Mietke harpsichord in Cöthen—whether it had a 16′ stop—remains
both unanswered and unanswerable.[2]

Despite the uncertainties about Bach's keyboard instruments and his use of
them, it is at least reasonable to assume that he and those around him did,
much of the time, play his *manualiter* works on harpsichords. Bach's estate
included five *Clavecins* at three levels of valuation: one instrument at eighty
talers, three at fifty, and one "smaller" instrument at twenty.[3] Although it has
been suggested that the major difference between the fifty- and eighty-taler instruments was one of smaller and larger keyboard compasses,[4] a few more keys
should not increase the value of a harpsichord by 60 percent.[5] If one assumes

that one or more of the fifty-taler harpsichords was a two-manual instrument with the "standard" three stops (i.e., 8′ + 8′ + 4′), then the additional valuation of the eighty-taler harpsichord might better be interpreted to have covered such features as a 16′ stop or a third 8′ register, if not merely some special decorative veneering. Thus Bach would have owned harpsichords of at least three different sizes and dispositions, ranging from a smallish single-manual instrument to a large two-manual.

It seems reasonable to assume that the variety of harpsichords within Bach's household reflected, to some degree, the variety of harpsichords found in those areas of Germany where Bach was active. Even if Bach, his patrons, and local colleagues did not own examples of every different model of harpsichord available in this area, he would doubtless have encountered and played most of them during his travels. Further, he would have expected his works, published or distributed in manuscript, to have been played on the various types of harpsichords that he had encountered. Thus the question of Bach's harpsichords is perhaps best answered by a survey of extant instruments made in his environs and of those rare contemporary documents that tell us something meaningful about them.[6]

THE OVERALL STATE OF HARPSICHORD MAKING
IN BACH'S GERMANY

The making of stringed keyboard instruments in Germany during Bach's lifetime was astonishingly rich and diverse, even if one chooses to disregard the many "expressive" *Claviere*[7] and considers only harpsichords. In contrast to the situation in France or England, where political and cultural life was focused around a central monarchy and harpsichord making was centered in one city (Paris or London), in Germany the political, cultural, and geographical conditions were such that harpsichord making was completely noncentralized. A history of Thuringia published the year before Bach's birth states proudly that "here they build in villages . . . stringed instruments such as violins, basses, viole da gamba, harpsichords, spinets, citterns."[8]

Such conditions in the German principalities had several important consequences for instrument making: (1) archaic practices of design and construction could long survive, here and there, unaffected by fashions established in more cosmopolitan centers of instrument making such as Antwerp, Paris, and London; nevertheless, (2) the nonexistence of a dominant national style allowed individual German makers to be freely innovative, whether under their own initiative, at the suggestion of individual musicians, or because of influence from elsewhere; therefore, (3) instrument making was subject to wide variation depending on each individual maker's circumstances at each particular time. Thus the diversity of German harpsichords evident from extant instruments and documents is to be expected, and the modern tendency to group German makers into schools is misleading. Frank Hubbard categorized German harpsichords into Hamburg and Saxon schools,[9] but even the superficially coherent Hamburg school, in which the instruments invariably have painted cases with round tails, falls apart when one looks more closely at the several Hamburg makers' individual design and construction practices. For example, each of the eight surviving harpsichords made by members of the Hass family of Hamburg is unique: they have one, two, or three manuals, six different compasses, and eight different dispositions of stops.[10] This may be compared with the work of three German-born makers working in Paris: Antoine Vater, his pupil Henri Hemsch, and the latter's brother, Guillaume. Their eight extant harpsichords all have two manuals of compass FF to e''' or FF to f''', with the standard French disposition.[11]

Historical harpsichord making is usually seen, following the pioneering work of Raymond Russell and Frank Hubbard, as having been polarized, since the middle of the sixteenth century, into two schools, the Italian and the Flemish.[12] Because eighteenth-century French harpsichord makers were strongly influenced by the Flemish Ruckers family, the work of these two adjacent regions is often grouped together as "Franco-Flemish." There is a certain historical validity to speaking of Italian and Franco-Flemish schools of harpsichord making, but difficulties often occur in categorizing instruments possessing both "Italianate" and "Franco-Flemish" features or features that fall between the two extremes. This eclectic or "intermediate" category includes virtually all extant German instruments.

A harpsichord by Christian Zell, Hamburg, 1728, for example, seems to bear out the statement in a recent discussion about the keyboard instruments available to Bach, that "German harpsichord makers borrowed elements of both French and Italian models."[13] The instrument has the standard French two-manual disposition: 8' + 4' stops on the lower keyboard, 8' on the upper, and a shove coupler. Moreover, its scaling, with the c'' string 347 mm. long, is close to Flemish and eighteenth-century French standards. On the other hand, its bridges are molded like Italian bridges, and its case walls are attached to the edges of the bottom board, as in Italian instruments. The thicknesses of the case walls—the spine of 12 mm. pine, the bent side and cheekpiece of 8 mm. maple—are intermediate between the typical Italian 4 mm. and Franco-Flemish 15 mm. Nevertheless, even if it is granted that the standard two-manual harpsichord disposition was first developed in mid-seventeenth-century France, it is not so absolutely clear that the other "Franco-Flemish" or "Italian" technical features were really adopted, directly or indirectly, from Italian, Flemish, or French models. There are, for example, only two ways to attach case walls to the bottom board: the "Italian" manner used by Zell, and the "Flemish" manner, used by another Hamburg maker, Carl Conrad Fleischer—whose widow Zell married—in which the bottom board is attached to the bottom edge of the walls.[14] If the joint is not done one way, it must be done the other; thus it is reasonable to hypothesize that Zell's tradition of harpsichord case construction arose independently in Germany. In general, it is useful to consider that any individual feature of harpsichord making might have arisen in Germany independently from its use by Italian, Flemish, or French makers, simply because there are a limited number of reasonable solutions to any particular technical requirement.

Edwin M. Ripin was perhaps the first to recognize the existence of a harpsichord-making tradition characterized mostly by features "intermediate" between Italian and Flemish practice, and to note that this style was prevalent throughout most of northern Europe until 1700.[15] Although Ripin, regarding this tradition as transitional between the Italian and Flemish styles, called it "intermediate," I have proposed to call it, more neutrally, an "international style."[16] This international style—perhaps better called a tradition, as it can be defined only as a set of various technical tendencies or possibilities—unfolded directly from an original "Gothic" tradition of making stringed keyboard instruments centered in Germany and the adjacent Burgundian Netherlands. In this interpretation, Italian harpsichord making is seen as a separate offshoot of the Gothic tradition. The earliest extant relic of that tradition is a late-fifteenth-century German upright harpsichord, now at the Royal College of Music in London.[17] This instrument, which predates all extant Italian stringed keyboard instruments, displays many of the "Italianate" features (e.g., a molded nut and thin case walls attached to the edges of the bottom) seen in some later German harpsichords. Thus German harpsichord making in Bach's time can, like organ building, be regarded as the culmination of an archaic native tradition that can be traced back as far as the fifteenth century.

An example of archaism is provided by an anonymous early-eighteenth-century Thuringian harpsichord now in the collection of the Bachhaus museum in Eisenach (pl.1).[18] The instrument's wrest plank is only a narrow piece near the nameboard, and what in a French or Flemish harpsichord would merely be veneer over a wide wrest plank is actually resonant soundboard wood. Thus the nut is acoustically active and functions as a second bridge. In general, this seems to promote the production of a comparatively loud but rapidly decaying tone with a full, fundamental quality. The same type of construction is found in several of the very few extant German harpsichords of the sixteenth and seventeenth centuries, including the earliest example, made by Hans Müller in Leipzig in 1537 (pl.2).[19]

That the Bachhaus harpsichord was, in its archaic wrest plank, not unusual among harpsichords in Bach's environs is suggested by Jacob Adlung's account of harpsichord making in *Musica mechanica organoedi*.[20] Adlung, who as an amateur clavichord maker obviously had a clear understanding of how instruments were constructed, habitually refers to wrest pins and harpsichord jacks as passing through the soundboard. In describing a harpsichord with a 4′ set of strings, he mentions that there must be an oak rail under the area of the soundboard through which the 4′ wrest pins are driven.[21] Thus, evidently, to Adlung the normal construction was like that of the Müller harpsichord of 1537, in which the soundboard, slotted for passage of the jacks, extends all the way to the nameboard.

Adlung's discussion of the harpsichord is particularly close to Bach's milieu. Although *Musica mechanica organoedi* was published posthumously in 1768, the text was written largely during Adlung's years in Jena (1723 to 1727). There he knew Johann Nicolaus Bach (1669–1753), organist, maker of stringed keyboard instruments, and a second cousin of J. S. Bach.[22] That Adlung maintained connections with the Bach family is suggested by his later work, *Anleitung zu der musikalischen Gelahrtheit* (Erfurt, 1758), with its preface by Johann Ernst Bach, a second cousin once removed and pupil of J. S. Bach. The text of *Musica mechanica organoedi* was edited for publication by Johann Lorenz Albrecht, who, together with Johann Friedrich Agricola—a former student of Bach—

Plate 1. Harpsichord, maker unknown, Thuringia, early eighteenth century (Bach-haus, Eisenach; Inv.-Nr. I 77).

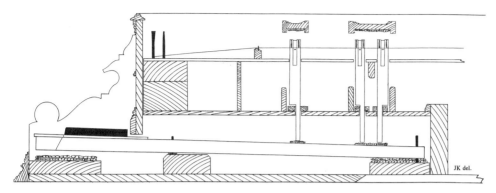

Plate 2. Harpsichord, Hans Müller, Leipzig, 1537 (Museo degli Strumenti Musicali, Rome): Elevation, showing contruction of the wrest plank and soundboard (some details of the action are conjectural).

contributed corrective and supplementary footnotes. Albrecht and Agricola left Adlung's remarks, with their implication about the construction of the wrest plank, to stand without further comment.

Here it should be emphasized that general characterizations of German harpsichord tone should be used with caution. The Thuringian harpsichord in the Bachhaus is, to my knowledge, the only extant eighteenth-century German harpsichord with the archaic wrest plank construction. My description of the timbral effect of the resonant nut is based on experience with only a few playable instruments of this type. The complex interactions of the various elements of harpsichord design and construction—of which some of the most important include string scaling and material, plucking points, soundboard material, and ribbing—and the variety of these elements in German harpsichords should be borne in mind when one reads that "individual tones on the older stringed instruments seem to take a bit longer to achieve full resonance than on the modern piano"[23] or that "brass strings . . . produced a relatively sustained 'organ-like' sonority."[24] Many scholars and harpsichord makers now assume that short-scaled German instruments were designed for brass strings.[25] There is some evidence, however, that short scalings (with c″ strings about 315 mm. long) might not always imply the use of brass strings, necessarily at a very low pitch. Rather, this might allow the use of iron strings either at a high pitch (i.e., *Chorton*, about a semitone above modern pitch) or at a stress significantly below the limits of the material's tensile strength.[26]

Another characteristic of German harpsichord making was the possibility of unfettered innovation. In most places there seems to have been no legal structure to regulate the making of stringed keyboard instruments. Thus Johann Nicolaus Bach, a musician, could become a part-time instrument maker, free to devise the lute-harpsichords and clever stop-changing mechanism described by Adlung.[27] By contrast, at about the same time in Paris the new keyboard instruments devised by the mechanical engineer Jean Marius were strenuously challenged in lawsuits brought by the guild of master musical instrument makers.[28]

A further important characteristic of German stringed keyboard instrument making is its close association with organ building. Many of the most notable harpsichord makers, such as Gottfried Silbermann and Zacharias Hildebrandt, were primarily organ builders, just as most professional harpsichordists were primarily organists. From this circumstance, which originated in the Gothic period and survived in Germany through the end of the eighteenth century, there was a natural tendency for concepts to be transferred from the organ to the harpsichord and other stringed keyboard instruments.[29]

FOREIGN PRESENCE AND INFLUENCE

In 1955 Friedrich Ernst concluded that Bach's harpsichords were primarily of Italian and Flemish origin.[30] Ten years later, Frank Hubbard emphasized that during the sixteenth and early seventeenth centuries most harpsichords in Germany were imported from Italy and Flanders, with French influence becoming predominant by the end of the seventeenth century.[31] More recently, the discovery and description of many previously unknown German harpsichords have made necessary a reevaluation of these views.[32] In this new interpretation, the importance of foreign influence on German makers is minimized, allowing only a few specific contributions. Italian harpsichords, for example, might have given Hans Müller, in 1537, or a predecessor the idea of making the soundboard of cypress. Thereafter, however, the occasional use of cypress in harpsichords made or used in Germany need not necessarily indicate direct Italian influence or presence. Thus, for example, the "*Clavicimbul* with two registers, of cypress with an ivory keyboard to GG," listed in an inventory of the electoral court in Dresden in 1681, might not have been made in Italy, as Hubbard assumed,[33] any more than the keyboard material—ivory, rarely found on Italian instruments—implies an African or Indian origin. During the same period

Joachim Tielke was making *Hamburger Cithrinchen* with cypress bellies.[34] Similarly, in 1746 the Berlin cabinetmakers Martin and Christoph Boehme provided a "cedar *Clavecin*" (or perhaps just cedar or cypress for a harpsichord) to the court of Frederick the Great.[35]

The use of, and significant direct influence from, harpsichords by the Ruckers or other Flemish makers seems to have been confined to the extreme northern portion of Bach's Germany. Several Flemish harpsichords are known to have been present there in the seventeenth and early eighteenth centuries, most notably the instrument shown in a group portrait including Johann Adam Reinken and Dietrich Buxtehude.[36] Ruckers harpsichords probably inspired some Hamburg makers, including members of the Fleischer and Hass families, to employ a few specific techniques: for example, the system of soundboard ribbing in which the bent side, 4′ hitch pin rail, and cutoff bar define areas of free soundboard around the bridges unencumbered by ribs crossing underneath.[37] Nevertheless, numerous equally important details were presumably derived purely from earlier German traditions—for example, the S-shaped bent sides and frequent unusual dispositions. An apparent amalgamation of the Flemish and the native international style can be seen in a harpsichord by Carl Conrad Fleischer, Hamburg, 1716, in which the 4′ hitch pin rail is of massive dimensions like those in Ruckers harpsichords.[38] Fleischer, however, chamfered its upper edges so that only a small surface, similar to that of the slender rails often found in international-style harpsichords, is actually glued to the soundboard.

Michael Mietke, toward the end of the seventeenth century, was said to have deceptively sold some of his earlier harpsichords as high-priced French imports.[39] This might indicate merely that instruments in his usual German style were decorated in the French fashion, but it is possible that one or two Parisian harpsichords had actually been brought to Berlin and might have influenced Mietke. These would have been seventeenth-century French instruments, made in the same international style practiced in Germany: Mietke would not have found anything about scaling, case construction, or soundboard ribbing that he could not have learned from German instruments. The most consistent and distinctive features of French harpsichords made from about 1650 to about 1690 are their dainty keyboards, with compass GG/BB to c‴, and their dispositions, most frequently with two manuals, which, from the best-preserved examples, seem usually or invariably to have had the standard disposition found later in eighteenth-century French instruments.[40] Mietke's keys are indeed rather dainty, and his "black" harpsichord (now in Schloß Charlottenburg, Berlin) has the French two-manual disposition.[41] Since Mietke is known, however, to have made at least two harpsichords with 16' stops,[42] which are never found on French instruments of the period, the French influence was obviously not all-pervasive, even in the instance of the one German maker who is specifically said to have imitated the French.

NONSTANDARD DISPOSITIONS

Because of the Bach-Cöthen-Mietke connection, extant harpsichords by Mietke or attributable to him, especially the "black" two-manual harpsichord and modern copies of it, have achieved a certain status as authentic Bach harpsichords. The black harpsichord happens to have what has been called the "simple, classic" disposition,[43] that is, the registrational format of the standard late-twentieth-century two-manual harpsichord derived from eighteenth-century French models. The introduction and acceptance of this standard modern classic harpsichord should largely be credited to the efforts and artistry of the Boston-based makers Frank Hubbard and William Dowd. Hubbard stated quite plainly "the extremely important fact that most German harpsichords show the same disposition as the French."[44] This was written before the discovery of many pertinent instruments and documents, but even confining ourselves to Hubbard's own tables of data about German harpsichords,[45] we find that only seven of the fifteen instruments in those tables have the standard French two-manual disposition; of the twelve two-manual instruments, no fewer than five are anomalous. Clearly, Hubbard allowed his own convictions about the characteristics of the ideal harpsichord to affect his informal statistical analysis. Although a fairly substantial number of extant German harpsichords have dispositions that seem normal to us (i.e., singles disposed 8' + 8' or 8' + 8' + 4' and doubles with the French disposition), an equally substantial number have dispositions that display an extraordinary degree of ingenuity. Two major propensities, sometimes bound together, can be observed: the idea of the harpsichord as a "color machine" and the influence of the organ.

The dispositions of Italian, Ruckers-period Flemish, and French harpsichords were generally quite "chaste," with their strings plucked by jacks in "normal" positions relative to the ends of the strings, so as to produce a "typical" harpsichord tone, varying only moderately within an instrument. In a

French harpsichord, for example, the difference between the plucking points of the lower-manual 8′ stop and the upper 8′ is only about 50 mm. In Germany, however, already in 1537, the Müller harpsichord, with two sets of strings plucked by two registers of jacks in the normal position, had an additional set of jacks plucking one set of strings very near the nut, producing a brilliant, reedy, nasal timbre. At c′ the difference in plucking points between the nearest and farthest registers is 101 mm.

That a single-manual disposition with 8′ + 8′ stringing and three registers, one of them nasal, is found on several of the very few extant seventeenth-century German harpsichords suggests that it was something of a standard feature.[46] Clearly, the purpose of this disposition, which arose at about the same time that organs were being provided with colorful new reed and flute stops, was to provide a variety of distinctive timbres. Occasionally, these three standard registers were supplemented by a 4′ stop.[47] In one instrument of about 1630 (pl. 3), the two sets of 8′ strings are plucked by five registers, including two nasal stops (one with metal plectra), two normal stops, and one exceptionally far from the nut.[48] Frequently, a buff stop also contributed to the tonal palette. The origin of the Müller harpsichord in Leipzig, the presence of a single-manual *Clavizimbul* with four registers in Dresden in 1681, and Adlung's familiarity with single-manual dispositions of this type suggest that such colorful instruments were known in Bach's environs.[49]

The concept of harpsichord as color machine certainly inhabits the registrations that C. P. E. Bach indicated for a sonata written in 1747 in Berlin (w. 69; h. 53).[50] Here, especially in the final movement (a set of variations), is a kaleidoscope of registrations, including upper-manual 8′ "damped" (i.e., with the buff stop) coupled to the lower-manual 4′; solo 4′ accompanied by upper-manual 8′ with buff; and 8′ + 8′ on the upper manual, accompanying 8′ + 4′ on the lower. Employing the stop names used by the composer, the disposition reconstructed from the registrations is as follows: lower manual with *Flöte* 8′ (i.e., a register with a relatively distant plucking point) and *Octav* 4′; upper manual with *Cornet* 8′ and *Spinet* 8′; buff stop affecting the *Cornet*. Because the registrations require both *Cornet* and *Spinet* to be coupled to the lower manual and to be used independently, there must have been an actual coupler (i.e., not a register of dogleg jacks shared between the two keyboards). In eighteenth-century Germany, the terms *Spinet* and *Cornet* were both used for registers in close proximity to the nut.[51] Because in this sonata the *Cornet* is used much

Plate 3. Harpsichord, maker unknown, southern Germany, about 1630 (Bayerisches Nationalmuseum, Munich; Inv.-Nr. Mu 78).

more frequently than the *Spinet*, it is likely that the latter was the more nasal stop, the too-frequent use of which would be likely to weary the ear. Thus the *Cornet* would have been the "normal" upper-manual 8′ register. Because both *Cornet* and *Spinet* were used while uncoupled to the lower manual with the *Flöte* stop engaged, neither of the upper-manual registers could have plucked the same set of strings as the *Flöte*, lest there be damper interference. Because the buff stop affected the *Cornet* but is not indicated for the *Spinet*, it is likely that the buff stop could not affect the *Spinet*, i.e., that the two upper-manual registers plucked different sets of strings.[52]

Thus the harpsichord called for by this sonata had four sets of strings and four registers, 8′ + 8′ + 8′ + 4′. This instrument can be regarded as an amalgamation of the archaic German single-manual multiple-8′ disposition, including a nasal register, and the standard French two-manual scheme. Moreover, it is likely that some of Bach's pupils (of whom his son Emanuel was the most prominent), if not J. S. Bach himself, would have applied such playful and colorful registrations to another set of variations also appearing in the 1740s: the "Goldberg" Variations.

Two-manual harpsichords like Emanuel Bach's, with more than the normal complement of two 8′ stops, might not have been utterly uncommon. One by Hieronymous Albrecht Hass, Hamburg, 1723, with three sets of 8′ strings and a 4′, has long been known.[53] Recently, Lance Whitehead has reconstructed the original disposition of another two-manual harpsichord by the same maker, dated 1721: this instrument seems almost certainly to have had five registers acting on three 8′ and two 4′ sets of strings.[54] Here the intention seems to have been to provide not only a variety of 8′ tone but also an independent 4′ register on each keyboard. Jacob Adlung, closer to the center of J. S. Bach's activity, describes somewhat similar harpsichords with two sets of 4′ strings in addition to two 8′ sets.[55]

Adlung also describes a slightly different type of harpsichord in which the same strings are plucked by different registers on two or even three keyboards:

> triple-strung [harpsichords] are mostly two 8′ and 4′, [but] sometimes an overspun 16′ string is found instead of an 8′. . . . It is very nice if a harpsichord has two keyboards, even if it has only three sets of strings. One can set it up so that the upper keyboard affects the front row of jacks, the lower controls the rest, and when all registers are to sound together the keyboards are to be coupled. However, one can also install extra rows of jacks, so that the lower manual can

play all the registers [i.e., sets of strings] without coupling, and the upper can be played single, double, or triple [i.e., with up to three registers].[56]

Elsewhere he writes: "One can, however, make harpsichords with two or three keyboards above each other: in which case it is best if the jacks of all the keyboards pluck the same strings."[57] Adlung then refers to his description of J. N. Bach's lute-harpsichords with such an arrangement, in which the upper manual, with its register plucking nearer to the nut and providing a brighter tone, is regarded as providing the instrument's *forte*.[58]

The final sentence of the first of these quotations suggests that Adlung or his contemporaries would not have been astonished to find a two-manual harpsichord with 8′ + 8′ + 4′ stringing and with 8′ + 8′ + 4′ registers on each keyboard. Even without a coupler, this would provide a wealth of registrational possibilities, limited only by the necessity of avoiding the simultaneous use of registers plucking the same sets of strings (lest the jacks on one keyboard damp the strings plucked by the other keyboard's jacks). Such a disposition and others in which there is more than one register on the upper manual might have facilitated the registration of works such as the Italian Concerto, in which passages marked *piano*, when played on a standard harpsichord with a single 8′ on the upper manual, are sometimes overwhelmed by the *forte* lower manual.

The influence of the organ on German harpsichord making has long been recognized in German makers' occasional provision of 16′ stops. A remarkable instance of such influence is a harpsichord owned by Bach's pupil and successor in Weimar, Johann Casper Vogler (1696–1763): it had a pedal disposed 32′ + 16′ + 8′ + 8′.[59] The two manuals had the standard 8′ + 8′ + 4′ disposition, but their compass was six octaves, CC to c″″. This would have allowed most of the contemporary keyboard literature, which largely falls within a four-octave C to c‴ compass, to be played an octave lower or higher, i.e., in effect with 16′ + 16′ + 8′ or 4′ + 4′ + 2′ registrations.

As for harpsichords of normal compass with conventional 16′ stops, these might not have been so rare as some modern writers have thought. Stauffer, for example, although admitting that middle-German makers occasionally provided 16′ stops, suggests that "they were nevertheless unusual enough to merit special mention, both in treatises and sales announcements."[60] To the contrary, however, one could argue by analogy that present-day advertisements for cars with four-wheel drive or air conditioning should not be taken by future historians as implying that these features were rare in the 1990s. In any case, one could point to an advertisement in Leipzig in 1731 for an undoubtedly unusual instrument, a hammer-action *Cymbal-Clavier,* which was described as being "in the form of a 16′ harpsichord," with which readers were obviously expected to be familiar.[61]

Perhaps the most remarkable document recently to have been discovered about harpsichords in Bach's environs is an advertisement, in the *Leipziger Intelligenzblatt* of 4 October 1775, for "a four-choired harpsichord [*Flügel*], beautifully veneered in walnut, by Zacharias Hildebrandt, for sale. This has two keyboards from FF to f‴. On the lower manual are a *Principal* 16′ and *Principal* 8′. On the upper are a *Cornet* 8′ and *Octava* 4′. For strengthening the bass there is a *Spinet* 8′ of two octaves, borrowed from the *Cornet.* Herewith are five registers with which, by using the coupler, very many variations can be made."[62] As Herbert Heyde, who discovered this document, points out, the harpsichord was probably made in Leipzig before 1750, since Hildebrandt (1688–1757), active there from the mid-1730s, left in 1750 to assist Gottfried Silbermann in building the monumental organ for the Catholic Schloßkirche in Dresden.[63] During the final period of Bach's life, no instrument maker is known to have worked in closer association with Bach than Hildebrandt. According to Agricola, the two collaborated in making a lute-harpsichord.[64] Hildebrandt also took care of instruments in Leipzig churches, including the harpsichord at St. Thomas.[65]

The disposition of the Hildebrandt harpsichord advertised in 1775 is remarkable in several ways. First is its organlike character: clearly, the intention was to provide resources analogous to those of an organ like that in the Dresden Schloßkirche, with a 16′ *Hauptwerk* "of large and massive [*gravitätischen*] scaling" and an 8′ *Oberwerk* "of sharp and penetrating scaling."[66] Second is the *Spinet*, presumably a close-plucking nasal register on the upper manual from FF to f, acting on the same strings as the normal upper-manual 8′ stop, the *Cornet.* This was probably intended to act as a foil to the 16′ stop, that is, to enrich the bass with bright harmonics, for the same reason that the Hass family occasionally included a 2′ stop in the lower part of the compass of harpsichords with 16′ stops. Third, the Hildebrandt harpsichord is extraordinary—or seems so to us—in that, except for the supplementary *Spinet*, it had the same disposition as the "Bach harpsichord" so admired by early modern harpsichord revivalists and so despised by later scholars and performers.[67]

Because the harpsichords in Bach's environs were diverse in their musical qualities and registrational resources, each performance would have involved some degree of adjustment in order to match the musical text to the characteristics of the particular instrument in use. Although it is not inappropriate for today's performers to employ, for Bach's works, the "classic" registrational possibilities available on the 8′ + 8′ + 4′ two-manual or 8′ + 8′ single-manual harpsichords that are most familiar in our time, neither is there any evidence to suggest that it is especially appropriate to do so.[68] Indeed, one might go so far as to say that it is entirely inappropriate for present-day interpretations to be restricted to the relatively limited variety of resources available on the harpsichords typically found in late-twentieth-century concert halls and recording studios.

NOTES

1. This is discussed further in John Koster, "The Quest for Bach's *Clavier:* An Historiographical Interpretation," *Early Keyboard Journal* 14 (1996): 65–84.

2. See Sheridan Germann, "The Mietkes, the Margrave, and Bach," in *Bach, Handel, Scarlatti: Tercentenary Essays*, ed. Peter Williams (Cambridge: Cambridge University Press, 1985), 119–48.

3. BR, 193.

4. See George B. Stauffer, "J. S. Bach's Harpsichords," in *Festa musicologica: Essays in Honor of George J. Buelow*, ed. Thomas J. Mathiesen and Benito V. Rivera (Stuyvesant, N.Y.: Pendragon Press, 1995), 304.

5. Jacob Adlung, *Anleitung zu der musikalischen Gelahrtheit* (Erfurt, 1758; facs. rpt., Kassel: Bärenreiter, 1953), 556, notes that extending the compass of harpsichords does not cost as much as doing so in organs.

6. In addition to Stauffer, "J. S. Bach's Harpsichords," important surveys include John Henry van der Meer, "Beiträge zur Cembalobau im deutschen Sprachgebiet bis 1700," *Anzeiger des Germanischen Nationalmuseums* (Nuremberg, 1966): 103–33, and Hubert Henkel, "Der Cembalobau der Bach-Zeit im sächsisch-thüringischen und im Berliner Raum," in *Bericht über die wissenschaftliche Konferenz zum III. Internationalen Bach-Fest der* DDR (Leipzig: Deutscher Verlag für Musik, 1977), 361–74.

7. These instruments—pianos, *Lautenwerke, Geigenwerke*, clavichords, etc.—are discussed in John Koster, "Pianos and Other 'Expressive' Claviere in J. S. Bach's Circle," *Early Keyboard Studies Newsletter* 7, no. 4 (October 1993): 1–11; 8, no. 1 (January 1994): 1–7; and 8, no. 2 (April 1994): 8–15.

8. August Boetius, *Merkwürdige und auserlesene Geschichte von der berühmten Landgrafschaft Thüringen* (Gotha, 1684), trans. in Karl Geiringer, *The Bach Family: Seven*

Generations of Creative Genius (London: Oxford University Press, 1954), 5 (slightly modified).

9. Frank Hubbard, *Three Centuries of Harpsichord Making* (Cambridge, Mass.: Harvard University Press, 1965), 172–91.

10. Lance Whitehead, "An Extraordinary Hass Harpsichord in Gothenburg," *Galpin Society Journal* 49 (1996): 95.

11. Several of the Vater and Hemsch instruments are discussed in John Koster, *Keyboard Musical Instruments in the Museum of Fine Arts, Boston* (Boston: Museum of Fine Arts, 1994), 88–96.

12. Russell, *The Harpsichord and Clavichord: An Introductory Study* (London: Faber & Faber, 1959); Hubbard, *Three Centuries of Harpsichord Making.*

13. David Schulenberg, *The Keyboard Music of J. S. Bach* (New York: Schirmer Books, 1992), 10. The Zell harpsichord of 1728 is in the Museum für Kunst und Gewerbe, Hamburg; I am grateful to the museum staff for the opportunity to examine it. The instrument is also described in Martin Skowroneck, "Das Cembalo von Christian Zell, Hamburg, 1728, und seine Restaurierung," *Organ Yearbook* 5 (1974): 79–87.

14. I am grateful to the late Hugh Gough for the opportunity to examine a Carl Conrad Fleischer harpsichord of 1716 before its sale to the Museum für Hamburgische Geschichte. For biographical details about Fleischer and Zell, see Donald H. Boalch, *Makers of the Harpsichord and Clavichord, 1440–1840,* 3d ed., ed. Charles Mould (Oxford: Clarendon Press, 1995), 61, 212.

15. See Edwin M. Ripin, "On Joes Karest's Virginal and the Origins of the Flemish Tradition," in *Keyboard Instruments: Studies in Keyboard Organology,* ed. Edwin M. Ripin (Edinburgh: Edinburgh University Press, 1971), 70.

16. John Koster, "The Importance of the Early English Harpsichord," *Galpin Society Journal* 33 (1980): 66. See also John Koster, *Early Netherlandish Harpsichord Making from Its Origins to 1600* (forthcoming).

17. See Elizabeth Wells, "The London Clavicytherium," *Early Music* 6 (1978): 568–71.

18. See Herbert Heyde, *Historische Musikinstrumente im Bachhaus Eisenach* (Eisenach: Bachhaus, 1976), 128–29; and Heyde, *Musikinstrumentenbau, 15.–19. Jahrhundert: Kunst, Handwerk, Entwurf* (Leipzig: Deutscher Verlag für Musik, 1986), 153 and pl. 63. I am grateful to the staff of the Bachhaus for the opportunity to examine this instrument.

19. See Luisa Cervelli and John Henry van der Meer, *Conservato a Roma il più antico clavicembalo tedesco* (Rome: Palatino, 1967). I am grateful to Antonio Latanza, Direc-

tor of the Museo Nazionale degli Strumenti Musicali, Rome, for the opportunity to examine this instrument.

20. Jacob Adlung, *Musica mechanica organoedi*, Berlin, 1768; facs. rpt., Kassel: Bärenreiter, 1961.

21. Ibid., 2:110.

22. See Adlung's autobiography, included as a preface to vol. 2 of *Musica mechanica organoedi*.

23. Schulenberg, *The Keyboard Music of J. S. Bach*, 10.

24. Robert L. Marshall, "Johann Sebastian Bach," in *Eighteenth-Century Keyboard Music*, ed. Robert L. Marshall (New York: Schirmer Books, 1994), 70. Brass strings, per se, do not result in any particular sonority. In some fine Italian harpsichords brass strings sound anything but organlike: that is, the tone is relatively short-sustained and "stringy."

25. See Stauffer, "J. S. Bach's Harpsichords," 317–18.

26. See John Koster, "The Stringing and Pitches of Historical Clavichords," in *De clavicordio* (Proceedings of the International Clavichord Symposium, Magnano, 1993), ed. Bernard Brauchli, Susan Brauchli, and Alberto Galazzo (Turin: Istituto per i Beni Musicali in Piemonte, 1994), 225–44; and Koster, "Some Remarks on the Relationship between Organ and Stringed-Keyboard Instrument Making," in *Harpsichord and Early Piano Studies*, ed. Charles Mould (Hebden Bridge, West Yorkshire: Peacock Press, forthcoming).

27. See *Musica mechanica organoedi* 2:108–9, 135–38.

28. See Albert Cohen, "Jean Marius' *Clavecin brisé* and *Clavecin à maillets* Revisited: The 'Dossier Marius' at the Paris Academy of Sciences," *Journal of the American Musical Instrument Society* 13 (1987): 23–38.

29. Further discussion in Koster, "Some Remarks."

30. Friedrich Ernst, *Der Flügel Johann Sebastian Bachs* (Frankfurt am Main: Peters, 1955), 31.

31. Hubbard, *Three Centuries of Harpsichord Making*, 165–66.

32. See especially van der Meer, "Beiträge zur Cembalobau," and Henkel, "Der Cembalobau der Bach-Zeit."

33. Hubbard, *Three Centuries of Harpsichord Making*, 170–71.

34. See Günther Hellwig, *Joachim Tielke, ein hamburger Lauten- und Violenmacher der Barockzeit* (Frankfurt am Main: Verlag Das Musikinstrument, 1980).

35. See Stauffer, "J. S. Bach's Harpsichords," 317, and Herbert Heyde, *Musikinstrumentenbau in Preussen* (Tutzing: Hans Schneider, 1994), 29, 242.

36. This painting by Johannes Voorhout, 1674, now in the Museum für Hamburgische Geschichte, is analyzed in Christoph Wolff, "The Hamburg Group Portrait with Reinken and Buxtehude: An Essay in Musical Iconography," trans. Thomson Moore, in *Boston Early Music Festival & Exhibition* (program book, 1987), 102–12. Another example of a Flemish harpsichord in northern Germany is one by Joannes Ruckers, 1618 (now in the Kulturhistoriska Museet, Lund University, Lund, Sweden), which was rebuilt by Johann Christoph Fleischer in Hamburg in 1724; see Grant O'Brien, *Ruckers: A Harpsichord and Virginal Building Tradition* (Cambridge: Cambridge University Press, 1990), 246.

37. On the other hand, the "Ruckers" soundboard stucture, with a crescent-shaped area of free soundboard around the bridge, is already present in the fifteenth-century German upright harpsichord at the Royal College of Music in London.

38. See note 14.

39. This information was written in a contemporary hand in a copy of Johann Mattheson's *Das neu-eröffnete Orchestre* (Hamburg, 1713); see C. F. Weitzmann, *Geschichte des Clavierspiels und der Clavierliteratur*, 2d ed. (Stuttgart: J. G. Cotta, 1879), 252.

40. See, for example, an anonymous Parisian harpsichord of 1667, described in Koster, *Keyboard Musical Instruments in the Museum of Fine Arts, Boston*, 39–46.

41. This instrument is described by William Dowd in an appendix to Germann, "The Mietkes, the Margrave, and Bach," 144–47, and by Dieter Krickeberg and Horst Rase, "Beiträge zur Kenntnis des mittel- und norddeutschen Cembalobaus um 1700," in *Studia organologica: Festschrift für John Henry van der Meer zu seinem fünfundsechzigsten Geburtstag*, ed. Freidemann Hellwig (Tutzing: Hans Schneider, 1987), 294–302.

42. See Germann, "The Mietkes, the Margrave and Bach," 138.

43. Ibid., 120.

44. Hubbard, *Three Centuries of Harpsichord Making*, 185.

45. Ibid., 178–81.

46. Examples are a harpsichord by Johann Mayer, Salzburg, 1619, described in John Henry van der Meer, "Die Kielklaviere im Salzburger Museum Carolino Augusteum," *Salzburger Museum Carolino Augusteum Jahresschrift* 12–13 (1966–67): 83–87, and an anonymous harpsichord in the Hungarian National Museum, Budapest, described in György Gábry, *Alte Musikinstrumente*, trans. Irene Kolbe, 2d ed. (Budapest: Corvina, 1976), 37 and pl. 3.

47. For example, in an upright harpsichord at the Germanisches Nationalmuseum,

Nuremberg (Inv.-Nr. MIR 1080). I am grateful to John Henry van der Meer for the opportunity to examine this instrument, which is described in his "Beiträge zur Cembalobau im deutschen Sprachgebiet bis 1700," 112–14.

48. This instrument, described by van der Meer, ibid., 109–10, is in the Bayerisches Nationalmuseum, Munich, to the staff of which I am grateful for the opportunity to examine it. Recently, evidence suggesting that this instrument was made about 1630, not 1700 (as van der Meer thought) has been discovered by Andreas Beurmann and Sabine Klaus, to whom I am grateful for a private communication of this information.

49. See Hubbard, *Three Centuries of Harpsichord Making*, 171; Adlung, *Anleitung*, 555–56.

50. Ed. Darrel M. Berg in *C. P. E. Bach, Klaviersonaten: Auswahl*, 3 vols. (Munich: Henle, 1986), vol. 1, no. 8. My analysis of the instrument's resources differs in detail from those in Darrell Berg's commentary to her facsimile edition, *The Collected Works for Solo Keyboard by Carl Philipp Emanuel Bach, 1714–1788*, 6 vols. (New York: Garland, 1985), 3:xii, and in David Schulenberg's review of the latter in *Journal of the American Musicological Society* 40 (1987): 111–12.

51. See Koster, "Some Remarks."

52. As on standard eighteenth-century English two-manual harpsichords, it would be possible for the *Cornet* and *Spinet* to pluck the same set of strings and to be used simultaneously to yield an interesting sort of 8′ + 8′ tone. Only C. P. E. Bach's failure to use the buff stop on the *Spinet* suggests that this register had its own strings.

53. This instrument, in the Musikhistorisk Museum, Copenhagen, is described in Hubbard, *Three Centuries of Harpsichord Making*, 331–32.

54. "An Extraordinary Hass Harpsichord in Gothenburg," 95–101.

55. Adlung, *Anleitung*, 554.

56. Ibid., 555 (my translation). Adlung states (30) that the text of the *Anleitung* was completed by 1754; thus the work was written, at the latest, not long after Bach's death.

57. Adlung, *Musica mechanica organoedi* 2:110 (my translation).

58. Ibid., 2:137.

59. The description of the instrument in an advertisement in the *Leipziger Intelligenz-Blatt* of 19 April 1766 is quoted in Carl G. Anthon, "An Unusual Harpsichord," *Galpin Society Journal* 37 (1984): 115. Vogler's widow advertised, along with the harpsichord, her late husband's "complete collection of music by J. S. Bach and other famous musicians."

60. Stauffer, "J. S. Bach's Harpsichords," 299.

61. The original text of the advertisement in the *Leipziger Post-Zeitungen* of 23 October 1731 is quoted in Christian Ahrens, "Pantaleon Hebenstreit und die Frühgeschichte des Hammerklaviers," *Beiträge zur Musikwissenschaft* 29 (1987): 42.

62. See Herbert Heyde, "Der Instrumentenbau in Leipzig zur Zeit Johann Sebastian Bachs," in *300 Jahre Johann Sebastian Bach* (exhibition catalogue, Internationale Bachakademie, Staatsgalerie, Stuttgart, 1985; Tutzing: Hans Schneider, 1985), 76 (my translation).

63. See Ulrich Dähnert, *Der Orgel- und Instrumentenbauer Zacharias Hildebrandt* (Leipzig: Breitkopf & Härtel, 1962), 121.

64. In Adlung, *Musica mechanica organoedi* 2:139.

65. See Dähnert, *Der Orgel- und Instrumentenbauer*, 80.

66. These descriptions of the scalings and their tonal effects were specified in the original contract for the organ, signed by Silbermann in 1750; see Werner Müller, *Gottfried Silbermann, Persönlichkeit und Werk: Eine Dokumentation* (Leipzig: Deutscher Verlag für Musik, 1982), 462.

67. See, in favor of the instrument, Erwin Bodky, *The Interpretation of Bach's Keyboard Works* (Cambridge, Mass.: Harvard University Press, 1960), 31; contra, see Hubbard, *Three Centuries of Harpsichord Making*, 184, and Ralph Kirkpatrick, "Fifty Years of Harpsichord Playing," *Early Music* 11 (1983): 37. The "Bach harpsichord" in the Musikinstrumenten-Museum des Staatlichen Instituts für Musikforschung Preußischer Kulturbesitz, Berlin (Kat.-Nr. 316), once thought to have been owned by J. S. Bach (in fact, there is only a tenuous connection between the instrument and W. F. Bach), has been partially rehabilitated; see Dieter Krickeberg and Horst Rase, "Beiträge zur Kenntnis," and *Das Berliner "Bach-Cembalo": Ein Mythos und seine Folgen*, ed. Konstantin Restle and Susanne Aschenbrandt (exhibition catalog; Berlin: Musikinstrumenten-Museum des Staatlichen Instituts für Musikforschung Preußischer Kulturbesitz, 1995). Now attributed to Johann Heinrich Harrass (1665–1714) of Großbreitenbach (or to one of his sons), the instrument appears originally to have been made with a 16′ stop (not with a third set of 8′ strings, as Hubbard concluded, *Three Centuries of Harpsichord Making*, 331–33).

68. Although 8′, 8′ single-manual harpsichords (e.g., the Thuringian harpsichord in the Bachhaus, Eisenach, mentioned above) seem to have been familiar in eighteenth-century Germany, these might primarily have been intended for accompaniment, not necessarily to provide the ideal minimal resources for solo use.

STYLE AT BERLIN

Because of its contrapuntal style, some have questioned whether the Musical Offering was a fitting presentation for the Prussian king. The question is founded in part upon eighteenth-century anecdotal evidence, especially that of Charles Burney. Discussions of the Musical Offering have perpetuated the following assumptions: that Frederick's rigid and conservative taste was for simple, gallant music; that Frederick performed on his flute only such unimaginative music as was composed by his favorite composer, Quantz, and by himself; and that Quantz's music did not vary, and therefore musical taste at the Prussian court remained conservative and unchanging from about 1740 until Frederick's death in 1786.[2] From these points follows the seemingly reasonable conclusion that Frederick eschewed the music of innovative composers at court, disliking in particular the music of Carl Philipp Emanuel Bach.[3] This view fails, however, to acknowledge the paucity of scholarly work on and editions of the Berlin repertory. Most of the music Frederick performed or knew during his life, including the vast majority of works by Quantz—not to mention operas by Hasse and Graun—remains virtually unknown. Published examples often do not represent the best or most interesting works of a given composer. Numerous extant flutes owned and played by Frederick have also long awaited a comprehensive assessment. Thus the time-honored conclusions based on what we "know" about Frederick's taste and musical abilities are open to question.

Not all of Quantz's compositions in Frederick's catalogs are written in stereotyped galant idioms with homophonic textures, simple harmony, and balanced, symmetrical phrases. A closer examination reveals that the writing is much more varied and uses a wide range of textures, tonalities, and harmonic procedures that are at times quite unusual by eighteenth-century standards. Quantz's concertos and solo sonatas for Frederick contain examples of canon and fugue, as well as double fugue, in all of which the bass usually participates as an equal partner.[4] Quantz published a *Zirkelcanon* for two flutes or flute and violin as part of his *Sei Duetti* (Berlin, 1759), perhaps having been inspired by Bach's use of the form in the Musical Offering. Quantz's *Duetti* do not appear in Frederick's catalogs, but we have no reason to doubt that Frederick played them. Most of Quantz's fugues are written in the older strict style, using minor keys, alla breve notation, and large note values—the type stemming from the Italian and Viennese traditions inherited by his teacher Jan

Dismas Zelenka.[5] Quantz's subjects are often chromatic and, like the majority of his melodic head motives, usually outline a rising minor sixth. Others employ a descending diminished seventh; sometimes the two intervals are used together (as in ex.1*a*), a characteristic as well of the "royal theme." Additionally, Quantz's fugues regularly incorporate a chromatic fourth either as a strict countersubject, as in ex.1*b*—note here also the outlining of a minor sixth by the subject—and ex.1*c*, or at some point in vertical combination with the fugue subject.[6] The fugue in ex.1*c* is excerpted in Quantz's *Solfeggi* and was therefore used pedagogically in Berlin.[7] Also worth noting is that the countersubject of QV 5:36 (ex.1*b*) is identical to the countersubject of another C-minor fugue, one for organ by J. S. Bach, BWV 537, mm. 57ff. Quantz invariably uses countersubjects that appear alongside the subject from the outset—especially in the flute concertos that contain fugues.[8] Use of the chromatic fourth appears regularly outside of fugal compositions as well. The most extreme case is the first movement of a flute sonata played by Frederick (ex.1*d*) in which the main motive, a chromatic fourth, is heard continuously in twenty-nine of forty-two measures.

That Frederick and other young musicians of his generation (including Emanuel Bach, Schaffrath, and both Grauns) were influenced by compositional ideas that Quantz brought along with him from Dresden can be seen, for example, in his use of instrumental recitative.[9] The second movement of a Dresden flute concerto in G major (QV 5:173), incorporated after 1741 into Frederick's collection, alternates between passages marked *Recit.*, *Lento*, and *Andante*. A concerto in E♭ (QV 5:89), also in Frederick's collection and of Dresden origin, features a central recitative movement in C minor. Similarly, a sonata in C minor by Frederick, cited below for its reliance on a fugue theme by Quantz, also opens with a movement that alternates between designated recitative and arioso passages. Thus, twice in one composition Frederick paid homage to his esteemed tutor. A solo sonata by Quantz (QV 1:116) composed in Dresden also features a recitative movement (Lento) as well as a fugue movement. As is well known, Emanuel Bach made use of instrumental recitative in the first of the Prussian Sonatas for keyboard, published with a dedication to the king in 1742. Emanuel's keyboard concerto in C minor of 1753 (w.31; H.441) likewise contains a second movement that employs operatic recitative alternating with adagio passages, and W. F. Bach made use of a similar device

Ex. 1. *a.* Quantz, Trio Sonata in C Minor for Two Flutes and Basso Continuo, QV 2:3, mvt. 4, mm. 1–5 (flute 1 part only), from DL, Mus. 2470-Q-35; *b.* Quantz, Concerto in C Minor for Flute, Strings, and Basso Continuo, QV 5:36, mvt. 2, mm. 1–6 (violin 1 and viola parts only), from SBB (Haus 1), KH M. 3544; *c.* Quantz, Trio Sonata in G Minor for Flute, Violin, and Basso Continuo, QV 2:34, mvt. 2, mm. 47–56, from DL, Mus. 2470-Q-34; *d.* Quantz, Sonata for Flute and Basso Continuo, QV 1:71, mvt. 1, mm. 6–16, SBB (Haus 1), KH M. 4219 and SBB (Haus 2), Mus. ms. 18020.

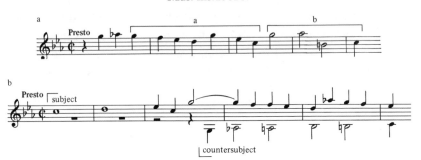

in his keyboard Fantasia F. 21, where dramatic recitative alternates with *furioso* passages. It is plausible that the Berlin taste for instrumental recitative derived from Quantz's music and not Emanuel's, as is commonly presumed.[10]

Frederick's musical education included studies in counterpoint that began with Gottlieb Heyne in 1718 and continued in 1726 with his Kapellmeister Carl Heinrich Graun, whom Friedrich Nicolai described as a strong contrapuntalist despite the composer's penchant for writing beautiful melodies.[11] According to Emanuel Bach, both Carl Heinrich Graun and his brother Johann Gottlieb were among the Berlin composers highly admired by Johann Sebastian Bach.[12] Frederick's training suggests that, although not adept at composing in learned forms of composition, he had not always been unfriendly toward counter-point.[13]

Quantz is not usually recognized as having composed strict counterpoint, but his solo sonatas and concertos as well as his trio sonatas contain genuine fugues.[14] Strict counterpoint continued to be cultivated by composers in midcentury Berlin and received extensive theoretical treatment by Wilhelm Friedrich Marpurg in his *Abhandlung von der Fuge* (1753). The source of Marpurg's one excerpt from Quantz can now be identified as the Trio Sonata in G Major for Flute, Violin, and Basso Continuo, QV 2:29, noted by Marpurg for its use of three-part canon.[15] Accounts of the music performed by Frederick generally discount trio sonatas as not being part of his repertory, as they survive mainly in Dresden manuscripts and were never included in the king's repertory catalogs. It is also assumed, based on these catalogs and late-eighteenth-century anecdotal evidence, that Frederick's musical diet did not include any repertory apart from solo sonatas and concertos of his own composition and those of Quantz. Frederick evidently played duets and trio sonatas, however, many of them in the learned style, by Quantz, the Grauns, Telemann, and others, both at Rheinsberg and during the early years in Berlin.

That Quantz and Frederick occasionally performed trios at court chamber concerts was testified to by the memoirist General Graf Isaak Franz Egmont von Chasot (1716–97).[16] The manuscript transmitted as Quantz's *Solfeggi* contains numerous examples from these kinds of pieces. The *Solfeggi* were probably begun and used as early as 1728, long before Frederick's catalogs were drawn up. Since the purpose of the catalogs, in which works were arranged according to a combination of key and order of composition, was ostensibly to serve as a rotational schedule of performances, the catalogs would not necessarily reflect pieces used pedagogically or those performed in more intimate or private settings. Two of J. G. Graun's compositions found their way into the catalogs, suggesting that other works were at hand.

Quantz, Frederick's tutor, remained an advocate of counterpoint in 1752, when he published the *Versuch*, insisting especially on its didactic merits.[17] Furthermore, eighteenth-century reports of the king's disposition toward counterpoint are not all negative. According to one source, "at the beginning of his reign [i.e., from 1740], the contrapuntal style was still not offensive to the king. The flute trios and quartets of Quantz, which he [Frederick] often played, especially in earlier times, are entirely in this taste. Among these the quartets are especially dry. Quantz's accompaniment in his concertos, and often the progression of his musical ideas, fundamentally originate from counterpoint, although with much diversity, naturalness, refinement, and beautiful song. Whoever, as did the king, heard such music daily, and also possessed a musical ear, could not be entirely ignorant of the principles of harmony."[18]

Ex. 2. *a.* J. S. Bach, *Ricercar a 3*, BWV 1079/1, mm. 1–9; *b.* Frederick the Great, Sonata in C Minor for Flute and Basso Continuo, mvt. 3, mm. 1–4 (flute part only), no. 2 in Philipp Spitta, ed., *Friedrich des Grossens Musicalische Werke* (Leipzig, 1889); *c.* Zelenka, *I penitenti al sepolchro del Redentore*, mvt. 1, mm. 24–32, from DL, Mus. 2358-D-73.

Christoph Wolff has called Frederick's "royal theme" (ex. 2*a*) a "deft and unprecedented" subject combining "two time-honored soggetto types."[19] The origin of this "royal theme" has been a favorite topic for speculation. Wolff suggests that Frederick may have been responsible for a "reduced form" of it, but he apparently rejects the hypothesis that someone at court might have advised him ahead of time. Frederick's only transmitted fugue, a weak composition forming the third movement of a flute sonata in C minor, has a subject that has been compared to the "royal theme" of the Musical Offering for its identical key and use of the descending diminished seventh (ex. 2*b*).[20] But a comparison of this subject with that of the C-minor fugue composed by Quantz (ex. 1*a*) demonstrates the striking resemblance that Frederick's subject bears to Quantz's fugue subject. Quantz's fugue forms the final movement of a four-movement trio for two flutes and basso continuo, QV 2:3 (composed in Dresden, most likely in the 1730s). This work was probably known to the king from his flute studies with Quantz during this period.[21] Frederick's fugue subject consists of two units, labeled here *a* and *b*, which correspond almost

85

note for note with those similarly labeled in Quantz's example. Quantz, while an oboist in Dresden, had studied counterpoint with Zelenka, whose C-minor trio sonata for two oboes and basso continuo might have served, in turn, as Quantz's model. The second movement of Zelenka's work is a C-minor fugue, whose subject features the descending chromatic fourth.[22]

Another of Zelenka's works, one that has not received attention in this context, may be of even greater import here. The oratorio *I penitenti al sepolchro del Redentore*, set in the appropriate key of C minor, opens with an Adagio scored for two flutes, two oboes, two violins, viola, and basso continuo. After the *pianissimo* ending of the mournful Adagio, there begins a fugue in C minor whose long, chromatic subject, played *unisono* by strings and continuo, contains the primary elements of the royal theme (see ex. 2c). Measure 3 resembles the royal theme in retrograde, followed by a sequential repetition of mm. 2–3. Measures 5–6 contain the descending chromatic fourth, identical in pitch and rhythm to the royal theme (Zelenka carefully marked "tenuto" under all chromatic portions of the subject, in stark contrast to the strokes or slurs above nonchromatic material). The chromatic fourth is followed by a lengthy and rhythmically complex tail (mm. 7–9) not unlike that of Bach's theme. The presence of the tail casts doubt on Wolff's "reduction" hypothesis: that the original form of the royal theme, as presented to Bach, ended simply with the chromatic fourth, and that Bach's version was an elaboration. Zelenka's autograph manuscript (DL Mus. 2358-D-73) is dated 29 March 1736 and was performed on Good Friday or Holy Saturday of that year, placing it well during the period when Quantz would have been one of the performers—the same year Sebastian Bach performed a recital at the Dresden Frauenkirche and received his official title in Dresden as court composer.[23]

If Frederick's theme was borrowed or, as is likely, based on a model, the source was probably the work of someone close to him. Not only did Quantz, who by this time had been a personal confidant of the king for nineteen years, hold by far the highest salary of all the court's instrumental musicians, but he also enjoyed privileges at court that would have made him the envy of any of his contemporaries.[24]

Neither the counterpoint of Bach's Trio Sonata nor the tonality, chromaticism, or remote key areas used—especially in the Andante in E♭ major—would have been unfamiliar to Frederick. Nor would he have found disturbing Bach's mixture of Baroque idioms and galant melodic motives.[25] That any of this

Ex. 3. Quantz, Sonata in G Minor for Flute and Basso Continuo, QV 1:114, mvt. 3, from SBB (Haus 1), KH M.4260: *a*. mm. 84–98; *b*. mm. 54–59.

would have displeased the king is predicated on the prevailing assumption that Quantz's "harmonies and melodies are innocuous, if not monotonous; and a single unchanging ideal is followed from year to year, from composition to composition—an ideal fostered and followed by his patron."[26] Remote keys and rapid harmonic modulation were in fact customary in certain movement types of Quantz's flute sonatas at Berlin, especially those that share the mournful affect of Bach's Trio Sonata. One of Quantz's earlier works for Frederick, a sonata in G minor, QV 1:114 (ex. 3), features passages not unlike that of the Andante from Bach's Trio Sonata, where the sigh motive undergoes lengthy sequencing and simultaneous rapid harmonic movement. Other sonatas for Frederick demonstrate the use of remote key areas; like the Andante of Bach's trio, the first movement of a sonata by Quantz also in E♭ (QV 1:52), labeled *Mesto*, moves through keys in the extreme flat direction, even touching on E♭ minor and the Neapolitan of B♭ minor (ex. 4). A sonata in C minor, QV 1:14 (ex. 5), opens again with a melancholy movement, labeled

Ex. 4. Quantz, Sonata in E♭ Major for Flute and Basso Continuo, QV 1:52, mvt. 1, mm. 65–70, from SBB (Haus 1), KH M. 4442.

Ex. 5. Quantz, Sonata in C Minor for Flute and Basso Continuo, QV 1:14, mvt. 1, mm. 1–16, from SBB (Haus 1), KH M. 4398.

Lamentabile. Notably, this sonata begins out of key, moving through a series of secondary dominants and postponing any perfect cadence in C minor until m. 66. The constantly shifting tonicizations pass through the remote key areas of B♭ minor, E♭ minor, and D♭ major (mm. 29–45).

Thus the tonalities and remote modulatory passages of the Trio Sonata in Bach's *Musical Offering*, with their corresponding cross-fingerings, present a style and level of difficulty for the flutist that was hardly unprecedented. Quantz regularly composed flute music for Frederick in keys with multiple flats and sharps; both sonatas and concertos in E♭ major and C minor are common, and most contain lengthy and difficult passagework in the related keys of F minor and A♭ major. An early Dresden sonata in F minor (QV 1:95) contains a slow binary movement in the unusual key of B♭ minor that modulates to Db major and back. Although the melodic gestures in the C Minor Sonata, QV 1:14 (ex. 5), are indeed "galant," that is, brief, symmetrical, and homophonic, Quantz's harmonic language is anything but simple and predictable, surpassing even what one encounters in the flute sonatas composed in Berlin by Carl Philipp Emanuel Bach. This, of course, challenges the notion that Frederick disliked Emanuel's flute music for its unconventional style and preferred Quantz's music because of its conventional simplicity.

J. S. Bach chose a mournful affect (*trauriger Affect*, as Quantz calls it) for his trio sonata. Far from being inappropriate in a chamber work for Frederick, this affect seems in fact to have been preferred by the king.[27] This is especially true of slow movements—if we are to judge by the high number of slow sonata and concerto movements by Quantz labeled *Lamentabile, Mesto, Con affetto mesto*, and so forth. These movements must have been effective in performance if it is true that Frederick was especially gifted at rendering sad, slow movements, often bringing his audience to tears.[28] The primacy of the mournful affect cultivated at Berlin is reflected in Quantz's *Versuch*, where he describes it in three separate chapters.[29] For such movements, Quantz, like Bach, not only introduces chromatic themes and harmony but reserves the keys (in order of frequency) of C minor, Eb major, and G minor, with one instance each of D minor and A major. Bach's trio employs Eb as the contrasting tonality for the internal slow movement; this is in keeping with Quantz's practice in the concertos for Frederick, where Eb is the tonality chosen most often for the slow inner movements of works in C minor, as is also the case in his trios. Conversely, in works set in Eb, C minor is the preferred contrasting key. These keys, along with the others mentioned above for the mournful slow movements, are also those used most frequently by Quantz for fugue. It is therefore probably not by chance that the archaic but traditional "royal theme" was presented in C minor, a key evidently associated at Berlin, at least in flute works, with fugue. Bach responded in kind by choosing for the Musical Offering a corresponding style and favorite affect for his trio sonata, setting it in what was, for Frederick, a familiar tonality, and employing its associated harmonic language.

THE INSTRUMENTS

If the repertory of Bach's dedicatee offers a new perspective on the Trio Sonata, we can learn even more about the precise instrumentation, temperament, and pitch standard of the latter by studying specific instruments played at Frederick's court. Performance at the Prussian court was a special circumstance, for which considerable organological and manuscript evidence survives. Frederick's frequent chamber soirées, as reported in various accounts, regularly featured himself as solo flutist accompanied by a contingent of strings and continuo. A total of four real parts was the norm early on (flute, violin I, violin II, basso continuo), five in the later period (flute, violin I, violin II, violetta, basso continuo), plus an occasional obbligato bassoon in the middle movements of concertos after 1763. The music performed at these concerts centered primarily on a flute repertory composed by Frederick himself and by Quantz, and as most of this repertory has survived we can glean from it much about Frederick's musical abilities as well as those of his instruments.

Bach's Trio Sonata was issued not in score but in parts designated for flute (*traversa*), violin, and "continuo," which were carefully laid out to avoid page turns during a movement.[30] From such a careful engraving of parts, it seems clear that Bach intended his trio sonata for performance, rather than for study, unlike the canons. Much discussion has arisen over the nature of Bach's clavier, and the case of the Musical Offering has been no exception. What is surprising is that discussions of the work have rarely given the flute more than a few passing remarks. In fact, the type of flute to be used in the piece deserves equal consideration. Because the scoring is indicated, the question of the type of flute might at first appear superfluous. But eighteenth-century flutes were as varied as the makers who built them, and modern descriptions of flutes owned by Frederick have been cursory or inaccurate. One author describes them as intolerable: "the crudity of the instruments which were available to Frederick is a real tribute to his aptitude and perseverance."[31] More recently, an article on Bach's flutes discredits the flutes that Quantz built for Frederick and rejects their appropriateness for the Musical Offering trio: "Though Quantz's flutes . . . were certainly used at Frederick's court after 1739 for the performance of his and Quantz's concertos . . . the rapid dynamic extremes, strongly accented appoggiaturas and agility between registers demanded by the more progressive style of music are hard to achieve on a Quantz flute; they are much more natural and effective on the newest instruments of the 1740s, which were quite probably at hand."[32] Yet a flutist well acquainted with Quantz's playing technique can execute such subtleties exceptionally well with Quantz's flutes. Quantz's highly variegated compositional style by no means excludes rapid dynamic extremes, strongly accented appoggiaturas, or agility between registers, and such traits occur already in his Dresden compositions before 1740.

Most of the flutes played by Frederick were two-keyed ebony flutes built by Quantz, who from 1726 had set out to improve the intonation of the instrument; all but two of those extant have been personally examined by the author (see table 1).[33] Quantz transformed flute design in numerous ways. At Berlin (about 1750) he divided the head joint by adding a tuning slide, which could accommodate variations in pitch level. However, Quantz's flutes differ most conspicuously from others of the time in that they have two keys for distinguishing the pitches of Eb and D♯, rather than a single Eb key (see pl. 1). Some fingering systems of Baroque flutes already employed enharmonic distinctions for other notes, with sharps sounding lower than flats,[34] but until Quantz's invention of 1726, the Eb and D♯ were compromised, as on the modern keyboard. String players probably also distinguished between sharps and flats, at least until the middle of the century.[35] Played in such a manner on a violin or flute, the chromaticism in the "royal theme" becomes anything but equal-tempered, and the assumption that the flute was challenged by such writing is easily refuted. Indeed, the chromaticism inherent in the theme, as well as in Bach's trio setting based on it, exploits this particular quality of Frederick's flute.

Quantz's invention has been dismissed by many as pedantry, since on the surface the distinction appears to be of limited use.[36] The new Dresden harpsichords of Gräbner did not have the split keys for D♯ and Eb, nor did the new Silbermann organs in Dresden. Split keys were common on earlier Italian organs and harpsichords, however, and older composers such as Zelenka may have been keen on the distinction in Dresden around 1725, when Quantz began thinking about flute design. In 1752 Quantz advised keyboard accompanists to hide the tempered subsemitones of their instruments in a middle or lower register, or to omit them entirely.[37] The two keys allow for an audible difference of twenty-two cents between Eb and D♯ (the human ear can hear distinctions of about four cents). Moreover, the additional key affects much more than simply two notes. The lower D♯ forms a relatively pure major third in B major, the dominant of E, in every octave within the compass of the instrument. Quantz's system also brings the otherwise troublesome perfect fifth from Eb to Bb into tune, as well as the normally too-wide major third from Eb to G and the too-narrow minor third from C to Eb. Apart from the added key,

TABLE 1. List of Frederick's flutes by (or attributed to) Quantz; those for which two entries are given include two head joints. Measurements (where known) are given in millimeters; complete sounding lengths (column **i**) are given only where the no.1 joint survives. For explanation of column headings, see below.

Present location and inventory number	a	b	c	d	e	f	g	h	i	j
Berlin, 5076, Musikinstrumentenmuseum des Staatlichen Instituts für Musikforschung, Preußischer Kulturbesitz	XVIII	–	5 (nos. 1–5)	113.05	40.0	188.1	139.5	110.0	590.65	10.0 × 8.8
				111.77	40.5	"	"	"	589.87	10.4 × 8.8
Berlin, Hz 1289, Kunstgewerbemuseum*	XVII	3837	1 (no.4)	110.85	41.4	–	140.3	110.8	–	9.9 × 8.6
same, with Sanssouci head joint and no.1 joint*	"			111.60	41.4	188.8	140.3	110.8	592.90	9.9 × 8.7
Halle, MS-577, Händel-Haus Instrumentenmuseum**	none	–	1? (no.1)	205.80	n.a.	201.0	197.0	125.5	729.30	10.4 × 9.3
Hamamatsu City Musical Instrument Museum (ex-Rosenbaum, not ex-Hohenzollern)	XV	–	5 (nos. 1–5)	111.15	40.1	189.0	139.0	109.8	589.05	9.9 × 8.9
				112.37	39.5	"	"	"	589.67	8.6 × 7.8
Hechingen, Burg Hohenzollern***	none	–	5? (nos. 1–3+)	108.65	40.4	–	139.0	101.7	–	9.9 × 8.8
Karlsruhe, private collection	III	–	5 (nos. 1–5)	112.32	40.15	188.1	140.3	190.74	590.61	9.4 × 8.5
				112.04	41.18	"	"	"	591.36	9.7 × 9.1
Leipzig, 1236n, Musikinstrumentenmuseum der Universität Leipzig†	IV	3838	5? (no.1?)	111.06	41.0	–	140.0	110.2	–	9.8 × 8.7
Paris, E.0614, Musée de Musique Instrumentale††	C.F.	–	1 (no.1)	159.52	n.a.	187.5	139.6	106.6	593.22	10.4 × 9.2
Potsdam, Schloß Sanssouci, Staatliche Schlößer und Gärten V 18†††	VI/XVII	3836	1 (no.1)	111.60	41.0	188.8	140.6	111.8	593.80	9.9 × 8.7

TABLE 1. (*continued*)

Present location and inventory number	a	b	c	d	e	f	g	h	i	j
Washington D.C., DCM 916, Library of Congress	XIII/II	–	5 (nos.1–6)††††	111.70	40.3	188.7	139.9	109.7	590.30	9.9 × 8.7
Lost, Berlin, ex-Hohenzollern Museum (amber flute, two gold keys)	1?	3841	3 (nos.1–3)	–	n.a.	–	–	–	–	–

Explanation of columns:

a. marking or opus number

b. inventory no. of the Hohenzollern Museum, Berlin, ca.1930; unpublished inventory held in the Neues Palais, Potsdam

c. original number of *corps de rechange*; those known or extant in parentheses

d. sounding length of head joint (distance from center of embouchure hole to end of head)

e. sounding length of tuning slide (measured when fully inserted)

f. sounding length of the long (no.1) upper middle joint (shoulder to shoulder), if extant

g. sounding length of lower middle joint

h. sounding length of foot joint

i. total sounding length (d + e + f + g + h)

j. embouchure size

*Currently with no.4 joint and lower middle joint from opus no. XVII; head joint, tuning slide, and foot joint unmarked.

**Alto flute attributed to Quantz; may have come from Frederick's collection. (See my forthcoming article, "Eine Quantz-Flöte in Halle? Zuordnung und Überlegungen zu Quantz als Flötenbauer" in *Scripta Artium*, Universität Leipzig)

***Unusually short, unmarked foot joint with only one key (original?); three unusually short upper middle joints marked 1–3; additional unmarked middle joint.

†All but foot joint unmarked.

††Copy after Quantz; perhaps by Christoph Freyer (?), who made flutes for Frederick's regiment after 1749; its provenance is uncertain.

†††Head joint and no.1 joint from opus no. XVII; foot joint from opus no. VI; tuning slide and lower middle joint unmarked.

††††Opus number II found on shortest joint (no.6), originally belonging to an earlier flute.

Plate 1. Flute of ebony and ivory, made by Johann Joachim Quantz for Frederick the Great, opus. no. XIII. The flute is part of the Dayton C. Miller Collection (inventory *916*) at the Library of Congress, Washington, D.C. It is displayed in its box of porcelain, painted with flowers and fruits, lined with pink velvet, and closed by a lock and key. In the lower portion of the box are four *corps de rechange*, while the vertically displayed upper tray holds (from top to bottom) the longest of the *corps de rechange*, the second longest, a head joint assembled with the tuning slide, and the right-hand middle joint assembled with the two-keyed foot joint. The long, curved key is used for D♯, the straight key for E♭. Photo courtesy of the Library of Congress, Music Division.

Quantz's extant flutes also feature a much lower, more stable F than on most other extant eighteenth-century flutes, providing a solid tonic for F major and F minor as well as a good subdominant in C major and C minor and a better scale overall in flat keys. The lower F is made possible by this tuning system's lower F♯, based on a purer major third to D.

Aside from the obvious advantages in navigating the C-minor tonality of Bach's Trio Sonata, the availability of a good F and a good E♭ is of great import in the Andante in E♭ major: a good F brings the dominant of E♭, B♭ major (as well as its parallel minor), into tune, allowing for a less perilous journey into the remote tonal regions exploited by Bach. The demands placed on the player with respect to intonation can be overcome on other flutes, but they are certainly more easily met by Quantz's design. In performing the trio, then, Frederick would not have had to struggle. Quantz's compositions suggest that both he and Frederick had flutes available to them that were capable of playing in keys not widely used for flute by other composers, and the extant instruments bear this out. Quantz advises beginners on the flute to learn to play in keys as remote as B♭ minor, even providing an *Anfangsstück* in that key.[38] Indeed, Quantz's flute music contains some of the most challenging passages, both technically and harmonically, found in the eighteenth-century flute literature. This not only demonstrates Frederick's own technical accomplishment and his ability to render Bach's trio, but it leads to the conclusion that Bach probably knew the flute for which he was writing the Musical Offering. Frederick's interest in technology probably made him proud to own such an unusual instrument; he commissioned over twenty of them.[39]

It may be that Johann Sebastian Bach had in mind such an instrument for another flute work as well: several sources for Bach's Flute Sonata in E Major, BWV 1035, bear inscriptions that connect that piece to Frederick's *Cammerdiener*, Michael Gabriel Fredersdorf (1708–58), and Bach's visit to Potsdam.[40] Fredersdorf had studied flute with his father, a *Stadtpfeifer* in Frankfurt. As Frederick's privy treasurer from 28 September 1740, Fredersdorf was responsible for remitting payment to Quantz for the king's flutes; he also acted as a liaison between Quantz and Frederick and kept flutes for Frederick while the latter was away at battle. Given the number of flutes that Quantz built for Frederick, it is probable that Fredersdorf had permission to play them, if not to own a similar instrument himself. BWV 1035, not unlike some of Quantz's sonatas, features a singing first movement and the *tierces coulées* favored in Berlin flute music, and it includes a siciliano—with canonic episodes—in C♯ minor. The tonality of this particular movement, which also modulates to F♯ minor, is far more unusual than the tonalities encountered by the flute in BWV 1079.

Not only do Quantz's flutes provide clues as to the intonation employed in Bach's trio and its suitability for performance at Berlin, but they also give us information about pitch and tone quality. The nine surviving flutes built by Quantz for Frederick show a remarkable degree of consistency in workmanship with regard to tuning, boring, materials, and general appearance. Archival evidence for instruments that have since disappeared or been destroyed further confirms this consistency. Quantz did not sign his instruments but rather engraved them with roman numerals to serve as opus numbers. Flutes with opus numbers from as early as II to as late as XVIII are extant and are all made from dense ebony (see table 1). They are significantly longer than other flutes, with thicker walls and a larger inner-bore dimension. A greater reduction (cone shape) of the bore yields a strong low register (especially d′, d♯′, and e′), while the wide undercutting of the blowhole on many of Quantz's head joints permits a good response in the high register, including f♯‴ and g‴; in other words, these flutes are especially capable of highlighting the large registral leaps encountered in the flute part of Bach's trio (e.g., second movement [Allegro], mm. 45ff.), and many of Quantz's own fast movements exploit this style of writing. As a result of their special design, these flutes not only produce a thicker, darker, and more powerful tone than other contemporary flutes—*dick, rund, [und] männlich,* as Quantz described it[41]—but they also were intended to play at a lower pitch.

The extant flutes all possessed at one time from five to six interchangeable middle pieces of varying length, giving the player some flexibility with regard to pitch (see pl. 2). The highest pitch at which most of the instruments will play is about a′ = 412–15 Hz; the lowest pitch, quite consistent among the surviving flutes, is about a′ = 385–87 Hz. This then represents the range available to Frederick: from low French chamber pitch up to what must have been Quantz's "German A pitch."[42] The flutes all play best at the lowest pitch, in terms of intonation and tone quality, and since Quantz used only a single reamer to construct the longest (lowest-sounding) joints, it seems beyond doubt that the instruments were intended to be played at the low chamber pitch whenever possible. The combined use of several shorter reamers for the shorter joints constitutes a compromise and is detrimental to the scale. For the end dimen-

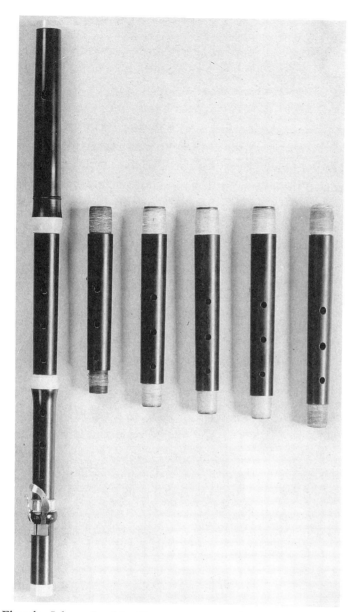

Plate 2. Flute by Johann Joachim Quantz, opus XIII, Dayton C. Miller Collection 916, Library of Congress, Washington, D.C. The flute is assembled with its no. 5 *corps de rechange*. The remaining, alternative *corps*, pictured from left to right, are nos. 6 (from opus II), 4, 3, 2, and 1. Each of the flute's original *corps*, from the shortest (no. 5) to longest (no. 1), produces an overall pitch five Herz lower than the previous. The longest, preferred, *corps* produces a pitch of ca. a′ = 387 Hz. Photo courtesy of the Library of Congress, Music Division.

sions of the joints to fit the remainder of the instrument, the bore must taper more rapidly than the ideal length of the longest joint. Signs of wear on these longer joints also seem to confirm that these were the ones most frequently used.[43] Since Quantz had begun constructing flutes already in Dresden, it is likely that Quantz established this pitch preference in Dresden; Bach might well have encountered such instruments prior to his trips to Berlin in the 1740s.

If the Musical Offering was performed at this low French chamber pitch, then what about the pitch of the keyboard instruments at Potsdam? We know that in December 1746 the Prussian court purchased a fortepiano by Gottfried Silbermann and that this was one of several in Frederick's collection.[44] A second fortepiano, discussed below, was purchased about the time of Bach's visit to Potsdam. The supposition that the *Ricercar a 3* from the Musical Offering was intended for fortepiano remains controversial,[45] but it is at least established that Frederick presented the "royal theme" to Bach on a fortepiano, probably one by Silbermann, on which Bach then improvised a three-part fugue. Whether or not the fortepiano was the instrument intended for the continuo part in the Trio Sonata of the Musical Offering, we should consider at what pitch keyboard instruments at court were tuned.

As is well known, the two court harpsichords now in Schloß Charlottenburg (possibly by Michael Mietke) have been altered and are thus problematical with regard to original scaling and pitch. In addition to fortepianos, Silbermann was paid by the court for a "Clavier" in June 1746. Three Silbermann fortepianos are extant today, two in Potsdam (one each in Frederick's palaces of Sanssouci and the Neues Palais) and one in the Germanisches National-museum in Nuremberg. The Sanssouci piano is dated 1746, and the one in the Neues Palais, undated, is probably the one purchased in 1747. The Nuremberg instrument is dated 1749. Two of these pianos (those in Nuremberg and the Neues Palais) feature transposers, that is, keyboards that slide to permit transposition—presumably for playing at both regular chamber pitch and low chamber pitch.[46] The "home" position of Silberman's keyboard (as indicated by the tuning pins, which are staggered into natural and accidental rows) is the upper position, presumably about $a' = 411$–15 Hz, which was the approximate pitch of Silbermann's organs in Dresden and the highest playing pitch of Quantz's flutes. Thus shifting the keyboard to the left would yield a pitch of about $a' = 385$–90 Hz.[47] This was possibly to accommodate other instruments used in Berlin and Potsdam, and it certainly would have accommodated the low pitch best suited to Frederick's flutes.

The unrestored piano in the Neues Palais provides striking evidence that this instrument was played primarily at the lower pitch: the grooves worn into the hammer heads' leathers correspond to wear caused by use of the keyboard manual in the lower position. The other Silbermann fortepiano with a transposing keyboard in Nuremberg also exhibits use mainly in the lower position.[48] What I believe to have been standard Berlin practice, that is, that keyboards were normally played at low *Kammerton* and were furnished with transposers to accommodate higher pitches when necessary, is supported by at least two contemporary accounts.

Jacob Adlung described the practice: "Usually they [harpsichords] are tuned to low chamber pitch, for the sake of flutes; but by shifting the keyboard it can be raised immediately a half tone and even a whole tone. . . . Transposition from low chamber pitch to the higher ones is even easier than on the clavichord."[49] Thus Adlung describes keyboards with single as well as double transposers. The reference to "higher" pitches suggests that flutes played at the lowest common form of pitch known to Adlung, that is, low French chamber pitch.

In 1786, in a discussion of Berlin manufacturers, Friedrich Nicolai described a royal keyboard produced by the Berlin maker Bauer. This instrument possessed a double transposer for playing at pitches one or two levels higher than *Kammerton*. Nicolai's description of its function is quite similar to Adlung's: "If one wants to play with wind instruments one or two [half] tones higher than *Kammerton*, one may change the pitch by a shift of the manual."[50] This fortepiano featured a double transposer and could thus accommodate three pitch levels, or the interval of a whole step. It was evidently intended to be played at the lowest of these pitches unless it was necessary to play with winds tuned to higher pitches.

From about 1763, in addition to the usual string complement, Frederick regularly performed concertos by Quantz with an obbligato bassoon in the central slow movements. In the outer movements the bassoon probably played as a ripieno bass instrument. This practice may account for a court purchase of a new low-pitch *basson* in 1774.[51] Whether or not this instrument was used for Frederick's chamber concerts, it seems that low *Kammerton* persisted throughout the eighteenth century in the Berlin circles in which Bach's as well as Quantz's music circulated.

Another Berlin keyboard instrument offers insights into the subject of pitch and performance practice in mid-eighteenth-century Berlin. Frederick's youngest sister, Princess Anna Amalia of Prussia (1723–87), received a house organ in 1755 for her personal use. Anna Amalia's enthusiasm for the instrument and her diligence in practicing on it are well documented by her letters. A report of 1783 indicates that the organ was tuned at chamber pitch.[52] The report does not specify which chamber pitch, but Anna Amalia offers a clue in a letter to her sister Wilhelmine: "The Gräfin Schwerin thought, naturally, that the organ is a little loud, but that its tone is charming. Please share this with my brothers. . . . The boys in the street did not stand there to listen, even though the balcony doors were open. That proves that the instrument does not have the usual power, as for a church. I want to practice so that I can accompany each of my brothers in a solo without losing a semitone in the bass."[53]

The curious statement about practicing her accompaniment for solos (presumably sonatas) may imply that the organ stood in the higher "German A-pitch" of around A = 412–15 Hz: if she were to accompany her brothers (including Frederick on the flute) at low chamber pitch, she would have needed to transpose downward by a semitone. As the lowest note on each of the organ's two manuals was C, Amalia would have needed to rework any bass line that descended below written C♯.

General Chasot, who witnessed Frederick's chamber music performances from 1734 onward, observed that the daily concerts in Potsdam "consisted of only a first and a second solo violin (seldom doubled), a viola, a violoncello, and as keyboard a fortepiano by Silbermann; one flute or two, when the king played trios with Quantz; one or two castrati; and from time to time . . . one of the best singers from the opera. One heard in the concerts only voices or flutes; all other instruments were there only for the accompaniment."[54] Both Silbermann pianos in Potsdam have what Stewart Pollens describes as "thick, woolly leather hammer coverings" that produce a sweet sound, as well as a mutation stop that produces "a bright, harpsichord-like" tonal quality; the sound of these pianos permits "discreet accompaniment for the Baroque flute or the human voice."[55]

From 1746, the date from which Frederick began owning Silbermann pianos, the latter may have been the preferred continuo instruments for his nightly chamber concerts. As the construction of Sanssouci was not finished until 1747 and the Neues Palais not yet begun, these concerts took place in the Stadt-schloß in Potsdam and in Schloß Charlottenburg. Flute manuscripts owned by Frederick from this period are labeled "pour Potsdam" or "pour Charlotten-bourg" accordingly. Archival documents from Frederick's payment accounts show that Quantz was responsible for the acquisition of numerous keyboards at court. At least one court fortepiano—acquired at the time of Bach's Potsdam visit—was purchased through Quantz. In May 1747 a payment of 373 talers, 12 groschen, was made "to the virtuoso Quantz for a Piano et Forte."[56] Frederick would have been keen to show off this brand-new acquisition; his enthusiasm might have been his motivation for presenting the royal theme on a fortepiano. Since the piano located in Sanssouci is dated 1746, the one purchased through Quantz is likely the undated, transposing instrument now held in the Neues Palais. Quantz's direct involvement in Frederick's major instrument purchases suggests that he controlled the nature of the court's keyboard instruments and was responsible for this instrument's transposing capabilities.

Indeed, Quantz's later Berlin sonatas seem to employ more numerous and varied dynamic indications, ranging from *pp* to *ff*, than do his earlier works. At least one flute concerto, QV 5:162, contains an obbligato continuo part des-ignated "Cimbalo, Piano e Forte."[57] Otherwise, figured continuo parts in the Berlin sources are routinely marked *Basso*. To judge from his remarks in the *Versuch*, Quantz clearly preferred the fortepiano as an accompaniment instru-ment.[58] Approximately half of his discussion of the duties of the keyboardist is concerned with dynamics, often with regard to portraying the various pas-sions (*Leidenschaften*) or to sensitivity in accompanying generally. By the 1740s Emanuel Bach, too, seems to have preferred the fortepiano and clavichord for providing "the best accompaniments in performances that require the most elegant taste."[59] J. S. Bach's Trio Sonata makes little use of explicit dynamic indications except in the Andante, where a fortepiano would be more effec-tive: numerous *piano* and *forte* indications occur, adding an echo effect to the perpetual dissonant "sigh" motives.

It is not known whether Quantz ever saw the trio sonata that Frederick re-ceived as part of Bach's Musical Offering. However, it may not be coincidental that Quantz's *Versuch* provides detailed explanation for more than a few of the difficult flute trills that Bach requires in the second movement (Allegro) of the Trio Sonata, many of which require special fingerings and techniques to be effective.[60] Could it be that Quantz was moved to address their difficulty after encountering them in Bach's trio? Quantz's special treatment of trills, especially with regard to their terminations, suggests, first of all, how important terminations were in performing trills; secondly, the level of virtuosity involved in Bach's flute part; and most importantly, that at least some players were equipped to tackle the difficulties presented by Bach's trio. There is little reason to doubt that Quantz was present at the time of Bach's visit; Quantz regularly presided over Frederick's chamber concerts, one of which immediately disbanded at Bach's arrival.[61] Given Bach's distribution of one hundred printed copies within fifteen months of its appearance and the great publicity accorded the event, it is likely that Quantz would have been curious about the work and had access to it.[62]

Johann Sebastian Bach appears to have been not only well informed about Frederick's musical tastes but also keenly aware of the special nature of his flute. Even if the elder Bach had not had the opportunity to hear this style of instrument on his trips to Dresden, where Quantz was employed before 1742, or on an earlier trip to Berlin, his son Emanuel Bach, one of Frederick's regular accompanists, would have known intimately the special qualities of the flutes that Quantz produced for Frederick and the character of music played on them. Emanuel Bach composed numerous sonatas for flute, both in Frankfurt an der Oder and at Berlin, as well as trios with flute and violin at Berlin and Potsdam in the 1740s. Having accompanied the king and probably Quantz and others at court, it is not hard to imagine that Emanuel would have related relevant information to his father, helping to ensure the special affinity of Bach's Trio Sonata with Frederick's instrument. Contrary to what has become the received wisdom about Bach's Musical Offering and its performance, musical and organological evidence confirm the extraordinary appropriateness of Bach's Trio Sonata while offering new insights into the performance of the work.[63]

NOTES

1. For reports of the work's origin, see BR, 176, 220, 260, and 305f.; BDOK 2:434-35.

2. See, e.g., Eugene Ernest Helm, *Music at the Court of Frederick the Great* (Norman: University of Oklahoma Press, 1960), 172: "The music of Quantz continued to please Frederick because it was unchanging"; Helm also speaks here of Quantz's "unconcern for counterpoint." Burney visited Potsdam in 1772, one year before Quantz's death; thus he gained his impression of Frederick during the nadir of musical life in Berlin. For a more recent perpetuation of such views, see Andrea Loewy, "Frederick

the Great: Flutist and Composer," *College Music Symposium* 30 (1992): 123–25. Charlotte Crockett, "The Berlin Flute Sonatas of Johann Joachim Quantz" (Ph.D. diss, University of Texas, 1982), did not have direct access to the majority of sources and thus does not acknowledge the breadth of style in Frederick's repertory over time.

3. Cf. Helm, *Music at the Court*, 175: "One of Emanuel [Bach]'s greatest disappointments was Frederick's failure to appreciate his compositions. Frederick, dedicated to the preservation of the cautious and correct aesthetic of Graun and Quantz, was repelled by the impetuous musical expressions of his cembalist. Burney suggests a further reason for Bach's neglect: 'his majesty having early attached himself to an instrument which, from its confined powers, has had less good music composed for it than any other in common use, was unwilling, perhaps, to encourage a boldness and variety in composition, in which his instrument would not allow him to participate.'"

4. Seven concertos from Frederick's repertory contain double fugues, i.e., with strictly recurring countersubjects. See Meike ten Brink, *Die Flötenkonzerte von Johann Joachim Quantz*, 2 vols. (Hildesheim: Georg Olms, 1995), 1:177–79. Warren Kirkendale, *Fuge und Fugato in der Kammermusik des Rokoko und der Klassik* (Tutzing: Hans Schneider, 1966), 126–27, incorrectly cites Quantz as having composed only fugues in which the bass does not participate: his example of the latter type, QV 2: ANH. 5, is a work of dubious attribution. Frederick's concert repertory is documented in thematic catalogs in which pieces were entered more or less in order of composition; see Horst Augsbach, *Thematisch-systematisches Verzeichnis der Werke von Johann Joachim Quantz* (Stuttgart: Carus, 1997), 270–87.

5. As Peter Williams notes in the preface to his edition, *Johann Sebastian Bach: Musicalisches Opfer* (London: Eulenburg, 1986), xxiv.

6. As in the second movement of QV 6:5, a Berlin concerto in G for two flutes (m. 65).

7. See Johann Joachim Quantz, *Solfeggi pour la Flute Traversiere avec l'enseignement. Par Monsr. Quantz*, ed. W. Michel and H. Teske (Winterthur: Amadeus, 1978), 68.

8. These concertos, although forming part of Frederick's collection, were most likely composed in Dresden and brought by Quantz to Berlin, as they are among the earliest concertos entered into Frederick's catalog. One of them, Concerto No. 59 (QV 6:3), exists in both Dresden and Berlin sources. Style attributes, together with the presence of Dresden scribal hands in these sources, seem to confirm this dating.

9. Jeanne Swack, "Quantz and the Sonata in E♭ Major for Flute and Cembalo, BWV 1031," *Early Music* 23 (1995): 31–53, has attempted to show that a few of Quantz's Dresden compositions were innovative and influential.

10. Helm, *Music at the Court*, 53 (following Philipp Spitta, ed., *Friedrich des Grossens*

Musicalische Werke, 3 vols. [Leipzig: Breitkopf & Härtel, 1889], 1:xii–xiii), maintains that Frederick's use of instrumental recitative was due to the influence of Emanuel Bach, who in turn had been inspired by Berlin opera. Other examples can be found in the music of J. C. F. Bach and Müthel.

11. Friedrich Nicolai, *Anekdoten von König Friedrich* II *von Preussen, und von einigen Personen, die um Ihn waren: Nebst Berichtigung einiger schon gedruckten Anekdoten*, vol. 3 (Berlin and Stettin, 1792), 253: "Dieser große Komponist war bekanntlich, obgleich der simpelste süsseste Gesang sein Hauptsache war, ein starker Kontrapunktist. Auch führte den König wieder einigermaßen auf den Kontrapunkt."

12. BDOK 3:288–90, and BR, 279: "In his last years he esteemed highly: Fux, Caldara, Händel, Kayser, Hasse, both Grauns, Telemann, Zelenka, Benda, and in general everything that was worthy of esteem in Berlin and Dresden." This statement makes it clear that J. S. Bach knew a great deal of Dresden and Berlin repertory.

13. It has been argued that Frederick forbade C. H. Graun to compose opera overtures in the French style because they contained fugal middle sections. Cf. Helm, *Music at the Court*, 144, and Michael Marissen, "The Theological Character of J. S. Bach's Musical Offering," in *Bach Studies 2*, ed. Daniel R. Melamed (Cambridge: Cambridge University Press, 1995), 91. But Frederick disliked French music in general, and French overtures were no longer in vogue; cf. Quantz: "The lot of the French with their overtures is almost the same as that of the Italians with their concertos. Since the overture produces such a good effect, however, it is a pity that it is no longer in vogue in Germany" (*Versuch einer Anweisung, die Flöte traversiere zu spielen* [Berlin, 1752], 18.42; trans. Edward R. Reilly as *On Playing the Flute*, 2d ed. [New York: Schirmer Books, 1985], 316).

14. See, for example, QV 2:3, QV 2:34, QV 2:42, QV 2:43, and QV 2: ANH.14.

15. Second mvt., mm. 60–72; DL, Mus. 2470-Q-6 (autograph score) and 2470-Q-7 (parts). See Friedrich Wilhelm Marpurg, *Abhandlung von der Fuge*, vol. 2 (Berlin: A. Haude & J. C. Spener, 1753), 12, and his table IV, fig. 3. Marpurg also quotes the "royal theme" from the *Ricercar a 3* in the Musical Offering, mm. 1–17, as an example of a chromatic fugue subject (see 1:79 and his table XII, fig. 5).

16. See ten Brink, *Die Flötenkonzerte*, 1:79 quoting Kurd von Schlözer; *General Graf Chasot: Zur Geschichte Friedrichs der Großen und seiner Zeit* (Berlin, 1878), 226–27.

17. Quantz, *Versuch*, 10.14; *On Playing the Flute*, 114.

18. Nicolai, *Anekdoten*, 253–54: "Dem Könige war auch im Anfang seiner Regierung der kontrapunktische Styl noch nicht zuwider. . . . Quantzens Flötentrios und Quatuors, die Er sonderlich in früheren Zeiten oft spielte, sind ganz in diesem Ge-

schmacke, und noch dazu die Quatuors ziemlich trocken. Quantzens Begleitung in seinen Koncerten, und oft die Fortschreitung seiner musikalischen Gedanken, entspringen im Grunde aus dem Kontrapunkte, obgleich mit vieler Mannigfaltigkeit, Ungezwungenheit, Feinheit, und schönem Gesange. Wer, wie der König, täglich solche Musik hörte, und dabey ein so seines musikalisches Ohr hatte, konnte wohl in den Grundsätzen der Harmonie nicht völlig unwissend seyn."

19. Christoph Wolff, "Apropos the Musical Offering: The Thema Regium and the Term Ricercar," in Wolff, *Bach: Essays on His Life and Music* (Cambridge, Mass.: Harvard University Press, 1991), 326.

20. Ibid., 325–26.

21. The vast majority of Quantz's trio sonatas, including QV 2:3, are preserved in Dresden manuscripts from the first half of the eighteenth century, held at the Sächsische Landesbibliothek (DL). Quantz states that from 1728 he set out to form a "personal style of composition" and that he departed Dresden for Berlin in December 1741; in 1728 Quantz also began his biannual trips to Berlin to teach Frederick lessons. See "Hrn. Johann Joachim Quanzens Lebenslauf, von ihm selbst entworfen," in Friedrich Wilhelm Marpurg's *Historische-kritische Beyträge zur Aufnahme der Musik*, 1 (1755; rpt., Amsterdam: Knuf, 1972): 197–250.

22. *Johann Dismas Zelenka: Sonata VI C-moll*, ed. Wolfgang Horn, Hortus Musicus 276 (Kassel: Bärenreiter, 1992).

23. See BDOK 2:388–90.

24. On Quantz's salary and privileges, see Helm, *Music at the Court*, 158–61. Jeanne Swack, "Quantz and the Sonata," 31–53, and Siegbert Rampe, "Bach, Quantz und das 'Musicalische Opfer,'" *Concerto* 10 (1993): 15–23, both attempt to link Quantz to Bach's trio through comparison with Quantz's trio QV 2:18. Both authors stress a comparison between the opening dotted theme of the second movement of Bach's Musical Offering trio and a theme in Quantz's first movement, but such motives are characteristic of numerous Berlin trios by, for example, the Grauns.

25. Marissen, "The Theological Character," 95–96, singles out the Andante of the Trio Sonata for its rapid motion "outside the ambitus to B♭ minor . . . and [later] E♭ minor," pointing to the "absurdly extended sequential passages of isolated appoggiaturas at mm. 20–8." Marissen finds this harmonic motion contradictory to "the galant melodic style."

26. Helm, *Music at the Court*, 167.

27. Marissen, "The Theological Character," 87, finds the "almost funereal" affect of the Musical Offering at odds with its presumed object of glorifying the king

and suggests that Frederick would have had little interest in studying or performing the work.

28. See the reports quoted by Helm, *Music at the Court*, 29–30.

29. Quantz, *Versuch*, 11.16, 14.6–8, and 17.2.17.

30. As pointed out by Peter Williams in the preface to his edition, *Johann Sebastian Bach: Musicalisches Opfer*, ix.

31. Helm, *Music at the Court*, 35. His chief source was an old pamphlet that reveals serious misunderstandings of eighteenth-century flutes and performance practice: Georg Müller, *Friedrich der Grosse: Seine Flöten und sein Flötenspiel* (Berlin: Parryhysius, 1932).

32. Ardal Powell with David Lasocki, "Bach and the Flute," *Early Music* 23 (1995): 18.

33. The flutes are documented in the following inventories: Michael Seyfrit, *Musical Instruments in the Dayton C. Miller Collection at the Library of Congress: A Catalog*, vol. 1, *Recorders, Fifes, and Simple System Flutes of One Key* (Washington, D.C.: Library of Congress, 1982), inventory no. 977, cat. no. 208, 210; *Kunstgewerbemuseum Berlin: Führer durch die Sammlungen* (Berlin: Staatliche Museen zu Berlin, 1988), inventory no. 1289, 101; Herbert Heyde, *Flöten: Musikinstrumenten-Museum der Karl-Marx-Universität Leipzig* (Leipzig: VEB Deutscher Verlag für Musik, 1978), 1:81; Berlin, Instrumentenmuseum, Preußischer Kulturbesitz, inventory no. 5076; Hamamatsu, Japan, instrument museum (unpublished photos and measurements kindly provided to me by Friedrich von Huene); Potsdam, Schloß Sanssouci (unpublished inventory); Hechingen, Burg Hohenzollern (no inventory no.); Karlsruhe, private collection (Ardal Powell kindly provided measured drawings). Additional information for both lost and surviving instruments is found in inventories (ca. 1930) from the former Hohenzollern Museum, Berlin (kindly made available to me by Thomas Kemper and Matthias Gärtner); see Mary Oleskiewicz, "A Museum, a World War, and a Rediscovery: Flutes by Quantz and Others from the Hohenzollern Museum," *Journal of the American Musical Instrument Society* 24 (1998): 107–45.

34. From as early as Jacques Hotteterre, *Principes de la flute traversière* (Amsterdam: Etienne Roger, 1707).

35. See, e.g., Patrizio Barbieri, "Violin Intonation: An Historical Survey," *Early Music* 19 (1991): 69–88, and John Hind Chestnut, "Mozart's Teaching of Intonation," *Journal of the American Musicological Society* 30 (1977): 254–71.

36. See, e.g., Dieter Krickeberg, "Studien zu Stimmung und Klang der Querflöte zwischen 1500 und 1850," *Jahrbuch des Staatlichen Instituts für Musikforschung Preus-*

sischer Kulturbesitz 1968, ed. Dagmar Droysen (Berlin: Walter de Gruyter, 1969), 99–118.

37. Quantz, *Versuch*, 17.6.20.

38. Ibid., 10.5. The *Anfangsstücke* (QV 1:177–8) are transmitted in Copenhagen, Det Kongelige Bibliotek, mu 6310.0860 (Gieddes samling 1:45) and are excerpted in the *Solfeggi*.

39. The total number is suggested by opus numbers (see table 1), extant receipts, and court records, none of which are complete. Receipts for flutes prior to 1747 are extant for December 1743 and March 1745; see Herbert Heyde, *Musikinstrumenten-bau in Preußen* (Tutzing: Hans Schneider, 1994), 29. Frederick's interest in technical innovation is evidenced by the elaborateness of the Berlin opera house, built in 1742, which had state-of-the-art acoustics and featured an in-house sprinkler system in case of fire.

40. NBA VI/3, KB, 22–24.

41. Quantz, *Versuch*, 4.3. Baroque flutes that feature, above all, an easily produced high range, such as copies of those by Rottenburgh, have thus become a common choice for performing Bach, but such flutes produce a light sound with correspondingly weak low notes.

42. Ibid., 17.7.7: "Ich will eben nicht die Parthey von dem ganz tiefen französischen Kammerton nehmen; *ob er gleich für die Flöte traversiere, den Hoboe, den Basson, und einige andere Instrumente der vortheilhafteste ist.* Ich halte deswegen den Deutschen sogennanten A-Kammerton, welcher eine kleine Terze tiefer ist, als der alte Chorten, für den besten" (italics added). Quantz recommends a compromise between the two extremes for general use, although this was clearly not his personal preference.

43. A number of the flutes listed in table 1 are still exant with their longest middle joint. These include those in Berlin, *5076*; Potsdam; Hamamatsu; Washington D.C., *916*; and Karlsruhe; and an alto flute, *MS-577*, in Halle.

44. See Stewart Pollens, *The Early Pianoforte* (Cambridge: Cambridge University Press, 1995).

45. Cf. Christoph Wolff, "Bach und das Fortepiano," in *Bach und die italienische Musik*, ed. Wolfgang Osthoff and Reinhard Wiesend (Venice: Centro Tedesco di Studi Veneziani, 1987), 197–209, and Williams, ed., *Johann Sebastian Bach: Musicalisches Opfer*, xii.

46. For descriptions of these fortepianos, see Pollens, *Early Pianoforte*, 175–84, and his table, 207. Silbermann received 200 talers for the "Clavier" (see Heyde, *Instrumentenbau in Preußen*, 29).

47. Communication from John Koster of the Shrine to Music Museum in Vermillion, S.D.

48. I would like to thank Barbara and Thomas Wolf for communicating this observation to me and for sharing their photos. Based on its close likeness to the Sanssouci piano, they suggest 1747 as the date for the one in the Neues Palais. They also generously provided photos showing the same evidence on the transposing Silbermann fortepiano in Nuremberg.

49. "Ordentlich stehen sie alle im tiefen Kammerton, um der Flöten willen; aber durch die Verrückung des Grifbrets kann man sie alsbald einen halben Ton erhöhen, auch wohl einen gantzen. . . . Die Transposition aus dem tiefen Kammerton in den Höhern ist noch leichter, als bey dem Clavichord" (Jakob Adlung, *Anleitung zu der musikalischen Gelahrtheit* [Erfurt, 1758], 570; translated in Bruce Haynes, "Pitch Standards in the Baroque and Classical Periods" [Ph.D. diss., University of Montreal, 1995], 227). Adlung also described an organ that played at both "low" and ordinary chamber pitch; see his *Musica mechanica organoedi*, ed. Johann Lorenz Albrecht (Berlin: F. W. Birnstiel, 1768), 260.

50. Friedrich Nicolai, "Beschreibung der Königliche Residenzstädte Berlin und Potsdam," in *Sämtliche Werke, Briefe, Dokumente*, vol. 8, part 1, ed. Ingeborg Spriewald (Berlin: Peter Lang, 1995), 404: "Wenn man mit blasenden Instrumenten, die einen oder zwey Töne höher sind als der Kammerton, spielen will, so kann man durch Schieben der Klaviatur den Ton verändern."

51. The account book entry reads: "Einen tieffen neuen Basson 65 Taler"; see Heyde, *Musikinstrumentenbau in Preußen*, 33.

52. "Dieses Werck ist auf Kammer Ton eingestimmt"; see Stefan Behrens and Uwe Pape, *Die Orgel der Prinzessin Anna Amalie von Preußen in der Kirche Zur frohen Botschaft in Berlin-Karlhorst* (Berlin: Pape, 1991), 12.

53. Letter dated 21 October 1755, in ibid., 13–14: "Die Gräfin Schwerin meinte, sie sei ein bißchen laut, was natürlich ist, aber der Ton ist charmant. Ich bitte sie, teilen Sie dies meinen Brüder mit. . . . Die Buben von der Straße sind nicht stehen geblieben um zu horschen, obwohl die Balkontüren offen waren, was beweist, daß dieses Instrument nicht die gewöhnliche Kraft hat wie für eine Kirche. Ich werde üben, daß ich jeden von meinen Brüdern in einem Solo begleiten kann, ohne daß ein Halbton von ihrem Bass verloren geht."

54. Quoted (in German translation from the original French) in ten Brink, *Die Flötenkonzerte* 1:79.

55. Pollens, *Early Pianoforte*, 182, 194.

56. Heyde, *Musikinstrumentenbau in Preußen*, 29. The payment for the Sanssouci instrument reads: "an dem Silbermann. vor Piano et Forte . . . 420 Thlr." The payment was made in December 1746. Heyde cites no additional payments for fortepianos. The king paid more than half this amount, 275 talers, for a Quantz flute.

57. A facsimile of the first page appears in Augsbach, *Thematisches Verzeichnis*, 294.

58. Quantz, *Versuch*, 17.6.17, trans. Reilly, *On Playing the Flute*, 259: "on a *pianoforte* everything required may be accomplished with the greatest convenience, for this instrument, of all those that are designated by the word keyboard, has the greatest number of qualities necessary for good accompaniment, and depends for its effect[iveness] only upon the player and his judgement. The same is true of a good clavichord with regard to playing, but not with regard to effect since it lacks the Fortissimo."

59. Carl Philipp Emanuel Bach, *Versuch über die wahre Art das Clavier zu spielen*, 2 vols. (Berlin, 1753–62), introduction to vol. 2; trans. William J. Mitchell as *Essay on the True Art of Playing Keyboard Instruments* (New York: Norton, 1949), 172. David Schulenberg, in his contribution to this volume, finds Emanuel Bach's music of the 1740s most idiomatic to the newer keyboard instruments.

60. Trills occur on twenty-three different notes, ranging from e♭' to e♭'''; all appear in Quantz's trill table, but fourteen are among those for which Quantz found it necessary to describe special fingerings and techniques for executing the trills and their terminations. Some of the most complex trills treated here include c" to d♭" with a termination (BWV 1079, mvt. 1, m. 43, described in *Versuch*, 9.12 and fig. 12); d♭" to e♭" (BWV 1079, mvt. 4, mm. 74, which requires a termination, described in *Versuch*, 9.12 and fig. 15); and d''' to e♭''' (BWV 1079, mvt. 2, mm. 19 and 132, described in *Versuch*, 9.10 and fig. 8), which is so troublesome that Quantz says it "should be used only in cases of necessity." Bach's trio makes frequent use of trills that require particular attention to tuning (see *Versuch*, 9.10, and figs. 5–9.). See also John Solum, "J. S. Bach's Trio Sonata from 'The Musical Offering': A Study in Trills?," in *Fluting and Dancing*, ed. David Lasocki (New York: McGinnis & Marx, 1992), 29–31.

61. BR, 305.

62. See J. S. Bach's letter to Johann Elias Bach, dated 6 October 1748 (BR, 182): "I cannot oblige you at present with the desired copy of the Prussian Fugue [from the Musical Offering], the edition having been exhausted just today, since I had only 100 printed, most of which were distributed *gratis* to good friends. But between now and the New Year's Fair I shall have some more printed."

63. A field and archival study permitting the author to examine the surviving flutes

Versions of Bach

Performing Practices in the Keyboard Works

David Schulenberg

My title is purposely ambiguous. It refers primarily to versions of Bach's music, not of Bach himself, although it is probably inevitable that ideas about what Bach was like or how he taught or played his works will to some degree enter into considerations of how we might perform them. By "keyboard works" I mean music played at one time or another on stringed keyboard instruments: harpsichord, clavichord, and fortepiano. By "versions" I have in mind three quite different things. First, there are the various compositional states in which Bach's works exist, or are thought to have existed. In addition, there may have been changes over the course of Bach's life in how he expected his music to be performed. Finally, it is clear that after Bach's death both the performing practices and the musical texts of his works continued to evolve, so that a work like the Chromatic Fantasy emerged as something very different—a new version, insofar as its sonorous and expressive qualities are concerned—in its late-eighteenth- and nineteenth-century guises.

BACH'S REVISIONS

Table 1 lists most of the keyboard works known to have undergone revision of one sort or another. It is not complete, and it omits the many works whose internal structure suggests that they underwent revision but whose sources provide no definite evidence for that. The most common types of revision, documented in nearly all of the major works, are, first, the addition or revision of signs for ornaments and articulation, and secondly, alterations of voice leading, minor melodic embellishment, and other changes of detail.[1] More radical types of alteration may have occurred frequently during the composing process, but such changes are rarely documented in the surviving material.

TABLE 1. J. S. Bach: Keyboard Works Surviving in Multiple Versions

BWV	Title	Form of revision*
772–801	Inventions and Sinfonias (all)	1, 3
	Inv., C	2
	Inv., c	5b
	Inv., E	5b
	Inv., e	2, 5a
	Inv., F	5a
	Inv., g	5a
	Inv., a	5a
	Inv., b	2
	Sinf., E♭	2
806–11	English Suites	1, 3
	Suite 1, A	1b (bourrée 2?), 5a (prelude), 6 (doubles 1–2)
	Suite 2, a	2 (sarabande)
	Suite 3, g	2 (sarabande), 5a (prelude)
	Suite 5, e	1b (courante)
812–17	French Suites	1, 3, 6
	Suite 2, c	1b (menuet 1?), 5a (allemande, courante), 6 (menuet 2)
	Suite 3, b	2 (sarabande), 6 (menuet 2)
	Suite 4, E♭	6 (prelude, menuet, gavotte 2)
	Suite 5, G	2 (sarabande), 6 (loure—deleted?)
818	Suite, a	1, 2 (sarabande), 3, 6 (double, menuet)
819	Suite, E♭	1, 3, 5b (allemande)
825–30	Partitas	1, 3 (especially Partitas 3, 6)
	Partita 3, a	5b (gigue?), 6 (scherzo)
	Partita 6, e	2 (sarabande), 5b (courante), 7 (gigue)
831	Ouverture in b	3, 7 (overture)
846–69	WTC, Part 1	1, 1b (prelude, d?), 2 (prelude, e), 3, 4 (preludes: c, D, d), 5a (preludes: C, c, C♯, c♯, D, d, G)
870–93	WTC, Part 2	1, 2 (fugue, G), 3, 5a (preludes: C, d, e; fugues: C, C♯, G, A♭), 6 (prelude, G), 7 (preludes: g?, b; fugue, b♭)

TABLE 1. *(continued)*

BWV	Title	Form of revision*
903	Chromatic Fantasy and Fugue, d	4 (fantasy)
912	Toccata, D	2 (adagios), 3, 7 (opening)
913	Toccata, d	2 (adagio), 3, 5a (fugue 1)
914	Toccata, e	5a (final fugue), 6
951	Fugue, b (Albinoni)	5a
957	Fughetta, G	3, 6 (final chorale)
971	Italian Concerto	3
988	Goldberg Variations	3
1079/2	Ricercar a 6	3
1080	Art of Fugue	3, 5a (Contrapuncti 1, 2, 3, 5, 10, 13; Augmentation Canon), 6, 7 (Contrap. 2?, 6; Aug. Canon)

*1—added or revised ornaments, articulation (1b)

2—added or revised embellishment

3—corrections and relatively small adjustments of compositional detail

4—insertion or revision of cadenzas

5—substantial compositional changes, revisions, or both, including (a) insertion of new material and (b) alteration of principal thematic material

6—addition, subtraction, or reordering of movements

7—rhythm or rhythmic notation altered

We may surmise, then, that Bach's keyboard pieces were initially notated in forms that still required the addition of ornaments and other performance signs, and in many cases minor alterations of compositional detail as well. In some works, more substantial alteration eventually followed. But other compositions, especially early ones that Bach passed over when assembling the famous collections, may never have undergone the complete process. These consequently may survive in states closer to their original drafts.

The picture is perhaps clearest in the French Suites, which the NBA prints in two versions: an early one preserved in a manuscript copy by Bach's student Johann Christoph Altnikol and a later version preserved in copies by other students.[2] The later version is designated in the NBA as the "ornamented" (*verzierte*) version, but this means only that the sources contain a greater number of ornament *signs*. Given the works' otherwise close imitation of the French keyboard style, it seems likely that Bach expected any performance of these works to include the idiomatic ornaments of the French harpsichord style. If so, it is historically inauthentic to play the earlier versions literally, in naked, unornamented form, simply because Bach had not yet entered all the ornaments into the text.[3]

Of course, Bach is famous for notating things that were normally left up to performers. But this does not mean that every ornament was specified in every piece. Bach's notational thoroughness, which seems to have been first mentioned in the famous polemical exchange between the critic Johann Adolph Scheibe and Bach's supporter Johann Abraham Birnbaum, must have applied primarily to finished works that were intended for public performance or dissemination.[4] The existence of numerous variant readings for ornament signs and other performance markings in his pupils' manuscript copies of many works suggests that Bach, or at least his students, allowed considerable leeway in the performance of such details.

Together with the evidence that Bach's revisions sometimes took the form of embellishment (see table 1), this may encourage more extensive ornamentation and embellishment of his music in performance than is usual today. But Bach seems to have left few keyboard pieces in which opportunities for significant embellishment were not eventually realized in notation. Apparent exceptions must be carefully scrutinized. For example, the B-minor prelude in Part 2 of the Well-Tempered Clavier contains a fermata at a point (m. 57) where one might wish to add a brief cadenza. Yet Bach had revised the movement at least once without seeing a need for any such elaboration.[5]

The care with which Bach selected embellishments for his works is evident from the sarabande of the E Minor Partita, perhaps the most heavily embellished movement in Bach's keyboard music. Although we do not possess an "original" unembellished form, we can at least examine the embellishment in two distinct versions. Both the nature of the decoration and its revision suggest that the embellishment can be understood as intensifying an essentially simple series of underlying progressions. Moreover, the embellishment plays a role in articulating not only the local harmonic motion but the structure of the movement as a whole, which resembles a simple sonata form.

The main theme can be understood as a few chords embellished through elaborate arpeggiation (ex. 1). Near the end of the movement this opening

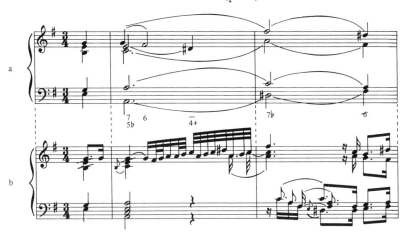

music is recapitulated in a somewhat differently embellished form; the passage leading into the recapitulation is embellished with particular vehemence, and it was this passage that was most heavily revised (ex. 2). The revisions were perhaps prompted by a compositional problem: the preceding passage comes to rest on a dominant chord with d♯″ in the upper voice (m. 28, second beat). But the main theme opens with a note that is separated from this d♯″ by the ungainly interval of a diminished fourth. This g″ in the top voice is then held over as a suspension, forming a seventh that resolves to f♯″.

The earlier version of the passage finesses the move from d♯″ to g″ with a sweeping scale through one and a half octaves (ex. 2*b*, m. 28). This version preserves the dotted rhythm on a repeated g″ as the first element of the recapitulated main theme, albeit in diminished note values and with the note g″ moved to the last half of the third beat. The revised version preserves the g″ in its original metrical position on the third beat, that is, as in the upbeat to m. 1; this is accomplished through the ascent of the upper voice from d♯″ through f♯″ on the second beat, as part of the embellishment of the dominant harmony that occupies beats 1 and 2. This version also enhances the unaccented (upbeat) character of the figure on the third beat by reversing the direction of the embellishment at that point; instead of beginning with an accented bass e′, the decorated arpeggio there now moves downward toward bass a on the following downbeat. The decoration of the 7 chord on that a is hardly altered, but the

Ex. 2. Partita No. 6 in E Minor, BWV 830, Sarabande, mm. 28–29: *a.* analysis;
b. earlier version (*Clavierbüchlein vor A. M. Bach*, 1725); *c.* final version.

suspended g″ now carries greater weight and therefore is likely to seem more expressive, the recapitulation stronger metrically.

POSSIBLE CHANGES IN BACH'S PERFORMANCE PRACTICES

Revisions like those shown in example 2 might well have arisen as consequences of initially unnotated changes in how Bach performed the passage. But even if they arose in improvisation, these changes were committed to paper only after careful forethought; this type of embellishment only seems impromptu. In any case, Bach's revisions here do not betoken a change in the underlying performing practice; both versions embellish the sarabande in the manner of an Italian adagio. Were there, however, more fundamental changes in how Bach played his music? Evidence for this might take the form of revisions that suggest substantially different ways of ornamenting, embellishing, or articulating notes, or changing intentions with regard to the instrumental medium and even the expressive character of particular works.

Unfortunately, Bach's students seem to have taken the same attitude toward his teaching that nineteenth-century editors took toward his works: Kirnberger, C. P. E. Bach, and others evidently saw in Bach's pedagogy one "true manner" (*wahre Art*) that was fixed and unvarying, at least in their redactions of it.[6] Even when reading between the lines, one can find little in their writings to suggest that Sebastian ever changed his approach to performance (or anything else), except of course during his early years, when he would have been discovering the principles later transmitted to his students.[7]

Thus we might expect to find the clearest evidence for such changes within the early works. And indeed some of the very earliest contain what would later appear as oddities, such as figured basses directing the realization of inner voices or repeat signs that cannot be honored without improvised adjustments to cover up discontinuities in the part writing.[8] Yet such things are as much indications of careless or incomplete compositional practice as of changing performance practice. They suggest that the young Bach took a relatively free approach toward notation, but we might have expected this during a period when the young composer had not yet acquired the habit of carefully notating his intentions in works prepared for publication or pedagogy. One would assume that his playing changed in the course of a career of almost half a century as a professional musician. Yet one can point only to occasional indications that his practice was not quite as consistent as his mature scores might suggest, or that younger musicians sometimes found his original notation difficult to interpret.

A favorite bone of contention in this regard has been the initial, dotted, section of the French overture in the harpsichord partita BWV 831. The work's published version, in B minor, introduced a number of revisions that have been interpreted as either an actual sharpening of the dotted rhythms of the earlier, C-minor, version, or merely a more precise way of notating the latter. Current consensus seems to be that the truth lies in some combination of these views,[9] but at any rate some alteration is apparent in performers' understanding of the notational convention, if not of the actual performance practice. Change in the latter is more clearly evident in the heavily embellished copy of the C-minor version preserved in a manuscript by Johann Gottlieb Preller, which points not only to a more ornamented performance but a considerably slower tempo than implied by the original notation.[10] Matthew Dirst, moreover, has pointed out an apparent shift in Bach's conception of the initial section of movements in French overture style from a rhythmic texture that accommodates contrapuntal motion in steady sixteenth notes—as is evident not only in BWV 831a but in works such as the C Major Orchestral Suite (BWV 1066)—to one characterized by *tirate* and "jerky" rhythms. This observation is consistent with a general pattern of sharpening rhythm and articulation and of increasingly vigorous, thoroughgoing dotting that is apparent over the hundred-year history of the genre. But to what degree Bach's understanding of the genre changed, and whether such a change can be dated to around 1730, seem open to question.[11]

Another problematic example occurs with the sarabande of the Sixth French Suite, which exists in versions distinguished by the very different ornament signs preserved in copies by two of Bach's students.[12] There is no way of determining which set of signs is the composer's, and both seem equally effective. A somewhat different case, although equally ambivalent, involves the Italian Concerto and the French Overture (Partita), which appeared together in Part 2 of the *Clavierübung* as pieces for two-manual harpsichord. The indications for changes of manual in both works are sometimes awkward to play, and they present some internal inconsistencies; they appear to have been afterthoughts, raising the possibility that Bach originally conceived the pieces for performance on a single-manual instrument.[13]

If Bach could add dynamic markings to these pieces in what was for him a fairly peremptory manner, perhaps he inserted changes of manual or registration in the performance of other works as well.[14] It is even conceivable that many of the early keyboard works—notably the *manualiter* toccatas—were originally written with the organ in mind but later came to be regarded primarily as "clavier" pieces, that is, works for stringed keyboard instruments. Evidence for this is sparse and ambivalent, however: for example, some ties in the early version of the D Major Toccata (BWV 912a) that suggest organ performance, additional virtuoso figuration in the later version (BWV 912) that might be more appropriate to the harpsichord.[15] But, whatever the instrument for which they were originally intended, the relatively early *manualiter* toccatas appear to have raised questions of interpretation for Bach's younger contemporaries, perhaps including his own students.

As no autograph sources survive, it is impossible to determine the authenticity of all the readings found in the manuscripts. But these sometimes give the impression of mid-eighteenth-century attempts to update music composed in what had already become an unfamiliar style. For example, a mildly chromatic passage in the D Major Toccata was rendered more conventional by the

Ex. 3. Well-Tempered Clavier, Prelude in F♯ Major, ʙᴡᴠ 882/1: *a*. m. 67; *b*. mm. 74–75.

elimination of several accidentals (mm. 61–62), and chord spacings and voice leading at several points were likewise brought into line with what appear to have been later notions of "correct" writing.[16] Moreover, a few details in the later version are reminiscent of several alterations of the text of the Chromatic Fantasy—discussed below—that were incorporated into nineteenth-century editions.[17] In addition, the early version of the toccata lacks many of the performance markings found in the later version—tempo marks, dynamics, a few ornament signs, and so-called cautionary accidentals—suggesting that freedoms of tempo and other (presumed) conventions of the Baroque *stylus fantasticus* had become unfamiliar before the end of the eighteenth century.

Since Bach is known to have added a few tempo indications to the generically similar preludes of the Well-Tempered Clavier and in free passages in other works,[18] it is conceivable that the markings in the toccatas possess similar authority. Yet, even if so, these markings provide evidence not of change in Bach's performing practice but rather of changing conditions of performance among his younger contemporaries. Similarly with another aspect of performance that was shifting during the eighteenth century: it seems unlikely that Sebastian Bach ever adopted the rules on the length of appoggiaturas given by Emanuel Bach in his *Essay*.[19] Although some of Sebastian's works employ the long appoggiaturas favored in the gallant style, these appoggiaturas seem always to be written out in regular notes; thus ex. 3*b* has a quarter note f♯′ on the second beat. Following the rules given by Emanuel Bach, the little note in m. 67 (ex. 3*a*) would also have been performed as a quarter note. But here as elsewhere Sebastian seems to have made a deliberate distinction between the two types of notation.[20] Indeed, Emanuel does not appear to have applied the rules to his own works prior to the issuance of the first volume of the *Versuch* in 1753.[21]

Ex. 4. English Suite No. 1 in A, Bourrée 1, mm. 1–4 (bass omitted): *a.* from early version, BWV 806a; *b.* from BWV 806.

But even if J. S. Bach remained consistent in his manner of performing appoggiaturas, he was not always consistent in his use of the signs indicating other ornaments. Thus a slanting line is used to mean both the measured breaking of a two-note chord and the insertion of an acciaccatura into a larger arpeggiated chord.[22] Conventions governing the notation of triplets and dotted rhythms also seem to be applied inconsistently or ambiguously in some instances.[23] But perhaps the most vexatious area involving inconsistent or ambiguous markings is that of articulation. For example, in an early version of the A Major English Suite, the steady eighth notes of the first bourrée are grouped consistently in pairs (ex. 4*a*), whereas most later copies give more varied articulation (ex. 4*b*).[24]

John Butt has demonstrated that, although some slurs sometimes appear to have been part of the essential (and first notated) motivic material of a given passage, Bach altered the slurring of other motives as they recurred through the course of a composition.[25] Nevertheless, each authentic slur in Bach's keyboard music, virtually without exception, can be understood as having the primary role of articulating a motive that arises as the embellishment of a single tone or chord. Different slurrings are possible, in effect, because the music permits multiple analyses.[26]

In the A-major bourrée, both sets of slurs are musically plausible. The two-note slurs in both versions represent simple neighbor motion. The four-note slurs of the later version represent, at one point (m. 4), a turn around one note (c♯″), and elsewhere arpeggiation of a third (g♯′/b′ or b′/d″) embellished by passing notes—what Kirnberger called an *accentuirte Brechung*.[27] The less homogeneous slurring of the later version can thus be attributed to more than a simple desire for variety; the melodic figuration varies from measure to measure, and the later slurs can be understood as reflecting greater insight not only into the varying motivic content of the surface but also into the underlying harmony or voice leading.

In short, Bach, upon reflection, might have performed this piece with articulation different from that taken for granted when it was first composed. But this remains a relatively minute element of performing practice. Although Butt has argued from certain markings in works of the 1720s and 1730s that the composer was then in the process of adopting "a new approach to articulation," he later qualifies this as an "*apparently* new approach."[28] Indeed, Bach's occasional use of relatively long slurs cannot offset the fact that articulation of all sorts is more thoroughly marked in later works (or in later versions). There may well have been a trend toward more flowing or legato keyboard playing in the course of the eighteenth century, but such changes in articulation as Bach specified in notation seem to have involved only the level of the most minute detail.

POSTHUMOUS CHANGES IN BACH PERFORMANCE

The same can hardly be said of the changes that Bach performance has undergone since his death. Changes are already evident in manuscript copies and early printed editions of Bach's music. Some may have arisen in connection with poor textual transmission or misunderstandings of Bach's notation. Often small in themselves, involving only the displacement of a slur or of a dynamic marking by a note or two, these errors nevertheless tended to favor the assimilation of performing practice in Bach's music to that of contemporary works. In so doing, these as well as other, more deliberate, changes in the interpretation of Bach's texts reflected developments in musical aesthetics that had been ongoing since the time of the works' composition.

Thus Preller's highly ornamented version of the overture of BWV 831a might reflect the same trend evident in what has been termed the mannerist style of C. P. E. and W. F. Bach and other midcentury German composers.[29] On the other hand, Johann Nicolaus Forkel, author of the first substantial Bach biography, supposed just a few decades later that the unembellished and often much shorter early versions of certain pieces were actually the final ones. By this reasoning, Bach not only had eliminated the cadenza-like codas and closing pedal points in the preludes in C, C minor, and others in Part 1 of the Well-Tempered Clavier but had also deleted the exquisitely embellished melody of the E-minor prelude.[30] Forkel printed these early versions as the principal text in his edition of the Well-Tempered Clavier; moreover, at least one other work, the D Minor Toccata, BWV 913, was issued at about the same time by the same publisher in a version that is distinctly simpler and presumably earlier than the one most familiar today.[31]

How could Forkel have regarded these early drafts as final versions "freed from all useless superfluities"?[32] Most likely his aesthetics colored his understanding of the philological evidence, despite his warm correspondence with Emanuel Bach and his contacts with Wilhelm Friedemann. Manuscripts as well as editions associated with Forkel consistently present texts of dubious authenticity, suggesting that Forkel frequently conflated his own opinions and performing practice with whatever he had learned from members of the Bach circle. Editions by Forkel's student Friedrich Conrad Griepenkerl, which the latter claimed to reflect the playing of Wilhelm Friedemann Bach, similarly contain poor texts as well as indications for ornaments, articulation, and other aspects of performance atypical of the first half of the eighteenth century.[33]

Nineteenth-century musicians already expressed their doubts about Forkel's dependability.[34] Yet Forkel has remained influential, particularly in his assertion that the clavichord was Bach's favorite keyboard instrument.[35] Moreover, Forkel evidently shared basic aesthetic positions with his Romantic contemporaries; his rejection of "useless superfluities" is reminiscent of the Romantic admiration for unaccompanied, unembellished Renaissance vocal polyphony.

Indeed, the Romantic distaste for Baroque complexity and rhetoric—including intense embellishment and complex articulation at the local level—can be seen as part of a trend that extended to all aspects of artistic life, including dance and other theatrical arts, where intricate and highly stylized Baroque types of movement were being replaced by what were thought to be more "natural" ones. The complex systems of short slurs characteristic of earlier instrumental music, rarely extending over a beat or a bar line, must have contributed to the impression of eighteenth-century keyboard playing as "choppy" (zerhackte), to use a term applied disparagingly in the early nineteenth century to music by C. P. E. Bach.[36] This impression would have been reinforced by an overly literal reading of eighteenth-century sources—not only musical scores, with their short or absent slurs, but also theoretical discussions, notably that of articulation in Emanuel Bach's *Versuch*. It is unclear whether C. P. E. Bach (and by extension, his father and other members of the Bach circle) really shortened unslurred notes by half their written value, and whether this necessarily leads to a choppy (as opposed to a clear and articulate) style. In any case, even Beethoven's slurs grew longer under editors such as Czerny.[37]

Thus the history of Bach's texts in later nineteenth-century editions resembles that of the Viennese Classical repertory. Not only popular or pedagogic editions were affected; when, for example, the English Suites appeared in 1863 in BG 13, edited by the pianist Franz Espagne, the latter apparently mistook certain appoggiatura signs for slurs and added further slurs in what he regarded as parallel passages (ex. 5).[38] The result was to introduce what Butt calls "cross-beat" slurs, whereas the original notation called for appoggiaturas or *ports de voix* that interrupt the smooth passage of the upper voice at the bar line.

The treatment of the slurs in ex. 5 recalls a type of alteration that occurred in the texts of some of Bach's cantatas. Robert Marshall has reported several instances of editorial tampering;[39] another likely instance occurs in Cantata 84, although the status of some stylistically anomalous slurs there remains uncertain.[40] At issue here are the little slurs from upbeat to downbeat in ex. 6 (mm. 0–1, 3–4, and 5–6), which, together with some of the other articulation signs present here, may represent unauthorized alterations to Bach's text.

Slurs of this type undeniably represent a version of Bach that was fully acceptable in the nineteenth century. Moreover, these short slurs are of a type common in the music of Haydn, Mozart, and Beethoven; this fact no doubt has continued to make them plausible to editors and performers to the present day. Most harpsichordists today, however, will regard these cross-beat slurs as contrary to what has come to be regarded as normal articulation in Baroque keyboard music. Bach assuredly did use such slurs, but only in exceptional instances (ex. 7). If genuine examples of such slurs occur in Bach's keyboard music, they are exceedingly rare. Their effect is to produce an agogic stress on the upbeat, a fixture of Classical and later styles; modern "historically informed" views of Bach interpretation, on the other hand, favor an agogic accent on practically every downbeat.

Although the readings of these little slurs are ostensibly a minor detail in the musical surface, the consistent adoption of one reading or another throughout a work will have a profound effect on the latter's character and rhythm — its *mouvement* or *Bewegung*, in eighteenth-century terms. Elimination of the regular agogic accentuation of the downbeat replaces a certain rhythmic formality — which has come to be understood as characteristic of Baroque in-

Ex. 5. English Suite No. 2 in A Minor, Prelude: *a.* mm. 55–57; *b.* mm. 70–72;
c. mm. 95–97. Top system: readings from NBA V/7; lower system:
readings from BG 13.

strumental music—with a nonchalance that is more typical of a later style.
Certainly the regular atomization of late-Baroque music into neatly ordered
metrical units starting on downbeats has become as important an element
of the rhythm and character of this music in modern performances as is the
proper "swing" in jazz.

Ex. 5. Continued

Ex. 6. Cantata *Ich bin vergnügt mit meinem Glücke*, BWV 84, aria, "Ich esse mit Freuden," mm. 1–11 (oboe part only).

Ex. 7. (a) Cantata *Süsser Trost, mein Jesus kommt*, BWV 151, aria, "In Jesu Demuth," mm. 1–5 (violin parts only). Main text: from original parts (SBB St 89); slurs added above: from autograph score (Coburg, Kunstsammlungen der Veste); slurs added beneath: from nonautograph second violin part (Coburg). From Butt, *Bach Interpretation*, ex. 39.

Within this performance tradition, the occasional cross-beat slurs that do occur in the music of Bach function as extraordinary, expressive exceptions to the rule. And if such was also the early-eighteenth-century tradition, then the minute slurs in ex. 5 represent a version of Bach that, at least at the local level, significantly assimilated the music to that of the mid-nineteenth century, when the edition appeared. An aspect of the music was rewritten, and with this came a distinct change in its expressive character.

Ex. 8. Chromatic Fantasy in D Minor, BWV 903/1: *a*. m. 30; *b*. mm. 74–77.
From Griepenkerl-Czerny edition.

Of all of Bach's keyboard works, the one that was most obviously affected by such a process was the Chromatic Fantasy. Griepenkerl's edition of this work (ex. 8) was followed by the now notorious one by Hans von Bülow.[41] Von Bülow's preface reveals that he accepted Griepenkerl's assertion that the numerous indications of dynamics, articulation, and embellishment in the latter's edition stemmed from W. F. Bach. Yet neither Sebastian's nor Friedemann's extant keyboard music contains anything like the variant figuration in ex. 8. The anticipation of the note bb'' at the end of the trill in m. 30 and the *prallende Doppelschläge* at the beginnings of the embellishments in m. 75 seem foreign to both composers' notation and use of ornaments. Still, something comparable to the little anticipatory notes found here occurs in two relatively early free fantasias of C. P. E. Bach, and at least this aspect of Griepen-

Ex. 9. C. P. E. Bach: Fantasia in E♭, H. 348.

kerl's version could therefore derive from an otherwise unattested Bach-circle practice in use at midcentury (ex. 9). Another seemingly anomalous figure, the Chopinesque chromatic scale in m. 76, in fact has approximate models in authentic works of J. S. Bach.[42] But the rhythmic displacement of the left-hand chords in mm. 76–78 seems antithetical to harpsichord style, in which full chords rarely accompany the resolutions of appoggiaturas.[43] And Bach's constantly varied arpeggio figuration on the even-numbered beats of mm. 75, 76, and 77 is replaced by new figures, of which four take essentially the same form. Although Griepenkerl might have had access, through Forkel, to some otherwise lost authentic version of the work, it is difficult to see his edition as anything other than an early-nineteenth-century revision of Bach.

Yet Romantic performance did not necessarily correspond to modern stereotypes, which tend to be based on what are actually the post-Romantic performance traditions of the earlier twentieth century. Griepenkerl, if not von Bülow, might have come somewhat closer to Bach's own performances in certain respects, such as the free substitution of one ornament for another and the use of what Teri Noel Towe characterizes as "relatively straightforward expression."[44] Even von Bülow, although seemingly far from Bach in many respects, may not have been any farther than we are.

Ex. 10. C. P. E. Bach, Sonata in G Minor, H. 47 (W. 65/17), mvt. 2, mm. 9–17.

CURRENT VERSIONS OF BACH

There exists more than one "version" of Bach today. Increasingly, however, the Bach of the late twentieth century has been one who played and composed for the harpsichord, to the exclusion of other stringed keyboard instruments. Still, the next generation of musicians, including Bach's sons and students, undoubtedly played most of their keyboard music—and his—on the newly available fortepianos and unfretted clavichords. C. P. E. Bach's works of the 1740s already evince an idiomatic clavichord or fortepiano style, most obviously in the occasional use of closely spaced dynamic markings. This music frequently seems to call as well for a more sustained, less articulate manner of playing than is now associated with the harpsichord. Certainly it is difficult to imagine a passage such as that shown in ex. 10, from a sonata composed in 1746, as being conceived with the harpsichord in mind.[45] Not only is the placement of the dynamic markings inappropriate to an instrument of fixed dynamic levels; in mm. 13–14 the music also seems to call for independent dynamic control over each note in each harmony as well as a sustained legato, both in order to give the principal melodic line (d″–c♯″–b′, g–f♯–e♮, etc.) a "singing" character apparently well suited to it. To be sure, this would not rule out the use of agogic accents as well (e.g., before the c♯″ on the downbeat of m. 12).

We might consider the possibility that by the 1740s, if not earlier, members of the Bach circle were at least sometimes playing keyboard instruments in a

Ex. 11. Goldberg Variations, BWV 988, var. 14, mm. 13–14.

way quite different from the cleanly articulate style to which many modern harpsichordists and organists have grown accustomed. Even Bach's own late works present occasional suggestions for the use of seemingly pianistic types of articulation. For instance, the dots in ex. 11 look very much like indications for accents, and a modern pianist will instinctively strike these notes with extra percussive force while making the surrounding notes relatively legato, perhaps even slurring them into the staccato notes in mm. 15–16. The work is explicitly for a two-manual harpsichord, on which performance in the manner described will not make the dotted notes sound any louder; if they seem accented, this is likely to stem from their registral isolation, not from any dynamic emphasis.

If Bach or members of the following generation employed a "pianistic" or "modern" keyboard technique not only here but in other contexts as well, then the crisply articulate style dependent on agogic accentuation that is currently favored by players of Bach's keyboard works might be a product of doubtful assumptions about historical performance practice—assumptions that have no doubt been influenced by current performance traditions and modern thinking about musical aesthetics. For instance, musicians today, unlike Bach and his students, frequently use his solo keyboard music for public performance, not solely for private study. Moreover, contemporary musicians, reflecting a modernist concern for clearly delineating musical structure, may place greater emphasis than did an eighteenth-century player on the clear projection of the meter (particularly in passages such as those shown in exx. 5–7). Articulate playing is often essential for conveying the meter to an audience when performing on a nondynamic keyboard instrument; hence, harpsichordists and organists may have arrived at a style of performance that is largely an artifact of current prejudices.

Still, there is reason to suppose that crisp, clear articulation of each beat was not atypical of Bach's practice. Most of his organ music and his harpsichord concertos were presumably composed for public presentation, yet their keyboard idiom does not differ fundamentally from that of his other keyboard works. In the concertos, however, the string parts—including the original solo violin parts of which the keyboard parts are transcriptions—employ slurs that tend to support the modern articulate style of performance, and there is further support in the evidence concerning eighteenth-century instrumental practice. For example, wind and string tutors of the period show that players of other instruments employed complex, highly rationalized systems of minute articulations, in which agogic emphasis of accented notes plays a crucial role. Still, although one might imagine that keyboard players adopted similar approaches to articulation, historical keyboard sources make no mention of them.[46] Moreover, even if we accept some version of this style as a historically attested norm, it does not follow that it applied in all works and in all passages. Evidence that Bach employed it is at best circumstantial, and there is no reason to think that he would have used any one practice throughout his career, or that his keyboard music requires the same. We in fact possess many versions of Bach—and so, in all likelihood, did he.

NOTES

1. I observe here a distinction between *ornaments*—small formulas that can be notated by signs—and *embellishments*, which involve more elaborate decoration that can be indicated only through actual written notes.

2. See NBA v/8. The NBA includes further versions of some of the French Suites: those from the *Clavierbüchlein vor Anna Magdalena Bach* (in NBA v/4), and alternate versions of Suites 3 and 4 (BWV 814a and 815a, in NBA v/8, Appendix).

3. Here I use the expression "historically inauthentic" to mean "not corresponding with a performing practice that can be demonstrated or inferred as being intended or employed by the composer and members of his immediate circle." Cf. my "Expression and Authenticity in the Harpsichord Music of J. S. Bach," *Journal of Musicology* 8 (1990): 464–66.

4. For Scheibe's criticism of Bach and the reply by Birnbaum, see BDOK 2:286–87, 296–306 (items 400 and 409); translation in BR, 238, 245–46. Birnbaum, citing several French composers as also indicating all ornaments, defends the practice as necessary in the absence of properly trained performers.

5. Emanuel Bach, whose B Minor Württemberg Sonata H.36 (W.49/6) pauses under a fermata in a very similar passage (mvt.1, m.64), likewise declined to fill in the

pause when he prepared an embellished version of the piece. The embellishments, catalogued separately under H.164 (W.68), can be consulted in Darrell Berg, ed., *The Collected Works for Solo Keyboard by Carl Philipp Emanuel Bach, 1714–1788* (New York: Garland, 1985), 6:161.

6. Carl Philipp Emanuel Bach, *Versuch über die wahre Art das Clavier zu spielen*, 2 vols. (Berlin, 1753–62), frequently appeals to his father as an authority; Johann Philipp Kirnberger claims to present J. S. Bach's pedagogy as the basis of his own in *Die wahren Grundsätze zum Gebrauch der Harmonie* (Berlin and Königsberg, 1773).

7. Thus C. P. E. Bach, *Versuch*, i.1.7, credits his father with devising a new approach to fingering; this evidently took place "in his youth" (*in seiner Jugend*), in response to a then ongoing "change in musical style" (*Veränderung mit dem musicalischen Geschmack*).

8. Figured bass: in the Capriccio BWV 992 and the Sonata BWV 967; problems at repeats: in the trio of the Ouverture BWV 820. See the discussions of these works in my *Keyboard Music of J. S. Bach* (New York: Schirmer Books, 1992).

9. Matthew Dirst, "Bach's French Overtures and the Politics of Overdotting," *Early Music* 25 (1997): 35, accepts this view, stated by the present author in *The Keyboard Music of J. S. Bach*, 305; Ido Abravaya, "A French Overture Revisited: Another Look at the Two Versions of BWV 831," *Early Music* 25 (1997): 47–61, reaches the same conclusion.

10. As I suggested in *The Keyboard of J. S. Bach*, 421, n.17, followed, with an extract from Preller's copy, by Dirst, "Bach's French Overtures," 39–40.

11. The dating of BWV 831a and other works is less certain than is suggested by Dirst's table of selected overture-style works ("Bach's French Overtures," 38). Dirst's table omits BWV 822, one of the earliest overtures attributed to Bach—it is characterized by *tirate* and "jerky" rhythms—as well as his last substantial movement in dotted overture style, Contrapunctus 6 *in stile francese* from the Art of Fugue, which employs running sixteenths in a number of passages.

12. The two copies are edited together in NBA v/8, as alternate texts for what is designated version B.

13. Further discussion in Schulenberg, *Keyboard Music*, 301–8. A previously unknown source that gives the first movement of the Italian Concerto in a substantially variant form appears to confirm the original absence of manual changes; see Kirsten Beißwenger, "An Early Version of the First Movement of the *Italian Concerto* BWV 971 from the Scholz Collection?" in *Bach Studies 2*, ed. Daniel R. Melamed (Cambridge: Cambridge University Press, 1995), 1–19.

14. Few other keyboard pieces, however, possess authentic dynamic markings, and there is no evidence that these were late additions. Examples include the gigue of the First English Suite and the Prelude in G♯ Minor from Part 2 of the Well-Tempered Clavier.

15. On the medium of the *manualiter* toccatas, see Robert Marshall, "Organ or 'Klavier'? Instrumental Prescriptions in the Sources of Bach's Keyboard Works," in *J. S. Bach as Organist: His Instruments, Music, and Performance Practices*, ed. George Stauffer and Ernest May (Bloomington: Indiana University Press, 1986), 212–39. On the Toccata in D, see also Schulenberg, *Keyboard Music*, 81–82.

16. For example, in mm. 16 and 40 the early version, BWV 912a, doubles the third of the chord on the second beat. See the edition by Robert Hill, *Keyboard Music from the Andreas Bach Book and the Möller Manuscript* (Cambridge, Mass.: Harvard University Press, 1991), 46–47 (this edition gives the tenor note on the third beat of m. 16 as a′; in the manuscript it is the third, c♯″). Hill, xxiv–xxv, suggests that the work was originally notated in tablature; evidence for this might be seen in the octave transpositions of notes in mm. 63 and 141 and in various readings suggesting uncertainty about accidentals, as well as in variants involving ties in mm. 1–6 and 83–84. If the later version indeed originated as a transcription of a tablature original, some new errors might have been introduced in the process, e.g., f♯′ for e′ in m. 175, a′ for g♯′ in m. 188, f𝄪″ for the first g♯′ in m. 226—although these could also have been intentional revisions.

17. See the revised scale figure at the end of m. 119, found in only a few late manuscripts, and the revised termination of the trill at the end of m. 121.

18. See, e.g., Christoph Wolff, "Text-Critical Comments on the Original Print of the Partitas," in *Johann Sebastian Bach: Essays on His Life and Music* (Cambridge, Mass.: Harvard University Press, 1991), 218.

19. Previously I suggested that Emanuel Bach's rules on the lengths of appoggiaturas did stem from his father's teaching; see my "Performing C. P. E. Bach: Some Open Questions," *Early Music* 16 (1988): 549.

20. For further examples, see Schulenberg, *Keyboard Music*, 157, 292–93. The small note in m. 67 is found only in copies; the autograph here has the sign for an *accent und trillo*.

21. The Prussian and Württemberg Sonatas (1740 and 1742, respectively), as well as many works preserved in manuscript, fail to employ many of the ornament signs and the precise values for *petites notes* recommended in the *Versuch*.

22. As in the First English Suite; see Schulenberg, *Keyboard Music*, 239–40.

23. Examples and further discussion in Schulenberg, *Keyboard Music*, 208–9, 218, 291.

24. Paired slurring occurs in version A of NBA v/7; many sources of version B, however, evidently continue to give the two-note slurring or do so inconsistently (see NBA v/7, KB, 120).

25. John Butt, *Bach Interpretation: Articulation Marks in Primary Sources of J. S. Bach* (Cambridge: Cambridge University Press, 1990), esp. 208.

26. For an early statement of this view of eighteenth-century slurs, see Heinrich Schenker, "Weg mit dem Phrasierungsbogen," in his *Das Meisterwerk in der Musik* (Munich: Drei Masken, 1925–26, 1930), 1:43–60.

27. Kirnberger, *Die Kunst des reinen Satzes*, vol. 1 (Berlin, 1771), 217.

28. Butt, *Bach Interpretation*, 166, 175, my emphasis.

29. The term is from Charles Rosen, "Bach and Handel," in *Keyboard Music*, ed. Denis Matthews (New York: Praeger, 1972), 105.

30. Johann Nicolaus Forkel, *Ueber Johann Sebastian Bachs Leben, Kunst und Kunstwerke* (Leipzig, 1802; facs. rpt., Frankfurt: Grahl, 1950), 55; translation in BR, 342.

31. The Leipzig firm of Kühnel and Hoffmeister—forerunner of Edition Peters—issued both Forkel's edition of the Well-Tempered Clavier and an edition of BWV 913 in 1801.

32. Forkel, 63 (BR, 348–49).

33. Beside the edition of the Chromatic Fantasy, discussed below, Griepenkerl published an edition of Friedemann's extraordinary twelve polonaises; both editions were claimed to present the Bach tradition as handed down to Griepenkerl through Forkel. The edition of the polonaises gives the first six in an early version; see Peter Wollny, "Studies in the Music of Wilhelm Friedemann Bach: Sources and Style" (Ph.D. diss., Harvard University, 1993), 205.

34. Carl Friedrich Zelter's sharply critical handwritten annotations are interleaved in his copy of Forkel's Bach biography, now in the Harvard University library; extracts in Hans-Joachim Schulze, "Johann Sebastian Bachs Konzertbearbeitungen nach Vivaldi und anderen: Studien- oder Auftragswerke?" *Deutsches Jahrbuch für Musikwissenschaft für 1973–1977* (Leipzig: Peters, 1978), 81. See also Franz Kroll's remarks (BG 14: 221) about the parallel octaves in Forkel's edition of the E Major Prelude of Part 1.

35. For the main arguments against Forkel's position, see the editorial footnote in BR, 311.

36. See George Barth, *The Pianist as Orator: Beethoven and the Transformation of Keyboard Style* (Ithaca, N.Y.: Cornell University Press, 1992), 41–45.

37. Ibid., 103–12. It is hard to believe that C. P. E. Bach meant the prescriptions in *Versuch* i.3.22 to be applied literally, but see Étienne Darbellay, "C. P. E. Bach's

Aesthetic as Reflected in His Notation," *C. P. E. Bach Studies*, ed. Stephen L. Clark (Oxford: Clarendon Press), 47–49.

38. The identity of the editor, not named in the volume, was established by Heinz Becker, "Ein unbekannter Herausgeber der Bach-Gesamtausgabe," *Die Musikforschung* 6 (1953): 356–57.

39. See Robert Marshall, " 'Editore traditore': Suspicious Performance Indications in the Bach Sources," in *The Music of Johann Sebastian Bach: The Sources, the Style, the Significance* (New York: Schirmer Books, 1989), 241–54. A "Postscript" (254) identifies performance markings in other Bach manuscripts as the work of Zelter—who was so scandalized by Forkel's misrepresentation of certain Bach works (see note 34 above).

40. Werner Neumann noted the peculiarity of certain markings but accepted them in his edition, as they occur in Bach's original performing parts (see NBA I/7, KB, 38). Butt, *Bach Interpretation*, 182, finds that certain of the slurs are "possibly not in Bach's hand," referring to the long slurs shown in mm. 8–10 of ex. 6. Such long slurs are unusual but by no means unknown in Bach's works; long slurs on what are essentially embellished arpeggiations of single chords occur elsewhere. Butt (183–84) gives further examples of this sort.

41. Lacking access to an exemplar of Griepenkerl's edition, I have used a copy of a reprint containing further alterations and annotations by Carl Czerny (Frankfurt: Peters, n.d.). Most of the dynamic markings in this edition are apparently Czerny's. Von Bülow's edition of Bach's works appeared at Berlin, 1859–65; the portion containing the Chromatic Fantasy and several other pieces is still available in reprints, e.g., that of G. Schirmer (New York, 1896).

42. Notably the Augmentation Canon from the Art of Fugue (mm. 15–16); also in the (probably authentic) keyboard arrangement of the Adagio from the C Major Violin Sonata (BWV 968, mm. 14, 32, etc.). On the fantasia illustrated in ex. 9, see Douglas A. Lee, "C. P. E. Bach and the Free Fantasia for Keyboard: Deutsche Staatsbibliothek Mus. Ms. Nichelmann 1N," in *C. P. E. Bach Studies*, ed. Stephen L. Clark (Oxford: Clarendon Press, 1988), 180.

43. Such chords make it difficult, on a nondynamic instrument, to give the impression that the resolution of the appoggiatura is softer than the appoggiatura itself. There is, of course, no certainty that the Chromatic Fantasy was written for harpsichord, although at least two eighteenth-century sources designate the medium as "cembalo" and one as "clavecin"; see the study of the sources by George Stauffer, " 'This fantasia . . . never had its like': On the Enigma and Chronology of Bach's

Chromatic Fantasia and Fugue in D Minor, BWV 903," in *Bach Studies*, ed. Don O. Franklin (Cambridge: Cambridge University Press), 160–82. For the quiet resolution of appoggiaturas, see C. P. E. Bach, *Versuch*, i.2.2.7.

44. Teri Noel Towe, "Present-Day Misconceptions about Bach Performance Practice in the Nineteenth Century: The Evidence of the Recordings," in *A Bach Tribute: Essays in Honor of William H. Scheide*, ed. Paul Brainard and Ray Robinson (Chapel Hill, N.C.: Hinshaw, 1993), 229.

45. Dates for C. P. E. Bach's works are given in the *Verzeichniß des musikalischen Nachlasses des verstorbenen Capellmeisters Carl Philipp Emanuel Bach* (Hamburg, 1790). This work may be one of several reportedly composed on a clavichord with a short octave, according to a much later letter from Emanuel Bach to Forkel; see *Carl Philipp Emanuel Bach Edition* 1/18 (Oxford: Oxford University Press, 1995): 110.

46. The information yielded by historical fingerings is, at best, ambiguous; for an example of the judicious application thereof, see Peter LeHuray, *Authenticity in Performance: Eighteenth-Century Case Studies* (Cambridge: Cambridge University Press, 1990), 8–12.

39. Praeludia et Fugen del Signor Johann Sebastian Bach?

The Langloz Manuscript, SBB Mus. ms. Bach P 296

William Renwick

Partimento fugue, a single-staff, figured-bass representation of keyboard fugue used as pedagogical material for thoroughbass accompaniment, improvisation, and composition, flourished in the decades around 1700.[1] SBB Mus. ms. Bach P 296, one of the largest extant Germanic collections of partimento fugues, is particularly intriguing because of its attribution to J. S. Bach. Despite its central position as a bridge between the theory and practice of figured bass and its possible connection to the Bach circle, P 296 has received scant critical attention.

Known as the Langloz manuscript after its scribe, P 296 is listed as item 22 in the preface to Schmieder's catalogue of Bach's works.[2] P 296 contains two sets of partimento compositions comprising sixty numbered items and seventy-five movements in all. Each set appears to consist of two gatherings of bifolios. Table 1 provides an inventory of the manuscript.

The cover of the 17 × 20.5 cm oblong octavo volume is marked *Bassi cifrati* in an unknown hand. The title page reads: "39. / PRAELUDIA *et* FUGEN / *del Signor* / Johann Sebastian Bach." In the lower right corner the same hand has inscribed: "Possessor / A. W. Langloz / ANNO 1763." According to Hans-Joachim Schulze, August Wilhelm Langloz (or Langlotz) (1745–1811) lived and worked in Erfurt and may have been a student of Bach's pupil Johann Christian Kittel (1732–1809).[3] The name Langloz has been stricken out, and a later "Possessor / J. C. Westphal" inscribed above. This would signify one of the two Hamburg organists and music publishers, Johann Christoph Westphal (1727–99) or, more likely, his son Johann Christian (1773–1828), sometimes also known as Johann Christoph.[4] To the left of these two is the notation

TABLE 1. Inventory of SBB Mus. ms. Bach P 296

page	item	length in measures
1	Fuga. 1. C. dur.	27
2–3	Fuga. 2. C. mol.	34
3	Fuga. 3. C. mol.	21
4–5	Fuga. 4. C. mol.	21
5	Fuga. 5. D. dur.	32
6	Fuga. 6. D. dur.	16
7	Fuga. 7. D. dur.	17
8–9	Fuga. 8. D. dur.	55
9	Fuga. 9. D. mol.	21
10–11	Fuga. 10. D. mol.	24
11	Fuga. 11. D. mol.	15
12–13	Fuga. 12. Dis. dur.	27
13	Fuga. 13. Dis. dur.	41
14	Fuga. 14. Dis. dur.	30
15	Fuga. 15. E. mol.	15
	Fuga. 16. E. dur.	20
16	Fuga. 17. E. dur.	29
17	Fuga. 18. E. mol.	49
18	Fuga. 19. F. dur.	16
18–19	Fuga. 20. F. dur.	66
20	Fuga. 21. F. dur.	22
21	Fuga. 22. F. dur.	29
22	Fuga. 23. F. dur.	24
23	Fuga. 24. G. mol.	17
24–25	Fuga. 25. F. mol.	43
	[no Fuga 26 appears]	
25	Fuga. 27. G. dur.	34
26–27	Fuga. 28. A. dur.	32
28–29	Fuga. 29. A. dur.	27
29	Fuga. 30. A. mol.	28
30	Fuga. 31. A. mol.	14
30–31	Fuga. 32. B. dur.	36
32	Fuga. 33. B. dur.	22

TABLE 1. (*continued*)

page	item	length in measures
33	Fuga. 34. B. dur.	20
34	Fuga. 35. B. dur.	20
34–35	Fuga. 36. H. mol.	34
36	Fuga. 37. H. mol.	19
36–37	Fuga. 38. H. mol.	22
38–39	Fuga. 39. H. mol.	59
40	Fuga. 40. H. mol.	
	[only the title and six blank staves appear]	
41	Praeludium et Fuga. 41. C. dur.	21
42–43	Praeludium et Fuga. 42. C. dur.	54
44–45	Fuga. 43. C. dur.	23
46–47	Praeludium et Fuga. 44. C. mol.	50
48–49	Praeludium et Fuga. 45. C. mol.	47
50–51	Praeludium et Fuga. 46. D. dur.	47
52–53	Praeludium et Fuga. 47. D. dur.	62
53	Praeludium et Fuga. 48. D. mol.	38
54–55	Praeludium et Fuga. 49. D. mol.	49
56–57	Praeludium et Fuga. 50. Dis. dur.	39
58–59	Praeludium et Fuga. 51. Dis. dur.	46
60–61	Praeludium et Fuga. 52. Dis. dur.	28
62–63	Praeludium et Fuga. 53. Dis. dur.	50
64–65	Praeludium et Fuga. 54. E. mol.	46
65	Praeludium 55. E. mol.	30
66–67	Praeludium et Fuga. 56. F. dur.	57
68–69	Fuga. 57. F. dur.	25
69	Aria	12
	[incipit: "Alles liebt und paart sich wieder"]	
70	Fuga. 58. F. dur.	21
71	Fuga. 59. F. dur.	22
72	Praeludium 60. G. dur.	35
73	Praeludium et Fuga. 61. G. dur.	32
74	Praeludium 62. A. mol.	25
75	[six compositional sketches]	4–12 each

"Voss / aus der Westphalschen / Auction," indicating that the manuscript was purchased by Graf von Voss-Buch in the 1830 auction of Westphal's Nachlass. "1326. Ad. No 4" in the lower left-center of the title page refers to the listing of this item in the auction catalogue. Graf von Voss-Buch (end of 18th cen.–mid-19th cen.) acquired much of Westphal's Bach *Nachlass* and developed what was to become the third largest collection of Bachiana to be acquired by the Staatsbibliothek zu Berlin, after those of Georg Polchau and the Singakademie. The Königliche Bibliothek, precursor of the SBB, obtained the Langloz manuscript in 1851 along with many others from the estate of Graf von Voss-Buch.[5]

Since the main body of the title page, the titles of the individual pieces, and the figures appear to be in a single hand, we can confidently identify the scribe as A. W. Langloz, and we can assume that he made the copy for his own purposes in 1763, probably while an eighteen-year-old student of Kittel in Erfurt. According to Yoshitake Kobayashi, no watermark appears.[6] The verso of the title page is blank, after which the music begins on the following recto. This and the following pages are numbered 1 through 75 in a later hand.

The majority of the pages have six staves; on the pages where seven staves appear (pp. 1, 5, 15, 25, 32, 52, and 53) all seven staves contain music, except on p. 1, where the seventh staff is blank. The layout is well planned, and only on pages 5 and 25 does a seventh stave appear to have been squeezed in at the bottom of the page. We can surmise that Langloz copied the layout of an earlier source, most likely in the possession of Kittel, page for page.

The first set of compositions, pages 1–40, contains thirty-eight fugues ordered according to an ascending series of the fifteen most familiar major and minor keys, from C major through B minor (see table 1). These pieces are numbered consecutively from 1 through 25 and 27 through 39—hence the number 39 on the title page.[7] Fuga 26 is missing. Of Fuga 40 appear only the title and the key indication *H mol* (B minor).

The second set of pieces (pp. 41–74) contains twenty-two works: fifteen preludes and fugues, three preludes, and four fugues, all numbered sequentially from 41 through 62 and arranged in an ascending sequence of only nine keys.[8] The less orderly nature of the second set and its omission of the higher keys G minor, A major, B♭ major, and B minor suggests that it is incomplete and may have been originally planned to include approximately thirty prelude-and-fugue pairs. Many of the preludes and fugues are arranged so as to span a verso and recto, as are several of the more lengthy independent fugues.

Page 75 contains six blank staves on which a later hand penned six short compositional drafts on a single theme for a treble melody instrument such as the violin.[9] The four blank staves at the bottom of page 69 were later used for an aria, "Alles liebt und paart sich wieder," seemingly in a different hand again.

The first set of pieces contains all of the white-key major and minor tonalities except B major, plus two flat keys, Bb major and Eb major, ordered for the most part in an ascending sequence of major and minor keys. The key sequence of the second set is an incomplete replica of that in the first set (see table 2). The selection of keys is identical to that found in Bach's Inventions and Sinfonias, and is also very similar to what Don Franklin identifies as the early-stage key schema for Part 2 of the Well-Tempered Clavier (WTC 2).[10] Other contemporaneous sources do not include exactly the same set of keys. Niedt's listing of keys in the *Musicalische Handleitung*, for example, omits Eb major, which was considered problematic on the organ, but includes both Bb minor and B major, although Niedt cautions against using the former on the organ. A priority for Niedt was the pairing of parallel major and minor for each key.[11] The key scheme represented in P 296 is entirely consistent with Bach's practice and with contemporaneous theory of the first decades of the eighteenth century.

Langloz, or the copyist or composer of his *Vorlage*, was careful to avoid page turns within pieces. Consideration of a page turn may account for an apparent reordering of Fugas 24 and 25 and may also have been a factor in the omission of Fuga 26. Fuga 24 is in G major and Fuga 25 is in F minor, breaking the established sequence of keys. Langloz may have reversed these pieces to accommodate the more lengthy Fuga 25 across a verso-recto pair and then used recto 23 for the next piece, the G major fugue.

The second set contains primarily *Praeludium et Fuga* combinations. These appear with considerable consistency from no. 41 through no. 54, following which the series concludes with isolated preludes and fugues and only two further prelude-and-fugue pairs, nos. 56 and 61, giving the impression of a score that was abandoned in an incomplete state.

Plate 1 illustrates some of the features of the Langloz manuscript. The piece shown also appears in Niedt's *Musicalische Handleitung*. The most obvious difference between the two versions is that in m. 21 the subject statement in the Langloz version is a fifth higher than Niedt's. Although this may be simply a scribal error of transposition, the result does make musical sense. The Langloz version also contains several small differences that could have arisen through

TABLE 2. Keys used in selected early-eighteenth-century works. To facilitate comparison, keys are listed from left to right in series of fifths from flats through sharps, with major and relative minor keys aligned vertically.

	G♭	D♭	A♭	E♭	B♭	F	C	G	D	A	E	B
Langloz manuscript, Set 1				E♭	B♭	F	C	G	D	A	E	
			f	c	g	d	a	e	b			
Langloz manuscript, Set 2				E♭		F	C	G	D			
				c		d	a	e				
Bach, Inventions and Sinfonias (ca. 1720)				E♭	B♭	F	C	G	D	A	E	
			f	c	g	d	a	e	b			
Bach's clavier and organ music, not including the Well-Tempered Clavier (the E♭ minor composition is the second minuet from the suite BWV 819)				E♭	B♭	F	C	G	D	A	E	
	e♭		f	c	g	d	a	e	b	f♯		
F. E. Niedt, *Musicalische Handleitung* vol. 1 (Hamburg, 1700) (Niedt cautions that B♭ minor sounds poor on organs)					B♭	F	C	G	D	A	E	B
		b♭	f	c	g	d	a	e	b			
Walther's *Musicalisches Lexicon* (Leipzig, 1732), *tabula* vii			A♭	E♭	B♭	F	C	G	D	A	E	B
	e♭		f	c	g	d	a	e	b			

error or intentional modification from Niedt's presumed original. The Langloz version incorporates eight 7–6 suspensions as against Niedt's three. These changes seem too systematic to be the haphazard work of a student copyist and more likely stem from some teacher's revision of Niedt's work.

Whereas the preludes are confined to the bass clef, except for two brief passages in Prelude 49, most of the fugues use soprano, alto, tenor, and bass clefs, just as continuo accompaniments to choral fugues do. Eight fugues include a

Plate 1. SBB Mus. ms. Bach P 296, No. 21. *FUGA. 22. F. dur.* By courtesy of the Staatsbibliothek zu Berlin–Preußischer Kulturbesitz, Musikabteilung.

treble clef in order to accommodate an extended range; all but one of these are in the first set. In none of the prelude-and-fugue pairs, and in no piece from no. 44 onward, does a treble clef appear. In some instances the word "Cant:," "Alt:," "Ten:," or "Bass:" appears in conjunction with a clef change. This practice occurs throughout Fuga 1, as if to establish a model, whereas in the majority of cases only one or two such indications appear.[12]

Fugas 14, 21, and 32 are set apart from the rest of the collection in that they use treble and bass clefs only. Two of these fugues are exceptional in other ways as well. The subject of Fuga 14 (see ex. 3*a* below) bears close rhythmic and intervalic relationships to the Fugue in G Minor from Part 1 of the Well-Tempered Clavier and to Fuga v in E♭ Major from Fischer's *Ariadne Musica* (1702). The imitative counterpoint of Fuga 14 is also rather more sophisticated than others in the manuscript: mm. 11–12 attempt a stretto at the octave, and m. 18 accommodates the subject above, since the countersubject occurs in the bass. Fuga 32 is unique in its adoption of a binary form with repeats and

Ex. 1. Selected incipits of fugues from SBB Mus. ms. Bach P 296: *a.* Fuga 32; *b.* Fuga 21; *c.* Fuga 20; *d.* Fuga 30; *e.* Fuga 37; *f.* Fuga 11; Buxtehude, Toccata in D Minor, BUXWV 155, mm. 29–30; *g.* Fuga 12; Bach, WTC 2, Fugue 16, mm 1–5.

projects something of a concerto style that is unusual in the collection. Each of the two parts of Fuga 32 uses a different subject (see ex. 1*a*); the second is very similar to the subjects of two of Handel's fugal partimenti.[13]

Errors in the manuscript include occasional missing notes, ties, and bar lines and, more frequently, missing figures or incorrect figure placement—to judge from the implied voice leading—and divergences between accidentals and key signatures. In plate 1, for instance, the final figure on the second line should appear on the penultimate eighth note, and the preceding figure should be 7. In m. 18 the first note of the lower part is missing, and in m. 24 the first figure should be on the first eighth note. Errors such as these occur throughout the work.

The fugue subjects may not be on the level of Bach's great fugue subjects, but they are by no means trifling either. Spitta's main argument against their authenticity, that "there is no single fugue theme which can be recognized as like anything of Bach's elsewhere, and the composition is so poor that I do not believe it to be by him,"[14] becomes weak indeed when these partimenti are seen in the context of other contemporaneous collections. The subjects of P 296 are more lengthy and complex than those found in the *Vorschriften und Grundsätze* attributed to Bach,[15] for example, or in the work of Bernardo Pasquini, and are entirely comparable with Handel's partimento subjects. Indeed, composed with pedagogical purposes in mind, partimento fugues predominantly contain commonplace motives rather than exceptional features.

Many of the subjects in P 296 have a repeated-note opening, as in Fuga 21 (ex. 1*b*). Longer ones such as Fuga 20 (ex. 1*c*) and Fuga 30 (ex. 1*d*) are often sequential. The subject of Fuga 37 (ex. 1*e*) is the only one that does not project a simple and immediately understandable tonal structure. Its initial ascent through the upper tetrachord of B natural minor suggests the Phrygian mode.

It is intriguing to try to link subjects of P 296 to other subjects in definitely attributable sources. The following represent some of the more compelling examples. The subject of Fuga 11 (ex. 1*f*) is similar to one of those in Buxtehude's Toccata in D Minor, BUXWV 155 (tenor, mm. 29–30), and the sequential subject of Fuga 12 (ex. 1*g*) is reminiscent of the underlying structure of the Fugue in G Minor, WTC 2. In addition, the latter fugue has the potential for invertible counterpoint at the tenth and the twelfth such as actually occurs in Bach's fugue. The subject of Fuga 17 resembles the C♯-major subject in WTC 2 (see ex. 3*b* below). Fuga 25 (see ex. 6 below) bears comparison with the middle section of the C-minor organ fugue BWV 537/2 (mm. 56ff.) as well as Pachelbel's Ricercar in C Minor. The subject of no. 42 resembles that of Bach's G-major organ fugue BWV 541/2, and the head of the fugue subject of no. 48 is the same as that of the Art of Fugue, as Schmieder has noted.[16] Despite these many resemblances, the propensity of composers to borrow subjects from one another during this period prevents us from inferring any definite attributions on this basis. Rather, these connections locate P 296 within a broadly conceived school of German and perhaps Thuringian fugal practice.

Although the great majority of the fugues contain opening expositions of four entries in the descending order soprano, alto, tenor, and bass, other patterns occasionally appear. Several fugues have five entries in the opening exposition, providing the formal structure subject-answer-subject-answer-subject (Fugas 1, 4, 8, 18, 39, 43). Only a handful of fugues begin with the alto (Fugas 7, 14, 21, 22 and 59). Fuga 7 (D major) appears to have only three entries, but it can accommodate a tenor entry in the realization immediately after the bass entry. In Fuga 21, only three entries appear in the opening exposition. Fuga 38 is the only one in which the opening exposition begins in the bass, marked *tasto solo*.

Partimento fugues can accommodate considerable freedom in their realization as to number of parts, complexity of texture, and degree of motivic imitation. The uppermost part in particular can be in a simple accompanimental style as might be done in the case of an accompanied choral fugue, or it can be elaborated into a more coherent voice with a well-developed contour. Example 2 illustrates one possible realization of Fuga 1 in which the added parts, for the most part in slower note values, join with the original to constitute simple yet genuinely contrapuntal four-part music.[17] The realized upper parts provide faster motion only where the given bass contains long notes, in mm. 12, 21, and 26. However, maintenance of strict four-part texture is by no means obligatory in this repertoire. Extensive use can be made of both three-part realization and fuller harmonies. Frequently the beginning of an upper-voice subject entry occurs simultaneously with a cadence in the bass, creating an elision. Typically in these cases the first few notes of the subject are not notated in the original, in order to accommodate the notated bass part. In ex. 2 this occurs at m. 13. (Fuga 32, shown in ex. 5b, contains a more extensive overlap at m. 28.) Because the bass in mm. 23–24 is essentially the same as the cantus of mm. 2–3, the suggested realization takes the opportunity to include an answer in invertible counterpoint in the cantus.

Example 2 is also representative of the way in which simple sequential episodes contribute to the clear expression of form in the fugues of P 296. Here the contrasting episodes delineate the tonal and formal divisions of the fugue in the simplest possible manner. Other fugues in P 296 contain episodes that are based directly on motives of the subject.

Although Fuga 1 is one of the simpler pieces in P 296, it nevertheless serves

Ex. 2. Fuga 1 from sbb Mus. ms. Bach p 296 (author's realization in small notes).

as an example of the collection's clear and well thought-out compositional method, with its decisive sequences and cadences and well-timed subject entries. P 296 as a whole is replete with a fine variety of styles and textures, yet it never strays from its focus on a traditional keyboard style. It thus emphasizes standard figuration and passagework, rather than exceptional or original ideas. But this characteristic, which Spitta and Schmieder have interpreted as a shortcoming of the work, is in fact its strength, for the ability to use standard figuration and textures is much more important for the development of a fluent improvisational ability than is the cultivation of unique qualities.

The average length of the fugues in P 296 is twenty-five to thirty measures. The shortest fugue, no. 41, is only thirteen measures in length, and the longest, no. 39—the concluding piece of the first set—occupies fifty-nine measures of common time. The most basic form which these fugues exhibit is an exposition of four entries (SATB) followed by a modulation and cadence on a closely related key, such as V (major keys) or III (minor keys), and a pair of additional entries in the order SB, continuing to a formal cadence on I at the end. Fugues 6, 11, 15, 16, 19, 31, 47, 50, 56, and 61 follow this plan precisely. This structure is sometimes expanded to accommodate additional entries, larger groups of entries (such as ASB or ATB), or more groups of entries, and perhaps a modulation and cadence in another related key. More elaborate fugues, such as Fuga 17,

Ex. 3. Selected design elements: *a.* Fuga 14, mm. 1–4, 18–19; *b.* Fuga 28, mm. 17–21; *c.* Fuga 17, mm. 21–24.

include additional complete sets of entries. Fuga 28 presents a rising series of entries (BTAS) in mm. 17–21—unusual among partimento fugues, where descending series are the norm (see ex. 3*b*). Stretto groupings are occasionally found, as in Fuga 17 (see ex. 3*c*), Fuga 21, and Fuga 30.

Subject statements occur only at the tonic and dominant levels throughout the fugues, with exceptions in only six fugues, all contained in the first set. In these cases additional subject entries occur in closely related keys, defining secondary harmonic areas. There are no plagal answers of the type that one frequently finds in Pasquini's work, for example.

Prelude-and-fugue pairs always share the same meter, and the similarity of their rhythmic values suggests that in performance these pairs should maintain a single tempo. In addition, in some instances prelude and fugue share motivic elements. The fugue subject of no. 41, for example, incorporates the eighth-note figure of its prelude, whereas in Fuga 44 the fugue subject uses the first four notes of its prelude (see ex. 4). Fuga 39, the final one in the first set, changes meter at the halfway point from common time to $\frac{6}{8}$ and continues with a rhythmically altered form of the subject, in the manner of the praeludia and toccatas of Buxtehude.

Ex. 4. Selected incipits of prelude-fugue pairs: *a.* no. 41; *b.* no. 44.

Ex. 5. Improvised accompaniment of upper part(s) (author's realization in small
notes): *a.* Fuga 27, mm. 17–22; *b.* Fuga 32, mm. 28–32.

In three or four treble passages of P 296, the addition of a simple accompaniment in a lower part seems warranted, even though none is indicated within the partimento score. One such example is notated in Fuga 4, where on two occasions block chords accompany a treble statement of the theme. Example 5 illustrates two other instances that invite the creative performer to respond to the context with imagination.

A most interesting facet of this manuscript is its frequent use of invertible counterpoint, whether actual or implied.[18] The combination of subject and countersubject that arises with the entry of the second part is often written in invertible counterpoint. Occasionally such a counterpoint is indicated at subsequent locations through figures such as 3 or 8, which would otherwise be superfluous. Invertible counterpoint is explicit in the subject-countersubject patterns of twelve fugues, in the stretto opening of Fuga 38, and in the episodes of three other fugues. Nine other fugues have a potential for invertible counterpoint that is never realized, as the countersubject never appears in the lowest-sounding part. Five other fugues imply but do not demand invertible counterpoint. Thus, fully thirty of the fifty-eight fugues include some form of invertible counterpoint.

Ex. 6. Fuga 25 in F Minor, mm. 1–28.

Fuga 25 is elaborately conceived in terms of invertible counterpoint that bears comparison to the second contrapuntal pattern of the fugue of BWV 537 (mm. 57 ff.), as well as to Pachelbel's Ricercar in C Minor (see ex. 6). Each of these pieces employs a similar two-part invertible counterpoint that operates in melodic inversion as well. The underlying structure is a simple alternation of sixths and thirds against a rising or descending chromatic line. Example 6 illustrates the deployment of this counterpoint through the first half of the fugue. Mattheson cited the identical structure and its contrapuntal extrapolations, apparently borrowed from the fugue of Bach's Sonata in C Major for Unaccompanied Violin, BWV 1005, as an example of what might be expected in an improvised fugue such as would be required in an examination for a major organ post like that of the Hamburg Cathedral.[19] An organist who had

Ex. 7. Similarities between subjects: *a.* Fugas 2 and 3; *b.* Fugas 16 (transposed from E to C) and 41; *c.* Fugas 28 and 57.

mastered the patterns embodied in p 296 would have excelled at this part of Mattheson's exam.

Several of the fugues in p 296 have unusual elements that merit attention. The subject of Fuga 3 appears to be an expansion of that of Fuga 2 (see ex. 7*a*), suggesting some sort of compositional relationship between the two and also illustrating an important facet of compositional technique: the borrowing and manipulation of preexisting materials. The fugue of no. 41 uses a shortened form of the subject of no. 16, although beginning with the answer (ex. 7*b*). The fugue of No. 49 is essentially the same as Fuga 9, the subject in No. 49 being differentiated only by the employment of a dotted rhythm that provides a motivic connection to the prelude. Fugues 9 and 49 also share the concluding figure of their subject with Fuga 54. The subject of Fuga 57 contains all the notes of the subject of Fuga 28 plus an additional four eighth notes interpolated in the middle (ex. 7*c*). The head of the subject of Fuga 45 is the retrograde of the head of the subject of Fuga 44. That many of these similarities involve pieces from both sets suggests that even if the two sets were originally separate they were largely the work of a single musician.

Fuga 4 contains a fermata in m. 11, at a full cadence in the relative major and preceding a direct return to the tonic and a restatement of the subject alone in the soprano. This unusual design creates a pronounced binary form. Fuga 6 contains repeat signs embracing mm. 3–14, similar to those noted above in Fuga 9. Although repeated passages such as this are most unusual in fugues, they do occur occasionally; Telemann employs the type of repetition found in Fuga 6 in nos. 3 and 15 of his xx *kleine Fugen* (Hamburg, 1731).[20]

Varying in length between eight measures (no. 41) and thirty-four measures (no. 60), the preludes suggest a full texture throughout, whether in block chords or arpeggiated patterns. The most significant design aspect of the preludes is that many of them follow the tonal plan used in the *Vorschriften*'s "Principles of Playing in Four Parts" (pp. 37–43): transposed repetitions of a given passage in tonic, dominant, and relative minor, followed by a restatement in the tonic. Fully ten of the eighteen preludes in the Langloz Manuscript are based on this type of plan: preludes 44, 45, 46, 49, 52, 53, 54, 55, 60, and 62. The opening passage shown in ex. 8 (mm. 1–5) is repeated in the dominant (mm. 6–10) and, following a brief sequence, in the relative major (mm. 17–21), after which it returns again in the tonic (mm. 22–26) in a written-out da capo. This pattern of repetitions, which establishes an effective if rudimentary form, is analogous to the major-key designs of the *Vorschriften*. Two preludes, nos. 55 and 60, use patterns of descending scales as a structural basis, again reminiscent of the patterns found in the same part of the *Vorschriften*.

The pedagogical value of the music of P 296 is manifold. It teaches harmony, key relationships, elementary form, transposition, imitation, invertible counterpoint, and style simultaneously. It in fact represents ideal material for an intermediate level of instruction in figured bass and improvisation, and it contains sufficient examples to reflect a considerable diversity of ideas and patterns.

At present, the only positive attribution that can be made concerning the contents of P 296 is for Fuga 22, which we must attribute to F. E. Niedt and date at 1700 or earlier. At the end of part 1 of his *Musicalische Handleitung*, Niedt explains that he intends to write a treatise on the extempore performance of fugues: "God willing, proper instruction on how Fugues are to be extemporized will be given to the kind Music Friend in the other [i.e., later] parts."[21] Perhaps P 296 contains material that was destined for Niedt's unfinished work. On the other hand, Spitta's opinion of P 296 may well be close to the truth: "Possibly they were pieces for practising figured-bass playing, collected by a pupil of Bach's, and transcribed by the said Langloz." Elsewhere Spitta adds: "There can scarcely be any doubt that [P 296] served as the continuation of his [Bach's] thoroughbass instructions."[22] Schulze views Spitta's comments as contradictory, the first denying, the second accepting, Bach's responsibility for

Ex. 8. Prelude 49 in D Minor, mm. 1–14 (author's realization in small notes).

the music of the Langloz manuscript, but this was surely not Spitta's intention.[23] Alfred Mann suggests that in P 296 "we might be dealing with a document preserving Bach's teaching as transmitted through the work of a pupil."[24]

The only indication that P 296 is the work of Bach is the attribution on the title page. However, no author that treats of Bach's teaching methods or compositional practice—neither C. P. E. Bach, nor Forkel, nor Kirnberger, nor Kittel—ever refers to this set of didactic pieces, even though it would be an obvious point for defense of Kirnberger's claim that in Bach "even the fugue originates in thoroughbass."[25] The possibility that each set is the work of a different composer might also be considered; likewise the possibility that it is an anthology compiled from a variety of sources. However, the general similarity of style between most of the pieces and the occasional close connections between pieces in both sets argue strongly for a single composer for the bulk of the work.

Gottfried Kirchhoff, too, ought to be considered. Born in Mühlbech in 1685, Kirchhoff was a pupil of Friedrich Wilhelm Zachow in Halle and later organist there until his death in 1746. Marpurg mentions that Kirchhoff had composed a set of partimento fugues, now lost, "to teach his students figured bass together with the manner of the various entries in a fugal composition."[26] The volume was entitled *L'ABC Musical: Praeludia und Fugen aus allen Tönen*, and it is not out of the question to consider the Langloz manuscript as a copy of all or a part of Kirchhoff's work, especially in that it includes all of the usual keys.[27] In this connection we may also consider the Fantasies and Fughettas in B♭ Major and D Major (BWV 907 and BWV 908), which have been credited to J. S. Bach, and apparently reattributed to "Kirchof" by Kirnberger.[28] Although these works are more extensive than any pieces in P 296, this does not rule out the possibility that the Langloz manuscript represents at least part of Kirchhoff's lost collection.

A pivotal figure in the history of P 296, whatever its genesis, is Kittel. Kittel was a pupil of Jakob Adlung in Erfurt and also studied with J. S. Bach in Leipzig from 1748 until the latter's death in 1750. Upon returning to his birthplace of Erfurt in 1756, Kittel attracted numerous pupils and became the center of an extensive group of organists, composers, and copyists, to whom he made much of Bach's keyboard music available for study. We can conjecture that Langloz was among this group of students.[29] Since Kittel's collection consisted partly of works in his own hand and partly of copies by his students, we can conclude that if Langloz was a student of Kittel, P 296 or its *Vorlage* might have belonged to Kittel at one time.

There is considerable evidence of connections between Kittel and the West-phal family. In 1794 the younger Westphal traveled with his father to Erfurt, where under Kittel's tutelage he undertook to learn to play the organ, return-ing to Hamburg in 1796.[30] At this time Langloz would have been age fifty. Already by 1774 Westphal senior was offering several of J. S. Bach's works for sale in Hamburg, either in print or in manuscript, indicating that the elder Westphal had made significant contact with the Thuringian keyboard school even before the pilgrimage of 1794.[31]

During 1800–1801 Kittel undertook an extensive concert tour through Göttingen and Hannover to Altona and Hamburg, where he paused for an entire year. While in Hamburg he carried out much of the preliminary work for his *Neues Choralbuch für Schleswig-Holstein*, which was published in 1803.[32]

During this time he saw many of his former students. This provides another, later, link between Kittel and Westphal. On the other hand, since Westphal junior was still collecting Bachiana as late as 1826,[33] he in fact could have obtained the manuscript at any point.

The lack of a definitive attribution at the present time does not diminish the central position that this collection holds in the understanding of the eighteenth-century approach to fugal composition through thoroughbass. For the eighteenth-century musician, performance, thoroughbass, improvisation, composition, and theory were aspects of a single art. Thoroughbass studies, including the partimenti of the Langloz manuscript, provide a wonderful bridge that unites theory and composition, performance and improvisation, in a manner that we may well envy in our age of specialization and diversity.

NOTES

1. David Schulenberg, "Composition and Improvisation in the School of J. S. Bach," BP 1 (1995): 13–16, and William Renwick, *Analyzing Fugue: A Schenkerian Approach* (Stuyvesant, N.Y.: Pendragon Press, 1995), 5–10, discuss partimento fugue and its relationship to improvisation and composition.

2. Schmieder gives the date as 1756. Paul Kast, *Die Bach-Handschriften der Berliner Staatsbibliothek* (Trossingen: Hohner, 1958), 21, lists P 296 as *Incerta 65*, and the scribe is identified as "W. Langloz."

3. Hans-Joachim Schulze, "Cembaloimprovisation bei Johann Sebastian Bach: Versuch einer Übersicht," in *Zu Fragen der Improvisation in der Instrumentalmusik der ersten Hälfte des 18. Jahrhunderts* (Blankenburg: Harz, 1980), 52.

4. Kast erroneously identifies the Westphal of P 296 as the Mecklenburg organist and collector Johann Jakob Heinrich Westphal (1774–1835), no relation to the Hamburg Westphals (*Bach-Handschriften*, 21, 148). Miriam Terry provides further information in "C. P. E. Bach and J. J. H. Westphal: A Clarification," *Journal of the American Musicological Society* 20 (1969): 106–15.

5. I am indebted to Dr. Joachim Jaenecke of the SBB for clarifying the transmission history of the manuscript.

6. Dr. Yoshitake Kobayashi (Johann-Sebastian-Bach-Institut, Göottingen), personal communication to the author, 9 September 1985.

7. The title page nevertheless refers to thirty-nine fugues with preludes; the latter are absent.

8. For this reason, Kast and others describe the collection as "62 Praeludien und Fugen."

9. Kast (*Bach-Handschriften*, 21) describes these sketches as belonging to the "Kittel-Schule."

10. Don O. Franklin, "Reconstructing the *Urpartitur* for WTC II," in *Bach Studies*, ed. Don O. Franklin (Cambridge: Cambridge University Press, 1989), 255–60. Bach's original ordering in the inventions was not the ascending sequence of its final presentation but an interspersion of ascending and descending major and minor keys. See NBA V/5, KB, 11–12.

11. Friederich Erhardt Niedt, *Musicalische Handleitung*, vol.1 (Hamburg, 1700), trans. Pamela L. Poulin and Irmgard C. Taylor as *The Musical Guide* (Oxford: Clarendon Press, 1989), 52–54.

12. These notations are distinct from the indications of upper-voice subject entries occasionally found in partimento fugues such as those of Handel.

13. See George Frideric Handel, *Aufzeichnungen zur Kompositionslehre*, Hallische Händel-Ausgabe, Supplement, Band 1, ed. Alfred Mann (Kassel: Bärenreiter, 1978), 49, 63.

14. Philipp Spitta, *Johann Sebastian Bach*, trans. Clara Bell and J. A. Fuller-Maitland (London: Novello, 1889), 2:107, n.153.

15. Brussels, Bibliothèque du Conservatoire Royal de Musique, 27.224. See *J. S. Bach's Precepts and Principles for Playing the Thorough-Bass or Accompanying in Four Parts*, trans. Pamela L. Poulin (Oxford: Clarendon Press, 1994). On the provenance of the manuscript, see Hans-Joachim Schulze, *Studien zur Bach-Überlieferung im 18. Jahrhundert* (Leipzig: Peters, 1984), 126.

16. The subject of the Fugue in E Minor, BWV 945 (of doubtful atribution), is also very similar in style to those of P 296. The subject of Fuga 31 begins in the same way as that in the spurious Fugue in D Minor, BWV ANH. II 98.

17. Heinichen illustrates an appropriate manner of realizing the figured bass of an accompanied fugue in *Der General-Bass in der Composition* (Dresden, 1728), 516–20.

18. Handel included examples of double fugue in his collection of partimenti. See Handel, *Aufzeichnungen zur Kompositionslehre*, 44–52. See also David Ledbetter, *Continuo Playing According to Handel* (Oxford: Oxford University Press, 1990). Heinichen's example of partimento fugue in *Der General-Bass in der Composition* (1728), 516–20, is also a double fugue. Invertible counterpoint is assumed in both Handel's and Heinichen's examples. See George J. Buelow, *Thorough-Bass Accompaniment According to Johann David Heinichen*, rev. ed. (Ann Arbor, Mich.: UMI Research Press, 1986), 208–10.

19. Johannes Mattheson, *Grosse General-Bass-Schule; oder, Der exemplarischen Organisten-Probe* (Hamburg: Johann Christoph Kistner, 1731), 36–39.

20. Ed. Walter Upmeyer, Nagels Musik-Archiv, 13 (Kassel: Bärenreiter, 1928).

21. *The Musical Guide*, 49. Niedt died without completing part 3, which would have included a section on fugues. Excerpts from Niedt's work recur in the *Vorschriften*, published as *J. S. Bach's Precepts and Principles* (see note 15).

22. Spitta, *Johann Sebastian Bach* 2:107, n.153; 3:120.

23. Schulze, "Cembaloimprovisation bei Johann Sebastian Bach," 52.

24. Alfred Mann, "Bach and Handel as Teachers of Thorough Bass," in *Bach, Handel, Scarlatti: Tercentenary Essays*, ed. Peter Williams (Cambridge: Cambridge University Press, 1985), 257.

25. Johann Philipp Kirnberger, *Gedanken über die verschiedenen Lehrarten in der Komposition, als Vorbereitung zur Fugenkenntniss* (Berlin, 1782), 4–5; trans. in BR, 262.

26. ". . . daß er seinen Schülern zugleich den Generalbass und die Art der verschiedenen Eintritte eines Fugensatzes beybrächte," *Abhandlung von der Fuge* (Berlin, 1753–54), 1:150. Marpurg's reference to Kirchhoff was noted by Schulze, *Studien zur Bach-Überlieferung*, 124–25.

27. Niedt published a music primer with a similar title: *Musicalisches* ABC (Hamburg: Benjamin Schiller, 1708).

28. See Schulze, *Studien zur Bach-Überlieferung*, 80–81.

29. As suggested by Schulze, "Cembaloimprovisation bei Johann Sebastian Bach," 52.

30. *Encyclopädie der gesammten musikalischen Wissenschaften, oder Universal-Lexicon der Tonkunst* (Stuttgart, 1838; facs. rpt., Hildesheim: Olms, 1974), 6:854.

31. Ludwig Finscher, "Bach in the Eighteenth Century," in *Bach Studies*, 291.

32. Albert Dreetz, *Johann Christian Kittel: Der letzte Bach-Schüler* (Leipzig: Kistner & Siegel, 1932), 24–25.

33. Schulze, *Studien zur Bach-Überlieferung*, 30, n.86.

Fugue in the Music-Rhetorical Analogy and Rhetoric in the Development of Fugue

Paul Walker

The sixteenth and seventeenth centuries are generally understood to belong to two different eras in the history of Western music: the Renaissance and the Baroque. In one important respect, however, they form a distinct era of their own, which one could with justification call the Age of Rhetoric. Before this time, during most of the fifteenth century, composers such as Dufay and Ockeghem worked to establish such fundamental techniques of Renaissance composition as functional bass lines, control of dissonance, and learned contrapuntal devices, but often left text underlay to chance while writing extremely long melodic lines for few syllables of text. By the end of the seventeenth century, Italian composers had developed a harmonic basis that served Western music until the beginning of the twentieth century and whose systematic nature allowed for such autonomous musical structures as ritornello structure and the so-called sonata-allegro form. In between, from the time of Josquin des Prez until that of Corelli and Vivaldi, composers had by contrast allowed their compositional decisions to be guided first and foremost by text. The musical means of achieving this expressive end might vary considerably during this two-hundred-year span, but Josquin's *Praeter rerum seriem*, Lassus's *Timor et tremor*, Marenzio's *Solo e pensoso*, Monteverdi's *Lamento d'Arianna*, Schütz's *Saul, was verfolgst du mich*, Carissimi's *Jephte*, and Purcell's *Hail, Bright Cecilia* all share the same principal goal of projecting both the individual words and the inherent meaning of the text to the listener. Here is musical rhetoric at its finest.

At the same time, these two centuries also witnessed the creation and establishment of fugue, widely recognized as one of the most abstract and purely

159

musical genres ever devised in Western music. On the surface, fugue would seem to have nothing to do with text-based composition or the discipline of rhetoric, and indeed the question of whether imitative counterpoint and text belonged together at all was periodically raised during these two centuries by musicians who worried that the words would not be apprehended and their expressiveness would be crushed beneath the burden of technical sophistication. Nevertheless, the first systematic fugal imitation, in the guise of point-of-imitation technique in the early sixteenth-century motet, was almost certainly devised as a way to bring compositional sophistication and textual clarity and expressiveness into balance, and the subsequent development that led ultimately to the late-Baroque fugue also included extramusical influence from the discipline of rhetoric.

One of those musicians to live through the transition from this Age of Rhetoric to the Age of Tonal Harmony was J. S. Bach, and in many ways he and his music straddle this divide. His early cantata *Gottes Zeit ist die allerbeste Zeit*, bwv 106, demonstrates mastery of the older, text-based approach to composition, but such later works as the St. Matthew Passion, with their ritornello structures and da capo arias, continue to emphasize the expressiveness of individual words and phrases. It is a difficult question of Bach scholarship, therefore, to determine the extent to which the master's compositional decisions rest on such purely musical considerations as counterpoint, harmony, or musical structure, and when they reflect such extramusical influences as rhetoric or theology. The purpose of this essay is to explore, for the music of Bach and his predecessors, the relationship between rhetoric and fugue.

This study is not a journey into uncharted waters; already twenty years ago Gregory G. Butler contributed an entire article on the topic.[1] Nevertheless, scholarly activity has in the meantime taught us much about both the development of fugue up to Bach's time and the Renaissance and Baroque understanding of rhetoric and music, and it is now time for a reevaluation of the evidence.[2] In particular, I would advocate that the nature of the relationship between rhetoric and fugue be stated somewhat more cautiously than Butler felt it necessary to do in 1977. Although it is true that many musicians of the time recognized such a relationship, that rhetoric played a role in the creation and development of the genre of fugue, and that the technique of fugal counterpoint played a role in musicians' thinking about the music-rhetorical analogy, I argue that the nature of these interrelationships was for all but a few musicians of the time simpler, more general, less detailed, and less extensive than Butler attempted to assert. A historical survey that follows the development of fugue and of contemporaneous thinking about the music-rhetorical analogy can illustrate these points most clearly.

* * *

In part 3 (On Counterpoint) of his *Institutioni harmoniche* (1558, rev. ed.1573), Gioseffo Zarlino places heavy emphasis on the purely technical aspects of writing contrapuntal music, without any rhetorical focus. Yet Zarlino bears considerable responsibility for much of the terminology that still today is associated with fugue.[3] Although most of his definitions failed to survive even his own century, many of the words and categories he codified are still with us, including the division of imitative counterpoint into fugue (*fuga*) and imitation (*imitatione*), the labeling of leading and answering voices as guide (*guida*) and follower (*consequente*)—these survive in their Latin synonyms *dux* and *comes*, as translated by Seth Calvisius in 1592—and his use of the word "subject" (*soggetto*) to label thematic material.[4] He was less successful in convincing his contemporaries to adopt "consequence" (*consequenza*) in place of the word *canon*, which, strictly speaking, meant "rule" and should be applied, in Zarlino's opinion, only to the rubric explaining how a canonic piece is realized, not the piece itself.

All of these words carry nonmusical meanings (*fugue*, for instance, refers to the act of chasing or fleeing), but three—*imitation*, *subject*, and *consequence*—also play a role in rhetorical treatises. Of greatest importance for our topic is *imitation*, which appears several times in Quintilian's *Institutio oratoria*.[5] The Latin *imitatio* means the same thing as its English cognate, and Quintilian uses the word when discussing the way in which a speaker might imitate the words or actions of another. Although other musicians used the word *imitation* in this sense, to describe the copying of other composers' styles or even specific works, Zarlino's definition suggests no specifically rhetorical connotations. Rather he uses the Italian words *fuga* and *imitatione* to denote his two principal subcategories of imitative counterpoint, which are defined in purely technical terms: *fuga* denotes imitative counterpoint in which all voices preserve exactly the rhythms and intervals of all other voices participating in the imitation, *imitatione* in which rhythms and intervals are not preserved by all voices. Zarlino gives us no reason to infer any underlying rhetorical meaning to the word *imitatione* or to doubt the commonsense presumption that musicians applied the word *imitation* to imitative counterpoint for much the same reason that they applied *fugue*. That is, in both cases the general, nonmusical, nonrhetorical meanings of the words ("to mimic" in the former case, "to flee or chase" in the latter) provide some sort of verbal analogy for the phenomenon of two or more voices producing the same or similar melodic lines in staggered fashion.[6]

Most of Zarlino's fugal terminology has survived to this day, but his distinction between exact and inexact imitation was already archaic in 1558 and failed to persuade his contemporaries. The wave of the future was not canonic writing of the sort found in his teacher Adrian Willaert's works, but the new motet style based on pervasive imitation and championed by Willaert's contemporaries Nicolas Gombert and Jacobus Clemens. For these northerners, the word *fugue* continued to refer to all sorts of imitative counterpoint just as it had before Zarlino tried to restrict its meaning. When applied to the new, noncanonic type, the word *fugue* might have two meanings: either the technique of noncanonic imitation or the principal manifestation thereof, the point of imitation.

The most important theorist to describe this style, the German Gallus Dressler, was also the first to bring rhetoric into writings about music in a significant way. His unpublished manuscript treatise *Praecepta musicae poeticae* (written in Magdeburg and dated 1563) introduced two aspects of rhetoric into the teaching of composition: *dispositio*, how to lay out a speech or essay, and *elocutio*, how to make its content effective through the use of figures of speech.[7] As Butler points out, sixteenth-century musicians were particularly fond of the second of these, and it has also received the most attention by twentieth-century scholars. When Dressler drew up his list of figures of music, however, he made no attempt to select particular figures of speech and search out a musical equivalent for each one, nor did he assign the names of any figures of speech to any musical phenomena. Instead, he kept the analogy quite general by relating the idea of figures of speech to the fundamental techniques of musical composition. He chose as his only three figures of music the basic building blocks of the motet style: suspensions (*syncopationes*), cadences (*clausulae*), and points of imitation (*fugae*). Butler speculates that fugue was "elevated to such a preeminent position as a musical-rhetorical element" primarily because the "movement [bringing together rhetoric and music] was largely highly learned and intellectual, even academic, in nature, and of course the *fuga* was looked upon as a highly learned element of composition."[8] Dressler's other musical figures, however, suggest that fugue was included simply as a result of its fundamental importance to the motet style of Clemens and Gombert.

Of ultimately greater importance for the history of fugue was Dressler's application of the rhetorical *dispositio* to the motet. Again he kept things simple and adopted the most basic design of beginning (*exordium*), middle (*medium*), and end (*finis*). The motet of Clemens and Gombert lacks unifying thematic material, of course, since each point of imitation comprises both a verbal phrase and a unique musical subject crafted to fit that phrase. Dressler's interpretation of the music-rhetorical analogy, therefore, expected the *exordium* merely to get the piece off to a good and proper start, not to introduce thematic material that would continue to be treated as the piece progresses. In musical terms he defined the *exordium* as the opening point of imitation and understood a proper start to be one that above all else presented the mode clearly. In practical terms, therefore, if a motet began with a fugue, then the voices of that fugue should begin on the proper modal notes of final and reciting tone, and their melodic motion should emphasize the most important modal notes. Fugues in the body of the piece, by contrast, could be handled more freely, with entrances on notes other than final and reciting tone, and with greater freedom in the handling of the imitation. At the end of the piece, the original mode should once again be clear as the final cadence approaches.

In sum, Dressler took a flexible and creative approach to the incorporation of rhetorical thought. On the one hand, be drew an analogy with figures of speech but chose for their musical counterparts purely musical techniques, with no attempt to match particular verbal phenomena with particular musical ones. On the other hand, he drew a direct parallel between the three parts of a good speech or essay and the three parts of a good musical composition, again without trying to relate specifically verbal techniques to musical ones. It is easy to believe that composers of the early sixteenth century were influenced in just this way by the ideals of their literary colleagues.

Most German writers on music in the century after Dressler's pioneering work remained content with this sort of general analogy, but Joachim Burmeister, a teacher of Latin grammar and composition in Rostock, did not.[9] Whereas Dressler had enumerated three figures of music, Burmeister in the first of his three books offered twenty-two; by the time of his third book the number of musical figures had grown to twenty-six, most of them borrowed from rhetoric. One can scarcely conceive of twenty-six fundamental techniques of musical composition comparable to Dressler's fugue, cadences, and suspensions, and in fact Burmeister took the analogy between figures of speech and figures of music far beyond this general model to the level of compositional surface detail.[10] Before Burmeister, theorists had largely focused their attention on the basics of writing music: how to handle the modes; how to write counterpoint in two, three, and four voices; how to set up suspensions; how to lay out a point of imitation. When it came time for the student to write real music of his own—that is, to set a text artistically with sensitivity and expression—the teacher directed the student, usually without further guidance or comment, to the works of highly respected composers. It was at precisely this level that Burmeister wished to offer guidance. Burmeister preferred the word *ornament* to describe his figures of music, highlighting their role in fleshing out or making more elegant the basic, skeletal framework of a musical composition. We might think of the use of these devices as that which separates the truly first-rate composer from the merely competent, just as the effective use of figures of speech separates the persuasive speaker from the rest of the pack. One could therefore make a case that Burmeister's musical ornaments provide a better analogy to Quintilian's figures of speech than do Dressler's fundamental compositional techniques.

When, however, one immerses oneself in the details of Burmeister's work, one becomes aware that the analogies are not entirely successful. One example will suffice to illustrate this. To the rhetorician, *anocope* is a figure in which a final letter or syllable is excised from a word. Lucas Lossius, one of Burmeister's teachers in Lüneburg, described it in his treatise on rhetoric as *abscisio dictionis in fine vel literae vel syllabae* (cutting off the end of an expression by either a letter or a syllable).[11] The Englishman Henry Peacham the Elder, who published a rhetoric text in 1577, gave as an example "Thus lovingly Dame Dian did" (for "Diana").[12] Burmeister's musical definition reads as follows:

> Apocope est Fuga, quae ex omni parte per omnes voces non absolvitur, sed cujus affectionis, quae in fugam abrepta est propter aliquam causam in una aliqua voce fit amputatio.
>
> *Apocope* is a fugue that is not completed in all [its] parts by all the voices. Instead, its subject, interrupted in mid-fugue, is cut off in one voice for some reason.[13]

Here Burmeister seems to describe a point of imitation in which a theme is presented several times but with one of those statements shortened. This is, in any event, the interpretation accepted by most other modern scholars (including Butler), but it does not fit Burmeister's favorite example, the beginning of the motet "Legem pone mihi" by Orlande de Lassus. The first eight measures of "Legem pone mihi" appeared in *Musica autoschediastike* (fols. 14v–K1r) in a version different from that of the familiar modern edition;[14] ex.1 reproduces Burmeister's version (originally notated in parts).

The theme of this point of imitation begins with a falling third (C–A in the discantus, F–D in the other four voices) but has no further melodic identity. That is, the altus follows this head motive with the upward leap of the fifth, tenor I with a downward second, tenor II with a downward third, and discantus and bassus with a unison. In short, beyond the opening two-note motive there is no consensus about the melodic identity of the theme, and thus there is no clearly defined theme that one of the voices "amputates." Instead, one might best describe the example as a fugue whose subject is truncated by its very nature—that is, consists of only two notes—rather than one whose subject is truncated by one voice. Burmeister offers other examples, all of which support this interpretation. The weight of evidence thus suggests that by *apocope* Burmeister understood a fugue constructed with a truncated subject. In the end, Burmeister's last definition is more reflective of its rhetorical counterpart than of the musical technique it is supposed to describe: the word *amputatio* suggests Lossius's *abscisio*, and both men refer to this amputation as happening in one place (i.e., a word or voice). One must conclude that Burmeister settled on this particular definition precisely because of its similarity to its rhetorical counterpart, not because of its value in deepening our understanding of the musical device.

The next important innovation in the music-rhetorical analogy came over half a century later, in the manuscript *Tractatus compositionis augmentatus* (ca.1660) of Christoph Bernhard. Bernhard's approach to the figures of music took as its starting point the dispute between Artusi and the Monteverdi brothers concerning dissonance treatment. In the arguments advocating daring dissonances to match expressive, emotional texts, Bernhard recognized an equivalent to the figures of speech and their role of moving and persuading the listener. He therefore replaced the traditional German analogy between

Ex.1. Lassus, "Legem pone mihi," mm.1–8 (Burmeister, *Musica autoschediastike*, fols. 14v–K1r). Text underlay is Burmeister's own. Italicized texts are editorial.

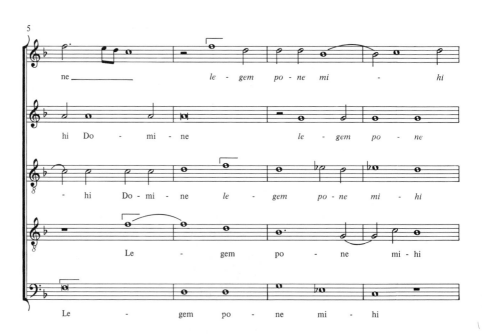

figures of speech and compositional techniques with a completely new one relating figures of speech to dissonance treatment; in doing so, he removed fugue entirely from the music-rhetorical analogy and gave it its own separate chapter. There he concentrated on purely technical phenomena, most prominently the relationship between fugal imitation and the modes, which, even at this late date, he discussed in the context of late-Renaissance motet style and especially the works of Palestrina.

Four recent advances in our understanding of fugue and its development during the seventeenth century bear particular significance. First, in the years after 1600 several German musicians introduced the word *fugue* for the first time as a genre designation for noncanonic pieces. The most important of these were extended pieces in learned style by Hans Leo Hassler, who almost certainly conceived them under the influence of his teacher Andrea Gabrieli. Gabrieli called such pieces ricercars, and Michael Praetorius, a colleague of Hassler, tells us that in fact the genre designations are equivalent. Praetorius's explanation dwells on the learned nature of the genres but makes no mention of any rhetorical influence.[15]

The second important development, from about the same time, was a codification of the theory of tonal answers. This theory can be traced to the Italian organists Girolamo Diruta and Adriano Banchieri and grew out of the kind of relationship between fugal imitation and mode that Dressler and other Renaissance musicians had stressed. Fugue's relationship to mode, one of its central defining characteristics throughout the sixteenth and seventeenth centuries, was presented by Diruta and Banchieri as a purely technical phenomenon, again without recourse to rhetorical language.[16]

Third, in the first half of the seventeenth century a group of northern Italian violinists that included Tarquinio Merula and Giovanni Legrenzi began to experiment in their sonatas with movements based on fugal counterpoint and organized like our modern fugue, that is, with an opening exposition followed by a series of groups of thematic statements, sometimes including one or more in closely related keys, all based on the same theme.[17] Compared to the grand keyboard ricercar/fugue of Hassler and Praetorius, these movements are much more modest in length, with relatively compact points of imitation and more quickly moving themes. Their approach to fugal structure was described, probably in the years after midcentury, by a northern Italian violinist working in Vienna, Antonio Bertali, who called it fugue.[18]

The fourth and final piece of the puzzle to be added in the seventeenth century was the countersubject. This idea grew out of experiments combining fugue with invertible counterpoint undertaken during the 1660s and 1670s by a circle of musicians in Hamburg and Lübeck that included Bernhard, Matthias Weckmann, Johann Adam Reinken, and Dietrich Buxtehude. Their inspiration seems to have been principally the writings on invertible counterpoint by Gioseffo Zarlino, whose work was transmitted to them through their teachers' teacher, Jan Pieterszoon Sweelinck.[19]

Of these four developments, only the third seems to have involved any significant influence from rhetoric. These northern Italian violinists took the old Renaissance motet model and began to experiment with an instrumental counterpart in which all points of imitation were based on the same theme. This thematic unity ensured musical coherence in the absence of text, but it also posed the obvious question of how to ensure sufficient variety in the body of the work. As described by Bertali, the composers devised a plan by which successive points of imitation, optimally totaling four or five, should differ from one another in some way. For instance, the voices should not always enter in the same order, and if they should happen to retain the same order in two successive points of imitation, they ought to swap starting notes. Later thematic statements might enter on other notes than final and dominant of the mode, just as Dressler had allowed for inner points of imitation in the motet. As for the end, Bertali particularly recommended the use of stretto, for, as he said, "Thus will the general proverb, desired in all the arts, also be verified in this one: Finis bonus."[20] Or, as we say in English, "All's well that ends well." Here, as in Dressler's writing, we find principles from the discipline of rhetoric applied to the art of composition but in the most general of ways. No attempt was made to draw specific analogies between verbal and musical techniques, but the overarching principles of a commanding beginning, a body characterized by variety and coherence, and an impressive conclusion remained the same.

By 1700, then, as Bach and Handel were poised to begin their careers, all elements of the modern textbook fugue, with the exception of the episode and the more systematic incorporation of tonal harmony, were in place. All available evidence suggests that the details of fugal writing—its relationship to mode, the rules of counterpoint by which it is written, and the technique of invertible counterpoint necessary for double fugue, countersubjects, and stretto—developed independently from any rhetorical influence. This influence exerted itself instead at the level of the whole piece, where the composer strove to create with notes a piece that, using its own means, could boast as great an effect on the listener as that of a great speech or essay. Butler cites several writers from the seventeenth and early eighteenth centuries who referred to the theme of the fugue as analogous to the theme of a speech and who likened fugal texture to a conversation or debate. In other words, analogies between fugue and rhetoric, if kept sufficiently general, worked well.

During the first half of the eighteenth century, however, interest in the music-rhetorical analogy seems to have intensified. Virtually all those taking an interest were Germans, and Butler characterizes their accomplishments as "rigorously apply[ing] the rhetorical disposition scheme in its complete form to such musical structures as fugue."[21] At the center of this renewed interest stood Johann Mattheson, who shortly before 1720 engaged in an extended quarrel with certain professional colleagues on the relative merits of fugue and canon. Among other things, Mattheson argued that these techniques were scarcely suitable for vocal music because they caused the words to be obscured, and to this the Dresden Capellmeister Johann Christoph Schmidt took great exception. Schmidt supported his counterargument by noting how important it was for a composer of fugue to understand and be able to apply the principles of rhetoric:

> For in treating a fugue, I must take my craft from the oratory just as [is done] in the modern style, even though harmony dominates [a fugue] more than words do. For the *dux* is the *propositio;* the *comes* the *aetiologia; oppositum* is the varied inversion of the fugue; *similia* give the altered figures of the *propositio* according to their value; *exempla* can refer to the fugal theme [stated] on other notes, with augmentation and diminution of the subject; *confirmatio* would be when I "canonize" on the subject; and *conclusio,* when I allow the subject to be heard near the [final] cadence in imitation above a pedal point; not to mention other artifices which can be introduced and observed in statements of the subject.[22]

The specific form of oratory that Schmidt chose for his analogy is generally known as a *chria,* a short essay whose thesis was most often some sort of famous saying. The author of a *chria* (1) stated the thesis (*propositio*), (2) gave a reason (*aetiologia*) for the validity of the thesis, then elaborated further on these reasons through (3) the refutation of statements to the contrary (*contrarium*) and the offering of (4) supportive examples (*exemplum*), (5) similes (*simile*), and (6) third-person testimony (*testimonium*) before (7) concluding the essay in appropriate fashion (*conclusio*). Schmidt felt that a composer of fugue faced the same task with respect to a particular theme. Its answer supplied the initial reason for the theme's existence, after which the theme was further elaborated upon through thematic statements in inversion (*contrarium*), with altered rhythm (*simile*), and at different pitches or in augmentation or diminution (*exemplum*). In place of the *testimonium*, which could scarcely be translated into fugal procedure, Schmidt chose the traditional "confirmation of the thesis" that often preceded the conclusion of a longer essay. He drew the analogy between it and the use of stretto near the end and suggested finally that the fugue close with freer use or stretto over a pedal point. In similar fashion to those who likened fugue to "conversation," Schmidt likened it to "explanation": not only was the theme of a vocal fugue "explained" and elaborated upon through its many varied statements, but the technique was an appropriate vehicle for text setting because it allowed the theme's text to be similarly "explained" through its varied repetitions.[23]

Mattheson similarly related rhetorical *dispositio* to a musical composition in the following passage from *Der vollkommene Capellmeister*: "Our musical Disposition differs from the rhetorical arrangement of an ordinary speech only in the subject, the matter at hand, the object. Hence it must observe the same six parts that are normally prescribed for the orator, namely: the *introduction*, the *narration*, the *proposition*, the *proof*, the *refutation*, and the *closing*, otherwise known as: Exordium, Narratio, Propositio, Confirmatio, Confutatia, & Peroratio."[24] At the end of this chapter, Mattheson led the reader to expect the detailed analogy between fugue and rhetoric that Butler postulates: "One more thing is to be mentioned, namely that among the great figures for elaboration, of which there are some thirty and which serve more for lengthening, amplification, embellishment, ornamentation, or show than for real persuasion of the intellect, the familiar and renowned clever device, the *fugue*, is quite properly to be classed, wherein the *Mimesis, Expolitio* [embellishing], *Distributio*, together with other little flowers which seldom ripen to fruit find their residence, as in a greenhouse. More instruction on this will follow in its place."[25]

In the treatment of fugue to be found later in the book, however, rhetoric plays a surprisingly small role. Mattheson divided the material on imitative counterpoint into four chapters devoted to simple fugue, imitation, invertible counterpoint, and double fugue, and he kept the focus overwhelmingly on such purely technical features as tonal answers and the writing of invertible counterpoint. He introduced no terminology from the classical *dispositio* and in fact laid out a model for fugal structure that is surprisingly close to the modern one. Mattheson's model began with an orderly exposition, to which he, like his predecessors, gave no special name, followed by a transition (*transitio*) of free counterpoint and then a series of groups of thematic statements (which he called *Durchführungen*) separated from one another by brief ornamental passages (called variously *Zwischenspiele*, *Schmückungen*, and *Zierrathen*). In short, the traditional tripartite disposition of Dressler and Bertali applies nicely, but Butler's attempt to subdivide further the body of the fugue into *confutatio*, *similia*, *exemplum*, and *confirmatio* finds no supporting evidence in Mattheson's work.

We might summarize the history of the relationship between fugue and rhetoric from the early sixteenth to the early eighteenth centuries as follows: In its early guise as a point of imitation in motet style, fugue first entered the music-rhetorical analogy as a compositional device analogous to a figure of speech. The only writer to try to match specific sorts of fugal counterpoint with specific figures of speech, however, was Joachim Burmeister, and his attempts, not entirely successful, remained without influence. During the course of the seventeenth century, the word *fugue* came to refer to a genre, and the characteristics by which we still define it today had largely come together by about 1700. Fugue in this guise never served as a figure of music, since just after midcentury Bernhard refocused the figure-of-speech analogy on dissonance treatment and thereby removed compositional techniques such as fugue from the analogy. Meanwhile, although most of the detail of fugal writing continued to develop in purely technical terms and without recourse to rhetorical ideas, fugal structure borrowed the tripartite design of *exordium*, *medium*, and *finis* from the classic rhetorical *dispositio*. By the time early-eighteenth-century musicians "rediscovered" or, more precisely, reacquired enthusiasm for a more detailed music-rhetorical analogy, the genre of fugue was already firmly established.

An exchange between Mattheson and the Bach pupil Lorenz Christoph Mizler sheds additional light on eighteenth-century approaches to the music-rhetorical analogy. In his *Kern melodischer Wissenschaft*, a preliminary draft of *Der vollkommene Capellmeister*, Mattheson used the classic *dispositio* as the basis for an analysis of an opera aria by Benedetto Marcello. In his review of the book, Mizler criticized this analysis as follows: "I do not know if the admirable Marcello would wish to apply the six parts of an oration here, in so much as it is not at all necessary to apply everything in every section of a piece. Rather, it is highly likely that the incomparable composer of this aria, while writing it, did not think about exordium, narratio, confutatio, confirmatio, or the order of how the said parts should follow upon one another. The matter thus seems forced, because Herr Mattheson uses one and the same [musical] phrase [*Satz*] for the introduction, the narration, and the proposition."[26] To this criticism Mattheson made the following response in the introduction to his *Vollkommene Capellmeister*: "Marcello, to be sure, has given as little thought to the six parts of an oration in composing the aria I quoted in the *Kern*, as in his other works: but one concedes that I have *quite plausibly* shown how they must be present in the melody. That is enough. Experienced masters proceed in an orderly manner, even when they do not think about it."[27]

In this exchange, Mizler and Mattheson are arguing a question that scholars still consider today: the role of analysis and its proper relationship to authorial intent.[28] Mattheson recognized in rhetoric a discipline that had exerted influence on the course of musical composition, and thus he found it an appropriate model with which to examine pieces. The purpose of this exercise was manifestly not to show how the composer conceived the piece but rather to deepen one's appreciation of it. From Mizler's objection we might surmise that his teacher, J. S. Bach, did not make much use of the rhetorical analogy in teaching composition to his students and that, if he used rhetorical models for his own composition, his students were not aware of it. Carl Philipp Emanuel Bach, in a letter of 1774 to Forkel, tells us further that when his father listened to other composers' fugues he focused first and foremost on the technical details of thematic material and counterpoint: "When [J. S. Bach] listened to a rich and many-voiced fugue, he could soon say after the first entries of the subjects, what contrapuntal devices it would be possible to apply, and which of them the composer by rights ought to apply, and on such occasions, when I was standing next to him, and he had voiced his surmises to me, he would joyfully nudge me when his expectations were fulfilled."[29]

C. P. E. Bach describes here the fugal phenomena that are the most purely musical and least obviously analogous to verbal language. The goal of rhetoric, however, is not merely to dazzle or impress but also to persuade and convince; in musical terms, we might say that the mere presence of contrapuntal devices does not guarantee an artistically successful fugue. It is at this point, where the anecdote leaves off, that rhetoric can make its contribution. To put it another way: if Emanuel Bach had asked his father after the performance for a subjective evaluation of the fugue—that is, whether the various contrapuntal devices added up to a terrific piece or an interminable bore—how would Johann Sebastian have articulated his answer?

Let us examine briefly one of J. S. Bach's own fugues with the aid of rhetorical principles. The Fugue in B♭ Minor, ʙᴡᴠ 867, from the first book of the Well-Tempered Clavier is, like most of the fugues in this collection, a masterpiece of compactness and artistry. Its technical basis is quickly summarized: five voices and a brilliantly devised subject that despite unremarkable rhythmic motion of half and quarter notes is made memorable through the upward leap of a minor ninth and that is well crafted to allow for its treatment in stretto. Quintilian writes that "the sole purpose of the *exordium* is to prepare our audience in such a way that they will be disposed to lend a ready ear to the rest of our speech," more specifically "by making the audience well-disposed [*benevolum*], attentive [*attentum*], and ready to receive instruction [*docilem*]."[30] Bach commands our attention in his opening exposition almost entirely through the theme itself, with its searing ninth, and the impressive fullness of five-voice texture. There is no countersubject, and Bach does not tip his hand regarding what he intends to do with the material. The audience is ready to learn.

It is in the body of a fugue that analogies with rhetoric become the trickiest to apply. Quintilian directs his remarks primarily to trial lawyers and hence concentrates to a large extent on two aspects of the lawyer's craft; the statement of facts (*narratio*) and the proof of those facts (*confirmatio*).[31] He allows a great deal of flexibility in the handling of this portion of the speech, and we may do the same in our fugal analysis. In place of statements of fact, fugue offers instead the potential for contrapuntal complexity and ingenuity, and Bach's B♭ Minor Fugue progresses inexorably to ever-greater levels of this complexity. Bach's mastery in the handling of this progression resides both in its incremental nature and in the manipulation of intensity and relaxation that allows the listener to prepare for its most important moments. In the first set of thematic entries after the exposition (mm. 25–33) the almost constant presence of stepwise quarter notes taken from the second half of the subject and the quick succession of thematic entries introduces the first level of complexity and suggests the stretto to come. The third set of entries (mm. 46–56) begins with two statements of the subject in proper succession but then introduces the first stretto, in the top voices where it can be readily perceived. After three statements in stretto, Bach concludes this set of entries with two final statements (mm. 53–56) that are not overlapped. The contrapuntal tour de force, which acts quite like Quintilian's "confirmation," appears in mm. 67–71, where all five voices bring in the subject in the tightest possible stretto.

Bach regulates the ebb and flow of tension in the body of the piece through the careful handling of episodes. The stepwise quarter notes of the second half of the subject provide him with sufficiently common material that he is able by incorporating them to drop the level of tension while retaining thematic unity. Also worthy of mention is his manipulation of range. To add interest to the second set of entries, before the introduction of stretto, Bach allows the texture to rise to the highest notes of the piece. For the entries in stretto, such highlighting through range is unnecessary. This set of entries is also distinguished harmonically through its beginning in the relative major, Db, followed by a relatively unstable series of harmonies.

Regarding the conclusion, Quintilian writes, "There are two kinds of peroration, for it may deal either with facts or with the emotional aspect of the case," and he maintains that it should be "as brief as possible."[32] One could make a case for the final set of entries as equivalent to Quintilian's conclusion dealing with facts, but I prefer to view these entries as the final confirmation of the fugue's body, and I see the conclusion as the closing few measures, where Bach "deals with the emotional aspect" of the piece. After the incredible sequence of stretto entries in mm. 67–71, the listener needs time, however brief, to "come down" before the final cadence sounds. No thematic statement burdens these measures, although the by now almost ubiquitous stepwise quarter notes remind us of the subject, and the fugue moves to a quiet close.

Whether or not Dressler and Burmeister originally introduced rhetoric to musical analysis because it lent legitimacy to the study of musical composition, its retention by later writers may have more to do with the way we humans express ourselves about music. Despite occasional attempts to create nonverbal analytical systems,[33] in the end most of us want to be able to express our reactions to music just as we express our reactions to most things in life: through words. Given that public speaking and musical performance share many of the same goals, the words we use to describe the effects of music and speech, though these effects are achieved through very different means, will ultimately be similar. Fugue puts on display everything that counterpoint and tonality have to offer, and it does so according to the nonverbal laws of musical notes. What separates the great fugue from the mediocre one, however, is rhetoric.

NOTES

1. "Fugue and Rhetoric," *Journal of Music Theory* 21 (1977): 49–109. Related to this article are two additional contributions by Butler from about the same time: "The Fantasia as Musical Image," *Musical Quarterly* 60 (1974): 602–15, and "Music and Rhetoric in Early Seventeenth-Century English Sources," *Musical Quarterly* 66 (1980): 53–64.

2. On fugue, see in particular the author's "Fugue in German Theory from Dressler to Mattheson" (Ph.D. dissertation, State University of New York at Buffalo, 1987), and his forthcoming book, *Theories of Fugue from the Age of Josquin to the Age of Bach*, to be published by the University of Rochester Press. Some scholars have urged a cautious approach to the topic of musical rhetoric in the Baroque; others express greater enthusiasm for it. Among the former are Peter Williams, "The Snares and Delusions of Musical Rhetoric: Some Examples from Recent Writings on J. S. Bach," in *Alte Musik: Praxis und Reflexion*, ed. Peter Reidemeister and Veronika Gutmann (Winterthur, Switzerland: Amadeus, 1983), 230–40, and Brian Vickers, "Figures of Rhetoric/Figures of Music?" *Rhetorica* 2 (1984): 1–44. Representative of the latter are Elaine R. Sisman, *Haydn and the Classical Variation* (Cambridge, Mass.: Harvard University Press, 1993), 21–22; Robert Toft, *Tune Thy Musicke to Thy Hart* (Toronto: University of Toronto Press, 1993), 159, n. 12; and Mark Evan Bonds, *Wordless Rhetoric: Musical Form and the Metaphor of the Oration* (Cambridge, Mass.: Harvard University Press, 1991), esp. 86–90.

3. Zarlino is not mentioned in any of Butler's three articles previously cited.

4. Seth Calvisius, *Melopoeia sive melodiae condendae ratio* (Erfurt: Georg Baumann, 1592), fol. H5r.

5. See *The Institutio oratoria of Quintilian* (Cambridge, Mass.: Harvard University Press, 1980), 4:540, for an index of all its appearances.

6. Certainly Zarlino was inclined to refer to a word's rhetorical meaning when he felt it important, as was the case when he redefined *consequenza* for the 1573 edition of *Le istitutioni*.

7. The *Praecepta* resides in SBB, Mus. ms. theor. 4° 84. A modern edition by Bernhard Engelke can be found in *Geschichts-Blätter für Stadt und Land Magdeburg* 49/50 (1914–15): 213–50; for fugue and rhetoric, see esp. 243–50.

8. Butler, "Fugue and Rhetoric," 50.

9. Burmeister's writings on fugue and rhetoric appeared in three books of overlapping content: (1) *Hypomnematum musicae poeticae* (Rostock: Stephan Myliander, 1599); (2) *Musica autoschediastike* (Rostock: Christoph Reusner, 1601), incorporating the first twelve chapters of the *Hypomnematum* (folio number citations from the *Hypomnematum* refer to this reprint); and (3) *Musica poetica* (Rostock: Stephan Myliander, 1606; facs. rpt., Kassel: Bärenreiter, 1955). The last of these has been translated into English under the title *Musical Poetics* by Benito Rivera (New Haven, Conn.: Yale University Press, 1993).

10. See Burmeister's introduction to the chapter on figures or ornaments of music in Rivera, *Musical Poetics*, 154–59.

11. Lucas Lossius, *Erotemata dialecticae et rhetoricae Philippi Melanchthonis* (Leipzig, 1562), quoted in Martin Ruhnke, *Joachim Burmeister: Ein Beitrag zur Musiklehre um 1600*, Schriften des Landesinstituts fur Musikforschung Kiel, no. 5 (Kassel: Bärenreiter, 1955), 150.

12. Henry Peacham, *The Garden of Eloquence* (London: H. Jackson, 1577; facs. rpt., Menston, England: Scolar Press 1971), fol. E2v.

13. Burmeister, *Musica poetica*, 59; the translation is adapted slightly from Rivera, *Musical Poetics*, 163, 165. The difficulties in interpreting Burmeister's Latin in this passage are characteristic. Burmeister uses the word *vox* in the preceding paragraph of *Musica poetica* to mean unequivocally "voice," and thus Rivera and I infer that meaning here. The word *affectio* Burmeister defined elsewhere (*Musica autoschediastike*, fol. O2v) as that which we understand by melodic subject or theme but with additional rhetorical connotation of "moving the hearts of men."

14. Orlando di Lasso, *Sämtliche Werke*, ed. Carl Proske and Franz Xaver Haberl (Leipzig: Breitkopf & Härtel, 1894–1926), 9:73–76.

15. Praetorius's description of the fugue/ricercar appears in his *Syntagma musicum*, vol. 3 (Wolfenbüttel: Elias Holwein, 1619; facs. rpt., Kassel: Bärenreiter, 1959), 21–22 (p. 22 is misnumbered 24). The entire topic is treated in greater detail in Paul Walker, "Fugue as a Genre Designation in the Early Seventeenth Century," unpublished paper delivered at the annual meeting of the American Heinrich Schütz Society, Washington University, St. Louis, April 1990.

16. See Paul Walker, "Modality, Tonality, and Theories of Fugal Answer in the Baroque," in *Church, Stage, and Studio: Music and Its Contexts in Seventeenth-Century Germany*, ed. Paul Walker (Ann Arbor, Mich.: UMI Research Press, 1990), 361–88, esp. 365–68.

17. See, e.g., the fugal movements in Merula's *Il primo libro delle canzoni a quattro voci* (1615), ed. Adam Sutkowski in *Opere complete*, vol. 1 (Brooklyn: Institute of Mediaeval Music, 1974), and in Legrenzi's op. 2 (1655), ed. Stephen Bonta in *The Instrumental Music of Giovanni Legrenzi: Sonate a due e tre, Opus 2, 1655* (Cambridge, Mass.: Department of Music, Harvard University, 1964).

18. See Paul Walker, "Vienna's Contribution to the Development of Fugue during the Seventeenth Century," in *Austria 996–1996: Music in a Changing Society*, forthcoming. Bertali's treatise survives in three manuscripts of overlapping but not identical content, all written in German. Two of these are attributed to Bertali, the third (wrongly) to Carissimi.

19. On this development, see Walker, "Zur Geschichte des Kontrasubjekts und zu seinen Gebrauch in den frühesten Klavier- und Orgelfugen Johann Sebastian Bachs," in *Das Frühwerk Johann Sebastian Bachs*, ed. Karl Heller and Hans Joachim Schulze (Cologne: Studio, 1995), 48–69. See also Walker, "Die Entstehung der Permutationsfuge," BJ 75 (1989), 21–42, and a slightly revised rendering into English as "The Origin of the Permutation Fugue," in *Studies in the History of Music 3: The Creative Process*, ed. by Ellen Beebe (Williamstown, Mass.: Broude Brothers, 1992), 51–91.

20. "und wird alss dann, das allgemeine proverbium so in ailer Künsten desideriret wird, nehmlich Finis bonus, auch in dieser verificirt werden" (Giacomo Carissimi [recte: Bertali], *Regulae compositionis*, Berlin Mus. ms. theor. 170, p. 17; the translation is mine).

21. Butler, "Fugue and Rhetoric," 68.

22. "Denn eine *Fugam* zu *tracti*ren, muss ich die *artificia* so wohl aus der *Oratoria*, als bey dem *Style moderno*, nehmen, ob gleich darinne mehr die *Harmonia* als *Oratio, domini*ret: Denn *Dux* ist *Propositio; Comes Aetiologia; Oppositum* ist *Inversio varia Fugae; Similia* geben die veränderten *Figu*ren der *Proposition, secundum valorem; Exempla* können heissen die *propositiones Fugae* in andern *Chord*en, *cum augmentatione & diminutione Subjecti; Confirmatio* wäre, wenn ich über das *Subjectum canoni*sire; und *Conclusio*, wenn ich das *Subject* gegen die *Cadenze, in Imitatione*, über eine *notam firmam* hören lasse, der andern *artificiorum* zu geschweigen, welche in Eintretung des *Subject*i anzubringen und zu *observi*ren sind" (Schmidt to Mattheson, 28 July 1718, published in "Die Orchester-Kanzeley," *Critica Musica* 2 [1725]: 267–68; the translation is my own).

23. Butler, "Fugue and Rhetoric," 72–99, seizes upon Schmidt's analogy and, after comparing it with the classic rhetorical disposition, which he identifies as *propositio*,

confutatio, similia, exemplum, confirmatio, and *conclusio,* tries to show how eighteenth-century musicians took the latter plan as the norm for fugal writing. It is important to recognize, however, that Schmidt's choice of a more detailed analogy than Bertali's came about primarily because he wished to show the common bonds between fugue and text.

24. "Unsere musicalische Disposition ist von der rhetorischen Einrichtung einer blossen Rede nur allein in dem Vorwurff, Gegenstand oder Objecto unterschieden: dannenhero hat sie eben diejenigen sechs Stücke zu beobachten, die einem Redner vorgeschieben werden, nemlich den Eingang, Bericht, Antrag, die Bekräfftigung, Wiederlegung und den Schluß. Exordium, Narratio, Propositio, Confirmatio, Confutatio & Peroratio" (*Der vollkommene Cappellmeister* [Hamburg: Christian Herold, 1739; facs. rpt., Kassel: Bärenreiter 1954], 235; the translation is by Bonds, *Wordless Rhetoric,* 85–86).

25. "Noch eins ist zu erinnern, daß nehmlich unter die grossen Erweiterungs-Figuren, deren etliche dreißig seyn werden, und die mehr zur Verlängerung, Amplification, zum Schmuck, Zierrath oder Gepränge, als zur gründlichen Uiberzeutung [*sic*] der Gemüther dienen, nicht mit Unrecht zu zehlen ist das bekannte und berühmte Kunst-Stück der *Fugen,* worin die Mimesis, Expolitio, Distributio samt andern Blümlein, die selten zu reiffen Früchten werden, ihre Residenz, als in einem Gewächs-Haus, antreffen. An seinem Orte wird davon mehr Unterricht folgen" (*Der vollkommene Capellmeister,* 244; the translation is by Ernest C. Harriss, *Johann Mattheson's Der vollkommene Capellmeister: A Revised Translation with Critical Commentary* [Ann Arbor, Mich.: UMI Research Press, 1981], 484).

26. "Ich weiß aber nicht ob der vortrefliche Marcello daselbst die erwähnte sechs Theile einer Rede anbringen wollen, indem es auch gar nicht nöthig ist, alles in allen Theilen eines Stückes anzubringen. Es ist vielmehr höchstwahrscheinlich, daß der unvergleichliche Verfasser besagter Arie, weder an *exordium, narrationem, confutationem, confirmationem,* noch an die Ordnung, wie besagte Theile nach einander folgen sollen, gedacht habe, wie er sie verfertiget. Die Sache scheinet auch daher gezwungen zu seyn, weil Herr Mattheson einen und denselben Satz zum Eingang, Erzehlung und Vortrag machet" (Mizler, review of Mattheson's *Kern melodischer Wissensahaft,* in Mizler's *Neu eröffnete musikalische Bibliothek,* vol.1 [Leipzig, 1738], part 6, 38–39; translated by Bonds, *Wordless Rhetoric,* 87).

27. "Marcello had freilich, bey Verfertigung der im Kern aus ihm angeführten Aria, so wenig, als bey seinem andern Wercken, wol schwerlich an die 6 Theile einer Rede gedacht, von welchen man doch gestehet, daß ich *gar wahrscheinlich* gezeiget

habe, wie sie in der Melodie vorhanden seyn müssen. Das ist genug. Gewiegte Meister verfahren ordentlich, wenn sie gleich nicht daran gedencken" (*Der vollkommene Capellmeister,* 25; the translation is adapted by Bonds from Harriss; see Bonds, *Wordless Rhetoric,* 87).

28. See the summary of current thinking on this topic in George Dickie and W. Kent Wilson, "The Intentional Fallacy: Defending Beardsley," *Journal of Aesthetics and Art Criticism* 53 (1995): 233–50.

29. "Bey Anhörung einer starck besetzten u. vielstimmigen Fuge, wuste er bald, nach den ersten Eintritten der *Thematum,* vorherzusagen, was für *contra*puncktische Künste möglich anzubringen wären u. was der Componist auch von Rechtswegen anbringen müste, u. bey solcher Gelegenheit, wenn ich bey ihm stand, u. er seine Vermuthungen gegen mich geäußert hatte, freute er sich u. stieß mich an, als seine Erwartungen eintrafen" (BDOK 3:285; translation from BR, 277).

30. "Causa principii nulla alia est, quam ut auditorem, quo sit nobis in ceteris partibus accommodatior, praeparemus. Id fieri tribus maxime rebus inter auctores plurimos constat, si benevolum, attentum, docilem fecerimus" (*Institutio oratoria of Quintilian* 2:8–9; the translation is by H. E. Butler).

31. On the former, see ibid., 48–121; on the latter, 154–311.

32. "Eius duplex ratio est posita aut in rebus aut in adfectibus." "In hac, quae repetemus, quam brevissime dicenda sunt" (both quotes ibid., 382–83; translation, H. E. Butler).

33. See Joseph Kerman, *Contemplating Music* (Cambridge, Mass.: Harvard University Press, 1985), 75–79 (on Hermann Keller) and 79–85 (on Heinrich Schenker).

Bach Recordings since 1980

A Mirror of Historical Performance

John Butt

In the two decades since 1980, "historically informed performance"—hereafter HIP—has been an unquestionable presence in classical performance (in the record catalogues, if not always in the concert hall). The present essay focuses on two issues: first, the trends that seem evident over this period—whether they suggest a general development in a particular direction or whether they demonstrate a pattern of action and reaction between recorded performers—and second, Richard Taruskin's bold argument that HIP is really not historical at all, but one of the last outposts of high modernism. Several subsidiary questions inform these central issues: How does the actual performance accord with the verbal claims made by the performers? How does scholarly hypothesis influence the actual practice of recorded performance? How influential are the development of the performers' technique and their growing familiarity with historical instruments? For data, I concentrate on recordings of certain key works, such as the Brandenburg Concertos and the Goldberg Variations, and on recordings that have had particular significance for HIP in the 1980s and 1990s: the final volumes of the complete cantata series recorded under the direction of Nikolaus Harnoncourt and Gustav Leonhardt, and choral recordings that show the direct or indirect influence of Joshua Rifkin's theory that Bach performed the majority of his choral music with but one singer to a part. This is, after all, by far the most extreme and contentious scholarly proposal regarding Bach performance in recent years.

Several scholars and critics have noted a development in HIP that began in the late 1980s and continues to the present (1997). Michelle Dulak, following Taruskin's claim that HIP has hitherto shown every sign of twentieth-century high modernism, observes a softening of the verbal rhetoric and a more luxuriant performing style: "The 'vinegar' that record reviewers once found in 'period' violin tone has turned to honey in the hands of the latest generation of players. . . . this new sound-quality is not just a retreat toward 'mainstream' ideals, but a distinct new timbre, gentler than the 'modern' string sound, more plaintive and more resonant, more suggestive of the physical gestures of performance."[1] In the field of Bach performance, Dulak notes one reviewer's slight embarrassment about enjoying Anner Bylsma's second recording of the cello suites (1992), which displays a degree of expressive "romanticism" that would be all but banned from "mainstream" performances.[2] Another reviewer attributes Bylsma's style more to a "sense of strain" that tends to detract from the spirit of the dances.[3] This observation might reflect just how unfamiliar certain forms of expression (whether or not labeled "romantic") have become. Bylsma's choice of instrument is also significant: an "original" instrument, to be sure, but as a Stradivari from the Smithsonian Institution it is not in its original state — no restorer would dare "put back" an instrument of such value. Interestingly, Elizabeth Blumenstock's recording of the violin sonatas with harpsichord was released at around the same time (1993) as Bylsma's, and for this she likewise uses an updated Stradivari, reequipped with gut strings and played with a Baroque bow.[4] These two instances of the use of "impure" yet superlative instruments would have been less readily admitted in HIP a decade before and add weight to the argument that we are becoming less squeamish about historical accuracy, particularly if there are expressive and sonic benefits to be gained. George Stauffer also observes a change of attitude in HIP interpretations of Bach, noting Nikolaus Harnoncourt's second recording of the Mass in B Minor (1986), for which he uses a mixed chorus, since, according to Harnoncourt, women's voices "bring the sensuous flair of adults to the music." Stauffer suggests that such a compromise may mark something new, an era "in which performers knowingly — and unabashedly — seek a middle ground between what they know of Bach's conventions and their own personal tastes."[5]

It is not difficult to find further examples to substantiate observations such as these. Jordi Savall's recording of the Brandenburg Concertos with the Concert des Nations is notable for its luxurious sound and very characterful interpretation.[6] We should also consider the latter volumes of the most impressive Bach recording project in recent decades, the complete HIP recording of Bach's sacred cantatas by Harnoncourt and Leonhardt, which was released by Teldec between 1971 and 1989. Both directors adopted an approach that stood in stark contrast to anything that was previously available: both took the meter and rhetoric of speech as a principal mode of interpretation, something that often ran in the face of conventional musical expression. On the other hand, their respective results differed markedly from one another: Harnoncourt tended to go for shock value, never afraid to let technical deficiencies contribute to the "grit" of the oration if this served the overall message; Leonhardt, by contrast, tended toward rather more musical elegance and metrical poise, although he was clearly not averse to syllabic weighting (particularly in chorales) that often verged on mannerism.

As the 1980s progress, both directors retain something of their respective styles, particularly in the choral sounds they seem to encourage. But whereas their earlier cantata recordings are striking for their dry, detached articulation, in the later recordings the note lengths are considerably longer, and the articulation, dynamic nuances, and tone are considerably more subtle. If anything, the two directors have become less easily distinguished from one another: Leonhardt takes some of the expressive force of Harnoncourt, and Harnoncourt in particular develops something close to the metrical pacing of Leonhardt. The last two cantatas of the set, BWV 198 (*Laß, Fürstin, laß noch einen Strahl*) and BWV 199 (*Mein Herze schwimmt im Blut*), are apportioned to Leonhardt and Harnoncourt respectively.[7] Both benefit from a more generous acoustic than the first recordings of the 1970s, and in both the performers seem to relish the sounds they produce. Harnoncourt calls on Barbara Bonney for the solo soprano part of BWV 199; she sounds a world apart from most of the boy soloists who grace virtually every disk in the collection (including the boy used for BWV 196, on the same disk). It is difficult to know how conscious the two directors were of the development; it is, after all, a persistent fault in recording reviews to attribute absolutely every element of a performance to the director's intention. What is certain here is that the performers (particularly the instrumentalists) have improved immensely since 1971, that they may well be able to offer expressive possibilities that were simply not available before. Directors will often develop their own interpretative style as much in response to what they hear as from their own abstracted viewpoint.

Although it is certainly possible to find many more recordings displaying a growing sensuousness in Bach performance and HIP in general, there are still plenty of examples to suggest that the more generic style of the early 1980s is still alive and well. Many recent releases of the Brandenburg Concertos are indistinguishable from one another in many respects, although virtually all show great technical advances over earlier recordings. I could not be confident of distinguishing in a blind test the Orchestra of the Age of Enlightenment (1989) from the Linde-Consort (1982/91), the Taverner Players (1989), the Brandenburg Consort (1991), or La Petite Bande (1995).[8] Even the latest "mainstream" recording, by the Bargemusic group, often approaches the same style, although the tempos are slower, the tone heavier, and the general mood more staid.[9] When HIP was young, critics often saw it as a pale substitute for what they considered "real," mainstream performance;[10] now it seems almost that the situation is reversed, with the mainstream offering little more than an imperfect facsimile of the HIP.

All these recordings have their striking moments, their star performers and slight variations of balance, but all seem to belong to the same family, and none speaks with a particularly individual voice. Of course, it is probably part of the intention behind these recordings that they should not present an overly individual interpretation: individual genius is, after all, the concept of an age later than Bach's. But one cannot help thinking that efficiency and conformity are more specifically virtues of a particular strain in the present age, one that sits opposite the trend toward greater expressivity. Moreover, Sigiswald Kuijken's notes to his recording with La Petite Bande could be used as a counterexample to the trend—noted above, with reference to Bylsma and Blumenstock —toward using instruments that are historical mongrels in order to gain a more sumptuous sonority. Kuijken explains that he uses horn instead of trumpet in Brandenburg Concerto No. 2 because he could not find a trumpet player with command of the historically correct playing technique ("without auxiliary valves and with the right bore"), whereas certain horn players can play without "the present practice of compromise when it comes to tromba playing." Thus it seems that the quest for instrumental purism was still so strong in 1995 that a director would rather opt for the wrong instrument at the wrong octave than for the right one played "wrongly" (to my ear the musical result, in matters other than octave and timbre, is essentially similar); there is almost a sense of historical bookkeeping or a moral imperative that works more or less independently of the empirical results.

Given, then, that not all Bach performance has unequivocally moved toward a freer, more luxurious style, perhaps the best way to examine recent recorded performances is by means of a reactive model, one in which some performances can be heard as reactions either to earlier performances or to a generic norm. Of course, it is not always possible to tell whether it is really the players who react to one another or the recording companies that choose the performances they think best suit the current market.

Glenn Gould's famous second recording of the Goldberg Variations on piano (1982) sets the benchmark for "objective," impersonal performance for the entire period under discussion.[11] His method of performance—totally eschewing any audience presence—conforms like no other to what many see as the worst aspect of HIP, a musical high modernism that presents much of the music in a mechanical, equally detached, and measured way. The variations occupy a single track on the CD—there is thus no opportunity to use the randomizer—and one is forced to listen to a continuous piece in which many of the tempos seem related in simple proportions to one another (this is perhaps the most productive insight of the performance). The primary human component is Gould's humming, which sounds almost as incongruous, eerie, and disembodied as the Ondes Martenot in Messiaen's *Turangalîla* symphony. The reactive element here is, I suggest, Gould's response to harpsichord and early-music culture, almost as if he is trying to beat harpsichordists at their own game (harpsichordists, that is, as seen in the popular imagination as inexpressive, twanging sewing-machine peddlers); whatever expressive potential the piano might have is virtually absent here. That such an ascetic style should have achieved cult status is, I suppose, grist to the mill for those who affirm that contemporary performance reflects a necessity of the modern, alienated age, but it does so to an extreme that would make the alleged sins of HIP pale into insignificance.[12]

A reaction to Gould can be found precisely a year later—perhaps too close to constitute an intended reaction—in the Goldberg Variations as recorded by Andras Schiff. This is virtually the polar opposite to Gould's.[13] Whereas Gould ignores the expressive potential of the piano, Schiff discovers sounds of which few pianists could conceive. Schiff, while he seemingly rides on Gould's success at having reestablished piano performance of the work, is now more free to exploit the possibilities of the medium. Schiff's achievement may lie in his attentive listening to what many of the greatest harpsichordists had achieved during the previous twenty years: techniques by which expression and musical sense can be conveyed without any absolute dynamic facility. One can almost hear the ghost of Gustav Leonhardt in the subtle delaying of certain notes and the infinite varieties of articulation and touch. Indeed, if one plays the recording at a very low level, the sound, which obviously involves subtle dynamic variation too, is not unlike that of a clavichord.

Ton Koopman's Goldberg recording was released in 1988, and, as with so many of his recordings, one can get the sense that this performer considers all the standard agogic and articulative devices of harpsichord playing to be exhausted, so he resorts to more radical solutions. If one compares Koopman's performances to those of his teacher, Gustav Leonhardt (or to the latter's pianistic equivalent Andras Schiff), one may perceive a classic case of the anxiety of influence. The basic playing style sometimes contains the same subtlety of timing and articulation, but sometimes not. What is immediately evident is the incessant ornamentation added to virtually every measure, often regardless of whether there is already obvious ornamentation in the notation.[14] Sometimes these seem intended to underline particular expressions and connections in the original music, but sometimes they almost seem random additions that virtually recast the original lines. There can be no doubt that in adding unwritten ornaments Koopman is realizing a particular historical style, one for which there is ample documentation (both in terms of positive advice and negative observation), but my most immediate reaction is often that this performance's principal message is "Not Leonhardt."

Another highly original response to the "Goldberg discussion" comes from Bob van Asperen (1991) who, in contrast to Koopman's ornamented road away from Leonhardt, takes the latter's rhythmic subtlety to a new extreme and perhaps presents the most rhythmically nuanced account of the work, one that will be ideal to some and mannered to others.[15] One of the most recent recordings, Christophe Rousset's (1995), comes from an artist who has received extremely favorable publicity in recent years.[16] This is a "meat and potatoes" account with steady rhythm, even articulation, and a matter-of-fact presentation with little extra ornamentation. In style it could be compared with Trevor Pinnock's 1980 recording (although the latter takes the fast movements considerably faster), suggesting that the pattern of action and reaction has come full circle, at least with regard to this work. On the other hand, it might belong to the relatively stable and generic style of HIP as evidenced in the group of Brandenburg recordings mentioned above; certainly Rousset does not seem to count among the "radical reactivists" such as Koopman and van Asperen.

"Radical reactivists" are evident in other areas of Bach performance, too. Most notable is the German violinist and director Reinhard Goebel (Musica

Antiqua Köoln), who is nothing less than a HIP fundamentalist, dismissing virtually all previous attempts in the movement as merely "a stylistic phenomenon of the twentieth century, and sometimes, in fact, far removed from historical truth." [17] Most specifically, this leads to his rejection of the uniform overdotting and coordination of short notes that has become standard practice for many in HIP, and to his view that the notation often gives us all we need to know. As Goebel remarks with regard to the Brandenburg Concertos: "The autograph score speaks a perfectly clear language: astringent, rough, surprising and sometimes unlike anything else, grandiose and startling." [18] Here there is not only a reaction to the received wisdom of performance practice (namely, to the rules he sees as abstracted from treatises postdating Bach's death) but also the attempt to remove Bach from the mainstream canon: "We must remember, too, that Bach, at thirty-five, was not yet the monument—three hundred years old and more—that we are inclined to take him for when we bid him welcome into our sitting rooms."

If Goebel's actual performances do indeed resonate with the historical environment of the younger Bach, it is not in purely musical matters but in their total avoidance of the political egalitarianism we associate with the latter part of the eighteenth century. The music is continually whipped forward, as if by a slave driver, and many of the trends notable in HIP style of the time seem more parodied than imitated, most particularly the predominantly fast tempos, which seem elevated almost beyond human capabilities (e.g., in the last movement of Brandenburg Concerto No. 3 or the first of Brandenburg Concerto No. 6). Goebel's fundamentalist dictatorship stands in direct contrast to a group such as the Orchestra of the Age of Enlightenment, which most represents the "enlightened," prodemocracy movement within HIP: their recordings flaunt the group's self-governing status, with no permament conductor (ironically, nothing could be further from the political system of Bach's own time). Although each of their Brandenburg Concertos (1989) is directed by whoever happens to be playing the most prominent solo part (and most of these are outstanding performers), the overall effect is one of agreeable neutrality, civilized but never too challenging.[19] In fact, the polarity between these two groups encapsulates one of the most fundamental dynamics working within the HIP movement over the last two decades or so, particularly with regard to instrumental groups. The antiauthoritarian, democratically oriented stream of HIP (often these are the English groups—which must surprise many American critics) provides a foil for those Continental groups that are driven more by the force of a single personality. With regard to Bach performance, the English stream often represents a tidied-up reaction to the characterful direction of Harnoncourt, whereas the "absolutists" either try to create their own difference with Harnoncourt (something Harnoncourt himself has done with his rerecordings of greater Bach works during the 1980s) or do something to shock the HIP democrats.

Perhaps the most interesting chain of influence and reaction is that stemming from Joshua Rifkin's theories of Bach's choral performance and his mildly notorious recording of the Mass in B Minor, released in 1982.[20] Here is the point at which exhaustive musicological research and HIP come closest together (i.e., in one person), where a specific hypothesis implies a radical revision of the existing HIP. This is something much more precise than Goebel's injunction that we should ignore the standard post-1750 lore, since it comes down to the specifics of how the performing materials were formatted, how many singers read from one part. Rifkin concludes that the vast majority of Bach's choral literature was sung by one singer per part. Furthermore—given that more singers were needed for the regular motet performance (often in eight voices), and that Bach seems to have tried performance with extra ripieno singers on his arrival in Leipzig but soon gave it up—he suggests that this was quite possibly Bach's preference.[21] The long, tortuous debates that have since transpired between Rifkin and his critics concerning Bach's specifications in the 1730 memorandum to the Leipzig council will probably elicit a groan from most informed readers today. But several developments in both scholarship and performance are worth noting, not least because the Rifkin theory represents a watershed in Bach performance, the most extreme challenge to tradition, and the most minimalist, sparse, and—to some—alienating moment in the movement as a whole. Whatever the academic arguments or the discussions of Rifkin's approach to performance, one thing comes across clearly in his performances: the vocal parts can be heard as strands within, but not dominating, the combined texture of vocalists and instrumentalists.

First, as I have noted elsewhere, Rifkin's single-voice performance of Bach's Mass in B Minor has led at least two subsequent directors to adopt a compromise solution.[22] Many years before, Wilhelm Ehmann had suggested that Bach's choruses in the Mass could be divided along concertino-ripieno lines, so that some choral sections could indeed be taken by soloists while the fuller textures would employ the full chorus.[23] As if Rifkin's more extreme conclusion had pushed Ehmann's into the middle ground, the latter's was the solution adopted by recordings of the Mass in B Minor by Andrew Parrott and John Eliot Gardiner.[24] Elsewhere, Parrott has followed the Rifkin scoring precisely, notably in a daring juxtaposition of two Easter cantatas, one from the Mühlhausen period (*Christ lag in Todes Banden*, BWV 4) and the other from the Leipzig era (the Easter Oratorio, BWV 249).[25] By emphasizing the enormous difference in instrumental forces required by the two works, he draws attention to the fact that the vocal forces remain precisely the same.

Parrott undertakes a further experiment with his recording of the St. John Passion.[26] In this case, as Rifkin acknowledges, Bach does seem to have used ripienists to double the solo singers. Parrott basically follows this model but takes the opportunity to test a remarkable idea with regard to the soprano and alto parts. He adds single boys to the soprano and alto parts as ripienists to boost the female soloists (both boys coming from the Tölzer Knabenchor). This scheme of adding a "modern" boy to a female voice is designed to suggest the kind of sound, agility, and insight that Bach might have expected from his students, who were still singing high parts in their late teens. Whatever the historical accuracy, this recording must rank as one of the most successful of the work, one that is lucid, dramatic, and spontaneous in every respect.

Whereas Parrott, and to some extent Gardiner, clearly take a positive stance toward Rifkin's theories, others set themselves in direct opposition. The first volumes from an entirely new series of the complete cantatas by Ton Koopman (which promises to be a vibrant and expressive set) present the early cantatas with choral forces of the proportions specified by Bach's "Entwurff" of 1730 (three to four singers per part). With their flaunting of Christoph Wolff as musicological consultant and lack of any reference to Rifkin, they seem virtually to defy the latter's theories.[27] In the booklet accompanying Philippe Herreweghe's B Minor Mass recording, there is also no doubt that Rifkin is the unspoken enemy as the director's notes begin with a discussion of the vocal forces at Leipzig (with all the usual quotes from the 1730 Memorandum).[28] This is followed by the following, extraordinarily contorted argument: "Going on the 1730 memorandum [in fact not, if it is read at face value], one might well envisage performances with only one singer per part, but if a minimalist approach of this kind were adopted for the Mass in B Minor, we feel that it could only create balance problems unacceptable outside the recording studio.

Modern musicology [meaning what?] thus enables one to put together a vocal and instrumental ensemble fairly close to what churchgoers would have heard in the Thomaskirche." Herreweghe goes on to remark that Baroque style has been hitherto largely dominated by instrumentalists, and that he adopts an approach based on a rhetorical system of organizing musical structure. This represents an obvious distancing from the (surely rhetorical) style of Leon-hardt, for whom Herreweghe prepared the chorus in the later issues of the complete cantata series. The difference with Leonhardt is clearly evident in the smooth, flat vocal lines although ironically, the somewhat understated choral texture is most strongly reminiscent of Rifkin's own Mass recording.

Rifkin has made several further recordings with the Bach Ensemble for the L'Oiseau-Lyre label, mainly of relatively well-known cantatas, all now performed with a vocal quartet. One of the tenor soloists on these recordings, Jeffrey Thomas, has formed the American Bach Soloists, a group that has consistently tried to gather the best Baroque performers in North America. Thomas seems to react to Rifkin in two almost diametrically opposed ways. First, the debut recording for the group presents cantatas for solo voices, thus resulting in roughly the same texture as Rifkin's performances, even though the full vocal quartet is not normally present (a four-part vocal choir makes an appearance for a single final chorale).[29] Thomas has proceeded to concentrate on the Mühlhausen and Weimar works, recorded with only one voice to a part.[30] His recording of the Mass in B Minor, on the other hand, represents the polar opposite to this practice. Here a full chorus makes an appearance, although the lead singers on each part are, in fact, the soloists, and even sections such as the Et iterum venturus (from the chorus Et resurrexit) are sung by the full complement.

In sound and musical interpretation, both the solo-style and choral-style approaches differ, in varying degrees, from Rifkin's. A useful comparison can be made between their respective recordings of Cantata 106, *Gottes Zeit ist die allerbeste Zeit*.[31] Rifkin tends toward fleetness, in a relatively dry acoustic with relatively short notes, whereas Thomas aims for a more sumptuous, resonant sonority, slightly slower tempos, and slightly longer notes. It sounds almost like a case of the single-voice idea's mellowing after the initial shock has passed. Although both these single-voice recordings of early cantatas have much in common, the differences between the two B Minor Mass recordings could hardly be greater. Thomas not only opts for the choral format but also aims for a much weightier, luxurious sound and approach. The slow tempo of the opening Kyrie has probably not been heard for a decade or two, and the highly evocative interpretation of the Crucifixus, nails and all, might recall the days when directors did not feel they always had to have the composer's notated direction before embarking on a vivid interpretation of the text.

The split between Thomas's approaches to the early cantatas and to the Mass might also underline Bach's odd status in contemporary culture, in which some works are unequivocally "mainstream" whereas others belong to the field of early music. The mainstream work thus receives the more "traditional," expansive performance, whereas the esoteric pieces are performed in a more intimate, HIP-inspired manner. Thomas's defiance of HIP norms is perhaps strongest in a work that does not really belong to the Bach canon at all, Bach's arrangement of Pergolesi's Stabat Mater, *Tilge, Höchster, meine Sünden*, with Benita Valente and Judith Malafronte as the soprano and alto soloists.[32] Here the singing style is virtually indistinguishable from mainstream opera singing, and the "period" string band plays as lusciously as possible.[33]

These last observations of vocal and choral style close the circle, joining the two approaches outlined earlier in this study: the reactive stance in this case leads directly to the more sumptuous, luxuriant style noted by Dulak and Stauffer. The move toward greater sonority can also be seen as a reaction against the dryer, fleeter idioms of the 1970s and 1980s. What is equally certain, however, is that HIP performing styles are diversifying: the Rifkin scoring is being developed at the same time that it is entirely contradicted.

Greater tolerance for Rifkin's views may reflect that many scholars and performers no longer feel compelled to approve of absolutely everything that Bach might have done (whether by volition or necessity) in performance. As soon as it becomes acceptable to dislike what Bach might have done, it is easier to allow that he might indeed have performed the majority of his choral music with single singers. If I am correct here, this would again suggest that there is a more liberal mood in the air with regard to HIP: historical evidence can be treated critically, and one can acknowledge that there is no absolute distinction between the choice of personal insight — or opinion — and historical accuracy.

Taruskin argues that HIP is hardly historical at all and, in fact, represents the most modern of performing practices.[34] According to him, virtually all the traits of HIP are precisely those that define the high modernism of Eliot and Pound as expounded by Ortega and musically exemplified in the writings, compositions, and performance style of Stravinsky. These characteristics include, above all, a depersonalizing attitude or one that at least defines the "personal" as irrelevant; modernism is concerned with objective order, precision, timeless constancy, geometric style, streamlining, and the equalization of tensions. Transmission takes precedence over interpretation, pathos is banned, and (as Adorno also complained) Bach is reduced and lightened to the average accomplishments of his age.[35]

Much of this will immediately strike a chord with both those who support and those who abhor HIP. Taruskin surely has a point when he notes that HIP performances are usually much closer in style to recent mainstream performance than both HIP and the mainstream are to the "vitalist" (i.e., late Romantic) style of a Strauss or a Furtwängler. By this token HIP is more an extension of, rather than a reaction to, the recent mainstream, and its countercultural credentials are, to a large degree, forged. The traits of HIP on which Taruskin most heavily pounces are its reliance on "objective" document (i.e., performance pretending to be a mode of accurate scholarship), its increasing lightness (which, in its commercialized form, easily becomes "liteness"), its equalization of beats, and its increasingly fleet tempos. The latter are neatly displayed in Taruskin's table of tempos for Brandenburg Concerto No. 5, showing a steady increase from Furtwängler to Hogwood, with the two HIP recordings merely evidencing the extreme continuation of a consistent pattern. However, Taruskin notes the "joyful results" and "human gait" of Leonhardt's recording of the concerto, as well as the remarkable character of Harnoncourt's, which differs radically from Leonhardt's and may even represent a reworking of the vitalist performance aesthetic of earlier twentieth-century performers.

These two approaches, together with that of Hogwood, which is Taruskin's main target, represent three streams of HIP. Surely both Leonhardt and Harnoncourt are central to contemporary Bach performance, and although both are clearly influenced by the modernist spirit, by no stretch of the imagination could they be considered more modernist than the mainstream. Thus, in modification of Taruskin, I would suggest that HIP has resulted in an extraordinary diversification of performance style. The three styles within HIP that even Taruskin acknowledges can be augmented with many more names in recent Bach performance; one could add Reinhard Goebel, Jordi Savall, Ton Koopman, and Anner Bylsma, to list the most idiosyncratic figures. Furthermore, in certain key mainstream performances, such as Gould's 1982 Goldberg recording, we have an extreme modernism that makes Taruskin's examples from HIP pale into insignificance. If one were to add another Brandenburg recording to Taruskin's survey, such as the Los Angeles Chamber Orchestra set (1980),[36] this would surely count as the most modernistic in terms of its rigid tempos, straightness of tone, and equalization of beats.

Another point is that what Taruskin would call "authentistic" rhetoric about historical accuracy in performance does not necessarily add up to the most modernistic, objective, and depersonalized performance. Goebel provides a case in point with his pseudo-scholarly remarks accompanying his Brandenburg recording; these point to a rigid fundamentalism based on the sacred text of the autograph (reverence toward the score, or course, being a characteristic of such high-modernist performers as Artur Schnabel and Arturo Toscanini). Yet the interpretations are the most bizarre on record, having nothing obvious to do with the letter of the score, and taking Taruskin's "modernist" tendencies toward fast tempos to such an extreme that this can no longer represent the tacit acceptance of an objectifying norm. This must be one of the most subjective, personalized reworkings of modernist signifiers available.

To cite a further example, Harnoncourt's first recording of the Bach Overtures (recorded in 1967 and rereleased in 1987) comes with the following note:

> For Bach differed in one important respect from all composers of his generation: he rejected the freedom of the performer, that essential feature of all baroque music, entirely. Perhaps it was just because he . . . knew the dangers that threatened the best compositions of his colleagues . . . that he left no place for this in his own works. . . . Just as he wrote out the execution of the ornaments in detail . . . he also laid down himself the final and unequivocal form.[37]

Although this rhetoric implies a new austerity, the sound of the set (admittedly stiffer and less sumptuous than the newer recording of 1984/85)[38] is certainly very characterful in comparison to other recordings of the time; it is surely an interpretation demonstrating the "freedom" of this talented performer and not merely the dutiful "reading" that the note may imply.

Exactly the same point can be made with an opposite example, Herreweghe's B Minor Mass recording (1989), where the HIP rhetoric of his liner note promises something new and exciting, whereas the results are fairly generic:

> For many years, Baroque style was defined by instrumentalists who had singers imitate the way they played; in so doing, they were of invaluable use to them in helping them question their style, which was so thoroughly rooted in nine-

teenth century tradition. But whether one likes it or not, the central element in [the] Baroque is the work itself, and particularly the work as shaped by the rhetorical system organising the overall musical structure. So for the past few years, our aim has been to move in the opposite direction, basing our approach on rhetoric, not only with the singers but with the instrumentalists as well.[39]

Nothing could sound less rhetorical than the beautiful, safe, and largely uninflected singing of the Collegium Vocale, the sort of sound and interpretation that one could have found in an English cathedral or college chapel for decades.

The fashionable rhetoric of restoration and authenticity covers a multitude of sins and, indeed, blessings. At its best, the movement toward HIP has resulted in newly imaginative approaches to musical interpretation; at its worst, it has merely helped to consolidate a preexistant style (what Taruskin defines as high modernism). Dulak has optimistically—and convincingly—described a more recent turn away from Taruskin's "authentisticity" that moves "toward the use of a newly expanded catalogue of expressive resources, developed in the shadow of the modernist mainstream—a set of resources whose applications will surely not long be confined to 'period' instruments."[40] She notes that this surely results from a discomfort with the "modern" and may represent the beginnings of a postmodern performance practice, while acknowledging the ambiguity and ever-expansive category of the "postmodern."

Dulak's diagnosis rings true for the field of Bach performance, although I believe there is still plenty of HIP in the generic "modernist" mode and even, in some instances, what I can describe only as "the new blandness." If postmodernism means a more liberated attitude toward historical evidence, a less guilty (and more conscious inclination) to follow one's own intuitions, then there are certainly more postmodern performers around than there were ten years ago. Taruskin very convincingly portrays a high-modernist strand within HIP (specifically in Bach performance), but he relegates the alternative strands to the end of his essay. None of these strands represents the polar opposite of modernism, but seen together, I believe, they point toward a postmodernism that represents a twist to, and a fragmentation of, high modernism.

Fredric Jameson shows how many features often associated with late modernism—pastiche and nostalgic art, the "death" of the subject or authorial personality—actually become functions of postmodernism in a symbiotic or a parasitic relationship.[41] The difference lies in the fact that such functions are no longer oppositional, or associated with autonomous cultural artifacts; high modernism is now conflated with mass culture. Many writers associate this postmodernism with the commercially aestheticized world of late capitalism, where nothing has absolute value, and culture—high and low—is reintegrated into everyday life. With this often comes a play of superficial surfaces, a reluctance to search for deep, unique meanings, and a belief that there is nothing more to uncover.

All this has much in common with many of the characterizations of HIP, most strikingly with Taruskin's complaint that HIP performers often forsake their own subjectivity and that they see nothing deep in great pieces of music. Furthermore, the movement would hardly have grown so powerful without its commercialization, the sophistication of recording technology, and the enticing packaging that advertises "authenticity." Perhaps the most pessimistic picture comes from Jean Baudrillard, with his concept of the simulacrum, a world in which everything is a copy (infinitely reproducible through technology) of a nonexistent original, where the saturation of media messages is such that the real and imaginary are frequently confused.[42] There is no need to point out here the close parallel with the HIP ideal of reproducing a historic performance, and with the extraordinary transmission of such "reproductions" through recording and the frequent duplications of performing style—resulting, for instance, in the illusion that one has an infinite choice between all those Brandenburg recordings, many of which are in fact virtually the same. The recording medium itself has been vital to the success of HIP: the CD is a token of the "original," the "authentic," when in fact it corresponds neither to an original historical performance (which today exists only in the realm of conjecture) nor even, in most cases of edited recording, to an actual contemporary performance; it is usually a collage invented by the sound engineer.

But there is a bright side too: the sheer diversity of value systems, the lack of a single standard for musical legitimation, is surely challenging and healthy. Jean-François Lyotard's injunction that we "wage war on totality" has been amply exercised by HIP,[43] even if some of the trends within the movement have been toward a totality more stifling than the last. Charles Jencks has taken an optimistic view of postmodernism (primarily in architecture) as an opportunity for the democratization of art and for its critique from within; both have been features of HIP from the time of its inception. Postmodernist HIP has helped to overcome one of the prime components of modernism, the division of labor in the cause of great efficiency of production (a heritage of the industrial revolution). In much performance of this century performers have been mere cogs—albeit expert ones—in musical production, parts of an extremely efficient machine of musical performance (Stravinsky being the most obvious advocate of this role). HIP has, at its best, caused performers to question their roles by studying instruments, composers, and notation. The best performers not only know where they stand in the process of production but profoundly influence that process itself.[44]

NOTES

1. Michelle Dulak, "The Quiet Metamorphosis of 'Early Music,'" *Repercussions* 2, no.2 (fall 1993): 39.

2. Ibid., 51–52. Dulak cites Nicholas Anderson's review in *Gramophone* 70 (January 1993): 49, of *J. S. Bach: Suites for Violoncello Solo*, Anner Bylsma (cello), Sony Classical, S2K 48047 (1992).

3. Malcolm Boyd, in *Early Music* 21 (1993): 319.

4. *J. S. Bach: Eight Sonatas for Violin and Harpsichord*, Elizabeth Blumenstock and John Butt, Harmonia Mundi, 907084.85 (1993).

5. George B. Stauffer, "Changing Issues of Performance Practice," in *The Cambridge Companion to Bach*, ed. John Butt (Cambridge: Cambridge University Press, 1997), 217. Harnoncourt's recording is on Teldec, 8.35716.

6. Astrée, E 8737 (1991).

7. *Johann Sebastian Bach: Das Kantatenwerk*, vol.45, Teldec, 244.194–2 (1989).

8. See, respectively, Virgin Classics, VCD 7 90747–2 (1989); EMI Classics, CMS 7 63434 2 (1982/1991); EMI, CDS 7 49806 2 (1989); Hyperion, CDA 7611/2 (1991); Deutsche Harmonia Mundi, 05472 77308 2 (1995).

9. Koch, 3-7294-2 Y6x2 (1996).

10. The most famous early critique of HIP performance of Bach is Paul Henry Lang's "Editorial" in *Musical Quarterly* 58 (1972): 117–27.

11. CBS Records, MK 37779 (1982).

12. In fairness to Gould's admirers, I note that most seem to prefer his earlier recording of 1955, rereleased on Columbia, MS 7096 and Chant du Monde, LDX 78799.

13. London, 417 116–2 (1983).

14. One of my students, Pamela Kamatani, also an outstanding professional pastry chef, described this style as "a bit like adding buttercream rosettes to whipped-cream decorations."

15. EMI, CDC 7 54209 2 (1991).

16. L'Oiseau-Lyre, 444 866-2 (1995).

17. Sleeve notes (1986) to Goebel's 1982/86 recording of Bach's Orchestral Suites on Archiv, 415671-2.

18. Archiv, 423 116-2 (1987).

19. For details of this recording, see note 8, above.

20. Nonesuch, 79036 (1982).

21. See Joshua Rifkin, "Bach's Chorus: A Preliminary Report," *Musical Times* 123 (1982): 747-54.

22. John Butt, *Bach: Mass in B Minor,* Cambridge Music Handbooks (Cambridge: Cambridge University Press, 1991), 40-41.

23. Wilhelm Ehmann, " 'Concertisten' und 'Ripienisten' in der h-moll-Messe J. S. Bachs," *Musik und Kirche* 30 (1960): 95-104, 138-47, 227-36, 255-73, and 298-309; reprinted in Ehmann, *Voce et tuba* (Kassel: Bärenreiter, 1976), 119-77.

24. On EMI Angel, CDCB47292 (1985), and Archiv, Polydor, 415 514-2 (1985), respectively.

25. Virgin Classics, 7 243 5 45011 2 8 (1994).

26. EMI, 7 54083 2 (1991).

27. *J. S. Bach: Complete Cantatas*, vols. 1 and 2, Erato, 4509-98536-2, 0630-12598-2 (1995).

28. Virgin Classics, 7 90757-2 (1989).

29. American Bach Soloists, *Solo Cantatas*, BWV *51, 54, 55, 82,* Koch, 3-7138-2 H1 (1992).

30. Ibid., vols. 3-5, Koch, 3-7164-2 H1 (1993), 3-7235-2H1 (1995), 3-7332-2H1 (1995).

31. Rifkin, on L'Oiseau-Lyre, 417 323-1 (1987); Thomas, on Koch, 3-7164-2 H1 (1993).

32. Koch, 3-7237-2H1 (1995).

33. It is interesting that virtually the only appearance of a modern (i.e., wobbly) soprano in a HIP recording during the 1980s occurs in Christopher Hogwood's recording of Handel's *Athalia*, on L'Oiseau-Lyre, 417 126-2 (1986), where the title role is taken by Joan Sutherland; it is perhaps no accident that this sound was chosen at that time for one of the most evil women in Hebrew history.

34. Taruskin lays out his thesis in greatest detail in "The Pastness of the Present and the Presence of the Past," in *Authenticity and Early Music*, ed. Nicholas Kenyon (Oxford: Oxford University Press, 1988), 137-210, reprinted with postscript in Taruskin, *Text and Act* (Oxford: Oxford University Press, 1995), 90-154. Harnoncourt was

perhaps the first to note that HIP is "modern," in the closing sentence of his essay on performance practice in vol.1 of the Bach cantata series (1971): "We do not in the least regard this new interpretation as a return to something that has long since passed, but as an attempt at releasing this great old music from its historical amalgamation with the classical-symphonic sound and, by means of the transparent and characteristic selection of old instruments, at finding a truly modern interpretation" (Telefunken–Das Alte Werke, SKW 1/1–2, 1971).

35. Theodor W. Adorno, "Bach Defended against His Devotees," in *Prisms*, trans. Samuel and Shierry Weber (Cambridge: MIT Press, 1981), 133–46.

36. Gerard Schwarz and the Los Angeles Chamber Orchestra, EMI Angel, DSSC 4504 5129568 1 (1980), rereleased on CD, EMI Angel, CDCB 7 47201 8 (1986).

37. Teldec, 8.43633/4 ZS (1967/87).

38. Teldec, 8.43051/2 ZS (1984/85).

39. Virgin Classics, 7 90757-2 (1989). Herreweghe seems to be unaware of the considerable degree of scholarly skepticism that has greeted earlier twentieth-century theories of rhetoric as the primary organizing factor of Baroque music. Furthermore, the concept of "the work itself" is a blatantly nineteenth-century invention that can hardly be "the central element" of Baroque composition, however skillful the musical writing.

40. Dulak, "The Quiet Metamorphsis," 60–61.

41. Fredric Jameson, "Periodising the 60s" (1984), in *The Ideologies of Theory: Essays 1971–86*, 2 vols. (London: Routledge, 1988), 2:178–208.

42. Jean Baudrillard, *Simulations*, trans. Paul Foss, Paul Patton, and Philip Beitchman (New York: Semiotext(e), 1983).

43. Jean-François Lyotard, *The Postmodern Condition: A Report on Knowledge*, trans. Geoff Bennington and Brian Massumi (Minneapolis: University of Minnesota Press, 1984), 82.

44. I am most grateful for the work of members of my 1996 seminar at the University of California at Berkeley, on historical performance: Alyson Ahern, Pamela Kamatani, Beth Levy, and Henry Spiller. They have funished me not only with much interesting information about recent recordings but also with some excellent observations and ideas. I am also most indebted to Michelle Dulak and Steven Lehning for their many suggestions.

CONTRIBUTORS

GREGORY BUTLER is Professor of Music in the School of Music at the University of British Columbia. He has recently brought to a conclusion a study of all the original editions of the compositions of J. S. Bach with an article on the Musical Offering. He is also author of *J. S. Bach's Clavierübung* III: *The Making of a Print.* Recently he has turned his attention to the concertos of J. S. Bach.

JOHN BUTT has held positions at Aberdeen University; Magdalene College, Cambridge; and the University of California at Berkeley. He is currently at King's College, Cambridge. His career combines performance and musicology; in addition to authoring four books he has edited *The Cambridge Companion to Bach* and has made numerous recordings on organ and harpsichord.

JOHN KOSTER is Conservator and Associate Professor of Museum Science at the University of South Dakota's Shrine to Music Museum. After receiving the A.B. with honors in music from Harvard College in 1971, he was for many years a professional harpsichord maker, producing a wide variety of instruments modeled closely after historical examples. In 1990–91 he held an Andrew W. Mellon senior fellowship at the Metropolitan Museum of Art in New York. His *Keyboard Musical Instruments in the Museum of Fine Arts, Boston* won the American Musical Instrument Society's Nicholas Bessaraboff Prize for 1994–95.

ALFRED MANN received his early training at the Academy of Music in Berlin, the Royal Conservatory in Milan, and the Curtis Institute of Music in Philadelphia. He took his M.A. and Ph.D. degrees from Columbia University and has served on the faculties of Rutgers University and the University of Rochester, where he remains active as Professor Emeritus at the Eastman School of Music. With Arthur Mendel, whom he had succeeded as conductor of the Cantata Singers in New York, he established in 1972 an American chapter of the Neue Bachgesellschaft (since 1986 the American Bach Society), and he served several terms on the board of the Georg-Friedrich-Händel-Gesellschaft. He contributed volumes for the complete works of Fux, Handel, Mozart, and Schubert, and his books include *The Study of Fugue, The Great Composer as Teacher and Student* (first published as *Theory and Practice*), *Handel: The Orchestral Works,* and *Bach and Handel: Choral Performance Practice.*

Contributors

MARY OLESKIEWICZ has recently been appointed Curator of Musical Instruments at The Shrine to Music Museum and Assistant Professor of Music at the University of South Dakota. Her Duke University doctoral dissertation is on Johann Joachim Quantz as flutist, flute maker, and composer at the Dresden court. Her field and archival work in Dresden and Berlin has been supported by two grants from the Deutscher Akademischer Austauschdienst; she has recently contributed articles on Quantz's flutes to the *Journal of the American Musical Instrument Society* and a Festschrift for Rainer Weber. She appears frequently as an invited speaker and performer on Baroque flutes and recorder in both the United States and Europe.

WILLIAM RENWICK is Associate Professor of Music in the School of Art, Drama and Music at McMaster University, Hamilton, Ontario. His major research is on aspects of voice leading and structure in music of the Baroque period. He is the author of *Analyzing Fugue: A Schenkerian Approach.*

DAVID SCHULENBERG is the author of *The Keyboard Music of J. S. Bach* and *The Instrumental Music of C. P. E. Bach.* He performs throughout the United States on early keyboard instruments and is preparing for publication a textbook on Baroque music history, together with an accompanying anthology.

JEANNE SWACK is Associate Professor of Musicology at the University of Wisconsin–Madison. Her research has centered around the music of Bach and Telemann, and she is currently writing a book on Telemann's chamber music. She has recently published an edition of Telemann's *Douze Solos* for violin or flute and continuo.

PAUL WALKER directs the University of Virginia Ensemble for Early Music and the ensemble Zephyrus, which has just released its first CD, of Renaissance motets for Christmas. He is also organist-choirmaster at Christ Episcopal Church in Charlottesville. His book *Theories of Fugue from the Age of Josquin to the Age of Bach* will be published by the University of Rochester Press, and he is contributing a new article on fugue for the next *Grove Dictionary of Music.*

GENERAL INDEX

Libraries and other collections are indexed under the cities in which they are located.

General Index

Baudrillard, Jean, 195
Bauer, Hofrath, 99
Beethoven, Ludwig van, 123
Berlin (*see also* sources)
  opera house, 107 n.39
  Königliche Bibliothek, 140
  Schloß Charlottenburg, 66
  Singakademie, 140
  Staatsbibliothek (SBB), 140
Bernhardt, Christoph, 165–67, 168, 171
Bertali, Antonio, 167, 168, 171
Birnbaum, Johann Abraham, 114, 130 n.4
Blumenstock, Elizabeth, 182, 184
Boehme, Christoph, 65
Boehme, Martin, 65
Bonney, Barbara, 183
Boyd, Malcolm, 9, 42
The Brandenburg Consort, 184
Bülow, Hans von, 126, 127, 134 n.41
Burmeister, Joachim, 163–66, 171, 174
Burney, Charles, 4, 80
Butler, Gregory G., 160, 162, 169, 171
Butt, John, 120, 121, 123, 125
Buxtehude, Dietrich, 65, 149, 168
  BUXWV 155: Toccata in D Minor, 144, 145
Bylsma, Anner, 182, 184, 192

cadenza, 5
Calvisius, Seth, 161
canon, in works of Quantz, 83–84
Carissimi, Giacomo, 159
Chasot, Isaak Franz Egmont von, 84, 100
clavichord, 122, 128, 135
Clemens, Jacobus, 162, 163
Collegium Musicum (Leipzig), 6
Collegium Vocale, 194
Concert des Nations, 182
concerto
  as genre, 15–16, 17–20, 22–23
  instrumentation and scoring, 4–7, 15–17,
    22–23, 42–43, 98. *See also* continuo
continuo, instrumentation of, 15, 24, 27, 29
  n.10, 99, 101. *See also* figured bass
Corelli, Arcangelo, 159
Cornet, 67–69, 71, 76 n.52
countersubject, in fugue, 168
Czerny, Carl, 123, 126, 134 n.41

Devise (motto), 16
  double *Devise*, 24–26
Devisenarie (motto aria), 24
Dirst, Matthew, 117
Diruta, Girolamo, 167
Dowd, William, 66
Dresden
  Frauenkirche, 86
  Sächsische Landesbibliothek, 105 n.21
  Schloßkirche, 71
Dressler, Gallus, 162–63, 168, 171, 174
Dreyfus, Laurence, 42
Dulak, Michelle, 181–82, 191, 194
Dufay, Guillaume, 159
dynamics, 101
  on flutes, 90–91
  on keyboard instruments, 118, 119, 128, 132
  n.14

Edition Peters, 133 n.31
Ehmann, Wilhelm, 188–89
Eisenach, Bachhaus, 61, 62, 63
Eliot, T. S., 191
Epilog, 22, 52 n.8
Ernst, Friedrich, 64
Erfurt, 155
Escher, M. C., 44, 52 n.21
Espagne, Franz, 123

figured bass, 117, 137
fingering, keyboard, 135 n.46
Fischer, Johann Caspar Ferdinand
  Ariadne musica, 143
Fischer, Wilhelm, 30 n.18, 52 n.8
Fleischer, Carl Conrad, 60, 65
Fleischer, Johann Christoph, 75 n.36
Fleischer family, 65
Flöte (keyboard stop), 67, 69
flute, 79, 90–98 (*see also* trills)
  intonation, 91–95
  keys, 91–95
  pitch, 96–98
Forkel, Johann Nicolaus, 6, 121–22, 127, 133
  nn.31–35, 172
fortepiano, 98–99, 100–101, 128
Fortspinnung, 22, 36, 52 n.8
Franklin, Don O., 141

INDEX OF BACH'S COMPOSITIONS

BACH PERSPECTIVES

VOLUME EIGHT

J. S. Bach and the
Oratorio Tradition

BACH PERSPECTIVES

VOLUME EIGHT

J. S. Bach and the
Oratorio Tradition

Edited by
Daniel R. Melamed

UNIVERSITY OF ILLINOIS PRESS
URBANA, CHICAGO, AND SPRINGFIELD

ISSN 1072-1924
ISBN 0-252-03584-4
ISBN 978-0-252-03584-5

Bach Perspectives is
sponsored by the
American Bach Society
and produced under the
guidance of its Editorial
Board. For information
about the American Bach
Society, please see its
Web site at this URL:
http://www.americanbachsociety.org.

CONTENTS

PREFACE

Versions of the first four essays in this collection were presented at the American Bach Society's conference "Bach and the Oratorio Tradition" held in Bethlehem, Pennsylvania, in May 2008, a meeting that emphasized the place of Bach's oratorios in their repertorial context. The expanded group approaches Bach's oratorios from a variety of perspectives: in relation to models, antecedents, and contemporary trends; from the point of view of the construction of musical and textual types; and from analytical vantage points as different as instrumental music and theology.

I want to thank the authors for their contributions to the volume; the anonymous readers for advice and suggestions; and Kerry O'Brien and Karen Anton for their excellent editorial assistance.

Daniel R. Melamed
Bloomington, Indiana

ABBREVIATIONS

BC   [Bach Compendium] Hans-Joachim Schulze and Christoph Wolff. *Bach Compendium: Analytisch-bibliographisches Repertorium der Werke Johann Sebastian Bachs.* Leipzig and Frankfurt, 1985–.

BWV   [Bach Werke-Verzeichnis] Wolfgang Schmieder. *Thematisch-systematisches Verzeichnis der musikalischen Werke von Johann Sebastian Bach.* Rev. ed. Wiesbaden: Breitkopf & Härtel, 1990.

BUXWV [Buxtehude Werke-Verzeichnis] Georg Karstadt. *Thematisch-systematisch Verzeichnis der musikalischen Werke von Dietrich Buxtehude.* 2nd ed. Wiesbaden: Breitkopf & Härtel, 1985.

TVWV   [Telemann Vokalwerke-Verzeichnis] Werner Menke. *Thematisches Verzeichnis der Vokalwerke von Georg Philipp Telemann.* 2nd ed. Frankfurt: Klostermann, 1988 and 1995.

Under the Spell of Opera?

Bach's Oratorio Trilogy

Christoph Wolff

The first summary catalogue of Johann Sebastian Bach's works from his obituary (1750/54) begins with a listing of the vocal compositions and sorts them into four groups. Whereas the first, third, and fourth consist of clearly defined types of compositions (church cantatas, passions, and motets), the second resembles a catch-all collection that lumps together "many oratorios, Masses, Magnificat, single Sanctus, Dramata, serenades, music for birthdays, name days, and funerals, wedding masses, and also several comic singing pieces."[1]

This random mixture of genres and works not only intermingles sacred and secular music, but also quantifies the pieces in a most general way. Beginning with oratorios, the adjective "many" refers equally to Masses, Magnificat, and the rest of the lot. This casual accounting suggests that the compiler of the summary catalogue, in all likelihood none other than Carl Philipp Emanuel Bach, either had no clear overview and no opportunity of surveying the pertinent repertory more closely, or lacked an interest in presenting a more accurate and differentiated picture. Regardless of the explanation, the above-mentioned catalogue entry does not, in fact, suggest that Bach composed many—in the sense of more than the three extant—oratorios, or that further oratorios, like so many other vocal works, must be considered lost.

The three known sacred works specifically designated by Bach as "oratorio" form a coherent and topically interrelated group of oratorios for Christmas, Easter, and Ascension Day, the three jubilant ecclesiastical feasts. Bach consistently designed Latin titles for all of them: "Oratorium Tempore Nativit: Xsti" (with corresponding subtitles for the individual feast days "Pars I [II, III, etc.] Oratorii"),[2] "Oratorium Festo Paschatos,"

---

1. *The New Bach Reader: A Life of Johann Sebastian Bach in Letters and Documents*, ed. Hans T. David and Arthur Mendel, revised and enlarged by Christoph Wolff (New York: W. W. Norton, 1998), no. 306.

2. In the *Christmas Oratorio* Bach fit "Oratorium" into the heading at a later point, making it correspond to the other two.

and "Oratorium Festo Ascensionis Xsti." If one adds to this trilogy of major works for the festivals of Christmas, Easter, and Ascension the traditional Good Friday Passion (for which Bach formulated Latin titles, as well: *Passio secundum Joannem / Matthaeum*), a grand overall design emerges in a musical series for the four principal Christological feast days of the ecclesiastical year, a series comprising large-scale compositions for narration and contemplation. They commemorate the major stations of the biblical story of the life of Jesus Christ that are singled out and emphasized in the Christian creed: his birth, suffering and death, resurrection, and ascension.

However, the overall triumphant character of the *Christmas, Easter,* and *Ascension Oratorios,* musically underlined by the sound of orchestral brass, separates them as a group from the passions and their focus on the suffering and death of Jesus. In addition, there are further reasons to distinguish them: liturgical function, chronological context, and considerations of genre.

Liturgical Function

The works composed and designated by Bach for Christmas, Easter, and Ascension Day deliberately conform to the general function, liturgical place, and proportions of the regular church cantata. Like a cantata, each oratorio was planned to be performed as festive *Haupt-Music* for the respective feast day at its proper place before the sermon in the principal morning service. Moreover, the Leipzig custom of repeat performances of the principal music on high feasts at the morning service in one church (alternating between the St. Nicholas and St. Thomas churches), at the vesper service of the other,[3] and then for the so-called old service of the University Church, resulted in three musical presentations on the same day.

The musical passions, on the other hand, had their unique place in the afternoon vesper service on Good Friday in just one of the main churches, alternating annually between St. Thomas's and St. Nicholas's. This special service, established in Leipzig only two years before Bach's arrival, assumed a musical character. Indeed, under Bach, with performances of multiple-hour works, the event turned into the musical pinnacle of the year; it was an absolute exception that a piece of music would dominate the liturgy and take up more time than the sermon, the traditional centerpiece of the Lutheran service. The shorter first part of the musical passion had to be timed in such a way that the sermon could start near the beginning of the second hour of the service, whereas there were no time restrictions for the longer second part.

Because the principal feasts of the ecclesiastical calendar from Christmas to Ascension focus on the main stations of the life of the biblical Jesus, Bach's oratorio trilogy and his passion settings are interrelated despite their differences in liturgical function

---

3. As applicable here on the First and Second days of Christmas, New Year's Day, Epiphany, First and Second days of Easter, and Ascension Day.

and musical design. The oratorios originating in the 1730s correspond to, continue, and complement (on a lesser scale) the role of the musical passions from the 1720s. In fact, Bach's work on the oratorios may also have prompted the major revisions to which he subjected the passions in 1736 and later, not only the two according to St. Matthew and St. John, but apparently also the *St. Mark Passion*.[4]

The question of why Bach did not plan a three-part oratorio for the three-day festival of Easter, analogous to the multipart design of the *Christmas Oratorio*, can easily be answered by the brevity of the biblical story of the resurrection. The traditional gospel reading for Easter Sunday consists of only the short lesson from Mark 16:1–8. However, Bach's *Easter Oratorio* compensates for its limitation to a single feast day by exceeding the ordinary half-hour limit adhered to by all six parts of the *Christmas Oratorio* and by the *Ascension Oratorio*, as well.

Chronological Context

Bach's Leipzig passions according to John, Matthew, and Mark were composed and presented between 1724 and 1731, that is, well before his oratorios originated. However, all three passions were slated for thorough revisions: the *St. Matthew* in 1736, the *St. John* in around 1739 (incomplete), and the *St. Mark* by 1744.[5] Bach's schedule for passion performances after 1733, when the performance was cancelled because of an official state mourning period, remains sketchy. However, Bach's only passion presentations documented by printed texts and other corroborating external evidence are his performances of Gottfried Heinrich Stölzel's "Ein Lämmlein geht und trägt die Schuld" in 1734, the second version of the *St. Matthew Passion* in 1736, and the expanded *St. Mark Passion* in 1744.[6]

Beginning with the first Sunday after Trinity in 1735, Bach apparently performed the entire annual cantata cycle "Das Saitenspiel des Herzens" by Stölzel in 1735–36. The extended pattern—uncovered by recent research[7]—of Bach performing music

---

4. Tatjana Schabalina, "'Texte zur Music' in St. Petersburg—Neue Funde," *Bach-Jahrbuch* 95 (2009): 11–48.

5. The thoroughly revised *St. Matthew Passion* was recorded in a calligraphic fair copy of 1736. The revision of the *St. John Passion* was undertaken in the late 1730s; an autograph fair copy of the score was begun in the late 1730s but left incomplete, apparently in 1739.

6. The 1743 and 1744 performances are evidenced by recently discovered dated original text booklets; see Tatjana Schabalina, "'Texte zur Music' in St. Petersburg. Neue Quellen zur Leipziger Musikgeschichte sowie zur Kompositions- und Aufführungstätigkeit Johann Sebastian Bachs," *Bach-Jahrbuch* 94 (2008): 33–98; and "'Texte zur Music' in St. Petersburg—Neue Funde." The 1736 performance was recorded in the church diary by the custodian Rost; see *New Bach Reader*, no. 114.

7. Schabalina, "'Texte zur Music' in St. Petersburg"; Marc-Roderich Pfau, "Ein unbekanntes Leipziger Kantatentextheft aus dem Jahr 1735—Neues zum Thema Bach und Stölzel," *Bach-Jahrbuch* 94 (2008): 99–122; Peter Wollny, "'Bekennen will ich seinen Namen'—Authentizität, Bestimmung und Kontext

by other composers during the mid-1730s may have implications for a better under-standing of the composer's creative activities in the same period, notably in regard to his liturgical music projects. He may have wanted to free up time to focus on revising and updating older large-scale works, as well as on borrowings and reworkings of ex-tant compositions. Works in this category include his passions, the five Kyrie-Gloria Masses BWV 232–36, and the three oratorios.

The first of these is the *Christmas Oratorio* from 1734–35, spanning six feast days from the First Day of Christmas 1734 through Epiphany 1735.[8] The *Christmas Oratorio* was followed within the same ecclesiastical year by the *Ascension Oratorio*, first performed on May 19, 1735.[9] Nothing indicates that the *Easter Oratorio* belongs between the two in narrative-liturgical sequence (Easter Sunday 1735). Source evidence rather points to a later year, most likely 1737 or perhaps also 1738.[10] At the same time, there can be no doubt about a relatively narrow time frame for the origin of the oratorio trilogy. In particular, the titles of the three works suggest that Bach intended a close interrelationship, as is obvious not only from a consistent linguistic phraseology, but also from a close match of the autograph handwriting.

Considerations of Genre

By focusing on the biblical narrative of the life of Jesus, Bach's oratorios offered an alternative to the regular cantatas composed for the same high feast days but based on non-narrating texts and ordinarily beginning with biblical verses containing theo-logical messages related to the prescribed liturgical readings or, in the case of chorale cantatas, consisting of the appropriate seasonal hymns. Biblical narrative as structural backbone links Bach's oratorio trilogy with his passions, even though the traditional *historia* format is far more pronounced in the passions because of their extended scrip-tural texts. Nonetheless, Bach's renewed interest in the *historia* concept that began with the *Christmas Oratorio* of 1734–35 may well have prompted his subsequent major revisions of his passions to complete and unify the large-scale musical cycle on the story of the biblical Jesus.[11]

---

der Arie BWV 200. Anmerkungen zu Johann Sebastian Bachs Rezeption von Werken Gottfried Hein-rich Stölzels," *Bach-Jahrbuch* 94 (2008): 123–58; Andreas Glöckner, "Ein weiterer Kantatenjahrgang Gottfried Heinrich Stölzels in Bachs Aufführungsrepertoire?" *Bach-Jahrbuch* 95 (2009): 95–115.

8. The date is in the published original libretto.

9. Dating based on scribal and paper evidence; BC D 9.

10. See BC D 8b.

11. It seems that Bach never treated his *St. Mark Passion* like those according to St. John and St. Matthew nor gave it the same weight.

At any rate, the *historia* tradition in sacred music provided a strong common denominator, and hence passion and oratorio represented for Bach essentially the same genre with respect to both text and music. The differences in their liturgical function pertained primarily to their assignment to different worship services in Leipzig. However, the term *Passion* or *Musicalische Passion* had long been firmly established in Lutheran Germany, whereas *Oratorium*, derived from the Italian oratorio, was (as the more modern term) only rarely applied and remained loosely defined for a long time.

The literary and musical genre of oratorio was, of course, familiar to Bach. To mention but one specific example, Christian Friedrich Henrici (alias Picander) published in 1725 a passion libretto under the heading *Erbauliche Gedanken . . . über den Leidenden Jesum, in einem Oratorio entworfen von Picandern* (Edifying reflections . . . on the suffering Jesus, drafted in an oratorio by Picander)—a publication well known to Bach, for it influenced the text of his *St. Matthew Passion* and perhaps encouraged his collaboration with Picander that began in 1725, if not before. However, Picander's passion oratorio did not make use of biblical narrative but, like most modern passion librettos, paraphrased it poetically. Another example of a similar libretto is found in the oratorio *Joseph* performed in Leipzig by the Collegium musicum under Georg Balthasar Schott prior to 1729, when Bach took over the directorship.[12]

Independent of the Italian oratorio tradition of the seventeenth century, the term *oratorio* came into use in protestant Germany after 1700, specifically in Hamburg and promoted there by Christian Friedrich Hunold and Erdmann Neumeister. Texts by these two prolific writers and leading exponents of sacred poetry were set to music by many composers, including Bach. From the very beginning, the term *oratorio* was not specifically defined by its German users and generally applied to various types of church composition. Telemann occasionally used it for regular cantatas. Even Johann Christoph Gottsched remained vague when he wrote in his *Versuch einer Critischen Dichtkunst*:

> Church pieces generally called oratorios—that is, prayer pieces—resemble cantatas in that they, too, contain arias and recitatives. They also generally introduce various speaking personae so that there might be variety amongst the singing voices. Here now the poet must introduce biblical persons, from the gospels or other texts, even Jesus and God himself, or allegorical figures representing religious functions such as Faith, Love, Hope, the Christian Church, Sacred Bride, Shulamite, Daughter Zion, or Faithful Soul, and the like in a speaking manner so that the outcome corresponds to purpose and place.[13]

---

12. Michael Maul, "Neues zu Georg Balthasar Schott, seinem Collegium musicum und Bachs Zerbster Geburtstagskantate," *Bach-Jahrbuch* 93 (2007): 61–104.

13. "Die Kirchenstücke, welche man insgemein Oratorien, das ist Bethstücke nennet, pflegen auch den Cantaten darin ähnlich zu seyn, daß sie Arien und Recitative enthalten. Sie führen auch insgemein

As this passage makes clear, however, oratorio was generally understood as a work of narrative or dramatic content based on a text that introduced dialogue of biblical or allegorical persons. Hence, opera invariably served as a point of reference. Accordingly, Johann Gottfried Walther, Bach's distant cousin, defines oratorio in the following way in his influential *Musicalisches Lexicon*:

> Oratorium . . . a sacred opera, or musical performance of a sacred historia in the chapels or chambers of great lords, consisting of dialogues, duos, trios, ritornellos, big choruses, etc. The musical composition must be rich in everything that art can muster in terms of ingenious and refined ideas.[14]

Oratorio as sacred opera—this definition posed a direct problem with respect to Bach's contractual obligations as cantor of St. Thomas's. Prior to his election as cantor, Town Councilor Steger had the town scribe record in the minutes of the meeting that he "voted for Bach, but he should make compositions that were not theatrical."[15] Moreover, and not surprisingly, Bach's final pledge to the town council of May 5, 1723, included a paragraph that specified that "the music . . . shall not last too long, and shall be of such a nature as not to make an operatic impression, but rather incite the listeners to devotion."[16]

How could Bach resolve this conflict? In passions, for example, there had been a tradition from medieval times, and continuing after the Reformation, of presenting the story of Christ's passion in dramatized form, with the Evangelist as musical narrator; the roles of Jesus, Peter, Pilate assigned to soliloquentes; and the crowds of the High Priests, the people, and soldiers as *turba* choruses. Bach's passions strictly adhered to this tradition by making use of the biblical narrative as structural backbone and by adding contemplative sacred poetry and congregational hymns. Therefore, the overall shape and character of the musical passion was clearly different from that of an opera. It is clearly for this reason that Walther modifies his definition by expressly adding to

---

verschiedene Personen redend ein, damit die Abwechslung verschiedener Singstimmen statt haben möge. Hier muß nun der Dichter entweder biblischen Personen, aus den Evangelien, oder andern Texten, ja Jesum, und Gott selbst; oder doch allegorische Personen, die sich auf die Religion gründen; als Glaube, Liebe, Hoffnung, die christliche Kirche, geistliche Braut, Sulamith, die Tochter Zion, oder die gläubige Seele, u.d.m. redend einführen: damit alles der Absicht und dem Orte gemäß herauskomme." (Leipzig, 1751), 728.

14. "Oratorium . . . eine geistliche Opera, oder musicalische Vorstellung einer geistlichen Historie in den Capellen oder Cammern gewisser großer Herrn, aus Gesprächen, Soli, Duo und Trio, Ritornellen, starcken Chören etc. bestehend. Die musicalische Composition muß reich an allen seyn, was nur die Kunst sinnreiches und gesuchtes aufzubringen vermag." (Leipzig, 1732), 451f.

15. *New Bach Reader*, no. 98.

16. *New Bach Reader*, no. 100.

"sacred opera" the reference to "sacred historia." Bach's use of the term *oratorio* for his trilogy of the 1730s goes in the same direction by conceptually adhering to the biblical *historia* tradition. However, as the genesis of the *Easter Oratorio* demonstrates, he originally came from someplace else and by no means drew a strict line between opera and oratorio.

The Experimental Background of the *Easter Oratorio*

What eventually became the *Easter Oratorio* in 1737–38 had first been performed—with the same number of movements, yet in a slightly different configuration—as a cantata on Easter Sunday, April 1, 1725. However, the Easter cantata of 1725 represented an arrangement of a secular piece, a "dramma per musica" commissioned by the court of Saxe-Weißenfels and presented as *Tafel-Music* for the birthday of Duke Christian and performed in Weißenfels on February 23, 1725. The time between the duke's birthday ceremony and Easter spanned not quite six weeks. On Palm Sunday, celebrated that year also as Annunciation Day, the last piece of the chorale cantata cycle, "Wie schön leuchtet der Morgenstern" BWV 1, had its premiere. A few days later, on Good Friday (March 30), the performance of the second version of the *St. John Passion* with the new opening movement of "O Mensch, bewein' dein' Sünde groß" took place. Considering this tight schedule, it seems plausible that adapting an occasional work of substantial proportions, performed out of town for a secular event, into a festive liturgical repertoire piece was premeditated by the composer and was neither an accident nor an emergency solution.

The libretto for the Weißenfels *dramma per musica*, a theatrical Arcadian scene involving four mythological characters (Doris, Sylvia, Menalcas, and Damoetas), was provided by Picander and marked the beginning of his collaboration with Bach. In the work the pastoral characters playfully serenade the duke. Its opening movement begins with the line "Entfliehet, verschwindet, entweichet, ihr Sorgen" (Flee, vanish, yield, ye sorrows), and the finale starts with the words "Glück und Heil, bleibe dein beständig Teil" (Luck and health will be steadily with you).

References in the text to the honored duke as "Großer Fürst" and "Großer Herzog," as well as the overall congratulatory quality and celebratory nature, made the piece entirely suitable for conversion into festal music in praise of the risen Lord. For the Easter cantata, the roles of the four pastoral characters were changed to fit the image of biblical figures—the disciples and their followers—running to the empty grave of Jesus risen from death: "Kommt, fliehet und eilet" (Come, flee and hurry) is now the opening line, and the entire text is adapted to the biblical early-morning scene after the resurrection. The roles of the four mythological characters are exchanged for the biblical figures of Mary, wife of James; Mary Magdalene; Peter; and John. All four voices maintain the vocal ranges of their models (see Table 1).

Table 1. Mythological and biblical characters

Tafel-Music February 23, 1725	*Easter Cantata* April 1, 1725
Doris (S)	Maria Jacobi (S)
Sylvia (A)	Maria Magdalena (A)
Menalcas (T)	Petrus (T)
Damoetas (B)	Johannes (B)

The music of the arias and choruses remained the same, as the metrical structure of the new text exactly follows the patterns of the secular model. Only the recitatives had to be newly composed, because the new dialogue, based on the biblical story, required extensive changes. The biblical text is not presented verbatim but rather is transformed into a narrative dialogue of the Hunold-Brockes variety—that is, a type that differs substantially from the literal scriptural recitatives of Bach's passions. Moreover, the newly created Easter cantata included not a single chorale, thereby making it truly exceptional within Bach's church cantatas. Because the work was so unusual in this regard, Bach apparently realized that it had to be balanced in the same Easter Sunday service by the performance of a second cantata. The work selected for this purpose consisted exclusively of chorale-based movements, a revision of the early cantata "Christ lag in Todes Banden" BWV 4.

The Easter cantata of 1725, a reworking of the Weißenfels *dramma per musica*, essentially matches the definition of oratorio as sacred opera, for *dramma per musica* was the eighteenth-century term for opera. Yet it should be noted that Bach did not call the 1725 cantata "oratorio." It is unlikely that the town councilors or anyone else took notice of Bach's contractual violation by making "an operatic impression," because the choruses, arias, and recitatives sounded like those of any other church cantata by Bach, and only chorales were missing. Nevertheless, Bach apparently put the Easter cantata aside for quite a while; in fact, it seems as if he withdrew the piece for at least a decade. Its secular model, however, was revived only one year later in the form of the *dramma per musica* "Die Feier des Genius" BWV 249b for the birthday in 1726 of Count Flemming, governor of Leipzig, with a reshaped libretto and new dramatis personae: Genius, Mercurius, Melpomene, and Minerva.

While there is no evidence that Bach performed the Easter cantata again between 1725 and 1735, he returned to it in the later 1730s after completing the *Christmas* and *Ascension* oratorios, and in doing so he made a few remarkable changes.[17] First of all, he gave the piece a new title: "Oratorium Festo Paschatos." In two stages, for a

17. For a detailed overview, see BC D 8a and 8b.

performance around 1738 and then for a re-performance in around 1743, he not only polished the text and refined the score quite significantly, but, in particular, eliminated the identification of the vocal solo parts with the roles of Peter, John, and the two Marys. Among the more notable changes are the opening "Aria Duetto," originally sung by Peter and John, which was retexted "Kommt, eilet und laufet" (from "Kommt, fliehet und eilet"), rescored for four parts, and designated "Chorus"; similarly, the concluding "Aria à 4" became a "Chorus," as well. Moreover and throughout the work, SATB entirely lost their role functions as dramatis personae. Thus, for example, the opening scene, with Peter and John cheering each other up with the words "Come, hasten, and race" to reach the empty grave, is stripped of its genuine theatrical flavor. Despite singing the same words, the four-part choir now neutralizes the function of the original operatic duet by simultaneously addressing and representing the congregational audience. The exhortation "Come, hasten, and race" to see the miracle of the empty grave is meant to involve all. Thereby—and in spite of the continuing absence of chorales—the character of the whole work deliberately changes from theatrical to devotional music. The choir gallery, once a quasi-operatic stage for the Easter cantata, returned to its proper place as a venue for musical sermons.

Even in its new guise, the *Easter Oratorio* still differs in some basic points from the other two oratorios, especially in the total absence of scriptural text and hymns. At the same time, the work and its prehistory serve as a reminder both of the close connections between opera and oratorio, and of Bach's development in the 1730s of a concept of a devotional oratorio based on a biblical story but largely without exchange of dramatic dialogue. Moreover, Bach seems to have become fond of the *Easter Oratorio* in its new version, for he re-performed it more than once, the last time on Easter Sunday 1749, some fifteen months before his death.

Biblical Stories without Dialogue

The conceptual change affecting the *Easter Oratorio* lines up well with the idea for the earlier *Christmas* and *Ascension* oratorios. In contrast to the passion story, the biblical accounts of Christmas, Easter, and Ascension in all four gospels contain little if any dialogue. The only soliloquentes who sing in Bach's *Christmas Oratorio*, for instance, are Angelus (the Angel, in BWV 248/13) and Herodes (King Herod, in BWV 248/55), both for only very short musical passages. The Angel in Part II (Luke 2:10–12, "Fear not: for, behold, I bring you good tidings") is assigned to the soprano voice, but the continuation of the angel's words (verse 12, "And this shall be a sign unto you") is taken up by the Evangelist, indicating that Bach here, too, intended a deemphasis of drama. The biblical text of the *Ascension Oratorio*, taken from the gospel harmony by Luther's colleague Johannes Bugenhagen, combines passages from Luke, Acts, and Mark. The short text is distributed over four recitatives and includes but a single dialogue: "Two men in white garments stood beside them, who also said: 'You men of Galilee, why do you stand and gaze up to heaven?'"

Major portions of the music in all three oratorios are borrowed, for the most part from secular *drammi per musica* in which the dramatis personae engage in dialogue. However, because Bach largely eliminated dialogue from the oratorios, what are the remaining typical features of the *dramma per musica?* There is, first of all, a general narrative quality—text and music join in presenting a biblical story. This story replaces the original mythological tale of the secular model, but, for the most part, connections remain. This is most obvious when a complete or nearly complete secular model is adapted, as, for instance, in the case of the *dramma per musica Herkules auf dem Schei-dewege* (Hercules at the Crossroads) BWV 213. Six out of seven arias and choruses from this work were incorporated in the *Christmas Oratorio*. The mythological tale of the young Hercules, destined to be the strongest man on earth, was written for the birthday of the young Saxon crown prince. The imagery could not have been more fitting for the original occasion (anticipating the future of the young prince as ruler of Saxony) or for the sacred parody (the Christ child as the ruler over heaven and earth)—again, most probably a case of premeditated reuse of the material to create a permanent repertoire piece.

For Bach, the connections between *dramma per musica* and oratorio manifest them-selves also in single arias, for these arias focus primarily on human virtues, qualities, and emotions and generally relate to the character of the original dramatis persona. For example, Fama, the mythological personification of popular rumor and the bass voice in the congratulatory drama BWV 214, pronounces the praise of the electoress: "Kron und Preiß gekrönter Damen" (crown and prize of crowned ladies). The same character, now a nameless bass voice, pronounces the Christ child in the *Christmas Oratorio* "Großer Herr und starker König" (great lord and strong king). "Die Scham-haftigkeit" (Chastity)—in dialogue with Natur (Nature), Tugend (Virtue), and Ver-hängnis (Destiny)—sings Gottsched's aria text "Unschuld, Kleinod reiner Seelen" (Innocence, jewel of pure souls) BWV Anh. 196/5 that also mentions "das Lilien Kleid unberührter Reinigkeit" (the lily-white gown of untouched purity). Its parody in the *Ascension Oratorio*, "Jesu, deine Gnadenblicke . . . deine Liebe bleibt zurücke" (Jesus, your mercy's glances . . . your love remains), is sung by the soprano, a voice that often represents the pure soul. Similarly, the soprano Doris of the Weißenfels Tafel-Music BWV 249a offers "Hunderttausend Schmeicheleien" (hundred thousand flatteries). The name of the Greek sea nymph Doris means pure or unmixed. This character remains behind the oratorio soprano who sings "Seele, deine Spezereien" (soul, your spices) with direct reference to the pure soul. This association of imagery may not be im-mediately perceived by the oratorio listener who does not know the secular original, but it definitely played a decisive role in the literary and musical process of parodying, for both the poet and the composer had an interest in preserving, if not intensifying, the intended character of expression.

Finally, chorale stanzas add a specifically sacred element to Bach's oratorios, but, as the absence of chorales in the *Easter Oratorio* demonstrates, they are by no means the principal or crucial distinguishing feature of his oratorios. Rather it is the extended sequence of choruses, recitatives, and arias and the presentation of (and reflection on) a self-contained biblical story that proves to be the difference between oratorio and cantata (see Table 2). For a regular church cantata not only typically has fewer movements, but ordinarily also arranges its texts in the form of a sermon, with a first part focusing on the exegesis of the text and a second on the application of the theological message for the conduct of Christian life. Therefore, it is misleading to label, for example, the six parts of the *Christmas Oratorio* as "cantatas."

Conclusion

I have referred to Bach's three oratorios as a trilogy, and would like to argue more specifically for this view. There is, first of all, the deliberate choice of the term *oratorium*. Beyond this, the three works are linked by another feature: The majority of all movements is taken over from occasional secular works, the texts of which had become obsolete after their performance. Bach therefore wanted to save the music for permanent use. This sets the oratorios of the 1730s apart from the passions of the 1720s[18] and their generally original music.

Table 2. Outlines of three oratorios and a "standard" church cantata by J. S. Bach

Christmas Oratorio I‡	Easter Oratorio	Ascension Oratorio	"Standard" Cantata
1. Chorus	1. Sinfonia	1. Chorus	1. Chorus
2. Recitative*	2. Adagio	2. Recitative*	2. Recitative
3. Recitative	3. Chorus	3. Recitative	3. Aria
4. Aria	4. Recitative	4. Aria	4. Recitative
5. Chorale	5. Aria	5. Recitative*	5. Aria
6. Recitative*	6. Recitative	6. Chorale	6. Chorale
7. Chorale + Recitative	7. Aria	7a. Recitative*	
8. Aria	8. Recitative	7b. Recitative	
9. Chorale	9. Aria	7c. Recitative*	
	10. Recitative	8. Aria	
	11. Chorus	9. Chorale	

‡ Parts II–VI contain 14, 13, 7, 11, and 11 movements, respectively.

* Biblical text

18. The *St. Mark Passion* of 1731 is different in that it incorporates many borrowings but, as far as can be determined, none from secular dramatic works.

It seems that in the 1730s Bach complemented the large number of his church cantatas from the 1720s with oratorios for the three major Christological feasts of the liturgical year, works that served as vehicles for accommodating music whose secular texts had fulfilled their onetime purpose. Besides, as most of these secular pieces were written for ceremonial functions such as birthdays of the royal-electoral family in Dresden, the elaborate scores and rich instrumentation would not make them practical for ordinary Sundays. Hence, the feast days of Christmas, Easter, and Ascension were particularly appropriate for the reuse of this music.

Moreover, the oratorios have yet another trait in common. Nearly all their model pieces were originally designed as "Drammi per musica," theatrical works involving dialogue of mythological or allegorical figures. As the contemporary term for opera was *dramma per musica*, as well, and as Bach's secular cantatas indeed represented genuine operatic scenes, the definition provided in Walther's *Lexicon* (for which Bach was not only a collaborator, but also the Leipzig sales agent) has particular relevance: "Oratorium . . . a sacred opera."

The dictionary of 1732 may even have given Bach the idea to devise, beginning in the summer of 1733 and subsequent to the dedication of the performing parts of the Missa BWV 232 to the Dresden court, a series of homage cantatas in the form of *drammi per musica* for an ultimate sacred destination. It remained for Bach to determine what a sacred opera should be, but his oratorio trilogy makes that clear. After the abortive attempt in 1725 of converting a dramatic dialogue through the simple exchange of mythological figures for biblical ones, a decade later he took a different approach and rejected converting biblical narration into a dramatic plot. Following the traditional model of the *historia*, he preserved the scriptural narrative, including, for the most part, the dialogue. In that respect the oratorio is different from the cantata, because cantatas ordinarily make no use of narrative dialogue. Similarly, choruses and arias were not conceived in a cantata-like manner, either—that is, not as personified pronouncements but as reflective and meditative contemplations.

Nevertheless, like cantatas and passions, the oratorios grew out of a delicate yet deliberate balancing act and were ultimately intended by Bach to fulfill one and the same purpose, namely that of arousing, inciting, and steering devotion—true to his pledge upon taking the office of cantor of St. Thomas. Perhaps not insignificantly, this pledge corresponds to a later account. For sometime after 1733, pondering the preconditions for invoking the presence of God's grace, Bach recorded two decisive words in the margins of his Calov Bible: "devotional *musique*." "Devotional" also signifies Bach's chief intention in the concept for his oratorios.

Johann Sebastian Bach
and Barthold Heinrich Brockes

Daniel R. Melamed

Johann Sebastian Bach never joined the likes of Reinhard Keiser, Georg Philipp Telemann, Georg Friedrich Händel, Johann Mattheson, Gottfried Heinrich Stölzel, and Johann Friedrich Fasch in setting the most influential passion text of the early eighteenth century, "Der für die Sünden der Welt gemarterte und sterbende Jesus" by Barthold Heinrich Brockes. Nonetheless, Brockes was arguably the most important textual influence on Bach's composition and performance of passion music. Bach had the opportunity of learning Brockes's text and several musical settings of it; he used movements drawn from one of those settings in a Leipzig passion performance; his *St. Matthew Passion* was influenced by it, perhaps even more than has been recognized; and his *St. John Passion* can be regarded as a Brockes setting adapted to the needs of a gospel oratorio.

The Brockes text and its early settings were widely circulated, and in Leipzig Bach had ample opportunity to encounter them. The original text printed in connection with the private Hamburg premiere in 1712 probably had only limited distribution.[1] But the revised version dating from 1713, with some additional texts, was published in 1715 as a supplement to Brockes's German translation of Giambattista Marino's *Slaughter of the Innocents.* That volume was frequently reprinted in the first half of the eighteenth century and appears to have been in wide circulation.[2]

Three of the four earliest musical settings of the *Brockes Passion* may also have been available to Bach. Keiser's complete setting was known in the region around Leipzig,

I had generous assistance in the research for this essay from Joshua Rifkin, Michael Marissen, Robin Leaver, Stephen Crist, Steven Zohn, and Ellen Exner.

1. See the chronology of the Brockes Passion and related works in the Appendix.

2. *Herrn Barthold Henrich Brockes . . . verteutschter Bethlehemitischer Kinder-Mord des Ritters Marino. Nebst etlichen von des herrn übersetzers eigenen Gedichten, mit Dessen Genehmhaltung ans licht Gestellet, Sammt einer Vorrede, Leben des Marino, und einigen Anmerckungen von König* (Cologne and Hamburg: B. Schillers Wittwe, 1715), a translation of Marino's "La strage degli innocenti." There is evidence of editions from 1715, 1725, 1727, 1734, 1739, 1740, 1742, and 1753.

having been performed in Sondershausen around 1727 under the direction of Johann Balthasar Christian Freislich. Freislich also composed his own version of the text, probably between 1721 and 1726.[3] Excerpts of Keiser's setting reduced for voice and continuo were published by the composer himself in 1714 under the title *Auserlesene Soliloquia aus dem . . . Oratorio gennant Der für die Sünde der Welt gemarterte und sterbende Jesus;* this print was available at the Leipzig book fair in the year of its publication. There is no overlap between the pieces in this collection and those used or adapted by Bach and his librettist in his *St. John Passion,* and this may not be a coincidence; they may have systematically avoided the texts in the *Auserlesene Soliloquia* as familiar and overused.[4] The Erfurt musician Johann Martin Klöppel performed Keiser's setting in that city's Barfüßerkirche in the first half of the 1730s.[5]

Georg Philipp Telemann's Brockes setting can be traced more directly to Leipzig. In a letter published in Johann Mattheson's *Grosse General-Baß-Schule,* Telemann refers to performances of his composition that must have taken place before September 14, 1718, the date of the letter, including one in Leipzig. The circumstances are unknown, though the Neukirche in 1717 or 1718 has been proposed as the venue.[6] There was also once a copy of Telemann's score in the library of the Thomasschule, to which

3. Irmgard Scheitler, *Deutschsprachige Oratorienlibretti. Von den Anfängen bis 1730,* Beiträge zur Geschichte der Kirchenmusik 12 (Paderborn: Ferdinand Schöningh, 2005), 212n165, 344n229. Karla Neschke, *Johann Balthasar Christian Freislich (1687–1764). Leben, Schaffen und Werküberlieferung. Mit einem thematisch-systematischen Verzeichnis seiner Werke,* Schriftenreihe zur Mitteldeutschen Musikgeschichte 3 (Oschersleben: Ziethen, 2000), 5off.

4. See Albert Göhler, *Verzeichnis der in den Frankfurter und Leipziger Messkatalogen der Jahre 1564 bis 1759 angezeigten Musikalien* (Leipzig: C. F. Kahnt, 1902), section 3, p. 9. The pieces in the *Auserlesene Soliloquia* were well known and were used in the assembling or pastiching of passion settings, for example, in a version of a Hamburg *St. Mark Passion* transmitted in a score now in Göttingen. See Daniel R. Melamed and Reginald Sanders, "Zum Text und Kontext der 'Keiser' Markuspassion," *Bach-Jahrbuch* 85 (1999): 41ff.

5. Klöppel's performance is documented in a printed libretto at Duke University overlooked by scholars. Both this presentation and in Nuremberg in 1729 (composer unknown, cited in Scheitler, *Deutschsprachige Oratorienlibretti,* 225) were presented in multiple parts spread over Lent, a striking parallel to J. S. Bach's performance of his *Christmas Oratorio* BWV 248 during the Christmas season 1734–35. I am preparing a study of the Erfurt libretto and of oratorio performances spread over several days.

6. Johann Mattheson, *Grosse General-Baß-Schule* (Hamburg: J. C. Kissner, 1731), 178. Telemann lists Frankfurt (the site of the well-documented premiere in 1716); Hamburg (where the earliest documented performance in 1719 was evidently preceded by an earlier one); Augsburg (about which there is no record), and Leipzig. Henning Friedrichs, *Das Verhältnis von Text und Musik in den Brockespassionen Keisers, Händels, Telemanns und Matthesons,* Musikwissenschaftliche Schriften 9 (Munich: Emil Katzbichler, 1975), 7, suggests an unconfirmed Hamburg date of 1716 following Richard Petzoldt, *Georg Philipp Telemann. Leben und Werk* (Leipzig: Deutscher Verlag für Musik, 1967), 47. On the

Bach presumably had access if it indeed dated from his time. Without knowing its age and origin we cannot be sure, but this further suggests that Telemann's setting was available to Bach.[7]

There is no evidence that J. S. Bach knew the Brockes setting by Johann Mattheson, a work that was evidently little circulated.[8] But Bach's knowledge of Georg Friedrich Händel's *Brockes Passion* is documented in a manuscript copy of the score begun by Bach circa 1746/47 and completed circa 1748/49 by his assistant J. N. Bammler.[9] We also know that Bach used movements from Händel's setting in his performance of a *St.*

Leipzig performance see Carsten Lange, "Georg Philipp Telemanns Passionsoratorium auf Worte von Barthold Heinrich Brockes," in *Telemanns Auftrags- und Gelegenheitswerke. Funktion, Wert und Bedeutung*, ed. Wolf Hobohm et al. (Oscherleben: Ziethen, 1997), 125n21; Lange points out that only the years 1717/1718 are possible. Andreas Glöckner, *Die Musikpflege an der Leipziger Neukirche zur Zeit Johann Sebastian Bachs*, Beiträge zur Bachforschung 9 (Leipzig: Nationale Forschungs- und Gedenkstätten Johann Sebastian Bach, 1990), 79, cites a report of a 1717 passion performance that evidently took place somewhere other than Leipzig's principal churches. He places it "zweifelsfrei in der Neukirche," probably under the direction of Johann Gottfried Vogler, and identifies it as likely having been Telemann's Brockes setting.

7. The Thomasschule copy is reported in Werner Menke, *Thematisches Verzeichnis der Vokalwerke von Georg Philipp Telemann*, 2 vols. (Frankfurt: Vittorio Klostermann, 1983). Glöckner and Lange (see note above) each acknowledge that it is unclear whether this copy was connected to the performance reported by Telemann. Glöckner earlier suggested that Bach may have made this copy for himself and proposed a possible connection with Bach's problems with his passion performance in 1739. "Bach and the Passion Music of His Contemporaries," *Musical Times* 116 (1975): 613–16. Kirsten Beißwenger has questioned whether the copy had any connection to Bach at all. *Johann Sebastian Bachs Notenbibliothek*, Catalogus Musicus 13 (Kassel: Bärenreiter, 1992), 69ff. C. P. E. Bach's estate catalogue, p. 87, lists "Die Broksche Passion von Telemann, in Partitur." That source, transmitted through Georg Poelchau (and listed in the catalogue of his collection), is Staatsbibliothek zu Berlin/Stiftung Preußischer Kulturbesitz Mus. ms. 21711. Although its title page (in Poelchau's hand) and its second title page (reportedly in pencil in C. P. E. Bach's) credit Telemann, the work is actually the pastiche of four Brockes settings discussed by Friedrichs, *Das Verhältnis von Text und Musik*, 55ff., not Telemann's integral setting.

8. Steffen Voss has raised the possibility that Bach may have performed Mattheson's church music in Leipzig, and if Bach really did have access to Mattheson's compositions the *Brockes Passion* could have been among the works he acquired, perhaps during his 1720 visit to Hamburg. But we do not know how closely the men were in contact; Mattheson made repeated public attempts to get biographical information from Bach, and one wonders how close their communication really was. See Steffen Voss, "Did Bach Perform Sacred Music by Johann Mattheson in Leipzig?" *Bach Notes* 3 (2005): 1–5, who cites a 1725 Leipzig Magnificat paraphrase that agrees with one performed by Mattheson in 1718. The autograph score of Mattheson's *Brockes Passion* returned to Hamburg in 1998 after its disappearance during World War II; Richard Charteris, "Thomas Bever and Some Rediscovered Sources in the Staats- und Universitätsbibliothek Hamburg," *Music & Letters* 81 (2000): 188—93.

9. Staatsbibliothek zu Berlin/Stiftung Preußischer Kulturbesitz Mus. ms. 9002/10. Full description and references to literature are in Kirsten Beißwenger, *Johann Sebastian Bachs Notenbibliothek*, 289ff.

Mark Passion in the late 1740s.[10] Bach's contact with Händel's setting is indisputable, but there are several questions. The first is that we do not know from what source Bach learned the piece. It had long been assumed that the movements he used in the pastiched *St. Mark Passion* came from his and Bammler's score, but Kirsten Beißwenger has demonstrated that they could not. Bach must have had another source[11] that could have come to him at any time after the work's composition in the late 1710s, and we should not take the date of the Bach/Bammler copy as an indication that Bach acquired Händel's setting only late in his life. He may well have learned the piece much earlier from a source that does not survive.[12]

A second question concerns the opening vocal text in Bach's copy of Händel's work, in which the two stanzas of the original poem (beginning "Mich vom Stricken meiner Sünden" and "Es muß meiner Sünden Flecken," respectively) have been replaced.[13] The new text consists of only a single verse, arguably a more modern construction than the strophic original.[14] It is also a much more explicit exordium; in fact, its exhorta-

---

On the dates of copying see Yoshitake Kobayashi, "Zur Chronologie der Spätwerke Johann Sebastian Bachs: Kompositions- und Aufführungstätigkeit von 1736 bis 1750," *Bach-Jahrbuch* 74 (1988): 57, 62. On the identification of Bammler as the second copyist see Peter Wollny, "Neue Bach-Funde," *Bach-Jahrbuch* 83 (1997): 44.

10. See Daniel R. Melamed, "Bachs Aufführung der Hamburger Markus-Passion in den 1740er Jahren," in *Bach in Leipzig—Bach und Leipzig. Konferenzbericht Leipzig 2000*, ed. Ulrich Leisinger, Leipziger Beiträge zur Bach-Forschung 5 (Hildesheim: Olms, 2002), 289–308.

11. Beißwenger, *Johann Sebastian Bachs Notenbibliothek*, 180. The one substantial performing part that survives was not copied from the score. It makes sense that Bach owned another source, given that the jointly copied score was completed by an assistant months or years after Bach began it; evidently he had long-term access to at least one model from which they worked. There may be a loose analogy to the fair copy of BWV 245, also begun by Bach and also completed by an assistant.

12. This possibility was suggested and ultimately dismissed—at least for the period before Bach's composition of BWV 245 and 244—by Bernd Baselt, "Händel und Bach: Zur Frage der Passionen," in *Johann Sebastian Bach und Georg Friedrich Händel—zwei führende musikalische Repräsentanten der Aufklärungsepoche*, ed. Walter Siegmund-Schulze (Halle, 1976), 58–66.

13. The new text is noted in Beißwenger, *Johann Sebastian Bachs Notenbibliothek*, 157n50; Friedrichs, *Das Verhältnis von Text und Musik*, 50; and Andreas Glöckner, "Johann Sebastian Bachs Aufführungen zeitgenössischer Passionsmusiken," *Bach-Jahrbuch* 63 (1977): 105. It was also mentioned by Friedrich Chrysander, *G. F. Händel*, vol. 1 (Leipzig: Breitkopf & Härtel, 1858), 440, who defended Händel against the apparently puzzling setting of "Bach's" text. We do not know whether Bach acquired Händel's *Brockes Passion* with this adapted text, but there is no evidence to suggest he was responsible for it.

14. The revised text has invited some speculation. Friedrichs, *Das Verhältnis von Text und Musik*, 50, called it "durchaus eine Verschlechterung" and proposed that Bach himself had made the change in connection with a performance of BWV 245 to disguise the connection with Brockes and the overlap with the alto aria BWV 245/7. There is, in fact, no evidence either way on Bach's responsibility for this

tions ("Kommet," "Seht," addressed outward to listeners) are exactly those of Picander and Bach's *St. Matthew Passion* BWV 244 ("Kommt, ihr Töchter," "Sehet!").[15] The new text reduces the original's emphasis on the first person even though individuality is an essential characteristic of Brockes's text, whose first word is, tellingly, "Me." In adapting this text in the *St. John Passion*, Bach and his collaborator similarly changed its focus, rearranging the syntax and moving the first-person pronoun away from the beginning. "Mich vom Stricken meiner Sünden" becomes "Von den Stricken meiner Sünden."

Opening text of the Brockes Passion

ORIGINAL

1. Mich vom Stricke meiner Sünden	From the ropes of my sins
Zu entbinden /	To unbind me
Wird mein Gott gebunden;	My God is bound;
Von der Laster Eyter-Beulen	From the putrifying vice-boils
Mich zu heilen /	To heal me
Läst er sich verwunden.	He allows himself to be wounded.
2. Es muß meiner Sünden Flecken	The stains of my sins
Zu bedecken /	To cover
Eignes Blut ihn färben;	He must be dyed in his own blood;
Ja / es will / ein ewig Leben	Yes, eternal life
Mir zu geben /	To give me
Selbst das Leben sterben.	Must Life itself die.

JSB COPY OF HÄNDEL'S SETTING

Kommet, ihr verworfnen Sünder,	Come, you rejected sinners,
Todeskinder;	Children of death;

---

new text. Bach's copy includes another correction that has gone unremarked. At the beginning of the aria "Erwäg, ergrimmte Natternbrut" Bach initially entered a different text. The underlay originally read, "Erwege doch" (like BWV 80/3?), then was corrected to "erweg, erweg." This is the very movement and exact passage in which someone, perhaps even Bach, added a continuo line to support the unaccompanied vocal opening. Beißwenger, *Johann Sebastian Bachs Notenbibliothek*, 182–83, stresses this passage as a significant variant whose origin appears to lie in an attempt to avoid an unaccompanied voice. The two issues—the musical revision and changed texts—may be related.

15. Perhaps a reference to John 4:29, "Kommt, seht einen Menschen, der mir gesagt hat alles, was ich getan habe, ob er nicht Christus sei!"; or to Psalms 66:5, "Kommet her und sehet an die Werke Gottes"; or to John 1:39, "Kommt und sehet's!"; or to Matthew 28:6, "Kommt her und seht die Stätte, da der Herr gelegen hat."

Seht, hier stirbt das Leben.	See, here Life dies.
Euer Tod soll mit ihm sterben;	Your death shall die with him;
Sein Verderben	His demise
Soll euch Rettung geben.	Shall give you rescue.

ADAPTATION IN BWV 245/7

Von den Stricken meiner Sünden	From the ropes of my sins
Mich zu entbinden,	To undbind me,
Wird mein Heil gebunden.	My salvation is bound.
Mich von allen Lasterbeulen	From all my vice-boils
Völlig zu heilen,	Fully to heal me
Läßt er sich verwunden.	He lets himself be wounded.
	(trans. M. Marissen)

The *Brockes Passion* text appeared in Leipzig at least once more in a performance in the Neukirche on April 15, 1729 (Good Friday), under the direction of C. G. Fröber. No musical sources survive, and it is unclear who composed the setting heard then, but the documented performance of the Brockes text further demonstrates Leipzig's familiarity with the libretto in the 1720s.[16] In all, Bach had ample opportunity to learn the text and one or more musical settings, and this exposure is reflected in music he performed in Leipzig.

In the mid-to-late 1740s he turned (for at least the third time in his career) to a *St. Mark Passion* setting from Hamburg, a work he attributed, perhaps incorrectly, to Reinhard Keiser. In that performance Bach incorporated seven arias from Händel's *Brockes Passion* as replacements or additions, inserting each in the equivalent spot in

---

16. The performance is documented in a printed text and a report. The work was considerably shortened, evidently omitting approximately half of the arias. In the absence of the church's former music director Georg Balthasar Schott (recently decamped for Gotha), the performance was led by Fröber, one of the applicants for the vacant position. See Andreas Glöckner, *Die Musikpflege an der Leipziger Neukirche*, 88, and Winfried Hoffmann, "Leipzigs Wirkungen auf den Delitzscher Kantor Christoph Gottlieb Fröber," *Beiträge zur Bachforschung* 1 (1982): 54–73. The title page and first page of the printed text are reproduced on p. 60. The text of the first movement is the original, not the replacement version found in Bach's copy of the Händel setting, but this libretto is clearly modeled on original print, so it is not out of the question that the text of the opening number was simply reproduced from the model libretto, whatever text might have been sung. Hoffmann reports that in the twelve-leaf text print, fourteen arias (of twenty-seven) were omitted, as were nine recitatives (of forty-eight), three ariosos (of six), and one duet (of two); one recitative and one chorale were added. Hoffmann suggested that it was Fröber's reworking of another composer's setting; Glöckner leans towards a piece of Fröber's own composition.

the narrative.[17] I have argued that in drawing movements from Händel's *Brockes Passion* Bach sought to make as thorough and systematic a use of that work as the context permitted.[18] His adoption of the material, typically seen from the perspective of the pastiched *St. Mark Passion*, is equally well viewed as his presentation of portions of the Brockes text—as a liturgical use of the *Brockes Passion*.

Bach's own *St. Matthew Passion* BWV 244 has a close relationship to Brockes's text, perhaps closer than has been acknowledged. Several of the work's poetic texts are derived from an earlier work by its poet Picander, his "Erbauliche Gedancken auf den Grünen Donnerstag und Charfreytag über den leidenden Jesum, in einem Oratorio entworffen," published in 1725. This text presents an abbreviated poetic narrative of the passion story in the voice of an Evangelist, along with poetry presented by allegorical characters (Zion, Gläubige Seele, Seele [possibly the same character]) and by figures in the narrative (Johannes, Petrus, Jesus, and Maria).[19] The text is the entry for Maundy Thursday/Good Friday in a cycle of reflective texts organized around the liturgical year. This one differs from the others in that it is cast as an oratorio, as the author himself wrote, and it is clearly modeled on the *Brockes Passion*.[20] At the least, Picander's reliance on Brockes for a work published in 1725 suggests his intensive engagement with the *Brockes Passion* text in Leipzig in the 1720s.

17. He used only arias that responded to Mark's gospel, avoiding more generally contemplative pieces. When his model and Händel's Brockes setting each offered interpolated movements, he favored arias over chorales and fuller textures over continuo arias. Most often he retained the tonality of the borrowed movements but adjusted either the surrounding material or the new aria when keys were too distant.

18. Melamed, "Bachs Aufführung der Hamburger Markus-Passion." I suggested there that one of Bach's motivations was the supposed impossibility of performing a poetic passion in the liturgy of the principal Leipzig churches, an assumption now upended by the documentation of a 1734 performance of just such a work in the Thomaskirche. See Tatjana Schabalina, "'Texte zur Music' in Sankt Petersburg. Neue Quellen zur Leipziger Musikgeschichte sowie zur Kompositions- und Aufführungstätigkeit Johann Sebastian Bachs," *Bach-Jahrbuch* 94 (2008): 77–84.

19. Elke Axmacher points out that Picander's text gives no words to antagonists of Jesus. "*Aus Liebe will mein Heyland sterben.*" *Untersuchungen zum Wandel des Passionsverständnisses im frühen 18. Jahrhundert*, Beiträge zur theologischen Bachforschung 2 (Stuttgart: Carus, 1984), 168n10. The text does not appear to have been written for musical setting, but see Scheitler, *Deutschsprachige Oratorienlibretti*, 345–47, who cites a libretto from a Nuremberg performance in 1729, and Hans-Joachim Schulze, "Bemerkungen zum zeit- und gattungsgeschichtlichen Kontext von Johann Sebastian Bachs Passionen," in *Johann Sebastian Bachs historischer Ort*, Bach-Studien 10, ed. Reinhard Szeskus (Wiesbaden: Breitkopf & Härtel, 1991), 209, 214, on a possible performance in the Leipzig Neukirche under Schott and one in Dresden under Christoph Ludwig Fehre.

20. Scheitler, *Deutschsprachige Oratorienlibretti*, 215, suggests that Picander's text is singular in the degree of its modeling on Brockes.

The connection is evident from the title of Picander's work, which resembles the title pages associated with early Brockes performances;[21] from the use of the term "soliloquium" for commentary texts;[22] and the assignment of every nonnarrative text to the voice of an allegorical or gospel character with no commentary by unidentified speakers, a characteristic of Brockes's text.[23] In fact, this is one of the features that aligns Picander's oratorio most closely with his Brockes model, and it is significant because allegorical characters (the very ones who appear in both Brockes and in the "Erbauliche Gedancken") are so important to his libretto for the *St. Matthew Passion*. In that work the voices of Daughter Zion and the Believers appear in prominent places, including effectively the opening and closing numbers of each half.[24] This has long been understood as an influence of the *Brockes Passion*.

In the reprinted libretto of the *St. Matthew Passion* that appeared in 1729, these allegorical characters are named only in dialogue numbers—that is, only when they are paired.[25] The standard interpretation has long been that the other recitatives and arias are presented by anonymous unidentified voices. But are they? It is at least plausible that all the poetic texts in the *St. Matthew Passion* are in the voices of Daughter Zion or the Believers. Nothing in the print specifically cancels the identification of Daughter Zion. There are no Evangelist or interlocutor identifications to shift the speaker, because the print includes only the poetry, omitting the gospel narrative, and

21. The title page of the 1716 Frankfurt performance of Telemann's setting, for example, reads, "Der Für die Sünde der Welt Leidende und Sterbende JESUS Aus Den IV. Evangelisten In einem PASSIONS ORATORIO Mit gebundener Rede vorgestellet."

22. Picander evidently used the term differently than Brockes. In the *Brockes Passion*, "Soliloquium" essentially means "scena" and can include arias, ariosos, and texts evidently meant as accompagnati. (For example, one sometimes finds the heading "Soliloquio" followed immediately by a textual label like "Arioso" identifying one of the constituent parts of the soliloquy.) Brockes's "Soliloquia" encompass many different combinations of arias, recitatives, and ariosos, but they always consist of multiple textual and musical units. Picander, in contrast (or in misunderstanding), evidently took "Soliloquium" to mean "recitative" or "accompagnato." Texts with this heading (always recitative-like blank verse) are sometimes found individually and never appear with a double label. Arias are always separately labeled, and there are two Soliloquium-Aria pairs corresponding to the kind of accompagnato/aria pairs found throughout Picander's text for the *St. Matthew Passion*.

23. Even the hymn stanzas are cast quasi-allegorically as "Choräle der christlichen Kirche."

24. No. 27a and b may well have originally been conceived as the conclusion of Part 1. Certainly they are the poetic end of that part, as a look at Picander's text print makes clear.

25. The text appears in the second collection of Picander's poetry, *Picanders Ernst-Schertzhaffte und Satÿrische Gedichte, Anderer Theil* (Leipzig, 1729), 101–12. Reproduced in Werner Neumann, ed., *Sämtliche von Johann Sebastian Bach vertonte Texte* (Leipzig: Deutscher Verlag für Musik, 1974), 321–24.

it is possible that all the poetic texts are in this voice (or perhaps that of the Believers, or of individual faithful souls).[26]

In this regard, the assignment to Zion of the recitative no. 59 "Ach, Golgotha," a movement for only one voice, is striking, because in this piece an allegorical character is identified outside the context of a dialogue. It is possible that the voice is labeled because of the accompagnato's pairing with the genuine dialogue aria no. 60 "Sehet, Jesus hat die Hand," in which both Zion and the Believers are indeed named. But it demonstrates that a solo number in this work can be connected with an allegorical voice. This leaves open the possibility that Picander conceived all the free poetry in the *St. Matthew Passion* for his (that is, Brockes's) allegorical figures. If so, the connection of the work to the Brockes model is even stronger than has been suspected. We would be justified in regarding BWV 244 as a biblical oratorio drawing heavily on the poetic type, and particularly on the *Brockes Passion*.[27] Bach's *St. Matthew Passion* is many things; one of them may be a Brockes setting once removed.

Picander evidently continued to take Brockes's passion poem as a model, even beyond his turn to the earlier "Erbauliche Gedancken" texts based on it. The ensemble poetic number BWV 244/27b "Sind Blitze, sind Donner" in the *St. Matthew Passion* appears to draw on the Brockes text, specifically an aria for Peter just after Judas's kiss and the capture of Jesus.[28]

BROCKES, ARIA [PETRUS]

Gifft und Gluht /	Poison and embers
Strahl und Fluht	Thunderbolts and floods,
Ersticke / verbrenne / zerschmettre / versencke	Smother, burn, smite, sink
Den falschen Verrähter / voll mördrische Rencke!	The false betrayer, full of murderous intrigue.

26. The matter is difficult to evaluate because the published text omits the gospel narrative that may well have been present in an original libretto connected with the liturgy.

27. Of course there is no mention of these characters in any musical source for BWV 244, so it is difficult to say whether this possibility, if true, had musical consequences. But from a textual point of view, if all the recitatives and arias are for Daughter Zion, that would mean that voices in Chorus 2, when functioning individually in recitatives and arias, represent that character just as the voices in Chorus 1 do; and that Chorus 2 stands for the Believers only when it is used as a four-voice group in dialogue pieces. This would certainly challenge interpretations that distinguish the words of the allegorical characters from other commentary movements.

28. This was noted at least as early as Philipp Spitta, *Johann Sebastian Bach*, 2 vols. (Leipzig: Breitkopf & Härtel, 1873–80), 2:386n106.

Man fesselt JESUM jämmerlich /	Jesus is pitiably bound
Und keine Wetter regen sich?	And the elements do not stir?
Auf dann / mein unverzagter Muht /	Up then, my undaunted courage
Vergieß das frevelhaffte Blut /	Shed the sacrilegious blood
Weil es nicht thut	Because they do not:
Gifft und Gluht /	Poison and embers,
Strahl und Fluht.	Thunderbolts and floods.

PICANDER, BWV 244/27B

Sind Blitze, sind Donner in Wolcken verschwunden!	Are lightning and thunder vanished in clouds?
Eröffne den feurigen Abgrund o Hölle!	Open up the fiery bottomless pit, o hell;
Zerdrümmre, verderbe, verschlinge, zerschelle.	Smash, ruin, swallow up, break to pieces
Mit plötzlicher Wuth	With sudden fury
Den falschen Verräther, das mördrische Blut.	That false betrayer, that murderous blood!
	(trans. M. Marissen)

Modern literature probably goes too far in citing Brockes as the author of the text of BWV 244/27b, but it is likely that Picander continued to be influenced by the *Brockes Passion* as he assembled the *St. Matthew Passion*.

Bach was not alone in his use of Brockes's text for liturgical passions, and settings by Georg Philipp Telemann are the most prominent examples. Telemann arrived in Hamburg in the fall of 1721 and began performing passions in the city's principal churches in the spring of 1722.[29] Text and music for his earliest passions there are lost, but outlines can be reconstructed from material used by Hans Hörner in his 1935 study.[30] Telemann's first passion, in 1722 (Table 1), was a St. Matthew setting incorporating eight free poetic texts, all drawn from the *Brockes Passion* (not just six, as incorrectly reported in most of the literature); one of the chorales specified by Brockes is also used in its original place. Telemann's next passion, the 1723 St. Mark setting

29. Stephen Zohn, "Telemann, Georg Philipp," *New Grove Dictionary of Music and Musicians* (London: Macmillan, 2000).

30. Hans Hörner, "Gg. Ph. Telemanns Passionsmusiken. Ein Beitrag zur Geschichte der Passionsmusik in Hamburg" (PhD diss., Kiel, 1933), 59ff. Hörner is incorrect in identifying only six of eight insertions in the 1722 passion as texts by Brockes; numerous authors have followed.

(Table 2), uses thirteen free poetic texts, nine from the *Brockes Passion* and four of un-known origin.[31] Telemann did not draw on the complete Brockes setting he already had—the arias were evidently newly composed—so his choice was not simply one of expediency.[32] Brockes represented his closest tie to the city both personally and by musical reputation, and his use of the poetry speaks to its continuing relevance.

One complete movement from these lost settings does survive in an unlikely place. In an effort to demonstrate the weakness of Telemann's Brockes settings compared to Bach's, Philipp Spitta included the aria "Mich vom Stricken meiner Sünden" from Telemann's 1723 passion in the musical appendix to the second volume of his Bach biography. This aria, which does not appear in the English translation, is a compact ritornello form with a repeat to accommodate the two stanzas of the text (Example 1).[33] The aria's characteristic syncopations and ties presumably reflect the words "ge-bunden" and "entbinden," just as Bach's setting does in a somewhat different way in the *St. John Passion*.

31. The last aria in Telemann's 1723 passion, "Zwölf Jünger folgten Jesu nach," attracted the atten-tion of Johann Mattheson, *Der vollkommene Capellmeister* (Hamburg, 1739), 200–201, who criticized a composer who set this piece with twelve canonic entries. Mattheson characteristically ridiculed this focus on the followers rather than on the one left behind. It is not clear whether he is refer-ring to Telemann's setting or that of some source composition from which Telemann may have taken the text. The passage is cited in Birger Petersen-Mikkelsen, *Die Melodielehre des "Vollkommenen Capellmeisters" von Johann Mattheson*, Eutiner Beiträge zur Musikforschung 1 (Norderstedt: Books on Demand, 2002), 157.

32. Perhaps characteristically, Telemann's 1722 and 1723 passions do not share any texts—the works are entirely complementary and systematic in their use of poems from the *Brockes Passion*. Proceed-ing in this way, Telemann could theoretically have produced a setting of all the Brockes arias over several years. Even though both the 1722 and 1723 scores are lost, we know that Telemann did not use the arias from his complete *Brockes Passion*, because incipits for 1723 were recorded by Hörner, and they show that the arias were not those of Telemann's earlier Brockes setting, but rather were distinct and presumably newly composed. The same is likely to have been true for the aria texts he used in 1722.

33. Spitta chose it from among the available Brockes settings because of its scoring as a solo aria, which made it a plausible comparison to "Von den Stricken" BWV 245/7 based on the same text. (All the other settings treat this as an aria tutti scored for multiple voices.) Philipp Spitta, *Johann Sebastian Bach: His Work and Influence on the Music of Germany, 1685–1750*, trans. Clara Bell and John Alexander Fuller-Maitland, 3 vols. (London, 1884—85), 2:533f: "There is hardly any interest to be found in comparing Bach's settings of Brockes' text with those of other composers. Not only do they surpass them immeasurably in richness and depth, but, in consequence of the profound church feeling [tiefinneren Kirchlichkeit] that prevades [sic] his style, they stand forth as something totally distinct when compared with the operatic religionism [opernhaften Religiosität] of the other Ger-man masters. The solitary grandeur in which Bach dwells as a composer of church music is only rendered more clear by a comparison with similar works by Keiser, Telemann, Mattheson, Stölzel,

Table 1. G. P. Telemann, *St. Matthew Passion* TVWV 5:7 (1722)

Gospel text/Chorale interpolations	Free poetic interpolations	Notes
Choral Wenn meine Sünd mich kränken		(also opens 1736, 1750)
Und es begab sich . . . zur Vergebung der Sünden	**O Gott, du Brunnquell alles Guten**	Brockes (TZ) [orig. 2nd v. of following]
Ich sage euch . . . meines Vaters Reich	**Aria Der Gott, dem alle Himmels-Kreise**	Brockes (TZ)
Choral Ach, wie hungert mein Gemüt [end of Alte Osterlamm]		
Und da sie den Lobgesang . . . sondern wie du willst		
Choral Wen seh ich dort an jenem Berge liegen	**Aria Brich, mein Hertz! Zerfließ in Tränen!**	Brockes (TZ)
Und er kam zu seinen Jüngern . . . dieselben Worte		
Choral Du Nacht voll Angst		
Da kam er zu seinen Jüngern . . . wer ist's, der dich schlug?	**Aria Was Bären-Tatzen, Löwen-Klauen**	Brockes (TZ)
Choral Du, auch du hast ausgestanden		
Petrus aber saß draußen . . . weinte bitterlich	**Arioso Welch ungeheurer Schmertz**	Brockes (Petrus)
Choral Ach Gott und Herr [end of Caiphas]	**Aria Heul du Schaum der Menschenkinder**	Brockes (Petrus)
Des Morgens aber . . . Landpfleger sich verwunderte		as in Brockes

Table 1. *Cont.*

Gospel text/Chorale interpolations	Free poetic interpolations	Notes
Auf das Fest aber . . . daß er gekreuzigt würde	**Aria (duetto) Sprichst du denn auf dies Verklagen/Nein, ich will euch itzo zeigen**	Brockes (TZ, Jesus)
Choral Herzliebster Jesu, was hast Du verbrochen		
Da nahmen die Kriegsknechte . . . schlugen damit sein Haupt		
Und da sie ihn verspottet hatten . . . wollte er nicht trinken	**Aria Laß doch diese herben Schmerzen**	Brockes (TZ)
Da sie ihn aber gekreuzigt hatten . . . einer zu Linken	**Aria Eilt, ihr angefochtenen Seelen**	Brockes (TZ, GS)
Choral O Welt, sieh hier dein Leben,		
Die aber vorübergingen . . . Ich bin Gottes Sohn		
Choral Du, ach du hast ausgestanden,		
Desgleichen schmähten ihn auch . . . und verschied		
Choral Ich danke dir/Wenn ich einmal/Erscheine mir		
Und siehe da . . . versiegelten den Stein		
Choral Nun ich danke dir von Hertzen,		
Choral Nun ich kann nicht viel geben/Ich wills vor Augen		

[Music and text lost; outline reconstructed from Hans Hörner, *Gg. Ph. Telemanns Passionsmusiken* (Leipzig, 1933).]

Table 2. G. P. Telemann, *St. Mark Passion* TVWV 5:8 (1723)

Gospel text/Chorale interpolations	Free poetic interpolations	Notes
[Sinfonia]		
Choral Ein Lämmlein geht [und trägt die Schuld/und weidete?]		
Und nach zweien Tagen war Ostern . . . [Aufruhr im Volk werde]	**Aria Mich vom Stricke meiner Sünden**	Brockes (GS); originally opening text
Und da es zu Bethanien war . . . [was sie jetzt getan hat]	Aria Laßt die mit Frieden	New (unknown)
Choral Ach höchster Gott verzeihe mir		
Und Judas Ischariot . . . [in dem Reich Gottes]	Aria Ach, Herr, ich habe dich verraten	New
Choral Jesus Christus unser Heiland [end of Alte Osterlamm]		
Und da sie den Lobgesang gesprochen . . . [sondern was du willst]		
Und kam und fand sie schlafend . . . [das Fleisch ist schwach]	**Aria Sünder schaut mit Furcht und Zagen**	Brockes (TZ)
Choral Wer fleißig betet und dir		
Und ging wieder hin und betete . . . [die Schrift erfüllt werde]		
Choral Nun er tut es herzlich gern [approx. end of Öleberg]		
Und die Jünger verließen . . . [und Schriftgelehrten]		
Petrus aber folgete ihm . . . [dass er des Todes schuldig wäre]	Aria Soll selbst der Herr und Richter aller Welt	New (unknown)
Da fingen an etliche ihn . . . [hob an zu weinen]		
Choral Erbarme dich, o Herre Gott [end of Caiphas]	**Aria Erwäg, ergrimmte Natternbrut**	Brockes (GS?)
Und bald am Morgen hielten . . . [überantworteten ihn dem Pilatus]		

Table 2. *Cont.*

Gospel text/Chorale interpolations	Free poetic interpolations	Notes
	Arioso Hat dies mein Heiland leiden müssen	Brockes (TZ)
	Aria Meine Laster sind die Stricke	Brockes (TZ)
Und Pilatus fragte ihn . . . [daß er gekreuzigt würde]		
	Soliloquio Besinne dich, Pilatus	Brockes (TZ)
	Aria Dein Bä [renherz ist felsenhart]	Brockes (TZ)
Die Kriegsknechte aber führeten . . . [und beteten ihn an]		
Choral Dass ihn, Gott, so [end of Pilatus]		
Und da sie ihn verspottet hatten . . . [er nahm's nicht zu sich]		
	Aria Heil der Welt, dein schmerzlich Leiden	Brockes (TZ)
Und da sie ihn gekreuziget hatten . . . [da sie ihn kreuzigten]		
Choral Wie wunderbarlich ist doch		
Und es war oben übergeschrieben . . . [von obenan bis untenaus]		
	Aria Bei Jesus Tod und Leiden	Brockes (GS)
Der Hauptmann aber . . . [gen Jerusalem gegangen waren]		
Choral O Jesu du mein Hilf [end of Creutz]		
Und am Abend dieweil es Rüsttag . . . [um den Leichnam Jesu]		
	Aria Zwölf Jünger folgten Jesu nach	New (unknown)
Choral O Jesu dessen Schmerzen		
Pilatus aber verwunderte sich . . . [?]		
Choral O hilf, Christe, Gottes Sohn [end of Sepulchrum]		
Choral Bleibt in Andacht meine Sinnen		

[Music and text lost; outline reconstructed from Hans Hörner, *Gg. Ph. Telemanns Passionsmusiken* (Leipzig, 1933).]

Table 3. G. P. Telemann, *St. Luke Passion* TVWV 5:9 (1724)

Gospel text/Chorale interpolations	Free poetic interpolations	Notes
Es war nahe das Fest der süßen Brot . . .		
. . . überantwortete ohne Lärmen [Rumor]	Aria Du Otter-Zucht, was soll der schnöde Raht?	unknown
. . . die fielen auf die Erde.	Aria Erweiche, diamantenes Herze	Hunold
. . . Petrus aber folgte von ferne.	Aria Schau, Se[e]l, auf deine Sünden	Hunold
. . . viele andere Lüsterungen sagten sie wider ihm.	Aria Süßer Trost, durch dieses Leiden	Hunold
. . . und sandte ihn wieder zu Pilatus.	Aria Fürst verklährter Engelsorden	Hunold
. . . so helf dir selber!	Aria Mein Herz, reiß aus dir die Lust	Hunold
. . . verschied er:	Aria Bebet, ihr Berge! zerberstet ihr Hügel	Postel
. . . den Sabbath über waren sie stille nach dem Gesetz.		
?	Aria "Gott läßt es nicht bey einer Wohltat bleiben/ Unzählig sind die Gaben seiner Hand"	unknown
?	[Aria]	unknown
?	[Aria]	unknown

[Music and text lost; partial outline reconstructed from Hans Hörner, *Gg. Ph. Telemanns Passionsmusiken* (Leipzig, 1933).]

Table 4. J. S. Bach, *St. John Passion* BWV 245 (1724)

Gospel text/Chorale interpolations	Free poetic interpolations	Notes
	1. Herr, unser Herrscher, dessen Ruhm	New (unknown); in place of orig. opening text
2. *Jesus ging mit seinen Jüngern . . . so lasset diese gehen!*		
3. O große Lieb, o Lieb ohn alle Maße		
4. *Auf dass das Wort . . . mein Vater gegeben hat?*		
5. Dein Will gescheh, Herr Gott, zugleich [end of Hortus]		
6. *Die Schar aber . . . umbracht für das Volk.*		
	7. Von den Stricken meiner Sünden	Brockes (GS); originally opening text, moved here
8. *Simon Petrus aber folgete Jesu nach und ein ander Jünger*		
	9. Ich folge dir gleichfalls	New (unknown)
10. *Derselbige Jünger war . . . was schlägest du mich?*		
11. Wer hat dich so geschlagen [2x]		
12. *Und Hannas sandte ihn . . . und weinete bitterlich.*		Interpolation from Mt
	13. Ach, mein Sinn	New (Weise) used in context
14. *Petrus, der nicht denkt zurück [end of Pontifices]*		
15. Christus, der uns selig macht		
16. *Da führeten sie Jesum . . . mein Reich nicht von dannen.*		
17. Ach großer König, groß zu allen Zeiten [2x]		
18. *Da sprach Pilatus zu ihm . . . geißelte ihn.*		
	19. Betrachte, meine Seel	Brockes (GS), used in place

Table 4. *Cont.*

Gospel text/Chorale interpolations	Free poetic interpolations	Notes
	20. Erwäge	Brockes (GS), used in place
21. Und die Kriegsknechte flochten . . . ihn losließe.		
	22. Durch dein Gefängnis	New (Postel) used in place
23. Die Jüden aber . . . auf Ebräisch: Golgatha		
	24. Eilt, ihr angefochtnen Seelen	Brockes (TZ/GS), used in place
25. Allda kreuzigten sie ihn . . . das habe ich geschrieben.		
26. In meines Herzens Grunde [approx. end of Pilatus]		
27. Die Kriegsknechte aber . . . das ist deine Mutter!		
28. Er nahm alles wohl in acht		
29. Und von Stund an . . . Es ist vollbracht!		
	30. Es ist vollbracht!	New (Postel?) used in place
31. Und neiget das Haupt und verschied		
	32. Mein teurer Heiland	Brockes (TZ/GS), used in place
33. Und der Vorhang im Tempel . . . von obenan bis untenaus.		Interpolation from Mk [later Mt]
	34. Mein Herz, in dem die ganze Welt	Brockes (GS), used in place
	35. Zerfließe, mein Herze	Brockes (GS), used in place
36. Die Jüden aber . . . sie gestochen haben		
37. O hilf, Christe, Gottes Sohn [end of Crux]		
38. Darnach bat Pilatum Joseph . . . das Grab nahe war		
	39. Ruht wohl, ihr heiligen Gebeine	Brockes (TZ), used in place [ending]
40. Ach Herr, lass dein lieb Engelein [end of Sepulcrum]		

Example 1. Aria from G. P. Telemann, *St. Mark Passion* (1723), as printed by Philipp Spitta

Example 1. *Cont.*

In his 1723 passion Telemann moved this text, originally the first number of the *Brockes Passion*, from its opening position to a spot a little later in the narrative where there is an explicit reference to Jesus's capture. Its poetic metaphor ("Mich vom Stricken meiner Sünden zu entbinden / Wird mein Gott gebunden") is thus treated more literally as a commentary on a specific event in the narrative; Telemann opens the 1723 work instead with a chorale stanza.

Telemann's 1724 *St. Luke Passion* (Table 3) follows a similar pattern, drawing on Christian Friedrich Hunold's influential poetic passion *Der blutige und sterbende Jesus* from circa 1704 for its interpolated movements. Once again a poetic passion oratorio supplied a substantial fraction of the aria texts; four more are from an unknown source, and one is from the infamous *St. John Passion* with aria texts by Christian Heinrich Postel, a work sometimes attributed to Händel. Telemann probably knew the Postel aria he used from Hunold, who printed three of Postel's aria texts with his libretto.[34] But there is, of course, a Bach connection here: Postel's work was the source of "Durch dein Gefängnis, Gottes Sohn" BWV 245/22, used at the center of the *St. John Passion*, and possibly indirectly also the origin of "Es ist vollbracht" BWV 245/30.[35] Both Bach and Telemann thus drew on this passion text in 1724. We do not know how Bach and his librettist learned the Postel text: from a libretto, a copy of the Hamburg setting,

---

or even by Handel." A footnote in the German original (2:364n85) adds: "Nonetheless, to provide the opportunity for such a comparison, the setting of the text 'Mich vom Stricke meiner Sünden' from Telemann's St. Mark Passion (B♭ major) is given as Music Example 2. I choose it because in the other passions this text is composed as a chorus, and thus cannot be easily compared with Bach's aria." This piece represents the only complete movement known to survive from any of Telemann's liturgical passions before 1728.

34. The Postel text Telemann employed, the aria "Bebet, ihr Berge! zerberstet, ihr Hügel," is in fact included in the published version of Hunold's libretto, which was evidently Telemann's source, so he did not need direct access to Postel's complete text. Three aria texts are reproduced (and the attribution to Postel made) in Christian Friedrich Hunold, *Der blutige und sterbende Jesus*, printed in his *Theatralische, galante und geistliche Gedichte* (Hamburg: G. Liebernickel, 1706), 34–35. This is pointed out by Scheitler, *Deutschsprachige Oratorienlibretti*, 188.

35. The work has been the subject of decades of scholarly debate. There is an overview and movement-by-movement discussion in Scheitler, *Deutschsprachige Oratorienlibretti*, 101–9. The latest entries are a forceful reclamation of the work for Händel in Rainer Kleinertz, "Zur Frage der Autorschaft von Händels *Johannespassion*," *Händel-Jahrbuch* 49 (2003): 341–76, and "Handel's *St John Passion*: A Fresh Look at the Evidence from Mattheson's *Critica Musica*," *The Consort* 61 (2005): 59–80; and a much more convincing argument that Reinhard Keiser is the "world-famous man" referred to by Mattheson in his notorious criticism of the work, and its likely composer, in John H. Roberts, "Placing 'Handel's St. John Passion,'" *Händel-Jahrbuch* 51 (2005): 153–77. The context of the work was evidently the presentation of St. John passions at Hamburg's St. Jacobi Church from approximately 1696/97.

or some other way. It is not out of the question that Bach came into contact with it through Hunold himself in Cöthen.

Telemann's 1722, 1723, and 1724 passion settings represent liturgical gospel oratorios that make use of aria texts from the *Brockes Passion* (or Hunold's poetic passion) presented essentially intact and largely in their original places in the narrative. The context is different—a biblical setting rather than an entirely poetic oratorio—so presumably the theological and even the esthetic perspective is distinct. But it is not difficult to see Telemann's use of these texts as a response to the popularity of this kind of religious poetry in general and to the fondness for Brockes's poems in particular, even when liturgical requirements did not permit the complete presentation of a poetic passion.

The appeal of Brockes's passion text is also reflected in J. S. Bach's *St. John Passion*, which uses numerous texts by Brockes either essentially intact or adapted (Table 4). It is widely accepted that Bach's work and the *Brockes Passion* are fundamentally different in construction and theological outlook.[36] It is also typical to view the text of the *St. John Passion* as heterogeneous—as a mixture drawn from various sources.[37] But it is also possible to see the *St. John Passion* as unified in its initial conception and as fundamentally a Brockes setting.

There are many points of contact between BWV 245 and the Brockes text. First, the allegorical characters so central to Brockes's passion, Daughter Zion and the Faithful Soul, evidently appear in the *St. John Passion* in no. 24, "Eilt, ihr angefochtnen Seelen," and no. 32, "Mein teurer Heiland"—at least, that is the implication of their adaptation from Brockes's dialogues cast for these voices.[38] We do not know if Bach and his

36. The former, as a biblical oratorio, conformed to the typical requirements of the Good Friday liturgy in Leipzig in Bach's time and may well reflect a conservative theological climate. Brockes's nonliturgical poetic oratorio provides many more interpolations, including some sung by characters in the drama; offers extended scenes of commentary labeled "Soliloquia"; and takes a different theological approach. That different outlook is, in fact, a principal thesis of Elke Axmacher's discussion of Bach's *St. John Passion* BWV 245, in which she is at pains to distinguish the two works, repeatedly emphasizing the ways in which the work differs from the *Brockes Passion*. *Aus Liebe will mein Heyland sterben*, 116–48. Other writers also point out the distinction, though less stridently. Michael Marissen, for example, contrasts the commentary in Bach's passions as exegesis, on the one hand, with that in the *Brockes Passion* as inviting the listener's participation in the narrative, on the other. *Lutheranism, Anti-Judaism, and Bach's* St. John Passion (New York: Oxford, 1998), 47n20.

37. Hans-Joachim Schulze has called it a "Florilegium," a careful selection from among the best available texts of the age. "Bemerkungen zum zeit- und gattungsgeschichtlichen Kontext von Johann Sebastian Bachs Passionen," in *Johann Sebastian Bachs historischer Ort*, Bach-Studien 10, ed. Reinhard Szeskus (Wiesbaden: Breitkopf & Härtel, 1991), 205.

38. On the consequences of these adaptations, see Daniel R. Melamed, "The Double Chorus in J. S. Bach's *St. Matthew Passion* BWV 244," *Journal of the American Musicological Society* 57 (2004): 3–50. It

librettist retained the characters in adapting these texts, but it seems likely: individual texts might be offered by unnamed characters, but dialogues almost certainly involve particular figures, allegorical or otherwise.

These movements possibly aside, named characters do not offer commentary in BWV 245 as Jesus, Peter, Judas, and Maria do in the *Brockes Passion*, but there is a suggestion of first-person reflection in the *St. John Passion*'s no. 13, "Ach, mein Sinn." That aria was sung in Bach's 1724 performance by the principal tenor, not the bass singer who delivered Peter's words. But its text, from Christian Weise's "Der weinende Petrus," can be read as a first-person lament of Peter, at least in its original context. Bach was capable of putting an aria in Peter's voice; in 1726 and after, in the equivalent spot in the anonymous *St. Mark Passion*, Bach assigned the mournful aria "Wein, ach wein itzt um die Wette" to the tenor who presented Peter's words, not the tenor concertist/ Evangelist. This tendency toward direct expression by characters is realized in the *St. Mark Passion* and hinted at in Bach's *St. John*, and it most likely reflects the influence of poetic oratorios like the *Brockes Passion*.

Another feature of "Ach, mein Sinn" also points to the influence of the *Brockes Passion*. The middle portion of the text contemplates inviting mountains to fall on the speaker, and the 1725 replacement no. 13^{II} "Zerschmettert mich" invokes the same image. This is a reference to scripture, but not from John's gospel. Rather it is from Luke; here the poetic portion of the libretto refers to a different narration of the passion story.

NO. 13 (1724), OPENING

Ach, mein Sinn,	O, my disposition,
Wo willt du endlich hin,	Where do you at last intend to go;
Wo soll ich mich erquicken?	Where shall I restore myself?
Bleib ich hier,	Shall I stay here,
Oder wünsch ich mir	Or do I wish
Berg und Hügel auf den Rücken?	Mountains and hills [to fall]
	upon my back?
	(trans. M. Marissen)

is also possible that some of the nondialogic pieces in BWV 245 were conceived in the voices of these characters, particularly Daughter Zion, but we have no original text sources to tell us, and the music sources of BWV 245 do not mention the characters.

NO. 13[11] (1725), OPENING

Zerschmettert mich, ihr Felsen und ihr Hügel,	Crush me, you rocks and you hills,
Wirf, Himmel, deinen Strahl auf mich!	Hurl, heaven, your thunderbolt upon me!

LUKE 23:30

Dann werden sie anfangen, zu sagen zu den Bergen: Fallet über uns! und zu den Hügeln: Decket uns!	Then they will begin to say to the mountains: Fall upon us! And to the hills, Cover us!

Borrowings from other gospels are a prominent feature of BWV 245, reflected not only in this aria, but also in the narrative itself. Peter's scene (no. 12c) incorporates words from Matthew 26:75 ending with "und weinete bitterlich," the cue for "Ach, mein Sin" (and in later versions for other pieces). The chorale stanza that follows the aria further refers to a passage from Luke's gospel.[39] Just after Jesus's death (no. 33), Bach and his collaborator originally inserted lines from Mark 15:38 that describe the rending of the temple veil and other events. In later versions this was further expanded by the substitution of most of the parallel passage from Matthew 27:51–52 that describes the scene in even more detail.[40] Listeners in the eighteenth century were thoroughly familiar with the tradition of the so-called Evangelienharmonie, a narration that combined features of all four gospels; the most famous exemplar was the *summa passionis* of Bugenhagen.[41] But in the early eighteenth century the conflation of gospels made itself most strongly felt in poetic passion texts like Brockes's, whose title page refers prominently to its construction "aus den IV. Evangelisten." Brockes's use of material from all the gospels was probably one of the models for this characteristic feature of Bach's *St. John Passion*.

39. Alfred Dürr, *Johann Sebastian Bach's* St. John Passion: *Genesis, Transmission, and Meaning*, trans. Alfred Clayton (Oxford: Oxford University Press, 2000), 38, connects the chorale line "Jesu, blicke mich auch an" with Luke 22:61, "Und der Herr wandte sich um und sah Petrus an."

40. These passages are the cues in the *Brockes Passion* for extensive commentary. The first is the occasion for a Soliloquio for Peter consisting of two recitatives and two arias (followed by a chorale) that emphasizes the themes of lament and remorse. The second triggers an aria ("Brich, brüllender Abgrund") that concentrates on earthquake imagery, and then (after some more narration) a large complex of concluding numbers that treat the cataclysms and the theme of lamenting.

41. Dürr, *Johann Sebastian Bach's* St. John Passion, 32, suggests that the tendency to listen in a synoptic manner and the desire to provide opportunities for the composition of affective commentary prompted the use of borrowed gospel material in BWV 245.

The most important evidence of the *Brockes Passion*'s influence on the *St. John Passion* lies in the sheer number and placement of its poems in Bach's setting. In all, eight poetic movements are used or adapted from the *Brockes Passion* out of a total of twelve (thirteen counting the problematic no. 22 "Durch dein Gefängnis," a free poetic text that Bach set to a chorale melody in a four-part cantional-style harmonization). These Brockes borrowings appear in six of the ten or eleven places selected for poetic commentary, including the final poetic number.[42] This is such a high proportion that we can fruitfully view BWV 245 as a Brockes setting using John's narrative. Each of the borrowed poetic texts is used in its original context except the adapted opening number, "Von den Stricken meiner Sünden mich zu entbinden . . . wird mein Heil gebunden," which was moved later in the story, where its metaphor of binding is literally suggested by events: "und die Diener der Jüden nahmen Jesum und bunden ihn" (and the servants of the Jews took Jesus and bound him). Aside from the new opening number supplied to replace it (a poetic Psalm paraphrase) there are only three new arias, four if you count "Durch dein Gefängnis." The use of textual sources other than Brockes has typically suggested a view of the *St. John Passion* as an assemblage most notable for its diversity, but it is equally compelling to see the Brockes texts as the starting point and as the basis of the work's interpolated movements.

This view is supported by the likelihood that the arias drawn from elsewhere were each calculated departures from the Brockes model. No. 13 "Ach, mein Sinn," which replaces Brockes's four-movement Soliloquium for Peter (Recit-Aria-Recit-Aria), might have had local significance: Its text by Christian Weise is reported to have been written to fit a composition by the Thomascantor Sebastian Knüpfer and was published in Leipzig.[43] At least one (and perhaps two) of the other non-Brockes interpolations are from the *St. John Passion* with poetic texts by Postel. No. 22 "Durch dein Gefängnis," inserted to comment on a detail (Pilate's contemplation of releasing Jesus) from John's narrative not taken up by Brockes, is certainly from that work. The aria no. 30 "Es is vollbracht" does not itself appear in the Postel passion, but Friedrich Smend observed that its poetic organization matches that of Postel's aria in the equivalent

---

42. This analysis suggests that chorales are used in this work largely for structural articulation, marking the beginning or end of each of the two parts, and closing off each of the actus. Only a fraction of them—nos. 3, 11, 17, and 28—are used in the manner of free poems to comment on moments within an actus.

43. Weise reported that he had constructed the text to fit an Intrada composed by his friend Sebastian Knüpfer. Knüpfer was already Thomascantor by the time of Weise's arrival at Leipzig University in 1660, and it is likely that the two men knew each other from there. *Der grünen Jugend nothwendige Gedanken* (Leipzig: Johann Fritzsche, 1675), 352. Weise was in Leipzig circa 1660–68, Knüpfer from 1657. George Buelow, "Weise, Christian" and "Knüpfer, Sebastian," *New Grove Dictionary*.

place, and it may be closely related.[44] Brockes's text at this point is a strophic poem, "O Donner-Wort," each of whose two stanzas ends with the words "Es ist vollbracht."

FROM THE POSTEL PASSION

O grosses Werk,

Im Paradies schon angefangen!

O Riesenstärk',

Die Christus lässt den Sieg erlangen!

Dass nach dem Streit in Siegespracht

Er sprechen kann:

Es ist vollbracht!

BWV 245/30

Es ist vollbracht!

O Trost vor die gekränkten Seelen!

Die Trauernacht

Läßt nun die letzte Stunde zählen.

Der Held aus Juda siegt mit Macht

Und schließt den Kampf.

Es ist vollbracht!

BROCKES PASSION AT "ES IST VOLLBRACHT"

1. O Donner-Wort! o schrecklich Schreyen

O Thon / den Tod und Hölle scheuen!

Der Ihre Macht zu Schanden macht.

Schall! der Stein und Felsen theilet /

Wovor der Teuffel bebt und heulet /

Wovor der düstre Abgrund kracht!

Es ist vollbracht!

44. Smend suggested that Bach derived "Es ist vollbracht" from Postel's original and implied that the new text was superior. *Bach in Köthen*, trans. John Page (St. Louis, Mo.: Concordia, 1985), 147ff. We should also consider the possibility that the aria in BWV 245 represents a second stanza of the original text, which we know only from the manuscript score that transmits the musical setting, D-B Mus. ms. 9001. Many of the poetic texts in the Postel Passion resemble stanzas of the kind of strophic "aria" common in Hamburg passions in the late seventeenth and early eighteenth centuries, particularly in their metrical organization and stanza construction. (Recall Bach's telling decision to set "Durch dein Gefängnis" to a chorale melody, with its implication of strophic construction, in BWV 245.) So it is possible that this aria was not only inspired by, but also adopted from, Postel's material.

2. O seeligs Wort! o heilsam Schreyen!

Nun darffst du Sünder nicht mehr scheuen

Des Teuffels und der Höllen Macht.

O schall! der unsern Schaden heilet /

Der uns die Seeligkeit ertheilet /

Die GOtt uns längst hat zugedacht!

Es ist vollbracht.

The similarity of the *St. John Passion*'s "Es ist vollbracht" to both Postel's and Brockes's texts is at least as striking as the substitution of a new poem. The one in BWV 245 is not far from the Brockes model.

These three new texts ("Ach, mein Sinn," "Durch dein Gefängnis," and "Es ist vollbracht") plus the fourth, no. 9 "Ich folge dir gleichfalls," which also responds to a detail not mentioned by Brockes, can be viewed as exceptions. Most of the aria texts in Bach's *St. John Passion* are from Brockes, and it appears that he and his collaborator chose texts from the *Brockes Passion* to fit John's gospel.[45] This perspective has been hinted at before. Philipp Spitta took John's narrative to be Bach's starting point. Regarding the work as having been composed in a hurry in Cöthen, he asserted that Bach had turned "naturally" to Brockes's text for commentary.[46] Friedrich Smend took the position that "for the production of the libretto Bach used the poetry of . . . Brockes."[47] Each writer emphasizes the changes of language and context and the distinctiveness of BWV 245, though. One commentator did consider BWV 245 fundamentally a Brockes setting: Albert Schweitzer wrote that the work was "founded on" Brockes's poem and that Bach "substitutes text of the fourth Gospel" in place of Brockes's "bombastic versified narrative."[48] This view goes a step further in suggesting that Bach started with the complete Brockes text, including its paraphrased narrative, and "substituted" gospel text.

I think Schweitzer was correct, at least about Brockes as the starting point. Bach and his anonymous collaborator found a way to make use of the *Brockes Passion*'s poetry even as they adapted and reworked it in a new (gospel) context. They moved its opening text to a location where its imagery was more literal, allowing a new exordium (no. 1 "Herr, unser Herrscher") to set the tone. In two significant places they turned to other

45. It is also possible that the Brockes adaptations and other texts predate Bach's use of the material; we simply do not know.

46. *Johann Sebastian Bach*, 2:520.

47. *Bach in Köthen*, 143.

48. The perspective here is striking: Bach begins with the Brockes text and "substitutes" the gospel narrative. Albert Schweitzer, *J. S. Bach*, 2 vols. (London: Breitkopf & Härtel, 1911), 2:174.

sources: to a poem with a Leipzig connection (no. 13 "Ach, mein Sinn") in place of Brockes's long Soliloquium for Peter, and possibly to another passion of Hamburg origin in place of Brockes's strophic aria on the words "Es ist vollbracht." In two places in which Brockes did not provide commentary they supplied no. 22 "Durch dein Gefängnis" from that same Hamburg passion and no. 9 "Ich folge dir gleichfalls" from an unknown source to amplify the commentary. This raises the question whether the *St. John Passion*, though admittedly different in outlook from the *Brockes Passion*, really contrasts as strongly as commentators have suggested. The many revisions to the borrowed Brockes texts—fundamental, in some commentators' views—actually makes the choice all the more striking; Bach and his librettist stuck largely with the *Brockes Passion* even though its poetry evidently required substantial changes for the new context. The critical focus on revisions and differences has come at the cost of recognizing the fundamental nature of BWV 245—it is a Brockes passion.[49]

It is worth recalling that Telemann did the same thing at almost the same time. His first two passions for Hamburg drew on Brockes's poetry, just as BWV 245 did. In 1722 Telemann exclusively used texts by Brockes. In 1723 he also borrowed from Brockes and moved the original opening text to connect directly with the narration,[50] in addition to incorporating four poems from other sources. In this regard the outlines of Telemann's 1723 *St. Matthew Passion* and Bach's 1724 *St. John* are strikingly similar; in fact, it is difficult to imagine a closer parallel.[51] I suspect that Telemann and Bach were each motivated by the pervasive influence and wide popularity of Brockes's text. Telemann began his tenure in Hamburg with two liturgical passions that drew on Brockes, then turned to another (even older) poetic text by Hunold. Bach did the same, drawing on Brockes in 1724 and 1725 with the two earliest versions of the *St. John Passion*, then indirectly relying on it again in 1727 in the *St. Matthew*. Even the work he presented in 1726—the Hamburg *St. Mark Passion*—was eventually brought around to the Brockes model many years later with the use of Händel's arias. Bach's own 1731 *St. Mark Passion* BWV 247, whose poetic texts were newly constructed to fit existing music, departs most significantly in this regard from Bach's other passion

---

49. Bach's 1725 revisions (version II) affect both Brockes and non-Brockes movements. His revisions around 1730 (version III) restore the Brockes pieces cancelled in version II but remove others. The last version (IV, 1749) restores most of the original movements; its revised texts involve both Brockes and non-Brockes movements.

50. Mark 14:1–2: "Und die Hohenpriester und Schriftgelehrten suchten, wie sie ihn mit List griffen und töteten. Sie sprachen aber: Ja nicht auf das Fest, daß nicht ein Aufruhr im Volk werde!"

51. See the brief but insightful comparison in Günther Massenkeil, *Oratorium und Passion*, part 1, *Handbuch der musikalischen Gattungen* 10/1 (Laaber: Laaber-Verlag, 1998), 210. Carl von Winterfeld, *Der evangelische Kirchengesang und sein Verhältnis zur Kunst des Tonsatzes*, 3 vols. (Leipzig, 1847), 368–72, makes a detailed comparison of Bach's BWV 245 and other composers' Brockes settings.

repertory. With its domination by chorale interpolations, it is clearly a different kind of setting. It may represent Bach's only departure from the Brockes text on which he otherwise relied so heavily throughout his career.

Appendix: Selective Chronology of the *Brockes Passion* and Related Works

c. 1704	Hunold/Menantes, *Der blutige und sterbende Jesus*
1712	R. Keiser, *Brockes Passion*, first performance (Hamburg) / first publication of text
1713	*Brockes Passion* revised text published
1714	Keiser, *Auserlesene Soliloquia* (*Brockes Passion* excerpts)
1715	*Brockes Passion* text published in *Bethlehemitischer Kinder-Mord*
1716	G. P. Telemann, *Brockes Passion*, Frankfurt premiere
1716	G. F. Händel, *Brockes Passion*, likely Hamburg premiere
c. 1717–18	Telemann, *Brockes Passion*, Hamburg/Augsburg/Leipzig performances
1718	J. Mattheson, *Brockes Passion*, Hamburg premiere
1720	J. S. Bach's visit to Hamburg
1722	Telemann, *St. Matthew Passion* TVWV 5:7
1723	Telemann, *St. Mark Passion* TVWV 5:8
1724	Telemann, *St. Luke Passion* TVWV 5:9
1724	Bach, *St. John Passion* BWV 245 (version I)
1725	Bach, *St. John Passion* BWV 245 (version II)
1725	Henrici/Picander, "Erbauliche Gedanken . . . in einem Oratorio entworffen"
c. 1721–26	J. B. C. Freislich, *Brockes Passion* (Sondershausen)
1727	Bach, *St. Matthew Passion* BWV 244
1727	Keiser, *Brockes Passion*, Sondershausen performance (under Freislich)
1729	*Brockes Passion* performance, Leipzig Neukirche (composer unknown)
c. 1730–37	Keiser, *Brockes Passion*, Erfurt Barfüßerkirche
1746/47	Bach's copy of Händel, *Brockes Passion* (completed by Bammler)
late 1740s	Bach's performance of *St. Mark Passion* w/ mvts. from Händel, *Brockes Passion*

Drama and Discourse

The Form and Function of Chorale Tropes in Bach's Oratorios

Markus Rathey

Musical Drama in Time and Space

Classical drama in the Aristotelian tradition demanded unity of time and space. Drama theorists in the eighteenth century emphasized this repeatedly in their treatises. The Leipzig poet Johann Christoph Gottsched (1700–1766) pointed out that tragedy had to avoid leaps in time and that the time in the dramatic narrative and in the action onstage must be congruent:

> Die Einheit der Zeit ist das andere, das der Tragödie unentbehrlich ist. Die Fabel eines Helden-Gedichtes kann viel Monate dauern . . . das macht, sie wird nur gelesen: Aber die Fabel eines Schau-Spieles, die mit lebendigen Personen in etlichen Stunden lebendig vorgestellet wird, kann nur einen Umlauf der Sonnen, wie Aristoteles spricht, das ist einen Tag dauren.[1]

> The unity of time is the other thing that is essential for the tragedy. The narrative of an epos can take several months . . . because it is only read: but the narrative of a drama, which is presented with living persons in several hours, can only take one circle of the sun, as Aristotle says, that is one day.

The same is true, Gottsched continued, for the unity of space:

> Zum dritten gehört zur Tragödie die Einheit des Ortes. Die Zuschauer bleiben auf einer Stelle sitzen, folglich müssen auch die spielenden Personen alle auf einem Platze bleiben.

> Thirdly is the unity of space essential for a tragedy. The members of the audience sit in one place; therefore, all acting persons have to stay at one place, as well.

Sulzer's *Theorie der schönen Künste* (1778), one of the fundamental works of aesthetics in the second half of the eighteenth century, reiterated this demand when it stated:

---

1. Johann Christoph Gottsched, "Versuch einer Critischen Dichtkunst vor die Deutschen," in *Schriften zur Literatur*, ed. Horst Steinmetz (Stuttgart: Reclam, 1972), 163.

Natürlicher Weise ist die Handlung auf eine gewisse Kürze der Zeit eingeschränkt. . . . Daher ist die Einrichtung des Drama gekommen, die überall beobachtet wird, dass ein paar Stunden hinlänglich sind, die ganze Handlung zu sehen.

Naturally, the action is limited to a certain span of time. . . . Therefore, the conception of drama came into being, which can be observed everywhere, that a few hours are enough to see the entire action.

Similarly, Sulzer says of the unity of space:

Soll die Handlung natürlich vorgestellt werden, so muss sie so beschaffen sein, dass auch in dem Orte, wo wir die handelnden Personen sehen, nichts widersprechendes sei. . . . Man muss eine sehr genaue Übereinkunft der Dinge, die geschehen, und der Orte, da sie geschehen, beobachten.[2]

If the action shall be presented in a natural way, it has to be of a kind that nothing contrary [= not natural] shall be at that place, where we see the acting characters. . . . One has to observe the exact congruence of the things that happen and the places where they happen.

Essential for both Gottsched and Sulzer were the credibility and the authenticity of the dramatic action onstage. If the drama was a reflection of reality, the means used had to conform to reality, as well.

The oratorio of the seventeenth and eighteenth centuries does not necessarily conform to this ideal, even though contemporary writers like Johann Gottfried Walther (1684–1748) emphasize its relationship to musical drama and opera. The texts of German Protestant oratorios combined dramatic and epic elements, which allowed for a freer disposition of the temporal structure of the text than contemporary drama. This is also true for Johann Sebastian Bach's oratorios, which grew out of the tradition of the protestant *historia*[3] and which interpolate the biblical text with pious reflections in arias and recitatives and with chorale stanzas. This created a three-layered texture of biblical narrative, reflections of the individual (arias, recitatives), and meditations by the congregation (hymns). Karol Berger has recently suggested the extent to which this multilayered fabric in the *St. Matthew Passion* differs from contemporary opera (which, as musical drama, had to conform to the Aristotelian ideals). Even though he focuses in his observations on one work, we can generalize his observations for all of Bach's oratorios: "The dramaturgy of the Passion closely resembles that of the contemporary *opera seria* in its practice of punctuating the action, set as simple recitative, with reflective and musically fully developed numbers, mostly arias, in which the action

2. Sulzer, "Drama," 275.

3. For the genre of the *historia* see Bernd Baselt, "Actus musicus und Historie um 1700 in Mitteldeutschland," *Hallesche Beiträge zur Musikwissenschaft*, Ser. G1 (1968/8): 77–103.

halts to allow the passion aroused by the most recent event to be expressed. However, whereas in an opera the job of passionate reflections is left to the protagonists of the drama, in the Passion the reflection comes from outside."[4] The reflections leave the unity of time and space intact and provide, to use Berger's terms, a "timeless moment of contemplation."[5] The librettos for Bach's oratorios violate the basic rules of classical drama to provide reflection from beyond the time (and the implied space) of the narrative. And the reflections provided justify this technique because they are presented from the perspective of the believer—an observer who shares the observing position with the devout listener.

Bach employs not only arias and recitatives in these reflective moments, but uses hymns, as well. However, while the arias focus on the perspective of the individual, the hymns provide the perspective of the Christian congregation. Berger suggests that "the chorales are the collective voice of the several generations of Lutheran faithful up to and including Bach's own congregation, and thus they represent the objective, authoritative utterance of the church."[6] In other words, breaking the rules of classical drama—which do not necessarily apply to a liturgical composition such as Bach's oratorios, but which still formed the aesthetic background for the reception of dramatic or quasidramatic pieces in Bach's time—served a dramatic purpose that included the listeners (as individuals and as a group) as part of the action.

A connection between two of these layers—the individual and the reflection of the community—is drawn in a type of chorale setting, the chorale trope, which combines a newly written text with a traditional hymn. The function of these settings is significantly different from other large-scale hymn settings in Bach's oratorios, which occur only at the beginning and the end of sections (like the framing movements of the 1725 version of the *St. John Passion*) and which are not integrated into the dramatic development. Chorale tropes appear at crucial moments, mostly at points where the doubt of the individual, ignited by the biblical narrative, must be overcome by the faith of the congregation. The individual and the community cease to be mere spectators and engage in the dramatic action themselves.

A chorale trope is the combination of a hymn with a free poem or a biblical text. The chorale can either sound simultaneously with a second text (a simultaneous trope), or the single lines of the hymn may be interrupted by the other text (an alternating trope).[7] Bach used this kind of polytextuality in approximately seventy-eight movements, from his time in Mühlhausen to the middle of the 1730s. Bach did not invent

4. Karol Berger, *Bach's Cycle, Mozart's Arrow: An Essay on the Origins of Musical Modernity* (Berkeley: University of California Press, 2007), 106.

5. Ibid., 106.

6. Ibid., 102.

7. A larger study of Bach's chorale tropes is in preparation by the author.

this technique; rather, he inherited it from the seventeenth century, when composers like Andreas Hammerschmidt (1611/12–1675), Wolfgang Carl Briegel (1626–1712), and members of Bach's own family used it extensively.[8] However, even though Bach borrows a historically established compositional model, it is remarkable how extensively he employs it in his vocal works. Different types of chorale tropes can be generally differentiated: some of them combine a hymn with a recitative, some with an aria, whereas others juxtapose the chorale with a motet-like texture. All of these types occur in Bach's oratorios.

The *St. John Passion*

The only combinations of aria and chorale in Bach's oratorios occur in the various versions of the *St. John Passion* BWV 245.[9] The thirty-second movement of the passion layers the text "Mein teurer Heiland" (My precious Savior) with a stanza from the hymn "Jesu Leiden, Pein und Tod." Bach added a second chorale trope during his revisions in 1725 when he inserted the aria "Himmel reiße, Welt erbebe" (Heaven, tear apart, world, quake) BWV 245/11[+], which features another stanza from the same hymn.[10] Even though both movements are arias with additional chorale layers, Bach's approach is significantly different.

The *aria con coro* "Mein teurer Heiland" from 1724 follows immediately after the death of Jesus, "Und neiget das Haupt und verschied" (And bowed his head and departed this life). The libretto layers two texts: the chorale and the words of the bass inquiring about the salvific meaning of Christ's death. The text of the aria layer is, as Alfred Dürr has pointed out,[11] based on an *aria à 2* by Barthold Heinrich Brockes (1680–1747).

Tochter	Sind meiner Seelen tieffe Wunden	Are the deep wounds of my
Zion		soul
	Durch deine Wunden nun verbunden?	Now dressed by his wounds?
	Kan ich durch deine Quaal	Can I, through his suffering
	und Sterben	and dying,

8. See Friedhelm Krummacher, "Traditionen der Choraltropierung in Bachs frühem Vokalwerk," in *Das Frühwerk Johann Sebastian Bachs. Kolloquium veranstaltet vom Institut für Musikwissenschaft der Universität Rostock*, ed. Karl Heller and Hans-Joachim Schulze (Cologne: Studio, 1995), 217–43.

9. For the versions of the *St. John Passion* see Daniel R. Melamed, *Hearing Bach's Passions* (Oxford: Oxford University Press, 2005), 66–77; and Arthur Mendel, *Neue Bach Ausgabe* II/4, Kritischer Bericht.

10. Regarding the genesis and chronology of this movement see Markus Rathey, "Weimar, Gotha oder Leipzig. Zur Chronologie der Arie 'Himmel, reiße' in der zweiten Fassung der Johannes-Passion (BWV 245/11+)," *Bach-Jahrbuch* 91 (2005): 291–300.

11. Alfred Dürr, *St John Passion: Genesis, Transmission, and Meaning*, trans. Alfred Clayton (Oxford: Oxford University Press 2000), 47.

	Nunmehr das Paradieß ererben?	Now inherit Paradise?
	Ist aller Welt Erlösung nah?	Is the salvation of the world close now?

Gläubige Seele	Dieß sind der Tochter Zion Fragen;	These are the questions of the Daughter Zion;
	Weil JEsus nun nichts kan vor Schmertzen sagen / So neiget er sein Haupt / und wincket: Ja!	Because Jesus cannot say anything for pain, He bows his head and indicates: Yes!

Whereas Brockes juxtaposes the questions of the Daughter Zion and the answers by the Faithful Soul, Bach's libretto assigns both the questions and the answers to the bass voice, who does not represent the Daughter Zion. Bach's libretto introduces a chorale stanza as a partner in the dialogue, sung in a four-part setting by the chorus and leading the bass from questions to the answers at the end. The chorale is the thirty-fourth stanza of the passion hymn "Jesu Leiden, Pein und Tod," a hymn also used in movements 14 (stanza 10) and 28 (stanza 20).

The two texts highlight the meaning of Christ's death from different angles:

Mein teurer Heiland, laß dich fragen,	My precious Savior. let me ask you:
Jesu, der du warest tot,	**Jesus, you who were dead,**
Da du nunmehr ans Kreuz geschlagen	Since you were nailed to the cross
Und selbst gesaget: Es ist vollbracht,	And have yourself said, "It is accomplished,"
Lebest nun ohn Ende,	**[But] now lives without end;**
Bin ich vom Sterben frei gemacht?	Have I been made free from death?
In der letzten Todesnot,	**In the final throes of death,**
Nirgend mich hinwende	**[I] turn myself nowhere**
Kann ich durch deine Pein und Sterben	Can I through your pain and death
Das Himmelreich ererben?	Inherit the kingdom of heaven?
Ist aller Welt Erlösung da?	Is the redemption of all the world here?
Als zu dir der mich versühnt,	**But to you, who reconciled me,**
O du lieber Herre!	**O you dear Lord!**
Du kannst vor Schmerzen zwar nichts sagen;	You can, in agony, it is true, say nothing;

Gib mir nur, was du verdient	Give me only what you
	have merited;
Doch neigest du das Haupt	But you bow your head
Und sprichst stillschweigend: ja.	And say in silence, "Yes."
Mehr ich nicht begehre!	**More do I not desire!**
	(trans. M. Marissen)

The aria layer does not look beyond the crucifixion; the bass expresses his lack of understanding and only toward the end comes to the conclusion "but you bow your head and say in silence 'yes.'" The hymn, representing the view of the Christian congregation, is already aware of Christ's resurrection and of the salvific and soteriological meaning of his death. In the course of the aria, the confidence of the congregation, expressed in the hymn, transforms the doubt of the individual (= bass) into understanding. The turning point from questions to answers is the third-to-last line, "Du kannst vor Schmerzen zwar nichts sagen."

In his setting, Bach establishes two distinct sonic layers. The primary layer is the solo for bass, accompanied by the basso continuo. The movement is a typical continuo aria; the thematic material is first presented by the continuo section in a short ritornello and then handed over to the vocalist in m. 3. As a second layer Bach introduces the four-part hymn setting in m. 4. The two layers are kept distinct throughout the movement. They are motivically independent (in contrast to earlier trope arias from Bach's Weimar period, such as BWV 161/1 and 163/5), and the two layers are in different meters, the aria in 12/8 and the chorale in C. For most of the movement, the chorale is sung simultaneously with the soloist; only during the words "O mein lieber Herre" is the chorale heard alone. Bach here highlights the doxological sentence "O you dear Lord" and also marks the turning point from question to answer. This is the very moment at which Brockes's model aria switched characters from the Daughter Zion to the Faithful Soul. Bach's compositional procedure, however, does more; he not only marks the transformation from doubt to understanding, but also inserts a line from the chorale into the text of the aria layer. The listener perceives—for the first time—the two layers in succession and thereby hears them as a single sentence, "O you dear Lord! You can, in agony, it is true, say nothing" (Example 1).

When Bach revised the *St. John Passion* for a performance on Good Friday 1725, he not only replaced the framing movements with two elaborated hymn settings, but also inserted two new arias, one of them a chorale trope, which was placed after movement 11: "Himmel reiße, Welt erbebe" (Heaven tear apart, world quake). The immediate context for the movement is the scourging of Jesus and reaction in the chorale "Wer

Example 1. J. S. Bach, *St. John Passion* BWV 245/32, mm. 27–32

hat dich so geschlagen" (Who has struck you so?). The aria, again sung by the bass, is combined with the chorale "Jesu deine Passion," the thirty-third stanza of the hymn "Jesu Leiden, Pein und Tod." The chorale is now sung by the soprano alone, and in contrast to the continuo texture of "Mein teurer Heiland," Bach furthermore uses two flutes as an accompaniment.[12] The most significant difference between the two trope arias in the 1725 *St. John Passion* is the closer relationship between the two texts in this later addition. The lines of the chorale are integrated into the rhyme scheme of the aria layer, and the two layers conceived as a poetic unity: "Trauerthon" rhymes with "Passion," "Freude" with "leide," and so on. Such a close connection would have been unusual in Bach's earlier cantatas, but it occurs frequently in his chorale cantata cycle,[13] composed in the months before the second version of the *St. John Passion*.

The text of the aria outlines a similar transformation as did movement 32 of the first version:[14]

Himmel reiße, Welt erbebe,	Heaven, tear apart; world quake;
fallt in meinen Trauerthon,	Fall in with my air of grief;
Jesu, deine Passion,	**Jesus, your Passion**
Ist mir lauter Freude,	**is pure joy to me;**
Sehet meine Qual und Angst,	Look at my sorrow and fear:
was ich, Jesu, mit dir leide!	What I suffer with you, Jesus!
Ja, ich zähle deine Schmerzen,	Yes, I do count up your agonies,
o zerschlagner Gottessohn,	O shattered Son of God;
Deine Wunden, Kron und Hohn	**your wounds, crown, and scorn**
Meines Herzens Weide.	**my heart's pasture.**
Ich erwähle Golgata	I choose Golgotha
vor dies schnöde Weltgebäude.	Before this vile earthly vault.
Werden auf den Kreuzeswegen	Should your thorns be sown
deine Dornen ausgesät,	On the path of the cross,
Meine Seel auf Rosen geht,	**My soul walks on roses,**
Wenn ich dran gedenke;	**when I reflect on it;**

12. Ulrich Leisinger has suggested that the flutes were added in 1725 to an existing movement. See "Die zweite Fassung der Johannes-Passion von 1725. Nur ein Notbehelf?," in *Bach in Leipzig—Bach und Leipzig. Konferenzbericht 2000*, Leipziger Beiträge zur Bachforschung 5, ed. Ulrich Leisinger (Hildesheim: Olms, 2002), 43.

13. See the overview in Markus Rathey, "Der zweite Leipziger Kantatenjahrgang—Choralkantaten," in *Bach-Handbuch 1*, ed. Reinmar Emans and Sven Hiemke (Laaber: Laaber, 2010).

14. Translation: Marissen, *Bach's Oratorios*, 129–30.

Weil ich in Zufriedenheit	Because I in contentment
mich in deine Wunden senke,	Submerge myself into your wounds,
So erblick ich in dem Sterben,	I will recognize, at my death,
wenn ein stürmend Wetter weht,	When a stormy tempest roars,
In dem Himmel eine Stätt	**grant me a place in heaven**
Mir deswegen schenke!	**because of it!**
Diesen Ort, dahin ich mich	This spot, where by faith I
täglich durch den Glauben lenke.	Daily direct myself.

The bass begins with an outburst of rage over the torture of Jesus ("Himmel reiße, Welt erbebe"), which turns into compassion ("Was ich, Jesu, mit dir leide") and leads finally to contentment ("Weil ich in Zufriedenheit mich in deine Wunden senke"). The chorale, on the other hand, expresses joy and contentment from the very beginning ("Jesu, deine Passion, ist mir lauter Freude"). The hymn, as the voice of the church, represents the state of contentment and confidence in salvation the bass must reach in the course of the aria. The two layers also differ in their musical character. The bass sings a virtuosic rage aria representing the tearing of heaven and the quaking of the earth, while the chorale melody proceeds in calm quarter notes, reflecting sonically the state of calm and contentment that is the goal of the movement.

The juxtaposition of the hymn stanza and the text sung by the bass conforms to the eighteenth-century understanding of this hymn. Johann Martin Schamelius (1671–1742)[15] published an extensive hymn commentary in Leipzig in 1724/25 and wrote that the appropriate reaction to Jesus's suffering in the stanza quoted in this movement was not mourning but rather joy. Schamelius criticizes the very attitude represented by the bass in Bach's aria:

> Ich bins versichert in meinem Heylande / ich thue ihm mehr Ehre, wenn ich mit gläubigen Hertzen mich über alle seine Pein freue / und in einer freudigen Liebe dancke und ihm diene / als wenn ich noch so viel Wehklagen darüber mache. Wer dies nicht mit mir thun will / der ist mir verdächtig. daß er weder die Krafft noch den Zweck dieses Leidens wise: sagt der seel. Hinckelmann Betr. von der Reinigung des Bluts Christi, p. 441.[16]

---

15. See Andreas Lindner, *Leben im Spannungsfeld von Orthodoxie, Pietismus und Frühaufklärung: Johann Martin Schamelius, Oberpfarrer in Naumburg*, Kirchengeschichtliche Monographien 3 (Gießen: Brunnen-Verlag, 1998), passim.

16. Johann Martin Schamelius, *Evangelischer Lieder-Commentarius, worinnen das glossirete Naumburgische Gesang-Buch weiter ausgeführet und verbessert wird und vornehmlich die alten Kirchen- und Kern-Lieder mit ... Anmerkungen versehen werden*, vol. 1 (Leipzig: Lankisch, 1724), 175. He quotes a treatise by

I trust in my savior that I do him more honor when I rejoice in his pain with a joyous heart, and when I thank him in joyful love and serve him than when I mourn over it. Whoever does not wish to do this with me is suspicious; he knows neither the power of this suffering nor it purpose; the late Hinckelmann says this in his *Reinigung des Bluts Christi*, p. 441.

The chorale trope in the second version of the *St. John Passion* juxtaposes the two possible reactions to the suffering: mourning and rage at the beginning of the bass part, and love in the text of the chorale. The transformation of the bass, again representing the faithful observer, is more gradual than in the earlier aria, and it lacks the clear "turning point" that was indicated by the presentation of one line of the chorale without the bass. However, both trope arias from the *St. John Passion* fulfill a similar dramatic (and theological) function as they demonstrate the reaction of the faithful believer to the suffering of Christ and outline the path of the individual from doubt to confidence and contentment by confronting him with the theological insights present in the congregational hymn.

The *St. Matthew Passion* I

In his *St. Matthew Passion* BWV 244, Johann Sebastian Bach employed two different types of chorale tropes. The first movement, arguably Bach's largest-scale chorale trope, is based on the model of the polychoral motet, and I will return to it later. No. 19 is an accompanied recitative for tenor and wind instruments of the *chorus primus* alternating with lines from the hymn "Was ist die Ursach aller solcher Plagen?" sung by *chorus secundus*.[17] The dramatic function of the movement is clear from its immediate context. The chorale trope is part of a sequence of movements consisting of a section from the passion narrative (no. 18) and its theological interpretation in a recitative (no. 19) and an aria (no. 20) both involving the tenor from *chorus primus* and the combined voices of the *chorus secundus* (Example 2). The narrative reports Jesus's fear in Gethsemane. The text is set—as are the other words of the "testo"—as a simple recitative; only the words of Christ (mm. 4–6 and 11–15) are, as is usual for the *vox Christi* in Bach's compositions, accompanied by the strings of the first chorus.[18] Initially the accompaniment of the words of Christ is limited to a halo-like extended

---

the theologian and Islam scholar Abraham Hinckelmann (1652–1695), *Christliche Betrachtungen von der Reinigung des Blutes Christi. 1 Joh. 1, v. 7* (Hamburg: Dose, 1687).

17. It is the third stanza of the chorale "Herzliebster Jesu." Picander and Bach use three stanzas of this Good Friday hymn in the *St. Matthew Passion* spread over the piece in nos. 3, 19, and 46. The other two settings are simple four-part harmonizations.

18. Cf. Martin Geck, "Die vox-Christi-Sätze in Bachs Kantaten," in *Bach und die Stile*, ed. Martin Geck, Dortmunder Bach Forschungen, 2 (Dortmund: Klangfarben Musikverlag, 1999), 79–101.

Example 2. J. S. Bach, *St. Matthew Passion* BWV 244/18,
mm. 12–15 and 244/19, mm. 1–3

chord, with eighth-note motion accentuating only the cadence. Later, the strings dissolve the chords in a sequence of obstinately repeated eighth notes depicting the fear and trembling of Jesus implied in the text.[19]

The following accompaganto for tenor elaborates musically and textually on the fear of Jesus in Gethsemane. The tenor of *chorus primus* laments, "O Schmerz! hier zittert das gequälte Herz" (O agony! How the afflicted heart trembles), and is accompanied by a web of sigh motives in the wind instruments and an organ point in the continuo group, which is subdivided into a chain of repeated sixteenth notes. The sixteenth-note motion (which is maintained in the recitative sections throughout the movement) sonically depicts the trembling of the heart. It also refers back to a similar motive in the preceding *vox Christi* section (there as eighth notes) and ties the two movements together motivically, realizing musically the textual connection between the two movements.

The trope-recitative finally leads to an aria for tenor solo (chorus 1) and choir (chorus 2), "Ich will bei meinem Jesus wachen" (I will stay awake beside my Jesus), continuing the combination of soloist and choir already established in the preceding recitative. The text of the aria elaborates on the contrast of sleep and being awake: Staying awake with Jesus makes sins fall asleep. The accompagnato therefore serves as a bridge between the aria and the biblical narrative (which urges the disciples to stay awake with Jesus), and as it points out that Jesus's afflictions were caused by the sins of the faithful ("Ach! meine Sünden haben dich geschlagen"). The movement features an alternation between recitative sections and lines of the chorale. Until the last statements the recitative sections have a length of four measures, while the lines of the chorale are three measures long. Only the last phrases in both layers are longer. This is in part because the very last line of the chorale is shorter (only five notes compared to the eleven in the unembellished versions of the other lines), prompting Bach to combine the last two lines of the hymn into one phrase of five measures, which is then followed by a similarly lengthened recitative section of seven measures. On a structural level, however, the expansion toward the end of the movement also creates the impression of a climax.

The setting of the chorale lines is simple and accompanied only *colla parte* by the strings of the *chorus secundus*, which creates an additional contrast to the wind instruments from *chorus primus* accompanying the tenor. The simplicity of the setting, however, is blurred by a highly chromatic harmonization and a continuous eighth-note motion that runs through the accompanying voices and that occasionally surfaces in

19. Bach's setting of the text stands in a long tradition of compositions that depict the trembling of Jesus in a similar way, like the passions by Valentin Meder and the anonymous passion formerly attributed to Keiser.

the melody as embellishments, emphasizing words like "Plagen" (torments), "dich geschlagen" (have struck you), and "was du erduldet" (that you endure). The eighth-note motion and the two-note melismas are taken over by Bach in the following aria, where they appear in the second choir. This ensures a motivic connection between the two movements. Thus the recitative not only serves as a theological bridge between the biblical narrative and the aria, but its motivic material also refers back to the narrative (repeated notes in the basso continuo) and forward (flowing eighth notes). This Janus-like character of the trope reinforces the contrast between the two layers within the recitative.

The contrast serves a distinct function in the passion, but it is unusual in comparison to similar combinations of recitative and chorale composed by Bach before 1727, in which Bach attempted to unify the chorale and the trope motivically. An early example is the cantata "Gleichwie der Regen und Schnee vom Himmel fällt" BWV 18, composed in Weimar around 1713/15. Four more examples originate from Bach's first year in Leipzig (1723–24),[20] during which BWV 18 saw another performance, as well. The majority of Bach's chorale trope recitatives were composed during his Chorale Cantata Cycle (1724–25).[21] After abandoning the cycle in February 1725, he only occasionally used the combination of recitative and chorale. The only extant example between 1725 and 1727 is the first movement of, "Wer weiß, wie nahe mir mein Ende" BWV 27 from October 1726. In other words, with nineteen previous examples, the movement in the *St. Matthew Passion* is by no means unique; however, Bach's compositional realization of this established model differs from its predecessors. In previous trope recitatives Bach attempts to integrate the two layers motivically. The earliest examples still exhibit a rather loose connection, for instance the second movement of "Erfreute Zeit im neuen Bunde" BWV 83 (February 2, 1724), which combines elements of an aria and a recitative. During the Chorale Cantata Cycle, Bach attempts more and more to unify the two layers. The last trope recitative in the cycle shows the closest integration of recitative and hymn setting. In the cantata "Mit Fried und Freud ich fahr' dahin" BWV 125 (February 2, 1725), the third movement is unified by a small motive that is continuously repeated at different pitch levels and that accompanies both the chorale and the recitative sections (Example 3). Although the chorale and the recitative are still distinguishable, the movement clearly appears as a unity.

The accompagnato recitative "O Schmerz" from the *St. Matthew Passion*, on the other hand, breaks with this earlier concept. While the recitative and the chorale layers themselves are each unified by consistent musical ideas, the two layers do not share musical material. Furthermore, the chorale and recitative are separated sonically

20. BWV 138/1–3, BWV 190/2, BWV 73/1, and BWV 83/2.

21. See the overview in Krummacher, *Choralkantaten*, 162.

Example 3. J. S. Bach, "Mit Fried und Freud ich fahr dahin" BWV 125/3, mm. 3–7

(woodwind versus string instruments), spatially (distinct ensembles), and in tessitura. The reasons for Bach's decision is the epic-dramatic concept of the passion, with its juxtaposition of the Daughter Zion (*chorus primus*) and the Faithful (*chorus secundus*), which is established in the first movement and which shapes the overall structure of the passion, as well. Within this polychoral concept of the work, the recitative no. 19 serves as a link between the biblical narrative (no. 18) and the theological interpretation in no. 20, and features both motivic material from the preceding movement and from the following one.

A second feature of the trope recitative that also differentiates it from earlier examples is also due to the concept of the passion. In seven earlier tropes, Bach juxtaposed recitative sections with lines from a hymn in four-part harmony. In most cases the recitative interpolations are sung by rotating soloists who then come together to sing the lines of the chorale (see Table 1). (The only exception seems to be BWV 138/1, but its opening sequence of recitatives and hymns is unusual; the first three movements, with recitative passages for several voices, should be seen as a unity.)[22] That this form of combination of a recitative and a chorale was familiar is shown by Friedrich Wilhelm Marpurg's *Anleitung zur Singekomposition* (1758), which devotes a large section to the composition of polychoral pieces. He "mentions explicitly that recitatives in settings for unequal choruses are sometimes distributed among all four soloists."[23] The *St. Matthew Passion* contains a similar movement, the recitative "Nun ist der Herr zur Ruh gebracht" (no. 67), which juxtaposes the soloists from one chorus with the ensemble of the second one; however, Bach does not use a chorale in that movement.

Table 1. Troped recitatives in J. S. Bach's cantatas before 1727

Movement (Year)	Text	Soloists in Recitative
18/3 (1713/15)	Mein Gott, hier wird mein Herze sein	S/T/B
138/1 (1723)	Warum betrübst du dich mein Herz	T
190/2 (1724)	Herr Gott, dich loben wir	A/T/B
73/1 (1724)	Herr, wie du willt	S/T/B
3/2 (1724)	Wie schwerlich läßt sich Fleisch und Blut	S/A/T/B
92/7 (1725)	Ei nun, mein Gott, so fall ich dir	S/A/T/B
27/1 (1726)	Wer weiß, wie nahe mir mein Ende	S/A/T

22. On the problems in dividing the movements in BWV 138, see Dürr, *Cantatas*, 134–35.

23. Ulrich Leisinger, "Forms and Functions of the Choral Movements in J. S. Bach's *St. Matthew Passion*," in *Bach Studies 2*, ed. Daniel R. Melamed (Cambridge: Cambridge University Press, 1995), 78.

In other words, Bach normally conceptualizes trope recitatives with four-part chorale settings as ensemble pieces in which the singers of the chorale step out of the
ensemble (figuratively speaking) to sing their lines of recitative and then reunite with
the other voices to sing the lines of the hymn. In the *St. Matthew Passion* Bach sacrifices
this unity on a micro level (and his model used in earlier cantatas) to emphasize the
juxtaposition of the two choruses and their respective epic-dramatic function on the
macro level of the passion.

The *Christmas Oratorio*

The last trope movements Bach composed appear in the *Christmas Oratorio* BWV 248
from 1734/35. The libretto for the oratorio was probably by Picander, who also provided the text for the *St. Matthew Passion*. While Bach borrowed about a third of the
movements of the oratorio from earlier (mostly secular) cantatas, the two tropes (no. 7
and no. 38/40) were, as far as we know, composed for this piece.[24]

The seventh movement of the first part of BWV 248 is a chorale trope that is close to
the compositional models employed in earlier cantatas. It is part of a sequence of movements that form the second half of the cantata. Whereas the first half focuses on the
interpretation of the advent and birth of Christ (nos. 2–5), the second half concentrates
on the relationship (or rather, paradoxical dichotomy) between the earthly poverty of
Jesus (symbolically visible in the image of the manger in the Gospel text from Luke 2)
and the spiritual wealth the believer gains from Christ's incarnation (nos. 6–8).[25] The
movements in the second half are an interpretation of the Gospel text, quoted in no. 6;
however, the polarity between "rich" and "poor" refers clearly to 2 Cor. 8:9, "For you
know the generous act of our Lord Jesus Christ, that though he was rich, yet for your
sakes he became poor, so that by his poverty you might become rich." The paradox of
God incarnate is also one of the underlying topics of Martin Luther's Christmas hymn
"Gelobet seist du Jesu Christ,"[26] and it was therefore appropriate that the librettist chose
a stanza from this hymn for the chorale trope that follows the biblical narrative.[27]

---

24. Cf. Walter Blankenburg, *Das Weihnachts-Oratorium von Johann Sebastian Bach* (Kassel: Bärenreiter,
1999), 47–48 and 98–105.

25. Cf. Martin Petzold, *Bach-Kommentar. Theologisch-musikalische Kommentierung der geistlichen Vokalwerke Johann Sebastian Bachs. Band II: Die geistlichen Kantaten vom 1. Advent bis zum Trinitatisfest* (Kassel:
Bärenreiter, 2007), 122.

26. Cf. the interpretation of the hymn in Gerhard Hahn, *Evangelium als literarische Anweisung. Zu
Luthers Stellung in der Geschichte des deutschen kirchlichen Liedes*, Münchner Texte und Untersuchungen
73 (Munich: Niemeier, 1981), 188–89.

27. "Gelobet seist du, Jesu Christ" was also one of the hymns prescribed by contemporary hymnbooks
for the first day of Christmas. We find this tradition also reflected in the cycle of hymn sermons

The trope movement juxtaposes the text (and the melody) of the hymn in the soprano with a newly written text in the bass. The two voices engage in a dialectic discourse, leading from questions sung by the bass, "Wer will die Liebe recht erhöhn?" (Who will properly extol the love?) to the confident statement, "So will er selbst als Mensch geboren werden" (That he himself wants to be born as man);[28] meanwhile, the chorale proclaims the meaning of Christ's incarnation in poverty. As in the *St. John Passion*, the two voices have distinct functions: the bass utters questions in recitative, while the hymn, the symbolic voice of the congregation, answers with confidence. Although the two voices in this movement engage in a discourse, they are also a multilayered commentary on the biblical narrative. The hymn comments on the paradoxical dichotomy of rich and poor in the Gospel, while the recitative questions this view and only toward the end agrees with the words of the chorale. The dialectic of rich-poor is continued in the following bass aria, "Großer Herr, o starker König" (Great Lord, o mighty King). The text of the aria continues the inner development of the bass from his initial questions to his confidence toward the end of the trope movement. Thus the aria serves as an emphatic confirmation of the belief in the paradox.

In his setting of the chorale trope, Bach alternates between lines of the chorale and recitative sections. With the different musical material he changes meter—the hymn is in 3/4 and the recitative in common time.[29] The contrast between the two layers is further emphasized by a change in the accompaniment. Whereas the chorale sections are accompanied by a trio of two oboi d'amore and continuo,[30] the recitative sections are mostly simple, with occasional ragged motives by the oboes. The short oboe motives are syntactically important because they connect the two otherwise

---

preached by Leipzig theologian Johann Benedict Carpzov in 1688/89; cf. Markus Rathey, "Schelle, Carpzov und die Tradition der Choralkantate in Leipzig" (forthcoming). The *Christmas Oratorio* uses only two stanzas from this hymn, but it is safe to assume that on Christmas Day 1734 the congregation sang the chorale in its entirety. Another example of Bach's use of the hymn is the chorale cantata "Gelobet seist du, Jesu Christ" BWV 91, composed for Christmas Day 1724 and performed again in the early 1730s.

28. Cf. Meinrad Walter, *Johann Sebastian Bach — Weihnachtsoratorium* (Kassel: Bärenreiter, 2006), 63.

29. Walter Blankenburg, *Das Weihnachts-Oratorium*, 48, has suggested that the triple meter in the chorale sections should be understood as a symbol for the Trinity. The text of the movement makes no reference to Trinitarian theology, and it is unlikely that the change of meter has any theological significance. Rather, it emphasizes the contrast between the chorale sections and the recitative.

30. The oboe motive foreshadows a similar one in the aria "Schlafe, mein Liebster" in the second part of the *Christmas Oratorio*. The aria was originally composed for the secular cantata BWV 213, and Bach uses the motive in both the aria and the chorale trope to depict the rocking of the child in the manger.

disjunct spheres of the chorale and the recitative by carrying over from the chorale sections into the recitative. The connection is not as tight as in the trope recitatives of the chorale cantata cycle, but the underlying concept is similar.

The entire movement is framed by a ritornello of twelve measures that provides the motivic material for both the short interludes between sections and for the accompaniment of the chorale. When the ritornello is played at the end of the movement in slightly modified form, the last phrase of the hymn melody ("Kyrieleis") is built into the beginning of the instrumental trio. In the course of the movement, the motivic material never appears in its original version, but it is transposed several times during the chorale sections and interludes, beginning in G major, then in E minor, D minor, A minor, and A minor, then finally back into C major and G. Ignace Bossuyt has recently suggested (based on Blankenburg's interpretation) that the "series of modulations moves constantly 'downwards,' as if to indicate that God had to lower himself to the level of humanity."[31] It should be added, however, that toward the end the modulations ascend again back to G major. Therefore, Bach uses descent and ascent to symbolize the incarnation as a process, in which Christ descends and the human heart ascends to God, the very idea that is expressed in the text of the hymn. Bach also uses a melodic descent in his setting of the words of the bass, "Des Höchsten Sohn kömmt in die Welt" (The son of the Most High comes into the world), which is set with a descending line from d' down to d (mm. 42–43); this is followed by a leap of an octave upward from e to e' on "Mensch" (man) in measure 53.

From a functional perspective, the movement prepares (like a normal recitative) the following aria. The two movements even share some motivic ideas, like the descending line from d' to d (mm. 42–43 in the recit and mm. 15–17 in the aria) and the brief oboe motive from the recitative sections that returns in the aria (for instance in m. 16). Because Bach originally composed the aria for another cantata and parodied it in the *Christmas Oratorio*, it is clear that he designed the material in the newly composed recitative to fit the following, preexisting aria.[32] The recitative therefore serves a syntactic purpose within the sequence of movements by connecting the preexisting aria with the rest of the piece, and a dramatic purpose by first staging and then resolving the dichotomy between "rich" and "poor."

The last chorale trope in the *Christmas Oratorio* is bipartite, framing the echo-aria "Flößt, mein Heiland" BWV 248/39. The two movements (38 and 40) share the same chorale stanza from a hymn by Johann Rist ("Jesu, du mein liebstes Leben"); the first

31. Ignace Bossuyt, *Johann Sebastian Bach: Christmas Oratorio. BWV 248*, trans. Stratton Bull (Leuven: Leuven University Press, 2004), 80; cf. Blankenburg, *Das Weihnachts-Oratorium*, 47.

32. Bach does this often in the *Christmas Oratorio*; the most obvious example is the first alto aria ("Bereite dich, Zion") and its preceding recitative, which quotes the beginning of the aria's vocal line.

half of the stanza is quoted in no. 38 and the second half in no. 40, both sung by the soprano and combined with a recitative layer assigned to the bass. Surprisingly, Bach uses the words of the chorale but not the melody that was traditionally associated with it and which must have been familiar to him. This is unusual for Bach and unique among his chorale tropes. The melody Bach composes resembles a song rather than a chorale and is not unlike the melodies in the *Schemelli Gesangbuch* published in 1736.[33] Bach's reason for composing his own melody was in part the highly emotional character of the text, which was only insufficiently captured in the original tune by Johann Schop (~1590–1667).[34] The newly composed melody also gives Bach the opportunity to disregard the AAB form of the original tune and to create a through-composed melody instead, one that can more closely follow the character and meaning of the individual words of the text. It is remarkable that Bach still loosely follows the "grammar" of a traditional hymn melody, by ending what was the end of the A section in no. 38 in the dominant C (m. 17) and modulating back to the tonic F in the B section in no. 40 (m. 16). Both parts of the melody are clearly conceived as a unity.

The sources for the *Christmas Oratorio* differ in their separation of the movements in the fourth cantata. The printed libretto suggests two separate recitatives instead of what is now no. 38. The first recitative was labeled only "Recit." and contained the litany-like praise of the name of Jesus (until "dein JEsu labet Herz und Brust"), followed by another movement headed "Choral und Recitat," containing the chorale trope and the following simple recitative of the bass. Bach decided instead to compose the entire text in one section so that the chorale trope stands framed by two simple recitative sections.

The fourth part of the *Christmas Oratorio* is a meditation on the power and meaning of the name of Jesus, elaborating on the Gospel reading for the day about his circumci-

---

33. Cf. Renate Steiger, *Gnadengegenwart. Johann Sebastian Bach im Kontext lutherischer Orthodoxie und Frömmigkeit*, Doctrina et Pietas. Zwischen Reformation und Aufklärung. Texte und Untersuchungen, II 2 (Stuttgart–Bad Cannstatt: Frommann-Holzboog, 2002), 177–85; Martin Geck refers to the melody as an example for the Pietist aria, '*Denn alles findet bei Bach statt*'. *Erforschtes und Erfahrenes* (Stuttgart: Metzler, 2000), 104–5. The association with Pietism made by Geck is problematic because this style, even though favored by some Pietist composers and theorists, was not limited to this religious camp. In fact, the *Schemelli Gesangbuch* was intended to serve as a more orthodox counterpart to the popular Pietistic songbooks of the time.

34. The concept of abandoning a preexisting chorale melody in order to better capture the emotional qualities of a hymn text has its models in the seventeenth century. Bach's predecessor as cantor at St. Thomas's in Leipzig, Johann Schelle (1648–1701), composed a setting of "Ach mein herzliebes Jesulein," the thirteenth stanza of Luther's hymn "Vom Himmel hoch," in which he replaces the familiar chorale melody with his own setting that emphasizes the emotive qualities of the text; cf. Markus Rathey, "Rezeption als Innovation. Zur Aktualisierung traditioneller geistlicher Texte durch die Musik im 17. und frühen 18. Jahrhundert," in *Aedificatio. Erbauung im interkulturellen Kontext der Frühen Neuzeit*, ed. Andreas Solbach (Tübingen: Niemeyer, 2005), 234–36.

sion and naming (Luke 2:21) in no. 37. No. 38 begins as a litany on the name of Jesus until the focus shifts to the meaning of this name for the individual ("pro me") in the hour of dying and in the face of death. This is the point where the soprano enters with the chorale. The relationship of the two simultaneous texts is unusual for a chorale trope by Bach. Instead of juxtaposing two texts that stand in some kind of tension (as in the *St. John Passion*), the two layers express similar ideas—the emotional closeness of the faithful believer and Christ in the time of death.[35] Bach's decision not to use the traditional melody of the chorale reflects this relationship, because the character of the voices is much more similar than in earlier trope movements. The difference between the bass and the soprano lines is small, with the bass more declamatory than the upper voice. A second feature that differentiates the movement from other trope recitatives is the simultaneous combination of recitative and chorale (or, in this case, a chorale-like melody). The two movements are not the first time that Bach used a simultaneous trope in a recitative. Between February 1723 and December 1725 he composed five movements of this type, but in each of the earlier examples the chorale is played by an instrument and never sung (see Table 2).

The combination of chorale and recitative is a difficult task. The first reason is that the regular meter of the hymn conflicts with the (more or less) free declamation of the recitative. The second is that the simultaneous presentation of texts makes it difficult for the listener to perceive both. This is less problematic in an aria, where text repetitions are common, and Bach makes sure in those arias that contain chorale tropes that the aria text is heard at least once without the chorale. To ensure that the texts are perceivable in the recitatives nos. 38 and 40, Bach employs a similar technique and repeats sections of the recitative text, breaking with a common principle of recitative composition.

In the fourth cantata of BWV 248, no. 38 functions as a preparation (like a regular recitative) for the following soprano aria, which elaborates further on the salvific significance of Jesus's name in the face of death. The melodic contour of the aria (which is a parody of an aria from BWV 213) resembles that of the trope recitative. Most of

Table 2. Simultaneous troped recitatives in Bach's cantatas

Movement (Year)	Poetic Text	Chorale	Scoring
23/2 (1723)	Ach! gehe nicht vorüber	Christe, du Lamm Gottes	T, str, ob I+II, bc
70/9 (1723)	Ach, soll nicht dieser große Tag	Es ist gewißlich an der Zeit	B, tr, str, bc
5/4 (1724)	Mein treuer Heiland tröstet mich	Wo soll ich fliehen hin	A, ob I, bc
38/4 (1724)	Ach! daß mein Glaube noch so schwach	Aus tiefer Not schrei ich zu dir	A, bc
122/3 (1724)	Die Engel, welche sich zuvor	Das neugeborne Kindelein	S, fl I–III, bc

35. This was pointed out by Martin Petzold, *Bach Kommentar II*, 317.

the time, the soprano sings in a songlike aria style without longer melismas; only twice (both times on "erfreuen" [rejoice]) does Bach compose more extensive melismas. It is therefore likely that Bach designed the soprano line in no. 38 (and later in no. 40) with the preexisting aria in mind.

The soprano aria is followed by the second half of the chorale trope in no. 40. The text continues the praise of the name of Jesus and emphasizes hope for those who carry his name in their hearts, "Dein Name soll allein . . . in meinem Herzen seyn." As in no. 38, the two texts do not stand in a dialectical relationship but basically express the same thing. This becomes especially clear toward the end of the movement when the two voices end with a question to Jesus, each culminating in a personal pronoun, *dir/dich*.

Bass	Doch, Liebster, sage mir:	But tell me, Most Beloved:
	Wie rühm ich dich, wie dank ich **dir**?	How may I glorify you, how may I thank **you**?
Soprano	Hirt und König, Licht und Sonne,	Shepherd and king, light and sun,
	Ach! wie soll ich würdiglich,	O! how shall I worthily
	Mein Herr Jesu, preisen **dich**?	Praise **you**, my Lord Jesus?

Ending with this open question, the recitative leads to the following tenor aria "Ich will nur dir zu Ehren leben" (For honor I will live only for you). Even though the trope recitatives nos. 38 and 40 are related and follow a similar idea, the realization of this idea is slightly different in each movement. In no. 38 the hymn text is embedded into a larger recitative text and is framed by passages of simple recitative. In no. 40 the two voices sing together almost from the beginning. Only four short recitative sections without the soprano interrupt the combination of the two texts. Furthermore, the character of the two voices in no. 40 is similar, with the bass singing in a more arioso-like tone, as well. The movement ceases to be a traditional chorale trope and dissolves instead into a real duet.

The *St. Matthew Passion* II

The culmination of Bach's chorale tropes based on the model of the motet is the first movement of the *St. Matthew Passion*, in which Bach combines a dialogue between two choruses with the chorale "O Lamm Gottes unschuldig" (O Lamb of God without guilt). Earlier examples of this type reach from his *Kyrie* BWV 233a, composed for Good Friday 1708,[36] to motets from Bach's tenure in Weimar like the funeral motet "Fürchte

36. Cf. Markus Rathey, "Zur Datierung einiger Vokalwerke Bachs in den Jahren 1707 und 1708," *Bach-Jahrbuch* 92 (2006): 73–77.

dich nicht" ʙᴡᴠ 228.[37] ʙᴡᴠ 228 is a polychoral motet featuring a chorale trope in the second half. The two choirs open the piece with a dialogue not much different from the first movement of the passion.[38] When the hymn enters in ʙᴡᴠ 228, Bach abandons the polychoral structure and continues with a trope motet that features the motet text in the lower three voices and the chorale in the soprano (Example 4).

Example 4. J. S. Bach, "Fürchte dich nicht" ʙᴡᴠ 228, mm. 75–81.

37. On the dating of this motet see Daniel R. Melamed, *J. S. Bach and the German Motet* (Cambridge: Cambridge University Press, 1995), 59–60.

38. In our context it is less relevant whether the passion has two equal choirs—as earlier research suggested—or rather reflects a *soli ripieni* structure, as Daniel R. Melamed, *Hearing Bach's Passions*, 49–65, has pointed out.

Example 4. *Cont.*

The reduction of voices with the entrance of the chorale melody conforms to traditions of the German motet in the late seventeenth century. Similar examples are known by other members of the Bach family, as in Johann Michael Bach's *Fürchtet euch nicht*.[39] His piece also begins with a polychoral dialogue that turns into a polytextual four-part setting when the chorale is introduced. The opening movement of the *St. Matthew Passion* is obviously based on these earlier models but surpasses them.

The dialogue between the two protagonists of the first movement can be read (and was probably conceived) as an elaboration on the text of the hymn, a German *Agnus Dei*. The Daughter Zion admonishes the Faithful to see the bridegroom (= Christ) like a lamb, and with the mention of the word "Lamm" the libretto inserts the first two lines of the hymn "O Lamm Gottes unschuldig." The next section of the dialogue instructs "Seht die Geduld," which is answered by the hymn with the phrase "allzeit erfunden geduldig." Finally, the last lines of the text by Picander use the words "Schuld" and "tragen," which correspond to the chorale's "Sünd" and "getragen."[40]

Instead of following Picander's suggestion of juxtaposing a soloist and choir, Bach conceived the part of the Daughter Zion for chorus, as well. Karol Berger has recently discussed this movement extensively and has pointed out the theological (or rather, dramaturgical) reasons for Bach's deviation from the libretto: "The Passion tells the story of the pivotal turning point of human history. From the start, therefore, the tone needs to be set high. The effect of epic monumentality that Bach undoubtedly sought to create here is not one that a solo, even one accompanied by a choir, could have provided."[41] In other words, the opening movement both sets the tone for the monumentality of the passion (which corresponds to the monumentality and audacity of the story told: God dies for the atonement of humankind) and sets the stage for further dialogues between the Daughter Zion and the Faithful in the movements to come. Like an exordium in a traditional passion setting, the first movement provides the hermeneutic key for understanding the following narrative both musically and theologically.

---

39. Cf. Rathey, "Rezeption als Innovation," 237–38.

40. Picander's decision to use the German *Agnus Dei* for the exordium of the passion, the very movement that traditionally provided the hermeneutic key for the following passion, conforms to the contemporary understanding of the hymn "O Lamm Gottes." Schamelius, quoting Simon Pauli, writes in his *Lieder-Commentarius* of 1724, 1:178: "Dis geistliche Lied singet unsere Kirche, wenn das heilige Abendmahl gehalten wird / unter der Verreichung und Niessung des wahren Leibes und Blutes JEsu Christi, und wenn die Paßion geprediget wird." Other authors of the sixteenth and seventeenth centuries call the song a "small passion" ("kleine Paßion") and a summary of the essence of Christ's suffering; see Johann Christoph Olearius, *Hymnologia Passionalis i.e. Homiletische Lieder-Remarques* (Arnstadt: Ehrt, 1709), 69.

41. Berger, *Bach's Cycle*, 47.

The compositional realization of Picander's libretto surpasses its predecessors and models in several respects. In this movement Bach blends two contradictory structures: the da capo form (ABA') of the two choirs and the XXY form of the chorale. The structural problem is solved by combining the hymn mostly with the two choirs in the B section while the A section does not quote the melody. The A' section (mm. 72–90) combines a shortened musical recapitulation of A, but instead of returning to the A text, Bach uses the last lines of the B text (here combined with the final line of the hymn). Only after the hymn has ended, the text of the A section returns.[42]

An aspect that contributes to the monumentality and the effect of the opening movement is the way the chorale is introduced into the polychoral texture. Traditionally, a polychoral movement would have abandoned its original texture, as seen both in Bach's motet BWV 228 and the earlier piece by Johann Michael Bach. Now, however, Bach maintains the polychoral juxtaposition even after the hymn has entered in m. 30. Instead of leading to a collapse of the polychorality, the chorale adds an additional layer to the already complex texture. Only toward the end of the movement, starting in m. 72, Bach abandons the distinction between the two ensembles and assigns the words of the Daughter Zion to both choirs, while the "Soprano in ripieno" sings the last phrase of the hymn, "Erbarm dich unser, o Jesu." The conflation of the forces, which would have been expected for the entrance of the hymn, is delayed until the final cry for God's mercy. With the short modified da capo, beginning in m. 83, Bach separates the two ensembles again for a brief call-and-response, but in the final cadence (mm. 89–90) the *chorus secundus* sings the same text as *chorus primus* (although with different notes).

The structural characteristics of the movement are significant. Viewed within the history of trope motets, the conflation of the two choirs toward the end (even though delayed) conforms to the conventions of the genre. The conflation, however, also has a semantic function. We have observed in earlier chorale tropes that they are often used to juxtapose the voice of a believer, often doubtful or at least full of questions, and the confident voice of the congregation, symbolized by the hymn. The opening movement features a similar dialogue carried out by the Daughter Zion, representing the confident part, and the Choir of the Faithful, who ask questions. In earlier tropes the doubts of the believer vanished and he/she was convinced by the confidence ex-

42. Karol Berger, noticeably in awe of Bach's compositional solution, writes: "In short, the opening is a varied da capo, but one with a most extraordinary ending, which conflates in a single phrase what normally is presented in successive ones—the end of the B section and the beginning of the A' section, as well as the recapitulations of the vocal phrase and the ritornello—and for good measure also blends the texts of the two protagonists into one. The effect is one not of impatient abbreviation or acceleration but, rather, of synthesizing culmination." *Bach's Cycle*, 59.

pressed in the chorale. Picander's libretto does not make this step from question to answers (the second chorus never stops asking questions), but Bach's composition goes a step further and combines the two choirs with the same text at exactly the moment at which the hymn has finished praising the salvific Lamb of God and culminates in a final cry for God's mercy, "Erbarm dich unser, o Jesu." Even though the two choirs split again for a moment, the movement ends with both ensembles singing the phrase "Als wie ein Lamm," a deliberate paraphrase of the beginning of the chorale.

It is clear that Bach erects this monumental movement from the blueprints of earlier chorale tropes, but at the same time he surpasses these models. The movement has a semantic and a syntactic function in the context of the *St. Matthew Passion*. On a syntactic level, the chorus serves as a grand portal to the passion. Furthermore, the conflation of the forces toward the end of the chorus anticipates a similar combination of forces at the end of each part of the passion in nos. 29 (after the revision of 1736) and 68.[43] On a semantic level, it presents the theological understanding of the passion narrative that is about to follow, combining the dialogue between the Daughter Zion and the questions of the Faithful with a traditional hymn. Even though the answers to the questions of the *chorus secundus* are given by the Daughter Zion (and not by the hymn), the words of the first chorus are clearly derived from the text of the chorale. The hymn (= the voice of the congregation) is, as in earlier movements, the final source of the answers.

Conclusions

Chorale tropes, the skillful combination of a hymn and free poetry, occur in Bach's works throughout his career, beginning in his earliest compositions for Mühlhausen and ending in Leipzig during the 1730s. Bach's contributions to this genre stand in the tradition of the seventeenth and early eighteenth centuries; however, he not only imitates earlier models, but deals intensely with the compositional challenges that are inherent in the combination of different musical and textual layers. Especially during his chorale cantata cycle from 1724/25, Bach worked out the compositional problems of integrating the two distinct layers and creating unity in diversity.[44]

In his oratorios, chorale tropes bridge the gap between individual reflection and response of the congregation. They serve especially as a means to juxtapose the confidence of the church and the doubt or questions of the individual. Bach uses the choral trope in most of his oratorios as a discursive element; two positions are juxtaposed in a dialectical way and lead to a conclusion. This is not really a true discourse, because

---

43. Cf. Berger, *Bach's Cycle*, 49.

44. See Krummacher, *Choralkantaten*, and Rathey, "Der zweite Leipziger Kantatenjahrgang."

the winner of the argument (the chorale) is predetermined. However, it is significant that Bach uses the model of the chorale trope in his oratorios almost consistently in this dramatic way.

The polarity of the two layers is reflected on a musical level by the fact that only one of the layers is newly composed while the other one is a chorale melody. More than in most discursive-dramatic dialogues in contemporary opera or in Bach's sacred cantatas, the two protagonists are clearly defined by their musical material. This is confirmed *ex negativo* by Bach's very last chorale trope, the bipartite movement in the fourth part of the *Christmas Oratorio:* the relationship between the texts of soprano and bass is not dialectical, and Bach therefore refrains from using the original melody and composes his own tune instead. The two characters are still musically distinct, but the musical realization makes clear that this is a juxtaposition of two individuals and not of an individual and the voice of the Christian community in the chorale. Even though the chorale trope loses its importance in Bach's cantatas in the later 1720s, we find several examples of this genre in his oratorios. At the same time, however, the trope is transformed. Bach abandons earlier compositional concepts like the motivic unity of the two layers in the trope-recitative in the *St. Matthew Passion* to emphasize the epic-dramatic concept of the passion as a juxtaposition of two distinct characters.

The chorale tropes in Bach's oratorios, even though they interrupt the flow of the narrative and break the unity of time and space in the story, contribute to the unification of the pieces by creating, at least for a moment, the illusion of a unity of time and space for the individual and communal response. The chorale tropes create their own dramatic moments in the epic interpolation into the biblical narratives of the oratorios. In most cases they transform the individual by contrasting his or her doubts about the paradox of the incarnation or Christ's suffering with the position and knowledge of the congregation as it is spelled out (and codified) in the congregational hymns. This goes beyond the use of chorale tropes in Bach's earlier cantatas, particularly in Weimar, where the introduction of a chorale (instrumental or vocal) served as an additional commentary to the primary text and had no dramatic function.

Oratorio on
Five Afternoons

From the Lübeck Abendmusiken
to Bach's Christmas Oratorio

Kerala J. Snyder

Most oratorios, like most operas, are performed within a single day as measured by real time in the theater, church, or oratory, regardless of the dramatic time that might be portrayed in their librettos. The Lübeck Abendmusiken and Bach's *Christmas Oratorio* BWV 248 form notable—although by no means unique—exceptions to this principle.[1] As is well known, the *Christmas Oratorio* consists of six parts, each similar to a cantata and first performed on the first, second, and third Christmas days of 1734 and on New Year's Day, the Sunday after New Year, and Epiphany of 1735. The Lübeck Abendmusiken, according to a guidebook from 1697, were "presented yearly on five Sundays between St. Martin's [November 11] and Christmas, following the Sunday vesper sermon, from 4 to 5 o'clock";[2] those five Sundays were the last two of Trinity and the second, third, and fourth of Advent.

Bach carefully timed his famous trip to visit Dieterich Buxtehude in Lübeck during the fall of 1705 to coincide with the Abendmusik season. He would have expected the regular performances to take place on November 15 and 22 and December 6, 13, and 20 of that year. From the Arnstadt archival records we know that he was back on February 7 and that he had been away for sixteen weeks, because "he had asked for only four weeks, but had stayed about four times as long."[3] That suggests that he

1. Another exception is Friedrich Funke's Christmas oratorio, its two parts performed in Lüneburg on December 25 and 26, 1693. See Peter Wollny, "Über die Beziehungen zwischen Oper und Oratorium in Hamburg im späten 17. und frühen 18. Jahrhundert," in *Il teatro musicale italiano nel Sacro Romano Impero nei secoli XVII e XVIII* (Como: Antiquae Musicae Italicae Studiosi, 1999), 172.

2. *Die Beglückte und Geschmückte Stadt Lübeck. Was ist Kurtze Beschreibung der Stadt Lübeck So wol Vom Anfang und Fortgang Derselben In ihrem Bau, Herrschafften und Einwohnern, Als sonderlich Merckwürdigen Begebenheiten und Veränderung* (Lübeck: Johann Gerhard Krüger, 1697), 114.

3. *Bach-Dokumente* II: *Fremdschriftliche und gedruckte Dokumente zur Lebensgeschichte Johann Sebastian Bachs 1685–1750*, ed. Werner Neumann and Hans-Joachim Schulze (Kassel: Bärenreiter, 1969), 19–20.

departed around October 18. From his obituary, we know that he "tarried" in Lübeck "for almost a quarter of a year,"[4] which would be about twelve weeks, leaving four weeks for the trip there and back, exactly what it would take to walk the 280 miles each way at an average of 20 miles a day (see Table 1).[5]

During the years in which Buxtehude served as organist of St. Mary's Church in Lübeck, from 1668 to 1707, he composed and directed three different types of Abendmusiken there: dramatic oratorios, ceremonial oratorios, and mixed programs of unrelated vocal works, as he did in the year 1700.[6] In 1705, while Bach was there,

Table 1. Hypothetical calendar of Bach's 1705–6 trip to Lübeck

	Sunday	Monday	Tuesday	Wednesday	Thursday	Friday	Saturday	Notes
October 1705	*18*	*19*	*20*	*21*	22	*23*	*24*	*Bach travels*
	25	*26*	*27*	*28*	29	*30*	*31*	*to Lübeck*
November	1	2	3	4	5	6	7	
	8	9	10	11	12	13	14	
	15	16	17	18	19	20	21	Sun.: *Abendmusik*
	22	23	24	25	26	27	28	Sun.: *Abendmusik*
December	29	30	1	2	3	4	5	Wed., Thurs.: Extraordinary Abendmusiken
	6	7	8	9	10	11	12	Sun.: *Abendmusik*
	13	14	15	16	17	18	19	Sun.: *Abendmusik*
	20	21	22	23	24	25	26	Sun.: *Abendmusik*
January 1706	27	28	29	30	31	1	2	
	3	4	5	6	7	8	9	
	10	11	12	13	14	15	16	
	17	18	19	20	21	22	23	
	24	*25*	*26*	*27*	*28*	*29*	*30*	*Bach returns*
February	*31*	*1*	*2*	*3*	*4*	*5*	6	*to Arnstadt*

4. *Bach-Dokumente* III: *Dokumente zum Nachwirken Johann Sebastian Bachs 1750–1800*, ed. Hans-Joachim Schulze (Kassel: Bärenreiter, 1972), 82.

5. See Kerala J. Snyder, "To Lübeck in the Steps of J. S. Bach," *Musical Times* 127 (1986): 672–77; German translation as *Nach Lübeck in den Fußstapfen von J. S. Bach*, trans. Martin Botsch (Lübeck: Stadtbibliothek Lübeck, 2005).

6. Listed in Snyder, *Dieterich Buxtehude: Organist in Lübeck*, rev. ed. (Rochester, N.Y.: University of Rochester Press, 2007), 425–26, and its German translation, *Dieterich Buxtehude: Leben, Werk, Aufführungspraxis*, trans. Hans-Joachim Schulze (Kassel: Bärenreiter, 2007), 467–68. References are to the revised English edition unless noted.

Buxtehude presented two ceremonial oratorios that he himself designated as "extra ordinaire": *Castrum doloris*, commemorating the death of the Holy Roman Emperor Leopold I and performed on Wednesday, December 2, and *Templum honoris*, celebrating the accession of his successor, Joseph I, performed the following evening, Thursday, December 3.[7] We have the librettos but not the music for these works.[8] Their characters are almost all allegorical: Fame, Fear of God, Righteousness, Grace, the Sciences, and a choir of lamenting women in *Castrum doloris*; Fame, Germany, Honor, Wisdom, Bravery, and Happiness in *Templum honoris*.

We cannot be certain that Buxtehude presented his "ordinary" five-concert Sunday series in 1705, but it appears likely that he did, since he so carefully positioned the "extraordinary" works on weekdays following the first Sunday of Advent (November 29 in 1705), when no Abendmusik concert ever took place. But since these "extraordinary" works required extraordinary resources, both musical and scenic, I suspect that those five ordinary concerts that year consisted of a mixture of unrelated works, as in 1700, requiring no new composition and little rehearsal. So Bach probably did not have the opportunity to hear a "classic" dramatic Lübeck Abendmusik series, in which, to quote the later Lübeck cantor Caspar Ruetz, "the poet uses a biblical story as the basis and constructs it according to the rules of theatrical poetics, dividing it into five parts, which are performed on as many Sundays."[9] But surely Buxtehude would have shown Bach some of his old scores, since the young man had walked so far to witness the Lübeck Abendmusiken.

Buxtehude had established this classic five-part structure no later than 1684, the year in which he announced the future publication of two Abendmusiken—most likely just their librettos—in the Frankfurt and Leipzig book fair catalogues. The first of these

7. Buxtehude's entry into the account book of St. Mary's Church; transcription in Snyder, *Buxtehude* (2007), 476.

8. *Castrum Doloris, Dero in Gott Ruhenden Römis. Käyserl. auch Königl. Majestäten Leopold dem Ersten, Zum Glorwürdigsten Andencken, In der Käyserl. Freyen Reichs-Stadt Lübecks Haupt-Kirchen zu St. Marien, Zur Zeit gewöhnlicher Abend-Music, Aus Aller-Unterthänigster Pflicht Musicalisch vorgestellet Von Diterico Buxtehuden, Organisten daselbst; Templum Honoris, Dero Regierenden Römis. Käyserl. auch Königl. Majestät Joseph Dem Ersten, Zu Unsterblichen Ehren, In der Käyserl. Freyen Reichs-Stadt Lübecks Haupt-Kirchen zu St. Marien, Im Jahr Christi 1705. Zu beliebter Zeit bey der gewöhnlichen Abend-Music, Aus Aller-Unterthänigster Pflicht Glückwünschend gewidmet Von Diterico Buxtehuden, Organisten daselbst* (Lübeck: Schmalhertzens Wittwe, 1705; facsimile reprint Lübeck: Bibliothek der Hansestadt, 2002; also in Georg Karstädt, *Die "extraordinairen" Abendmusiken Dietrich Buxtehudes* [Lübeck: Max Schmidt-Römhild, 1962]).

9. Caspar Ruetz, *Widerlegte Vorurtheile von der Beschaffenheit der heutigen Kirchenmusic und von der Lebens-Art einiger Musicorum* (Lübeck: Peter Böckmann, 1752), 44. For a translation of the complete passage, see Snyder, *Buxtehude*, 55–56; for the original German text see the German edition, 79–81.

was listed as *"Heavenly Joy of the Spirit on Earth over the Incarnation and Birth of Our Dearest Savior Jesus Christ,* in five separate acts, in opera style, with many arias and ritornelli, brought into a musical harmony for six concerted voices, various instruments and capella voices."[10] This must have been Buxtehude's own Christmas oratorio, and it has disappeared without a further trace. The preserved librettos and scores of the eighteenth-century Lübeck Abendmusiken composed by Buxtehude's successors Johann Christian Schieferdecker, Johann Paul Kunzen, Adolf Carl Kunzen, and Johann Wilhelm Cornelius von Königslöw adhere to Buxtehude's five-part structure.[11]

Buxtehude's Abendmusik *Die Hochzeit des Lamms*

All the music for Buxtehude's known Abendmusiken is lost,[12] and we have just one other extant libretto, that of his first known Abendmusik, *Die Hochzeit des Lamms* BUXWV 128, a dramatic oratorio in two parts, presented on December 8 and 15, 1678, the second and third Sundays in Advent that year. Its title page (Figure 1) reads in part:

> *The Wedding of the Lamb and the Joyful Reception of the Bride to It in the Five Wise [Maidens] and the Exclusion of the Ungodly from It in the Five Foolish Maidens, as It is Told by the Bridegroom of the Soul, Christ Himself, in Matthew 25, and in Other Passages of Scripture . . . to Be Presented by Dieterico Buxtehude, Organist of [St.] Mary in Lübeck, in the Customary Time of the Abend-Musik on the second and third Sundays of Advent in the Main Church of St. Mary from four until five o'clock. Lübeck . . . 1678.*[13]

It is clear from this title that by 1678, Buxtehude's presentation of concerts known as Abendmusiken on certain Sunday afternoons had become customary, but those earlier concerts most likely consisted of unrelated offerings of vocal and instrumental music. His predecessor, Franz Tunder, had presented such concerts on Thursday

---

10. "Himml. Seelenlust auf Erden über die Menschwerdung u. Geburt unsers allerliebsten Heil. u. Seligm. J. Chr. [in 5. unterschiedenen Abhandlungen auf der Operen Art mit vielen Arien u. Ritornellen, in einer musikal. Harmonia à 6 voc. concert. nebst divers. Instr. u. Capell-Stimmen gebracht.];" listed in Albert Göhler, *Verzeichnis der in den Frankfurter und Leipziger Messkatalogen der Jahre 1564 bis 1759 angezeigten Musikalien* (Leipzig, 1902; reprint Hilversum: Knuf, 1965), part 2, p. 12.

11. For a list of titles and present locations see Volker Scherliess and Arndt Schnoor, eds., *"Theater-Music in der Kirche": Zur Geschichte der Lübecker Abendmusiken* (Lübeck: Bibliothek der Hansestadt Lübeck–Musikhochschule Lübeck, 2003), 73–75.

12. I have argued that the anonymous oratorio *Wacht! Euch zum Streit gefasset macht* is Buxtehude's Abendmusik from 1683 (see Snyder, *Buxtehude,* 68–69), but that work does not figure in the present discussion.

13. *SUu* vmhs 6:8. The complete libretto appears in facsimile in Erik Kjellberg and Kerala J. Snyder, eds., *The Düben Collection Database Catalogue,* http://www.musik.uu.se/duben/Duben.php.

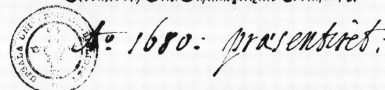

Die Hochzeit des Lamms/
Und die
Freuden-volle Einholung der Braut
zu derselben
In den 5. klugen
Und die Außschliessung der Gottlosen von derselben
In den 5. thörichten

Jungfrauen/

Welche wie sie
Von dem Seelen-Bräutigam Christo selbst beym
Matth. 25. an die Hand gegeben/.

Auch nach Anleitung andrer Orther in der Heil. Schrifft den Frommen und nach der Zukunfft ihres Seelen-Bräutigams hertzlich sehnenden zum innerlichen Seelen-Trost und süssten Freude; den Gottlosen aber zum Schrecken; Beides zu Gottes hohen Ehren; Christ-wollmeinend in der gewöhnlichen Zeit der Abend-Music am 2. und 3. Advents-Sontage in der Haupt-Kirchen St. Mariæ von 4. biß 5. Uhr soll vorgestellet werden
von
Dieterico Buxtehuden/
Organista Mariæ Lubec.

Lübeck/
Gedruckt bey Seel. Schmalhertzens Erben/1678.

A° 1680: præsentiret:

Figure 1. Buxtehude, *Die Hochzeit des Lamms* BUXWV 128, title page of libretto (Uppsala Universitetsbibliotek)

afternoons.[14] It is probably no accident that this first *dramatic* Lübeck Abendmusik of which we know occurred in 1678; at the beginning of that year, the Hamburg Opera had opened its doors with an opera by Buxtehude's friend Johann Theile. Buxtehude himself characterized his 1684 Abendmusik *Heavenly Joy* as "in opera style, with many arias and ritornelli," and Ruetz could still write in 1752 that "these Abendmusiken . . . are not just theatrical, but a complete *Drama per Musica*, as the Italians say, and the singers would only need to act for it to be a sacred opera."[15] Buxtehude's contemporary Hinrich Elmenhorst, preacher at St. Catherine's church in Hamburg and a librettist for the Hamburg Opera, wrote in 1688 that "Musicians understand the word *operas* to mean the compositions of poets and composers performed not only in theaters, but also in churches. . . . In this connection I must mention how the world-famous Lübeck musician Diedericus Buxtehude has performed more than one such opera in public churches there in the Abendmusik customary at a certain time of year, whose poetry has been published."[16] Two years before Bach composed his *Christmas Oratorio*, Johann Gottfried Walther defined oratorio as "sacred opera."[17]

The libretto for *Die Hochzeit des Lamms* "uses a biblical story as the basis," just as the eighteenth-century Abendmusiken did, in this case the parable of the wise and foolish maidens found in Matthew 25:

> [1]Then the kingdom of heaven shall be compared to ten maidens who took their lamps and went to meet the bridegroom. [2]Five of them were foolish, and five were wise. [3]For when the foolish took their lamps, they took no oil with them; [4]but the wise took flasks of oil with their lamps. [5]As the bridegroom was delayed, they all slumbered and slept. [6]But at midnight there was a cry, "Behold, the bridegroom! Come out to meet him." [7]Then all those maidens rose and trimmed their lamps. [8]And the foolish said to the wise, "Give us some of your oil, for our lamps are going out." [9]But the wise replied, "Perhaps there will not be enough for us and for you; go rather to the dealers and buy for yourselves." [10]And while they went to buy, the bridegroom came, and those who were ready went in with him to the marriage feast; and the door was shut. [11]Afterward the other maidens came also, saying "Lord, lord, open to us." [12]But

14. See Snyder, "Franz Tunder's Stock-Exchange Concerts: Prelude to the Lübeck Abendmusiken," *GOArt Research Reports* 2 (2000): 41–57.

15. Ruetz, *Widerlegte Vorurtheile*, 44.

16. Hinrich Elmenhorst, *Dramatologia Antiquo-Hodierna* (Hamburg: Georg Rebenl. Wittwe, 1688; facsimile reprint Leipzig: Zentralantiquariat der deutschen demokratischen Republik, 1978), 100–101; translation from Snyder, *Buxtehude*, 65; original in German edition, 91.

17. Johann Gottfried Walther, *Musicalisches Lexicon* (Leipzig: Wolffgang Deer, 1732; facsimile reprint, ed. Richard Schaal (Kassel: Bärenreiter, 1953), 451.

he replied, "Truly, I say to you, I do not know you." [13]Watch therefore, for you know neither the day nor the hour.[18]

As with the later Abendmusiken, the poet constructed the story "according to the rules of theatrical poetics," dividing it not yet into five parts, but into only two at this early date. The scenario can be divided into two acts, not designated as such, but clearly separated by sonatas and printed stars (fol. 4r):

Act I [2nd Sunday in Advent]

Scene 1: Betrothal, Christ and the Church (fols. 1v–2v)

Scene 2: Wise and foolish maidens sleep (fols. 2v–3v)

Scene 3: The Bridegroom approaches (fols. 3v–4r)

Act II [3rd Sunday in Advent]

Scene 1: Foolish maidens ask for oil (fols. 4r–4v)

Scene 2: Christ invites wise maidens and angels into the feast (fols. 4v–5v)

Scene 3: Christ rejects foolish maidens (fols. 5v–6r)

Conclusion: The moral of the story (fols. 6r–6v)

The characters are both biblical (Christ, the wise maidens, the foolish maidens, the angels) and allegorical (the church, as the bride, who is entirely missing from the biblical story).[19] Christ is always a bass, but the role of the church is variously played by a soprano (fol. 2r), an alto (fol. 2r), and an entire chorus of voices and instruments (fol. 1v). This varied scoring artfully reflects the church as a collection of individual believers; in her role as a bride, however, all the pronouns are singular, even when the whole chorus is singing. The angels, too, have varied scorings, but the wise maidens are always represented by two sopranos and the foolish maidens by two altos.

This libretto embroiders upon the biblical narrative considerably, beginning with the addition of a betrothal scene. Christ proposes with the words of Hosea 2:19: "I will betroth you to me forever; I will betroth you to me in righteousness and in justice, in steadfast love and in mercy." The church responds with a verse from Isaiah, "I rejoice in the Lord . . . as a bridegroom decks himself with a garland, and as a bride adorns herself with her jewels" (both fol. 1v). They then sing a love duet, to which I shall return. In the second scene both the wise and foolish maidens fall asleep, but the

---

18. *The Holy Bible, Revised Standard Version* (New York: Thomas Nelson & Sons, 1952), New Testament, 31.

19. The *Revised Standard Version* has a footnote to verse 1: "Other ancient authorities add *and the bride*."

wise maidens frame an aria sung by an angel with words from the Song of Solomon: "I sleep, but my heart is awake" (fol. 3v). As the bridegroom approaches in scene 3, the wise maidens awaken, and the act closes as the angels announce that the wedding day has arrived.

As the plot resumes a week later, the foolish maidens ask for oil from the wise maidens, who refuse to give it to them. When Christ, the bridegroom, appears in the second scene, he speaks with words from the Song of Solomon: "Arise, my love, my fair one, and come away; for lo, the winter is past, the rain is over and gone. The flowers appear on the earth. . . . Let me see your face, let me hear your voice, for your voice is sweet, and your face is comely" (fol. 4v). Yet, as in the biblical text, the bride is missing from this scene. The wise maidens enter the wedding hall amid great rejoicing from angels and a heavenly choir. In the final scene, Christ rejects the foolish maidens with the words "I do not know you," spoken only once in Matthew 25:12 but eight times in the libretto (fols. 5v–6r), after which the foolish maidens descend into the flames of hell. A concluding section draws the moral of this drama: woe to those who disdain the word of the Lord; joy to the righteous. It differs considerably from that of the biblical parable in Matthew 25:13, "Watch therefore, for you know neither the day nor the hour."

Although the entire plot is based on the parable narrated in Matthew 25:1–13, the only words from this biblical passage that actually appear in the libretto are those of the direct quotations, sometimes repeated: "Behold, the bridegroom! Come out to meet him" (fols. 3v, 4r); "Give us some of your oil, for our lamps are going out"; "Perhaps there will not be enough for us and for you; go rather to the dealers and buy for yourselves" (fol. 4r); "Lord, Lord, open to us" (fol. 5v); and finally, "Truly, I say to you, I do not know you" (fols. 5v–6r). The story is filled in with numerous other biblical passages, all of which are meticulously identified. For example, because the parable text gives no direct lines to Christ, the bridegroom, when he invites the wise maidens into the wedding feast the libretto borrows words for him from Isaiah 26:2, "Open the gates, that the righteous nation which keeps faith may enter in," and Genesis 24:31, "Come in, O blessed of the Lord; why do you stand outside?" (fols. 4v–5r).

At the celebration that follows, a heavenly choir sings the biblical passage from which the title *Die Hochzeit des Lamms* had been drawn: "Hallelujah! For the Lord our God the Almighty reigns. Let us rejoice and exult and give him the glory, for the marriage of the Lamb has come, and his Bride has made herself ready" (Revelation 19:6–7; fol. 5r). Up to this climactic point, the image of Jesus as lamb and bridegroom had appeared only twice, but now it becomes incorporated into a refrain that occurs four times: "Wonne Wonne über Wonne! Gottes Lamm ist unsre Sonne" (fols. 5r, 5v, 6r).

Three familiar chorales are integrated into the plot. Verse 7 of "Wie schön leuchtet der Morgenstern" ("Wie bin ich doch so herzlich froh") forms part of the love duet (fol. 2r), and verse 6 ("Zwingt die Saiten in Cithara," fol. 5r) is sung as the wise maidens enter the wedding hall. An undesignated soloist sings the first verse of "Jesu meine Freude" (fol. 2v) before the maidens fall asleep, but its text points to the bride as the character who is singing: "Jesu meine Freude . . . Gottes Lamm, mein Bräutigam." The presence of all three verses of "Wachet auf, ruft uns die Stimme" comes as no surprise, since it paraphrases the parable of the wise and foolish maidens. The wise maidens sing the first two verses as the bridegroom arrives (fol. 3v), and a heavenly choir sings the final verse after the wise maidens have entered the wedding hall (fol. 5v).

Biblical verses and chorales have no place in opera; to be in operatic style an Abend-musik must have, in Buxtehude's words, "many arias and ritornelli." Three poems are specifically designated "Aria" (fols. 3r, 4r, 6v), two of them with numbered strophes articulated by ritornelli. Buxtehude may also have set the librettos numerous other poems in aria style, and ritornelli abound throughout.

Unlike many opera librettos of the day, the title page of *Die Hochzeit des Lamms* prominently displays Buxtehude's name but makes no mention of the poet responsible for the text. Caspar Ruetz wrote in 1752 that Karl Heinrich Lange, the *Conrector* of the Katharineum, Lübeck's renowned Latin school, was the usual Abendmusik poet,[20] but no similar documentation exists for Buxtehude's time. Nevertheless, his librettist for *Die Hochzeit des Lamms* can be identified with reasonable certainty as Johann Wilhelm Petersen, based on Petersen's subsequent publication of a devotional treatise with a remarkably similar title: *Die Hochzeit Des Lammes und der Braut*.[21]

Johann Wilhelm Petersen (1649–1727) grew up in Lübeck and attended the Katha-rineum until 1669, the year after Buxtehude's arrival in the city. Petersen studied philosophy and theology at the universities of Gießen and Rostock, and, following a short stint as professor of poetry in Rostock, he embarked upon a career as an ortho-dox Lutheran pastor with appointments as pastor of the Aegidienkirche in Hannover (1677), court preacher and superintendent in Eutin (1678), and superintendent in Lüneburg (1688). He had established contact with Philipp Jakob Spener during his student years, and Spener officiated at his marriage to Johanna Eleonora von und

---

20. Ruetz, *Widerlegte Vorurtheile*, 44.

21. Johann Wilhelm Petersen, *Die Hochzeit Des Lammes und der Braut Bey Der herannahenden Zunkunfft Jesu Christi Durch ein Geschrey in dieser Mitternacht, zur heiligen Wache: Beweglich vorgestellet, und mit vielen Kupffern, auch dreyen Registern außgezieret*. Offenbach am Mayn, Bonaventura de Launoy, n.d. [1701]. I first noted the similarity of titles in the first edition of *Dieterich Buxtehude: Organist in Lübeck* (New York: Schirmer, 1987), 147. Jürgen Heidrich investigated the matter further and iden-tified Petersen as the librettist in "Andachts- und Erbauungsliteratur als Quelle zur norddeutschen Musikgeschichte um 1700: Dieterich Buxtehude, Johann Wilhelm Petersen und die 'Hochzeit des Lamms,'" in *Bach, Lübeck und die norddeutsche Musiktradition: Bericht über das Internationale Symposon der Musikhochschule Lübeck April 2000*, ed. Wolfgang Sandberger (Kassel: Bärenreiter, 2002), 86–100.

zu Merlau (1644–1724), a member of Spener's congregation in Frankfurt, in 1680. As husband and wife their theology moved increasingly toward radical pietism and millenarianism, and in 1692 Johann Wilhelm was dismissed for this reason from his position as superintendent and ordered to leave Lüneburg.[22] A hymnal published that year, *Andächtig Singender Christen-Mund*, contains a strophic text by Petersen that Buxtehude set to music (BUXWV 90).[23] Its first verse reads:

O wie selig sind, die zu dem Abendmahl	Oh how blessed are those who are
des Lammes berufen sind.	called to the communion of the Lamb.
Liebster Jesu, liebstes Leben,	Dearest Jesus, dearest life,
Der du bist das Gotteslamm,	Who is the Lamb of God,
Das die Sünde auf sich nahm,	That took sin upon himself,
Dir hab' ich mich ganz ergeben.	I have devoted myself to you completely.
Dich will ich den Bräut'gam nennen,	I will call you the Bridegroom,
Den ich bin ja deine Braut,	For I am your bride,
Die du ewig dir vertraut.	To whom you pledged your troth
	eternally.
Nichts soll unsre Liebe trennen.	Nothing shall separate our love.

As evidence for Petersen's authorship of Buxtehude's *Hochzeit* libretto, Jürgen Heidrich advances Petersen's composition of a now lost wedding poem for Buxtehude in 1668;[24] the fact that Petersen and another pupil at the Katharineum had taken the roles of the Church and Christ in a poetic paraphrase of the Song of Solomon that they had written, memorized, and performed; and similarities in theme and wording between the libretto, the text of "O wie selig," and the foreword to his 1701 treatise.

---

22. Both Johann Wilhelm and Johanna Eleonora Petersen wrote autobiographies. The information from Johann Wilhelm's *Lebens-Beschreibung* (1719) up to 1692 is included in Markus Matthias, *Johann Wilhelm und Johanna Eleonora Petersen* (Göttingen: Vandenhoeck & Ruprecht, 1993); *Leben Frauen Joh. Eleonora Petersen* (1718) is translated as *The Life of Lady Johanna Eleonora Petersen, Written by Herself: Pietism and Women's Autobiography in Seventeenth-century Germany*, ed. and trans. Barbara Becker-Cantarino (Chicago: University of Chicago Press, 2005), 59–98.

23. *Andächtig Singender Christen-Mund, Das ist: Wahrer Kinder Gottes Geheiligte Andachten, bestehende In einem dreyfachen Christlichen Hand- und Gesang-Buche* (Wesel: Andreas Luppius, 1692), 150–51. It contains hymns by Petersen and others and is dedicated to Philip Jacob Spener, August Herman Franck, and Petersen, among others. I have seen only the title page and dedication; Martin Geck identified it as the source for the text of BUXWV 90 in *Die Vokalmusik Dietrich Buxtehudes und der frühe Pietismus* (Kassel: Bärenreiter, 1965), 214. See also Snyder, *Buxtehude*, 344–45.

24. Heidrich, 87–89; for a list of similar poems by Petersen see Matthias, 385–86.

This treatise consists of a detailed exegesis of the parable of the wise and foolish maidens, with a chapter devoted to each biblical verse, preceded by a foreword, with each illustrated by an engraving containing an excerpt from that verse.[25] The biblical verse accompanying the foreword, "the marriage of the Lamb has come, and his Bride has made herself ready," comes from Revelation 19:7, from which the titles of both the libretto and the treatise are derived. But the foreword does not offer an exegesis of this verse; rather, it considers the entire parable, giving the complete text of Matthew 25:1–13 in both Greek and German.

To Heidrich's evidence I would add one further point of similarity between the libretto and Petersen's 1701 treatise: the addition of a bride to the biblical story. As mentioned in note 19, some ancient manuscripts add "and the bride" to the bridegroom in verse 1 (although not to his appearances in subsequent verses). Martin Luther's translation does not include this phrase in verse 1, but Petersen's foreword has it in both the Greek and German versions, and he devotes a portion of chapter 2 to a discussion of its omission by the early church fathers.[26] A bride appears with the bridegroom in the engraved illustrations preceding both the foreword and chapter 2; in both cases they are seen in clouds above the earth (Figure 2). Petersen also includes the bride in his title for the 1701 treatise. The betrothal scene at the beginning of Buxtehude's libretto definitely includes a bride, although she does not reappear as the plot moves on to the narrative of the wise and foolish maidens, just as she disappears from the illustrations in Petersen's treatise after chapter 2.

Petersen declares his millenarianism in the full title of his treatise:

The Wedding of the Lamb and the Bride at the Approaching Future of Jesus Christ, through a Cry in this Midnight to Holy Watchfulness, Movingly Presented, and Decorated with Many Engravings and Three Indexes.

One can see a hint of it in the much earlier libretto's full title:

The Wedding of the Lamb and the Joyful Reception of the Bride to It in the Five Wise [Virgins] and the Exclusion of the Ungodly from It in the Five Foolish Virgins, as It is Told by the Bridegroom of the Soul, Christ Himself, in Matthew 25, and in Other Passages of Scripture, [to provide] Inner Consolation of the Soul and Sweetest Joy to the Pious and Those who Heartily Long for the Future of their Bridegroom of the Soul, but Fright to the Ungodly.

But whereas the millennium (*Zukunfft Jesu Christi*) is fast approaching in the treatise title, the pious are still longing for it in the libretto.

---

25. Listed in Heidrich, 91–92; the engravings illustrating chapters 3, 5, and 6 appear in facsimile in his appendix, pp. 95–97. The chapters do not correspond exactly to verses of the parable; verse 1, for example, is divided between chapters 1 and 2.

26. Petersen, *Hochzeit*, 50–57.

Sie nahmen ihre Lampen und giengen
dem Bräutigam entgegen

Figure 2. Illustration for chapter 2 of J. W. Petersen, *Die Hochzeit des Lammes und der Braut,* opposite page 40. The five wise maidens are on the left, with garlands on their heads. (Beinecke Rare Book and Manuscript Library, Yale University)

Bach's *Christmas Oratorio* and Buxtehude's Abendmusiken

In choosing a biblical story and dividing it into a specified number of parts to be performed on different days, the librettist of Bach's *Christmas Oratorio*—also anonymous[27]—appears to have followed the pattern of the Lübeck Abendmusiken as Ruetz described it in 1752. The story is lengthy—the account of the birth of Jesus and the visit by the wise men, as narrated in Luke 2:1–21 and Matthew 2:1–12—and so familiar that a summary will suffice (see Table 2). These selections follow generally, but by no means exactly, the Leipzig lectionary readings for these days.[28] By contrast, the biblical text that forms the basis of Buxtehude's *Die Hochzeit des Lamms* is specified for the 27th Sunday after Trinity in the Lübeck lectionary, not the second and third Sundays in Advent, when this Abendmusik was performed.

An even greater difference between Bach's *Christmas Oratorio* and Buxtehude's *Hochzeit* comes to light when one considers how these biblical texts function within their respective libretti. As noted above, only the direct quotations from the chosen text appear in *Die Hochzeit*, whereas in the *Christmas Oratorio* the entire text is present, most of it narrated in simple recitative by the tenor Evangelist. The direct quotations are handled in three different ways. In only three instances, named characters sing them: in Part II an angel (soprano, no. 13): "Fear not! Look, I announce to you great joy, which will come to all people; for to you this day is born in the city of David the Savior, who is Christ, the Lord," and a choir of angels (chorus, no. 21): "May honor be to God on high, and peace on earth, and to humankind [God's] great pleasure"; and in Part VI Herod (bass, no. 55): "Set out and search diligently for the little child,

27. According to Walter Blankenburg and Alfred Dürr, Christian Friedrich Henrici (Picander) is generally considered the author, although it appears in none of his printed works (Johann Sebastian Bach, *Neue Ausgabe sämtlicher Werke, Serie II, Band 6: Weihnachts-Oratorium, Kritischer Bericht* [Kassel: Bärenreiter, 1962], 190). But in 2006, Hans-Joachim Schultze describes the librettist as "leider unbekannt" (*Die Bach-Kantaten: Einführungen zu sämtlichen Kantaten Johann Sebastian Bachs* [Leipzig: Evangelische Verlagsanstalt, 2006], 634).

28. The Leipzig lectionary readings were Luke 2:1–14 for Christmas 1; Luke 2:15–20 for Christmas 2 (or an alternate for St. Stephen's Day); John 1:1–14 for Christmas 3 (or an alternate for St. John's Day); Luke 2:21 for New Year's Day; Matthew 2:13–23 for the Sunday after New Year; and Matthew 2:1–12 for Epiphany. See Alfred Dürr, *Die Kantaten von Johann Sebastian Bach* (Kassel: Bärenreiter/Deutscher Taschenbuch Verlag, 1975), for each day. The Lübeck lectionary from 1703 divides Luke 2:1–20 among the three days of Christmas just as Bach's *Christmas Oratorio* does. See "Anweisung Wie die Gesänge Sonntäglich nach den Evangelischen und Epistalischen Texten können gebraucht werden," in *Lübeckisches Gesang-Buch . . . Auff Verordnung Eines Hoch-Edlen Hochweisen Raths Von Einem Ehrwürdigen MINISTERIO Ausgegeben* (Lübeck: Christian Ernest Wiedemeyer, 1729), fols. (b)3–4.

Table 2. The six days of Bach's *Christmas Oratorio* BWV 248
and their gospel readings

Date	Gospel	Events
Christmas 1 Dec. 25, 1734	Luke 2:1, 3–7	Mary and Joseph travel to Bethlehem, and Mary gives birth to a son
Christmas 2 Dec. 26, 1734	Luke 2:8–14	The angels appear to the shepherds and tell them of the child; the heavenly host proclaim "Glory to God"
Christmas 3 Dec. 27, 1734	Luke 2:15–20	The shepherds go to the child and tell Mary and Joseph what the angels had said; Mary ponders their words
New Year Jan. 1, 1735	Luke 2:21	After eight days, the circumcision and naming of Jesus
Sunday after NY Jan. 2, 1735	Matt. 2:1–6	The wise men see the star and inquire of King Herod in Jerusalem about the child
Epiphany Jan. 6, 1735	Matt. 2:7–12	The wise men follow the star to Bethlehem, pay the child homage, and return without informing Herod

and when you find it, report this to me, so that I, too, may come and worship it." The words spoken by groups of humans in the biblical text are for the most part assigned simply to the chorus, although the text itself identifies them: the shepherds in Part III (no. 26): "Let's go, now, into Bethlehem and see what the story is that's taking place there, which the Lord has made known to us;" and the wise men in part V (no. 45): "Where is the newborn King of the Jews? We have seen his star in the Orient and have come to worship him." But the chief priests and scripture experts whom Herod consulted do not give their answer as a chorus; the evangelist alone recites their quotation (no. 50): "at Bethlehem in the Jewish region; for so it stands written by the prophet . . ." In one other instance the Evangelist sings words that are ascribed in the text to a specific character: the continuation of the Angel's address to the shepherds in Part II (no. 16): "And take this for a sign: you will find the child wrapped in bands of cloth and lying in a manger."[29]

Unlike Buxtehude's *Hochzeit des Lamms*, Bach's *Christmas Oratorio* names no characters for any of the accompanied recitatives or arias set to newly composed poetry. Most of them are contemplative and appear to be the words of a believing soul commenting

29. All translations from the *Christmas Oratorio* are from Michael Marissen, *Bach's Oratorios: The Parallel German-English Texts with Annotations* (Oxford: Oxford University Press, 2008), 5–28.

upon the action and at times even addressing the characters, as the bass does in the recitative (no. 17) "So go forth, then, you shepherds" in Part II and the soprano to King Herod in Part VI (no. 56): "You deceitful one, just try to bring down the Lord." Two arias, both for alto, appear however to flow naturally from the lips of Mary. In Part III, following the Evangelist's recitation of Luke 2:19, "But Mary kept all these words and tossed them about within her heart," the alto sings, "Schließe, mein Herze, dies selige Wunder fest in deinem Glauben ein" (no. 31, My heart, include this blessed marvel steadfastly in your faith). The lullaby in Part II, "Schlafe, mein Liebster, genieße der Ruh" (no.19, Sleep, my Most Beloved, enjoy your rest), is even more convincing as a song for Mary, even though the bass recitative that precedes it tells the shepherds to sing the lullaby as a choir. The parodied aria that lies behind it, "Schlafe, mein Liebster, und pflege der Ruh," which the soprano "Wollust" (sensual pleasure) sings to Hercules in *Herkules auf dem Scheidewege* BWV 213 is also a lullaby. The fact that the *Christmas Oratorio* lullaby occurs in Part II, after the angel has told the shepherds that they will find the child in a manger, rather than in Part III, when they actually arrive at the stable, does not present a serious problem; a baroque illustration might have put the manger scene in a cloud, just as Petersen's illustrator did with the bride and groom, who had not yet arrived.

Using the alto arias "Schließe, mein Herze" and "Schlafe, mein Liebster" as his point of departure, Walter Blankenburg concluded that the alto voice represents Mary throughout the *Christmas Oratorio*.[30] Renate Steiger followed with the identification of the bass/soprano duets as representing dialogues between the faithful soul and faith.[31] More recently, Ernst Koch has proposed that the alto part further represents "the voice of the Holy Spirit speaking in the faithful heart."[32] These varied attempts to identify voices in the *Christmas Oratorio* all underline the fact that Bach and his librettist refused to do so. Clearly, their model was not the same as that of the poets of the Lübeck Abendmusiken, who sought to construct the biblical story according to the rules of theatrical poetics.

All these differences between Buxtehude's *Hochzeit des Lamms* and Bach's *Christmas Oratorio*—the latter's use of an Evangelist to recite the complete biblical story, including some of the direct quotations, its correspondence to the lectionary, and its lack of

---

30. Walter Blankenburg, "Die Bedeutung der solistischen Alt-Partien im Weihnachts-Oratorium, BWV 248," in *Studies in Renaissance and Baroque Music in Honor of Arthur Mendel*, ed. Robert L. Marshall (Kassel: Bärenreiter, 1974), 139–48.

31. Renate Steiger, "Die Einheit des Weihnachtsoratoriums von J. S. Bach," *Musik und Kirche* 51 (1981): 273–80; 52 (1982): 9–15.

32. Ernst Koch, "Die Stimme des Heiligen Geistes: Theologische Hintergründe der solistischen Altpartien in der Kirchenmusik Johann Sebastian Bachs," *Bach-Jahrbuch* 81 (1995): 76.

specific characters—can be ascribed to the greatest disparity between the two oratorios: each of the six parts of the *Christmas Oratorio* took the place of the cantata within the liturgy at St. Thomas's or St. Nicholas's church, whereas the Lübeck Abendmusiken occurred outside the liturgy, as concerts following the afternoon vesper services at St. Mary's. And in avoiding the assignment of specific characters to the singers of the nonbiblical portions of the *Christmas Oratorio*, Bach may have been remembering that he had signed a pledge to the Leipzig town council on May 5, 1723, that included the requirement that his music should be "of such a nature as not to make an operatic impression."[33] Nevertheless, powerful dramatic forces lie beneath the non-operatic impression that Bach may have been seeking to convey, and these can be illuminated by a further comparison between the *Christmas Oratorio* and Buxtehude's Lübeck Abendmusiken. Their points of similarity go beyond their serial nature to include their mutual use of the love duet, of chorale dialogues, and of trumpets and timpani associated with nobility.

In the libretto for *Die Hochzeit des Lamms*, in the opening betrothal scene, Christ and the church (bass and alto) sing:

Ich bin dein und du bist mein	I am thine and thou art mine,
Du bist mein und ich bin dein,	thou art mine and I am thine,
Ewig sol die Liebe seyn.	our love shall be eternal.

This elemental expression of love goes back to the Minnesänger:

Du bist mein, ich bin dein:	Thou art mine, I am thine:
Des sollst du gewiss sein.[34]	of that you should be certain.

and long before that to the Song of Solomon:

Mein Freund ist mein, und ich bin sein.	My friend is mine, and I am his.
	(Song of Solomon 2:16)

We can get a suggestion of how Buxtehude might have set this love poetry from the soprano-bass duet in one of his compositions based on the Song of Solomon, *Dialogus inter Christum et fidelem animam* (Dialogue between Christ and the faithful soul BUXWV 111). The text of this work consists of six strophes of poetry that loosely paraphrase

---

33. *The New Bach Reader: A Life of Johann Sebastian Bach in Letters and Documents*, ed. Hans T. David and Arthur Mendel, revised and enlarged by Christoph Wolff (New York: Norton, 1998), 105.

34. Modern German version in Calvin Thomas, ed., *An Anthology of German Literature* (Boston: D. C. Heath, 1909), 84.

the narrative in the Song of Solomon of the lover lost and then found, followed by a single strophe of a second poem celebrating the love between Jesus and the soul. The lovers find each other during strophes 3 and 4, which Buxtehude set as a lyrical interlude in triple time and E♭ tonality (Example 1), contrasting with the common time and B♭ or g-minor tonality of the surrounding strophes. One can imagine that the bride and groom in *Die Hochzeit des Lamms* might similarly have begun by singing separately and then coming together in parallel motion. One layer beneath this allegorical love duet for Jesus and the faithful soul, in which the contrast in register between bass and soprano reflects the polarity between male and female, could lie a love duet between actual lovers on the stage of the Hamburg Opera.

Bach traces the same trajectory of lovers apart and then together in the two duets for soprano and bass that separate the three strophes of the chorale in his cantata "Wachet auf, ruft uns die Stimme" BWV 140, first performed November 25, 1731, on the 27th Sunday after Trinity. Just as in Buxtehude's *Hochzeit des Lamms*, the unknown librettist of BWV 140 brings together the parable of the wise and foolish maidens, its chorale paraphrase, and imagery from the Song of Solomon and Revelation. The recitatives preceding the duets introduce the interlocutors as bridegroom and bride; the text of the first duet identifies them further as Jesus and the soul (*liebliche Seele*); and the text of the second quotes from the Song of Solomon:

Mein Freund ist mein und ich bin sein,	My friend is mine and I am his,
die Liebe soll nichts scheiden.	Nothing shall separate our love.
Ich will mit dir / Du sollst mit mir in	I will with you / you shall with me feed
Himmels Rosen weiden,	among heaven's roses,
Da Freude die Fülle, da Wonne	Where fullness of joy and delight
wird sein.	will be.

E. Ann Matter proposes that in keeping the third-person construction from the Song of Solomon (Ich bin sein—I am *his*) instead of turning it into a true dialogue (Ich bin dein—I am *thine*), the bridegroom is distancing himself somewhat. This gives the story an apocalyptic edge, suggesting that this bridegroom is the Christ of the Last Days, in keeping with the theme of the last Sunday in Trinity.[35] The lovers do address each other in the second person in the B section, but in the future tense. Buxtehude's lovers, by contrast, speak to each other directly in the second person

---

35. E. Ann Matter, "The Love between the Bride and the Bridegroom in Cantata 140 'Wachet auf!' from the Twelfth Century to Bach's Day," in *Die Quellen Johann Sebastian Bachs: Bachs Musik im Gottesdienst*, ed. Renate Steiger (Heidelberg: Manutius, 1998), 116.

Example 1. Buxtehude, *Dialogus inter Christum et fidelem animam*
BUXWV 111, mm. 84–95

and the present tense in both the "Ich bin dein" duet of *Die Hochzeit* and throughout the *Dialogus*.

Bach composed another love duet to a remarkably similar text in *Herkules auf dem Scheidewege* BWV 213 between Hercules (alto) and Virtue (tenor):

Ich bin deine, Du bist meine,	I am thine, thou art mine,
Küsse mich, ich küsse dich.	Kiss me, I kiss thee.
Wie Verlobte sich verbinden,	As betrothed couples unite,
Wie die Lust, die sie empfinden,	As the desire that they feel
Treu und zart und eiferig,	Is true and tender and passionate,
So bin ich.	So am I.

Here the lovers speak in the second person and in the present tense. Bach designated this work a "Drama per musica,"[36] and he performed it with his Collegium musicum at Zimmerman's coffeehouse on September 5, 1733, honoring the birthday of Crown Prince Friedrich Christian of the Dresden court. The following year he parodied

36. See the facsimile of the libretto in Werner Neumann, *Sämtliche von Johann Sebastian Bach vertonte Texte* (Leipzig: VEB Deutscher Verlag für Musik, 1974), 353.

it for the third part of the *Christmas Oratorio*, with a text emphasizing compassion, mercy, and love:

Herr, dein Mitleid, dein Erbarmen	Lord, your compassion, your mercy
Tröstet uns und macht uns frei.	Comforts us and makes us free.
Deine holde Gunst und Liebe,	Your pleasing favor and love,
Deine wundersamen Triebe	Your wondrous desires,
Machen deine Vatertreu	Make your Fatherly faithfulness
Wieder neu.	New again.

With his transposition of the original aria up a third from F major to A major, Bach changed the voice parts of this duet from alto and tenor to soprano and bass, as in the love duets of the cantata "Wachet Auf" and Buxtehude's *Dialogus*. The concomitant shift from the violas of *Herkules* to two oboes d'amore also calls to mind the oboe obbligato of the second duet in bwv 140, "Mein Freund ist mein." This transposition may have been necessary in order to attain tonal symmetry, as Blankenburg suggests,[37] but with it Bach also obtained the typical pairing of bass and soprano for Jesus and the faithful soul, his bride. The new text does not suggest this pairing in a love duet, but the layers beneath it, in *Herkules* and "Wachet Auf," do. The text for the *Herkules* duet, and Bach's music for it, is far more erotic than one would expect for a conversation between a mythical man and an allegorical character named "Virtue" in an unstaged coffeehouse production; lurking beneath it is a love duet for a human man and woman on the operatic stage. In its *Christmas Oratorio* version it moves even further away from opera, but its dramatic power is still present.

In the betrothal scene of Buxtehude's *Die Hochzeit des Lamms*, the sensuous "Ich bin dein/du bist mein" love duet between Christ and the Church is immediately followed by another duet, this time in dialogue and with the Church now represented by a soprano.

Die Kirche	Wie bin ich doch so hertzlich froh!	How heartily joyful I am
	Das mein Schatz ist das A und O,	That my treasure is the alpha
		and omega,
	Der Anfang und das Ende.	The beginning and the end.

---

37. Blankenburg, "Alt-Partien," 139, and Walter Blankenburg, *Das Weihnachts-Oratorium von Johann Sebastian Bach* (Kassel: Bärenreiter/Deutscher Taschenbuch Verlag, 1982), 82. See also Ulrich Siegele, "Das Parodieverfahren des Weihnachtsoratoriums von J. S. Bach als dispositionelles Problem," in *Studien zur Musikgeschichte: Eine Festschrift für Ludwig Finscher*, ed. Annegrit Laubenthal (Kassel: Bärenreiter, 1995), 263.

JESUS	In meines Vaters Hause sind viel Wohnungen, und ich wil wieder kommen, und euch zu mir nehmen, auff daß ihr seyd wo ich bin, Joh 14:2–3.	In my Father's house are many rooms; . . . and I will come again and will take you to myself, that where I am you may be also. (John 14:2–3)
Die Kirche	Er wird mich doch zu seinem Preiß, Auffheben in daß Paradeiß	As his reward, He will lift me up into Paradise,
	Des klopff ich in die Hände.	For which I clap my hands.
JESUS	Ich komme bald, Offenb. 22/20	I am coming soon. (Revelation 22:20)
Die Kirche	Amen, Amen Komm du schöne Freuden Krohne, Bleib nicht lange, Deiner wart ich mit Verlangen	Amen, Amen, Come, you lovely crown of joy, do not delay. I am waiting for you with longing.

The Church's lines come from the final verse of the chorale "Wie schön leuchtet der Morgenstern," while Jesus's scriptural words are identified in the libretto. As the voice part for the Church changes from alto to soprano, and the source of the text moves from the duet's free poetry to scripture, its theme changes, too, from erotic to eschatological, from present love to the second coming of Christ. The characters no longer address one another, but speak only in the first person. Presumably the soprano sang this poetry to the chorale melody, and the bass in the lyrical recitative style that Buxtehude typically used for words of scripture assigned to a bass soloist. His extant vocal works contain no similar interruption of a chorale verse, but the dialogue "Wo soll ich fliehen hin" BUXWV 112 opens with an alternation between the soprano singing two complete verses of that chorale and the bass responding to each with words of scripture:

S: Wo soll ich fliehen hin?	S: Whither shall I flee?
Weil ich beschweret bin	For I am laden down
Mit vielen großen Sünden:	With many grievous sins;
Wo sol ich Rettung finden?	Where shall I find rescue?
Wenn alle Welt herkähme,	If all the world came here
Mein Angst sie nicht wegnehme.	It could not take away my anguish.

B: Kombt her zu mir alle, die ihr
mühselich und beladen seid,
ich will euch erquicken.
Nehmet auf euch mein Joch,
und lernet von mir; den ich bin
sanftmühtig und von Herzen
demühtig.

B. Come to me, all who are
weary and heavy laden,
and I will give you rest.
Take my yoke upon you,
and learn from me; for I
am gentle and lowly in
heart.
(Matthew 11:28–29)

The words of the bass are spoken by Jesus in the biblical text; the soprano implicitly represents the faithful soul.

Bach's *Christmas Oratorio* contains three chorale/recitative dialogues (nos. 7, 38, and 40), each also scored with the soprano singing the chorale and the bass responding, but with poetry rather than the scriptural quotations that appear in Buxtehude's chorale dialogues. In the first of these (no. 7), the soprano sings a verse added by Luther to an even older Christmas hymn, "Gelobet seist du, Jesu Christ":

Er ist auf Erden kommen arm,
Daß er unser sich erbarm,
Und in dem Himmel mache reich,
Und seinen lieben Engeln gleich.

Kyrieleis.

He has come on earth poor,
That he might have mercy on us,
And might make [us] rich, in heaven,
And [might make us] equal to his
dear angels.

Lord have mercy.

The soprano takes the lead, singing the chorale melody nearly unadorned, and the bass then comments upon it line by line:

Wer will die Liebe recht erhöhn,
Die unser Heiland vor uns hegt?

Who will properly extol the love
That our Savior feels for us?

His answering recitative contrasts strongly with the arioso of the chorale and its accompanying oboes d'amore. In this dialogue the voices have exchanged roles; the bass unexpectedly represents not Jesus but rather the faithful soul, the individual responding to the collective faith stated by the soprano with a chorale from the Reformation era.

The soprano reassumes the role of the faithful soul in the other two soprano/bass duets (nos. 38 and 40) and addresses Jesus as her bridegroom in the words of a hymn by Johann Rist, first published in 1642 in part 5 of his *Himlische Lieder*:

38

Jesu, du mein liebstes Leben,	Jesus, you, my most beloved life,
Meiner Seelen Bräutigam,	My soul's bridegroom,
Der du dich vor mich gegeben	You who has given himself for me
An des bittern Kreuzes Stamm!	On the beam of the bitter cross!

40

Jesu, meine Freud und Wonne,	Jesus, my joy and gladness,
Meine Hoffnung, Schatz und Teil,	My hope, treasure, and portion,
Mein Erlösung, Schmuck und Heil,	My redemption, adornment, and salvation,
Hirt und König, Licht und Sonne,	Shepherd and king, light and sun,
Ach! Wie soll ich würdiglich,	Oh! How shall I worthily
Mein Herr Jesu, preisen dich?[38]	Praise you, my Lord Jesus?

These ten lines that Bach or his librettist divided between two chorale-recitative dialogues form the first strophe of Rist's thirteen-verse hymn. The two parts have different rhyme schemes: abab / cddcee, and Johann Schop's setting in the *Himlische Lieder* articulates this division with binary form. Schop's melody appears in numerous hymnals, including Gottfried Vopelius's *Das Neu Leipziger Gesangbuch* of 1682,[39] but Bach did not use it here. Instead he wrote a new melody, completely through-composed, and more in the style of a spiritual song than a church chorale, with many syllables set to two notes of music. The two dialogues form a frame—textually, tonally, and stylistically—around the soprano's echo aria "Flößt, mein Heiland" (no. 39).

The bass assumes a complex role in these latter two dialogues. This time he begins the conversation with his recitative, and at first it appears that he still represents the faithful soul:

Immanuel, o süßes Wort!	"Emanuel," O sweet word!
Mein Jesus heißt mein Hort,	My Jesus is called "my refuge,"
Mein Jesus heißt mein Leben.	My Jesus is called "my life."
Mein Jesus hat sich mir ergeben;	My Jesus has submitted himself to me;

38. Johann Rist, *Himlische Lieder, Mit sehr anmuthigen, von dem weitberühmten, Herrn Johann: Schopen gesetzten Melodeyen, Das Fünffte und letzte Zehn* (Lüneburg: Johann und Heinrich Sternen, 1642), 19–20. Facsimile of all five parts ed. Siegfried Kross (Hildesheim: Georg Olms, 1976). The text given here is that of the *Christmas Oratorio*, which contains slight variants from the original.

39. See Johannes Zahn, *Die Melodien der deutschen evangelischen Kirchenlieder*, 6 vols. (Gütersloh: C. Bertelsmann, 1888–93; reprint, Hildesheim: Georg Olms, 1963), no. 7891.

But when the soprano enters with the chorale, the bass does not stop to listen; instead, he joins in arioso style and metamorphoses into the bridegroom that the soprano, as bride, is invoking:

Komm! Ich will dich mit Lust umfassen,	Come! With delight I will embrace you,
Mein Herze soll dich nimmer lassen.	My heart shall never leave you.

With this, two formerly separate genres have merged; the chorale-recitative dialogue has briefly become a love duet (Example 2).

Finally, Buxtehude and Bach each made dramatic use of trumpets to represent the nobility. Buxtehude dedicated his two "extraordinary" Abendmusiken of 1705 to the very highest nobility—the Holy Roman Emperor—and scored for trumpets in both of them. In *Castrum doloris*, dedicated to the memory of Emperor Leopold I, who had died May 5, 1705, he used muted trumpets; in *Templum honoris*, honoring his successor, Emperor Joseph I, he specified two choirs of trumpets and timpani. In 1673 Buxtehude had purchased two of the six trumpets that St. Mary's Church owned and described them as "for the embellishment of the Abendmusik, made in a special way, the likes of which have not been heard in the orchestra of any prince."[40]

Templum honoris begins with an "Intrada" for the double choir of trumpets and timpani. We can get an idea of how this opulent music might have sounded from a cantata that Buxtehude had composed for the wedding of Joachim von Dalen and Catharine Margarethe Brauer von Hachenburg in1681. Von Dalen was a lawyer, and his bride the daughter of a Bürgermeister. Both belonged to the nobility, which occupied a small but privileged position in Lübeck society. The social classes in seventeenth-century Lübeck were highly stratified, and sumptuary laws governed the conduct of weddings: how many guests one could invite, how many musicians could play, and what sort of food and drink one could serve. Von Dalen, as a member of the highest class, was permitted 120 guests (not including those from out of town); wine; a meal of four courses including pastry, fish, game, and roasted meat; and a large ensemble of musicians, including players of trumpets and drums.[41] Thus Buxtehude scored this wedding cantata for four singers (two sopranos, alto, and bass), two violins and violone, two trumpets with timpani, and continuo, and he began it by referring to the work's scoring: "Schlagt, Künstler! die Pauken" BUXWV 122. Its printed libretto

---

40. Snyder, *Buxtehude*, 58, 465.

41. *Ordnung Eines Erbahren Raths der Keiserlichen Freyen, und des heiligen Reichß Stadt LÜBECK Darnach sich hinführo dieser Stadt Bürger und Einwohner bey Verlöbnüssen, Hochzeiten, in Kleydungengen, Kindbetten, Gefatterschafften, Begräbnissen, und was denselben allen angengig sampt ihren Frawen, Kindern und Gesinde, verhalten sollen* (Lübeck, 1619).

Example 2. Bach, *Christmas Oratorio* BWV 248/38
"Recitativo con Chorale," mm. 10–13

specifies that it, too, begins with an Intrada for trumpets and timpani,[42] but that section may have been improvised, because the preserved parts do not contain a separate opening instrumental movement. The opening vocal movement does, however, begin with eleven measures of music for trumpets and timpani alone in the style of a fanfare (Example 3). Its text makes explicit the relationship between the instruments and the nobility of its dedicatees:

Schlagt, Künstler! Die Paucken und Saiten auffs best,	Strike the drums, you artists, and the strings at your best!
Stosst eilend zusammen in eure weitschallende Silber-Trompeten:	Rush to bring together your broadly ringing silver trumpets;
Vermischet das Trummeln auff Kupfernen Trummeln mit klaren Klareten	Blend the drumming of copper drums with the clear clarions,
Heut feyren zwey Edle ihr Ehliches Fest.	Today two nobles celebrate their wedding feast.

Bach drew similarly on the association of trumpets and timpani with the nobility in "Tönet ihr Pauken! Erschallet, Trompeten!" BWV 214, which he composed in 1733 for the birthday of the Electress Maria Josepha of Saxony, who was also queen of Poland and the daughter of Emperor Joseph I. Its opening movement names the musical instruments and directly addresses the queen:

Tönet ihr Pauken! Erschallet, Trompeten!	Sound, you drums! Ring out, you trumpets!
Klingende Saiten, erfüllet die Luft!	Resonant strings, fill the air!
Singet itzt Lieder, ihr muntren Poeten,	Sing songs now, you lively poets!
"Königin lebe!" Wird fröhlich geruft.	"Long live the Queen" is joyfully cried.

This chorus became the opening movement of the *Christmas Oratorio*, which celebrates the birth of a king. "Großer Herr, o starker König," the only aria with trumpet obbligato in the *Christmas Oratorio* (no. 8), also emanates from "Tönet ihr Pauken." Klaus Hofmann has noted that the fanfare theme that first appears against the bass voice in m. 15 of both this aria and its parodied original, "Kron und Preiß gekrönter Damen, Königin!" might have been used in ceremonies at the Dresden court.[43] Bach designated

---

42. Facsimile in *The Düben Collection Database Catalogue*, http://www.musik.uu.se/duben/display Facsimile.php?Select_Path=vmhso50,015_p12_01v.jpg (accessed October 15, 2009).

43. Klaus Hofmann, "'Großer Herr, o starker König': Ein Fanfarenthema bei Johann Sebastian Bach," *Bach-Jahrbuch* 81 (1995): 31–46.

Example 3. Buxtehude, *Schlagt, Künstler! die Pauken* BUXWV 122, mm. 1–11

"Tönet ihr Pauken" a "Drama per musica,"[44] with the four singers assigned the roles of the antique goddesses Irene, Bellona, and Pallas and the allegorical character Fame.

Court ceremonies are inherently dramatic, and trumpets play no small role in the drama. But in free imperial cities such as Lübeck and Mühlhausen there was no court; the city council answered directly to the Holy Roman Emperor. In addressing his "extraordinary" Abendmusiken of 1705 directly to the emperors, dead and alive, Buxtehude was celebrating this fact. Bach was in Lübeck for those performances, most likely playing a violin or continuo instrument, and it is unlikely that he had ever witnessed ceremonial music as elaborate as this. He soon had the opportunity to emulate it, when it fell to him to compose the music for the inauguration of the city council of Mühlhausen in 1708. Richly scored for four choirs of instruments, including trumpets and timpani, with both solo and capella voices, "Gott ist mein König" BWV 71 demonstrates the young composer's grasp of the ceremonial genre.

By 1734, Buxtehude's vocal music had become much too old-fashioned to serve as a direct model for new composition. It is quite possible, however, that his radical but long-lived concept of the dramatic Abendmusik series, in which a story is stretched out over five performances in as many weeks, inspired the structure of Bach's *Christmas Oratorio*, with its six performances produced in a more reasonable time span of under two weeks. But that raises the question of why it took him twenty-nine years to

44. See facsimile in Neumann, *Sämtliche vertonte Texte*, 406–7.

implement this concept. Perhaps the answer lies in events of Bach's life during the late 1720s and early 1730s: his interest in the Dresden court and the opera there, including his attendance at the 1731 premiere of Hasse's *Cleofide;* his application in 1733 for the position of *Hofkapellmeister;* and his assumption of the leadership of the Leipzig Collegium musicum, which gave him the means to produce *drammi per musica* honoring members of the electoral court. These works in turn provided the building blocks for a larger, multipartite dramatic structure, the *Christmas Oratorio.* Both the Lübeck Abendmusiken and the Dresden opera may have inspired Bach's *Christmas Oratorio,* just as the Hamburg Opera had spawned Buxtehude's dramatic Abendmusiken. Although Bach's *Christmas Oratorio* lacks the named characters that populate Buxtehude's Abendmusiken, and its venue lay in the liturgy of the church rather than in public concerts, it nonetheless displays drama in music of the very highest art.

The Triumph of "Instrumental Melody"

Aspects of Musical Poetics in Bach's St. John Passion

Laurence Dreyfus

How does J. S. Bach set poetry to music? It is not a question one asks very often. Yet if we want to understand Bach's aims in his vocal music, we need to pay attention to his attitudes toward poetic verse, querying the compositional actions he takes with respect to it. It is fair to say—despite the proliferating interpretations treating Bach's passions and cantatas—that this methodological concern has been given relatively short shrift in the literature. It is often tacitly assumed, for example, that one can ignore the specific poetic articulation of madrigalian verse, yet at the same time have direct access to its meaning. Instead of engaging with the poetry, we are often content to devise a condensed digest of its import, and then—moving on to what really interests us—observe how the musical conduit of Bach's craft, genius, and religiosity conveys this sense into a legible amalgam of words and sounds.

Things are never that simple, however, and I suggest that Bach was in fact an unusually wayward setter of texts, a composer whose musical praxis both obscures and undermines a straightforward translation of literary ideas. For if one exhibits even the slightest sympathy for the poetry that precedes the compositional invention, it is easy to show that Bach defies virtually every rule of musical propriety advocated by his contemporaries, whether literati or musicians. We need, therefore, to confront his obstructive attitude toward language and diction, and ask what it signifies in the early eighteenth century. Far from wishing to deprive anyone of aesthetic pleasure or theological edification found in Bach's vocal music, I try to peel off a veneer of misplaced respect attached to Bach's compositions so as to grasp what is so extraordinary about music that has outlived its original function. Some arias from the *St. John Passion* suggest how Bach not only fails to reflect his texts in a conventionally appropriate manner, but has an unusual way of overshadowing—even eclipsing—the representation of their assembled and explicit meanings. In the interplay between musical processes and the poetic verse, one can see how Bach's music invariably "says" something different from the accompanying words. To the extent that Bach has crafted a distinctly new experience, therefore, it is worth assessing the curious features of his musical poetics.

Before turning to Bach's peculiarity, it is useful to describe a conventional and respectful attitude toward poetry. To this end, I turn briefly to an aria from Handel's *Giulio Cesare in Egitto* (1724), where the linking of text and music differs so strikingly from Bach's. The text for the first part of an aria sung by Sesto (act 1, scene 4) reads as follows:

Svegliatevi nel core	Awaken in my heart
Furie d'un alma offesa,	Ye furies of an offended soul,
A far d'un traditor	To take upon a traitor
Aspra vendetta!	Bitter vengeance!

When Sesto enters, he closely shadows the first four bars of the opening ritornello represented in Example 1. The music skillfully mimics key aspects of the poetic structure, rushing headlong from the first line into a syncopated emphasis on the "furie"—the furies or the wrath—of the second line. The music even helps the emphatic rendition of the fourth line, setting it off by inserting a short breath after "traditor." The elaboration in sixteenth notes in the remaining bits of the ritornello—one finds out later—serves, not surprisingly, to depict the "furore"—a furious backdrop against which the stage character declaims his incensed imperative to cease lamentations and turn to avenging his father. Even the continuo line subsequently sets the word "svegliatevi" in a clear echo of the singer. There can be no doubt that the music not only elaborates, but also adheres to the text. The notes become a transparent cipher for the words: we hear the music but think the meaning of the poetry. So when literal repetitions or reformulated passages occur later in the aria, Handel refers us back to the aria text as a primary source of meaning.

This effective representation and enhancement of the text is exactly what enlightened critics of the time demanded and precisely what Handel supplies. If one follows Johann Mattheson's rules of clarity in composing arias found in *Der vollkommene Capellmeister* (1739), for example, one can see how, barring a liberty taken here and there, Handel fulfils every critical desideratum. The first rule is that one must strictly observe the caesuras and punctuation in the poetry. "It is mind-boggling [*fast nicht glaublich*]"— Mattheson continues—"how even the greatest masters defy this rule, expending all their efforts in rousing the ears [*die Ohren aum Aufstande zu bringen*] with booming and noisy figurations which in no way satisfy the senses, much less move the heart."[1] Next, Handel complies with Mattheson's strict rule to observe the accent and empha-

---

1. Johann Mattheson, *Der vollkommene Capellmeister* (Hamburg, 1739; facsim. Kassel, 1980), 141, 145. Translations are my own unless otherwise indicated.

Example 1. G. F. Handel, "Svegliatevi nel cuore" from *Giulio Cesare*, idealized ritornello and opening vocal line compared

sis of the words. "The actual emphasis," he writes, "always calls for a precise type of musical accent: the chief thing is to know which words take musical accents."[2] One never really attains clarity, moreover, unless each melody contains (no more than) one emotion (*Gemütsbewegung*).[3] Mixing and matching affects in one and the same melody, he implies, is bound to be confusing. As one might expect of Mattheson, he provides a host of practical examples and elaborations to illustrate these prescriptions.

Mattheson's final rule of clarity insists that the composer base settings of poetry on the "sense and meaning" (*Sinn und Verstand*) of the words rather than on any one of them individually: the aim is "communicative sounds" (*redende Klänge*) rather than "colorful notes."[4] He amplifies this rule later on with a crucial distinction between aria melodies for singing and those for playing (*Vom Unterschiede zwischen den Sing- und Spiel-Melodien*), to which he devotes an entire chapter. Vocal melody is indisputably the mother, while instrumental melody is her daughter. Vocal melody not only "claims rank and privilege, but also instructs the daughter how best to fulfil her mother's wishes so as to make everything lyrical and fluent whereby one can tell whose child she is." There is even some fear of illegitimacy: "We can easily tell which among the instrumental melodies are the real daughters and which are, as it were, produced out of wedlock."[5]

Mattheson's key point is that when instruments and voices collaborate, "the instruments must not predominate [*hervorragen*]." "Many a beautiful painting is obscured in this way when fitted with a gold carved frame which alone diverts the eye and detracts from the painting. Any connoisseur of painting will prefer to choose a dark over a bright frame. The same thing applies to instruments," which provide no more than a frame for the words set to music.[6] Relying on these prescriptions, one can see why Handel's text settings were commended by those even occasionally critical of him who praised his exceptional powers. Writing about expression in vocal works, one such critic, Charles Avison, confesses in 1752 that he has "chosen to give all [his] illustrations on this Matter from the works of Mr Handel, because no one has exercised this talent more universally, and because these instances must also be most universally understood."[7]

From several passages in Mattheson's *Capellmeister* one can infer that Bach was a special irritant, but even fourteen years earlier, Mattheson had subjected Bach to a

2. Ibid., 148.

3. Ibid., 145.

4. Ibid., 141.

5. Ibid., 204.

6. Ibid., 207.

7. Charles Avison, *Essay on Musical Expression* (1752; 2nd ed. London, 1753), 65.

scathing criticism of his text setting at an early stage in his career as a church composer. In a passage in the *Critica Musica* of 1725 Mattheson notes:

> In order that good old Zachau may have company and not be quite so alone, let us set beside him an otherwise excellent practicing musician of today, who for a long time does nothing but repeat: — "I, I, I, I had much grief, I had much grief, in my heart, in my heart. I had much grief, etc., in my heart, etc., etc., I had much grief, etc., in my heart, etc., I had much grief, etc., in my heart etc., etc., etc., etc. I had much grief, etc., in my heart, etc., etc.[8]

It is paradoxical that Mattheson singles out the first fugal chorus from Bach's "Ich hatte viel Bekümmernis" BWV 21, a cantata written for Weimar in 1714, because here Bach has taken the syllabic declamation of the text more literally than is often his practice. The problem is not only the initial repetitions that Mattheson finds irksome, but also that the fugal subject fails to set the phrase "in meinem Herzen" with a convincing or audible declamation.

The arias from the *St. John Passion* were composed in the same year as Handel's *Giulio Cesare* and were performed only months before Mattheson penned his poisonous jibe about Cantata 21. But in them Bach is working to a completely different plan. No. 13 "Ach, mein Sinn" is the shortest aria in the *St. John Passion* but is long on musical substance by any reckoning. Peter has just repeated his denial of Jesus in recent recitatives, and the aria text (an adaptation of the first verse of a poem by Christian Weise) comments on the biblical verses in which Peter is said to have "gone out and wept bitterly" (*ging hinaus und weinte bitterlich*).

		End rhyme	Stresses
1	**Ach, mein Sinn, wo willt du endlich hin?** [V_1]	[a]	5
2	**Wo soll ich mich erquicken?** [V_2]	[b]	3
3	Bleib ich hier? oder wünsch ich mir	[c]	4
4	Berg und Hügel auf den Rücken?	[b]	4
5	Bei **der Welt ist gar kein Rat** [*part of* V_1]	[d]	4
6	Und im Herzen stehn die Schmerzen	[e]	4
7	Meiner Missetat,	[d]	3
8	Weil der Knecht den Herrn ver**leugnet hat**. [E_1–*end*]	[d]	5

boldfaced text = words set to ritornello subject

8. Hans T. David and Arthur Mendel, rev. and enlarged Christoph Wolff, *The New Bach Reader: A Life of Johann Sebastian Bach in Letters and Documents* (New York: Norton, 1998), 325, document 319.

(Oh my soul, where do you wish to go, where should I find relief? / Should I stay here or do I wish mountains and hills [to fall] upon my back? / There's no answer in the world and the pains of my misdeed remain in my heart, because the servant has denied his Lord.)

The poem consists of one strophe of eight lines, with end rhymes abcb dedd that break the octave into two quatrains and with additional internal rhymes in lines 1, 3, and 6 (*Sinn/hin; hier/mir; Herzen/Schmerzen*). The first quatrain is held together by its repeating scheme of pentameter followed by a trimeter and by its grammatical questions. The second quatrain breaks new ground by answering the questions posed in the first four lines but without abandoning a desperate tone of hopelessness. Its stresses form a kind of mirror image to the first quatrain, so that the final two lines replicate in reverse order the stresses of the two first lines of the poem, binding the two quatrains in a subtly balanced unit. The insistent end rhymes on *Rat, Missetat*, and *verleugnet hat* in lines 5, 7, and 8 are punctuated by the internal rhymes *Herzen* and *Schmerzen*—heart and pains—which themselves mirror the internal rhyme in line 3 and drive the poem forward speedily toward its concluding explanation, stark in its literal recall of Peter's denial but terse in contrasting "servant" (*Knecht*) with "Lord" (*Herr*) in powerful monosyllables. Not *too* bad a poem, in fact, were it not for too many contrived end rhymes. The surprise is that that the poet and theorist Christian Weise (1642–1708)—on whose version the *St. John Passion* text is based—composed his original five-stanza poem around 1675 in an introduction to the art of poetry and rhetoric so as to show how a poet can add words to a preexisting instrumental work.[9] The musical piece for which it provided a singable text—an intrada by Sebastian Knüpfer—is lost, but the musical incipit of the treble line survives, as shown in Example 2. Although the notation without barlines and with ambiguous fermatas is a bit obscure—each fermata seems to be merely a *signum congruentiae* corresponding to the commas in the text—Weise shows clearly how his metrical accents in the first line match the rhythmic stresses in, as he puts it, Knüpfer's "nimble entry music [*bewegliche Intrade*]."[10]

9. In Christian Weise's version the poem was called Weeping Peter (*Der weinende Petrus*); the first strophe, which includes all the text Bach eventually used, is laid out in eight lines. "Ach, mein Sinn, wo denkstu weiter hin" is one line, for example. Strophes 2–5 were ignored by Bach's poetic collaborator, whose identity remains unknown. See Alfred Dürr, *Johann Sebastian Bach's* St. John Passion: *Genesis, Transmissions and Meaning*, trans. Alfred Clayton (Oxford: Oxford University Press, 2002), 43.

10. Christian Weise, *Der grünen Jugend Nothwendigen Gedancken* [Necessary Thoughts for an Inexperienced Youth] (Leipzig, 1675), 352. I'm grateful to Daniel Melamed for providing me with a facsimile of the original.

Ach mein Sinn, wo denks-tu wei-ter hin?

Example 2. Christian Weise, "Ach, mein Sinn," as
hypothetically underlaid to Knüpfer's Intrada

So how did Bach engage with this poetic structure? Not terribly well, as one quickly discovers. (A reduction of Bach's ritornello for "Ach, mein Sinn" is shown in Example 3.) The harmony, as one can see, features a prominent bass line that chromaticizes a falling tetrachord from the tonic F♯ down to C♯, and stays in the close proximity of the tonic and dominant for the next few bars, before initiating (on the second line of the sketch) the linear intervallic pattern 10–7–10, 10–7–10. This sequence works well with a progression of fifths in the bass before landing on the dominant. This dominant chord on C♯ is prolonged for a few bars, cadences in the minor tonic, and is extended via diminished harmonies long enough to raise the third in the final F♯ minor chord from A♮ to A♯.

It is clear that Bach designed only part of the ritornello melody to be sung: just the first two lines fit the music, and some words fit far better than others. So the first problem is that the instrumental melody overwhelms the vocal line. Far worse, the emphatic declamation of the line "Ach, mein Sinn," with its willful emphasis on the possessive pronoun "mein," breaks the fundamental rule about music observing poetic accents: Bach's first musico-poetic act is to slap the trochee (long-short-long) in the face, as well as to insert an unnecessary textual repetition. Rather than respect the prosody of "Ach, mein Sinn," he accentuates the word "my," reinforcing a conventional trope of passion sermons in which Peter's sin and remorse are applied to the modern Christian. He also seems to have alighted on the declamatory possibilities of "wo willt du endlich hin," which evoke the gently swinging rhythmic inequality of French dance types, especially those with three beats to the bar. The most suitable candidate, given Peter's departure (in lines 3 and 4) following his shameful denial of Christ, was the French chaconne, not only because of its metrical scheme and fast tempo, but also because—in the minor mode—it boasted a venerable link to the gravitas of falling lamento bass lines. The proliferation of accents on the second beat (in mm. 1, 3, 5, 6, 11, and 15) confirms, moreover, that the implied dance type is the tragic if spirited chaconne rather than the more grandiose and slower sarabande grave marked by a conventional second-beat stress only in the first measure and a *mouvement* that wafts over rather than drives the music's pulse. (The absence of a caesura or feminine ending in the fourth measure also points away from the sarabande.) The result was Bach's genial idea for a ritornello comprising two quick eight-measure

Example 3. J. S. Bach, *St. John Passion* BWV 245/13, ritornello and vocal line compared

periods of chaconne overlying an initial lamento bass with a tagged-on (if curtailed) *petite reprise* at the end.

None of the bright ideas and pointed associations found in the ritornello can mask the fact that the setting of the end of line 2 is less than poetically inspired: in a common failing of Bach's text settings, the composer assigns too many notes to the end of the poetic line. Whereas the music fits "wo willt du endlich hin" hand in glove, it is wide of the mark on "wo sóll ich mích erquícken," with the rhythmic punch on the word "erquicken" both garbled and drawled. Because the remainder of the ritornello is virtually devoid of text, Bach seems to have followed the impulse of his already devised instrumental melody rather than return to the poetry. For only at the very end does he invite the voice to join the instruments for the closing phrase, with its final rhyme and grammatical period, before concluding—again, instrumentally—with a valedictory afterword and dancelike *reprise.*[11]

To select some words as inspiration and blatantly ignore the rhythm of others suggests an odd approach to setting texts. What is more, few words of the poem are sung to the ritornello subject (these are in boldface above). Apart from the words in the musical sketch, only a bit of line 5, "Bei der Welt ist gar kein Rat," sounds to the strain of the theme. Yet even here, the words can hardly be said to fit the music: they have been pasted onto the melodic line as best Bach could, but not persuasively so. As a result, these lines project less conviction than those for which the composer thought out a compelling declamation in advance. (How different is the Handel aria, where the opening of the ritornello sets the entire text conforming to the rule of predominant vocal melody!) Everything else the tenor sings in the entire Bach aria is, in fact, in free counterpoint that makes a point of never repeating itself. As a result, one can guess which words were most important to Bach: they are the ones set to the ritornello. After all, there is good evidence that they served as the topic of invention for some aspects of the ritornello, since they have been assigned a clear declamation that others words lack.

The design of the aria as a whole also helps explain Bach's unusual attitude toward the poetry. Although his arias and choruses display several different constructive methods, the harmonic functions of this ritornello closely resemble those he had developed earlier in several fast movements of his instrumental concertos.[12] Just as there are the two opening sections that define the key—Vordersatz 1 and 2 [V_1 and V_2]—there is a middle, "wandering" Fortspinnung that withholds the key [F], as well as two Epilog segments that confirm and close in the tonic. The individual segments, no matter what one calls them, are not merely analytic constructs, but discrete objects of Bach's invention, for each one of them becomes detached and repeated during the course of the piece. The segmentation, moreover, occurs during the course of an alternation between ideas belonging to the ritornello and those called episodes, which, unlike ritornello segments, are not strung together as a syntactic unit. Indeed, one might

11. A related association between chaconne and lamento is found in the opening chorus of Bach's cantata "Jesu, der du meine Seele" BWV 78 (composed five months later in 1724) and is discussed in Dreyfus, "Bachian Invention and Its Mechanisms," in *The Cambridge Companion to Bach*, ed. John Butt (Cambridge: Cambridge University Press, 1997), 184–92. In "Ach, mein Sinn," the reprise, which I have labeled a second Epilog, is attached to the ritornello only in its last statement at the end of the aria.

12. The concerto processes developed from the works of Antonio Vivaldi are discussed in Dreyfus, *Bach and the Patterns of Invention* (Cambridge: Cambridge University Press, 1996), esp. 43–94. An analysis of an aria from the *St. John Passion* with another segmentable ritornello, "Eilt, ihr angefochtnen Seelen," can be found on pp. 94–101.

consider how, for Bach, the higher the style of an aria or chorus, the greater number and depth of paradigmatic inflections he crafts—the more, in other words, he pays attention to the working out of the music.

These paradigms are represented in Table 1, a "ritornellogram" that represents in shorthand one kind of constructive thinking that went into the composition of the movement. The main part of the table identifies each appearance of ritornello segments in order of their occurrence within the piece, R_1 through R_9. As the table shows, this is music saturated with ritornellos. For each ritornello occurrence, moreover, the table details the scale degree on which the ritornello recurs, the mode (minor or major), whether the voice is participating at the time, and the identity and order of segments. An inspection across and down reveals that not one ritornello is identical to another—even the first and last differ. We are dealing with a composer obsessed with permutations and reformulations of his musical material.

The musical permutations are far from a random act of juggling, however, because the function of each ritornello segment is laden with affective associations. The Vordersatz in "Ach, mein Sinn" is, for example, translated into major mode to mark a moment of hope at the beginning of the question "Bleib ich hier?" But if the Epilog had been translated into the major mode—a procedure Bach would have taken pains to include in a concerto—the operation would have sent an unmistakably pastoral message of galant tranquility and comforting closure. It is easy to devise a perfectly grammatical example of what I elsewhere have called a Bachian MODESWITCH by playing the Epilog segments in F♯ major,[13] but the translation is utterly inappropriate to this aria. Because this message would contradict the dramatic situation of the aria, an Epilog in major was unacceptable, so Bach omits it.

It is also Bach's habit to seek out connective links between segments, researching how he can forge new connections, as one can see in the last column that lists three unexpected linkages. Between R_2 and R_3 (at m. 26), the composer has noticed a clever if seamless connection between the end of the second Vordersatz segment in the tonic and the second Epilog in the dominant that produces a caesura prolonging C♯ major. Similar kinds of RESEARCH investigating possible joins between nonadjacent segments occur between R_3 and R_4 (at m. 32), a transition that moves from a varied Fortspinnung to the Vordersatz at the upper fifth (the dominant); and in a parallel move, this time from the major to the minor at m. 63 from a Fortspinnung in E major to an opening Vordersatz in B minor.

To appreciate this mind-boggling Bachian musicianship, one can dismantle the aria and listen for the paradigms rather than follow the nominal order of the piece, hearing it as a set of variations of its fundamental segments. Taking the two Vordersatz

13. See Dreyfus, *Bach and the Patterns of Invention*, esp. 18–19, 72–77.

Table 1. Ritornellogram of J. S. Bach, *St. John Passion* BWV 245/13

Rit	Mm.	Degree	Mode	Voice	V_1	V_2	F	E_1	E_2	Notes
R_1	1–16	I	minor		V_1	V_2	F	E_1		
R_2	17–24	I	minor	X	V_1	V_2				
	24–26	I	minor	X		V_2				
R_3	26–28	V	minor						E_2	RESEARCH [V_2(I)–E_2(V)]
R_4	28–32	I	minor	X			F^*			RESEARCH [F(I)–V/V)]
R_5	32–47	V	minor	X	V_1	V_2	F	E_1		NB m.42 diatonic substitution
R_6	47–50	V	minor	X	V_1^*					absent melodic subject, decorations from [F]
R_7	52–59	VII	MAJOR	X	V_1	V_2	F			RESEARCH [F(VII)–V_1(IV)]
	59–63	VII	MAJOR			V_2				
R_8	63–74	IV	minor	X	V_1	V_2	F			
R_9	74–89	I	minor	X	V_1^*	V_2	F	E_1		
	89–91	I	minor						E_2	

Segment	Mm.	Text
V_1	1–6	Ach, mein Sinn, wo willt du endlich hin
V_2	6–8	wo soll ich mich erquicken
F	8–12	
E_1	12–16	(ver)leugnet hat
E_2	89–91	

R	Ritornello
V	Vordersatz
F	Fortspinnung
E	Epilog
*	varied segment
X	voice present

[V$_1$–V$_2$] segments together, one hears the second segment vocalized on its in own in the tonic, as well as both segments played on the fourth and fifth scale degrees in the minor and on the seventh scale degree in the major; the vocal lines in each case never repeat themselves. Listening down the occurrences of the F segment, one hears it arrayed on four different scale degrees: the first, fifth, seventh, and fourth. Like the Vordersatz segments, the Fortspinnung can also be translated into the major, which Bach undertakes at m. 59. The first Epilog, as mentioned, is permissible only in the minor and occurs at the beginning of the aria, in the very middle, and at the end. The second Epilog, more interestingly, occurs first on the dominant at m. 26, where its function as a prolongation of a cadential gesture is not yet clearly defined with respect to the ritornello; E$_2$ is then attached in its correct syntactic relation to E$_1$ only in the final measures of the piece.

One would think that the ritornellos in "Ach, mein Sinn" constituted only the basic scaffolding of the aria. In fact, in charting the ritornello segments out of order, one has accounted—amazingly—for every measure of the piece. So dense and self-sustaining are Bach's ritornello procedures that he has composed virtually nothing episodic in the entire aria. What might be considered structurally equivalent to something free and episodic is, strikingly, the elaboration of the vocal line, which could not be further from a submission of instrumental to vocal melody in Mattheson's terms. If anything, this kind of saturated permutation of strictly identified materials signals a clear if anarchic revolt of the instrumental realm over and against the vocal.

This musical thicket of continuous variations therefore has implications for an understanding of Bach's poetics. For given the inordinate attention paid to musical reworkings in "Ach, mein Sinn," Bach has done serious violence to the text as a work of poetry. As a setting of a poem, the music shows so little respect for the structure as to make one wonder why a poem with a meter and rhyme scheme was necessary in the first place. Even the simplest poetic parallelisms are ignored, as in the rhymes of the first quatrain or the metrical scheme in lines 3 and 4. Nor does the punctuated question ending line 4, for example, even coincide with a local cadence, an obvious enough point that is stressed by Bach's cousin Johann Gottfried Walther in his article "Aria" in the *Musicalisches Lexicon* of 1732.[14] Even the second Epilog segment occurs as an arbitrary medial close just before Bach returns to repeat the opening text "Ach, mein Sinn" once again. As a champion of poetry, one has to be grateful for those moments when Bach makes a point of setting a word with a clear accentuation, as in the evocative declamation of "meine Missetat" near the end of the aria, or when the second quatrain repeats the first Vordersatz in B minor.

14. Johann Gottfried Walther, *Musicalisches Lexicon* (Leipzig, 1732; facsim. ed. Richard Schaal, Kassel, 1953), 46–47.

For these reasons, it makes more sense to claim that the poetic text largely accompanies the music, not the other way round. To extend Mattheson's imagery, one can even suggest that in eighteenth-century terms the composer has fathered a bastard child incapable of demonstrating its filial duty to the words and their sense. If, on the other hand, one hears the ritornello as key to Bach's rendition of thoughts underlying the text, then one can see how the ritornello acts as a microcosm for Bach's partial reading of the text, in which part substitutes for whole. The ritornello also filters this partial experience through the prism of its musical associations, together with all they can evoke, so that the act of confronting the singer in this aria (a personage universalized from the situation of Peter) is not remotely the same as reading his words. Even though the vocalist recites all the words of the text, he does not, if you will, communicate all of them. Most are drowned out by the music, by all the attention Bach has paid to the ritornello. Even words that emerge with some clarity from the vocal texture are outbursts contained within a ritornello that one has already come to know rather well. The words are not so much framed or embellished by music, but rather confirm and expand the affective sense already assigned to the emblem of the ritornello, which evoke a group of metaphors through which one Bach recasts his selective experience of the poem.[15]

We might also think about the ritornello's recastings in terms of an unusual and inappropriate mode of "work" that Bach is all too happy to display in his music. Having no doubt read Abraham Birnbaum's defense of Bach in the dispute with Johann Adolph Scheibe, Mattheson even makes a point of taking to task Bach's aesthetic of musical *Fleiß*—industriousness or diligence—as reported even in the form of a modest admission. As reported by Birnbaum, "that which I [Bach] have achieved by industry and practice, anyone else with tolerable natural gift and ability can also achieve."[16] Mattheson phrases Bach's words slightly differently, slightly garbling the original:

I have recently read an opinion of a master which reads as follows: "What I've been able to achieve myself through diligence and practice [*durch Fleiß und Übung*], someone else who possesses only half the natural talent must also be able to achieve." At that I thought, if this were true, then why is such a master the only one in the world without equal? Pieces difficult to play can be excused in another way, but because most men who want [to compose this way] in fact utterly lack the necessary natural talent, hard work is little use to them. This is indisputably true and borne out by adverse experience.[17]

---

15. The issue of nonlinguistic metaphors in music has become a fruitful topic in recent aesthetics. I have entered this debate in "Christopher Peacocke's 'The Perception of Music: Sources of Significance,'" *British Journal of Aesthetics* 49 (2009): 293–97.

16. Wolff, *New Bach Reader*, 346.

17. Mattheson, *Vollkommene Capellmeister*, 144–45.

So even if Bach as musical master is unique in his command of difficult works, hard work as a compositional value is actually overvalued because it more often than not leads to an excess of art, something artificial and wholly unnatural. As Mattheson (obviously struggling with this conundrum) continues in a footnote: "All excellent things possess a certain difficulty, but difficult things aren't all excellent."

With Bach's difficult and excellent aria "Ach, mein Sinn," we therefore come across something very different from a conventional musical setting of a poem. Rather, we encounter a metamorphosis of ideas, images, and affects into music that has, as it turned out, claimed rather an unexpected afterlife. Whereas Handel achieved an admirable musical transparency in his setting of the text, boasting, as it were, how clearly the text and its meaning had been enhanced and transmitted, Bach is busy focusing in his anti-literary way on a peculiarly personal and pointedly self-authorized rendering. Right from the start, this "performance" of the text targets an experience that asserts Bach's own favored reading of the text, a reading that subverts and transcends the point of departure. By crafting a remarkable ritornello configuring the experience of the first two lines of the poem, Bach has turned a quick chaconne and grave lament into a dance of desperation from which one cannot escape. As for the words, the gesture and sense surrounding the phrase "wo willt du endlich hin" become the aria's leading motive, if you will. No wonder, then, that professors of literature such as Gottsched took pains to develop critical theories that urged managerial restraint over the excesses of unruly composers, Bach chief among them.

Bach as an uncontrollable spirit isn't perhaps an especially pleasant characterization, and for theologically inclined writers in particular, Bach is never allowed to be unruly. Instead, he has to be seen to toe some line grounded in specifiable doctrine. But how does one specify the doctrine? The usual route is to examine a poetic text as a whole, condense its sense into a verbal gloss that the music can then represent and adorn. From the perspective of my analysis of "Ach, mein Sinn," this method seems peculiarly anathema to an adequate treatment of Bach's music and can lead to some exaggerated interpretations. In his monograph on the *St. John Passion*, Michael Marissen suggests that "Bach's music [for 'Ach, mein Sinn'] conveys the message that all is not lost. The noble dance rhythms," he asserts, "underlying the aria's tortured mood can be understood as God's Yes behind his No, Luther's way of expressing the paradoxical coexistence of God's condemning wrath and merciful grace."[18] Yet how does the music even begin to represent this kind of complex theological paradox? Despite its theological credentials, the reading proves unconvincing precisely because the supposed sign of God's grace—the noble dance Marissen mistakenly labels

18. Michael Marissen, *Lutheranism, Anti-Judaism, and Bach's* St. John Passion (Oxford: Oxford University Press, 1998), 17.

a sarabande—can be understood only conceptually via theological explanations that are seen to "amplify and deepen the verbal messages of the [passion] libretto."[19]

It is significant that Marissen, a sensitive critic willing to celebrate an active interpretative voice for the composer, falls into a similar trap when he claims that "the melodic shape of the soprano aria, 'Ich folge dir gleichfalls mit freudigen Schritten,' captures an irony extremely well. . . . The listener to the narrative, like Peter, cheerfully declare[s] to Jesus that I am his follower; but actually, just as Peter is about to do, I will continually deny my discipleship and *not* follow Jesus." Bach's joyous music, in other words, is not telling the truth and asserts the exact opposite of what it represents. This interpretation may be plausible theologically but is completely at odds with the affective character of the aria. Based likewise on a three-part ritornello, it is the charming opening line, "I follow you likewise with joyous steps," in which the Vordersatz played by the flute revels. (The Vordersatz also works as a lighthearted and not entirely serious canon at the unison.) The only break from following in the joyous steps of the Savior as Simon Peter and an anonymous disciple did, we are told in the previous recitative, is found in the setting of the words "und höre nicht auf" (and do not cease), which, like the running patterns of sixteenth notes in the Fortspinnung and Epilog, spin out a conceit of continuous melodic pleasure, so desirous is the happy soul to tag along in what has temporarily become a rather galant garden party festooned with the pastoral costume of characters dancing a passepied in B♭ major. We might just have to live with the anomalous, even tasteless placement of this aria: the Evangelist had recounted in the previous recitative how Simon Peter also "followed" Jesus, and the aria text puns inappropriately on a joyful and universal "following" of Jesus with joyful steps, oblivious to the serious and dramatic context of Peter's denial that has already been introduced. Already in the 1870s, Philipp Spitta was in no doubt that this aspect of the *St. John Passion* text "leaves much to be desired. . . . We cannot always consider the places where the free poetry is brought in," Spitta notes, "as well chosen. . . . Whereas the incident [of Peter's denial] leads to one of contemptible weakness and cowardly retraction, it needs no very subtle sense of fitness to perceive that a transient feeling is made prominent at the cost of the whole effect."[20]

19. Ibid., 8. Several other writers, including Doris Finke-Hecklinger, author of *Tanzcharactere in Johann Sebastian Bachs Vokalmusik* (2nd ed., Bloomington: Indiana University Press, 2001), cited by Marissen, oddly misidentify the dance type as a sarabande. The mistaken identity is repeated in Bernard Sherman, "Notation of Tempo and Early-Music Performance: Some Reconsiderations," *Early Music* 28 (2000): 458. Sherman worries (having subscribed to the sarabande reference) that contemporary performances of the piece are too fast and "lack historical justification." Marissen even goes so far as to maintain that the performance of the aria need not "be rendered in sarabande tempo." The problem disappears as soon as one appreciates the marked difference between the French sarabande and chaconne.

20. Philipp Spitta, *Johann Sebastian Bach: His Work and Influence on the Music of Germany, 1685–1750*, trans. Clara Bell (New York: London: Novello, 1889), 2:523–24.

For Marissen to propose an ironic reading for this aria not only proceeds from the questionable notion of Bach as a persuasive "musical preacher," but, more generally, from an inflated sense of confidence in the potential of poetic texts to articulate clear theological arguments to which Bach's music must subscribe. Quite the opposite turns out to be true: that Bach's music reveals with some precision exactly what he took the texts to mean, which is the same as saying that the actual value of words in the Bachian musical universe is best assessed by his actions in setting them. Especially in works in which Bach was handed a text that dictated the outline of his actions, it is important to realize that we are dealing with music far removed from a Wagnerian *Gesamtkunstwerk*. It also will not do to cite Bach's underlinings in the Calov Bible as keys to his musical interests in his sacred music, because Bach did not acquire the Calov Bible until 1733, when the passions and the bulk of the cantatas had already been written: this crucial point of historical fact is often forgotten in theological accounts of Bach's texted music.[21]

What is downplayed in these kinds of readings, it seems to me, is Bach's supplemental and often suprarepresentational approach to musical invention. Naturally there will be theological implications that one is welcome to read into Bach's compositional practice, but to be credible, they need proceed from the musical evidence rather than from some superimposed theological intentions of the text to which music has easy access.[22] Even as a devout believer—or better, because he was a devout believer—Bach can be shown to have ignored through his musical actions certain sanctioned doctrinal views so as to treat aspects of the experience he found especially compelling. Needless to say, if the music only parrots ideas from Luther, one might as well dispense with the music. Yet Luther provides little support for Bach's compositional practice. In his famous poem titled "Frau Musica," Luther personifies music and "singing" as a lady "who gives God more joy and mirth / than all the pleasures of the earth."[23] More valuable even than "the precious nightingale," God created Music to be his true songstress (*sein rechte sengerin*) and mistress (*meisterin*) who tirelessly offers thanks:

Denn singt und springt sie tag und nacht	For she sings and dances day and night
Seines lobs sie nichts müde macht.	Never tiring [of singing] His praise.

21. Marissen, *Lutheranism*, 19. For the date of Bach's acquisition of the Calov Bible, see Christoph Wolff, *Johann Sebastian Bach: The Learned Musician* (New York: Norton, 2000), 335.

22. Theological superimpositions on readings of Bach's vocal music are the subject of Rebecca Lloyd's "Bach among the Conservatives: The Quest for Theological Truth" (PhD diss., King's College London, 2006).

23. Robin A. Leaver, *Luther's Liturgical Music: Principles and Implications* (Grand Rapids, Mich.: William B. Eerdmans, 2007), 74–75.

A "fine art" rather than a discrete discourse or a vehicle for interpretation, "the notes," as Luther puts it in the *Tischreden*, "make the words live," which is rather different from claiming that music comments on the words.[24] This mistress who enlivens words to sing praises scarcely evokes a character authorized to wander into a theological seminar to lecture on hermeneutics. Ultimately, Lutheran principles of music may even be inhospitable to Bach's unusual approach to composing sacred works, for Luther was obviously in no position to anticipate the expressive possibilities of much later music.

Another telling example of Bach's selective poetics is the aria "Es ist vollbracht!" no. 30 ("It is accomplished") that occurs just before Jesus's final words sung at the end of the preceding recitative. Here the unknown poet sings of "consolation for grieving souls" and of "the funereal night" that "now counts [its] final hour." Apart from Christ's words "Es ist vollbracht!" that accompany the Epilog, none of the words in the main part of the aria are set to the ritornello.

	End rhyme
Es ist vollbracht!	[a]
O Trost vor die gekränkten Seelen!	[b]
Die Trauernacht	[a]
Läßt nun die letzte Stunde zählen.	[b]
Der Held aus Juda siegt mit Macht,	[a]
Und schließt den Kampf. $[F_3?]$	[c]
Es ist vollbracht! $[E_2]$	[a]

In fact, all these potent images play a marginal role in the emotional state depicted by the music. Only in the wildly contrasting middle section of the aria, marked *vivace*, in which the "hero of Judah ends his victorious fight," does the contrasting heroic music evoke a Handelian setting of the text with "Der Held aus Juda siegt mit Macht." If anything, this section shows that Bach knows how to write a pleasing and conventional vocal melody not eclipsed by the instruments, though he once again ignores the end rhymes. Yet it is also true that in the latest autograph part, the gamba obbligato doubles the vocalist at the lower octave, no doubt hindering the comprehension of the text.[25] Yet just in this exciting patch of passagework, Bach dispenses with an underlying

24. Ibid., ix.

25. This instrumental doubling of a vocal line at the lower octave is a rarity in Bach's works. One antecedent that Bach is unlikely to have known is found in Handel's early *La Resurrezione* (1708), in which the viola da gamba doubles a soprano voice (Maddalena) in the aria "Ferma l'ali, e sù miei lumi." There the doubling uncannily suits the pastoral tone and references to shepherd's pipes; Bach's odd shadowing of the heroic victor of Judah is inventive but not easy to decipher.

Example 4. J. S. Bach, *St. John Passion* BWV 245/30, ritornello and vocal line compared

ritornello or any structurally repeating material, apart from a subtle melodic reference to the ritornello in the linking line "und schließt den Kampf." One can see a sketch of the ritornello in the main part of the aria and its relation to the text in Example 4.

More interesting for the focus on Bachian poetics is, again, the concentrated density of the ritornello processes, which, as can be seen from Table 2, decompose this mournful dirge played by the viola da gamba into seven discrete bits deployed with remarkable variety on five separate scale degrees. As in "Ach, mein Sinn," there is scarcely more than a brief episodic moment: the saturation with the musical ideas of the ritornello is well nigh complete. The setting of the alto vocalist's words, by contrast, weaves a tissue of free counterpoint around the mesh of ritornello segments in the viol part, and only in the last notes of the aria does he sing the haunting opening words to the second Epilog, the same sighing phrase we had heard in the final moments of the preceding recitative.

Table 2. Ritornellogram of J. S. Bach, *St. John Passion* BWV 245/30

Rit	Mm.	Degree	Mode	Voice	V_a	V_b	F_1	F_2	F_3	E_1	E_2
R_0 No. 29, mm.13–14		V	minor	SOLO							E_2
R_1	1–5	I	minor		V_a	V_b	F_1	F_2	F_3	E_1	E_2
R_2	5–8	I	minor	X	V_a	V_b	F_1	F_2	F_3		
R_3	8–9	I	minor	X		V_b	F_1				
R_4	10–12	III	MAJOR		V_a	V_b	F_1	F_2			
R_5	12–13	IV	minor	x	V_a^*	V_b^*					
R_6	13–17	V	minor	X	V_a	V_b	F_1	F_2	F_3	E_1	E_2
R_7	18–19	VII	MAJOR				F_1	F_2			
R_8	40	I	minor	SOLO							E_2
R_9	40–44	I	minor	X	V_a	V_b	F_1	F_2	F_3	E_1	E_2

Recurrent solo episodes

	Mm.	Degree	Mode	Voice
S_1	5	I	minor	X
S_2	17–18	V	minor	instrumental

Segments	Mm.	Text
V_a	1	
V_b	1	
F_1	2	
F_2	2–3	
F_3	3–4	und schliesst den Kampf
E_1	4	
E_2	4–5	Es ist vollbracht!

The inventive possibilities Bach devises for this ritornello are especially rich: whereas the tonal process opens and closes in the same key of B minor, the second Fortspinnung [F2] (first heard in mm. 2–3) concludes with an unusual full cadence in IV before pressing on to the expected dominant chord to end the Fortspinnung and begin the Epilog. This medial cadential figure amid the flow of the ritornello allows Bach to conclude the MODESWITCH of R$_4$ in G major in m. 12, permitting a glimmer of autonomous instrumental hope unprompted by the text. Perhaps this is compensation for having ignored any sympathetic depiction of the word "Trost" in the previous measures: instead Bach despairs of any "comfort" by his ravaged declamations of that word setting. He also takes advantage of the cadence in F$_2$ to set R$_7$ on the seventh scale degree, thereby preparing a proper move to III for the victorious *vivace* section. The concentration of reused and reworked musical material in the *molt'adagio* is astounding when one considers its brevity and the number of tonal areas toward which it beckons.

But how is one to understand the expressive content of the ritornello? By convention, an instrumental ritornello was meant to accord with the poetic ideas in the text subsequently to be sung. As Johann Adolph Scheibe writes in the *Critischer Musikus:* "As for what concerns the ritornello in particular, one should note that the words and [musical] content of the aria should suit one another [*gemäß seyn soll*]." Naturally the instruments may play some independent role even in this model, and, as he puts it, may participate "in a kind of pleasant competition [with the vocal melody] which always gives church music a special beauty as long as one does not go too far and obscure the understanding of the words."[26] Yet a darkening (*Verdünkelung*) of the perception of the words is exactly what Bach has triggered. One may forgive Bach because of the slant he takes to the words in all their experiential *musical* complexity, but this post-Wagnerian, romanticized reception of Bach—in which one subordinates the goal of transparency of words in a poem to a poetic vagueness—cannot hide the consequence of these kinds of compositional actions in an alien eighteenth-century context hostile to the remotest whiff of obfuscation.

If Bach can hardly be said to set the words of the poetic text in his instrumental ritornello for "Es ist vollbracht," we have a right to ask what he *is* doing. Here, in an act of creative borrowing from instrumental genres, Bach seems to have appealed to a musical fantasia or tombeau that takes the gestural sighs of Christ's dying words, disregards the poetic reckoning of time (as in counting the last hour), ignores the funereal night (but for an exaggerated slow tempo), and instead performs a soliloquy on a musical hexachord—the descent of six notes—that repeatedly depicts Christ's poignant

---

26. J. A. Scheibe, *Critischer Musikus: Neue, vermehrte und verbesserte Auflage* (1745; facsim. ed. Hildesheim, 1970), 432–33.

sigh. One cannot know for sure, but Bach might have intended an oblique reference to Marin Marais's two eloquent tombeaux for Lully and Ste. Colombe printed in the second book of his *Pièces de violes* (1701). This "incomparable viola da gambist," J. G. Walther noted in 1732, had printed works that were "known all through Europe."[27] In both tombeaux (the openings are shown in Examples 5a and 5b), Marais spins out elegies in B minor and E minor that keep returning to altered restatements of exclamatory tragic figures with which the pieces each begin. The theme and treatment of the viola da gamba line in "Es ist vollbracht" are rather similar, especially if one imagines Bach's notation according to French conventions in augmented note values.

Whatever the intention of the viola da gamba part, the affective logic of Bach's ritornello is compelling: the high-level, aristocratic diction of the French ornaments expressing the *grands sentiments* of tragedy; the notated dotted figures evoking royal overtures and *entrées*; the two rhetorical questions punctuated by gasping breaths, the first hopeful (in pointing the major mode), the second pathetic in its leap of a seventh onto a painful appoggiatura; finally, the dotted descent through the octave portending the bitterness

Example 5a. Marin Marais, *Tombeau pour Monsr. Lully*, opening

Example 5b. Marin Marais, *Tombeau po[ur] Mr. de Ste. Colombe*, opening

27. Walther, *Musicalisches Lexicon*, 382.

of resignation. The *vivace* interjection challenges this view with a contrasting fantasy of heroic triumph, but as it dissolves into fragments of the ritornello, Bach suggests—in the very looseness of his construction—that, at least for the moment, the messianic dream of a hero's redemption is but sound and fury signifying nothing. So as one succumbs to the dominant mood in the *molto adagio*, and confronts the satisfying if wildly unconventional ending—where the mute vocalist dare not utter even a word until the final exclamation—it is evident that Bach's music results neither from setting a poetic text nor from sending a theological message, but rather from a musician taking the law into his own hands, defining his own, more amorphous theological and poetic space.

As a tool for observing ruptures and disparities between text and music, filtering the poetry through the lens of a ritornello, this kind of musico-poetic analysis tries to pinpoint Bach's demonstrable aims in a particular aria, that is, which aspects of the poetry he wished to emphasize and which he was happy to overlook. In "Von den Stricken" no. 7, for example, the crucial theological punch line about salvation at the end of the first strophe is perversely severed from any connection with the ritornello. The Evangelist has just related how the army, the captain and the servant of the Jews had taken Jesus and bound him to take him before the High Priest. The text of the aria begins with two punning references to the binding—"my salvation is bound [i.e., bound up] with the unbinding or disengagement from the ropes of my sins." The allegorical point of the poetry implies that because Jesus was bound and brought to trial and crucifixion, the sinning Christian gains salvation and forgiveness of sins. Bach's music, on the other hand, is rather too preoccupied with the binding—in the form of a musical canon in the Vordersatz of this three-part ritornello, a sign of what was called the bound style or *der gebundene Styl*. The musical emblem of the aria—to borrow a useful historical term—prompts a canonic fantasy on bondage to the exclusion of any serious treatment of salvation.

Bach gains little by diminishing the notion of salvation. Certainly he is not trying to deny its theology. What he asserts instead is a metaphorical highlighting of only segments of the poetic text. It is the depiction of the ropes of sin as a canon (the "Stricken," which are lavishly embellished and emphasized throughout the aria) and the desire to unravel them so as "to release me" (mich zu entbinden), which constitute the two foci of musico-poetic interest. So even as the poem moves into the second, parallel strophe—with its grim hyperbole speaking graphically of Christ's body, which will "heal all the running sores of vice" (von allen Lasterbeulen völlig zu heilen)— the oboes and basso continuo patiently chirp out fragments related to the "cordal" or ropelike disengagement from the first stanza. In fact, the word "Lasterbeulen" is set so melismatically that no one hears it properly. Who can recall Bach's music for "the running sores of vice"? The music has not only overshadowed the poetry, but has monopolized the commanding images about which it generates its own compelling fantasy. If one needs evidence to support this view, it is found surely in Bach's habitual revisiting of ritornello segments and related fragments in the aria: the more frequently the composer forces upon us his associations—expressed musically through a mechanism that disparages the poetic form—the less one takes each word of the poetry seriously, at least those relatively neglected by Bach.

This pattern, which highlights some words and downplays others, is widespread in Bach's oeuvre but has not been taken seriously in criticism of his arias. Bach's native piety is commonly supposed to have engendered music that serves as a dutiful if intelligent receptacle for theological ideas conscripted from the often mediocre poetic texts with which the composer mostly had to contend. Perhaps it would be more fruitful to assert that the poor quality of the poetry takes the blame for some less than wholly inspired music. For not every note of the music for the *St. John Passion* inhabits the same exalted plane. There are, if one is honest, substantial *longeurs* in certain arias and choruses when Bach lands himself in some evident compositional trouble. For example, the huge investment in displaying the work of invertible counterpoint for the two viole d'amore in the tenor aria "Erwäge" no. 20 prompts an elegant but very protracted three-part ritornello that has little to do with the cryptic opening lines of poetry, which ask the Christian to "ponder how his blood-stained back resembles heaven in all its parts." (Only on the words "dem Himmel gleich" [resembling heaven], which see a jump up of a widened interval, does the tenor double—seemingly trivially—the ritornello's Epilog.) One needs to await an episode in the lengthy second section of the aria both to hear what the cryptic natural simile signifies and to confirm that the watery waves of sins have poured down (in the form of a wearying dactyl of sixteenth and thirty-second notes) to reveal the most beautiful rainbow marking God's sign of grace. But this we learn only in the last line of the poem. As functional *poesia per la musica*, the text is particularly lame, and Bach's poetic response is perhaps equally so, since his music does little more than discourse at great length on the watery waves of sin, while painting an arched rainbow figure marking God's grace, which we are repeatedly told to "consider" seriously at the beginning of the poem. In this case Bach's inventive fantasy got the better of him, in that he fashioned an elaborate and discursive ritornello forced to bear the weight of the many strenuous repetitions needed to clear a path through the poetic thicket.

A similar mishap can be said to occur, I think, in the protracted final chorus "Ruht wohl, ihr heiligen Gebeine" no. 39. Despite an auspicious start with touchingly simple minuet phrasing, and wonderful cascading descents into what is no doubt the comforting "grave [that] no longer contains suffering" (Das Grab, [daß] ferner keine Not umschließt), the formal disposition of the chorus—a kind of *menuet en rondeau* in which a static ritornello structure is unvaryingly repeated on the same scale degree—offers, in the end, a depiction of weariness verging dangerously on undiluted gloominess, the reigning affect of the entire work identified by Philipp Spitta. It was a brilliant risk to take in the conclusion of this journey of suffering—albeit in only one of the four versions of the passion—but one that may have betrayed first principles in failing to construct musical materials allowing both syntactic and semantic alteration. For to return to some of the greatest achievements in this massive work, Bach is at his best when he doesn't stand to rapt attention admiring a poetic image from afar, but engages actively with its meaning and dances around it to sing praises with the most vivid musical figures.

This is the kind of musical invention and elaboration one sees, for example, in the soprano aria "Zerfließe, mein Herze in Fluten der Zähren" no. 35 (Dissolve my heart in floods of tears), in which a ritornello that refuses to be translated from the minor into the major mode creates a musical world rich in contrasting affects: no matter how slowly the *molt'adagio* is taken, one encounters ideas both similar and yet always different. In fact, Bach liked his invention for this aria so much that he recast it for the *St. Matthew Passion* as a siciliano for "Erbarme dich."

To sum up my main argument: Bach discloses his musical point of view in the *St. John Passion* by composing arias that clearly flout reasonable eighteenth-century standards of text setting. Not only does he develop selective ideas from his texts that spark a dominating instrumental melody, but he also attaches signs, genres, and styles foreign to the text that impose, by way of a kind of performance or execution of the text, an obscuring palimpsest on the poetry. Rather than subscribe to the transparency of music, Bach's musical diligence and ever-inventive permutations teach listeners to see one experience through the focused lens of another, rejecting long-established notions of musical propriety and resemblance. This is not to say that Bach succeeds at every moment of this rather wild and willful process of discovery: it can't, after all, be a good thing to thumb one's nose at perfectly lucid principles of poetry any more than it would have been sensible to throw overboard established principles of harmony and voice leading. Instead, one admires the courage of Bach's actions and the often stirring musical result.

In the end, my consideration of Bach's musical poetics is not much more than a return to Philipp Spitta, whose critical edge in writing about the *St. John Passion* drives a useful wedge between poetry and music. Despite his hagiographic baggage, Spitta strikes a fresh and irreverent critical pose in his celebrated biography, which feels free to slate poetic inconsistencies and musical indulgences while never ignoring the religious depth of the music. As mentioned earlier, Spitta was not greatly impressed with much of the passion text and inveighs against "sacred poetry which . . . had sunk, under the successors of Neumeister to be a false and hollow mockery. It would not be too much to say that the influence of the cantata-poem upon the development of poetry at that time was really ruinous" and that "those who chiefly threw themselves into this branch of poetry were persons who either had no poetic faculty at all, or in whom whatever talent there might be inclined to another kind of work."[28] Of course Spitta marvels at the music, asserting that the arias in the *St. John Passion*, with a few exceptions, "are among the best that Bach ever wrote," with "the solitary grandeur in which Bach dwells as a composer of church music . . . only rendered more clear by a comparison with similar works by Keiser, Telemann, Mattheson, Stölzel, or even Handel . . . which lack the profound church feeling that pervades [Bach's style]."[29] For "Ach, mein Sinn," for example, he notes the aria's "novelty and captivating ingenuity," its "ingenious construction" and its "superiority to that which subsequently took its place, . . . [how] we are insensibly led on from the second part into the third, which here consists only of the opening ritornello, while the vocal line continues its course independently."[30] Yet Spitta is fearless when it comes to criticizing some of Bach's text setting, especially the passion's recitatives:

> The composer wanders through the realm of musical imagery and gives himself up to realizing it, now in one way and now in another—prompted to do so now by some important factor, and now by something wholly unimportant. . . . We can find no reason in the nature of things why in one place he should devote all the means at his command to an exhaustive illustration of some emphatic word, while in another he passes it over with complete indifference; it was his good pleasure, so he did it.[31]

Bach, he claims, displays a cavalier disregard of textual coherence and superiority. Instead,

> the supreme and sole principle of form that governs [recitatives of the *St. John Passion*] throughout is the result of [Bach's] own innate tendency towards vigorous melodic movement. Everything else is merely a means to this end; if it were not so it would be inconceivable why Bach should sometimes introduce picturesque details which have no dramatic musical purpose, and which, in themselves, are mere sport of the composer—e.g. when the word "Pavement" [*Hochpflaster*] in German is declaimed in such a pronounced way [i.e. emphasizing a dramatic leap downwards of a sixth].[32]

Perhaps Spitta goes too far in suggesting Bach's treatment is so arbitrary, but his critical intelligence, on balance, is surely preferable to readings that treat Bach's text setting as if it were the most natural thing in the world. What became an indigenous nine-

28. Spitta, *Bach*, 2:347–48.

29. Ibid., 2:532, 534.

30. Ibid., 2:533.

31. Ibid., 2:531.

32. Ibid., 2:530.

teenth-century *topos*—the triumph of musical autonomy over a servitude to words—is foreshadowed in Bach in ways not easily tolerated by his contemporary thought or historical categories. Bach's struggles with his texts are much like his struggles with music generally: they expose imperfections while they achieve remarkable things. In the end, we are left with a not unexpected but attractive paradox: the more human, even flawed, our image of Bach, the more riveting his musical thought and the more justified his status as inimitable icon.

Bach's *Ascension Oratorio*

God's Kingdoms and Their Representation

Eric Chafe

A s is well known, Bach's *Ascension Oratorio*, "Lobet Gott in seinen Reichen" BWV 11, composed in all probability in 1735, follows a pattern that is very close to that of its much more extended sister work, the *Christmas Oratorio*, composed a few months earlier for the 1734–35 Christmas season. In part it is parodied from earlier secular cantatas, and its movement layout resembles that of the *Christmas Oratorio* closely in its sequences of biblical recitatives for voice(s) and basso continuo only, nonbiblical accompanied recitatives, arias, and chorales (see Table 1).

Although the *Ascension Oratorio* has been studied from both the theological and musical standpoints, there has been no close coordination of the two approaches.[1] The musical and textual design of the oratorio relates closely to the liturgical and scriptural background for Ascension Day, and to contemporary theological perspectives that can be gleaned from writings by Lutheran authors of the seventeenth and eighteenth centuries. The tonal plan of the oratorio reflects its theological meaning. Bach's structure can be described as consisting of two parallel halves (as shown in Table 1), with framing movements in D major and two arias that feature somewhat unusual qualities: "Ach, bleibe doch," in the relatively rare key of the dominant minor, and "Jesu, deine Gnadenblicke," belonging to the very small number of arias without basso continuo in Bach's oeuvre. The theological meaning of the oratorio revolves around the relationship of the two arias and their placement in the design of the whole. In their different ways the two halves of the oratorio mirror the theological presentation of God's kingdoms as worlds "above" and "below," united for the faithful through Jesus's ascension.

---

1. Two commentaries are particularly valuable: Walter Hindermann, *Johann Sebastian Bach: Himmelfahrts-Oratorium: Gestalt und Gehalt* (Hofheim: F. Hofmeister, 1985), and Martin Petzoldt, *Bach-Kommentar*, vol. 2, *Die Geistlichen Kantaten vom 1. Advent bis zum Trinitatisfest* (Kassel: Bärenreiter, 2007), 920–37.

Table 1. Outline of the *Ascension Oratorio*

Chorus: "Lobet Gott in seinen Reichen"
(SATB, 3 tpts., timp., fl. 1 & 2, ob. 1 & 2, str., b.c.)
D major

Recitative (Evangelist): "Der Herr hub seine Hände auf"
(T, b.c.) [Luke 24:50–51a]
B minor to A major

Accompagnato: "Ach, Jesu, ist dein Abschied schon
so nah?"
(B, fl. 1 & 2, b.c.)
V/F♯ minor to A minor

Aria: "Ach, bleibe doch, mein liebstes Leben"
(A, vn. 1 & 2, b.c.)
A minor

Recitative (Evangelist): "Und war aufgehaben zusehends"
(T, b.c.) [Acts 1:9a; Luke 24:51b; Acts 1:9b; Mark 16:19c]
E minor to F♯ minor

Chorale: "Nun lieget alles unter dir"
(SATB doubled by ww. and str., b.c.)
D major

6. Chorale: "Nun lieget alles unter dir"
(SATB doubled by ww. and str., b.c.)
D major

7a. Recitative (Evangelist, Two Men from Galilee):
"Und da sie ihm nachsahen gen Himmel fahren"
(Tenor, Bass, b.c.) [Acts 1:10–11]
D major

7b. Accompagnato: "Ach ja! so komme bald zurück"
(Alto, fl. 1 & 2, b.c.)
G major to B minor

7c. Recitative (Evangelist): "Sie aber beteten ihn an"
(Tenor, b.c.) [Luke 24:52; Acts 1:12; Luke 24:52b]
V/D major to G major

8. Aria: "Jesu deine Gnadenblicke"
(S, fl. 1 & 2, ob. 1, unison vn. and va., no b.c.)
G major

9. Chorale: "Wann soll es doch geschehen"
(Same instrumentation as no. 1)
D major

The Liturgical and Scriptural Background

The initial words of the *Ascension Oratorio*, "Lobet Gott in seinen Reichen," urge praise of God in his kingdoms ("Reichen," dative plural), a detail that, as Martin Petzoldt remarks, refers to the "streitende Kirche" (church militant) on earth and the "triumphirende Kirche" (church triumphant) of the "heiligen Engel und Menschen" (angels and saints) in heaven.[2] Petzoldt associates the plural with passages from the book of Revelation, of which chapter 11, verse 15 is the most direct (in the sense that it alone employs the plural "Reiche"): "And the seventh angel blew his trumpet and there arose great voices in heaven, which said, The kingdoms [Reiche] of this world are become the kingdoms of our Lord, and of his Christ; and he shall reign for ever and ever." Petzoldt is undoubtedly correct in making this association, although in commentaries other than that of Johann Olearius (on which Petzoldt bases his discussion), it is not necessary to go beyond the readings for Ascension Day itself to understand what underlies the reference to God's kingdoms. These commentaries suggest a different interpretation. The reference to "Reiche" arises primarily from

2. Martin Petzoldt, *Bach-Kommentar*, 2:923.

the Epistle for the day (Acts 1:1–11), where we read, "He also showed himself as the living one with many proofs to them [that is, the apostles, as mentioned in the previous verse] after his passion, and was seen among them for forty days, and spoke with them of the kingdom of God" [verse 3]. A little later, in verse 6, the disciples ask, "Lord, will you at this time restore again the kingdom to Israel?" The words "at this time" refer to the preceding verse (5), in which the author of Acts reports Jesus as saying, "but you shall be baptized with the Holy Spirit not long after these days." The references to the kingdom of God in verse 3 and the kingdom of Israel in verse 6 underlie the meaning of Ascension Day for the faithful as it is discussed in many Lutheran theological treatises and commentaries between the time of the reformer and that of Bach (and beyond).[3] In those discussions we find copious references (explicit or implicit) to the distinction between heavenly (or spiritual) versus worldly (or physical) kingdoms. The passage from Revelation 11, cited by Petzoldt, most likely suggests in its particular wording ("kingdoms of this world") only the latter, not both heavenly and earthly realms.

The Epistle for Ascension Day plays a major part not only in the text of the *Ascension Oratorio*, but also in the formation of the liturgical year itself, in which Ascension Day (although not one of the three principal feasts of Christmas, Easter, and Pentecost) is only a notch lower in importance. The placement of Ascension Day on the fortieth day after Easter (always a Thursday), ten days before Pentecost, is directly owing to the reference to "forty days" in the passages from Acts 1:3–5 cited earlier.[4] Pentecost itself was derived, of course, from the Jewish Pentecost (the feast of "first fruits" or feast of "weeks": 7 × 7 days, origin of the early Christian term "great Sunday"), celebrated on the fiftieth day after Passover to commemorate the Israelites reach-

---

3. See, for example, Johann Arndt, *Postille. Das ist Auslegung der Sonn- und Fest-Tage Evangelien durchs gantze Jahr* (Frankfurt, 1713), part 3 (Easter through Pentecost), 164–68 (on Jesus's visible ascension), 168–74 (on Jesus's invisible ascension, further subdivided into three levels or Kingdoms), 176–78 (on Jesus's "königliche Ampt," his removing the faithful from the "Reich der Finsternüs" to the "Reich der Gnaden und Seligkeit"). Among the writers who followed, and made similar distinctions among God's kingdoms, see Joachim Lütkemann, *Apostolischer Hertzens-Wekker*, published along with Heinrich Müller's *Evangelischer Hertzens-Spiegel* (Stade, 1736), 754; Heinrich Müller, *Apostolischer Schluß-Kette* (Frankfurt, 1671), 505–8; August Hermann Francke, *Predigten über die Sonn- und Fest-Tags Episteln* (Halle, 1726), 705–9; Johann Jacob Rambach, *Evangelische Betrachtungen über die Sonn- und Fest-Tags-Evangelia des gantzen Jahrs* (Halle, 1732), 646–48 (on Jesus's "Reich der Natur" and "Reich der Gnaden"). Behind all these discussions lies the (sometimes unspoken) belief that God's kingdom is actually one—that it is the human perspective that speaks of it in plural terms.

4. All the sources cited in the preceding note make this point, several characterizing the forty-day span as a "Spiegel [or 'Vorbild'] des ewigen Lebens."

ing Mount Sinai and the giving of the Law, as God had commanded (Exodus 34:22; Leviticus 23:15–16).[5] In the Christian church, Pentecost celebrated the coming of the Holy Spirit, which was viewed as a counterpart of the Jewish celebration of the giving of the Law. In his Pentecost sermon from the *Kirchenpostille*, Luther explained Pentecost in terms of the giving of a "new law," that of the Spirit as described by St. Paul in 2 Corinthians 3:6, where the apostle juxtaposes it to the law of Moses, opposing "letter" (or "flesh") and "spirit."[6]

The part of the year from Easter to Pentecost, known as the "great fifty days," is the oldest part of the Christian liturgy, the climactic fulfillment of the first half of the year, centered on the life of Jesus. Within it Ascension Day marks the end of Jesus's time on Earth, following the resurrection and forty days of post-resurrection appearances to the disciples and others (sometimes known as the "great forty days").[7] The gospel readings for most of the Sundays and feast days from the Sunday after Easter to Pentecost and Trinity are drawn from John, an association that suggested to some Lutheran authors that Jesus's discourse with the disciples on "the kingdom of God" would have involved essentially the same content as that of the greatest discourse of this kind in all of New Testament scripture, the so-called farewell discourse of John (chapters 14–17).[8] The single exception is Ascension Day, because John has no narrative of the ascension per se. But the very quality of spirituality that led to Pentecost and ran throughout the farewell discourse is bound up with the absence of a specific ascension

5. Oddly, Arndt (*Postille*, part 3, 165) equates the Jewish Pentecost with the fortieth day, viewing Jesus's teaching the disciples of his kingdom in Acts 1 with baptism, the Holy Spirit, and their preparation for Pentecost.

6. For an English translation of Luther's sermon see *The Complete Sermons of Martin Luther*, vol. 4.1, *Sermons on Epistle Texts for Epiphany, Easter and Pentecost* (Grand Rapids, Mich.: Baker Books, 2000), 330.

7. The Lutheran tradition retained the much older practice of relating the forty days of Jesus's post-resurrection appearances to one or more of the following: the forty hours that Jesus was dead between the crucifixion and resurrection (commonly cited), the forty days of Lent, the forty years of the Israelites wandering in the wilderness, and the forty days between Jesus's birth and his presentation in the temple (with a parallel between the temple "built by hands" and the temple of God's Kingdom). See the sources cited in note 2.

8. Strictly speaking, the farewell discourse consists of chapters 14 to 16 of John, whereas the seventeenth chapter is addressed by Jesus to God rather than to the disciples. Some authors include the seventeenth chapter within the discourse; some do not. August Hermann Francke, for example, makes this point in his *Predigten über die Sonn- und Fest-Tags Episteln*, 704, interpreting Jesus's command that the disciples wait in Jerusalem for the "promise of the Father" as the promise made in John 14, 15, and 16, in which Jesus spoke of the Holy Spirit. For some modern authors the seventeenth chapter has been understood as the equivalent for John of Jesus's ascension.

narrative in John. For most theologians Jesus's ascension is, as Stephen Smalley puts it, "'built in' to every part of John's theological line," and for some, notably C. H. Dodd, the seventeenth chapter of John (in which, following the farewell discourse to the disciples Jesus anticipates the "glorification" of the passion) is understood as the equivalent for John of Jesus's ascension.[9] In other words, Ascension Day is embedded within the context of a season permeated by Johannine gospel readings, particularly those of the farewell discourse, chosen to reflect what Jesus might have said to the disciples during the great forty days.[10] Its gospel and epistle readings, from Mark (16:14–20) and Acts (1:1–11), were chosen because of their narrative character, whereas their full meaning is supplied by the Johannine context.[11]

In the farewell discourse, and throughout John's gospel, the "transfigured nature" of Jesus mentioned by Smalley is associated particularly with one of John's most famous dualistic oppositions, that of "above" and "below."[12] Jesus not only descends and ascends, but he speaks often of the two spheres after the following manner (8:23): "And he said unto them, You are from below; I am from above: you are of this world; I am not of this world." In the farewell discourse Jesus makes many references to his going and returning, the return suggesting at times the second coming, but more often his return through the Holy Spirit. Such passages seem, like the epistle for Ascension Day itself, to have determined the relationship of Ascension Day to Easter and Pentecost. That is, Ascension Day completes the triumphant "upswing" of the resurrection, and its own meaning is completed with the coming of the Holy Spirit (Pentecost). In this view, Ascension Day was an extension of Jesus's Easter victory, predicted, as was believed, in Psalms 3, 47, 68, and 104 and described as such by St. Paul in Colossians 2:15. It celebrated Jesus's triumphant return to the world above from which he came, his victorious work now completed, after which Pentecost commemorated his return

9. Stephen S. Smalley, *John Evangelist and Interpreter* (Exeter: Paternoster Press, 1978), 237; C. H. Dodd, *The Interpretation of the Fourth Gospel* (Cambridge: Cambridge University Press, 1960), 419.

10. As is well known, John was Luther's favorite gospel because of its emphasis on Jesus's words rather than his works; and within the fourth gospel the farewell discourse was Luther's favorite part. The set of sermons he preached on it between Easter and Pentecost 1537 he later declared his best book. See *Luther's Works*, vol. 35, ed. E. Theodore Bachmann (Philadelphia: Muhlenberg Press, 1960), 361–62. For a concise assessment of this topic, see Victor C. Pfitzner, "Luther as Interpreter of John's Gospel: With Special Reference to His Sermons on the Gospel of St. John," *Lutheran Theological Journal* 18 (1984): 65–73.

11. Petzoldt alludes to this in his commentary on the word "Abschied" in the text of the *Ascension Oratorio* ("Abschiedsreden" = farewell discourse). Petzoldt, *Bach-Kommentar*, 2:924.

12. See Miroslav Volf, "Johannine Dualism and Contemporary Pluralism," in *The Gospel of John and Christian Theology*, ed. Richard Bauckham and Carl Mosser (Grand Rapids, Mich.: Wm. B. Eerdman, 2008), 19–50.

and continued presence through the Holy Spirit. Many Lutheran commentaries retained the ancient threefold interpretation of Easter, Ascension Day, and Pentecost as celebrating three aspects of Jesus's work, as "Überwinder" (conqueror), "Durchbrecher" (breaker of barriers), and "Tröster" (giver of life to the faithful through the word, the sacraments and the Holy Spirit).[13] In this sequence the "upswing" of Jesus's resurrection and ascension to God's kingdom has as its counterpart the establishing of another kingdom, that of the church and the faithful below.

Aligned as Jesus's references to his ascending/descending character are with John's other well-known sets of dualistic oppositions—good/evil, spirit/flesh, light/darkness, and the like, such passages often create the impression of two simultaneously existing worlds and of humanity as belonging intrinsically to one or the other. This "vertical" view of salvation is usually described in terms of John's tendency toward realized eschatology, according to which humans are saved or judged by God in the present. Two passages, from the gospel for Ascension Day and the second day of Pentecost respectively, make clear the difference between John and the synoptic gospels in this regard. In the gospel for Ascension Day, Jesus says to the disciples, "Whoever believes and is baptized shall be saved; but whoever does not believe will be damned" (Mark 16:16). And in the gospel for the second day of Pentecost, Jesus says, "Whoever believes in him [the Son of God] is not judged: but whoever does not believe is judged already, because he does not believe in the name of the only begotten Son of God."

We can only speculate whether those who originally formed the gospel readings for this time period intended a specific association between these two apparently contradictory passages, which come so close together in the liturgical calendar. But in the interpretation of Ascension Day by Lutheran theologians between the time of Luther and Bach, we find that there is a substantial emphasis, if not exactly on fully realized eschatology, then at the very least on the verifying of the hope of salvation in the present for the faithful, even at times of its certainty. In fact, among all the feast days of the year, those qualities were associated with Ascension Day in particular. In this regard, the most widely cited metaphor (a very ancient one) for the above/below view of salvation was that of Haupt and Glieder, or head and body (members), which can be found in several Bach cantatas.[14] According to the metaphor, Jesus, the head of the church,

13. In addition to the sources cited in note 2, good discussions can be found in August Pfeiffer, *Evangelische Schatz-Kammer*, part 1 (Nuremberg, 1697), 523–27: and Martin Moller, *Praxis Evangeliorum*, part 2 (Görlitz, 1614), 258. Pfeiffer also uses the traditional Latin terms for Jesus's three aspects: *mortis triumphatio, coeli referatio,* and *vitae aeterniae donatio* (523–24). For a still more detailed description of Jesus as *Überwinder* and *Durchbrecher* (the latter based, as are all such characterizations, on Micah 2:13), see Valerius Herberger, *Epistolische Herz-Postilla*, part 1 (Leipzig, 1736), 46–54.

14. Nearly all the sources cited in note 2 draw on this metaphor. Among Bach's Ascension Day cantatas it is prominent in the first movement of Cantata 128, "Auf Christi Himmelfahrt allein" (1725).

is joined to the members as a head to a body; when he ascends, therefore, the head is in heaven, while the body remains below, to be fetched up at the right time, usually identified with the second coming. In the interpretation of the metaphor, therefore, its vertical aspect (above/below) is tempered by the horizontal (temporal) element. Although the relationship between the vertical and horizontal views of salvation may vary in emphasis from author to author, one thing never does: that Jesus's ascension provided the assurance of salvation for the faithful who constituted his body. The meaning of Ascension Day could be said to lift the believer, in spirit, out of the world.

There is another, more doctrinal aspect to Jesus's ascension that the Lutheran authors almost never fail to bring up in their commentaries: that Jesus's ascent was a visible one, not a simple disappearance or sudden vanishing, as the phrase "schied er von ihnen" (he departed from them) might be taken to mean. The difference, for August Pfeiffer, was one between Calvinists and Lutherans; and the latter staunchly opposed what they viewed as a purely metaphysical interpretation of the ascension.[15] In the Lutheran view, Jesus ascended in his human nature, a matter of central concern in the interpretation of the certainty of salvation for the faithful below. Thus Lutheran interpretations often describe the ascension in terms of degrees, inherited from much older authors, that pass from the physical to the spiritual spheres, the lowest one completely visible to the human senses. The upward progression passed through higher stages of physical bodies (e.g., the stars) until the point, no longer physical, where Jesus sat at the right hand of God, as described by Luke.[16] The place where physical seeing changed to spiritual seeing (faith) corresponded to the moment narrated in scripture at which a cloud concealed the ascent from the eyes of those below.[17] The latter part of the ascent was then an instantaneous one, beyond the senses.

Nevertheless, in Mariane von Ziegler's text for "Auf Christi Himmelfahrt allein" (Upon Christ's ascension alone) BWV 128, for Ascension Day 1725, we hear the believer proclaim, "Ich sehe durch die Sterne, daß er sich schon von ferne zur Rechten Gottes zeigt" (I see through the stars that he already shows himself in the distance at the right hand of God). There is, of course, no contradiction between this passage and the line

15. August Pfeiffer, *Evangelische Schatz-Kammer*, 1:518. See also Lütkemann, *Apostolischer Hertzens-Wekker*, 656; Müller, *Hertzens-Spiegel*, 646; Rambach, *Evangelische Betrachtung*, 659; Arndt, *Postille*, 163–66.

16. Usually such discussions speak of four stages of the ascent: through the air (*Luft*), the stars (*Sterne*), the souls (*Seele*), and the divinely majestic, the right hand of God. See, for example, Pfeiffer, *Evangelische Schatz-Kammer*, 1:519; Müller, *Apostolische Schluß-Kette*, 510; idem, *Hertzens-Spiegel*, 646.

17. Pfeiffer, *Evangelische Schatz-Kammer*, 1:519; Lütkemann, *Apostolischer Hertzens-Wekker*, 656–57; Müller, *Apostolische Schluß-Kette*, 511; Rambach, *Evangelische Betrachtung*, 640.

"Ich sehe schon im Geist, wie er zu Gottes Rechten auf seine Feinde schmeißt. . . . Ich stehe hier am Weg und schau ihm sehnlich nach" (I see already in the Spirit how at God's right hand he strikes out at his enemies. . . . I stand here on the path and look longingly after him) from Bach's Ascension Day cantata for 1726, "Gott fähret auf mit Jauchzen" (God ascends with rejoicing), BWV 43. In such passages it is clear that for Lutherans, even the purely spiritual seeing of faith has a physical dimension, essential to the view that through the ascension of his human nature Jesus remains connected to the fleshly beings below who constitute his body.

The sense of continuity from the physical to the spiritual that was associated with Jesus's ascension thus became equivalent to the seeing through faith of those who, while remaining on earth, were joined "in the Spirit" with Jesus and the world above. That meant that Jesus was present "continuously" (beständig) on earth even as he sat at the right hand of God in heaven. This is the ancient view of Jesus as the "Durchbrecher" (one who breaks through), who in his ascension penetrated the barrier between heaven and earth, permitting the faithful to see with the eyes of faith into the spiritual sphere (above), and at the same time to experience Jesus's "Gnadengegenwart" (presence through grace, that is, his presence below).[18] Of course, for most Lutherans the fulfillment of Jesus's ascension would be the second coming, when the faithful would be physically resurrected and ascend as Jesus had before them. (This is the meaning of Paul's naming Jesus the "first fruits of them that slept.") But within the pietist sphere there was a tendency to emphasize the presentness of salvation still more. Thus August Hermann Francke (1663–1727), in a sermon for Ascension Day titled "Die samt Christo in das himmlische Wesen versetzte Gläubigen" (The faithful, transferred into the heavenly condition along with Christ), sets forth, as the background to his delineation of the meaning of the ascension, the idea that the faithful are transferred ("versetzt") to the heavenly condition ("himmlische Wesen") already, in advance of the second coming. Noting that Paul, in the first and second chapters of Ephesians, had used the same Greek verb for Jesus's ascension and the raising up of humanity, Francke argues:

---

18. In this emphasis on Jesus's *Gnadengegenwart*, the ascension is the other side of Jesus's return through the Holy Spirit, as predicted by him in the farewell discourse (and set to music by Bach in Cantatas 108 and 74). Heinrich Müller (*Apostolischer Schluß-Kette*, 505, 511, 513) makes this clear in his use of the expression "Gnadengegenwart" and synonymous expressions such as "wahrhafftig anwesende Gegenwart," associating the latter with Jesus's words from the gospel for Pentecost (John 14:28), "You have heard that I have said unto you, I go away and come again unto you." See also Renate Steiger, "'Gnadengegenwart': Johann Sebastian Bachs Pfingstkantate BWV 172 'Erschallet, ihr Lieder, erklinget, ihr Saiten,'" in *Die Quellen Johann Sebastian Bachs. Bach's Musik im Gottesdienst*, ed. Renate Steiger (Heidelberg: Manutius Verlag, 1998), 15–57.

Without doubt the apostle again (in the following second chapter, sixth verse) uses this very word with great care concerning the faithful, when he says of them, that they are transferred along with him into the heavenly condition . . . into the heavenly things, into the heavenly blessings, into the heavenly glory and splendor. Accordingly, God shows just the same degree of his power, just the same working of his mighty strength, as he showed with Christ when he resurrected him from the dead and placed him in the heavens, also with the faithful members of Jesus Christ, that they not only on the day of judgment, but already in this world are transferred into the heavenly condition along with and in Christ. . . . Thus you see clearly that already here you shall rejoice in such blessedness as members of heaven, there, however you shall enjoy the same eternally and fully. In this, therefore, the truly blossoming power of faith shall demonstrate in you that your heart is continually occupied with heavenly things, that you are better known in heaven than on earth, that for you everything in the entire world is foreign and bitter, and your greatest joy and bliss consists in the fact that you have your head in heaven and are united with the same in faith.[19]

Later in the same sermon, Francke emphasizes that Paul does not speak of the transferring of the faithful to heaven in the future "but in the past. He does not say 'you shall one day be transferred with Christ in the heavenly condition,' but 'you are already transferred along with Christ into the heavenly condition.'"[20]

---

19. August Hermann Francke, *Sonn- und Fest-Tags Predigten* (Halle, 1724), 862–63: "Eben dieses Wort nun hat der Apostel ohne Zweifel mit allem Fleiß im nachfolgendem 2 Cap. V. 6 wieder gebrauchet von denen Gläubigen, wenn er von ihnen saget; daß sie samt ihm **in das himmlische Wesen,** . . . in die himmlische Dinge, in die himmlische Güter, in die himmlische Glorie und Herrlichkeit versetzet sind. Es erzeiget demnach GOTT eben dieselbe Grösse seiner Kraft, eben dieselbe Wirckung seiner mächtigen Stärcke, die er an CHristo erzeiget hat, da er ihn von den Todten auferwecket und ihn in den Himmel gesetzet, auch an allen gläubigen Gliedern JEsu CHristi, daß sie nicht erst am jüngsten Tage, sondern bereits in dieser Welt in das himmlische Wesen samt und in CHristo gesetzet sind . . . . So sehet ihr ja, daß ihr euch solcher Seligkeit, als Genossen des Himmels, schon hier erfreuen, dort aber derselben ewig und völlig geniessen sollet. Darinnen soll sich also die rechte grünende Kraft des Glaubens bey euch beweisen, daß euer Hertz beständig mit himmlischen Dingen umgehe, daß ihr besser im Himmel als auf Erden bekant seyd, daß euch alles in der gantzen Welt fremde und bitter sey, und eure höchste Freude und Wonne darinnen bestehe, daß ihr euer Haupt im Himmel habet, und mit demselben in Glauben vereiniget seyd." Johann Jacob Rambach (*Evangelische Betrachtungen*, 650) follows Francke in this regard.

20. Francke, *Sonn- und Fest-Tage Predigten*, 865: "Denn es redet ja, wie schon erinnert worden, und mit Fleiß abermal erinnert wird, Paulus nicht in der zukünftigen Zeit, sondern in der **vergangenen.** Er spricht nicht: ihr sollt einmal mit Christo ins himmlische Wesen versetzet werden, sondern, ihr seyd bereits samt Christo ins himmlische Wesen versetzet."

The *Ascension Oratorio*: **Musical and Textual Design**

How does Bach's *Ascension Oratorio* relate to the questions I have outlined? Can we discern any theological position reflected in the music? We must first consider the textual and musical design. As Table 1 shows, the textual structure is a variant of that of the *Christmas Oratorio*, first performed a few months earlier; it has been outlined in more or less the same way by many writers. I have given no. 6 double duty, not to insist that the oratorio be thought of as divided into two parts but to bring out the parallel between its two stages of meditation.[21] That is, nos. 1–6 are preparatory to nos. 7–9 in that they deal with the narrative of the ascension, which is completed in no. 5 and meditated on in no. 6. This part of the oratorio then serves as background to the remaining movements, which deal with the human response. Of course, the first accompanied recitative and aria (nos. 3 and 4) also represent the human response, but it is a different kind of response from that in nos. 7b and 8. The difference is that in the scriptural passages on which the second half is based, the meaning of the ascension is already interpreted for the faithful (by the two "men in white" who appear to the disciples), whereas in the first half the response is unmediated by scripture. Bach's structure pivots around this distinction.

Table 1 makes clear that the *Ascension Oratorio* is solidly anchored in D major, as are, to varying degrees, its great counterparts, the *Christmas Oratorio* and the *Easter Oratorio*. Within each half, however, there is a significant pattern of digression from D, in association with the human response to events. The first is to the ascension itself in nos. 3 and 4, the first accompanied recitative and the aria "Ach, bleibe doch," which urge Jesus to remain. In the second half the reaction is to the explanation given the disciples by the "two men in white" who appear while the disciples are still looking upward. This occurs in no. 7b, in which the believer cries for Jesus to return soon, and (following no. 7c, another biblical recitative narrating the disciples' return to Jerusalem "mit großer Freude" [with great joy]) in the aria no. 8 "Jesu, deine Gnadenblicke," in which the idealized believer voices the primary meaning of the ascension, the "seeing" of Jesus "continually" through the Spirit (i.e., Jesus's "Gnadengegenwart") and the experience of his love in the present.

---

21. The NBA's numbering of movements 7a, 7b, 7c, 8, and 9 (rather than as 7, 8, 9, 10, and 11) of the Ascension Oratorio is illogical and inconsistent with the practice followed in the passions. No. 7b is a madrigal-texted movement set as an accompanied recitative and, following the practice of the other oratorios, should have been assigned a new number (8). Also, the biblical recitatives 7a and 7c do not form a continuous biblical recitative, since 7a is from Acts, whereas 7c begins and ends with excerpts based on Luke. Numbering the movements from 7 through 11 would make the correspondence between the two halves much clearer.

If we were to understand the first of these two arias, "Ach, bleibe doch," in the strict theological terms that Elke Axmacher has applied to several movements of the St. Matthew Passion (the aria "Gebt mir meinen Jesum wieder," for example), we would have to conclude that it is inappropriate, in that it cries out for the halting of God's plan for the salvation of humanity.[22] That is, of course, not the intention, which is that of depicting two human responses in the two arias. Nevertheless, the fact that the first aria is in minor and the second in major is a telling detail, reflecting the different characters of the two points of meditation. The former, "Ach, bleibe doch," is entirely sorrowful, whereas the latter, "Jesu, deine Gnadenblicke," affirms the believer's joy in the certainty or presentness of salvation. This lifting of the believer out of the framework of physical sorrow to spiritual joy is also a feature of many Ascension Day commentaries. Heinrich Müller (1631–1675), for example, in the introduction to his sermon on the gospel for Ascension Day from the *Evangelischer Herzens-Spiegel*, says:

> If one friend of the heart journeys away from the other, then this does not occur without mourning, tears and lamenting. For departure, one says, brings suffering. What one possesses in joy one loses with weeping. David and Jonathan wept as they departed from one another. The very dearest friend of our soul, Jesus, also took his departure from us a thousand and several hundred years ago on this day and withdrew his visible presence from us, but not that he would thereby cast us into sorrow, but much more into joy. For He is not removed from us, but only gone before, so that he prepares the way and opens the door of heaven. . . . To be sure, he has withdrawn his visible presence, yet he has remained with us and remains with us until the end of the world with His invisible consolation, with his grace. Therefore we should rejoice much more than be sorrowful on this day. If the head has gone up, then also the members will not remain here below but follow after; we rejoice and sing for joy: "Christ ascended to heaven," etc.[23]

22. Elke Axmacher, *"Aus Liebe will mein Heyland sterben": Untersuchungen zum Wandel des Passionsverständnisses im frühen 18. Jahrhundert* (Neuhausen-Stuttgart: Hänssler-Verlag, 1984), 195–96.

23. Heinrich Müller, *Herzens-Spiegel*, 739: "Wenn ein Hertzens-Freund von dem andern abreiset, da gehet es nicht ab ohne Trauren, Thränen und Klagen; Denn Scheiden, saget man, bringet Leiden. Was man mit Lust besitzet, das verleuret man mitWeinen. David und Jonathan weineten als sie von einander schieden. Unser allertheurester Seelen-Freund JESUS, hat auch vor tausend und etlichen hundert Jahren auff diesen Tag seinen Abschied von uns genommen, und uns seine sichtbare Gegenwart entzogen, nicht aber, daß er uns dadurch in Leid, sondern vielmehr in Freude, versetze. Denn er ist uns nicht entzogen, sondern nur vorhin gegangen, daß er uns den Weg bahne, und die Himmels-Thür öffne . . . . Er hat uns zwar seine sichtbare Gegenwart entzogen, doch ist er bey uns geblieben, und bleibet bey uns bis ans Ende der Welt mit seinem unsichtbahren Trost, mit seiner Gnade. Darum freuen wir uns vielmehr am heutigen Tage, als daß wir trauren sollten. Ist das Haupt hinauff, so werden auch

Directly following this introduction, Müller introduces the theme of love, foremost in most of his writings, as the key to human participation in Jesus's ascension. It is this response of joy, replacing the immediate response of sorrow, that "Jesu, deine Gnadenblicke" represents, along with the ideas of seeing Jesus continuously (beständig) through faith, and experiencing his "Gnadengegenwart" as the love that remains behind:

Jesu, deine Gnadenblicke	Jesus, your glance of grace
Kann ich doch beständig sehn.	I can still see continuously.
Deine Liebe bleibt zurücke,	Your love remains behind,
Daß ich mich hier in der Zeit	So that I, here in the present time,
An der künftgen Herrlichkeit	Already refresh myself in the Spirit
Schon voraus im Geist erquicke,	With the coming splendor,
Wenn wir einst dort vor dir stehn.	When we will finally stand there
	before you.

To set up the joy that belongs to the completed Ascension Day message, the librettist of the *Ascension Oratorio* added, as the final recitative (no. 7c), a compound of parts of two verses from Luke and Acts. The twelfth verse of the first chapter of Acts (that is, one verse beyond the Epistle reading, which ends with verse 11) is embedded within the two halves of Luke 24:52 (the postscript to Luke's ascension narrative, not among the readings for the day but, like Acts 1:12, cited frequently in Lutheran commentaries). This enabled the recitative to accomplish two things. First, it confirms the shift of focus of the biblical narrative itself to the disciples and the effect of the resurrection on them, so that with "Jesu, deine Gnadenblicke," the believer, by extension of the situation of the disciples to that of the contemporary faithful, could express the "great joy" with which the disciples returned to Jerusalem. Second, it introduces the information that the ascension took place on the Mount of Olives, a "Sabbath-Day's" journey from Jerusalem.[24] As we might expect, virtually all Lutheran commentaries from Bach's time and earlier carried forward the much older tradition of drawing a parallel between Jesus's suffering on the Mount of Olives in the passion and his ascen-

---

die Glieder nicht hienieder bleiben, sondern nachfolgen, wir freuen uns, und singen für Freuden: Christ fuhr gen Himmel, u."

24. "Sie aber beteten ihn an, wandten um gen Jerusalem von dem Berge, der da heißet der Ölberg, welcher ist nahe bei Jerusalem und liegt einen Sabbater-Weg davon, und sie kehreten wieder gen Jerusalem mit großer Freude" (They however prayed to him, turned around toward Jerusalem from the mountain which is known there as the mount of olives, which is near to Jerusalem and lies a Sabbath day's journey away, and returned to Jerusalem with great joy.) (Based on Acts 1:12.)

sion from the Mount of Olives. Johann Jacob Rambach, for example, refers to it in at least two treatises, making the point narrated throughout scripture that God chose high and low places to emphasize the character of events (Mount Sinai, the Sermon on the Mount, and the like). In this case, to bring out the "Niedrigkeit" (humiliation, abasement) of the passion and the "Herrlichkeit" (gloriousness, splendor) of the ascension, Rambach emphasized that Gethsemane was a low place, whereas the Mount of Olives was a high one.[25]

"Jesu, deine Gnadenblicke," as is well known, is one of the very select number of pure *bassetchen* arias in Bach's oeuvre. That is, it has no basso continuo realization, and its bass line is at high pitch, played by unison violins and violas (Example 1). The practice it represents is described in thoroughbass treatises throughout the baroque period with the terms *bassetto*, *petit basse*, or *bassetchen* (sometimes *bassetgen*), all meaning "little bass," a designation that is particularly applicable to Bach's examples, in which the high bass line always mimics the character of a normal low bass. And Bach often causes the accompanimental instrumental lines to move in parallel thirds, sixths, tenths, and the like, all of which gives the impression that harmonic completeness is essential. The primary meaning therefore seems to be that the entire pitch framework is transferred temporarily to a higher sphere. There is often a substantial contrast between the bassetchen movement or section of a movement and the music that surrounds it, as, for example, in the best-known instance, the aria "Aus Liebe will mein Heiland sterben" from the *St. Matthew Passion*. In fact, underlying all Bach's uses of the technique is the immediate impact of the contrast of high and low pitch spheres. This contrast may be almost purely pictorial in nature, but it may also be the background for theological ideas, such as God's judgment (above) and his mercy or love (below), Jesus's taking away (above) the sins of the world (below), and the like.[26]

One instance that is both close to "Jesu, deine Gnadenblicke" in time and comparable to it in meaning is found in the first and last movements of the second cantata of the *Christmas Oratorio*, which are musically related in their thematic material. In the introductory Sinfonia, Bach distinguishes between two instrumental choirs, one

25. Rambach, *Evangelische Betrachtungen*, 639–40; *idem*, *Betrachtungen über das gantze Leiden Christi* (Jena, 1730), 5. The sources cited in notes 2 and 12 all give similar interpretations of the Mount of Olives.

26. Alfred Dürr, *The Cantatas of J. S. Bach*, rev. and trans. Richard D. P. Jones (Oxford: Oxford University Press, 2005), 435, says the following of Bach's omitting the basso continuo: "As a rule, its omission by Bach has a symbolic character and refers either to someone who does not need this support or else to someone who has lost it, who no longer has the ground under his feet and has withdrawn from God." Dürr is certainly correct in viewing the device as symbolic. But Bach's use of the *bassetchen* technique is subtler than Dürr's commentary indicates, with background (high/low) and foreground (theological) dimensions that encompass a much wider range of theological associations.

Example 1. J. S. Bach, *Ascension Oratorio* BWV 11/8, mm. 1–8

of which has a bassetchen part, the other the normal basso continuo. The former, as Albert Schweizer argued many years ago, seems to be associated with the angels of the incarnation and the latter with the shepherds, a simple above/below pictorialism that is amplified by the pastoral style and instrumentation: transverse flutes and strings for the shepherds, pairs of oboes d'amore and oboes da caccia for the angels (with the second oboe da caccia playing the bassetchen part, a sustained g (Example 2).[27] The melody of the angelic music begins with a descending line, then settles on a decorated perfect fifth—g'-d''—as if to suggest a hovering quality, whereas the shepherd music always has an upward direction. If there is any doubt about these associations, it is dispelled at the end of the cantata, where in the final recitative, following the chorus "Glory to God in the highest and on earth peace and goodwill toward humanity," a bass recitative proclaims, "Just so, you angels; rejoice and sing that it has turned out so well for us today! Up, then! We will join in with you; it can make us joyful just like you." The bass voice is, of course, that of the contemporary believer who projects his identity "through" that of one of the shepherds. It is as if one of the shepherds of the incarnation stepped forward to address the angels, to announce the joining of shepherds below and angels above in the hymn with which the cantata ends. And in his setting of the subsequent chorale, Bach brings back the angelic music from the Sinfonia as the interludes between the chorale phrases, its bassetchen texture now

27. Albert Schweizer, *J. S. Bach* (1905), trans. Ernest Newman (London: Breitkopf & Härtel, 1911), 80.

Example 2. J. S. Bach, *Christmas Oratorio* BWV 248/10, mm. 9–12

contrasting with the chorale lines, which are all set with basso continuo and which all feature the rising theme associated with the shepherds as the bass line.

The meaning seems clear: The final chorale represents a joining, a unanimity of the shepherds representing the world below and the angels representing that above (in the purely pictorial, physical senses of those words). The pastorale style, however, as Renate Steiger has argued, projects an additional eschatological character that emerges most clearly in the aria "Beglückte Herde, Jesu Schafe, die Welt ist euch ein Himmelreich" (Fortunate flock, Jesus's sheep, the world is a heavenly kingdom for you), from Cantata 104.[28] In that aria (not a bassetchen piece), the pastoral style suggests that the world (below) is transformed into a "heavenly kingdom" by the presence of Jesus, the "good shepherd." This is the underlying meaning of the ending of the second part of the *Christmas Oratorio*. And it underlies the meaning of "Jesu, deine Gnadenblicke" in the *Ascension Oratorio*, as well. In the *Christmas Oratorio* the angels come down to announce Jesus's incarnation; in "Jesu, deine Gnadenblicke" the believer, mimicking the upward-looking disciples, sees in the Spirit Jesus's ascension, his return to the kingdom above, and through his or her faith perceives continuity of that kingdom with the one below.

The Tonal Design of the *Ascension Oratorio*

There is another aspect to the design of the *Christmas Oratorio* that applies to the *Ascension Oratorio*, as well. As is well known from studies of the former work, the pastorale-centered second cantata seems to associate its subdominant tonality, G, with the world into which Jesus is incarnated, a world whose relative darkness is projected in the motion toward its subdominant, C, in which the chorale "Schaut hin, dort liegt im finstern Stall" (Look there, he lies in a dark stable) is set. And this association has its opposite number in the fifth cantata of the oratorio, the only one in the dominant key, A.[29] In that cantata the star of Bethlehem is interpreted as bringing light to the world, first in the recitative "Wohl euch, die ihr dies Licht gesehen, es ist zu eurem Heil geschehen! Mein Heiland, du bist das Licht, das auch den Heiden scheinen sollen" (Blessed are you who have seen this light; it has appeared for your salvation); then in the chorale, "Dein Glanz all Finsternis verzehrt" (Your brilliance consumes all darkness), virtually the opposite association (but not the opposite meaning) to that of

---

28. Renate Steiger, "'Die Welt ist euch ein Himmelreich': Zu J. S. Bachs Deutung des Pastoralen," *Musik und Kirche* 41 (1971): 1–8, 69–79.

29. See Walter Blankenburg, *Das Weihnachts-Oratorium von Johann Sebastian Bach* (Kassel: Bärenreiter, 1982), 64, 109; Dürr, *The Cantatas of J. S. Bach*, 121, also brings out the fact that "Schaut hin, dort liegt im finstern Stall" sounds in a low register, a fifth below the pitch at which the same chorale melody sounds at the end of the cantata.

"Schaut hin, dort liegt im finstern Stall," then in the aria "Erleucht auch meine finstre Sinnen" (Illuminate also my dark senses). Throughout the cantata the emphasis on light imagery projects the sense that the dominant (sharp) tonality is a kind of opposite to the subdominant of the second cantata.

In the *Ascension Oratorio*, however, we find that the subdominant G major tonality of "Jesu, deine Gnadenblicke" has a place in the design of the whole that is comparable to the role of the subdominant in Bach's other festive D major works.[30] That is, it depicts a vision from below (the subdominant) of the world above (the *bassetchen* texture, associated with the ascended Jesus) through faith, a vision according to which the believer is joined with Jesus or sees "continually" (beständig) Jesus's glance of grace through the love that remains behind.[31] This is the final and most important message of the ascension within the Lutheran framework.

But how does the vision projected in "Jesu, deine Gnadenblicke" relate musically to that of its counterpart in the first half of the oratorio, "Ach, bleibe doch"? Their relationship is a key to understanding the design of the oratorio as a whole. For "Ach, bleibe doch" is in the unusual key of the dominant minor, following a recitative that makes a pronounced tonal descent from the initial announcement of Jesus's ascension in the first recitative, "The Lord Jesus raised up his hands and blessed his disciples, and it took place that as he blessed them he departed from them," which had ended in A major. In the opening chorus, the kingdoms of the first line of the text seem to be associated respectively with the two principal sections, the first of which is in D major, ending in A major on its first sounding (the A section), whereas the second is in B minor, ending in F♯ minor. The former segment is festive, dominated by the trum-

30. What I have said of the role of the subdominant is true of the supertonic, as well. A few movements to consider in this context would be the "Et in terra pax" of the Gloria of the Mass in B Minor (which moves from the initial D major to G major and E minor), the "Qui tollis" of the Glorias of all three major-key Missae Breves (all in the supertonic of the keys of their respective masses); the G major "Et in unum Dominum Jesum Christum" of the Credo of the Mass in B minor; the G major aria "Sanfte soll mein Todeskummer" of the *Easter Oratorio;* and the G major aria "Wo zwei und drei versammlet sind" of Cantata 42. In these and a great many similar instances, the key sequence moves from the tonic major to the subdominant or supertonic to project an affect of contrast that mirrors an above/below element in the text. Within the second part of the *Christmas Oratorio* an outstanding instance of the association of tonal directions (flat/sharp) with earth and heaven appears in the choral setting of the song of the heavenly hosts, "Ehre sei Gott in der Höhe und Friede auf Erden" (Glory be to God on high and peace on earth) origin of the beginning of the Gloria. For the first half of the text ("Ehre sei Gott in der Höhe"), Bach modulates progressively by the circle of fifths in the sharp direction (G, D, a, e, b), then immediately reverses the direction for "Friede auf Erden" (B, e, a, d). Such devices are ubiquitous among the vocal works.

31. August Hermann Francke, *Predigten über die Sonn- und Fest-Tags Episteln*, 712, describes, on the basis of the original Greek ("used for kinds of diligent and zealous contemplations"), that the narrative of the disciples' looking upward in the Epistle means to "ignite the affect of heartfelt love."

pets and kettledrums, whereas the latter, in addition to emphasizing minor keys, drops the trumpets and drums and begins with syncopated music, projecting a considerably less definite and majestic character. After the pronounced praise of God in the first segment, the text of the second sets the lines "sucht sein Lob recht zu vergleichen wenn ihr mit gesamten Chören ihm ein Lied zu Ehren macht" (Seek to match his praise when you make a song to his honor with entire choirs). As Petzoldt points out, the verb "vergleichen" here retains a meaning it shares with an archaic meaning of "vergelten," used frequently in scripture; it urges those below to provide a response or counterpart to the heavenly praise of God.[32] The "gesamten Chören" do not sound in this segment—the trumpets and drums are out. The text refers to their return directly following the central segment in response to it. The movement as a whole is not to be thought of as corresponding directly to the praise of God that occurs in the heavenly kingdom, but rather as an earthly counterpart of which the first and last segments represent a self-consciously human imagining of what the heavenly praise might be like. In theological terms it parallels the idea that music can provide a foretaste of the kingdom of God, a topic that was taken up by Heinrich Müller in his *Himmlischer Liebeskuß* and was given a more directly musical twist in Christoph Raupach's treatise *Veritophili*, published by Johann Mattheson along with the third part of Friedrich Niedt's *Musicalische Handleitung*.[33] The foretaste is, of course, an entirely theological concept; but following Luther's remarks on the capacity of music to provide such a foretaste, it was invoked by Lutherans to justify concerted church music.[34]

32. Petzoldt, *Bach-Kommentar*, 1:924. Petzoldt cites the Grimm brothers' *Deutches Wörterbuch* on the older meaning, which he relates to the use of the word "vergelten" in Psalms 116:12. The Bible with concordances published in Halle from the time of August Hermann Francke to the mid-nineteenth century (with preface by Francke) gives still better instances of this usage with reference to the apocryphal book of Tobias (chapter 12, verses, 2, 5, and 7), which, citing psalm 116, also projects a striking sense of the praise of God (verses 7 and 8). See *BIBLIA, Da ist: Die gantze Heil. Schrift, Altes und Neues Testaments, Nach der Teutschen Übersetzung D. Martin Luthers . . . Die XIX. Auflage* (Halle, 1725). 614.

33. Heinrich Müller, *Himmlischer Liebeskuß oder Übung des wahren Christenthumbs* (Frankfurt and Leipzig, 1686), 786. Raupach's treatise *VERITOPHILI Deutliche Beweis-Grunde / Worauf der rechte Gebrauch der MUSIC, beydes in den Kirchen / als ausser denselben / beruhet, . . . Samt einer Vorrede / heraus gegeben von Mattheson*, was sent anonymously to Mattheson, who published it along with the third part of Niedt's *Musicalische Handleitung* (Hamburg, 1717). It has been issued in facsimile, along with the three parts of the *Musicalische Handleitung* (Hildesheim: Georg Olms, 2002). Chapter 7 of Raupach's treatise, titled "Von dem Nützen der Kirchen-Music, krafft welcher man den Vorschmack des dwigen Freuden-Lebens empfindet," cites Müller and Luther (and other theologians such as Christian Scriver, as well as musicians such as Werckmeister) on the quality in question.

34. An illustration from Heinrich Müller's *Göttliche Liebes-Flamme* (the alternate title of the *Himmlischer Liebes-Kuß*) published by Renate Steiger, "'Gnadengegenwart': Johann Sebastian Bachs Pfingstkantate bwv 172," 55, depicts the union of harmonies above and below, the latter showing organ with sing-

Bach's opening chorus subtly suggests God's kingdoms of heaven and earth by the musical means just described, after which the first recitative moves from b to A, narrating first Jesus's blessing of the disciples, traditionally viewed as a manifestation of his "priestly office" (priesterliches Amt), concerned with present life, followed by his ascension, traditionally viewed as his "kingly office" (königliches Amt).[35] The modulation is direct, centering entirely on the fifth-related harmonies B minor, E major, and A major. The voice rises to its highest pitch for the cadence to A, while the basso continuo outlines rising, then falling, thirty-second-note groups that frame the phrase that narrates Jesus's blessing as if mimicking the gesture itself.

The unusual tonal motion within the recitative no. 3 that follows suggests a shift in perspective from the upward direction of the ascension itself and its A major cadence, to the initial response of sorrow from those left below (Example 3). Whereas the relationship of G major to D major in "Jesu, deine Gnadenblicke" and the final movement of the oratorio is not in any sense one of opposition, the shift from A major to A minor that leads to "Ach, bleibe doch" is. Here the believer resists (or, like the disciples misunderstanding Jesus's reference to the Kingdom in Acts 1, has not yet grasped) the true meaning of the ascension, focusing, as in Heinrich Müller's description cited earlier, on the sorrow that corresponds to a physical loss rather than on the beneficial meaning of the ascension. "Ach, bleibe doch," as is well known, is a parody of a lost aria, from which the Agnus Dei of the Mass in B minor was also parodied.[36] The Agnus, in G minor, is the only flat-key movement in the mass, serving as a kind of symbolic plagal cadence to the D major of the final Dona nobis pacem. This may or may not have been intended in the Mass as a reminder of the world below, but as

ers and instruments within a representation of the human heart, while above, the vista opens up to reveal the heavenly choirs, again with organ, singers, and instrumentalists. The accompanying poem ends with the lines "Der Himmel lobet dich, den Himmel hier auf Erden / hab ich wann ich dich lob so muß man Englisch werden" (Heaven praises you; I have heaven here on earth when I praise you; thus one becomes like the angels). This is an exact illustration of the "Himmel in Hertzen" described by Müller with respect to the Epistle for Ascension Day (*Apostolischer Schluß Kette*, 505): "Das ist das Reich Gottes in uns / der Himmel im Hertzen . . . . In einem andächtigen Gespräch vom Reich Gottes ist offt ein lieblicher Vorschmack des Himmels" (That is the kingdom of God within us, heaven within our hearts . . . . In a devout conversation on the kingdom of God there is often a lovely foretaste of heaven). It depicts all that underlies God's "kingdoms" and the verb "vergleichen" in the opening chorus of the Ascension Oratorio.

35. In nearly all the Lutheran commentaries on Ascension Day cited in this article, Jesus is often described in terms of his two or three "offices" (*Ämter*), of prophet, priest, and king (sometimes just the second and third).

36. The opening chorus and second aria were also parodied from occasional works. See Dürr, *Cantatas*, 338.

Example 3. J. S. Bach, *Ascension Oratorio* BWV 11/3

Example 3. *Cont.*

the final cry for mercy it certainly partakes of an above/below element,[37] and the Neapolitan inflections in the main melody might be taken to suggest something similar.

After "Ach, bleibe doch," however, the narrative of the ascension picks up again, this time from the Epistle for the day (Acts 1:9), which is much more specific about the ascent being a visible one, about the cloud that hid Jesus from the disciples' eyes (in the Lutheran interpretation only the upper stages were hidden, whereas the adverb "zusehends" [visibly] made the question of a visible ascent clear), and about Jesus's sitting on the right hand of God: "Und ward aufgehaben zusehends und fuhr auf gen Himmel, eine Wolke nahm ihn weg vor ihren Augen, und er sitzet zur rechten Hand Gottes" (And was visibly lifted up and journeyed up toward heaven; a cloud removed him from their eyes; and he sits at the right hand of God). Once again the modulation is a straightforward circle of fifths, now in the opposite direction; after the a of "Ach, bleibe doch," it picks up on e and moves from there through b to F♯ minor. The D major chorale "Nun lieget alles unter dir" (Now everything lies beneath you) provides the affirmation of Jesus's ascent into his "königliches Amt" (kingly office).

From this point what remains is the all-important revelation of the tropological meaning of Jesus's ascent, its benefit for the faithful below. The narrative of the two men in white introduces this theme in their questioning of the disciples' upward gaze; since they (the two men) were traditionally understood to be angels, their meaning is one given as if from above. It is that, since Jesus will return exactly as the disciples have just seem him ascend—that is, in a cloud, as in Jesus's prediction of his second coming (well known from the *St. Matthew Passion*)—it is futile to seek him in physical form until that day. Rather, it is in his Gnadengegenwart, his presence through the Holy Spirit, in word and sacraments that he must be sought. In keeping with the other pillars of the structure of the oratorio and their association with God's kingdom, this movement is set solidly in D major.

But in the subsequent accompanied recitative no. 7a, another very human affective response suggests torment and instability once again, even though the range of the tonal ground it traverses from beginning to ending is not wide: it begins from a D 4/2 chord (immediately suggesting a turn downward after the D of the preceding movement) and ends in B minor (Example 4). Its bass line, however, is a continuously descending chromatic scale from c' to e♯ (leading tone to the dominant of B minor), while its harmonies (after the initial one) outline mostly diminished-seventh chords changing to dominant sevenths and moving according to the circle of fifths in the flat direction until the arrival on the first B minor chord in m. 5. That pattern was used

---

37. A similar conception perhaps underlies the C minor tonality of Cantata 6, "Bleib bei uns," for Easter Monday 1725, which marks a striking shift in tone from the D major Easter cantata of the preceding day (BWV 249, "Kommt, fliehet und eilet").

in a more straightforward (less chromatic) fashion in the recitative no. 3 preceding "Ach, bleibe doch" (see Example 3), which began on an E♯ diminished-seventh chord that changed to a dominant seventh on C♯, then basically followed that pattern (with only slight variations) for two additional degrees of progressive flattening (i.e., A♯ diminished followed by F♯ dominant, then a brief B minor and Phrygian cadence to F♯ major followed by D♯ diminished and B dominant seventh, and finally, G♯ diminished and E dominant seventh, closing in A minor).[38] In the later recitative (Example 4), the harmony, following the initial D 4/2 chord, introduced the E♯ diminished-seventh chord again, changing to a C♯ 4/2 chord, followed by an A♯ diminished seventh, changing (only on the last sixteenth note of the harmony) to an F♯ dominant harmony and a B 4/2 chord, before chromatically inflecting what could have been an E major harmony, to E♯ instead (for the move to the B minor cadence).

I have given this much detail to make clear that the two accompanied recitatives that respond to Jesus's ascension both follow circle-of-fifths patterns, although the second is more hidden, chromatic, and tortured than the first. The text of this recitative, instead of urging Jesus to remain, cries for him to return soon and remove the believer's sorrowful demeanor (Gebärde); otherwise, every moment (of waiting) will be hateful and seem to last years. The meaning is that, as other Bach cantatas argue, taking a sorrowful approach to life simply augments one's torment. After the B minor cadence the final narrative recitative, no. 7c, continues the downward tonal motion from its initial B minor to an E minor cadence for the narrative of the disciples' descent from the Mount of Olives and on to C major (now about to become the subdominant of G major) for their return to Jerusalem. The arrival on C is at very low pitch, after which the voice leaps up an octave to complete the arrival on G "mit grosser Freude." The turn toward E minor, beginning on "Ölberg," was perhaps intended as a reminder of the passion, whereas the shift to G major, affirmed of course by "Jesu, deine Gnadenblicke," is aligned with the disciples' finally coming to a true understanding of the ascension.

In all this Bach uses modulation from D major in the flat (or subdominant) direction to depict two different kinds of relationship of the world to Jesus's ascension. "Ach, bleibe doch" is Müller's more literal, physical response of sorrow and "Jesu, deine Gnadenblicke" his tropological understanding of the joy of Jesus's ascension. "Ach, bleibe doch" retains a degree of antithesis, while "Jesus, deine Gnadenblicke" does not. In the recitatives Bach utilizes circle-of-fifths modulations to move in continuous step-by-step fashion between the perspectives of above and below. Throughout the oratorio Bach of course also lavishes attention on figurational details that amplify

38. I cannot agree with Alfred Dürr's designation of the beginning key of this recitative as F♯ minor (*Cantatas*, 336). There is no cadence to F♯ and no F♯ harmony in the entire movement. The first cadence is a Phrygian cadence to F♯ major; but this is a movement dominated by the circle-of-fifths motion, that is, a continual process of transition, not by specific keys (until, of course, the A minor final cadence).

Example 4. J. S. Bach, *Ascension Oratorio* BWV 11/7b

the sense of upward/downward directions that I have discussed in terms of the tonal design. The long upward sequences on "sehn" in "Jesu, deine Gnadenblicke" are perhaps the culmination of what the Lutheran theologians viewed as the primary message of Ascension Day: that the faithful learn to direct their lives upward to God—to see him continually in the Spirit—and the future that awaits them. I think it likely that in the final chorale, which returns to D major and the instrumentation of the opening chorus, Bach intended a representation of the praise of God that is called for in the middle section of the opening movement. That is, the final movement is a "Lied" for "gesamten Chören," but one that now centers entirely on the longing of the faithful for God's kingdom. The chorale itself is in B minor, but it is embedded within the D major framework of the instrumental parts, particularly the trumpets, which project a strikingly eschatological quality, the tonal dualism invoking the idea of God's two kingdoms and the awaiting of the faithful for fulfillment in the one above.

CONTRIBUTORS

ERIC CHAFE is the Victor and Gwendolyn Beinfield Professor of Musicology at Brandeis University.

LAURENCE DREYFUS is professor of music at Oxford University and a fellow of Magdalen College.

DANIEL R. MELAMED is professor of musicology at the Indiana University Jacobs School of Music.

MARKUS RATHEY is associate professor of music history at Yale University.

KERALA J. SNYDER is professor emerita of musicology at the Eastman School of Music, University of Rochester.

CHRISTOPH WOLFF is Adams University Professor at Harvard University.

GENERAL INDEX

INDEX OF BACH'S COMPOSITIONS

INDEX OF OTHER
COMPOSITIONS

The University of Illinois Press
is a founding member of the
Association of American University Presses.

———————————————————————

Composed in 10/14 Janson Text
by Jim Proefrock
at the University of Illinois Press
Manufactured by Sheridan Books, Inc.

University of Illinois Press
1325 South Oak Street
Champaign, IL 61820-6903
www.press.uillinois.edu